PETER HAINING has written and edited a number of bestselling books on the supernatural, notably the widely acclaimed *Ghosts: The Illustrated History* (1975) and *A Dictionary of Ghosts* (1982), which have been translated into several languages including French, German, Russian and Japanese. His companion volume to this anthology, *Haunted House Stories*, was published by Carroll & Graf in 2005. A former journalist and publisher, he lives in a sixteenth-century timber frame house in Suffolk that is haunted by the ghost of a Napoleonic prisoner of war.

Also available

The Mammoth Book of Awesome Comic Fantasy
The Mammoth Book of Best New Erotica 5
The Mammoth Book of Best New Manga
The Mammoth Book of Climbing Adventures
The Mammoth Book of Comic Crime
The Mammoth Book of Egyptian Whodunnits
The Mammoth Book of Endurance and Adventure
The Mammoth Book of Explorers
The Mammoth Book of Eyewitness America
The Mammoth Book of Eyewitness Battles
The Mammoth Book of Eyewitness Everest
The Mammoth Book of Fantasy
The Mammoth Book of Fighter Pilots
The Mammoth Book of Funniest Cartoons of All Time
The Mammoth Book of Future Cops
The Mammoth Book of Great Detective Stories
The Mammoth Book of Hard Men
The Mammoth Book of Haunted House Stories
The Mammoth Book of Heroes
The Mammoth Book of Heroic and Outrageous Women
The Mammoth Book of Historical Whodunnits
The Mammoth Book of Humor
The Mammoth Book of Illustrated Crime
The Mammoth Book of Jacobean Whodunnits
The Mammoth Book of Journalism
The Mammoth Book of Killers at Large
The Mammoth Book of Legal Thrillers
The Mammoth Book of Lesbian Erotica
The Mammoth Book of Maneaters
The Mammoth Book of Men O'War
The Mammoth Book of Mountain Disasters
The Mammoth Book of Murder and Science
The Mammoth Book of Native Americans
The Mammoth Book of Perfect Crimes and Locked Room Mysteries
The Mammoth Book of Private Eye Stories
The Mammoth Book of Prophecies
The Mammoth Book of Pulp Action
The Mammoth Book of Roaring Twenties Whodunnits
The Mammoth Book of Roman Whodunnits
The Mammoth Book of Science Fiction
The Mammoth Book of Sex, Drugs and Rock 'n' Roll
The Mammoth Book of Short Erotic Novels
The Mammoth Book of Special Ops
The Mammoth Book of Tales from the Road
The Mammoth Book of the Titanic
The Mammoth Book of UFOs
The Mammoth Book of Vampires
The Mammoth Book of War Comics
The Mammoth Book of War Correspondents
The Mammoth Book of Women Who Kill

THE MAMMOTH BOOK OF
Modern Ghost Stories

Great Supernatural Tales of
The Twentieth Century

Edited by PETER HAINING

CARROLL & GRAF PUBLISHERS
NEW YORK

Carroll & Graf Publishers
An Imprint of Avalon Publishing Group, Inc.
245 W. 17th Street, 11th Floor
New York, NY 10011-5300
www.carrollandgraf.com

AVALON
publishing group incorporated

First published in the UK by Robinson,
an imprint of Constable & Robinson Ltd 2007

First Carroll & Graf edition 2007

ISBN-13: 978-0-78671-960-0
ISBN-10: 0-7867-1960-5

Printed and bound in the EU

For my wife
Philippa
– who has shared a lifetime with ghosts

"Ghosts, to make themselves manifest, require two conditions abhorrent to the modern mind: silence and continuity."

Edith Wharton, 1937

"The modern ghost story appears to be as much about longing as it is about dread."

Sinclair McKay, 2001

Contents

ACKNOWLEDGMENTS   xiii

FOREWORD   xvii

1. RAISING SPECTRES: The Modern Tradition

"OH WHISTLE, AND I'LL COME TO YOU, MY LAD"
M. R. James   3

THE HOUSE AT TREHEALE
A. C. Benson   21

THE RICHPINS
E. G. Swain   45

THE EVERLASTING CLUB
Arthur Gray   59

NUMBER SEVENTY-NINE
A. N. L. Munby   66

2. GHOST WRITERS: The "Golden Era"

PLAYING WITH FIRE
Sir Arthur Conan Doyle   75

THE HOUSE SURGEON
Rudyard Kipling   88

THE GROVE OF ASHTAROTH
John Buchan   110

A MAN FROM GLASGOW
Somerset Maugham   131

THE LAST LAUGH
D. H. Lawrence   141

THE VISIT TO THE MUSEUM
Vladimir Nabokov   157

3. PHANTOM RANKS: Supernatural at War

THE BOWMEN
Arthur Machen   169

THE GHOST OF *U65*
George Minto   173

"VENGEANCE IS MINE"
Algernon Blackwood   180

THE PUNISHMENT
Lord Dunsany   212

THE HAUNTED CHATEAU
Dennis Wheatley   216

PINK MAY
Elizabeth Bowen   229

A GREMLIN IN THE BEER
Derek Barnes   237

MONEY FOR JAM
Sir Alec Guinness   243

4. THE GHOST-FEELERS: Modern Gothic Tales

THE LADY'S MAID'S BELL
Edith Wharton   257

THE DUENNA
Marie Belloc Lowndes   276

CLYTIE
Eudora Welty   289

THE POOL
Daphne du Maurier   301

A SPOT OF GOTHIC
Jane Gardam   328

5. ENTERTAINING SPOOKS: Supernatural High Jinks

THE INEXPERIENCED GHOST
H. G. Wells   341

FULL FATHOM FIVE
Alexander Woollcott   353

THE NIGHT THE GHOST GOT IN
James Thurber   356

SIR TRISTRAM GOES WEST
Eric Keown   362

WHO OR WHAT WAS IT?
Kingsley Amis   370

ANOTHER FINE MESS
Ray Bradbury   380

6. CHRISTMAS SPIRITS: Festive Season Chillers

ONLY A DREAM . . .
Rider Haggard   391

THE HAUNTED HOUSE
Edith Nesbit   398

THE LIGHT IN THE GARDEN
E. F. Benson   410

THE PRESCRIPTION
Marjorie Bowen   419

CHRISTMAS HONEYMOON
Howard Spring   435

SOUTH SEA BUBBLE
Hammond Innes   453

RINGING IN THE GOOD NEWS
Peter Ackroyd   460

7. HAUNTING TIMES: Tales of Unease

SMOKE GHOST
Fritz Leiber   469

THE GHOST
A. E. Van Vogt   484

THE PARTY
William F. Nolan   516

UNDERGROUND
J. B. Priestley   526

HAUNTED
Joyce Carol Oates   535

VIDEO NASTY
Philip Pullman   554

MY BEAUTIFUL HOUSE
Louis de Bernières   563

APPENDIX: A Century of Ghost Novels 1900–2000   569

Acknowledgments

Acknowledgment is made to the following authors, agents and publishers for permission to reprint the stories in this collection.

"Ringing in the Good News" by Peter Ackroyd © 1985. Originally published in *The Times*, 24 December 1985. Reprinted by permission of Sheil Land Associates Ltd.

"Who or What was It?" by Kingsley Amis © 1972. Originally published in *Playboy* magazine, November 1972. Reprinted by permission of PFD.

"A Gremlin in the Beer" by Derek Barnes © 1942. Originally published in *The Spectator*, June 1942 and reprinted by permission of the magazine.

"The Light in the Garden" by E. F. Benson © 1921. Originally published in *Eve*, December 1921. Reprinted by permission of the Executors of K. S. P. MacDowall.

"Vengeance is Mine" by Algernon Blackwood © 1921. Originally published in *Wolves of God*, 1921. Reprinted by permission of A. P. Watt Ltd.

"Pink May" by Elizabeth Bowen © 1945. Originally published in *The Demon Lover*, 1945. Reprinted by permission of Curtis Brown Ltd.

"The Prescription" by Marjorie Bowen © 1928. Originally published in the *London Magazine*, December 1928. Reprinted by permission of the Penguin Group.

"Another Fine Mess" by Ray Bradbury © 1995. Originally published in *The Magazine of Fantasy & Science Fiction*, April 1995. Reprinted by permission of Abner Stein.

"My Beautiful House" by Louis de Bernières © 2004. Originally published in *The Times*, 18 December 2004. Reprinted by permission of Lavinia Trevor Agency.

"The Pool" by Daphne du Maurier © 1959. Originally published in *Breaking Point*, 1959. Reprinted by permission of Curtis Brown Ltd.

"The Punishment" by Lord Dunsany © 1918. Originally published in *Tales of War*, 1918. Reprinted by permission of Curtis Brown Ltd.

"A Spot of Gothic" by Jane Gardam © 1980. Originally published in *The Sidmouth Letters*, 1980. Reprinted by permission of David Higham Associates.

"The Everlasting Club" by Arthur Gray © 1919. Originally published in *Tedious Brief Tales of Granta and Gramarye*, 1919. Reprinted by permission of W. Heffer & Sons.

"Money for Jam" by Alec Guinness © 1945. Originally published in *Penguin New Writing*, 1945 and reprinted by permission of Christopher Sinclair-Stevenson.

"South Sea Bubble" by Hammond Innes © 1973. Originally published in *Punch magazine*, December 1973. Reprinted by permission of the Estate of Ralph Hammond Innes.

"Sir Tristram Goes West" by Eric Keown © 1935. Originally published in *Punch* magazine, May 1935. Reprinted by permission of the Estate of Eric Keown.

"Smoke Ghost" by Fritz Leiber © 1941. Originally published in *Unknown Worlds*, October 1941. Reprinted by permission of Arkham House.

"The Duenna" by Marie Belloc Lowndes © 1926. Originally published in *The Ghost Book*, 1926. Reprinted by permission of the Executors of M. B. Lowndes.

"The Bowmen" by Arthur Machen © 1914. Originally published in *London Evening News*, 29 September, 1914. Reprinted by permission of A. M. Heath Ltd.

"A Man From Glasgow" by Somerset Maugham © 1944. Originally published in *Creatures of Circumstance*, 1944. Reprinted by permission of William Heinemann.

"The Ghost of *U65*" by George Minto © 1962. Originally published in *Blackwood's Magazine*, July 1962. Reprinted by permission of William Blackwood & Sons.

"Number Seventy-Nine" by A. N. L. Munby © 1949. Originally published in *The Alabaster Hand*, 1949. Reprinted by permission of the Estate of A. N. L. Munby.

"A Visit to the Museum" by Vladimir Nabokov © 1963. Reprinted by permission of *Esquire* Publications Inc.

"The Party" by William F. Nolan © 1967. Originally published in *Playboy*, April 1967. Reprinted by permission of the author.

"Haunted" by Joyce Carol Oates © 1987. Originally published in *The Architecture of Fear*, 1987. Reprinted by permission of Sara Menguc Literary Agency.

"Underground" by J. B. Priestley © 1974. Originally published in *Collected Stories of J. B. Priestley*, 1974. Reprinted by permission of PFD.

"Video Nasty" by Philip Pullman © 1985. Originally published in *Cold Feet*, 1985. Reprinted by permission of A. P. Watt Ltd.

"Christmas Honeymoon" by Howard Spring © 1940. Originally published in the London *Evening Standard*, December 1940. Reprinted by permission of PFD.

"The Richpins" by E. G. Swain © 1912. Originally published in *The Stoneground Ghost Tales*, 1912. Reprinted by permission of W. Heffer & Sons.

"The Night the Ghost Got In" by James Thurber © 1933. Originally published in the *New Yorker*, September 1933. Reprinted by permission of the Estate of James Thurber.

"The Inexperienced Ghost" by H. G. Wells © 1902. Originally published in the *Strand* magazine, March 1902. Reprinted by permission of A. P. Watt Ltd.

"The Ghost" by A. E. Van Vogt © 1942. Originally published in *Unknown Worlds*, October 1942. Reprinted by permission of Forrest J. Ackerman.

"Clytie" by Eudora Welty © 1941. Originally published in *The Southern Review*, Number 7, 1941. Reprinted by permission of the Penguin Group.

"The Haunted Chateau" by Dennis Wheatley © 1943. Originally published in *Gunmen, Gallants and Ghosts*, 1943. Reprinted by permission of Hutchinson Publishers and the Estate of Dennis Wheatley.

"Full Fathom Five" by Alexander Woollcott © 1938. Originally published in the *New Yorker*, October 1938. Reprinted by permission of the *New Yorker*.

Foreword

I Have Been Ghost Hunting

Cambridge has the reputation of being a city of ghosts. With its centuries' old colleges, streets of ancient buildings and a maze of small alleyways, the spirits of the men and women who once lived and died in the area are almost tangible. Legends have long circulated about wandering spooks, numerous eyewitness reports exist in newspapers and books about restless phantoms – the internet can also be employed to summon up details of several more – and a nocturnal "ghost tour" is a regular feature of the city's tourist trail.

A story that is associated with one particular property, the Gibbs' Building on The Backs, has intrigued me for years. The Gibbs is an imposing, three-story edifice, standing in the shadow of King's College Chapel; that wonderful example of Gothic architecture built in three stages over a period of 100 years. King's itself was founded in 1441 by King Henry VI as an ostentatious display of royal patronage and intended for boys from Eton College. It has, of course, boasted some distinguished if varied *alumni* over the years, including E. M. Forster, John Bird and, most recently, Zadie Smith, when the college became one of the first to admit women.

Gibbs' Building lies on the banks of the River Cam which, as its name suggests, gave the city its name. The area was first settled by the Romans at the southern edge of the Fens, a stretch of countryside consisting mostly of marshes and swamps that were not properly drained until the 17th century. Cambridge evolved at the northern-most point, where the traveller was first confronted by the ominous, dank Fens. Even then, stories were already swirling in from the darkness of strange figures and unearthly sounds that only the very brave – or foolish – would think of investigating.

Today, of course, the whole countryside from Cambridge to the coast of East Anglia is very different. But a story persists in King's College that a ghostly cry is still sometimes heard on a staircase in Gibbs' Building. The main authority for this is the ghost story writer,

M. R. James, who came from Eton to Kings at the end of the 19th century and was allotted a room close to the staircase. *He* never heard the cry, James explained in his autobiography, *Eton and King's* (1926), but he knew of other academics who had. Out of a similar interest, I have visited Cambridge on a number of occasions hoping to get to the bottom of the haunting. I had one fascinating discussion with a local author and paranormal investigator, T. C. Lethbridge, who suggested a novel reason why the city had so many ghosts. It was due to being near the Fen marshes, he said. During his research, Lethbridge had discovered that ghosts were prevalent in damp areas and came to the conclusion that they might be the result of supernatural "discharges" being conducted through water vapour. It was – and is – an intriguing concept.

But to return to the story of the Gibbs' Building Ghost. Certainly there is some further evidence about it in the form of brief reports in the archives of the Society for Psychical Research, which were given to the Cambridge University Library in 1991. However, though like M. R. James I have neither heard nor seen anything during my visits, there is a possible explanation as to its cause of the phenomena.

On 'O' Staircase

It seems that a certain Mr Pote once occupied a set of ground floor rooms at the south end of Gibbs' Building. He was, it appears, "a most virulent person", compared by some who crossed his path to Charles Dickens' dreadful Mr Quilp. Ultimately, Pote was banned from the college for his outrageous behaviour and sending "a profane letter to the Dean". As he was being turned out of the university, Pote cursed the college "in language of ineffaceable memory", according to M. R. James. Was it, then, *his* voice that has been occasionally heard echoing around the passageways where he once walked? I like to think it might an explanation for a mystery that has puzzled me all these years – but as is the way of ghost stories, I cannot be *sure*.

It comes as no great surprise to discover that M. R. James, who is now acknowledged to be the "Founding Father of the Modern Ghost Story", should have garnered much of his inspiration while he was resident in Cambridge. He was a Fellow at King's and, as an antiquarian by instinct, could hardly fail to have been interested in the city's enduring tradition of the supernatural. Indeed, it seems that he was so intrigued by the accounts of ghosts that he discovered in old documents and papers – a number of them in the original Latin – as well as the recollections of other academics, that he began to adapt them into stories to read to his friends. He chose the Christmas season as an appropriate time to tell these stories and such was the reaction from his colleagues that the event became an annual gathering.

When James was later encouraged by his friends into publishing his first collection of these tales, *Ghost Stories of an Antiquary*, in 1904, the public response was equally enthusiastic. Within a few years the scholarly and retiring academic had effectively modernized the traditional tale of the supernatural into one of actuality, plausibility and malevolence well suited for 20th century readers – banishing the old trappings of antique castles, terrified maidens, evil villains and clanking, comic spectres – and provided the inspiration for other writers who, in the ensuing years, would develop the ghost story into the imaginative, varied and unsettling genre we know and enjoy today.

This book is intended to be a companion to my earlier anthology, *Haunted House Stories* (2005), as well as a celebration of the Modern Ghost Story ranging from the groundbreaking tales of M. R. James to the dawn of the 21st century. A collection that demonstrates how and why the ghost has survived the march of progress that some critics once believed would confine it to the annals of superstition. Defying, as it did so, the very elements that were expected to bring about its demise: the electric light, the telephone, cars, trains and aeroplanes, not forgetting modern technology and psychology and, especially, the growth of human cynicism towards those things that we cannot explain by logic or reason.

I have deliberately divided the book into seven sections in order to try and show just how diversified it has become in the hands of some very accomplished and skilful writers, a considerable number of them not specifically associated with the genre. After the landmark achievements of James and his circle, readers of supernatural fiction soon found the story-form attracting some of the most popular writers of the first half of the 20th century – notably Conan Doyle, Kipling, Buchan, Somerset Maugham, D. H. Lawrence and Vladimir Nabokov – who created what amounted to a "Golden Era" of ghost stories. However, the occurrence of two world wars in the first half of the century saw the emergence of a group of writers exploring the idea of life after death as personified by ghosts, which offered an antidote to the appalling slaughter and suffering caused by the conflicts. Some of these stories were read as literally true by sections of the population, obviously desperate for some form of comfort after the loss of dear ones. Among my contributors to this particular section you will find Arthur Machen with his famous story of "The Bowmen", Algernon Blackwood, Dennis Wheatley and Elizabeth Bowen. Plus one name I believe will be quite unexpected: that of Sir Alec Guinness, whose evocative ghost story at sea, "Money For Jam", I am delighted to be returning to print here for the first time since 1945!

The Gothic Story also returned revitalized to address new generations, thanks to the work of an excellent school of female writers, loosely categorized as "Ghost Feelers". At the forefront was the American Edith Wharton, who claimed it was a conscious act more than a belief to write about the supernatural. "I don't believe in ghosts," she said, "but I'm afraid of them." Even with this reservation, Wharton and others went ahead to create the "new gothic" of claustrophobia, disintegration and terror of the soul, notably Marie Belloc Lowndes, Eudora Welty, Daphne du Maurier and Jane Gardam. The humorous ghost story which Dickens had first interjected to entertain the readers of *Pickwick Papers*, the previous century, got a life of its own thanks to a typically innovative story from H. G. Wells in 1902. His lead was followed by others of a similar sense of humour such as Alexander Woollcott, James Thurber, Kingsley Amis and Ray Bradbury.

The book would, of course, be incomplete without a section devoted to the Christmas Ghost Story. Over the years, dozens of newspapers and magazines have echoed the words of the editor of *Eve* magazine addressing his readers in 1921: "Ghosts prosper at Christmas time: they like the long evenings when the fire is low and the house hushed for the night. After you have sat up late reading or talking about them they love to hear your heart beating and hammering as you steal upstairs to bed in the dark . . ." Here you will find Rider Haggard, Marjorie Bowen, Hammond Innes, Peter Ackroyd and their seasonal compatriots vying to keep you firmly in your seat by the fireside.

The final selection sees the ghost story come of age as the 21st century dawns. It has now completed its evolution from the Medieval Tradition through the Gothic Drama and the Victorian Parlour Tale. In a group of unique stories by Fritz Leiber, J. B. Priestley, Joyce Carol Oates, Philip Pullman and Louis de Bernières you will encounter ghosts no longer confined in any way but existing in the most everyday situations of modern living: inhabiting flats and houses, using the transport system, the phone, even the latest IT technology, for self-expression. You will find them emancipated in a way no one could have imagined a century ago. As L. P. Hartley observed recently, "Ghosts have emancipated themselves from their disabilities, and besides being able to do a great many things that human beings can't do, they can now do a great many that human beings *can* do. Immaterial as they are or should be, they have been able to avail themselves of the benefits of our materialistic civilisation." A sobering thought, it seems to me, as technology presses ahead even faster and further in the 21st century.

I started my remarks with M. R. James and I will end with him, as he has been so influential on the ghost story genre. As he was dying, the great man was asked by another writer of supernatural fiction, the Irishman Shane Leslie, to answer a question that had long been bothering him. Did James *really* believe in ghosts? The old man smiled slightly, lifted his white head and looked his visitor straight in the eyes. "Depend upon it!" he said. "Some of these things are so, but we do not know the *rules*." I suggest we may still be looking for those rules at the end of the 21st century.

Peter Haining
June 2007

1

Raising Spectres

The Modern Tradition

"Oh, Whistle, And I'll Come to You, My Lad"

M. R. James

Location: Burnstow Beach, Suffolk.
Time: Spring, 1900.
Eyewitness Description: *"It would stop, raise arms, bow itself toward the sand, then run stooping across the beach to the water-edge and back again; and then, rising upright, once more continue its course forward at a speed that was startling and terrifying . . ."*

Author: Montague Rhodes James (1862–1936) only wrote just over two dozen ghost short stories during the early years of the 20th century, but they have continued to haunt each new generation of readers and inspire writers ever since. The son of a clergyman, he was raised in Suffolk, discovered traditional ghost tales while at his prep school, and then decided to try his own interpretation of the genre when he became a Fellow of King's College in 1887. By the dawn of the century, he was telling stories to friends at Christmas gatherings in his room, jovially referred to as "meetings of the Chitchat Society" – though they were evidently anything *but* chatty in the shadowy, candle-lit gloom. All James' narratives bore out his conviction about ghosts: "I am prepared to consider evidence and accept it if it satisfies me." The reader is invited to see whether he finds James convincing in this opening story that is undoubtedly one of his most eerie and frightening.

"I suppose you will be getting away pretty soon, now Full term is over, Professor," said a person not in the story to the Professor of Ontography, soon after they had sat down next to each other at a feast in the hospitable hall of St James's College.

The Professor was young, neat, and precise in speech.

"Yes," he said; "my friends have been making me take up golf this term, and I mean to go to the East Coast – in point of fact to Burnstow – (I dare say you know it) for a week or ten days, to improve my game. I hope to get off tomorrow."

"Oh, Parkins," said his neighbour on the other side, "if you are going to Burnstow, I wish you would look at the site of the Templars' preceptory, and let me know if you think it would be any good to have a dig there in the summer."

It was, as you might suppose, a person of antiquarian pursuits who said this, but, since he merely appears in this prologue, there is no need to give his entitlements.

"Certainly," said Parkins, the Professor: "if you will describe to me whereabouts the site is, I will do my best to give you an idea of the lie of the land when I get back; or I could write to you about it, if you would tell me where you are likely to be."

"Don't trouble to do that, thanks. It's only that I'm thinking of taking my family in that direction in the Long, and it occurred to me that, as very few of the English preceptories have ever been properly planned, I might have an opportunity of doing something useful on off-days."

The Professor rather sniffed at the idea that planning out a preceptory could be described as useful. His neighbour continued:

"The site – I doubt if there is anything showing above ground – must be down quite close to the beach now. The sea has encroached tremendously, as you know, all along that bit of coast. I should think, from the map, that it must be about three-quarters of a mile from the Globe Inn, at the north end of the town. Where are you going to stay?"

"Well, *at* the Globe Inn, as a matter of fact," said Parkins; "I have engaged a room there. I couldn't get in anywhere else; most of the lodging-houses are shut up in winter, it seems; and, as it is, they tell me that the only room of any size I can have is really a double-bedded one, and that they haven't a corner in which to store the other bed, and so on. But I must have a fairly large room, for I am taking some books down, and mean to do a bit of work; and though I don't quite fancy having an empty bed – not to speak of two – in what I may call for the time being my study, I suppose I can manage to rough it for the short time I shall be there."

"Do you call having an extra bed in your room roughing it, Parkins?" said a bluff person opposite. "Look here, I shall come down and occupy it for a bit; it'll be company for you."

The Professor quivered, but managed to laugh in a courteous manner.

"By all means, Rogers; there's nothing I should like better. But I'm afraid you would find it rather dull; you don't play golf, do you?"

"No, thank Heaven!" said rude Mr Rogers.

"Well, you see, when I'm not writing I shall most likely be out on the links, and that, as I say, would be rather dull for you, I'm afraid."

"Oh, I don't know! There's certain to be somebody I know in the place; but, of course, if you don't want me, speak the word, Parkins; I shan't be offended. Truth, as you always tell us, is never offensive."

Parkins was, indeed, scrupulously polite and strictly truthful. It is to be feared that Mr Rogers sometimes practised upon his knowledge of these characteristics. In Parkins's breast there was a conflict now raging, which for a moment or two did not allow him to answer. That interval being over, he said:

"Well, if you want the exact truth, Rogers, I was considering whether the room I speak of would really be large enough to accommodate us both comfortably; and also whether (mind, I shouldn't have said this if you hadn't pressed me) you would not constitute something in the nature of a hindrance to my work."

Rogers laughed loudly.

"Well done, Parkins!" he said. "It's all right. I promise not to interrupt your work; don't you disturb yourself about that. No, I won't come if you don't want me; but I thought I should do so nicely to keep the ghosts off." Here he might have been seen to wink and to nudge his next neighbour. Parkins might also have been seen to become pink. "I beg pardon, Parkins," Rogers continued; "I oughtn't to have said that. I forgot you didn't like levity on these topics."

"Well," Parkins said, "as you have mentioned the matter, I freely own that I do *not* like careless talk about what you call ghosts. A man in my position," he went on, raising his voice a little, "cannot, I find, be too careful about appearing to sanction the current beliefs on such subjects. As you know, Rogers, or as you ought to know; for I think I have never concealed my views—"

"No, you certainly have not, old man," put in Rogers *sotto voce*.

"—I hold that any semblance, any appearance of concession to the view that such things might exist is to me a renunciation of all that I hold most sacred. But I'm afraid I have not succeeded in securing your attention."

"Your *undivided* attention, was what Dr Blimber actually *said*,"*

---

* Mr Rogers was wrong, *vide* "Dombey and Son", chapter xii.

Rogers interrupted, with every appearance of an earnest desire for accuracy. "But I beg your pardon, Parkins: I'm stopping you."

"No, not at all," said Parkins. "I don't remember Blimber; perhaps he was before my time. But I needn't go on. I'm sure you know what I mean."

"Yes, yes," said Rogers, rather hastily – "just so. We'll go into it fully at Burnstow, or somewhere."

In repeating the above dialogue I have tried to give the impression which it made on me, that Parkins was something of an old woman – rather henlike, perhaps, in his little ways; totally destitute, alas! of the sense of humour, but at the same time dauntless and sincere in his convictions, and a man deserving of the greatest respect. Whether or not the reader has gathered so much, that was the character which Parkins had.

On the following day Parkins did, as he had hoped, succeed in getting away from his college, and in arriving at Burnstow. He was made welcome at the Globe Inn, was safely installed in the large double-bedded room of which we have heard, and was able before retiring to rest to arrange his materials for work in apple-pie order upon a commodious table which occupied the outer end of the room, and was surrounded on three sides by windows looking out seaward; that is to say, the central window looked straight out to sea, and those on the left and right commanded prospects along the shore to the north and south respectively. On the south you saw the village of Burn-stow. On the north no houses were to be seen, but only the beach and the low cliff backing it. Immediately in front was a strip – not considerable – of rough grass, dotted with old anchors, capstans, and so forth; then a broad path; then the beach. Whatever may have been the original distance between the Globe Inn and the sea, not more than sixty yards now separated them.

The rest of the population of the inn was, of course, a golfing one, and included few elements that call for a special description. The most conspicuous figure was, perhaps, that of an *ancien militaire*, secretary of a London club, and possessed of a voice of incredible strength, and of views of a pronouncedly Protestant type. These were apt to find utterance after his attendance upon the ministrations of the Vicar, an estimable man with inclinations towards a picturesque ritual, which he gallantly kept down as far as he could out of deference to East Anglian tradition.

Professor Parkins, one of whose principal characteristics was pluck, spent the greater part of the day following his arrival at

Burnstow in what he had called improving his game, in company
with this Colonel Wilson: and during the afternoon – whether the
process of improvement were to blame or not, I am not sure – the
Colonel's demeanour assumed a colouring so lurid that even Parkins
jibbed at the thought of walking home with him from the links. He
determined, after a short and furtive look at that bristling moustache
and those incarnadined features, that it would be wiser to allow the
influences of tea and tobacco to do what they could with the Colonel
before the dinner-hour should render a meeting inevitable.

"I might walk home to-night along the beach," he reflected – "yes,
and take a look – there will be light enough for that – at the ruins of
which Disney was talking. I don't exactly know where they are, by
the way; but I expect I can hardly help stumbling on them."

This he accomplished, I may say, in the most literal sense, for in
picking his way from the links to the shingle beach his foot caught,
partly in a gorse-root and partly in a biggish stone, and over he went.
When he got up and surveyed his surroundings, he found himself in a
patch of somewhat broken ground covered with small depressions
and mounds. These latter, when he came to examine them, proved to
be simply masses of flints embedded in mortar and grown over with
turf. He must, he quite rightly concluded, be on the site of the
preceptory he had promised to look at. It seemed not unlikely to
reward the spade of the explorer; enough of the foundations was
probably left at no great depth to throw a good deal of light on the
general plan. He remembered vaguely that the Templars, to whom
this site had belonged, were in the habit of building round churches,
and he thought a particular series of the humps or mounds near him
did appear to be arranged in something of a circular form. Few
people can resist the temptation to try a little amateur research in a
department quite outside their own, if only for the satisfaction of
showing how successful they would have been had they only taken it
up seriously. Our Professor, however, if he felt something of this
mean desire, was also truly anxious to oblige Mr Disney. So he paced
with care the circular area he had noticed, and wrote down its rough
dimensions in his pocketbook. Then he proceeded to examine an
oblong eminence which lay east of the centre of the circle, and
seemed to his thinking likely to be the base of a platform or altar. At
one end of it, the northern, a patch of the turf was gone – removed by
some boy or other creature *ferae naturae*. It might, he thought, be as
well to probe the soil here for evidences of masonry, and he took out
his knife and began scraping away the earth. And now followed
another little discovery: a portion of soil fell inward as he scraped,

and disclosed a small cavity. He lighted one match after another to help him to see of what nature the hole was, but the wind was too strong for them all. By tapping and scratching the sides with his knife, however, he was able to make out that it must be an artificial hole in masonry. It was rectangular, and the sides, top, and bottom, if not actually plastered, were smooth and regular. Of course it was empty. No! As he withdrew the knife he heard a metallic clink, and when he introduced his hand it met with a cylindrical object lying on the floor of the hole. Naturally enough, he picked it up, and when he brought it into the light, now fast fading, he could see that it, too, was of man's making – a metal tube about four inches long, and evidently of some considerable age.

By the time Parkins had made sure that there was nothing else in this odd receptacle, it was too late and too dark for him to think of undertaking any further search. What he had done had proved so unexpectedly interesting that he determined to sacrifice a little more of the daylight on the morrow to archæology. The object which he now had safe in his pocket was bound to be of some slight value at least, he felt sure.

Bleak and solemn was the view on which he took a last look before starting homeward. A faint yellow light in the west showed the links, on which a few figures moving towards the club-house were still visible, the squat martello tower, the lights of Aldsey village, the pale ribbon of sands intersected at intervals by black wooden groynings, the dim and murmuring sea. The wind was bitter from the north, but was at his back when he set out for the Globe. He quickly rattled and clashed through the shingle and gained the sand, upon which, but for the groynings which had to be got over every few yards, the going was both good and quiet. One last look behind, to measure the distance he had made since leaving the ruined Templars' church, showed him a prospect of company on his walk, in the shape of a rather indistinct personage in the distance, who seemed to be making great efforts to catch up with him, but made little, if any, progress. I mean that there was an appearance of running about his movements, but that the distance between him and Parkins did not seem materially to lessen. So, at least, Parkins thought, and decided that he almost certainly did not know him, and that it would be absurd to wait until he came up. For all that, company, he began to think, would really be very welcome on that lonely shore, if only you could choose your companion. In his unenlightened days he had read of meetings in such places which even now would hardly bear thinking of. He went on thinking of them, however, until he reached home, and particularly of one which catches most people's fancy at some time of their childhood. "Now I saw in my dream that Christian had gone but a very little way when he saw a foul fiend coming over the field to meet him." "What should I do now," he thought, "if I looked back and caught sight of a black figure sharply defined against the yellow sky, and saw that it had horns and wings? I wonder whether I should stand or run for it. Luckily, the gentleman behind is not of that kind, and he seems to be about as far off now as when I saw him first. Well, at this rate he won't get his dinner as soon as I shall; and, dear me! it's within a quarter of an hour of the time now. I must run!"

Parkins had, in fact, very little time for dressing. When he met the Colonel at dinner, Peace – or as much of her as that gentleman could manage – reigned once more in the military bosom; nor was she put to flight in the hours of bridge that followed dinner, for Parkins was a more than respectable player. When, therefore, he retired towards twelve o'clock, he felt that he had spent his evening in quite a satisfactory way, and that, even for so long as a fortnight or three weeks, life at the Globe would be supportable under similar conditions – "especially," thought he, "if I go on improving my game."

As he went along the passages he met the boots of the Globe, who stopped and said:

"Beg your pardon, sir, but as I was a-brushing your coat just now there was somethink fell out of the pocket. I put it on your chest of drawers, sir, in your room, sir – a piece of a pipe or somethink of that, sir. Thank you, sir. You'll find it on your chest of drawers, sir – yes, sir. Good-night, sir."

The speech served to remind Parkins of his little discovery of that afternoon. It was with some considerable curiosity that he turned it over by the light of his candles. It was of bronze, he now saw, and was shaped very much after the manner of the modern dog-whistle; in fact it was – yes, certainly it was – actually no more nor less than a whistle. He put it to his lips, but it was quite full of a fine, caked-up sand or earth, which would not yield to knocking, but must be loosened with a knife. Tidy as ever in his habits, Parkins cleared out the earth on to a piece of paper, and took the latter to the window to empty it out. The night was clear and bright, as he saw when he had opened the casement, and he stopped for an instant to look at the sea and note a belated wanderer stationed on the shore in front of the inn. Then he shut the window, a little surprised at the late hours people kept at Burnstow, and took his whistle to the light again. Why, surely there were marks on it, and not merely marks, but letters! A very little rubbing rendered the deeply-cut inscription quite legible, but the Professor had to confess, after some earnest thought, that the meaning of it was as obscure to him as the writing on the wall to Belshazzar. There were legends both on the front and on the back of the whistle. The one read thus:

$$\text{FUR} \quad \begin{matrix} \text{FLA} \\ \text{FLE} \end{matrix} \quad \text{BIS}$$

The other:

QUIS   EST   ISTE   QUI   VENIT

"I ought to be able to make it out," he thought; "but I suppose I am a little rusty in my Latin. When I come to think of it, I don't believe I even know the word for a whistle. The long one does seem simple enough. It ought to mean, 'Who is this who is coming?' Well, the best way to find out is evidently to whistle for him."

He blew tentatively and stopped suddenly, startled and yet pleased at the note he had elicited. It had a quality of infinite distance in it, and, soft as it was, he somehow felt it must be audible for miles round. It was a sound, too, that seemed to have the power (which many scents possess) of forming pictures in the brain. He saw quite clearly for a moment a vision of a wide, dark expanse at night, with a fresh wind blowing, and in the midst a lonely figure – how employed, he could not tell. Perhaps he would have seen more had not the picture been broken by the sudden surge of a gust of wind against his casement, so sudden that it made him look up, just in time to see the white glint of a sea-bird's wing somewhere outside the dark panes.

The sound of the whistle had so fascinated him that he could not help trying it once more, this time more boldly. The note was little, if at all, louder than before, and repetition broke the illusion – no picture followed, as he had half hoped it might. "But what is this? Goodness! what force the wind can get up in a few minutes! What a tremendous gust! There! I knew that window-fastening was no use! Ah! I thought so – both candles out. It is enough to tear the room to pieces."

The first thing was to get the window shut. While you might count twenty Parkins was struggling with the small casement, and felt almost as if he were pushing back a sturdy burglar, so strong was the pressure. It slackened all at once, and the window banged to and latched itself. Now to relight the candles and see what damage, if any, had been done. No, nothing seemed amiss; no glass even was broken in the casement. But the noise had evidently roused at least one member of the household: the Colonel was to be heard stumping in his stockinged feet on the floor above, and growling.

Quickly as it had risen, the wind did not fall at once. On it went, moaning and rushing past the house, at times rising to a cry so desolate that, as Parkins disinterestedly said, it might have made fanciful people feel quite uncomfortable; even the unimaginative, he thought after a quarter of an hour, might be happier without it.

Whether it was the wind, or the excitement of golf, or of the researches in the preceptory that kept Parkins awake, he was not sure. Awake he remained, in any case, long enough to fancy (as I am afraid I often do myself under such conditions) that he was the victim of all manner of fatal disorders: he would lie counting the beats of his heart, convinced that it was going to stop work every moment, and would entertain grave suspicions of his lungs, brain, liver, etc. – suspicions which he was sure would be dispelled by the return of daylight, but which until then refused to be put aside. He found a little vicarious comfort in the idea that someone else was in the same boat. A near neighbour (in the darkness it was not easy to tell his direction) was tossing and rustling in his bed, too.

The next stage was that Parkins shut his eyes and determined to give sleep every chance. Here again over-excitement asserted itself in another form – that of making pictures. *Experto crede*, pictures do come to the closed eyes of one trying to sleep, and often his pictures are so little to his taste that he must open his eyes and disperse the images.

Parkins's experience on this occasion was a very distressing one. He found that the picture which presented itself to him was continuous. When he opened his eyes, of course, it went; but when he shut them once more it framed itself afresh, and acted itself out again, neither quicker nor slower than before. What he saw was this:

A long stretch of shore – shingle edged by sand, and intersected at short intervals with black groynes running down to the water – a scene, in fact, so like that of his afternoon's walk that, in the absence of any landmark, it could not be distinguished therefrom. The light was obscure, conveying an impression of gathering storm, late winter evening, and slight cold rain. On this bleak stage at first no actor was visible. Then, in the distance, a bobbing black object appeared; a moment more, and it was a man running, jumping, clambering over the groynes, and every few seconds looking eagerly back. The nearer he came the more obvious it was that he was not only anxious, but even terribly frightened, though his face was not to be distinguished. He was, moreover, almost at the end of his strength. On he came; each successive obstacle seemed to cause him more difficulty than the last. "Will he get over this next one?" thought Parkins; "it seems a little higher than the others." Yes; half climbing, half throwing himself, he did get over, and fell all in a heap on the other side (the side nearest to the spectator). There, as if really unable to get up again, he remained crouching under the groyne, looking up in an attitude of painful anxiety.

So far no cause whatever for the fear of the runner had been shown; but now there began to be seen, far up the shore, a little flicker of something light-coloured moving to and fro with great swiftness and irregularity. Rapidly growing larger, it, too, declared itself as a figure in pale, fluttering draperies, ill-defined. There was something about its motion which made Parkins very unwilling to see it at close quarters. It would stop, raise arms, bow itself toward the sand, then run stooping across the beach to the water-edge and back again; and then, rising upright, once more continue its course forward at a speed that was startling and terrifying. The moment came when the pursuer was hovering about from left to right only a few yards beyond the groyne where the runner lay in hiding. After two or three ineffectual castings hither and thither it came to a stop, stood upright, with arms raised high, and then darted straight forward towards the groyne.

It was at this point that Parkins always failed in his resolution to keep his eyes shut. With many misgivings as to incipient failure of eyesight, overworked brain, excessive smoking, and so on, he finally resigned himself to light his candle, get out a book, and pass the night waking, rather than be tormented by this persistent panorama, which he saw clearly enough could only be a morbid reflection of his walk and his thoughts on that very day.

The scraping of match on box and the glare of light must have startled some creatures of the night – rats or what not – which he heard scurry across the floor from the side of his bed with much rustling. Dear, dear! the match is out! Fool that it is! But the second one burnt better, and a candle and book were duly procured, over which Parkins pored till sleep of a wholesome kind came upon him, and that in no long space. For about the first time in his orderly and prudent life he forgot to blow out the candle, and when he was called next morning at eight there was still a flicker in the socket and a sad mess of guttered grease on the top of the little table.

After breakfast he was in his room, putting the finishing touches to his golfing costume – fortune had again allotted the Colonel to him for a partner – when one of the maids came in.

"Oh, if you please," she said, "would you like any extra blankets on your bed, sir?"

"Ah! thank you," said Parkins. "Yes, I think I should like one. It seems likely to turn rather colder."

In a very short time the maid was back with the blanket.

"Which bed should I put it on, sir?" she asked.

"What? Why, that one – the one I slept in last night," he said, pointing to it.

"Oh yes! I beg your pardon, sir, but you seemed to have tried both of 'em; leastways, we had to make 'em both up this morning."

"Really? How very absurd!" said Parkins. "I certainly never touched the other, except to lay some things on it. Did it actually seem to have been slept in?"

"Oh yes, sir!" said the maid. "Why, all the things was crumpled and throwed about all ways, if you'll excuse me, sir – quite as if anyone 'adn't passed but a very poor night, sir."

"Dear me," said Parkins. "Well, I may have disordered it more than I thought when I unpacked my things. I'm very sorry to have given you the extra trouble, I'm sure. I expect a friend of mine soon, by the way – a gentleman from Cambridge – to come and occupy it for a night or two. That will be all right, I suppose, won't it?"

"Oh yes, to be sure, sir. Thank you, sir. It's no trouble, I'm sure," said the maid, and departed to giggle with her colleagues.

Parkins set forth, with a stern determination to improve his game.

I am glad to be able to report that he succeeded so far in this enterprise that the Colonel, who had been rather repining at the prospect of a second day's play in his company, became quite chatty as the morning advanced; and his voice boomed out over the flats, as certain also of our own minor poets have said, "like some great bourdon in a minster tower."

"Extraordinary wind, that, we had last night," he said. "In my old home we should have said someone had been whistling for it."

"Should you, indeed!" said Parkins. "Is there a superstition of that kind still current in your part of the country?"

"I don't know about superstition," said the Colonel. "They believe in it all over Denmark and Norway, as well as on the Yorkshire coast; and my experience is, mind you, that there's generally something at the bottom of what these country-folk hold to, and have held to for generations. But it's your drive" (or whatever it might have been: the golfing reader will have to imagine appropriate digressions at the proper intervals).

When conversation was resumed, Parkins said, with a slight hesitancy:

"Apropos of what you were saying just now, Colonel, I think I ought to tell you that my own views on such subjects are very strong. I am, in fact, a convinced disbeliever in what is called the 'supernatural'."

"What!" said the Colonel, "do you mean to tell me you don't believe in second-sight, or ghosts, or anything of that kind?"

"In nothing whatever of that kind," returned Parkins firmly.

"Well," said the Colonel, "but it appears to me at that rate, sir, that you must be little better than a Sadducee."

Parkins was on the point of answering that, in his opinion, the Sadducees were the most sensible persons he had ever read of in the Old Testament; but, feeling some doubt as to whether much mention of them was to be found in that work, he preferred to laugh the accusation off.

"Perhaps I am," he said; "but— Here, give me my cleek, boy! – Excuse me one moment, Colonel." A short interval. "Now, as to whistling for the wind, let me give you my theory about it. The laws which govern winds are really not at all perfectly known – to fisherfolk and such, of course, not known at all. A man or woman of eccentric habits, perhaps, or a stranger, is seen repeatedly on the beach at some unusual hour, and is heard whistling. Soon afterwards a violent wind rises; a man who could read the sky perfectly or who possessed a barometer could have foretold that it would. The simple people of a fishing-village have no barometers, and only a few rough rules for prophesying weather. What more natural than that the eccentric personage I postulated should be regarded as having raised the wind, or that he or she should clutch eagerly at the reputation of being able to do so? Now, take last night's wind: as it happens, I myself was whistling. I blew a whistle twice, and the wind seemed to come absolutely in answer to my call. If anyone had seen me—"

The audience had been a little restive under this harangue, and Parkins had, I fear, fallen somewhat into the tone of a lecturer; but at the last sentence the Colonel stopped.

"Whistling, were you?" he said. "And what sort of whistle did you use? Play this stroke first." Interval.

"About that whistle you were asking, Colonel. It's rather a curious one. I have it in my— No; I see I've left it in my room. As a matter of fact, I found it yesterday."

And then Parkins narrated the manner of his discovery of the whistle, upon hearing which the Colonel grunted, and opined that, in Parkins's place, he should himself be careful about using a thing that had belonged to a set of Papists, of whom, speaking generally, it might be affirmed that you never knew what they might not have been up to. From this topic he diverged to the enormities of the Vicar, who had given notice on the previous Sunday that Friday would be the Feast of St Thomas the Apostle, and that there would be service at eleven o'clock in the church. This and other similar proceedings constituted in the Colonel's view a strong presumption that the Vicar was a concealed Papist, if not a Jesuit; and Parkins, who could not very readily follow the Colonel in this region, did not disagree with him. In fact, they got on so well together in the morning that there was no talk on either side of their separating after lunch.

Both continued to play well during the afternoon, or, at least, well enough to make them forget everything else until the light began to fail them. Not until then did Parkins remember that he had meant to do some more investigating at the preceptory; but it was of no great importance, he reflected. One day was as good as another; he might as well go home with the Colonel.

As they turned the corner of the house, the Colonel was almost knocked down by a boy who rushed into him at the very top of his speed, and then, instead of running away, remained hanging on to him and panting. The first words of the warrior were naturally those of reproof and objurgation, but he very quickly discerned that the boy was almost speechless with fright. Inquiries were useless at first. When the boy got his breath he began to howl, and still clung to the Colonel's legs. He was at last detached, but continued to howl.

"What in the world *is* the matter with you? What have you been up to? What have you seen?" said the two men.

"Ow, I seen it wive at me out of the winder," wailed the boy, "and I don't like it."

"What window?" said the irritated Colonel. "Come, pull yourself together, my boy."

"The front winder it was, at the 'otel," said the boy.

At this point Parkins was in favour of sending the boy home, but the Colonel refused; he wanted to get to the bottom of it, he said; it was most dangerous to give a boy such a fright as this one had had, and if it turned out that people had been playing jokes, they should suffer for it in some way. And by a series of questions he made out this story: The boy had been playing about on the grass in front of the Globe with some others; then they had gone home to their teas, and he was just

going, when he happened to look up at the front winder and see it a-
wiving at him. *It* seemed to be a figure of some sort, in white as far as he
knew – couldn't see its face; but it wived at him, and it warn't a right
thing – not to say not a right person. Was there a light in the room? No,
he didn't think to look if there was a light. Which was the window?
Was it the top one or the second one? The seckind one it was – the big
winder what got two little uns at the sides.

"Very well, my boy," said the Colonel, after a few more questions.
"You run away home now. I expect it was some person trying to give
you a start. Another time, like a brave English boy, you just throw a
stone – well, no, not that exactly, but you go and speak to the waiter,
or to Mr Simpson, the landlord, and – yes – and say that I advised
you to do so."

The boy's face expressed some of the doubt he felt as to the
likelihood of Mr Simpson's lending a favourable ear to his com-
plaint, but the Colonel did not appear to perceive this, and went on:

"And here's a sixpence – no, I see it's a shilling – and you be off
home, and don't think any more about it."

The youth hurried off with agitated thanks. and the Colonel and
Parkins went round to the front of the Globe and reconnoitred.
There was only one window answering to the description they had
been hearing.

"Well, that's curious," said Parkins; "it's evidently my window the
lad was talking about. Will you come up for a moment, Colonel
Wilson? We ought to be able to see if anyone has been taking liberties
in my room."

They were soon in the passage, and Parkins made as if to open the
door. Then he stopped and felt in his pockets.

"This is more serious than I thought," was his next remark. "I
remember now that before I started this morning I locked the door. It
is locked now, and, what is more, here is the key." And he held it up.
"Now," he went on, "if the servants are in the habit of going into
one's room during the day when one is away, I can only say that –
well, that I don't approve of it at all." Conscious of a somewhat weak
climax, he busied himself in opening the door (which was indeed
locked) and in lighting candles. "No," he said, "nothing seems
disturbed."

"Except your bed," put in the Colonel.

"Excuse me, that isn't my bed," said Parkins. "I don't use that one.
But it does look as if someone had been playing tricks with it."

It certainly did: the clothes were bundled up and twisted together
in a most tortuous confusion. Parkins pondered.

"That must be it," he said at last: "I disordered the clothes last night in unpacking, and they haven't made it since. Perhaps they came in to make it, and that boy saw them through the window; and then they were called away and locked the door after them. Yes, I think that must be it."

"Well, ring and ask," said the Colonel, and this appealed to Parkins as practical.

The maid appeared, and, to make a long story short, deposed that she had made the bed in the morning when the gentleman was in the room, and hadn't been there since. No, she hadn't no other key. Mr Simpson he kep' the keys; he'd be able to tell the gentleman if anyone had been up.

This was a puzzle. Investigation showed that nothing of value had been taken, and Parkins remembered the disposition of the small objects on tables and so forth well enough to be pretty sure that no pranks had been played with them. Mr and Mrs Simpson furthermore agreed that neither of them had given the duplicate key of the room to any person whatever during the day. Nor could Parkins, fair-minded man as he was, detect anything in the demeanour of master, mistress, or maid that indicated guilt. He was much more inclined to think that the boy had been imposing on the Colonel.

The latter was unwontedly silent and pensive at dinner and throughout the evening. When he bade good-night to Parkins, he murmured in a gruff undertone:

"You know where I am if you want me during the night."

"Why, yes, thank you, Colonel Wilson, I think I do; but there isn't much prospect of my disturbing you, I hope. By the way," he added, "did I show you that old whistle I spoke of? I think not. Well, here it is."

The Colonel turned it over gingerly in the light of the candle.

"Can you make anything of the inscription?" asked Parkins, as he took it back.

"No, not in this light. What do you mean to do with it?"

"Oh, well, when I get back to Cambridge I shall submit it to some of the archæologists there, and see what they think of it; and very likely, if they consider it worth having, I may present it to one of the museums."

"'M!" said the Colonel. "Well, you may be right. All I know is that, if it were mine, I should chuck it straight into the sea. It's no use talking, I'm well aware, but I expect that with you it's a case of live and learn. I hope so, I'm sure, and I wish you a good-night."

He turned away, leaving Parkins in act to speak at the bottom of the stair, and soon each was in his own bedroom.

By some unfortunate accident, there were neither blinds nor curtains to the windows of the Professor's room. The previous night he had thought little of this, but to-night there seemed every prospect of a bright moon rising to shine directly on his bed, and probably wake him later on. When he noticed this he was a good deal annoyed, but, with an ingenuity which I can only envy, he succeeded in rigging up, with the help of a railway-rug, some safety-pins, and a stick and umbrella, a screen which, if it only held together, would completely keep the moonlight off his bed. And shortly afterwards he was comfortably in that bed. When he had read a somewhat solid work long enough to produce a decided wish for sleep, he cast a drowsy glance round the room, blew out the candle, and fell back upon the pillow.

He must have slept soundly for an hour or more, when a sudden clatter shook him up in a most unwelcome manner. In a moment he realized what had happened: his carefully-constructed screen had given way, and a very bright frosty moon was shining directly on his face. This was highly annoying. Could he possibly get up and reconstruct the screen? or could he manage to sleep if he did not?

For some minutes he lay and pondered over the possibilities; then he turned over sharply, and with all his eyes open lay breathlessly listening. There had been a movement, he was sure, in the empty bed on the opposite side of the room. To-morrow he would have it moved, for there must be rats or something playing about in it. It was quiet now. No! the commotion began again. There was a rustling and shaking: surely more than any rat could cause.

I can figure to myself something of the Professor's bewilderment and horror, for I have in a dream thirty years back seen the same thing happen; but the reader will hardly, perhaps, imagine how dreadful it was to him to see a figure suddenly sit up in what he had known was an empty bed. He was out of his own bed in one bound, and made a dash towards the window, where lay his only weapon, the stick with which he had propped his screen. This was, as it turned out, the worst thing he could have done, because the personage in the empty bed, with a sudden smooth motion, slipped from the bed and took up a position, with outspread arms, between the two beds, and in front of the door. Parkins watched it in a horrid perplexity. Somehow, the idea of getting past it and escaping through the door was intolerable to him; he could not have borne – he didn't know why – to touch it; and as for its touching him, he would sooner dash himself through the window than have that happen. It stood for the moment in a band of dark shadow, and he had not seen what its face was like. Now it began to move, in a stooping posture, and all at once the spectator realized, with some horror and some relief, that it must be blind, for it seemed to feel about it with its muffled arms in a groping and random fashion. Turning half away from him, it became suddenly conscious of the bed he had just left, and darted towards it, and bent and felt over the pillows in a way which made Parkins shudder as he had never in his life thought it possible. In a very few moments it seemed to know that the bed was empty, and then, moving forward into the area of light and facing the window, it showed for the first time what manner of thing it was.

Parkins, who very much dislikes being questioned about it, did once describe something of it in my hearing, and I gathered that what he chiefly remembers about it is a horrible, an intensely horrible, face *of crumpled linen*. What expression he read upon it he could not or would not tell, but that the fear of it went nigh to maddening him is certain.

But he was not at leisure to watch it for long. With formidable quickness it moved into the middle of the room, and, as it groped and waved, one corner of its draperies swept across Parkins's face. He could not, though he knew how perilous a sound was – he could not keep back a cry of disgust, and this gave the searcher an instant clue. It leapt towards him upon the instant, and the next moment he was halfway through the window backwards, uttering cry upon cry at the utmost pitch of his voice, and the linen face was thrust close into his own. At this, almost the last possible second, deliverance came, as you will have guessed: the Colonel burst the door open, and was just in time to see the dreadful group at the window. When he reached the figures only one was left. Parkins sank forward into the room in a faint, and before him on the floor lay a tumbled heap of bed-clothes.

Colonel Wilson asked no questions, but busied himself keeping everyone else out of the room and in getting Parkins back to his bed; and himself, wrapped in a rug, occupied the other bed, for the rest of the night. Early on the next day Rogers arrived, more welcome than he would have been a day before, and the three of them held a very long consultation in the Professor's room. At the end of it the Colonel left the hotel door carrying a small object between his finger and thumb, which he cast as far into the sea as a very brawny arm could send it. Later on the smoke of a burning ascended from the back premises of the Globe.

Exactly what explanation was patched up for the staff and visitors at the hotel I must confess I do not recollect. The Professor was somehow cleared of the ready suspicion of delirium tremens, and the hotel of the reputation of a troubled house.

There is not much question as to what would have happened to Parkins if the Colonel had not intervened when he did. He would either have fallen out of the window or else lost his wits. But it is not so evident what more the creature that came in answer to the whistle could have done than frighten. There seemed to be absolutely nothing material about it save the bed-clothes of which it had made itself a body. The Colonel, who remembered a not very dissimilar occurrence in India, was of opinion that if Parkins had closed with it it could really have done very little, and that its one power was that of frightening. The whole thing, he said, served to confirm his opinion of the Church of Rome.

There is really nothing more to tell, but, as you may imagine, the Professor's views on certain points are less clear cut than they used to be. His nerves, too, have suffered: he cannot even now see a surplice hanging on a door quite unmoved, and the spectacle of a scarecrow in a field late on a winter afternoon has cost him more than one sleepless night.

The House at Treheale

A. C. Benson

Location: Grampound, Cornwall.
Time: October, 1903.
Eyewitness Description: *"Something seemed to rush up the stairs and past me; a strange, dull smell came from the passage: I know that there fell on me a sort of giddiness and horror, and I went back into the room with hands outstretched, like Elymas the sorcerer, seeking someone to guide me . . ."*

Author: Arthur Christopher Benson (1862–1925) was one of M. R. James' closest friends at Cambridge and like him wrote only a handful of ghost stories, notably "The House at Treheale" which he read at the Christmas gathering in 1903. One of three writing sons of E. W. Benson, an Archbishop of Canterbury, Arthur trained as a teacher and after a period as a housemaster at Eton moved to Cambridge in 1903 where he was later appointed Master of Magdalene College. A curiously nervous and melancholic man, he loved music and its use in this story of a musician whose personality is warped by his contact with the supernatural is also interesting because Benson composed the words for a number of songs including "Land of Hope and Glory" for Edward Elgar's *Pomp and Circumstance* march. It is known that he wrote a number of other ghost stories – several of which were read to his university friends – but the manuscripts disappeared after his death. Had they survived they would surely have enhanced his reputation as an equal of M. R. James.

It was five o'clock in the afternoon of an October day that Basil Netherby's letter arrived. I remember that my little clock had just given its warning click, when the footsteps came to my door; and just as the clock began to strike, came a hesitating knock. I called out, "Come in," and after some fumbling with the handle there stepped into the room I think the shyest clergyman I have ever seen. He shook hands like an automaton, looking over his left shoulder; he would not sit down, and yet looked about the room, as he stood, as if wondering why the ordinary civility of a chair was not offered him; he spoke in a husky voice, out of which he endeavoured at intervals to cast some viscous obstruction by loud hawkings; and when, after one of these interludes, he caught my eye, he went a sudden pink in the face.

However, the letter got handed to me; and I gradually learnt from my visitor's incoherent talk that it was from my friend Basil Netherby; and that he was well, remarkably well, quite a different man from what he had been when he came to Treheale; that he himself (Vyvyan was his name) was curate of St Sibby. Treheale was the name of the house where Mr Netherby lived. The letter had been most important, he thought, for Mr Netherby had asked him as he was going up to town to convey the letter himself and to deliver it without fail into Mr Ward's own hands. He could not, however, account (here he turned away from me, and hummed, and beat his fingers on the table) for the extraordinary condition in which he was compelled to hand it to me, as it had never, so far as he knew, left his own pocket; and presently with a gasp Mr Vyvyan was gone, refusing all proffers of entertainment, and falling briskly down – to judge from the sounds which came to me – outside my door.

I, Leonard Ward, was then living in rooms in a little street out of Holborn – a poor place enough. I was organist of St Bartholomew's, Holborn; and I was trying to do what is described as getting up a connection in the teaching line. But it was slow work, and I must confess that my prospects did not appear to me very cheerful. However, I taught one of the Vicar's little daughters, and a whole family, the children of a rich tradesman in a neighbouring street, the piano and singing, so that I contrived to struggle on.

Basil Netherby had been with me at the College of Music. His line was composing. He was a pleasant, retiring fellow, voluble enough and even rhetorical in tête-à-tête talk with an intimate; but dumb in company, with an odd streak of something – genius or eccentricity – about him which made him different from other men. We had drifted into an intimacy, and had indeed lodged together for some months. Netherby used to show me his works – mostly short studies – and though I used to think that they always rather oddly broke down in unexpected places, yet there was always an air of aiming high about them, an attempt to realize the ideal.

He left the College before I did, saying that he had learnt all he could learn and that now he must go quietly into the country somewhere and work all alone – he should do no good otherwise. I heard from him fitfully. He was in Wales, in Devonshire, in Cornwall; and then some three months before the day on which I got the letter, the correspondence had ceased altogether; I did not know his address, and was always expecting to hear from him.

I took up the letter from the place where Mr Vyvyan had laid it down; it was a bulky envelope; and it was certainly true that, as Mr Vyvyan had said, the packet was in an extraordinary condition. One of the corners was torn off, with a ragged edge that looked like the nibbling of mice, and there were disagreeable stains both on the front and the back, so that I should have inferred that Mr Vyvyan's pocket had been filled with raspberries – the theory, though improbable, did not appear impossible. But what surprised me most was that near each of the corners in front a rough cross of ink was drawn, and one at the back of the flap.

I had little doubt, however, that Mr Vyvyan had, in a nervous and absent mood, harried the poor letter into the condition in which I saw it, and that he had been unable to bring himself to confess to the maltreatment.

I tore the letter open – there fell out several pages of MS. music, and a letter in which Basil, dating from Treheale, and writing in a bold firm hand – bolder and firmer, I thought, than of old – said that he had been making a good deal of progress and working very hard (which must account for his silence), and he ventured to enclose some of his last work which he *hoped* I would like, but he wanted a candid opinion. He added that he had got quarters at a delightful farmhouse, not far from Grampound. That was all.

Stay! That was not all. The letter finished on the third side; but, as I closed it, I saw written on the fourth page, very small, in a weak loose hand, and as if scribbled in a ferocious haste, as a man might write (so it came oddly into my head) who was escaped for a moment from the vigilance of a careful gaoler, a single sentence. "Vyvyan will take this; and for God's sake, dear Leonard, if you would help a friend who is on the edge (I dare not say of what), come to me tomorrow, UNINVITED. You will think this very strange, but do not mind that – only come – *unannounced*, do you see . . ."

The line broke off in an unintelligible flourish. Then on each corner of the last page had been scrawled a cross, with the same ugly and slovenly haste as the crosses on the envelope.

My first thought was that Basil was mad; my next thought that he had drifted into some awkward situation, fallen under some unfortunate influence – was perhaps being blackmailed – and I knew his sensitive character well enough to feel sure that whatever the trouble was it would be exaggerated ten times over by his lively and apprehensive mind. Slowly a situation shaped itself. Basil was a man, as I knew, of an extraordinary austere standard of morals, singularly guileless, and innocent of worldly matters.

Someone, I augured, some unscrupulous woman, had, in the remote spot where he was living, taken a guileful fancy to my poor friend, and had doubtless, after veiled overtures, resolved on a bolder policy and was playing on his sensitive and timid nature by some threat of nameless disclosures, some vile and harrowing innuendo.

I read the letter again – and still more clear did it seem to me that he was in some strange durance, and suffering under abominable fears. I rose from my chair and went to find a time-table, that I might see when I could get to Grampound, when again a shuffling footstep drew to my door, an uncertain hand knocked at the panel, and Mr Vyvyan again entered the room. This time his confusion was even greater, if that were possible, than it had previously been. He had forgotten to give me a further message; and he thereupon gave me a filthy scrap of paper, nibbled and stained like the envelope, apologized with unnecessary vehemence, uttered a strangled cough and stumbled from the room.

It was difficult enough to decipher the paper, but I saw that a musical phrase had been written on it; and then in a moment I saw that it was a phrase from an old, extravagant work of Basil's own, a *Credo* which we had often discussed together, the grim and fantastic accompaniment of the sentence "He descended into hell."

This came to me as a message of even greater urgency, and I hesitated no longer. I sat down to write a note to the father of my family of pupils, in which I said that important business called me away for two or three days. I looked out a train, and found that by catching the 10 o'clock limited mail I could be at Grampound by 6 in the morning. I ordered a hasty dinner and I packed a few things into a bag, with an oppressive sense of haste. But, as generally happens on such occasions, I found that I had still two or three hours in hand; so I took up Netherby's music and read it through carefully.

Certainly he had improved wonderfully in handling; but what music it was! It was like nothing of which I had ever even dreamed.

There was a wild, intemperate voluptuousness about it, a kind of evil relish of beauty which gave me a painful thrill. To make sure that I was not mistaken, owing to the nervous tension which the strange event had produced in me, I put the things in my pocket and went out to the house of a friend, Dr Grierson, an accomplished and critical musician who lived not far away.

I found the great man at home smoking leisurely. He had a bird-like demeanour, like an ancient stork, as he sat blinking through spectacles astride of a long pointed nose. He had a slight acquaintance with Netherby, and when I mentioned that I had received some new music from him, which I wished to submit to him, he showed obvious interest. "A promising fellow," he said, "only of course too transcendental." He took the music in his hand; he settled his spectacles and read. Presently he looked up; and I saw in the kind of shamefaced glance with which he regarded me that he had found something of the same incomprehensible sensuality which had so oddly affected myself in the music. "Come, come," he said rather severely, "this is very strange stuff – this won't do at all, you know. We must just hear this!" He rose and went to his piano; and peering into the music, he played the pieces deliberately and critically.

Heard upon the piano, the accent of subtle evil that ran through the music became even more obvious. I seemed to struggle between two feelings – an over-powering admiration, and a sense of shame at my own capacity for admiring it. But the great man was still more moved. He broke off in the middle of a bar and tossed the music to me.

"This is filthy stuff," he said. "I should say to you – burn it. It is clever, of course – hideously, devilishly clever. Look at the progression – F sharp against F natural, you observe" (and he added some technical details with which I need not trouble my readers).

He went on: "But the man has no business to think of such things. I don't like it. Tell him from me that it won't do. There must be some reticence in art, you know – and there is none here. Tell Netherby that he is on the wrong tack altogether. Good heavens," he added, "how could the man write it? He used to be a decent sort of fellow."

It may seem extravagant to write thus of music, but I can only say that it affected me as nothing I had ever heard before. I put it away and we tried to talk of other things; but we could not get the stuff out of our heads. Presently I rose to go, and the Doctor reiterated his warnings still more emphatically. "The man is a criminal in art," he said, "and there must be an end once and for all of this: tell him it's abominable!"

I went back; caught my train; and was whirled sleepless and excited to the West. Towards morning I fell into a troubled sleep, in which I saw in tangled dreams the figure of a man running restlessly among stony hills. Over and over again the dream came to me; and it was with a grateful heart, though very weary, that I saw a pale light of dawn in the east, and the dark trees and copses along the line becoming more and more defined, by swift gradations, in the chilly autumn air.

It was very still and peaceful when we drew up at Grampound station. I enquired my way to Treheale; and I was told it was three or four miles away. The porter looked rather enquiringly at me; there was no chance of obtaining a vehicle, so I resolved to walk, hoping that I should be freshened by the morning air.

Presently a lane struck off from the main road, which led up a wooded valley, with a swift stream rushing along; in one or two places the chimney of a deserted mine with desolate rubbish-heaps stood beside the road. At one place a square church-tower, with pinnacles, looked solemnly over the wood. The road rose gradually. At last I came to a little hamlet, perched high up on the side of the valley. The scene was incomparably beautiful; the leaves were yellowing fast, and I could see a succession of wooded ridges, with a long line of moorland closing the view.

The little place was just waking into quiet activity. I found a bustling man taking down shutters from a general shop which was also the post-office, and enquired where Mr Netherby lived. The man told me that he was in lodgings at Treheale – "the big house itself, where Farmer Hall lives now; if you go straight along the road," he added, "you will pass the lodge, and Treheale lies up in the wood."

I was by this time very tired – it was now nearly seven – but I took up my bag again and walked along a road passing between high hedges. Presently the wood closed in again, and I saw a small plastered lodge with a thatched roof standing on the left among some firs. The gate stood wide open, and the road which led into the wood was grass-grown, though with deep ruts, along which heavy laden carts seemed to have passed recently.

The lodge seemed deserted, and I accordingly struck off into the wood. Presently the undergrowth grew thicker, and huge sprawling laurels rose in all directions. Then the track took a sudden turn; and I saw straight in front of me the front of a large Georgian house of brown stone, with a gravel sweep up to the door, but all overgrown with grass.

I confess that the house displeased me strangely. It was substantial, homely, and large; but the wood came up close to it on all sides, and it seemed to stare at me with its shuttered windows with a look of dumb resentment, like a great creature at bay.

I walked on, and saw that the smoke went up from a chimney to the left. The house, as I came closer, presented a front with a stone portico, crowned with a pediment. To left and right were two wings which were built out in advance from the main part of the house, throwing the door back into the shadow.

I pulled a large handle which hung beside the door, and a dismal bell rang somewhere in the house – rang on and on as if unable to cease; then footsteps came along the floor within, and the door was slowly and reluctantly unbarred.

There stood before me a little pale woman with a timid, downcast air. "Does Mr Netherby live here?" I said.

"Yes; he lodges here, sir."

"Can I see him?" I said.

"Well, sir, he is not up yet. Does he expect you?"

"Well, not exactly," I said, faltering; "but he will know my name – and I have come a long way to see him."

The woman raised her eyes and looked at me, and I was aware, by some swift intuition, that I was in the presence of a distressed spirit, labouring under some melancholy prepossession.

"Will you be here long?" she asked suddenly.

"No," I said; "but I shall have to stay the night, I think. I travelled all last night, and I am very tired; in fact I shall ask to sit down and wait till I can see Mr Netherby."

She seemed to consider a moment, and then led me into the house. We entered a fine hall, with stone flags and pillars on each side. There hung, so far as I could see in the half-light, grim and faded portraits on the walls, and there were some indistinct pieces of furniture, like couched beasts, in the corners. We went through a door and down a passage and turned into a large rather bare room, which showed, however, some signs of human habitation. There was a table laid for a meal.

An old piano stood in a corner, and there were a few books lying about; on the walls hung large pictures in tarnished frames. I put down my bag, and sat down by the fire in an old armchair, and almost instantly fell into a drowse. I have an indistinct idea of the woman returning to ask if I would like some breakfast, or wait for Mr Netherby. I said hastily that I would wait, being in the oppressed condition of drowsiness when one's only idea is to get a respite from the presence of any person, and fell again into a heavy sleep.

I woke suddenly with a start, conscious of a movement in the room. Basil Netherby was standing close beside me, with his back to the fire, looking down at me with a look which I can only say seemed to me to betoken a deep annoyance of spirit. But seeing me awake, there came on to his face a smile of a reluctant and diplomatic kind. I started to my feet, giddy and bewildered, and shook hands.

"My word," he said, "you sleep sound, Ward. So you've found me out? Well, I'm very glad to see you; but what made you think of coming? and why didn't you let me know? I would have sent something to meet you."

I was a good deal nettled at this ungenial address, after the trouble to which I had put myself. I said, "Well, really, Basil, I think that is rather strong. Mr Vyvyan called on me yesterday with a letter from you, and some music; and of course I came away at once."

"Of course," he said, looking on the ground – and then added rather hastily, "Now, how did the stuff strike you? I have improved, I think. And it is really very good of you to come off at once to criticize the music – *very* good of you," he said with some emphasis; "and, man, you look wretchedly tired – let us have breakfast."

I was just about to remonstrate, and to speak about the postscript, when he looked at me suddenly with so peculiar and disagreeable a glance that the words literally stuck in my throat. I thought to myself that perhaps the subject was too painful to enter upon at once, and that he probably wished to tell me at his own time what was in the background.

We breakfasted; and now that I had leisure to look at Basil, I was surprised beyond measure at the change in him. I had seen him last a pale, rather haggard youth, loose-limbed and untidy. I saw before me a strongly-built and firmly-knit man, with a ruddy colour and bronzed cheek. He looked the embodiment of health and well-being. His talk, too, after the first impression of surprise wore off, was extraordinarily cheerful and amusing. Again and again he broke out into loud laughter – not the laughter of an excited or hectic person, but the firm, brisk laugh of a man full to the brim of good spirits and health.

He talked of his work, of the country-people that surrounded him, whose peculiarities he seemed to have observed with much relish; he asked me, but without any appearance of interest, what I thought about his work. I tried to tell him what Dr Grierson had said and what I had felt; but I was conscious of being at a strange disadvantage before this genial personality. He laughed loudly at our criticisms. "Old Grierson," he said, "why, he is no better than a clergyman's widow: he would stop his ears if you read Shakespeare to him. My dear man, I have travelled a long way since I saw you last; I have found my tongue – and what is more, I can say what I mean, and as I mean it. Grierson indeed! I can see him looking shocked, like a pelican with a stomach-ache."

This was a felicitous though not a courteous description of our friend, but I could find no words to combat it; indeed, Basil's talk and whole bearing seemed to carry me away like a swift stream and in my wearied condition I found that I could not stand up to this radiant personality.

After breakfast he advised me to have a good sleep and he took me, with some show of solicitude, to a little bedroom which had been got ready for me. He unpacked my things and told me to undress and go to bed, that he had some work to do that he was anxious to finish, and that after luncheon we would have a stroll together.

I was too tired to resist, and fell at once into a deep sleep. I rose a new man; and finding no one in Basil's room, I strolled out for a moment on to the drive, and presently saw the odd and timid figure of Mrs Hall coming along, in a big white flapping sort of sun-bonnet, with a basket in her hand. She came straight up to me in a curious, resolute sort of way, and it came into my mind that she had come out for the very purpose of meeting me.

I praised the beauty of the place, and said that I supposed she knew it well. "Yes," she said; adding that she was born in the village and her mother had been as a girl a servant at Treheale. But she went on to tell me that she and her husband had lived till recently at a farm down in the valley, and had only been a year or so in the house itself. Old Mr Heale, the last owner, had died three or four years before, and it had proved impossible to let the house. It seemed that when the trustees gave up all idea of being able to get a tenant, they had offered it to the Halls at a nominal rent, to act as caretakers. She spoke in a cheerless way, with her eyes cast down and with the same strained look as of one carrying a heavy burden. "You will have heard of Mr Heale, perhaps?" she said with a sudden look at me.

"The old Squire, sir," she said; "but I think people here are unfair to him. He lived a wild life enough, but he was a kind gentleman in his way – and I have often thought it was not his fault altogether. He married soon after he came into the estate – a Miss Tregaskis from down to St Erne – and they were very happy for a little; but she died after they had been married a couple of years, and they had no child; and then I think Mr Heale went nearly mad – nothing went right after that. Mr Heale shut himself up a good deal among his books –

he was a very clever gentleman – and then he got into bad ways; but it was the sorrow in his heart that made him bad – and we must not blame people too much, must we?" She looked at me with rather a pitiful look.

"You mean," I said, "that he tried to forget his grief, and did not choose the best way to do it."

"Yes, sir," said Mrs Hall simply. "I think he blamed God for taking away what he loved, instead of trusting Him; and no good comes of that. The people here got to hate him – he used to spoil the young people, sir – you know what I mean – and they were afraid of seeing him about their houses. I remember, sir, as if it were yesterday, seeing him in the lane to St Sibby. He was marching along, very upright, with his white hair – it went white early – and he passed old Mr Miles, the church-warden, who had been a wild young man too, but he found religion with the Wesleyans, and after that was very hard on everyone.

"It was the first time they had met since Mr Miles had become serious; and Mr Heale stopped in his pleasant way, and held out his hand to Mr Miles; who put his hands behind him and said something – I was close to them – which I could not quite catch, but it was about fellowship with the works of darkness; and then Mr Miles turned and went on his way; and Mr Heale stood looking after him with a curious smile on his face – and I have pitied him ever since. Then he turned and saw me; he always took notice of me – I was a girl then; and he said to me,

" 'There, Mary, you see that. I am not good enough, it seems, for Mr Miles. Well, I don't blame him; but remember, child, that the religion which makes a man turn his back on an old friend is not a good religion"; but I could see he was distressed, though he spoke quietly – and as I went on he gave a sigh which somehow stays in my mind. Perhaps sir, you would like to look at his picture; he was painted at the same time as Mrs Heale in the first year of their marriage."

I said I should like to see it, and we turned to the house. She led me to a little room that seemed like a study. There was a big bookcase full of books, mostly of a scientific kind; and there was a large kneehole table much dotted with inkspots. "It was here," she said, "he used to work, hour after hour." On the wall hung a pair of pictures – one, that of a young woman, hardly more than a girl, with a delightful expression, both beautiful and good. She was dressed in some white material, and there was a glimpse of sunlit fields beyond.

Then I turned to the portrait of Mr Heale. It represented a young man in a claret-coloured coat, very slim and upright. It showed a face of great power, a big forehead, clear-cut features, and a determined chin, with extraordinarily bright large eyes; evidently the portrait of a man of great physical and mental force, who would do whatever he took in hand with all his might. It was very finely painted, with a dark background of woods against a stormy sky.

I was immensely struck by the picture; and not less by the fact that there was an extraordinary though indefinable likeness to Mrs Hall herself. I felt somehow that she perceived that I had noticed this, for she made as though to leave the room. I could not help the inference that I was compelled to draw. I lingered for a moment looking at the portrait, which was so lifelike as to give an almost painful sense of the presence of a third person in the room. But Mrs Hall went out, and I understood that I was meant to follow her.

She led the way into their own sitting-room, and then with some agitation she turned to me. "I understand that you are an old friend of Mr Netherby's, sir," she said.

"Yes," I said; "he is my greatest friend."

"Could you persuade him, sir, to leave this place?" she went on. "You will think it a strange thing to say – and I am glad enough to have a lodger, and I like Mr Netherby – but do you think it is a good thing for a young gentleman to live so much alone?"

I saw that nothing was to be gained by reticence, so I said, "Now, Mrs Hall, I think we had better speak plainly. I am, I confess, anxious about Mr Netherby. I don't mean that he is not well, for I have never seen him look better; but I think that there is something going on which I don't wholly understand."

She looked at me suddenly with a quick look, and then, as if deciding that I was to be trusted, she said in a low voice, "Yes, sir, that is it; this house is not like other houses. Mr Heale – how shall I say it? – was a very determined gentleman, and he used to say that he never would leave the house – and – you will think it very strange that I should speak thus to a stranger – I don't think he has left it."

We stood for a moment silent, and I knew that she had spoken the truth. While we thus stood, I can only say what I felt – I became aware that we were not alone; the sun was bright on the woods outside, the clock ticked peacefully in a corner, but there was something unseen all about us which lay very heavily on my mind. Mrs Hall put out her hands in a deprecating way, and then said in a low and hurried voice, "He would do no harm to me, sir – we are too near for that" – she looked up at me, and I nodded; "but I can't help it, can I, if he is different with other people? Now, Mr Hall is not like that, sir – he is a plain good man, and would think what I am saying no better than madness; but as sure as there is a God in Heaven, Mr Heale is here – and though he is too fine a gentleman to take advantage of my talk, yet he liked to command other people, and went his own way too much."

While she spoke, the sense of oppression which I had felt a moment before drew off all of a sudden; and it seemed again as though we were alone.

"Mrs Hall," I said, "you are a good woman; these things are very dark to me, and though I have heard of such things in stories, I never expected to meet them in the world. But I will try what I can do to get my friend away, though he is a wilful fellow, and I think he will go his own way too." While I spoke I heard Basil's voice outside calling me, and I took Mrs Hall's hand in my own. She pressed it, and gave me a very kind, sad look. And so I went out.

We lunched together, Basil and I, off simple fare; he pointed with an air of satisfaction to a score which he had brought into the room, written out with wonderful precision. "Just finished," he said, "and you shall hear it later on; but now we will go and look round the place. Was there ever such luck as to get a harbourage like this? I have been here two months and feel like staying for ever. The place is in Chancery. Old Heale of Treheale, the last of his stock – a rare old blackguard – died here. They tried to let the house, and failed, and put Farmer Hall in at last. The whole place belongs to a girl ten years old. It is a fine house – we will look at that tomorrow; but today we will walk round outside. By the way, how long can you stay?"

"I must get back on Friday at latest," I said. "I have a choir practice and a lesson on Saturday."

Basil looked at me with a good-natured smile. "A pretty poor business, isn't it?" he said. "I would rather pick oakum myself. Here I live in a fine house, for next to nothing, and write, write, write – there's a life for a man."

"Don't you find it lonely?" said I.

"Lonely?" said Basil, laughing loud. "Not a bit of it. What do I want with a pack of twaddlers all about me? I tread a path among the stars – and I have the best of company, too." He stopped and broke off suddenly.

"I shouldn't have thought Mrs Hall very enlivening company," I said. "By the way, what an odd-looking woman! She seems as if she were frightened."

At that innocent remark Basil looked at me suddenly with the same expression of indefinable anger that I had seen in his face at our first meeting; but he said nothing for a moment. Then he resumed: "No, I want no company but myself and my thoughts. I tell you, Ward, if you had done as I have done, opened a door into the very treasure-house of music, and had only just to step in and carry away as much as one can manage at a time, you wouldn't want company."

I could make no reply to this strange talk; and he presently took me out. I was astonished at the beauty of the place. The ground fell sharply at the back, and there was a terrace with a view over a little valley, with pasture-fields at the bottom, crowned with low woods – beyond, a wide prospect over uplands, which lost themselves in the haze. The day was still and clear; and we could hear the running of the stream below, the cooing of doves and the tinkling of a sheepbell. To the left of the house lay large stables and barns, which were in the possession of the farmer.

We wandered up and down by paths and lanes, sometimes through the yellowing woods, sometimes on open ground, the most perfect views bursting upon us on every side, everything lying in a rich still peace, which came upon my tired and bewildered mind like soft music.

In the course of our walk we suddenly came upon a churchyard surrounded by a low wall; at the farther end, beyond the graves, stood a small church consisting of two aisles, with a high perpendicular tower. "St Sibby," said Basil, "whether he or she I know not, but no doubt a very estimable person. You would like to look at this? The church is generally open."

We went up a gravel path and entered the porch; the door was open, and there was an odd, close smell in the building. It was a very plain place, with the remains of a rood-loft, and some ancient woodwork; but the walls were mildewed and green and the place looked neglected.

"Vyvyan is a good fellow," said Basil, looking round, "but he is single-handed here; the Rector is an invalid and lives at Penzance, and Vyvyan has a wretched stipend. Look here, Leonard; here is the old Heale vault." He led me into a little chapel near the tower, which opened on to the church by a single arch. The place was very dark; but I could see a monument or two of an ancient type and some brasses. There were a couple of helmets on iron supports and the remains of a mouldering banner. But just opposite to us was a tall modern marble monument on the wall. "That is old Heale's monument," said Basil, "with a long, pious inscription by the old rector. Just look at it – did you ever see such vandalism?"

I drew near – then I saw that the monument had been defaced in a

hideous and horrible way. There were deep dints in the marble, like
the marks of a hammer; and there were red stains over the inscription, which reminded me in a dreadful way of the stains on the letter
given me by Vyvyan.

"Good Heavens!" I said, "what inconceivable brutality! Who on
earth did this?"

"That's just what no one can find out," said Basil, smiling. "But
the inscription was rather too much, I confess – look at this: '*who
discharged in an exemplary way the duties of a landowner and a
Christian.*' Old Heale's idea of the duties of a landowner was to
screw as much as he could out of his farmers – and he had, moreover,
some old ideas, which we may call feudal, about his relations with
the more attractive of his tenants: he was a cheerful old boy – and as
to the Christian part of it, well, he had about as much of that, I
gather, as you take up on a two-pronged fork. Still, they might have
left the old man alone. I daresay he sleeps sound enough in spite of it
all." He stamped his foot on the pavement as he did so, which
returned a hollow sound. "Are you inside?" said Basil, laughingly;
"perhaps not at home?"

"Don't talk like that," I said to Basil, whose levity seemed to me
disgusting. "Certainly not, my boy," he said, "if you don't like it. I
daresay the old man can look after himself." And so we left the
church.

We returned home about four o'clock. Basil left me on the terrace
and went into the house to interview Mrs Hall on the subject of
dinner. I hung for a time over the balustrade, but, getting chilly and
still not feeling inclined to go in; I strolled to the farther end of the
terrace, which ran up to the wood. On reaching the end, I found a
stone seat; and behind it, between two yews, a little dark sinister path
led into the copse.

I do not know exactly what feeling it was which drew me to enter
upon the exploration of the place; the path was slippery and overgrown with moss, and the air of the shrubbery into which it led was
close and moist, full of the breath of rotting leaves. The path ran with
snakelike windings, so that at no point was it possible to see more
than a few feet ahead. Above, the close boughs held hands as if to
screen the path from the light. Then the path suddenly took a turn to
the left and went straight to the house.

Two yews flanked the way and a small flight of granite steps, slimy
and mildewed, led up to a little door in the corner of the house – a
door which had been painted brown, like the colour of the stone, and
which was let into its frame so as to be flush with the wall. The upper

part of it was pierced with a couple of apertures like eyes filled with glass to give light to the passage within. The steps had evidently not been trodden for many months, even years; but upon the door, near the keyhole, were odd marks looking as if scratched by the hoofs of some beast – a goat, I thought – as if the door had been impatiently struck by something awaiting entrance there.

I do not know what was the obsession which fell on me at the sight of this place. A cold dismay seemed to spring from the dark and clutch me; there are places which seem so soaked, as it were, in malign memories that they give out a kind of spiritual aroma of evil. I have seen in my life things which might naturally seem to produce in the mind associations of terror and gloom. I have seen men die; I have seen a man writhe in pain on the ground from a mortal injury; but I never experienced anything like the thrill of horror which passed through my shuddering mind at the sight of the little door with its dark eye-holes.

I went in chilly haste down the path and came out upon the terrace, looking out over the peaceful woods. The sun was now setting in the west among cloud-fiords and bays of rosy light. But the thought of the dark path lying like a snake among the thickets dwelt in my mind and poisoned all my senses.

Presently I heard the voice of Basil call me cheerfully from the corner of the house. We went in. A simple meal was spread for us, half tea, half dinner, to which we did full justice. But afterwards, though Basil was fuller than ever, so it seemed to me, of talk and laughter, I was seized with so extreme a fatigue that I drowsed off several times in the course of our talk, till at last he laughingly ordered me to bed.

I slept profoundly. When I awoke, it was bright day. My curtains had been drawn, and the materials for my toilette arranged while I still slept. I dressed hastily and hurried down, to find Basil awaiting me.

That morning we gave up to exploring the house. It was a fine old place, full from end to end of the evidences of long and ancestral habitation. The place was full of portraits. There was a great old dining-room – Basil had had the whole house unshuttered for my inspection – a couple of large drawing-rooms, long passages, bed-rooms, all full of ancient furniture and pictures, as if the family life had been suddenly suspended. I noticed that he did not take me to the study, but led me upstairs.

"This is my room," said Basil suddenly; and we turned into a big room in the lefthand corner of the garden-front. There was a big fourpost bedroom here, a large table in the window, a sofa, and some fine chairs. But what at once attracted my observation was a low door in the corner of the room, half hidden by a screen. It seemed to me, as if by a sudden gleam of perception, that this door must communicate with the door I had seen below; and presently, while I stood looking out of the great window upon the valley, I said to Basil, "And that door in the corner – does that communicate with the little door in the wood?"

When I said this, Basil was standing by the table, bending over some MSS. He suddenly turned to me and gave me a very long, penetrating look; and then, as if suddenly recollecting himself, said, "My dear Ward, you are a very observant fellow – yes, there is a little staircase there that goes down into the shrubbery and leads to the terrace. You remember that old Mr Heale of whom I told you – well, he had this room, and he had visitors at times whom I daresay it was not convenient to admit to the house; they came and went this way; and he too, no doubt, used the stairs to leave the house and return unseen."

"How curious!" I said. "I confess I should not care to have this room – I did not like the look of the shrubbery door."

"Well," said Basil, "I do not feel with you; to me it is rather agreeable to have the association of the room. He was a loose old fish, no doubt, but he lived his life, and I expect enjoyed it, and that is more than most of us can claim."

As he said the words he crossed the room, and opening the little door, he said, "Come and look down – it is a simple place enough."

I went across the room, and looking in, saw a small flight of stairs going down into the dark; at the end of which the two square panes of the little shrubbery door were outlined in the shadow.

I cannot account for what happened next; there was a sound in the passage, and something seemed to rush up the stairs and past me; a strange, dull smell came from the passage; I know that there fell on me a sort of giddiness and horror, and I went back into the room with hands outstretched, like Elymas the sorcerer, seeking someone to guide me. Looking up, I saw Basil regarding me with a baleful look and a strange smile on his face.

"What was that?" I said. "Surely something came up there . . . I don't know what it was."

There was a silence; then, "My dear Ward," said Basil, "you are behaving very oddly – one would think you had seen a ghost." He looked at me with a sort of gleeful triumph, like a man showing the advantages of a house or the beauties of a view to an astonished friend. But again I could find no words to express my sense of what I had experienced. Basil went swiftly to the door and shut it, and then said to me with a certain sternness, "Come, we have been here long enough – let us go on. I am afraid I am boring you."

We went downstairs; and the rest of the morning passed, so far as I can remember, in a species of fitful talk. I was endeavouring to recover from the events of the morning; and Basil – well, he seemed to me like a man who was fencing with some difficult question. Though his talk seemed spontaneous, I felt somehow that it was that of a weak antagonist endeavouring to parry the strokes of a persistent assailant.

After luncheon Basil proposed a walk again. We went out on a long ramble, as we had done the previous day; but I remember little of what passed. He directed upon me a stream of indifferent talk, but I laboured, I think, under a heavy depression of spirit, and my conversation was held up merely as it might have been as a shield against the insistent demands of my companion. Anyone who has been through a similar experience in which he wrestles with some tragic fact, and endeavours merely to meet and answer the sprightly suggestions of some cheerful companion, can imagine what I felt. At last the evening began to close in; we retraced our steps: Basil told me that we should dine at an early hour, and I was left alone in my own room.

I became the prey of the most distressing and poignant reflections. What I had experienced convinced me that there was something about the whole place that was uncanny and abnormal. The attitude of my companion, his very geniality, seemed to me to be forced and unnatural; and my only idea was to gain, if I could, some notion of how I should proceed. I felt that questions were useless, and I committed myself to the hands of Providence. I felt that here was a situation that I could not deal with and that I must leave it in stronger hands than my own. This reflection brought me some transitory comfort, and when I heard Basil's voice calling me to dinner, I felt that sooner or later the conflict would have to be fought out, and that I could not myself precipitate matters.

After dinner Basil for the first time showed some signs of fatigue, and after a little conversation he sank back in a chair, lit a cigar, and presently asked me to play something.

I went to the piano, still, I must confess, seeking for some possible opportunity of speech, and let my fingers stray as they moved along the keys. For a time I extemporized and then fell into some familiar music. I do not know whether the instinctive thought of what he had scrawled upon his note to me influenced me but I began to play Mendelssohn's anthem *Hear my prayer*. While I played the initial phrase, I became aware that some change was making itself felt in my companion; and I had hardly come to the end of the second phrase when a sound from Basil made me turn round.

I do not think that I ever received so painful a shock in my life as that which I experienced at the sight that met my eyes. Basil was still in the chair where he had seated himself, but instead of the robust personality which he had presented to me during our early interviews, I saw in a sudden flash the Basil that I knew, only infinitely more tired and haggard than I had known him in life. He was like a man who had cast aside a mask, and had suddenly appeared in his own part. He sat before me as I had often seen him sit, leaning forward in an intensity of emotion. I stopped suddenly wheeled round in my chair, and said, "Basil, tell me what has happened."

He looked at me, cast an agitated glance round the room – and then all on a sudden began to speak in a voice that was familiar to me of old.

What he said is hardly for me to recount. But he led me step by step through a story so dark in horrors that I can hardly bring myself to reproduce it here. Imagine an untainted spirit, entering cheerfully upon some simple entourage, finding himself little by little within the net of some overpowering influence of evil.

He told me that he had settled at Treheale in his normal frame of mind. That he had intended to tell me of his whereabouts, but that there had gradually stolen into his mind a sort of unholy influence. "At first," he said, "I resisted it," but it was accompanied by so extraordinary an access of mental power and vigour that he had accepted the conditions under which he found himself. I had better perhaps try to recount his own experience.

He had come to Grampound in the course of his wanderings and had enquired about lodgings. He had been referred to the farmer at Treheale. He had settled himself there, only congratulating himself upon the mixture of quiet and dignity which surrounded him. He had arranged his life for tranquil study, had chosen his rooms, and had made the best disposition he could of his affairs.

"The second night," he said, "that I was here, I had gone to bed thinking of nothing but my music. I had extinguished my light and was lying quietly in bed watching the expiring glimmer of the embers on my hearth. I was wondering, as one does, weaving all kinds of fancies about the house and the room in which I found myself, lying with my head on my hand, when I saw, to my intense astonishment, the little door in the corner of the bedroom half open and close again.

"I thought to myself that it was probably Mrs Hall coming to see whether I was comfortable, and I thereupon said, 'Who is there?' There was no sound in answer, but presently, a moment or two after, there followed a disagreeable laughter, I thought from the lower regions of the house in the direction of the corner. 'Come in, whoever you are,' I said; and in a moment the door opened and closed, and I became aware that there was someone in the room.

"Further than that," said Basil to me in that dreadful hour, "it is impossible to go. I can only say that I became aware in a moment of the existence of a world outside of and intertwined with our own; a world of far stronger influences and powers – how far-reaching I know not – but I know this, that all the mortal difficulties and dilemmas that I had hitherto been obliged to meet melted away in the face of a force to which I had hitherto been a stranger."

The dreadful recital ended about midnight; and the strange part was to me that our positions seemed in some fearful manner to have been now reversed. Basil was now the shrinking, timorous creature, who only could implore me not to leave him. It was in such a mood as this that he had written the letter. I asked him what there was to fear. "Everything," he said with a shocking look. He would not go to bed; he would not allow me to leave the room.

Step by step I unravelled the story, which his incoherent statement had only hinted at. His first emotion had been that of intense fright; but he became aware almost at once that the spirit who thus so unmistakably came to him was not inimical to him; the very features of the being – if such a word can be used about so shadowy a thing – appeared to wear a smile. Little by little the presence of the visitant had become habitual to Basil: there was a certain pride in his own fearlessness, which helped him.

Then there was intense and eager curiosity; "and then, too," said the unhappy man, "the influence began to affect me in other ways. I will not tell you how, but the very necessaries of life were provided for me in a manner which I should formerly have condemned with the utmost scorn, but which now I was given confidence to disregard. The dejection, the languorous reflections which used to hang about me, gradually drew off and left me cheerful, vigorous, and, I must say it, delighting in evil imaginations; but so subtle was the evil influence, that it was not into any gross corruption or flagrant deeds that I flung myself; it was into my music that the poison flowed.

"I do not, of course, mean that evil then appeared to me, as I can humbly say it does now, *as* evil, but rather as a vision of perfect beauty, glorifying every natural function and every corporeal desire. The springs of music rose clear and strong within me and with the fountain I mingled from my own stores the subtle venom of the corrupted mind. How glorious, I thought, to sway as with a magic wand the souls of men; to interpret for each all the eager and leaping desires which maybe he had dully and dutifully controlled. To make all things fair – for so potent were the whispers of the spirit that talked at my ear that I believed in my heart that all that was natural in man was also permissible and even beautiful, and that it was nothing but a fantastic asceticism that forbids it; though now I see, as I saw before, that the evil that thwarts mankind is but the slime of the pit out of which he is but gradually extricating himself."

"But what *is* the thing," I said, "of which you speak? Is it a spirit of evil, or a human spirit, or what?"

"Good God!" he said, "how can I tell?" and then with lifted hand he sang in a strange voice a bar or two from Stanford's *Revenge*.

"Was he devil or man? he was devil for aught they knew."

This dreadful interlude, the very flippancy of it, that might have moved my laughter at any other time, had upon me an indescribably sickening effect. I stared at Basil. He relapsed into a moody silence with clasped hands and knotted brow. To draw him away from the nether darkness of his thoughts, I asked him how and in what shape the spirit had made itself plain to him.

"Oh, no shape at all," said he; "he is *there*, that is enough. I seem sometimes to see a face, to catch the glance of an eye, to see a hand raised to warn or to encourage; but it is all impossibly remote; I could never explain to you *how* I see him."

"Do you see him now?" I asked.

"Yes," said Basil, "a long way off – and he is running swiftly to me, but he has far to go yet. He is angry; he threatens me; he beats the air with his hands."

"But *where* is this?" I asked, for Basil's eyes were upon the ground.

"Oh, for God's sake, man, be silent," said Basil. "It is in the region of which you and others know little; but it has been revealed to me. It lies all about us – it has its capes and shadowy peaks, and a leaden sea, full of sound; it is there that I ramble with him."

There fell a silence between us. Then I said, "But, dear Basil, I must ask you this – how was it that you wrote as you did to me?"

"Oh! he made me write," he said, "and I think he overreached himself – or my angel, that beholds the Father's face, smote him down. I was myself again on a sudden, the miserable and abject wretch whom you see before you, and knowing that I had been as a man in a dream. Then I wrote the despairing words, and guarded the letter so that he could not come near me; and then Mr Vyvyan's visit to me – that was not by chance. I gave him the letter and he promised to bear it faithfully – and what attempts were made to tear it from him I do not know; but that my adversary tried his best I do not doubt. But Vyvyan is a good man and could not be harmed.

"And then I fell back into the old spell; and worked still more abundantly and diligently and produced this – this accursed thing which shall not live to scatter evil abroad." As he said these words he rose, and tore the score that lay on the table into shreds and crammed the pieces in the fire. As he thrust the last pieces down, the poker he was holding fell from his hands.

I saw him white as a sheet, and trembling. "What is the matter?" I said.

He turned a terrible look on me, and said, "He is here – he has arrived."

Then all at once I was aware that there was a sort of darkness in the room; and then with a growing horror I gradually perceived that in and through the room there ran a thing like the front of a precipice, with some dark strand at its foot on which beat a surge of phantom waves. The two scenes struggled together. At one time I could plainly see the cliff-front, close beside me – and then the lamp and the firelit room was all dimmed even to vanishing; and then suddenly the room would come back and the cliff die into a steep shadow.

But in either of the scenes Basil and I were there – he standing irresolute and despairing, glancing from side to side like a hare when the hounds close in. And once he said – this was when the cliff loomed up suddenly – "There are others with him." Then in a moment it seemed as if the room in which we sat died away altogether and I was in that other place; there was a faint light as from under a stormy sky; and a little farther up the strand there stood a group of dark figures, which seemed to consult together.

All at once the group broke and came suddenly towards us. I do not know what to call them; they were human in a sense – that is, they walked upright and had heads and hands. But the faces were all blurred and fretted, like half-rotted skulls – but there was no sense of comparison in me. I only knew that I had seen ugliness and corruption at the very source, and looked into the darkness of the pit itself.

The forms eluded me and rushed upon Basil, who made a motion as though to seize hold of me, and then turned and fled, his arms outstretched, glancing behind him as he ran – and in a moment he was lost to view, though I could see along the shore of that formless sea something like a pursuit.

I do not know what happened after that. I think I tried to pray; but I presently became aware that I was myself menaced by danger. It seemed – but I speak in parables – as though one had separated himself from the rest and had returned to seek me. But all was over, I knew; and the figure indeed carried something which he swung and shook in his hand, which I thought was a token to be shown to me. And then I found my voice and cried out with all my strength to God to save me; and in a moment there was the fire-lit room again, and the lamp – the most peaceful-looking room in England.

But Basil had left me; the door was wide open; and in a moment the farmer and his wife came hurrying along with blanched faces to ask who it was that had cried out, and what had happened.

I made some pitiful excuse that I had dozed in my chair and had awoke crying out some unintelligible words. For in the quest I was about to engage in I did not wish that any mortal should be with me.

They left me, asking for Mr Netherby and still not satisfied. Indeed, Mrs Hall looked at me with so penetrating a look that I felt that she understood something of what had happened. And then at once I went up to Basil's room. I do not know where I found the courage to do it; but the courage came.

The room was dark, and a strong wind was blowing through it from the little door. I stepped across the room, feeling my way; went down the stairs, and finding the door open at the bottom, I went out into the snake-like path.

I went some yards along it; the moon had risen now. There came a sudden gap in the trees to the left, through which I could see the pale fields and the corner of the wood casting its black shadow on the ground.

The shrubs were torn, broken, and trampled, as though some heavy thing had crashed through. I made my way cautiously down, endowed with a more than human strength – it was a steep bank covered with trees – and then in a moment I saw Basil.

He lay some distance out in the field on his face. I knew at a glance that all was over; and when I lifted him I became aware that he was in some way strangely mangled, and indeed it was found afterwards that though the skin of his body was hardly contused, yet that almost every bone of the body was broken in fragments.

I managed to carry him to the house. I closed the doors of the staircase; and then I managed to tell Farmer Hall that Basil had had, I thought, a fall and was dead. And then my own strength failed me, and for three days and nights I lay in a kind of stupor.

When I recovered my consciousness, I found myself in bed in my own room. Mrs Hall nursed me with a motherly care and tenderness which moved me very greatly; but I could not speak of the matter to her, until, just before my departure, she came in, as she did twenty times a day, to see if I wanted anything. I made a great effort and said, "Mrs Hall, I am very sorry for you. This has been a terrible business, and I am afraid you won't easily forget it. You ought to leave the house, I think."

Mrs Hall turned her frozen gaze upon me, and said, "Yes, sir, indeed, I can't speak about it or think of it. I feel as if I might have prevented it; and yet I have been over and over it in my mind and I can't see where I was wrong. But my duty is to the house now, and I shall never leave it; but I will ask you, sir, to try and find a thought of pity in your heart for *him*" – I knew she did not mean Basil – "I don't think he clearly knows what he has done; he must have his will, as he always did. He stopped at nothing if it was for his pleasure; and he did not know what harm he did. But he is in God's hands; and though I cannot understand why, yet there are things in this life which He allows to be; and we must not try to be judges – we must try to be merciful. But I have not done what I could have done; and if God gives me strength, there shall be an end of this."

A few hours later Mr Vyvyan called to see me; he was a very different person to the Vyvyan that had showed himself to me in Holborn.

I could not talk much with him but I could see that he had some understanding of the case. He asked me no questions, but he told me a few details. He said that they had decided at the inquest that he had fallen from the terrace. But the doctor, who was attending me, seems to have said to Mr Vyvyan that a fall it must have been, but a fall of an almost inconceivable character. "And what is more," the old doctor had added, "the man was neither in pain nor agitation of mind when he died." The face was absolutely peaceful and tranquil; and the doctor's theory was that he had died from some sudden seizure before the fall.

And so I held my tongue. One thing I did: it was to have a little slab put over the body of my friend – a simple slab with name and date – and I ventured to add one line, because I have no doubt in my own mind that Basil was suddenly delivered, though not from death. He had, I supposed, gone too far upon the dark path, and he could not, I think, have freed himself from the spell; and so the cord was loosed, but loosed in mercy – and so I made them add the words:

"And in their hands they shall bear thee up."

I must add one further word. About a year after the events above recorded I received a letter from Mr Vyvyan, which I give without further comment.

St Sibby, Dec, 18, 189–.

"Dear Mr Ward,

"I wish to tell you that our friend Mrs Hall died a few days ago. She was a very good woman, one of the few that are chosen. I was much with her in her last days, and she told me a strange thing, which I cannot bring myself to repeat to you. But she sent you a message which she repeated several times, which she said you would understand. It is simply this: 'Tell Mr Ward I have prevailed.' I may add that I have no doubt of the truth of her words, and you will know to what I am alluding.

"The day after she died there was a fire at Treheale: Mr Hall was absolutely distracted with grief at the loss of his wife, and I do not know quite what happened. But it was impossible to save the house; all that is left of it is a mass of charred ruins, with a few walls standing up. Nothing was saved, not even a picture. There is a wholly inadequate insurance, and I believe it is not intended to rebuild the house.

"I hope you will bear us in mind; though I know you so little, I shall always feel that we have a common experience which will hold us together. You will try and visit us some day when the memory of what took place is less painful to you. The grass is now green on your poor friend's grave; and I will only add that you will have a warm welcome here. I am just moving into the Rectory, as my old Rector died a fortnight ago, and I have accepted the living. God bless you, dear Mr Ward.

"Yours very sincerely,
"James Vyvyan."

The Richpins

E. G. Swain

Location: Stoneground, East Anglia.

Time: December, 1912.

Eyewitness Description: *"Her information
was precise and her story perfectly coherent.
She preserved a maidenly reticence about his
trousers, if she had noticed them; but added
a new fact, and a terrible one, in her description of the eyeless
sockets. No wonder she had screamed . . ."*

Author: Edmund Gill Swain (1861–1938) was Chaplain at King's
College, Cambridge and like M. R. James drawn to the rich vein
of antiquarian and supernatural lore in East Anglia. In his
capacity as Reverend Canon and proctor at the University, he
had ample opportunity to study the ghostly tradition of the eerie
wastes of The Fens where several of his best stories are located.
"The Richpins" is set near Yarmouth and there are strong
similarities between this tale with its Napoleonic echoes and my
own "Peyton House Ghost," set in nearby Suffolk, which I wrote
about in the companion volume, *Haunted House Stories* (2005).
Swain read this gruesome little yarn at one of the Christmas
gatherings just before the outbreak of the First World War and
he dedicated his only collection of supernatural tales,
Stoneground Ghost Stories (1912), subtitled "From the
recollections of the Reverend Roland Batchel" to M. R. James,
"For Twenty Pleasant Years Mr Batchel's Friend and the
Indulgent Parent of Such Tastes as these Pages Indicate."

S omething of the general character of Stoneground and its people
has been indicated by stray allusions in the previous narratives.
We must here add that of its present population only a small part is
native, the remainder having been attracted during the recent pros-

perous days of brickmaking, from the nearer parts of East Anglia and
the Midlands. The visitor to Stoneground now finds little more than
the signs of an unlovely industry, and of the hasty and inadequate
housing of the people it has drawn together. Nothing in the place
pleases him more than the excellent train-service which makes it easy
to get away. He seldom desires a long acquaintance either with
Stoneground or its people.

The impression so made upon the average visitor is, however,
unjust, as first impressions often are. The few who have made further
acquaintance with Stoneground have soon learned to distinguish
between the permanent and the accidental features of the place, and
have been astonished by nothing so much as by the unexpected
evidence of French influence. Amongst the household treasures of the
old inhabitants are invariably found French knick-knacks: there are
pieces of French furniture in what is called "the room" of many
houses. A certain ten-acre field is called the "Frenchman's meadow."
Upon the voters' lists hanging at the church door are to be found
French names, often corrupted; and boys who run about the streets
can be heard shrieking to each other such names as Bunnum,
Dangibow, Planchey, and so on.

Mr Batchel himself is possessed of many curious little articles of
French handiwork – boxes deftly covered with split straws, arranged
ingeniously in patterns; models of the guillotine, built of carved meat-
bones, and various other pieces of handiwork, amongst them an
accurate road-map of the country between Stoneground and Yarmouth, drawn upon a fly-leaf torn from some book, and bearing
upon the other side the name of Jules Richepin. The latter had been
picked up, according to a pencilled-note written across one corner,
by a shepherd, in the year 1811.

The explanation of this French influence is simple enough. Within
five miles of Stoneground a large barracks had been erected for the
custody of French prisoners during the war with Bonaparte. Many
thousands were confined there during the years 1808–14. The
prisoners were allowed to sell what articles they could make in
the barracks; and many of them, upon their release, settled in the
neighbourhood, where their descendants remain. There is little
curiosity amongst these descendants about their origin. The events
of a century ago seem to them as remote as the Deluge, and as
immaterial. To Thomas Richpin, a weakly man who blew the organ
in church, Mr Batchel shewed the map. Richpin, with a broad, black-
haired skull and a narrow chin which grew a little pointed beard, had
always a foreign look about him: Mr Batchel thought it more than

possible that he might be descended from the owner of the book, and told him as much upon shewing him the fly-leaf. Thomas, however, was content to observe that "his name hadn't got no E," and shewed no further interest in the matter. His interest in it, before we have done with him, will have become very large.

For the growing boys of Stoneground, with whom he was on generally friendly terms, Mr Batchel formed certain clubs to provide them with occupation on winter evenings; and in these clubs, in the interests of peace and good-order, he spent a great deal of time. Sitting one December evening, in a large circle of boys who preferred the warmth of the fire to the more temperate atmosphere of the tables, he found Thomas Richpin the sole topic of conversation.

"We seen Mr Richpin in Frenchman's Meadow last night," said one.

"What time?" said Mr Batchel, whose function it was to act as a sort of fly-wheel, and to carry the conversation over dead points. He had received the information with some little surprise, because Frenchman's Meadow was an unusual place for Richpin to have been in, but his question had no further object than to encourage talk.

"Half-past nine," was the reply.

This made the question much more interesting. Mr Batchel, on the preceding evening, had taken advantage of a warmed church to practise upon the organ. He had played it from nine o'clock until ten, and Richpin had been all that time at the bellows.

"Are you sure it was half-past nine?" he asked.

"Yes," (we reproduce the answer exactly), "we come out o' night-school at quarter-past, and we was all goin' to the Wash to look if it was friz."

"And you saw Mr Richpin in Frenchman's Meadow?" said Mr Batchel.

"Yes. He was looking for something on the ground," added another boy.

"And his trousers was tore," said a third.

The story was clearly destined to stand in no need of corroboration.

"Did Mr Richpin speak to you?" enquired Mr Batchel.

"No, we run away afore he come to us," was the answer.

"Why?"

"Because we was frit."

"What frightened you?"

"Jim Lallement hauled a flint at him and hit him in the face, and he didn't take no notice, so we run away."

"Why?" repeated Mr Batchel.

"Because he never hollered nor looked at us, and it made us feel so funny."

"Did you go straight down to the Wash?"

They had all done so.

"What time was it when you reached home?"

They had all been at home by ten, before Richpin had left the church.

"Why do they call it Frenchman's Meadow?" asked another boy, evidently anxious to change the subject.

Mr Batchel replied that the meadow had probably belonged to a Frenchman whose name was not easy to say, and the conversation after this was soon in another channel. But, furnished as he was with an unmistakeable *alibi*, the story about Richpin and the torn trousers, and the flint, greatly puzzled him.

"Go straight home," he said, as the boys at last bade him good-night, "and let us have no more stone-throwing." They were reckless boys, and Richpin, who used little discretion in reporting their misdemeanours about the church, seemed to Mr Batchel to stand in real danger.

Frenchman's Meadow provided ten acres of excellent pasture, and the owners of two or three hard-worked horses were glad to pay three shillings a week for the privilege of turning them into it. One of these men came to Mr Batchel on the morning which followed the conversation at the club.

"I'm in a bit of a quandary about Tom Richpin," he began.

This was an opening that did not fail to command Mr Batchel's attention. "What is it?" he said.

"I had my mare in Frenchman's Meadow," replied the man, "and Sam Bower come and told me last night as he heard her gallopin' about when he was walking this side the hedge."

"But what about Richpin?" said Mr Batchel.

"Let me come to it," said the other. "My mare hasn't got no wind to gallop, so I up and went to see to her, and there she was sure enough, like a wild thing, and Tom Richpin walking across the meadow."

"Was he chasing her?" asked Mr Batchel, who felt the absurdity of the question as he put it.

"He was not," said the man, "but what he could have been doin' to put the mare into that state, I can't think."

"What was he doing when you saw him?" asked Mr Batchel.

"He was walking along looking for something he'd dropped, with his trousers all tore to ribbons, and while I was catchin' the mare, he made off."

"He was easy enough to find, I suppose?" said Mr Batchel.

"That's the quandary I was put in," said the man. "I took the mare home and gave her to my lad, and straight I went to Richpin's, and found Tom havin' his supper, with his trousers as good as new."

"You'd made a mistake," said Mr Batchel.

"But how come the mare to make it too?" said the other.

"What did you say to Richpin?" asked Mr Batchel.

"Tom," I says, "when did you come in? 'Six o'clock,' he says, 'I bin mendin' my boots'; and there, sure enough, was the hobbin' iron by his chair, and him in his stockin'-feet. I don't know what to do."

"Give the mare a rest," said Mr Batchel, "and say no more about it."

"I don't want to harm a pore creature like Richpin," said the man, "but a mare's a mare, especially where there's a family to bring up." The man consented, however, to abide by Mr Batchel's advice, and the interview ended. The evenings just then were light, and both the man and his mare had seen something for which Mr Batchel could not, at present, account. The worst way, however, of arriving at an explanation is to guess it. He was far too wise to let himself wander into the pleasant fields of conjecture, and had determined, even before the story of the mare had finished, upon the more prosaic path of investigation.

Mr Batchel, either from strength or indolence of mind, as the reader may be pleased to determine, did not allow matters even of this exciting kind, to disturb his daily round of duty. He was beginning to fear, after what he had heard of the Frenchman's Meadow, that he might find it necessary to preach a plain sermon upon the Witch of Endor, for he foresaw that there would soon be some ghostly talk in circulation. In small communities, like that of Stoneground, such talk arises upon very slight provocation, and here was nothing at all to check it. Richpin was a weak and timid man, whom no one would suspect, whilst an alternative remained open, of wandering about in the dark; and Mr Batchel knew that the alternative of an apparition, if once suggested, would meet with general acceptance, and this he wished, at all costs, to avoid. His own view of the matter he held in reserve, for the reasons already stated, but he could not help suspecting that there might be a better explanation of the name "Frenchman's Meadow" than he had given to the boys at their club.

50   E. G. SWAIN

Afternoons, with Mr Batchel, were always spent in making pastoral visits, and upon the day our story has reached he determined to include amongst them a call upon Richpin, and to submit him to a cautious cross-examination. It was evident that at least four persons, all perfectly familiar with his appearance, were under the impression that they had seen him in the meadow, and his own statement upon the matter would be at least worth hearing.

Richpin's home, however, was not the first one visited by Mr Batchel on that afternoon. His friendly relations with the boys has already been mentioned, and it may now be added that this friendship was but part of a generally keen sympathy with young people of all ages, and of both sexes. Parents knew much less than he did of the love affairs of their young people; and if he was not actually guilty of match-making, he was at least a very sympathetic observer of the process. When lovers had their little differences, or even their greater ones, it was Mr Batchel, in most cases, who adjusted them, and who suffered, if he failed, hardly less than the lovers themselves.

It was a negotiation of this kind which, on this particular day, had given precedence to another visit, and left Richpin until the later part of the afternoon. But the matter of the Frenchman's Meadow had, after all, not to wait for Richpin. Mr Batchel was calculating how long he should be in reaching it, when he found himself unexpectedly there. Selina Broughton had been a favourite of his from her childhood; she had been sufficiently good to please him, and naughty enough to attract and challenge him; and when at length she began to walk out with Bob Rockfort, who was another favourite, Mr Batchel rubbed his hands in satisfaction. Their present difference, which now brought him to the Broughtons' cottage, gave him but little anxiety. He had brought Bob half-way towards reconciliation, and had no doubt of his ability to lead Selina to the same place. They would finish the journey, happily enough, together.

But what has this to do with the Frenchman's Meadow? Much every way. The meadow was apt to be the rendezvous of such young people as desired a higher degree of privacy than that afforded by the public paths; and these two had gone there separately the night before, each to nurse a grievance against the other. They had been at opposite ends, as it chanced, of the field, and Bob, who believed himself to be alone there, had been awakened from his reverie by a sudden scream. He had at once run across the field, and found Selina sorely in need of him. Mr Batchel's work of reconciliation had been there and then anticipated, and Bob had taken the girl home in a condition of great excitement to her mother. All this was explained, in breathless sentences, by Mr Broughton, by way of accounting for the fact that Selina was then lying down in "the room".

There was no reason why Mr Batchel should not see her, of course, and he went in. His original errand had lapsed, but it was now replaced by one of greater interest. Evidently there was Selina's testimony to add to that of the other four; she was not a girl who would scream without good cause, and Mr Batchel felt that he knew how his question about the cause would be answered, when he came to the point of asking it.

He was not quite prepared for the form of her answer, which she gave without any hesitation. She had seen Mr Richpin "looking for his eyes". Mr Batchel saved for another occasion the amusement to be derived from the curiously illogical answer. He saw at once what had suggested it. Richpin had until recently had an atrocious squint, which an operation in London had completely cured. This operation, of which, of course, he knew nothing, he had described, in his own way, to anyone who would listen, and it was commonly believed that his eyes had ceased to be fixtures. It was plain, however, that Selina had seen very much what had been seen by the other four. Her information was precise, and her story perfectly coherent. She preserved a maidenly reticence about his trousers, if she had noticed them; but added a new fact, and a terrible one, in her description of the eyeless sockets. No wonder she had screamed. It will be observed that Mr Richpin was still searching, if not looking, for something upon the ground.

Mr Batchel now proceeded to make his remaining visit. Richpin lived in a little cottage by the church, of which cottage the Vicar was the indulgent landlord. Richpin's creditors were obliged to shew some indulgence, because his income was never regular and seldom sufficient. He got on in life by what is called "rubbing along", and appeared to do it with surprisingly little friction. The small duties about the church, assigned to him out of charity, were overpaid. He succeeded in attracting to himself all the available gifts of masculine clothing, of which he probably received enough and to sell, and he had somehow wooed and won a capable, if not very comely, wife, who supplemented his income by her own labour, and managed her house and husband to admiration.

Richpin, however, was not by any means a mere dependant upon charity. He was, in his way, a man of parts. All plants, for instance, were his friends, and he had inherited, or acquired, great skill with fruit-trees, which never failed to reward his treatment with abundant crops. The two or three vines, too, of the neighbourhood, he kept in fine order by methods of his own, whose merit was proved by their success. He had other skill, though of a less remunerative kind, in fashioning toys out of wood, cardboard, or paper; and every correctly behaving child in the parish had some such product of his handiwork. And besides all this, Richpin had a remarkable aptitude for making music. He could do something upon every musical instrument that came in his way, and, but for his voice, which was like that of the peahen, would have been a singer. It was his voice that had secured him the situation of organ-blower, as one remote from all incitement to join in the singing in church.

Like all men who have not wit enough to defend themselves by argument, Richpin had a plaintive manner. His way of resenting injury was to complain of it to the next person he met, and such complaints as he found no other means of discharging, he carried home to his wife, who treated his conversation just as she treated the singing of the canary, and other domestic sounds, being hardly conscious of it until it ceased.

The entrance of Mr Batchel, soon after his interview with Selina, found Richpin engaged in a loud and fluent oration. The fluency was achieved mainly by repetition, for the man had but small command of words, but it served none the less to shew the depth of his indignation.

"I aren't bin in Frenchman's Meadow, am I?" he was saying in appeal to his wife – this is the Stoneground way with auxiliary verbs – "What am I got to go there for?" He acknowledged Mr Batchel's entrance in no other way than by changing to the third person in his discourse, and he continued without pause – "if she'd let me out o' nights, I'm got better places to go to than Frenchman's Meadow. Let policeman stick to where I am bin, or else keep his mouth shut. What call is he got to say I'm bin where I aren't bin?"

From this, and much more to the same effect, it was clear that the matter of the meadow was being noised abroad, and even receiving official attention. Mr Batchel was well aware that no question he could put to Richpin, in his present state, would change the flow of his eloquence, and that he had already learned as much as he was likely to learn. He was content, therefore, to ascertain from Mrs Richpin that her husband had indeed spent all his evenings at home, with the single exception of the one hour during which Mr Batchel had employed him at the organ. Having ascertained this, he retired, and left Richpin to talk himself out.

No further doubt about the story was now possible. It was not twenty-four hours since Mr Batchel had heard it from the boys at the club, and it had already been confirmed by at least two unimpeachable witnesses. He thought the matter over, as he took his tea, and was chiefly concerned in Richpin's curious connexion with it. On his account, more than on any other, it had become necessary to make whatever investigation might be feasible, and Mr Batchel determined, of course, to make the next stage of it in the meadow itself.

The situation of "Frenchman's Meadow" made it more conspicuous than any other enclosure in the neighbourhood. It was upon the edge of what is locally known as "high land"; and though its elevation was not great, one could stand in the meadow and look sea-wards over many miles of flat country, once a waste of brackish water, now a great chess-board of fertile fields bounded by straight dykes of glistening water. The point of view derived another interest from looking down upon a long straight bank which disappeared into the horizon many miles away, and might have been taken for a great railway embankment of which no use had been made. It was, in fact, one of the great works of the Dutch Engineers in the time of Charles I, and it separated the river basin from a large drained area called the "Middle Level," some six feet below it. In this embankment, not two hundred yards below "Frenchman's Meadow", was one of the huge water gates which admitted traffic through a sluice, into the lower level, and the picturesque thatched cottage of the sluice-keeper formed a pleasing addition to the landscape. It was a view with which Mr Batchel was naturally very familiar. Few of his surroundings were pleasant to the eye, and this was about the only place to which he could take a visitor whom he desired to impress favourably. The way to the meadow lay through a short lane, and he could reach it in five minutes: he was frequently there.

It was, of course, his intention to be there again that evening: to spend the night there, if need be, rather than let anything escape him. He only hoped he should not find half the parish there also. His best hope of privacy lay in the inclemency of the weather; the day was growing colder, and there was a north-east wind, of which Frenchman's Meadow would receive the fine edge.

Mr Batchel spent the next three hours in dealing with some arrears of correspondence, and at nine o'clock put on his thickest coat and boots, and made his way to the meadow. It became evident, as he walked up the lane, that he was to have company. He heard many voices, and soon recognised the loudest amongst them. Jim Lallement was boasting of the accuracy of his aim: the others were not disputing it, but were asserting their own merits in discordant chorus. This was a nuisance, and to make matters worse, Mr Batchel heard steps behind him.

A voice soon bade him "Good evening." To Mr Batchel's great relief it proved to be the policeman, who soon overtook him. The conversation began on his side.

"Curious tricks, sir, these of Richpin's."

"What tricks?" asked Mr Batchel, with an air of innocence.

"Why, he's been walking about Frenchman's Meadow these three nights, frightening folk and what all."

"Richpin has been at home every night, and all night long," said Mr Batchel.

"I'm talking about where he was, not where he says he was," said the policeman. "You can't go behind the evidence."

"But Richpin has evidence too. I asked his wife."

"You know, sir, and none better, that wives have got to obey. Richpin wants to be took for a ghost, and we know that sort of ghost. Whenever we hear there's a ghost, we always know there's going to be turkeys missing."

"But there are real ghosts sometimes, surely?" said Mr Batchel.

"No," said the policeman, "me and my wife have both looked, and there's no such thing."

"Looked where?" enquired Mr Batchel.

"In the 'Police Duty' Catechism. There's lunatics, and deserters, and dead bodies, but no ghosts."

Mr Batchel accepted this as final. He had devised a way of ridding himself of all his company, and proceeded at once to carry it into effect. The two had by this time reached the group of boys.

"These are all stone-throwers," said he, loudly.

There was a clatter of stones as they dropped from the hands of the boys.

"These boys ought all to be in the club instead of roaming about here damaging property. Will you take them there, and see them safely in? If Richpin comes here, I will bring him to the station."

The policeman seemed well pleased with the suggestion. No doubt he had overstated his confidence in the definition of the "Police Duty". Mr Batchel, on his part, knew the boys well enough to be assured that they would keep the policeman occupied for the next half-hour, and as the party moved slowly away, felt proud of his diplomacy.

There was no sign of any other person about the field gate, which he climbed readily enough, and he was soon standing in the highest part of the meadow and peering into the darkness on every side.

It was possible to see a distance of about thirty yards; beyond that it was too dark to distinguish anything. Mr Batchel designed a zigzag course about the meadow, which would allow of his examining it systematically and as rapidly as possible, and along this course he began to walk briskly, looking straight before him as he went, and pausing to look well about him when he came to a turn. There were no beasts in the meadow – their owners had taken the precaution of removing them; their absence was, of course, of great advantage to Mr Batchel.

In about ten minutes he had finished his zig-zag path and arrived at the other corner of the meadow; he had seen nothing resembling a man. He then retraced his steps, and examined the field again, but arrived at his starting point, knowing no more than when he had left it. He began to fear the return of the policeman as he faced the wind and set upon a third journey.

The third journey, however, rewarded him. He had reached the end of his second traverse, and was looking about him at the angle between that and the next, when he distinctly saw what looked like Richpin crossing his circle of vision, and making straight for the sluice. There was no gate on that side of the field; the hedge, which seemed to present no obstacle to the other, delayed Mr Batchel considerably, and still retains some of his clothing, but he was not long through before he had again marked his man. It had every appearance of being Richpin. It went down the slope, crossed the plank that bridged the lock, and disappeared round the corner of the cottage, where the entrance lay.

Mr Batchel had had no opportunity of confirming the gruesome observation of Selina Broughton, but had seen enough to prove that the others had not been romancing. He was not a half-minute behind the figure as it crossed the plank over the lock – it was slow going in the darkness – and he followed it immediately round the corner of the house. As he expected, it had then disappeared.

Mr Batchel knocked at the door, and admitted himself, as his custom was. The sluice-keeper was in his kitchen, charring a gate post. He was surprised to see Mr Batchel at that hour, and his greeting took the form of a remark to that effect.

"I have been taking an evening walk," said Mr Batchel. "Have you seen Richpin lately?"

"I see him last Saturday week," replied the sluice-keeper, "not since."

"Do you feel lonely here at night?"

"No," replied the sluice-keeper, "people drop in at times. There was a man in on Monday, and another yesterday."

"Have you had no one today?" said Mr Batchel, coming to the point.

The answer showed that Mr Batchel had been the first to enter the door that day, and after a little general conversation he brought his visit to an end.

It was now ten o'clock. He looked in at Richpin's cottage, where he saw a light burning, as he passed. Richpin had tired himself early, and had been in bed since half-past eight. His wife was visibly annoyed at the rumours which had upset him, and Mr Batchel said such soothing words as he could command, before he left for home.

He congratulated himself, prematurely, as he sat before the fire in his study, that the day was at an end. It had been cold out of doors, and it was pleasant to think things over in the warmth of the cheerful fire his housekeeper never failed to leave for him. The reader will have no more difficulty than Mr Batchel had in accounting for the resemblance between Richpin and the man in the meadow. It was a mere question of family likeness. That the ancestor had been seen in the meadow at some former time might perhaps be inferred from its traditional name. The reason for his return, then and now, was a matter of mere conjecture, and Mr Batchel let it alone.

The next incident has, to some, appeared incredible, which only means, after all, that it has made demands upon their powers of imagination and found them bankrupt.

Critics of story-telling have used severe language about authors who avail themselves of the short-cut of coincidence. "That must be reserved, I suppose," said Mr Batchel, when he came to tell of Richpin, "for what really happens; and that fiction is a game which must be played according to the rules."

"I know," he went on to say, "that the chances were some millions to one against what happened that night, but if that makes it incredible, what is there left to believe?"

It was thereupon remarked by someone in the company, that the credible material would not be exhausted.

"I doubt whether anything happens," replied Mr Batchel in his dogmatic way, "without the chances being a million to one against it. Why did they choose such a word? What does 'happen' mean?"

There was no reply: it was clearly a rhetorical question.

"Is it incredible," he went on, "that I put into the plate last Sunday the very half-crown my uncle tipped me with in 1881, and that I spent next day?"

"Was that the one you put in?" was asked by several.

"How do I know?" replied Mr Batchel, "but if I knew the history of the half-crown I did put in, I know it would furnish still more remarkable coincidences."

All this talk arose out of the fact that at midnight on the eventful day, whilst Mr Batchel was still sitting by his study fire, he had news that the cottage at the sluice had been burnt down. The thatch had been dry; there was, as we know, a stiff east-wind, and an hour had sufficed to destroy all that was inflammable. The fire is still spoken of in Stoneground with great regret. There remains only one building in the place of sufficient merit to find its way on to a postcard.

It was just at midnight that the sluicekeeper rung at Mr Batchel's door. His errand required no apology. The man had found a night-fisherman to help him as soon as the fire began, and with two long sprits from a lighter they had made haste to tear down the thatch, and upon this had brought down, from under the ridge at the South end, the bones and some of the clothing of a man. Would Mr Batchel come down and see?

Mr Batchel put on his coat and returned to the place. The people whom the fire had collected had been kept on the further side of the water, and the space about the cottage was vacant. Near to the smouldering heap of ruin were the remains found under the thatch. The fingers of the right hand still firmly clutched a sheep bone which had been gnawed as a dog would gnaw it.

"Starved to death," said the sluice-keeper, "I see a tramp like that ten years ago."

They laid the bones decently in an outhouse, and turned the key, Mr Batchel carried home in his hand a metal cross, threaded upon a cord. He found an engraved figure of Our Lord on the face of it, and the name of Pierre Richepin upon the back. He went next day to make the matter known to the nearest Priest of the Roman Faith, with whom he left the cross. The remains, after a brief inquest, were interred in the cemetery, which the rites of the Church to which the man had evidently belonged.

Mr Batchel's deductions from the whole circumstances were curious, and left a great deal to be explained. It seemed as if Pierre Richepin had been disturbed by some premonition of the fire, but had not foreseen that his mortal remains would escape; that he could not return to his own people without the aid of his map, but had no perception of the interval that had elapsed since he had lost it. This map Mr Batchel put into his pocket-book next day when he went to Thomas Richpin for certain other information about his surviving relatives.

Richpin had a father, it appeared, living a few miles away in Jakesley Fen, and Mr Batchel concluded that he was worth a visit. He mounted his bicycle, therefore, and made his way to Jakesley that same afternoon.

Mr Richpin was working not far from home, and was soon brought in. He and his wife shewed great courtesy to their visitor, whom they knew well by repute. They had a well-ordered house, and with a natural and dignified hospitality, asked him to take tea with them. It was evident to Mr Batchel that there was a great gulf between the elder Richpin and his son; the former was the last of an old race, and the latter the first of a new. In spite of the Board of Education, the latter was vastly the worse.

The cottage contained some French kick-shaws which greatly facilitated the enquiries Mr Batchel had come to make. They proved to be family relics.

"My grandfather," said Mr Richpin, as they sat at tea, "was a prisoner – he and his brother."

"Your grandfather was Pierre Richepin?" asked Mr Batchel.

"No! Jules," was the reply. "Pierre got away."

"Shew Mr Batchel the book," said his wife.

The book was produced. It was a Book of Meditations, with the name of Jules Richepin upon the title-page. The fly-leaf was missing. Mr Batchel produced the map from his pocket-book. It fitted exactly. The slight indentures along the torn edge fell into their place, and Mr Batchel left the leaf in the book, to the great delight of the old couple, to whom he told no more of the story than he thought fit.

The Everlasting Club

Arthur Gray

Location: Jesus College, Cambridge.
Time: 2 November 1918.
Eyewitness Description: *"From ten o'clock to midnight a hideous uproar went on in the chamber of Bellasis. Who were his companions none knew. Blasphemous outcries and ribald songs, such as had not been heard for twenty years past, aroused from sleep or study the occupants of the court . . ."*
Author: Sir Arthur Gray (1852–1940) who wrote under the pseudonym "Ingulphus" for *The Cambridge Review, Chanticlere* and other literary periodicals of the early years of the 20th century, was the Master of Jesus College and another important figure in the "James Circle". He, too, was an antiquary, though his interests focused very much on his own college with its long, lurid and occasionally bloody history. The stories which he wrote under his pen-name were often given intriguing titles like "To Two Cambridge Magicians", "The Necromancer" and "The Burden of Dead Books". However, Sir Arthur's rich and mellifluous tones were apparently best heard at the Christmas gathering in 1918 when he presented the grisly story of "The Everlasting Club" – and, after reading it, one can only guess at the effect it might have had on the circle of men in James' candle-lit room. This tale, like several of the best works by "Ingulphus", was subsequently collected in a volume curiously entitled, *Tedious Brief Tales of Granta and Gramarye* (1919), now one of the rarest volumes of ghost stories from its period.

There is a chamber in Jesus College the existence of which is probably known to few who are now resident, and fewer still have penetrated into it or even seen its interior. It is on the right hand of the landing on the top floor of the precipitous staircase in the angle of the cloister next the Hall – a staircase which for some forgotten story connected with it is traditionally called "Cow Lane". The padlock which secures its massive oaken door is very rarely unfastened, for the room is bare and unfurnished. Once it served as a place of deposit for superfluous kitchen ware, but even that ignominious use has passed from it, and it is now left to undisturbed solitude and darkness. For I should say that it is entirely cut off from the light of the outer day by the walling up, some time in the eighteenth century, of its single window, and such light as ever reaches it comes from the door, when rare occasion causes it to be opened.

Yet at no extraordinarily remote day this chamber has evidently been tenanted, and, before it was given up to darkness, was comfortably fitted, according to the standard of comfort which was known in college in the days of George II. There is still a roomy fireplace before which legs have been stretched and wine and gossip have circulated in the days of wigs and brocade. For the room is spacious and, when it was lighted by the window looking eastward over the fields and common, it must have been a cheerful place for a sociable don.

Let me state in brief, prosaic outline the circumstances which account for the gloom and solitude in which this room has remained now for nearly a century and a half.

In the second quarter of the eighteenth century the University possessed a great variety of clubs of a social kind. There were clubs in college parlours and clubs in private rooms, or in inns and coffee-houses: clubs flavoured with politics, clubs clerical, clubs purporting to be learned and literary. Whatever their professed particularity, the aim of each was convivial. Some of them, which included undergraduates as well as seniors, were dissipated enough, and in their limited provincial way aped the profligacy of such clubs as the Hell Fire Club of London notoriety.

Among these last was one which was at once more select and of more evil fame than any of its fellows. By a singular accident, presently to be explained, the Minute Book of this Club, including the years from 1738 to 1766, came into the hands of a Master of Jesus College, and though, so far as I am aware, it is no longer extant, I have before me a transcript of it which, though it is in a recent handwriting, presents in a bald shape such a singular array of facts that I must ask you to accept them as veracious. The original book is described as a stout duodecimo volume bound in red leather and fastened with red silken strings. The writing in it occupied some 40 pages, and ended with the date 2 November 1766.

The Club in question was called the Everlasting Club – a name sufficiently explained by its rules, set forth in the pocket-book. Its number was limited to seven, and it would seem that its members were all young men, between 22 and 30. One of them was a Fellow-Commoner of Trinity: three of them were Fellows of Colleges, among whom I should specially mention a Fellow of Jesus, named Charles Bellasis: another was a landed proprietor in the county, and the sixth was a young Cambridge physician. The Founder and President of the Club was the Honourable Alan Dermot, who, as the son of an Irish peer, had obtained a nobleman's degree in the University, and lived in idleness in the town. Very little is known of his life and character, but that little is highly in his disfavour. He was killed in a duel at Paris in the year 1743, under circumstances which I need not particularise, but which point to an exceptional degree of cruelty and wickedness in the slain man.

I will quote from the first pages of the Minute Book some of the laws of the Club, which will explain its constitution:

"1. This Society consisteth of seven Everlastings, who may be Corporeal or Incorporeal, as Destiny shall determine.

2. The rules of the Society, as herein written, are immutable and Everlasting.

3. None shall hereafter be chosen into the Society and none shall cease to be members.

4. The Honourable Alan Dermot is the Everlasting President of the Society.

5. The Senior Corporeal Everlasting, not being the President, shall be the Secretary of the Society, and in this Book of Minutes shall record its transactions, the date at which any Everlasting shall cease to be Corporeal, and all fines due to the Society. And when such Senior Everlasting shall cease to be Corporeal he shall, either in person or by some sure hand, deliver this Book of Minutes to him who shall be next Senior and at the time Corporeal, and he shall in like manner record the transactions therein and transmit it to the next Senior. The neglect of these provisions shall be visited by the President with fine or punishment according to his discretion.

6. On the second day of November in every year, being the Feast of All Souls, at ten o'clock *post meridiem*, the Everlasting shall meet at supper in the place of residence of that Corporeal member of the Society to whom it shall fall in order of rotation to entertain them,

and they shall all subscribe in this Book of Minutes their names and present place of abode.

7. It shall be the obligation of every Everlasting to be present at the yearly entertainment of the Society, and none shall allege for excuse that he has not been invited thereto. If any Everlasting shall fail to attend the yearly meeting, or in his turn shall fail to provide entertainment for the Society, he shall be mulcted at the discretion of the President.

8. Nevertheless, if in any year, in the month of October and not less than seven days before the Feast of All Souls, the major part of the Society, that is to say, four at the least, shall meet and record in writing in these Minutes that it is their desire that no entertainment be given in that year, then, notwithstanding the two rules last rehearsed, there shall be no entertainment in that year, and no Everlasting shall be mulcted on the ground of his absence."

The rest of the rules are either too profane or too puerile to be quoted here. They indicate the extraordinary levity with which the members entered on their preposterous obligations. In particular, to the omission of any regulation as to the transmission of the Minute Book after the last Everlasting ceased to be "Corporeal," we owe the accident that it fell into the hands of one who was not a member of the society, and the consequent preservation of its contents to the present day.

Low as was the standard of morals in all classes of the University in the first half of the eighteenth century, the flagrant defiance of public decorum by the members of the Everlasting Society brought upon it the stern censure of the authorities, and after a few years it was practically dissolved and its members banished from the University. Charles Bellasis, for instance, was obliged to leave the college, and, though he retained his fellowship, he remained absent from it for nearly twenty years. But the minutes of the society reveal a more terrible reason for its virtual extinction.

Between the years 1738 and 1743 the minutes record many meetings of the Club, for it met on other occasions besides that of All Souls Day. Apart from a great deal of impious jocularity on the part of the writers, they are limited to the formal record of the attendance of the members, fines inflicted, and so forth. The meeting on 2 November in the latter year is the first about which there is any departure from the stereotyped forms. The supper was given in the house of the physician. One member, Henry Davenport, the former Fellow-Commoner of Trinity, was absent from the entertainment, as he was then serving in Germany, in the Dettingen campaign. The minutes contain an entry, "Mulctatus propter absentiam per Presidentem, Hen. Davenport." An entry on the next page of the book runs, "Henry Davenport by a Cannonshot became an Incorporeal Member, 3 November 1743."

The minutes give in their own handwriting, under date 2 November, the names and addresses of the six other members. First in the list, in a large bold hand, is the autograph of "Alan Dermot, President, at the Court of His Royal Highness." Now in October Dermot had certainly been in attendance on the Young Pretender at Paris, and doubtless the address which he gave was understood at the time by the other Everlastings to refer to the fact. But on October 28, five days *before* the meeting of the Club, he was killed, as I have already mentioned, in a duel. The news of his death cannot have reached Cambridge on 2 November, for the Secretary's record of it is placed below that of Davenport, and with the date 10 November: "this day was reported that the President was become an Incorporeal by the hands of a French chevalier." And in a sudden ebullition, which is in glaring contrast with his previous profanities, he has dashed down "The Good God shield us from ill."

The tidings of the President's death scattered the Everlastings like a thunderbolt. They left Cambridge and buried themselves in widely parted regions. But the Club did not cease to exist. The Secretary was still bound to his hateful records: the five survivors did not dare to neglect their fatal obligations. Horror of the presence of the President made the November gathering once and for ever impossible: but horror, too, forbade them to neglect the precaution of meeting in October of every year to put in writing their objection to the celebration. For five years five names are appended to that entry in the minutes, and that is all the business of the Club. Then another member died, who was not the Secretary.

For eighteen more years four miserable men met once each year to deliver the same formal protest. During those years we gather from the signatures that Charles Bellasis returned to Cambridge, now, to appearance, chastened and decorous. He occupied the rooms which I have described on the staircase in the corner of the cloister.

Then in 1766 comes a new handwriting and an altered minute: "27 Jan., on this day Francis Witherington, Secretary, became an Incorporeal Member. The same day this Book was delivered to me, James Harvey." Harvey lived only a month, and a similar entry on 7 March states that the book has descended, with the same mysterious celerity, to William Catherston. Then, on 18 May, Charles Bellasis writes that on that day, being the date of Catherston's decease, the

Minute Book has come to him as the last surviving Corporeal of the Club.

As it is my purpose to record fact only I shall not attempt to describe the feelings of the unhappy Secretary when he penned that fatal record. When Witherington died it must have come home to the three survivors that after twenty-three years' intermission the ghastly entertainment must be annually renewed, with the addition of fresh incorporeal guests, or that they must undergo the pitiless censure of the President. I think it likely that the terror of the alternative, coupled with the mysterious delivery of the Minute Book, was answerable for the speedy decease of the two first successors to the Secretaryship. Now that the alternative was offered to Bellasis alone, he was firmly resolved to bear the consequences, whatever they might be, of an infringement of the Club rules.

The graceless days of George II had passed away from the University. They were succeeded by times of outward respectability, when religion and morals were no longer publicly challenged. With Bellasis, too, the petulance of youth had passed: he was discreet, perhaps exemplary. The scandal of his early conduct was unknown to most of the new generation, condoned by the few survivors who had witnessed it.

On the night of 2 November 1766, a terrible event revived in the older inhabitants of the College the memory of those evil days. From ten o'clock to midnight a hideous uproar went on in the chamber of Bellasis. Who were his companions none knew. Blasphemous outcries and ribald songs, such as had not been heard for twenty years past, aroused from sleep or study the occupants of the court; but among the voices was not that of Bellasis. At twelve a sudden silence fell upon the cloisters. But the Master lay awake all night, troubled at the relapse of a respected colleague and the horrible example of libertinism set to his pupils.

In the morning all remained quiet about Bellasis' chamber. When his door was opened, soon after daybreak, the early light creeping through the drawn curtains revealed a strange scene. About the table were drawn seven chairs, but some of them had been overthrown, and the furniture was in chaotic disorder, as after some wild orgy. In the chair at the foot of the table sat the lifeless figure of the Secretary, his head bent over his folded arms, as though he would shield his eyes from some horrible sight. Before him on the table lay pen, ink and the red Minute Book. On the last inscribed page, under the date of 2 November, were written, for the first time since 1742, the autographs of the seven members of the Everlasting Club, but without address. In the same strong hand in which the President's name was written there was appended below the signatures the note, "Mulctatus per Presidentem propter neglectum obsonii, Car. Bellasis."

The Minute Book was secured by the Master of the College, and I believe that he alone was acquainted with the nature of its contents. The scandal reflected on the College by the circumstances revealed in it caused him to keep the knowledge rigidly to himself. But some suspicion of the nature of the occurrences must have percolated to students and servants, for there was a long-abiding belief in the College that annually on the night of 2 November sounds of unholy revelry were heard to issue from the chamber of Bellasis. I cannot learn that the occupants of the adjoining rooms have ever been disturbed by them. Indeed, it is plain from the minutes that owing to their improvident drafting no provision was made for the perpetuation of the All Souls entertainment after the last Everlasting ceased to be Corporeal. Such superstitious belief must be treated with contemptuous incredulity. But whether for that cause or another the rooms were shut up, and have remained tenantless from that day to this.

Number Seventy–Nine

A. N. L. Munby

Location: Red Lion Square, London.
Time: Autumn, 1935.
Eyewitness Description: *"I saw something else emerge from his room. At least I can't say that I saw it; I thought I discerned a shadowy figure come through the doorway, but apart from an impression of grey colouring I could not describe it"*
Author: Alan Noel Latimer Munby (1913–74) has been described as "the man who came closest to inheriting the mantle of M. R. James" by Mike Ashley. The son of an architect, he was educated at King's College, Cambridge, where his fascination with antiquarian books began, and he later became librarian of the college. Munby also became a leading figure in the antiquarian book trade and for many years was associated with the legendary dealer, Bernard Quaritch. He wrote several bibliographical studies as well as a number of stories featuring books and book dealers. "Number Seventy-Nine" combines Munby's interest in books and the supernatural and is written in an elegant and scholarly style reminiscent of his model. Curiously, Munby's subsequent collection of ghost stories, *The Alabaster Hand*, published in 1949, were largely written to pass the time away while he was a German POW at Eichstatt in Upper Franconia from 1943–5. This collection also acknowledged the author's debt to his inspiration with a dedication to M. R. James: *Collegii Nostri Olim Praepositi Huiusce Generis Fabularum Sine Aemulo Creatoris.*

"I'm sorry, sir, but number seventy-nine isn't available."
The bookseller's young assistant shook his head complacently as he pronounced the words. I was bitterly disappointed. It wasn't as

though I had wasted any time. The catalogue had reached my breakfast-table only half an hour before, and I had gulped down my coffee and made a beeline for Egerton's bookshop, an old firm whose premises were situated in one of the passages just off Red Lion Square. The item which had so aroused my interest was a manuscript of the mid-seventeenth century, dealing with the sombre subject of necromancy. From the cataloguer's description it seemed possible to me that it was a transcript of one of the lost manuscripts of Dr John Dee, the Elizabethan astrologer. If this were the case, the price of fifteen pounds was by no means excessive, and I had set my heart on securing the book. Hence my disappointment.

"Was it sold before the catalogue was sent out?" I asked.

The young man shook his head again.

"If it's been ordered but is still on the premises, perhaps I could see it?" I continued eagerly. The assistant seemed embarrassed.

"I am afraid it isn't available," he repeated evasively. "I can't tell you any more than that." Then his face lit up with relief.

"Ah, here is Mr Egerton coming in now," he said. "You'd better ask him about it."

I turned to greet the proprietor as he came through the shop door.

"What's all this mystery about number seventy-nine?" I said, waving my catalogue at him. "I gather it hasn't been sold yet. Can I have a look at it? Surely that's not much to ask, after all the years I've dealt with you."

The bookseller's usually genial face clouded over, and he hesitated before replying. Finally he said:

"Will you come upstairs to my room?"

I accompanied him through the shop and past the little cataloguer's room behind it, and we mounted the stairs together. I'd always liked the firm of Egerton. The bulk of their business was in legal books, but their catalogues usually had something in them of interest to me, and over a period of fifteen years I'd bought a number of books from them. Egerton himself had become quite a personal friend. We often met in the reading-room of the British Museum. We entered his room on the first floor lined with reference books, and he waved me into a chair.

"The manuscript you want to see has been destroyed," he said.

"I'm very sorry to hear that," I replied. "What an unfortunate accident!"

"It wasn't an accident," he said abruptly; "it was burned by – myself."

I looked at him. He was obviously upset and reluctant to discuss the matter, but why on earth a businessman like Egerton should have destroyed a book worth fifteen pounds was beyond my comprehension.

He realised that some explanation was due, but seemed to be undecided whether to give it to me. Finally he said:

"I'll tell you about it, if you like. In fact, it's rather more in your line than mine."

He paused, and I waited hopefully.

"You knew Merton?" he resumed.

"Your cataloguer?" I said. "Why, of course I know him – you've had him with you for years."

Merton was one of those enigmatic figures that one occasionally meets in the rare-book business – a man of considerable ability and apparently not the slightest ambition.

"I don't think I've ever told you his history," said Egerton. "He came down from Oxford in 1913, and got caught up in the war before he'd settled down to anything. He was badly shell-shocked in France, and when he got his discharge in 1918 he was a nervous wreck. He came to me temporarily while he was looking round for something to do, and stayed for twenty years. Of course he was eccentric, but extremely able. In fact, he was so eccentric that I tried never to let him deal with customers, but if he kept in his room behind the shop he did really excellent work. I think I can justifiably claim a very high standard for our catalogues, and this was due to Merton. Of course he was undeniably odd – he was normally moody, but sometimes he'd get fits of depression for weeks on end, during which he literally would hardly speak a word to a soul. He wasn't a very cheerful member of the firm, but his excellence at his job compensated for his other failings.

"About a year ago he came to me one morning and announced that he was engaged to be married. I was astounded, but also delighted for his sake. I felt that if anything could help him to overcome his moodiness and eccentricity, married life would do it for him. I congratulated him warmly and agreed to raise his salary. His fiancée came to the shop several times and he introduced her to me. She struck me as being just the sort of wife he needed – about twenty-five and obviously extremely capable and sensible. He was devoted to her and became a new man. I've never seen such a transformation as his. You would never have recognized him as the shy, tongue-tied recluse that he was before."

I shifted uneasily in my chair, wondering what all this had to do with the book I wanted. Egerton must have sensed my unspoken impatience, for he continued:

"Don't think that all this is irrelevant. You'll see soon how the manuscript fits into the story. But first I must tell you more about Merton.

"Four months ago his fiancée was killed – in a motoring accident. Naturally any man would be deeply upset in such circumstances, but you've no conception of the effect it had on Merton. All his past depression returned a hundred-fold accentuated. He'd sit in his room for hours on end with his head buried in his hands. He seemed to have lost all interest in life. I got seriously concerned about him, and tried to persuade him to see a doctor. I offered him a month's holiday by the sea, but he refused to take it. If he hadn't been such an old and tried member of the firm, I should really have had to consider getting rid of him.

"From a conversation I had with him at this time I learned that some quack medium had got hold of him and that he was attending séances. He asked me my view on spiritualism on one occasion, and from his remarks I gathered that he wasn't himself deriving much solace from it. The medium had, of course, promised that he should be put in touch with his dead fiancée, but the contact had still to be established. It was really pitiful to see a grown man taking such stuff seriously.

"Merton's state of mind was particularly unfortunate at this time, as I had bought a private library in Shropshire early in the summer. The catalogue I sent you last night represents only about half of it – I had hoped to have offered the whole collection for sale by now. I don't suppose Merton catalogued more than a third of the items. I did the rest; the boy down in the shop isn't up to such work yet. I expect you noticed a small section of occult books, of which number seventy-nine was one. Those were the only books in which Merton showed any interest – he spent hours on them, far more time than their value justified, but I didn't mind. I was so glad to see him at work again, and hoped it would be a prelude to returning to his normal output.

"One night about a week ago Merton came up to my room at closing time, and made me an offer of ten pounds for the manuscript. I was surprised at this – he wasn't a collector, and I knew that he couldn't afford it. I refused – rather brusquely, I'm afraid. When he had gone I had a good look at it. It was full of the usual cabbalistic mumbo-jumbo, the pentacle, the secrets of Solomon, and the like, but the section on necromancy, which comprised the bulk of the book, was much fuller than I've seen in other manuscripts of this class, and included a lot of the dog-Latin incantations and conjurations to be employed by the practitioner of the black art to invoke the spirits of the dead. I put it away in the safe and thought no more about it.

"The day before yesterday Merton asked me for the key of the safe at lunch-time. This was such a common occurrence that I gave it to him quite automatically, without asking him what he wanted. There are always a few good things in there awaiting cataloguing, and I assumed that he was going to make a start on one of them.

"Now, although we close at six o'clock, if I'm busy I'm very often on the premises until eight or even later. The boy goes off at six sharp, but Merton used to stay on for another half hour or so. I was always the last to leave. That evening I was hard at work trying to trace an obscure coat-of-arms on a German binding. I never could find my way about Rietstap. It was about half-past seven, and I assumed that Merton had gone home, although I usually heard the door when he let himself out. It was, of course, quite dark outside. Suddenly I heard a cry from downstairs. It was Merton's voice, and I don't think I've ever heard such a degree of fear infused into a single scream; it expressed the very essence of terror. I opened my door quickly and looked down over the bannisters into the well of the staircase. The switch is at the foot of the stairs and the light was off. I could hear him pulling the door handle of his room, and as I watched the door was flung open. His room too was in darkness so I got only a glimpse of what happened then; for the light coming over my shoulder from the open door behind me shone only halfway down the stairs. Merton ran through the shop, and I heard the bell ring as he opened the outer door. I was going to shout after him, when I saw something else emerge from his room. At least I can't say that I saw it; I thought I discerned a shadowy figure come through the doorway, but apart from an impression of grey colouring I could not describe it. But it wasn't what I saw that made me shudder, it was a smell – one that I had met only once before in my life, and that was forty years ago. When I was a boy, we had an exhumation in the village churchyard, and being an inquisitive child I crept up between the tombstones as the grave-diggers were raising the coffin. I only got a glimpse because the village policeman spotted me, and I got a clout on the side of the head for my pains. But I smelt a smell that I didn't meet again until it floated up the well of these stairs on the night before last – a dank, sickening, fœtid reek of rottenness and decay. I nearly fainted with revulsion. In a second I was back in my room with the door shut. I sat here for a few minutes, and then I thought of Merton and wondered what had become of him. I plucked up courage and went downstairs – the place was deserted and the shop door still open. I went outside and hurried down the passage towards Holborn. I remember thinking, as I did so, how quiet everything seemed. When I emerged into Holborn I discovered the reason. The traffic was stationary and in the middle of the road a group of people were gathered round a prone figure. I pushed my way through the crowd and saw that it was Merton. A policeman told me that he had run headlong from the passage straight under the wheels of a bus, and had been killed instantly.

"You can imagine how shaken I was when I came back to the shop. I went into Merton's room and there on his desk was that damned manuscript. From the place at which it was open and from some notes on his pad, it was obvious that the poor devil had been experimenting with one of the formulæ set out there. Something had occurred to frighten him out of his wits, and in his nervous state this wasn't perhaps surprising. I suppose that some obscure telepathy communicated his panic to me – at least I prefer to believe that than credit the implications of what I thought I sensed at the foot of the stairs. Anyhow, I was taking no chances, and before I went home I burned every particle of the manuscript and of Merton's notes. I'm sorry to disappoint you, but there it is. And although I've always found occult books a lucrative sideline, it's a class of literature that I shall be avoiding for the future."

2

Ghost Writers

The "Golden Era"

Playing With Fire

Sir Arthur Conan Doyle

Location: Badderly Gardens, Merton, Surrey.
Time: 14 April 1900.
Eyewitness Description: *"Then suddenly a
sound came out of the darkness – a low,
sibilant sound, the quick, thin breathing of a
woman. Quicker and thinner yet it came, as
between clenched teeth, to end in a loud gasp with a dull rustle
of cloth . . ."*

Author: Sir Arthur Conan Doyle (1859–1930), the creator of
Sherlock Holmes, gave the detective story genre one of its
enduring masterpieces, *The Hound of the Baskervilles*, just as
the 20th century dawned. The fame of the Great Detective has,
of course, overshadowed much of his other writing, in
particular his contribution to the modern ghost story. Doyle
had been fascinated by "ghosts, haunted houses, sepulchral
voices, materializations and mysterious sounds and lights since
his early days as a doctor," according to his biographer,
Hesketh Pearson, and he turned this fascination into a number
of short stories that featured scientific enquiry into the
supernatural, especially the new cult of spiritualism. "Playing
With Fire", was one of the first of these tales and it was to
inspire a number of similar tales by ghost story writers as well
as challenge other distinguished literary figures to tackle the
genre. Collectively, the stories by these luminaries helped to
create what is now regarded as a "Golden Era" of the ghost
story. This tale of a medium, Mrs Delamere, and *what* she
conjures up in a suburban house is told with Conan Doyle's
typical skill, added to which is the kind of detail only he as
someone who had been an actual eyewitness to séances could
possibly offer.

I cannot pretend to say what occurred on the 14th of April last at No. 17, Badderly Gardens. Put down in black and white, my surmise might seem too crude, too grotesque, for serious consideration. And yet that something did occur, and that it was of a nature which will leave its mark upon every one of us for the rest of our lives, is as certain as the unanimous testimony of five witnesses can make it. I will not enter into any argument or speculation. I will only give a plain statement, which will be submitted to John Moir, Harvey Deacon, and Mrs Delamere, and withheld from publication unless they are prepared to corroborate every detail. I cannot obtain the sanction of Paul Le Duc, for he appears to have left the country.

It was John Moir (the well-known senior partner of Moir, Moir, and Sanderson) who had originally turned our attention to occult subjects. He had, like many very hard and practical men of business, a mystic side to his nature, which had led him to the examination, and eventually to the acceptance, of those elusive phenomena which are grouped together with much that is foolish, and much that is fraudulent, under the common heading of spiritualism. His researches, which had begun with an open mind, ended unhappily in dogma, and he became as positive and fanatical as any other bigot. He represented in our little group the body of men who have turned these singular phenomena into a new religion.

Mrs Delamere, our medium, was his sister, the wife of Delamere, the rising sculptor. Our experience had shown us that to work on these subjects without a medium was as futile as for an astronomer to make observations without a telescope. On the other hand, the introduction of a paid medium was hateful to all of us. Was it not obvious that he or she would feel bound to return some result for money received, and that the temptation to fraud would be an overpowering one? No phenomena could be relied upon which were produced at a guinea an hour. But, fortunately, Moir had discovered that his sister was mediumistic – in other words, that she was a battery of that animal magnetic force which is the only form of energy which is subtle enough to be acted upon from the spiritual plane as well as from our own material one. Of course, when I say this, I do not mean to beg the question; but I am simply indicating the theories upon which we were ourselves, rightly or wrongly, explaining what we saw. The lady came, not altogether with the approval of her husband, and though she never gave indications of any very great psychic force, we were able, at least, to obtain those usual phenomena of message-tilting which are at the same time so puerile and so inexplicable. Every Sunday evening we met in Harvey Deacon's studio at Badderly Gardens, the next house to the corner of Merton Park Road.

Harvey Deacon's imaginative work in art would prepare anyone to find that he was an ardent lover of everything which was *outré* and sensational. A certain picturesqueness in the study of the occult had been the quality which had originally attracted him to it, but his attention was speedily arrested by some of those phenomena to which I have referred, and he was coming rapidly to the conclusion that what he had looked upon as an amusing romance and an after-dinner entertainment was really a very formidable reality. He is a man with a remarkably clear and logical brain – a true descendant of his ancestor, the well-known Scotch professor – and he represented in our small circle the critical element, the man who has no prejudices, is prepared to follow facts as far as he can see them, and refuses to theorize in advance of his data. His caution annoyed Moir as much as the latter's robust faith amused Deacon, but each in his own way was equally keen upon the matter.

And I? What am I to say that I represented? I was not the devotee. I was not the scientific critic. Perhaps the best that I can claim for myself is that I was the dilettante man about town, anxious to be in the swim of every fresh movement, thankful for any new sensation which would take me out of myself and open up fresh possibilities of existence. I am not an enthusiast myself, but I like the company of those who are. Moir's talk, which made me feel as if we had a private pass-key through the door of death, filled me with a vague contentment. The soothing atmosphere of the séance with the darkened lights was delightful to me. In a word, the thing amused me, and so I was there.

It was, as I have said, upon the 14th of April last that the very singular event which I am about to put upon record took place. I was the first of the men to arrive at the studio, but Mrs Delamere was already there, having had afternoon tea with Mrs Harvey Deacon. The two ladies and Deacon himself were standing in front of an unfinished picture of his upon the easel. I am not an expert in art, and I have never professed to understand what Harvey Deacon meant by his pictures; but I could see in this instance that it was all very clever and imaginative, fairies and animals and allegorical figures of all sorts. The ladies were loud in their praises, and indeed the colour effect was a remarkable one.

"What do you think of it, Markham?" he asked.

"Well, it's above me," said I. "These beasts – what are they?"

"Mythical monsters, imaginary creatures, heraldic emblems – a sort of weird, bizarre procession of them."

"With a white horse in front!"

"It's not a horse," said he, rather testily – which was surprising, for he was a very good-humoured fellow as a rule, and hardly ever took himself seriously.

"What is it, then?"

"Can't you see the horn in front? It's a unicorn. I told you they were heraldic beasts. Can't you recognize one?"

"Very sorry, Deacon," said I, for he really seemed to be annoyed. He laughed at his own irritation.

"Excuse me, Markham!" said he; "the fact is that I have had an awful job over the beast. All day I have been painting him in and painting him out, and trying to imagine what a real live, ramping unicorn would look like. At last I got him, as I hoped; so when you failed to recognise it, it took me on the raw."

"Why, of course it's a unicorn," said I, for he was evidently depressed at my obtuseness. "I can see the horn quite plainly, but I never saw a unicorn except beside the Royal Arms, and so I never thought of the creature. And these others are griffins and cockatrices, and dragons of sorts?"

"Yes, I had no difficulty with them. It was the unicorn which bothered me. However, there's an end of it until tomorrow." He turned the picture round upon the easel, and we all chatted about other subjects.

Moir was late that evening, and when he did arrive he brought with him, rather to our surprise, a small, stout Frenchman, whom he introduced as Monsieur Paul Le Duc. I say to our surprise, for we held a theory that any intrusion into our spiritual circle deranged the conditions, and introduced an element of suspicion. We knew that we could trust each other, but all our results were vitiated by the presence of an outsider. However, Moir soon reconciled us to the innovation. Monsieur Paul Le Duc was a famous student of occultism, a seer, a medium, and a mystic. He was travelling in England with a letter of introduction to Moir from the President of the Parisian brothers of the Rosy Cross. What more natural than that he should bring him to our little séance, or that we should feel honoured by his presence?

He was, as I have said, a small, stout man, undistinguished in appearance, with a broad, smooth, clean-shaven face, remarkable only for a pair of large, brown, velvety eyes, staring vaguely out in front of him. He was well dressed, with the manners of a gentleman, and his curious little turns of English speech set the ladies smiling. Mrs Deacon had a prejudice against our researches and left the room,

upon which we lowered the lights, as was our custom, and drew up
our chairs to the square mahogany table which stood in the centre of
the studio. The light was subdued, but sufficient to allow us to see
each other quite plainly. I remember that I could even observe the
curious, podgy little square-topped hands which the Frenchman laid
upon the table.

"What a fun!" said he. "It is many years since I have sat in this
fashion, and it is to me amusing. Madame is medium. Does madame
make the trance?"

"Well, hardly that," said Mrs Delamere. "But I am always conscious of extreme sleepiness."

"It is the first stage. Then you encourage it, and there comes the
trance. When the trance comes, then out jumps your little spirit and
in jumps another little spirit, and so you have direct talking or
writing. You leave your machine to be worked by another. *Hein?* But
what have unicorns to do with it?"

Harvey Deacon started in his chair. The Frenchman was moving
his head slowly round and staring into the shadows which draped the
walls.

"What a fun!" said he. "Always unicorns. Who has been thinking
so hard upon a subject so bizarre?"

"This is wonderful!" cried Deacon. "I have been trying to paint
one all day. But how could you know it?"

"You have been thinking of them in this room."

"Certainly."

"But thoughts are things, my friend. When you imagine a thing
you make a thing. You did not it, *hein?* But I can see your unicorns
because it is not only with my eye that I can see."

"Do you mean to say that I create a thing which has never existed
by merely thinking of it?"

"But certainly. It is the fact which lies under all other facts. That is
why an evil thought is also a danger."

"They are, I suppose, upon the astral plane?" said Moir.

"Ah, well, these are but words, my friends. They are there –
somewhere – everywhere – I cannot tell myself. I see them. I could
touch them."

"You could not make *us* see them."

"It is to materialise them. Hold! It is an experiment. But the power
is wanting. Let us see what power we have, and then arrange what
we shall do. May I place you as I wish?"

"You evidently know a great deal more about it than we do," said
Harvey Deacon; "I wish that you would take complete control."

"It may be that the conditions are not good. But we will try what we can do. Madame will sit where she is, I next, and this gentleman beside me. Meester Moir will sit next to madame, because it is well to have blacks and blondes in turn. So! And now with your permission I will turn the lights all out."

"What is the advantage of the dark?" I asked.

"Because the force with which we deal is a vibration of ether and so also is light. We have the wires all for ourselves now – *hein*? You will not be frightened in the darkness, madame? What a fun is such a séance!"

At first the darkness appeared to be absolutely pitchy, but in a few minutes our eyes became so far accustomed to it that we could just make out each other's presence – very dimly and vaguely, it is true. I could see nothing else in the room – only the black loom of the motionless figures. We were all taking the matter much more seriously than we had ever done before.

"You will place your hands in front. It is hopeless that we touch, since we are so few round so large a table. You will compose yourself, madame, and if sleep should come to you you will not fight against it. And now we sit in silence and we expect – *hein*?"

So we sat in silence and expected, staring out into the blackness in front of us. A clock ticked in the passage. A dog barked intermittently far away. Once or twice a cab rattled past in the street, and the gleam of its lamps through the chink in the curtains was a cheerful break in that gloomy vigil. I felt those physical symptoms with which previous séances had made me familiar – the coldness of the feet, the tingling in the hands, the glow of the palms, the feeling of a cold wind upon the back. Strange little shooting pains came in my forearms, especially as it seemed to me in my left one, which was nearest to our visitor – due no doubt to disturbance of the vascular system, but worthy of some attention all the same. At the same time I was conscious of a strained feeling of expectancy which was almost painful. From the rigid, absolute silence of my companions I gathered that their nerves were as tense as my own.

And then suddenly a sound came out of the darkness – a low, sibilant sound, the quick, thin breathing of a woman. Quicker and thinner yet it came, as between clenched teeth, to end in a loud gasp with a dull rustle of cloth.

"What's that? Is all right?" someone asked in the darkness.

"Yes, all is right," said the Frenchman. "It is madame. She is in her trance. Now, gentlemen, if you will wait quiet you will see something, I think, which will interest you much."

Still the ticking in the hall. Still the breathing, deeper and fuller now, from the medium. Still the occasional flash, more welcome than ever, of the passing lights of the hansoms. What a gap we were bridging, the half-raised veil of the eternal on the one side and the cabs of London on the other. The table was throbbing with a mighty pulse. It swayed steadily, rhythmically, with an easy swooping, scooping motion under our fingers. Sharp little raps and cracks came from its substance, file-firing, volley-firing, the sounds of a faggot burning briskly on a frosty night.

"There is much power," said the Frenchman. "See it on the table!"

I had thought it was some delusion of my own, but all could see it now. There was a greenish-yellow phosphorescent light – or I should say a luminous vapour rather than a light – which lay over the surface of the table. It rolled and wreathed and undulated in dim glimmering folds, turning and swirling like clouds of smoke. I could see the white, square-ended hands of the French medium in this baleful light.

"What a fun!" he cried. "It is splendid!"

"Shall we call the alphabet?" asked Moir.

"But no – for we can do much better," said our visitor.

"It is but a clumsy thing to tilt the table for every letter of the alphabet, and with such a medium as madame we should do better than that."

"Yes, you will do better," said a voice.

"Who was that? Who spoke? Was that you, Markham?"

"No, I did not speak."

"It was madame who spoke."

"But it was not her voice."

"Is that you, Mrs Delamere?"

"It is not the medium, but it is the power which uses the organs of the medium," said the strange, deep voice.

"Where is Mrs Delamere? It will not hurt her, I trust."

"The medium is happy in another plane of existence. She has taken my place, as I have taken hers."

"Who are you?"

"It cannot matter to you who I am. I am one who has lived as you are living, and who has died as you will die."

We had heard the creak and grate of a cab pulling up next door. There was an argument about the fare, and the cabman grumbled hoarsely down the street. The green-yellow cloud still swirled faintly over the table, dull elsewhere, but glowing into a dim luminosity in the direction of the medium. It seemed to be piling itself up in front of her. A sense of fear and cold struck into my heart. It seemed to me that lightly and flippantly we had approached the most real and august of sacraments, that communion with the dead of which the fathers of the Church had spoken.

"Don't you think we are going too far? Should we not break up this séance?" I cried.

But the others were all earnest to see the end of it. They laughed at my scruples.

"All the powers are made for use," said Harvey Deacon. "If we *can* do this, we *should* do this. Every new departure of knowledge has been called unlawful in its inception. It is right and proper that we should inquire into the nature of death."

"It is right and proper," said the voice.

"There, what more could you ask?" cried Moir, who was much excited. "Let us have a test. Will you give us a test that you are really there?"

"What test do you demand?"

"Well, now – I have some coins in my pocket. Will you tell me how many?"

"We come back in the hope of teaching and elevating, and not to guess childish riddles."

"Ha, ha, Meester Moir, you catch it that time," cried the Frenchman. "But surely this is very good sense what the Control is saying."

"It is a religion, not a game," said the cold, hard voice.

"Exactly – the very view I take of it," cried Moir. "I am sure I am very sorry if I have asked a foolish question. You will not tell me who you are?"

"What does it matter?"

"Have you been a spirit long?"

"Yes."

"How long?"

"We cannot reckon time as you do. Our conditions are different."

"Are you happy?"

"Yes."

"You would not wish to come back to life?"

"No – certainly not."

"Are you busy?"

"We could not be happy if we were not busy."

"What do you do?"

"I have said that the conditions are entirely different."

"Can you give us no idea of your work?"

"We labour for our own improvement and for the advancement of others."

"Do you like coming here tonight?"

"I am glad to come if I can do any good by coming."

"Then to do good is your object?"

"It is the object of all life on every plane."

"You see, Markham, that should answer your scruples." It did, for my doubts had passed and only interest remained.

"Have you pain in your life?" I asked.

"No; pain is a thing of the body."

"Have you mental pain?"

"Yes; one may always be sad or anxious."

"Do you meet the friends whom you have known on earth?"

"Some of them."

"Why only some of them?"

"Only those who are sympathetic."

"Do husbands meet wives?"

"Those who have truly loved."

"And the others?"

"They are nothing to each other."

"There must be a spiritual connection?"

"Of course."

"Is what we are doing right?"

"If done in the right spirit."

"What is the wrong spirit?"

"Curiosity and levity."

"May harm come of that?"

"Very serious harm."

"What sort of harm?"

"You may call up forces over which you have no control."

"Evil forces?"

"Undeveloped forces."

"You say they are dangerous. Dangerous to body or mind?"

"Sometimes to both."

There was a pause, and the blackness seemed to grow blacker still, while the yellow-green fog swirled and smoked upon the table.

"Any questions you would like to ask, Moir?" said Harvey Deacon.

"Only this – do you pray in your world?"

"One should pray in every world."

"Why?"

"Because it is the acknowledgment of forces outside ourselves."

"What religion do you hold over there?"

"We differ exactly as you do."

"You have no certain knowledge?"

"We have only faith."

"These questions of religion," said the Frenchman, "they are of interest to you serious English people, but they are not so much fun. It seems to me that with this power here we might be able to have some great experience – *hein*? Something of which we could talk."

"But nothing could be more interesting than this," said Moir.

"Well, if you think so, that is very well," the Frenchman answered, peevishly. "For my part, it seems to me that I have heard all this before, and that tonight I should weesh to try some experiment with all this force which is given to us. But if you have other questions, then ask them, and when you finish we can try something more."

But the spell was broken. We asked and asked, but the medium sat silent in her chair. Only her deep, regular breathing showed that she was there. The mist still swirled upon the table.

"You have disturbed the harmony. She will not answer."

"But we have learned already all that she can tell – *hein*? For my part I wish to see something that I have never seen before."

"What then?"

"You will let me try?"

"What would you do?"

"I have said to you that thoughts are things. Now I wish to *prove* it to you, and to show you that which is only a thought. Yes, yes, I can do it and you will see. Now I ask you only to sit still and say nothing, and keep ever your hands quiet upon the table."

The room was blacker and more silent than ever. The same feeling of apprehension which had lain heavily upon me at the beginning of the séance was back at my heart once more. The roots of my hair were tingling.

"It is working! It is working!" cried the Frenchman, and there was a crack in his voice as he spoke which told me that he also was strung to his tightest.

The luminous fog drifted slowly off the table, and wavered and flickered across the room. There in the farther and darkest corner it gathered and glowed, hardening down into a shining core – a strange, shifty, luminous, and yet non-illuminating patch of radiance, bright itself, but throwing no rays into the darkness. It had changed from a greenish-yellow to a dusky sullen red. Then round this centre there coiled a dark, smoky substance, thickening, hardening, growing denser and blacker. And then the light went out, smothered in that which had grown round it.

"It has gone."

"Hush – there's something in the room."

We heard it in the corner where the light had been, something which breathed deeply and fidgeted in the darkness.

"What is it? Le Duc, what have you done?"

"It is all right. No harm will come." The Frenchman's voice was treble with agitation.

"Good heavens, Moir, there's a large animal in the room. Here it is, close by my chair! Go away! Go away!"

It was Harvey Deacon's voice, and then came the sound of a blow upon some hard object. And then . . . And then . . . how can I tell you what happened then?

Some huge thing hurtled against us in the darkness, rearing, stamping, smashing, springing, snorting. The table was splintered. We were scattered in every direction. It clattered and scrambled amongst us, rushing with horrible energy from one corner of the room to another. We were all screaming with fear, grovelling upon our hands and knees to get away from it. Something trod upon my left hand, and I felt the bones splinter under the weight.

"A light! A light!" someone yelled.

"Moir, you have matches, matches!"

"No, I have none. Deacon, where are the matches? For God's sake, the matches!"

"I can't find them. Here, you Frenchman, stop it!"

"It is beyond me. Oh, *mon Dieu*, I cannot stop it. The door! Where is the door?"

My hand, by good luck, lit upon the handle as I groped about in the darkness. The hard-breathing, snorting, rushing creature tore past me and butted with a fearful crash against the oaken partition. The instant that it had passed I turned the handle, and next moment we were all outside, and the door shut behind us. From within came a horrible crashing and rending and stamping.

"What is it? In Heaven's name, what is it?"

"A horse. I saw it when the door opened. But Mrs Delamere –?"

"We must fetch her out. Come on, Markham; the longer we wait the less we shall like it."

He flung open the door and we rushed in. She was there on the ground amidst the splinters of her chair. We seized her and dragged her swiftly out, and as we gained the door I looked over my shoulder into the darkness. There were two strange eyes glowing at us; a rattle of hoofs, and I had just time to slam the door when there came a crash upon it which split it from top to bottom.

"It's coming through! It's coming!"

"Run, run for your lives!" cried the Frenchman.

Another crash, and something shot through the riven door. It was a long white spike, gleaming in the lamp-light. For a moment it shone before us, and then with a snap it disappeared again.

"Quick! Quick! This way!" Harvey Deacon shouted. "Carry her in! Here! Quick!"

We had taken refuge in the dining-room, and shut the heavy oak door. We laid the senseless woman upon the sofa, and as we did so, Moir, the hard man of business, drooped and fainted across the hearthrug. Harvey Deacon was as white as a corpse, jerking and twitching like an epileptic. With a crash we heard the studio door fly to pieces, and the snorting and stamping were in the passage, up and down, up and down, shaking the house with their fury. The Frenchman had sunk his face on his hands, and sobbed like a frightened child.

"What shall we do?" I shook him roughly by the shoulder. "Is a gun any use?"

"No, no. The power will pass. Then it will end."

"You might have killed us all – you unspeakable fool – with your infernal experiments."

"I did not know. How could I tell that it would be frightened? It is mad with terror. It was his fault. He struck it."

Harvey Deacon sprang up. "Good heavens!" he cried.

A terrible scream sounded through the house.

"It's my wife! Here, I'm going out. If it's the Evil One himself I am going out!"

He had thrown open the door and rushed out into the passage. At the end of it, at the foot of the stairs, Mrs Deacon was lying senseless, struck down by the sight which she had seen. But there was nothing else.

With eyes of horror we looked about us, but all was perfectly quiet and still. I approached the black square of the studio door, expecting with every slow step that some atrocious shape would hurl itself out of it. But nothing came, and all was silent inside the room. Peeping and peering, our hearts in our mouths, we came to the very threshold, and stared into the darkness. There was still no sound, but in one direction there was also no darkness. A luminous glowing cloud, with incandescent centre, hovered in the corner of the room. Slowly it dimmed and faded, growing thinner and fainter, until at last the same dense, velvety blackness filled the whole studio. And with the last flickering gleam of that baleful light the Frenchman broke into a shout of joy.

"What a fun!" he cried. "No one is hurt, and only the door broken, and the ladies frightened. But, my friends, we have done what has never been done before."

"And as far as I can help," said Harvey Deacon, "it will certainly never be before again."

And that was what befell on the 14th of April last at No. 17 Badderly Gardens. I began by saying that it would seem too grotesque to dogmatise as to what it was which actually did occur; but I give my impressions, *our* impressions (since they are corroborated by Harvey Deacon and John Moir), for what they are worth. You may, if it pleases you, imagine that we were the victims of an elaborate and extraordinary hoax. Or you may think with us that we underwent a very real and a very terrible experience. Or perhaps you may know more than we do of such occult matters, and can inform us of some similar occurrence. In this latter case a letter to William Markham, 146M, The Albany, would help to throw a light upon that which is very dark to us.

The House Surgeon

Rudyard Kipling

Location: Holmescroft, Sussex.
Time: April, 1909.
Eyewitness Description: *"I had no theory to
go on, except a vague idea that I had come
between two poles of discharge and had
taken a shock meant for someone else. I
waited cautiously on myself, expecting to be overtaken by
horror and the supernatural . . ."*
Author: Joseph Rudyard Kipling (1865–1936) was born in
Bombay and undoubtedly heard his first ghost stories there
while still a child. His years as a journalist on the Indian
national paper, the *Pioneer*, helped him to gather the material
for his classic works, the two *Jungle Books* (1894–5) and the
Just So Stories (1902). It was after his return to England as a
feted author, that Kipling wrote his little series of supernatural
stories including "The House Surgeon" in which several
influences are noticeable. It has been suggested that the haunted
house may have been based on Rock House near Torquay
"which mysteriously depressed him, but nine years later
produced his best psychic story", according to his biographer,
Angus Wilson; or alternately could have been his later Sussex
home, Bateman's, which was known to have caused "psychic
discomforts" to some visitors. A less debateable influence was
Sir Arthur Conan Doyle who lived close by. "The House
Surgeon" is obviously a psychic detective story in the Doyle
style and apart from the references to the Great Detective and
his companion, Dr Watson, Kipling even names the haunted
house at the centre of the story after his hero.

On an evening after Easter Day, I sat at a table in a homeward bound steamer's smoking-room, where half a dozen of us told ghost stories. As our party broke up, a man, playing Patience in the next alcove, said to me: "I didn't quite catch the end of that last story about the Curse on the family's first-born."

"It turned out to be drains," I explained. "As soon as new ones were put into the house the Curse was lifted, I believe. I never knew the people myself."

"Ah! I've had *my* drains up twice; I'm on gravel too."

"You don't mean to say you've a ghost in your house? Why didn't you join our party?"

"Any more orders, gentlemen, before the bar closes?" the steward interrupted.

"Sit down again and have one with me," said the Patience player. "No, it isn't a ghost. Our trouble is more depression than anything else."

"How interesting! Then it's nothing any one can see?"

"It's – it's nothing worse than a little depression. And the odd part is that there hasn't been a death in the house since it was built – in 1863. The lawyer said so. That decided me – my good lady, rather – and he made me pay an extra thousand for it."

"How curious. Unusual, too!" I said.

"Yes, ain't it? It was built for three sisters – Moultrie was the name – three old maids. They all lived together; the eldest owned it. I bought it from her lawyer a few years ago, and if I've spent a pound on the place first and last, I must have spent five thousand. Electric light, new servants' wing, garden – all that sort of thing. A man and his family ought to be happy after so much expense, ain't it?" He looked at me through the bottom of his glass.

"Does it affect your family much?"

"My good lady – she's a Greek by the way – and myself are middle-aged. We can bear up against depression; but it's hard on my little girl. I say little; but she's twenty. We send her visiting to escape it. She almost lived at hotels and hydros last year, but that isn't pleasant for her. She used to be a canary – a perfect canary – always singing. You ought to hear her. She doesn't sing now. That sort of thing's unwholesome for the young, ain't it?"

"Can't you get rid of the place?" I suggested.

"Not except at a sacrifice, and we are fond of it. Just suits us three. We'd love it if we were allowed."

"What do you mean by not being allowed?"

"I mean because of the depression. It spoils everything."

"What's it like exactly?"

"I couldn't very well explain. It must be seen to be appreciated, as the auctioneers say. Now, I was much impressed by the story you were telling just now."

"It wasn't true," I said.

"My tale is true. If you would do me the pleasure to come down and spend a night at my little place, you'd learn more than you would if I talked till morning. Very likely 'twouldn't touch your good self at all. You might be – immune, ain't it? On the other hand, if this influenza-influence *does* happen to affect you, why, I think it will be an experience."

While he talked he gave me his card, and I read his name was L. Maxwell M'Leod, Esq., of Holmescroft. A City address was tucked away in a corner.

"My business," he added, "used to be furs. If you are interested in furs – I've given thirty years of my life to 'em."

"You're very kind," I murmured.

"Far from it, I assure you. I can meet you next Saturday afternoon anywhere in London you choose to name, and I'll be only too happy to motor you down. It ought to be a delightful run at this time of year – the rhododendrons will be out. I mean it. You don't know how truly I mean it. Very probably – it won't affect you at all. And – I think I may say I have the finest collection of narwhal tusks in the world. All the best skins and horns have to go through London, and L. Maxwell M'Leod, he knows where they come from, and where they go to. That's his business."

For the rest of the voyage up-channel Mr M'Leod talked to me of the assembling, preparation, and sale of the rarer furs; and told me things about the manufacture of fur-lined coats which quite shocked me. Somehow or other, when we landed on Wednesday, I found myself pledged to spend that weekend with him at Holmescroft.

On Saturday he met me with a well-groomed motor, and ran me out in an hour-and-a-half to an exclusive residential district of dustless roads and elegantly designed country villas, each standing in from three to five acres of perfectly appointed land. He told me land was selling at eight hundred pounds the acre, and the new golf links, whose Queen Anne pavilion we passed, had cost nearly twenty-four thousand pounds to create.

Holmescroft was a large, two-storied, low, creeper-covered residence. A verandah at the south side gave on to a garden and two tennis courts, separated by a tasteful iron fence from a most park-like meadow of five or six acres, where two Jersey cows grazed. Tea was ready in the shade of a promising copper beech, and I could see groups on the lawn of young men and maidens appropriately clothed, playing lawn tennis in the sunshine.

"A pretty scene, ain't it?" said Mr M'Leod. "My good lady's sitting under the tree, and that's my little girl in pink on the far court. But I'll take you to your room, and you can see 'em all later."

He led me through a wide parquet-floored hall furnished in pale lemon, with huge cloisonné vases, an ebonised and gold grand piano, and banks of pot flowers in Benares brass bowls, up a pale oak staircase to a spacious landing, where there was a green velvet settee trimmed with silver. The blinds were down, and the light lay in parallel lines on the floors.

He showed me my room, saying cheerfully: "You may be a little tired. One often is without knowing it after a run through traffic. Don't come down till you feel quite restored. We shall all be in the garden."

My room was rather close, and smelt of perfumed soap. I threw up the window at once, but it opened so close to the floor and worked so clumsily that I came within an ace of pitching out, where I should certainly have ruined a rather lop-sided laburnum below. As I set about washing off the journey's dust, I began to feel a little tired. But, I reflected, I had not come down here in this weather and among these new surroundings to be depressed, so I began to whistle.

And it was just then that I was aware of a little grey shadow, as it might have been a snowflake seen against the light, floating at an immense distance in the background of my brain. It annoyed me, and I shook my head to get rid of it. Then my brain telegraphed that it was the forerunner of a swift-striding gloom which there was yet time to escape if I would force my thoughts away from it, as a man leaping for life forces his body forward and away from the fall of a wall. But the gloom overtook me before I could take in the meaning of the message. I moved toward the bed, every nerve already aching with the foreknowledge of the pain that was to be dealt it, and sat down, while my amazed and angry soul dropped, gulf by gulf, into that horror of great darkness which is spoken of in the Bible, and which, as auctioneers say, must be experienced to be appreciated.

Despair upon despair, misery upon misery, fear after fear, each causing their distinct and separate woe, packed in upon me for an unrecorded length of time, until at last they blurred together, and I heard a click in my brain like the click in the ear when one descends in a diving bell, and I knew that the pressures were equalised within and without, and that, for the moment, the worst was at an end. But I knew also that at any moment the darkness might come down anew; and while I dwelt on this speculation precisely as a man torments a raging tooth with his tongue, it ebbed away into the little grey shadow on the brain of its first coming, and once more I heard my brain, which knew what would recur, telegraph to every quarter for help, release, or diversion.

The door opened, and M'Leod reappeared. I thanked him politely, saying I was charmed with my room, anxious to meet Mrs M'Leod, much refreshed with my wash, and so on and so forth. Beyond a little stickiness at the corners of my mouth, it seemed to me that I was managing my words admirably, the while that I myself cowered at the bottom of unclimbable pits. M'Leod laid his hand on my shoulder, and said: "You've got it now already, ain't it?"

"Yes," I answered, "it's making me sick!"

"It will pass off when you come outside. I give you my word it will then pass off. Come!"

I shambled out behind him, and wiped my forehead in the hall.

"You mustn't mind," he said. "I expect the run tired you. My good lady is sitting there under the copper beech."

She was a fat woman in an apricot-coloured gown, with a heavily powdered face, against which her black long-lashed eyes showed like currants in dough. I was introduced to many fine ladies and gentlemen of those parts. Magnificently appointed landaus and covered motors swept in and out of the drive, and the air was gay with the merry outcries of the tennis players.

As twilight drew on they all went away, and I was left alone with Mr and Mrs M'Leod, while tall men-servants and maid-servants took away the tennis and tea things. Miss M'Leod had walked a little down the drive with a light-haired young man, who apparently knew everything about every South American railway stock. He had told me at tea that these were the days of financial specialisation.

"I think it went off beautifully, my dear," said Mr M'Leod to his wife; and to me: "You feel all right now, ain't it? Of course you do."

Mrs M'Leod surged across the gravel. Her husband skipped nimbly before her into the south verandah, turned a switch, and all Holmescroft was flooded with light.

"You can do that from your room also," he said as they went in. "There is something in money, ain't it?"

Miss M'Leod came up behind me in the dusk. "We have not yet been introduced," she said, "but I suppose you are staying the night?"

"Your father was kind enough to ask me," I replied.

She nodded. "Yes, *I* know; and you know too, don't you? I saw your face when you came to shake hands with mamma. You felt the depression very soon. It is simply frightful in that bedroom sometimes. What do you think it is – bewitchment? In Greece, where I was a little girl, it might have been; but not in England, do you think? Or *do* you?"

"I don't know what to think," I replied. "I never felt anything like it. Does it happen often?"

"Yes, sometimes. It comes and goes."

"Pleasant!" I said, as we walked up and down the gravel at the lawn edge. "What has been your experience of it?"

"That is difficult to say, but – sometimes that – that depression is like as it were" – she gesticulated in most un-English fashion – "a light. Yes, like a light turned into a room – only a light of blackness, do you understand? – into a happy room. For sometimes we are so happy, all we three, – so very happy. Then this blackness, it is turned on us just like – ah, I know what I mean now – like the head-lamp of a motor, and we are eclipsed. And there is another thing –"

The dressing gong roared, and we entered the over-lighted hall. My dressing was a brisk athletic performance, varied with outbursts of song – careful attention paid to articulation and expression. But nothing happened. As I hurried downstairs, I thanked Heaven that nothing had happened.

Dinner was served breakfast fashion; the dishes were placed on the sideboard over heaters, and we helped ourselves.

"We always do this when we are alone, so we talk better," said Mr M'Leod.

"And we are always alone," said the daughter.

"Cheer up, Thea. It will all come right," he insisted.

"No, papa." She shook her dark head. "Nothing is right while *it* comes."

"It is nothing that we ourselves have ever done in our lives – that I will swear to you," said Mrs M'Leod suddenly. "And we have changed our servants several times. So we know it is not *them*."

"Never mind. Let us enjoy ourselves while we can," said Mr M'Leod, opening the champagne.

But we did not enjoy ourselves. The talk failed. There were long silences.

"I beg your pardon," I said, for I thought some one at my elbow was about to speak.

"Ah! That is the other thing!" said Miss M'Leod. Her mother groaned.

We were silent again, and, in a few seconds it must have been, a live grief beyond words – not ghostly dread or horror, but aching, helpless grief – overwhelmed us, each, I felt, according to his or her nature, and held steady like the beam of a burning-glass. Behind that pain I was conscious there was a desire on somebody's part to explain something on which some tremendously important issue hung.

Meantime I rolled bread pills and remembered my sins; M'Leod considered his own reflection in a spoon; his wife seemed to be praying, and the girl fidgeted desperately with hands and feet, till the darkness passed on – as though the malignant rays of a burning glass had been shifted from us.

"There," said Miss M'Leod, half rising. "Now you see what makes a happy home. Oh, sell it – sell it, father mine, and let us go away!"

"But I've spent thousands on it. You shall go to Harrogate next week, Thea dear."

"I'm only just back from hotels. I am *so* tired of packing."

"Cheer up, Thea. It is over. You know it does not often come here twice in the same night. I think we shall dare now to be comfortable."

He lifted a dish-cover, and helped his wife and daughter. His face was lined and fallen like an old man's after debauch, but his hand did not shake, and his voice was clear. As he worked to restore us by speech and action, he reminded me of a grey-muzzled collie herding demoralized sheep.

After dinner we sat round the dining-room fire – the drawing-room might have been under the Shadow for aught we knew – talking with the intimacy of gipsies by the wayside, or of wounded comparing notes after a skirmish. By eleven o'clock the three between them had given me every name and detail they could recall that in any way bore on the house, and what they knew of its history.

We were to bed in a fortifying blaze of electric light. My one fear was that the blasting gust of depression would return – the surest way, of course, to bring it. I lay awake till dawn, breathing quickly and sweating lightly, beneath what De Quincey inadequately describes as "the oppression of inexpiable guilt." Now as soon as the lovely day was broken, I fell into the most terrible of all dreams – that joyous one in which all past evil has not only been wiped out of our lives, but has never been committed; and in the very bliss of our assured innocence, before our loves shriek and change countenance, we wake to the day we have earned.

It was a coolish morning, but we preferred to breakfast in the south verandah. The forenoon we spent in the garden, pretending to play games that come out of boxes, such as croquet and clock golf. But most of the time we drew together and talked. The young man who knew all about South American railways took Miss M'Leod for a walk in the afternoon, and at five M'Leod thoughtfully whirled us all up to dine in town.

"Now, don't say you will tell the Psychological Society, and that you will come again," said Miss M'Leod, as we parted. "Because I know you will not."

"You should not say that," said her mother. "You should say, "Good-bye, Mr Perseus. Come again.'"

"Not him!" the girl cried. "He has seen the Medusa's head!"

Looking at myself in the restaurant's mirrors, it seemed to me that I had not much benefited by my weekend. Next morning I wrote out all my Holmescroft notes at fullest length, in the hope that by so doing I could put it all behind me. But the experience worked on my mind, as they say certain imperfectly understood rays work on the body.

I am less calculated to make a Sherlock Holmes than any man I know, for I lack both method and patience, yet the idea of following up the trouble to its source fascinated me. I had no theory to go on, except a vague idea that I had come between two poles of a discharge, and had taken a shock meant for some one else. This was followed by a feeling of intense irritation. I waited cautiously on myself, expecting to be overtaken by horror of the supernatural, but my self persisted in being humanly indignant, exactly as though it had been the victim of a practical joke. It was in great pains and upheavals – that I felt in every fibre – but its dominant idea, to put it coarsely, was to get back a bit of its own. By this I knew that I might go forward if I could find the way.

After a few days it occurred to me to go to the office of Mr J. M. M. Baxter – the solicitor who had sold Holmescroft to M'Leod. I explained I had some notion of buying the place. Would he act for me in the matter?

Mr Baxter, a large, greyish, throaty-voiced man, showed no enthusiasm. "I sold it to Mr M'Leod," he said. "It 'ud scarcely do for me to start on the running-down tack now. But I can recommend –"

"I know he's asking an awful price," I interrupted, "and atop of it he wants an extra thousand for what he calls your clean bill of health."

Mr Baxter sat up in his chair. I had all his attention.

"Your guarantee with the house. Don't you remember it?"

"Yes, yes. That no death had taken place in the house since it was built. I remember perfectly."

He did not gulp as untrained men do when they lie, but his jaws moved stickily, and his eyes, turning towards the deed boxes on the wall, dulled. I counted seconds, one, two, three – one, two, three – up to ten. A man, I knew, can live through ages of mental depression in that time.

"I remember perfectly." His mouth opened a little as though it had tasted old bitterness.

"Of course *that* sort of thing doesn't appeal to me." I went on. "*I* don't expect to buy a house free from death."

"Certainly not. No one does. But it was Mr M'Leod's fancy – his wife's rather, I believe; and since we could meet it – it was my duty to my clients – at whatever cost to my own feelings – to make him pay."

"That's really why I came to you. I understood from him you knew the place well."

"Oh yes. Always did. It originally belonged to some connections of mine."

"The Misses Moultrie, I suppose. How interesting! They must have loved the place before the country round about was built up."

"They were very fond of it indeed."

"I don't wonder. So restful and sunny. I don't see how they could have brought themselves to part with it."

Now it is one of the most constant peculiarities of the English that in polite conversation – and I had striven to be polite – no one ever does or sells anything for mere money's sake.

"Miss Agnes – the youngest – fell ill" (he spaced his words a little), "and, as they were very much attached to each other, that broke up the home."

"Naturally. I fancied it must have been something of that kind. One doesn't associate the Staffordshire Moultries' (my Demon of Irresponsibility at that instant created 'em), "with – with being hard up."

"I don't know whether we're related to them," he answered importantly. "We may be, for our branch of the family comes from the Midlands."

I give this talk at length, because I am so proud of my first attempt at detective work. When I left him, twenty minutes later, with instructions to move against the owner of Holmescroft with a view to purchase, I was more bewildered than any Doctor Watson at the opening of a story.

Why should a middle-aged solicitor turn plover's egg colour and drop his jaw when reminded of so innocent and festal a matter as that no death had ever occurred in a house that he had sold? If I knew my

English vocabulary at all, the tone in which he said the youngest sister "fell ill" meant that she had gone out of her mind. That might explain his change of countenance, and it was just possible that her demented influence still hung about Holmescroft; but the rest was beyond me.

I was relieved when I reached M'Leod's City office, and could tell him what I had done – not what I thought.

M'Leod was quite willing to enter into the game of the pretended purchase, but did not see how it would help if I knew Baxter.

"He's the only living soul I can get at who was connected with Holmescroft," I said.

"Ah! Living soul is good," said M'Leod. "At any rate our little girl will be pleased that you are still interested in us. Won't you come down some day this week?"

"How is it there now?" I asked.

He screwed up his face. "Simply frightful!" he said. "Thea is at Droitwich."

"I should like it immensely, but I must cultivate Baxter for the present. You'll be sure and keep him busy your end, won't you?"

He looked at me with quiet contempt. "Do not be afraid. I shall be a good Jew. I shall be my own solicitor."

Before a fortnight was over, Baxter admitted ruefully that M'Leod was better than most firms in the business. We buyers were coy, argumentative, shocked at the price of Holmescroft, inquisitive, and cold by turns, but Mr M'Leod the seller easily met and surpassed us; and Mr Baxter entered every letter, telegram, and consultation at the proper rates in a cinematograph-film of a bill. At the end of a month he said it looked as though M'Leod, thanks to him, were really going to listen to reason. I was many pounds out of pocket, but I had learned something of Mr Baxter on the human side. I deserved it. Never in my life have I worked to conciliate, amuse, and flatter a human being as I worked over my solicitor.

It appeared that he golfed. Therefore, I was an enthusiastic beginner, anxious to learn. Twice I invaded his office with a bag (M'Leod lent it) full of the spelicans needed in this detestable game, and a vocabulary to match. The third time the ice broke, and Mr Baxter took me to his links, quite ten miles off, where in a maze of tramway lines, railroads, and nursery-maids, we skelped our divoted way round nine holes like barges plunging through head seas. He played vilely and had never expected to meet any one worse; but as he realized my form, I think he began to like me, for he took me in hand by the two hours together. After a fortnight he could give me no more than a stroke a hole, and when, with this allowance, I once managed to beat him by one, he was honestly glad, and assured me that I should be a golfer if I stuck to it. I was sticking to it for my own ends, but now and again my conscience pricked me; for the man was a nice man. Between games he supplied me with odd pieces of evidence, such as that he had known the Moultries all his life, being their cousin, and that Miss Mary, the eldest, was an unforgiving woman who would never let bygones be. I naturally wondered what she might have against him; and somehow connected him unfavourably with mad Agnes.

"People ought to forgive and forget," he volunteered one day between rounds. "Specially where, in the nature of things, they can't be sure of their deductions. Don't you think so?"

"It all depends on the nature of the evidence on which one forms one's judgment," I answered.

"Nonsense!" he cried. "I'm lawyer enough to know that there's nothing in the world so misleading as circumstantial evidence. Never was."

"Why? Have you ever seen men hanged on it?"

"Hanged? People have been supposed to be eternally lost on it," his face turned grey again. "I don't know how it is with you, but my consolation is that God must know. He *must*! Things that seem on the face of 'em like murder, or say suicide, may appear different to God. Heh?"

"That's what the murderer and the suicide can always hope – I suppose."

"I have expressed myself clumsily as usual. The facts as God knows 'em – may *be* different – even after the most clinching evidence. I've always said that – both as a lawyer and a man, but some people won't – I don't want to judge 'em – we'll say they can't – believe it; whereas *I* say there's always a working chance – a certainty – that the worst hasn't happened." He stopped and cleared his throat. "Now, let's come on! This time next week I shall be taking my holiday."

"What links?" I asked carelessly, while twins in a perambulator got out of our line of fire.

"A potty little nine-hole affair at a Hydro in the Midlands. My cousins stay there. Always will. Not but what the fourth and the seventh holes take some doing. You could manage it, though," he said encouragingly. "You're doing much better. It's only your approach shots that are weak."

"You're right. I can't approach for nuts! I shall go to pieces while you're away – with no one to coach me," I said mournfully.

"I haven't taught you anything," he said, delighted with the compliment.

"I owe all I've learned to you, anyhow. When will you come back?"

"Look here," he began. "I don't know your engagements, but I've no one to play with at Burry Mills. Never have. Why couldn't you take a few days off and join me there? I warn you it will be rather dull. It's a throat and gout place – baths, massage, electricity, and so forth. But the fourth and the seventh holes really take some doing."

"I'm for the game," I answered valiantly, Heaven well knowing that I hated every stroke and word of it.

"That's the proper spirit. As their lawyer I must ask you not to say anything to my cousins about Holmescroft. It upsets 'em. Always did. But speaking as man to man, it would be very pleasant for me if you could see your way to "

I saw it as soon as decency permitted, and thanked him sincerely. According to my now well-developed theory he had certainly misappropriated his aged cousins' monies under power of attorney, and had probably driven poor Agnes Moultrie out of her wits, but I wished that he was not so gentle, and good-tempered, and innocent-eyed.

Before I joined him at Burry Mills Hydro, I spent a night at Holmescroft. Miss M'Leod had returned from her Hydro, and first we made very merry on the open lawn in the sunshine over the manners and customs of the English resorting to such places. She knew dozens of hydros, and warned me how to behave in them, while Mr and Mrs M'Leod stood aside and adored her.

"Ah! That's the way she always comes back to us," he said. "Pity it wears off so soon, ain't it? You ought to hear her sing 'With mirth, thou pretty bird.'"

We had the house to face through the evening, and there we neither laughed nor sang. The gloom fell on us as we entered, and did not shift till ten o'clock, when we crawled out, as it were, from beneath it.

"It has been bad this summer," said Mrs M'Leod in a whisper after we realized that we were freed. "Sometimes I think the house will get up and cry out – it is so bad."

"How?"

"Have you forgotten what comes after the depression?"

So then we waited about the small fire, and the dead air in the room presently filled and pressed down upon us with the sensation (but words are useless here) as though some dumb and bound power were striving against gag and bond to deliver its soul of an articulate word. It passed in a few minutes, and I fell to thinking about Mr Baxter's conscience and Agnes Moultrie, gone mad in the well-lit bedroom that waited me. These reflections secured me a night during which I rediscovered how, from purely mental causes, a man can be physically sick; but the sickness was bliss compared to my dreams when the birds waked. On my departure, M'Leod gave me a beautiful narwhal's horn, much as a nurse gives a child sweets for being brave at a dentist's.

"There's no duplicate of it in the world," he said, "else it would have come to old Max M'Leod," and he tucked it into the motor. Miss M'Leod on the far side of the car whispered, "Have you found out anything, Mr Perseus?"

I shook my head.

"Then I shall be chained to my rock all my life," she went on. "Only don't tell papa."

I supposed she was thinking of the young gentleman who specialized in South American rails, for I noticed a ring on the third finger of her left hand.

I went straight from that house to Burry Mills Hydro, keen for the first time in my life on playing golf, which is guaranteed to occupy the mind. Baxter had taken me a room communicating with his own, and after lunch introduced me to a tall, horse-headed elderly lady of decided manners, whom a white-haired maid pushed along in a bath-chair through the park-like grounds of the Hydro. She was Miss Mary Moultrie, and she coughed and cleared her throat just like Baxter. She suffered – she told me it was the Moultrie castemark – from some obscure form of chronic bronchitis, complicated with spasm of the glottis; and, in a dead flat voice, with a sunken eye that looked and saw not, told me what washes, gargles, pastilles, and inhalations she had proved most beneficial. From her I was passed on to her younger sister, Miss Elizabeth, a small and withered thing with twitching lips, victim, she told me, to very much the same sort of throat, but secretly devoted to another set of medicines. When she went away with Baxter and the bath-chair, I fell across a major of the Indian army with gout in his glassy eyes, and a stomach which he had taken all round the Continent. He laid everything before me; and him I escaped only to be confided in by a matron with a tendency to follicular tonsilitis and eczema. Baxter waited hand and foot on his cousins till five o'clock, trying, as I saw, to atone for his treatment of the dead sister. Miss Mary ordered him about like a dog.

"I warned you it would be dull," he said when we met in the smoking-room.

"It's tremendously interesting," I said. "But how about a look round the links?"

"Unluckily damp always affects my eldest cousin. I've got to buy her a new bronchitis-kettle. Arthurs broke her old one yesterday."

We slipped out to the chemist's shop in the town, and he bought a large glittering tin thing whose workings he explained.

"I'm used to this sort of work. I come up here pretty often," he said. "I've the family throat too."

"You're a good man," I said. "A very good man."

He turned towards me in the evening light among the beeches, and his face was changed to what it might have been a generation before.

"You see," he said huskily, "There was the youngest – Agnes. Before she fell ill, you know. But she didn't like leaving her sisters. Never would." He hurried on with his odd-shaped load and left me among the ruins of my black theories. The man with that face had done Agnes Moultrie no wrong.

We never played our game. I was waked between two and three in the morning from my hygienic bed by Baxter in an ulster over orange and white pyjamas, which I should never have suspected from his character.

"My cousin has had some sort of a seizure," he said. "Will you come? I don't want to wake the doctor. Don't want to make a scandal. Quick!"

So I came quickly, and led by the white-haired Arthurs in a jacket and petticoat, entered a double-bedded room reeking with steam and Friar's Balsam. The electrics were all on. Miss Mary – I knew her by her height – was at the open window, wrestling with Miss Elizabeth, who gripped her round the knees. Her hand was at her throat, which was streaked with blood.

"She's done it. She's done it too!" Miss Elizabeth panted. "Hold her! Help me!"

"Oh, I say! Women don't cut their throats," Baxter whispered.

"My God! Has she cut her throat?" the maid cried, and with no warning rolled over in a faint. Baxter pushed her under the wash-basins, and leaped to hold the gaunt woman who crowed and whistled as she struggled towards the window. He took her by the shoulder, and she struck out wildly.

"All right! She's only cut her hand," he said. "Wet towel – quick!"

While I got that he pushed her backward. Her strength seemed almost as great as his. I swabbed at her throat when I could, and found no mark; then helped him to control her a little. Miss Elizabeth leaped back to bed, wailing like a child.

"Tie up her hand somehow," said Baxter. "Don't let it drip about the place. She" – he stepped on broken glass in his slippers, "She must have smashed a pane."

Miss Mary lurched towards the open window again, dropped on her knees, her head on the sill, and lay quiet, surrendering the cut hand to me.

"What did she do?" Baxter turned towards Miss Elizabeth in the far bed.

"She was going to throw herself out of the window," was the answer. "I stopped her, and sent Arthurs for you. Oh, we can never hold up our heads again!"

Miss Mary writhed and fought for breath. Baxter found a shawl which he threw over her shoulders.

"Nonsense!" said he. "That isn't like Mary"; but his face worked when he said it.

"You wouldn't believe about Aggie, John. Perhaps you will now!" said Miss Elizabeth. "I *saw* her do it, and she's cut her throat too!"

"She hasn't," I said. "It's only her hand."

Miss Mary suddenly broke from us with an indescribable grunt, flew, rather than ran, to her sister's bed, and there shook her as one furious schoolgirl would shake another.

"No such thing," she croaked. "How dare you think so, you wicked little fool?"

"Get into bed, Mary," said Baxter. "You'll catch a chill."

She obeyed, but sat up with the grey shawl round her lean shoulders, glaring at her sister. "I'm better now," she crowed. "Arthurs let me sit out too long. Where's Arthurs? The kettle."

"Never mind Arthurs," said Baxter. "*You* get the kettle." I hastened to bring it from the side table. "Now Mary, as God sees you, tell me what you've done."

His lips were dry, and he could not moisten them with his tongue.

Miss Mary applied herself to the mouth of the kettle, and between indraws of steam said: "The spasm came on just now, while I was asleep. I was nearly choking to death. So I went to the window. I've done it often before, without waking any one. Bessie's such an old maid about draughts. I tell you I was choking to death. I couldn't manage the catch, and I nearly fell out. That window opens too low. I cut my hand trying to save myself. Who has tied it up in this filthy handkerchief? I wish you had had my throat, Bessie. I never was nearer dying!" She scowled on us all impartially, while her sister sobbed.

From the bottom of the bed we heard a quivering voice: "Is she dead? Have they took her away? Oh, I never could bear the sight o' blood!"

"Arthurs," said Miss Mary, "you are an hireling. Go away!"

It is my belief that Arthurs crawled out on all fours, but I was busy picking up broken glass from the carpet.

Then Baxter, seated by the side of the bed, began to cross-examine in a voice I scarcely recognized. No one could for an instant have doubted the genuine rage of Miss Mary against her sister, her cousin, or her maid; and that the doctor should have been called in – for she did me the honour of calling me doctor – was the last drop. She was choking with her throat; had rushed to the window for air; had near pitched out, and in catching at the window bars had cut her hand. Over and over she made this clear to the intent Baxter. Then she turned on her sister and tongue-lashed her savagely.

"You mustn't blame me," Miss Bessie faltered at last. "You know what we think of night and day."

"I'm coming to that," said Baxter. "Listen to me. What *you* did, Mary, misled four people into thinking you – you meant to do away with yourself."

"Isn't one suicide in the family enough? Oh God, help and pity us! You *couldn't* have believed that!" she cried.

"The evidence was complete. Now, don't you think," Baxter's finger wagged under her nose – "*can't* you think that poor Aggie did the same thing at Holmescroft when she fell out of the window?"

"She had the same throat," said Miss Elizabeth. "Exactly the same symptoms. Don't you remember, Mary?"

"Which was her bedroom?" I asked of Baxter in an undertone.

"Over the south verandah, looking on to the tennis lawn."

"I nearly fell out of that very window when I was at Holmescroft – opening it to get some air. The sill doesn't come much above your knees," I said.

"You hear that, Mary? Mary, do you hear what this gentleman says? Won't you believe that what nearly happened to you must have happened to poor Aggie that night? For God's sake – for her sake – Mary, *won't* you believe?"

There was a long silence while the steam kettle puffed.

"If I could have proof – if I could have proof," said she, and broke into most horrible tears.

Baxter motioned to me, and I crept away to my room, and lay awake till morning, thinking more specially of the dumb Thing at Holmescroft which wished to explain itself. I hated Miss Mary as perfectly as though I had known her for twenty years, but I felt that, alive or dead, I should not like her to condemn me.

Yet at mid-day, when I saw Miss Mary in her bath-chair, Arthurs behind and Baxter and Miss Elizabeth on either side, in the park-like grounds of the Hydro, I found it difficult to arrange my words.

"Now that you know all about it," said Baxter aside, after the first strangeness of our meeting was over, "it's only fair to tell you that my poor cousin did not die in Holmescroft at all. She was dead when they found her under the window in the morning. Just dead."

"Under that laburnum outside the window?" I asked, for I suddenly remembered the crooked evil thing.

"Exactly. She broke the tree in falling. But no death has ever taken place *in* the house, so far as we were concerned. You can make yourself quite easy on that point. Mr M'Leod's extra thousand for what you called the 'clean bill of health' was something towards my cousins' estate when we sold. It was my duty as their lawyer to get it for them – at any cost to my own feelings."

I know better than to argue when the English talk about their duty. So I agreed with my solicitor.

"Their sister's death must have been a great blow to your cousins," I went on. The bath-chair was behind me.

"Unspeakable," Baxter whispered. "They brooded on it day and night. No wonder. If their theory of poor Aggie making away with herself was correct, she was eternally lost!"

"Do you believe that she made away with herself?"

"No, thank God! Never have! And after what happened to Mary last night, I see perfectly what happened to poor Aggie. She had the family throat too. By the way, Mary thinks you are a doctor. Otherwise she wouldn't like your having been in her room."

"Very good. Is she convinced now about her sister's death?"

"She'd give anything to be able to believe it, but she's a hard woman, and brooding along certain lines makes one groovy. I have sometimes been afraid for her reason – on the religious side, don't you know. Elizabeth doesn't matter. Brain of a hen. Always had."

Here Arthurs summoned me to the bath-chair and the ravaged face, beneath its knitted Shetland wool hood, of Miss Mary Moultrie.

"I need not remind you, I hope, of the seal of secrecy – absolute secrecy – in your profession," she began. "Thanks to my cousin's and my sister's stupidity, you have found out –" she blew her nose.

"Please don't excite her, sir," said Arthurs at the back.

"But, my dear Miss Moultrie, I only know what I've seen, of course, but it seems to me that what you thought was a tragedy in your sister's case, turns out, on your own evidence, so to speak, to have been an accident – a dreadfully sad one – but absolutely an accident."

"Do you believe that too?" she cried. "Or are you only saying it to comfort me?"

"I believe it from the bottom of my heart. Come down to Holmescroft for an hour – for half an hour – and satisfy yourself."

"Of what? You don't understand. I see the house every day – every night. I am always there in spirit – waking or sleeping. I couldn't face it in reality."

"But you must," I said. "If you go there in the spirit the greater need for you to go there in the flesh. Go to your sister's room once more, and see the window – I nearly fell out of it myself. It's – it's awfully low and dangerous. That would convince you," I pleaded.

"Yet Aggie had slept in that room for years," she interrupted.

"You've slept in your room here for a long time, haven't you? But you nearly fell out of the window when you were choking."

"That is true. That is one thing true," she nodded. "And I might have been killed as – perhaps – Aggie was killed."

"In that case your own sister and cousin and maid would have said you had committed suicide, Miss Moultrie. Come down to Holmescroft, and go over the place just once."

"You are lying," she said quite quietly. "You don't want me to come down to see a window. It is something else. I warn you we are Evangelicals. We don't believe in prayers for the dead. "As the tree falls –' "

"Yes. I daresay. But you persist in thinking that your sister committed suicide –"

"No! No! I have always prayed that I might have misjudged her."

Arthurs at the bath-chair spoke up: "Oh, Miss Mary! you *would* 'ave it from the first that poor Miss Aggie 'ad made away with herself; an', of course, Miss Bessie took the notion from you. Only Master – Mister John stood out, and – and I'd 'ave taken my Bible oath *you* was making away with yourself last night."

Miss Mary leaned towards me, one finger on my sleeve.

"If going to Holmescroft kills me," she said, "you will have the murder of a fellow-creature on your conscience for all eternity."

"I'll risk it," I answered. Remembering what torment the mere reflection of her torments had cast on Holmescroft, and remembering, above all, the dumb Thing that filled the house with its desire to speak, I felt that there might be worse things.

Baxter was amazed at the proposed visit, but at a nod from that terrible woman went off to make arrangements. Then I sent a telegram to M'Leod bidding him and his vacate Holmescroft for that afternoon. Miss Mary should be alone with her dead, as I had been alone.

I expected untold trouble in transporting her, but to do her justice, the promise given for the journey, she underwent it without murmur, spasm, or unnecessary word. Miss Bessie, pressed in a corner by the window, wept behind her veil, and from time to time tried to take hold of her sister's hand. Baxter wrapped himself in his newly-found happiness as selfishly as a bridegroom, for he sat still and smiled.

"So long as I know that Aggie didn't make away with herself," he explained, "I tell you frankly I don't care what happened. She's as hard as a rock – Mary. Always was. *She* won't die."

We led her out on to the platform like a blind woman, and so got her into the fly. The half-hour crawl to Holmescroft was the most racking experience of the day. M'Leod had obeyed my instructions. There was no one visible in the house or the gardens; and the front door stood open.

Miss Mary rose from beside her sister, stepped forth first, and entered the hall.

"Come, Bessie," she cried.

"I daren't. Oh, I daren't."

"Come!" Her voice had altered. I felt Baxter start. "There's nothing to be afraid of."

"Good heavens!" said Baxter. "She's running up the stairs. We'd better follow."

"Let's wait below. She's going to the room."

We heard the door of the bedroom I knew open and shut, and we waited in the lemon-coloured hall, heavy with the scent of flowers.

"I've never been into it since it was sold," Baxter sighed. "What a lovely restful place it is! Poor Aggie used to arrange the flowers."

"Restful?" I began, but stopped of a sudden, for I felt all over my bruised soul that Baxter was speaking truth. It was a light, spacious, airy house, full of the sense of well-being and peace – above all things, of peace. I ventured into the dining-room where the thoughtful M'Leods had left a small fire. There was no terror there, present or lurking; and in the drawing-room, which for good reasons we had never cared to enter, the sun and the peace and the scent of the flowers worked together as is fit in an inhabited house. When I returned to the hall, Baxter was sweetly asleep on a couch, looking most unlike a middle-aged solicitor who had spent a broken night with an exacting cousin.

There was ample time for me to review it all – to felicitate myself upon my magnificent acumen (barring some errors about Baxter as a thief and possibly a murderer), before the door above opened, and Baxter, evidently a light sleeper, sprang awake.

"I've had a heavenly little nap," he said, rubbing his eyes with the backs of his hands like a child. "Good Lord! That's not *their* step!"

But it was. I had never before been privileged to see the Shadow turned backward on the dial – the years ripped bodily off poor human shoulders – old sunken eyes filled and alight – harsh lips moistened and human.

"John," Miss Mary called, "I know now. Aggie didn't do it!" and "She didn't do it!" echoed Miss Bessie and giggled.

"I did not think it wrong to say a prayer," Miss Mary continued. "Not for her soul, but for our peace. Then I was convinced."

"Then we got conviction," the younger sister piped.

"We've misjudged poor Aggie, John. But I feel she knows now. Wherever she is, she knows that we know she is guiltless."

"Yes, she knows. I felt it too," said Miss Elizabeth.

"I never doubted," said John Baxter, whose face was beautiful at that hour. "Not from the first. Never have!"

"You never offered me proof, John. Now, thank God, it will not be the same any more. I can think henceforward of Aggie without sorrow." She tripped, absolutely tripped, across the hall. "What ideas these Jews have of arranging furniture!" She spied me behind a big cloisonné vase.

"I've seen the window," she said remotely. "You took a great risk in advising me to undertake such a journey. However, as it turns out . . . I forgive you, and I pray you may never know what mental anguish means! Bessie! Look at this peculiar piano! Do you suppose, Doctor, these people would offer one tea? I miss mine."

"I will go and see," I said, and explored M'Leod's new-built servants' wing. It was in the servants' hall that I unearthed the M'Leod family, bursting with anxiety.

"Tea for three, quick," I said. "If you ask me any questions now, I shall have a fit!" So Mrs M'Leod got it, and I was butler, amid murmured apologies from Baxter, still smiling and self-absorbed, and the cold disapproval of Miss Mary, who thought the pattern of the china vulgar. However, she ate well, and even asked me whether I would not like a cup of tea for myself.

They went away in the twilight – the twilight that I had once feared. They were going to an hotel in London to rest after the fatigues of the day, and as their fly turned down the drive, I capered on the doorstep, with the all-darkened house behind me.

Then I heard the uncertain feet of the M'Leods, and bade them not to turn on the lights, but to feel – to feel what I had done; for the Shadow was gone, with the dumb desire in the air. They drew short, but afterwards deeper, breaths, like bathers entering chill water, separated one from the other, moved about the hall, tiptoed upstairs, raced down, and then Miss M'Leod, and I believe her mother, though she denies this, embraced me. I know M'Leod did.

It was a disgraceful evening. To say we rioted through the house is to put it mildly. We played a sort of Blind Man's Buff along the darkest passages, in the unlighted drawing-room, and little dining-room, calling cheerily to each other after each exploration that here, and here, and here, the trouble had removed itself. We came up to *the* bedroom – mine for the night again – and sat, the women on the bed, and we men on chairs, drinking in blessed draughts of peace and comfort and cleanliness of soul, while I told them my tale in full, and received fresh praise, thanks, and blessings.

When the servants, returned from their day's outing, gave us a supper of cold fried fish, M'Leod had sense enough to open no wine. We had been practically drunk since nightfall, and grew incoherent on water and milk.

"I like that Baxter," said M'Leod. "He's a sharp man. The death wasn't in the house, but he ran it pretty close, ain't it?"

"And the joke of it is that he supposes I want to buy the place from you," I said. "Are you selling?"

"Not for twice what I paid for it – now," said M'Leod. "I'll keep you in furs all your life, but not our Holmescroft."

"No – never our Holmescroft," said Miss M'Leod. "We'll ask *him* here on Tuesday, mamma." They squeezed each other's hands.

"Now tell me," said Mrs M'Leod – "that tall one I saw out of the scullery window – did *she* tell you she was always here in the spirit? I hate her. She made all this trouble. It was not her house after she had sold it. What do you think?"

"I suppose," I answered, "she brooded over what she believed was her sister's suicide night and day – she confessed she did – and her thoughts being concentrated on this place, they felt like a – like a burning glass."

"Burning glass is good," said M'Leod.

"I said it was like a light of blackness turned on us," cried the girl, twiddling her ring. "That must have been when the tall one thought worst about her sister and the house."

"Ah, the poor Aggie!" said Mrs M'Leod. "The poor Aggie, trying to tell every one it was not so! No wonder we felt Something wished to say Something. Thea, Max, do you remember that night –"

"We need not remember any more," M'Leod interrupted. "It is not our trouble. They have told each other now."

"Do you think, then," said Miss M'Leod, "that those two, the living ones, were actually told something – upstairs – in your – in the room?"

"I can't say. At any rate they were made happy, and they ate a big tea afterwards. As your father says, it is not our trouble any longer – thank God!"

"Amen!" said M'Leod. "Now, Thea, let us have some music after all these months. 'With mirth, thou pretty bird,' ain't it? You ought to hear that."

And in the half-lighted hall, Thea sang an old English song that I had never heard before.

> With mirth, thou pretty bird, rejoice
>   Thy Maker's praise enhanced;
> Lift up thy shrill and pleasant voice,
>   Thy God is high advanced!
> Thy food before He did provide,
> And gives it in a fitting side,
>   Wherewith be thou sufficed!
> Why shouldst thou now unpleasant be,
>   Thy wrath against God venting,
> That He a little bird made thee,
>   Thy silly head tormenting,
> Because He made thee not a man?
> Oh, Peace! He hath well thought thereon,
>   Therewith be thou sufficed!

The Grove of Ashtaroth

John Buchan

Location: Welgevonden, South Africa.
Time: June, 1910.
Eyewitness Description: *"And then I honestly
began to be afraid. I, a prosaic modern
Christian gentleman, a half-believer in
casual faiths, was in the presence of some
hoary mystery of sin far older than creeds or Christendom.
There was fear in my heart."*
Author: John Buchan (1875–1940) was another man for whom
the start of the 20th century would mean a significant shift in his
fortunes from "half barrister and half writer", to quote his own
words. The early years of the new century were spent in South
Africa, which would provide the raw material for some of his
later books, notably the fantasy adventure *Prester John* (1910),
and the spur five years later for his immortal spy thriller, *The 39
Steps*. "The Grove of Ashtaroth" draws on his knowledge of
South African supernaturalism to tell the story of a young man
who falls under the spell of an old temple dedicated to the
worship of an ancient goddess. It is a significant story among
Buchan's work in that critics have in the past used the part-
Jewish hero as an example of his anti-Semitism. In fact, although
Buchan did make the occasional tasteless remark about Jews in
his fiction – as did many other leading writers of the period – he
numbered several among his friends and was one of the first
important literary figures to denounce Hitler's persecution of the
race during his rise to power.

W e were sitting around the camp fire, some thirty miles north of
a place called Taqui, when Lawson announced his intention of
finding a home. He had spoken little the last day or two, and I had

guessed that he had struck a vein of private reflection. I thought it
might be a new mine or irrigation scheme, and I was surprised to find
that it was a country house.

"I don't think I shall go back to England," he said, kicking a
sputtering log into place. "I don't see why I should. For business
purposes I am far more useful to the firm in South Africa than in
Throgmorton Street. I have no relations left except a third cousin,
and I have never cared a rush for living in town. That beastly house
of mine in Hill Street will fetch what I gave for it, – Isaacson cabled
about it the other day, offering for furniture and all. I don't want to
go into Parliament, and I hate shooting little birds and tame deer. I
am one of those fellows who are born Colonial at heart, and I don't
see why I shouldn't arrange my life as I please. Besides, for ten years I
have been falling in love with this country, and now I am up to the
neck."

He flung himself back in the camp-chair till the canvas creaked,
and looked at me below his eyelids. I remember glancing at the lines
of him, and thinking what a fine make of a man he was. In his
untanned field-boots, breeches, and grey shirt he looked the born
wilderness-hunter, though less than two months before he had been
driving down to the City every morning in the sombre regimentals of
his class. Being a fair man, he was gloriously tanned, and there was a
clear line at his shirt-collar to mark the limits of his sunburn. I had
first known him years ago, when he was a broker's clerk working on
half commission. Then he had gone to South Africa, and soon I heard
he was a partner in a mining house which was doing wonders with
some gold areas in the North. The next step was his return to London
as the new millionaire – young, good-looking, wholesome in mind
and body, and much sought after by the mothers of marriageable
girls. We played polo together, and hunted a little in the season, but
there were signs that he did not propose to become the conventional
English gentleman. He refused to buy a place in the country, though
half the Homes of England were at his disposal. He was a very busy
man, he declared, and had not time to be a squire. Besides, every few
months he used to rush out to South Africa. I saw that he was restless,
for he was always badgering me to go big-game hunting with him in
some remote part of the earth. There was that in his eyes, too, which
marked him out from the ordinary blonde type of our countrymen.
They were large and brown and mysterious, and the light of another
race was in their odd depths.

To hint such a thing would have meant a breach of friendship,
for Lawson was very proud of his birth. When he first made his

fortune he had gone to the Heralds to discover his family, and those obliging gentlemen had provided a pedigree. It appeared that he was a scion of the house of Lowson or Lowieson, an ancient and rather disreputable clan on the Scottish side of the Border. He took a shooting in Teviotdale on the strength of it, and used to commit lengthy Border ballads to memory. But I had known his father, a financial journalist who never quite succeeded, and I had heard of a grandfather who sold antiques in a back street at Brighton. The latter, I think, had not changed his name, and still frequented the synagogue. The father was a progressive Christian, and the mother had been a blonde Saxon from the Midlands. In my mind there was no doubt, as I caught Lawson's heavy-lidded eyes fixed on me. My friend was of a more ancient race than the Lowsons of the Border.

"Where are you thinking of looking for your house?" I asked. "In Natal or in the Cape Peninsula? You might get the Fishers' place if you paid a price."

"The Fishers' place be hanged!" he said crossly. "I don't want any stuccoed overgrown Dutch farm. I might as well be at Roehampton as in the Cape."

He got up and walked to the far side of the fire, where a lane ran down through thornscrub to a gully of the hills. The moon was silvering the bush of the plains, forty miles off and three thousand feet below us.

"I am going to live somewhere hereabouts," he answered at last.

I whistled. "Then you've got to put your hand in your pocket, old man. You'll have to make everything, including a map of the countryside."

"I know," he said; "that's where the fun comes in. Hang it all, why shouldn't I indulge my fancy? I'm uncommonly well off, and I haven't chick or child to leave it to. Supposing I'm a hundred miles from a railhead, what about it? I'll make a motor-road and fix up a telephone. I'll grow most of my supplies, and start a colony to provide labour. When you come and stay with me, you'll get the best food and drink on earth, and sport that will make your mouth water. I'll put Lochleven trout in these streams – at 6,000 feet you can do anything. We'll have a pack of hounds, too, and we can drive pig in the woods, and if we want big game there are the Mangwe flats at our feet. I tell you I'll make such a country-house as nobody ever dreamed of. A man will come plumb out of stark savagery into lawns and rose-gardens." Lawson flung himself into his chair again and smiled dreamily at the fire.

"But why here, of all places?" I persisted. I was not feeling very well and did not care for the country.

"I can't quite explain. I think it's the sort of land I have always been looking for. I always fancied a house on a green plateau in a decent climate looking down on the tropics. I like heat and colour, you know, but I like hills too, and greenery, and the things that bring back Scotland. Give me a cross between Teviotdale and the Orinoco, and, by Gad! I think I've got it here."

I watched my friend curiously, as with bright eyes and eager voice he talked of his new fad. The two races were very clear in him – the one desiring gorgeousness, the other athirst for the soothing spaces of the North. He began to plan out the house. He would get Adamson to design it, and it was to grow out of the landscape like a stone on the hillside. There would be wide verandahs and cool halls, but great fireplaces against winter time. It would all be very simple and fresh – "clean as morning" was his odd phrase; but then another idea supervened, and he talked of bringing the Tintorets from Hill Street. "I want it to be a civilised house, you know. No silly luxury, but the best pictures and china and books . . . I'll have all the furniture made after the old plain English models out of native woods. I don't want second-hand sticks in a new country. Yes, by Jove, the Tintorets are a great idea, and all those Ming pots I bought. I had meant to sell them, but I'll have them out here."

He talked for a good hour of what he would do, and his dream grew richer as he talked, till by the time we went to bed he had sketched something liker a palace than a country-house. Lawson was by no means a luxurious man. At present he was well content with a Wolseley valise, and shaved cheerfully out of a tin mug. It struck me as odd that a man so simple in his habits should have so sumptuous a taste in bric-à-brac. I told myself, as I turned in, that the Saxon mother from the Midlands had done little to dilute the strong wine of the East.

It drizzled next morning when we inspanned, and I mounted my horse in a bad temper. I had some fever on me, I think, and I hated this lush yet frigid table-land, where all the winds on earth lay in wait for one's marrow. Lawson was, as usual, in great spirits. We were not hunting, but shifting our hunting-ground, so all morning we travelled fast to the north along the rim of the uplands.

At midday it cleared, and the afternoon was a pageant of pure colour. The wind sank to a low breeze; the sun lit the infinite green spaces, and kindled the wet forest to a jewelled coronal. Lawson gaspingly admired it all, as he cantered bareheaded up a bracken-clad slope. "God's country," he said twenty times. "I've found it." Take a piece of Saxon downland; put a stream in every hollow and a patch of wood; and at the edge, where the cliffs at home would fall to the sea, put a cloak of forest muffling the scarp and dropping thousands of feet to the blue plains. Take the diamond air of the Görnergrat, and the riot of colour which you get by a West Highland lochside in late September. Put flowers everywhere, the things we grow in hothouses, geraniums like sun-shades and arums like trumpets. That will give you a notion of the countryside we were in. I began to see that after all it was out of the common.

And just before sunset we came over a ridge and found something better. It was a shallow glen, half a mile wide, down which ran a blue-grey stream in linns like the Spean, till at the edge of the plateau it leaped into the dim forest in a snowy cascade. The opposite side ran up in gentle slopes to a rocky knoll, from which the eye had a noble prospect of the plains. All down the glen were little copses, half moons of green edging some silvery shore of the burn, or delicate clusters of tall trees nodding on the hill brow. The place so satisfied the eye that for the sheer wonder of its perfection we stopped and stared in silence for many minutes.

Then "The House," I said, and Lawson replied softly, "The House!"

We rode slowly into the glen in the mulberry gloaming. Our transport waggons were half an hour behind, so we had time to explore. Lawson dismounted and plucked handfuls of flowers from the water-meadows. He was singing to himself all the time – an old French catch about *Cadet Rousselle* and his *trois maisons*.

"Who owns it?" I asked.

"My firm, as like as not. We have miles of land about here. But whoever the man is, he has got to sell. Here I build my tabernacle, old man. Here, and nowhere else!"

In the very centre of the glen, in a loop of the stream, was one copse which even in that half light struck me as different from the others. It was of tall, slim, fairy-like trees, the kind of wood the monks painted in old missals. No, I rejected the thought. It was no Christian wood. It was not a copse, but a "grove," – one such as Diana may have flitted through in the moonlight. It was small, forty or fifty yards in diameter, and there was a dark something at the heart of it which for a second I thought was a house.

We turned between the slender trees, and – was it fancy? – an odd tremor went through me. I felt as if I were penetrating the *temenos* of some strange and lovely divinity, the goddess of this pleasant vale. There was a spell in the air, it seemed, and an odd dead silence.

Suddenly my horse started at a flutter of light wings. A flock of doves rose from the branches, and I saw the burnished green of their plumes against the opal sky. Lawson did not seem to notice them. I saw his keen eyes staring at the centre of the grove and what stood there.

It was a little conical tower, ancient and lichened, but, so far as I could judge, quite flawless. You know the famous Conical Temple at Zimbabwe, of which prints are in every guide-book. This was of the same type, but a thousand-fold more perfect. It stood about thirty feet high, of solid masonry, without door or window or cranny, as shapely as when it first came from the hands of the old builders. Again I had the sense of breaking in on a sanctuary. What right had I, a common vulgar modern, to be looking at this fair thing, among these delicate trees, which some white goddess had once taken for her shrine?

Lawson broke in on my absorption. "Let's get out of this," he said hoarsely, and he took my horse's bridle (he had left his own beast at the edge) and led him back to the open. But I noticed that his eyes were always turning back, and that his hand trembled.

"That settles it," I said after supper. "What do you want with your mediaeval Venetians and your Chinese pots now? You will have the finest antique in the world in your garden – a temple as old as time, and in a land which they say has no history. You had the right inspiration this time."

I think I have said that Lawson had hungry eyes. In his enthusiasm they used to glow and brighten; but now, as he sat looking down at the olive shades of the glen, they seemed ravenous in their fire. He had hardly spoken a word since we left the wood.

"Where can I read about these things?" he asked, and I gave him the names of books.

Then, an hour later, he asked me who were the builders. I told him the little I knew about Phoenician and Sabaean wanderings, and the ritual of Sidon and Tyre. He repeated some names to himself and went soon to bed.

As I turned in, I had one last look over the glen, which lay ivory and black in the moon. I seemed to hear a faint echo of wings, and to see over the little grove a cloud of light visitants. "The Doves of Ashtaroth have come back," I said to myself. "It is a good omen. They accept the new tenant." But as I fell asleep I had a sudden thought that I was saying something rather terrible.

*   *   *

Three years later, pretty nearly to a day, I came back to see what
Lawson had made of his hobby. He had bidden me often to
Welgevonden, as he chose to call it – though I do not know why
he should have fixed a Dutch name to a countryside where Boer
never trod. At the last there had been some confusion about dates,
and I wired the time of my arrival, and set off without an answer. A
motor met me at the queer little wayside station of Taqui, and after
many miles on a doubtful highway I came to the gates of the park,
and a road on which it was a delight to move. Three years had
wrought little difference in the landscape. Lawson had done some
planting, – conifers and flowering shrubs and such-like – but wisely
he had resolved that Nature had for the most part forestalled him. All
the same, he must have spent a mint of money. The drive could not
have been beaten in England, and fringes of mown turf on either
hand had been pared out of the lush meadows. When we came over
the edge of the hill and looked down on the secret glen, I could not
repress a cry of pleasure. The house stood on the farther ridge, the
viewpoint of the whole neighbourhood; and its brown timbers and
white rough-cast walls melted into the hillside as if it had been there
from the beginning of things. The vale below was ordered in lawns
and gardens. A blue lake received the rapids of the stream, and its
banks were a maze of green shades and glorious masses of blossom. I
noticed, too, that the little grove we had explored on our first visit
stood alone in a big stretch of lawn, so that its perfection might be
clearly seen. Lawson had excellent taste, or he had had the best
advice.

The butler told me that his master was expected home shortly, and
took me into the library for tea. Lawson had left his Tintorets and
Ming pots at home after all. It was a long, low room, panelled in teak
half-way up the walls, and the shelves held a multitude of fine
bindings. There were good rugs on the parquet floor, but no orna-
ments anywhere, save three. On the carved mantelpiece stood two of
the old soapstone birds which they used to find at Zimbabwe, and
between, on an ebony stand, a half moon of alabaster, curiously
carved with zodiacal figures. My host had altered his scheme of
furnishing, but I approved the change.

He came in about half-past six, after I had consumed two cigars
and all but fallen asleep. Three years make a difference in most men,
but I was not prepared for the change in Lawson. For one thing, he
had grown fat. In place of the lean young man I had known, I saw a
heavy, flaccid being, who shuffled in his gait, and seemed tired and
listless. His sunburn had gone, and his face was as pasty as a city

clerk's. He had been walking, and wore shapeless flannel clothes, which hung loose even on his enlarged figure. And the worst of it was, that he did not seem over-pleased to see me. He murmured something about my journey, and then flung himself into an arm-chair and looked out of the window.

I asked him if he had been ill.

"Ill! No!" he said crossly. "Nothing of the kind. I'm perfectly well."

"You don't look as fit as this place should make you. What do you do with yourself? Is the shooting as good as you hoped?"

He did not answer, but I thought of heard him mutter something like "shooting be damned."

Then I tried the subject of the house. I praised it extravagantly, but with conviction. "There can be no place like it in the world," I said.

He turned his eyes on me at last, and I saw that they were as deep and restless as ever. With his pallid face they made him look curiously Semitic. I had been right in my theory about his ancestry.

"Yes," he said slowly, "there is no place like it – in the world."

Then he pulled himself to his feet. "I'm going to change," he said. "Dinner is at eight. Ring for Travers, and he'll show you your room."

I dressed in a noble bedroom, with an outlook over the garden-vale and the escarpment to the far line of the plains, now blue and saffron in the sunset. I dressed in an ill temper, for I was seriously offended with Lawson, and also seriously alarmed. He was either very unwell or going out of his mind, and it was clear, too, that he would resent any anxiety on his account. I ransacked my memory for rumours, but found none. I had heard nothing of him except that he had been extraordinarily successful in his speculations, and that from his hill-top he directed his firm's operations with uncommon skill. If Lawson was sick or mad, nobody knew of it.

Dinner was a trying ceremony. Lawson, who used to be rather particular in his dress, appeared in a kind of smoking suit with a flannel collar. He spoke scarcely a word to me, but cursed the servants with a brutality which left me aghast. A wretched footman in his nervousness spilt some sauce over his sleeve. Lawson dashed the dish from his hand, and volleyed abuse with a sort of epileptic fury. Also he, who had been the most abstemious of men, swallowed disgusting quantities of champagne and old brandy.

He had given up smoking, and half an hour after we left the dining-room he announced his intention of going to bed. I watched him as he waddled upstairs with a feeling of angry bewilderment.

Then I went to the library and lit a pipe. I would leave first thing in the morning – on that I was determined. But as I sat gazing at the moon of alabaster and the soapstone birds my anger evaporated, and concern took its place. I remembered what a fine fellow Lawson had been, what good times we had had together. I remembered especially that evening when we had found this valley and given rein to our fancies. What horrid alchemy in the place had turned a gentleman into a brute? I thought of drink and drugs and madness and insomnia, but I could fit none of them into my conception of my friend. I did not consciously rescind my resolve to depart, but I had a notion that I would not act on it.

The sleepy butler met me as I went to bed. "Mr Lawson's room is at the end of your corridor, sir," he said. "He don't sleep over well, so you may hear him stirring in the night. At what hour would you like breakfast, sir? Mr Lawson mostly has his in bed."

My room opened from the great corridor, which ran the full length of the front of the house. So far as I could make out, Lawson was three rooms off, a vacant bedroom and his servant's room being between us. I felt tired and cross, and tumbled into bed as fast as possible. Usually I sleep well, but now I was soon conscious that my drowsiness was wearing off and that I was in for a restless night. I got up and laved my face, turned the pillows, thought of sheep coming over a hill and clouds crossing the sky; but none of the old devices were any use. After about an hour of make-believe I surrendered myself to facts, and, lying on my back, stared at the white ceiling and the patches of moonshine on the walls.

It certainly was an amazing night. I got up, put on a dressing-gown, and drew a chair to the window. The moon was almost at its full, and the whole plateau swam in a radiance of ivory and silver. The banks of the stream were black, but the lake had a great belt of light athwart it, which made it seem like a horizon, and the rim of land beyond it like a contorted cloud. Far to the right I saw the delicate outlines of the little wood which I had come to think of as the Grove of Ashtaroth. I listened. There was not a sound in the air. The land seemed to sleep peacefully beneath the moon, and yet I had a sense that the peace was an illusion. The place was feverishly restless.

I could have given no reason for my impression, but there it was. Something was stirring in the wide moonlit landscape under its deep mask of silence. I felt as I had felt on the evening three years ago when I had ridden into the grove. I did not think that the influence, whatever it was, was maleficent. I only knew that it was very strange, and kept me wakeful.

By-and-by I bethought me of a book. There was no lamp in the corridor save the moon, but the whole house was bright as I slipped down the great staircase and over the hall to the library. I switched on the lights and then switched them off. They seemed a profanation, and I did not need them.

I found a French novel, but the place held me and I stayed. I sat down in an arm-chair before the fireplace and the stone birds. Very odd those gawky things, like prehistoric Great Auks, looked in the moonlight. I remember that the alabaster moon shimmered like translucent pearl, and I fell to wondering about its history. Had the old Sabaeans used such a jewel in their rites in the Grove of Ashtaroth?

Then I heard footsteps pass the window. A great house like this would have a watchman, but these quick shuffling footsteps were surely not the dull plod of a servant. They passed on to the grass and died away. I began to think of getting back to my room.

In the corridor I noticed that Lawson's door was ajar, and that a light had been left burning. I had the unpardonable curiosity to peep in. The room was empty, and the bed had not been slept in. Now I knew whose were the footsteps outside the library window.

I lit a reading-lamp and tried to interest myself in "La Cruelle Enigme". But my wits were restless, and I could not keep my eyes on the page. I flung the book aside and sat down again by the window. The feeling came over me that I was sitting in a box at some play. The glen was a huge stage, and at any moment the players might appear on it. My attention was strung as high as if I had been waiting for the advent of some world-famous actress. But nothing came. Only the shadows shifted and lengthened as the moon moved across the sky.

Then quite suddenly the restlessness left me, and at the same moment the silence was broken by the crow of a cock and the rustling of trees in a light wind. I felt very sleepy, and was turning to bed when again I heard footsteps without. From the window I could see a figure moving across the garden towards the house. It was Lawson, got up in the sort of towel dressing-gown that one wears on board ship. He was walking slowly and painfully, as if very weary. I did not see his face, but the man's whole air was that of extreme fatigue and dejection.

I tumbled into bed and slept profoundly till long after daylight.

The man who valeted me was Lawson's own servant. As he was laying out my clothes I asked after the health of his master, and was told that he had slept ill and would not rise till late. Then the man, an anxious-faced Englishman, gave me some information on his own account. Mr Lawson was having one of his bad turns. It would pass away in a day or two, but till it had gone he was fit for nothing. He advised me to see Mr Jobson, the factor, who would look to my entertainment in his master's absence.

Jobson arrived before luncheon, and the sight of him was the first satisfactory thing about Welgevonden. He was a big, gruff Scot from Roxburghshire, engaged, no doubt, by Lawson as a duty to his Border ancestry. He had short grizzled whiskers, a weatherworn face, and a shrewd, calm blue eye. I knew now why the place was in such perfect order.

We began with sport, and Jobson explained what I could have in the way of fishing and shooting. His exposition was brief and business-like, and all the while I could see his eye searching me. It was clear that he had much to say on other matters than sport.

I told him that I had come here with Lawson three years before, when he chose the site. Jobson continued to regard me curiously. "I've heard tell of ye from Mr Lawson. Ye're an old friend of his, I understand."

"The oldest," I said. "And I am sorry to find that the place does not agree with him. Why it doesn't I cannot imagine, for you look fit enough. Has he been seedy for long?"

"It comes and goes," said Mr Jobson. "Maybe once a month he has a bad turn. But on the whole it agrees with him badly. He's no' the man he was when I first came here."

Jobson was looking at me very seriously and frankly. I risked a question.

"What do you suppose is the matter?"

He did not reply at once, but leaned forward and tapped my knee. "I think it's something that doctors canna cure. Look at me, sir. I've always been counted a sensible man, but if I told you what was in my head you would think me daft. But I have one word for you. Bide till tonight is past and then speir your question. Maybe you and me will be agreed."

The factor rose to go. As he left the room he flung me back a remark over his shoulder – "Read the eleventh chapter of the First Book of Kings."

After luncheon I went for a walk. First I mounted to the crown of the hill and feasted my eyes on the unequalled loveliness of the view. I saw the far hills in Portuguese territory, a hundred miles away, lifting up thin blue fingers into the sky. The wind blew light and fresh, and the place was fragrant with a thousand delicate scents. Then I descended to the vale, and followed the stream up through the garden. Poinsettias and oleanders were blazing in coverts, and there was a paradise of tinted water-lilies in the slacker reaches. I saw good trout rise at the fly, but I did not think about fishing. I was searching my memory for a recollection which would not come. By-and-by I found myself beyond the garden, where the lawns ran to the fringe of Ashtaroth's Grove.

It was like something I remembered in an old Italian picture. Only, as my memory drew it, it should have been peopled with strange figures – nymphs dancing on the sward, and a prick-eared faun peeping from the covert. In the warm afternoon sunlight it stood, ineffably gracious and beautiful, tantalizing with a sense of some deep hidden loveliness. Very reverently I walked between the slim trees, to where the little conical tower stood half in sun and half in shadow. Then I noticed something new. Round the tower ran a narrow path, worn in the grass by human feet. There had been no such path on my first visit, for I remembered the grass growing tall to the edge of the stone. Had the Kaffirs made a shrine of it, or were there other and stranger votaries?

When I returned to the house I found Travers with a message for me. Mr Lawson was still in bed, but he would like me to go to him. I found my friend sitting up and drinking strong tea – a bad thing, I should have thought, for a man in his condition. I remember that I looked over the room for some sign of the pernicious habit of which I believed him a victim. But the place was fresh and clean, with the windows wide open, and, though I could not have given my reasons, I was convinced that drugs or drink had nothing to do with the sickness.

He received me more civilly, but I was shocked by his looks. There were great bags below his eyes, and his skin had the wrinkled puffy appearance of a man in dropsy. His voice, too, was reedy and thin. Only his great eyes burned with some feverish life.

"I am a shocking bad host," he said, "but I'm going to be still more inhospitable. I want you to go away. I hate anybody here when I'm off colour."

"Nonsense," I said; "you want looking after. I want to know about this sickness. Have you had a doctor?"

He smiled wearily. "Doctors are no earthly use to me. There's nothing much the matter, I tell you. I'll be all right in a day or two, and then you can come back. I want you to go off with Jobson and hunt in the plains till the end of the week. It will be better fun for you, and I'll feel less guilty."

Of course I pooh-poohed the idea, and Lawson got angry. "Damn it, man," he cried, "why do you force yourself on me when I don't want you? I tell you your presence here makes me worse. In a week I'll be as right as the mail, and then I'll be thankful for you. But get away now; get away, I tell you."

I saw that he was fretting himself into a passion. "All right," I said soothingly; "Jobson and I will go off hunting. But I am horribly anxious about you, old man."

He lay back on his pillows. "You needn't trouble. I only want a little rest. Jobson will make all arrangements, and Travers will get you anything you want. Good-bye."

I saw it was useless to stay longer, so I left the room. Outside I found the anxious-faced servant. "Look here," I said, "Mr Lawson thinks I ought to go, but I mean to stay. Tell him I'm gone if he asks you. And for Heaven's sake keep him in bed."

The man promised, and I thought I saw some relief in his face.

I went to the library, and on the way remembered Jobson's remark about 1st Kings. With some searching I found a Bible and turned up the passage. It was a long screed about the misdeeds of Solomon, and I read it through without enlightenment. I began to re-read it, and a word suddenly caught my attention –

For Solomon went after Ashtaroth, the goddess of the Zidonians.

That was all, but it was like a key to a cipher. Instantly there flashed over my mind all that I had heard or read of that strange ritual which seduced Israel to sin. I saw a sunburnt land and a people vowed to the stern service of Jehovah. But I saw, too, eyes turning from the austere sacrifice to lonely hill-top groves and towers and images, where dwelt some subtle and evil mystery. I saw the fierce prophets, scourging the votaries with rods, and a nation penitent before the Lord; but always the backsliding again, and the hankering after forbidden joys. Ashtaroth was the old goddess of the East. Was it not possible that in all Semitic blood there remained, transmitted through the dim generations, some craving for her spell? I thought of the grandfather in the back street at Brighton and of those burning eyes upstairs.

As I sat and mused my glance fell on the inscrutable stone birds. They knew all those old secrets of joy and terror. And that moon of alabaster! Some dark priest had worn it on his forehead when he worshipped, like Ahab, "all the host of Heaven." And then I honestly began to be afraid. I a prosaic, modern Christian gentleman, a half-believer in casual faiths, was in the presence of some hoary mystery of sin far older than creeds or Christendom. There was fear in my heart, – a kind of uneasy disgust, and above all a nervous eerie disquiet. Now I wanted to go away, and yet I was ashamed of the cowardly thought. I pictured Ashtaroth's Grove with sheer horror. What tragedy was in the air? what secret awaited twilight? For the night was coming, the night of the Full Moon, the season of ecstasy and sacrifice.

I do not know how I got through that evening. I was disinclined for dinner, so I had a cutlet in the library and sat smoking till my tongue ached. But as the hours passed a more manly resolution grew up in my mind. I owed it to old friendship to stand by Lawson in this extremity. I could not interfere – God knows, his reason seemed already rocking – but I could be at hand in case my chance came. I determined not to undress, but to watch through the night. I had a bath, and changed into light flannels and slippers. Then I took up my position in a corner of the library close to the window, so that I could not fail to hear Lawson's footsteps if he passed.

Fortunately I left the lights unlit, for as I waited I grew drowsy, and fell asleep. When I woke the moon had risen, and I knew from the feel of the air that the hour was late. I sat very still, straining my ears, and as I listened I caught the sound of steps. They were crossing the hall stealthily, and nearing the library door. I huddled into my corner as Lawson entered.

He wore the same towel dressing-gown, and he moved swiftly and silently as if in a trance. I watched him take the alabaster moon from the mantelpiece and drop it in his pocket. A glimpse of white skin showed that the gown was his only clothing. Then he moved past me to the window, opened it, and went out.

Without any conscious purpose I rose and followed, kicking off my slippers that I might go quietly. He was running, running fast, across the lawns in the direction of the grove – an odd shapeless antic in the moonlight. I stopped, for there was no cover, and I feared for his reason if he saw me. When I looked again he had disappeared among the trees.

I saw nothing for it but to crawl, so on my belly I wormed my way over the dripping sward. There was a ridiculous suggestion of deer-stalking about the game which tickled me and dispelled my uneasiness. Almost I persuaded myself I was tracking an ordinary sleep-walker. The lawns were broader than I imagined, and it seemed an age before I reached the edge of the grove. The world was so still that I appeared to be making a most ghastly amount of noise. I remember that once I heard a rustling in the air, and looked up to see the green doves circling about the treetops.

There was no sign of Lawson. On the edge of the grove I think that all my assurance vanished. I could see between the trunks to the little tower, but it was quiet as the grave, save for the wings above. Once more there came over me the unbearable sense of anticipation I had felt the night before. My nerves tingled with mingled expectation and dread. I did not think that any harm would come to me, for the powers of the air seemed not malignant. But I knew them for powers, and felt awed and abased. I was in the presence of the "host of Heaven," and I was no stern Israelitish prophet to prevail against them.

I must have lain for hours waiting in that spectral place, my eyes riveted on the tower and its golden cap of moonshine. I remember that my head felt void and light, as if my spirit were becoming disembodied and leaving its dew-drenched sheath far below. But the most curious sensation was of something drawing me to the tower, something mild and kindly and rather feeble, for there was some other and stronger force keeping me back. I yearned to move nearer, but I could not drag my limbs an inch. There was a spell somewhere which I could not break. I do not think I was in any way frightened now. The starry influence was playing tricks with me, but my mind was half asleep. Only I never took my eyes from the little tower. I think I could not, if I had wanted to.

Then suddenly from the shadows came Lawson. He was stark-naked, and he wore, bound across his brow, the half moon of alabaster. He had something, too, in his hand – something which glittered.

He ran round the tower, crooning to himself, and flinging wild arms to the skies. Sometimes the crooning changed to a shrill cry of passion, such as a maenad may have uttered in the train of Bacchus. I could make out no words, but the sound told its own tale. He was absorbed in some infernal ecstasy. And as he ran, he drew his right hand across his breast and arms, and I saw that it held a knife.

I grew sick with disgust – not terror, but honest physical loathing. Lawson, gashing his fat body, affected me with an overpowering repugnance. I wanted to go forward and stop him, and I wanted, too, to be a hundred miles away. And the result was that I stayed still. I believe my own will held me there, but I doubt if in any case I could have moved my legs.

The dance grew swifter and fiercer. I saw the blood dripping from Lawson's body, and his face ghastly white above his scarred breast.

And then suddenly the horror left me; my head swam; and for one second – one brief second – I seemed to peer into a new world. A strange passion surged up in my heart. I seemed to see the earth peopled with forms – not human, scarcely divine, but more desirable than man or god. The calm face of Nature broke up for me into wrinkles of wild knowledge. I saw the things which brush against the soul in dreams, and found them lovely. There seemed no cruelty in the knife or the blood. It was a delicate mystery of worship, as wholesome as the morning song of birds. I do not know how the Semites found Ashtaroth's ritual; to them it may well have been more rapt and passionate than it seemed to me. For I saw in it only the sweet simplicity of Nature, and all riddles of lust and terror soothed away as a child's nightmares are calmed by a mother. I found my legs able to move, and I think I took two steps through the dusk towards the tower.

And then it all ended. A cock crew, and the homely noises of earth were renewed. While I stood dazed and shivering, Lawson plunged through the Grove towards me. The impetus carried him to the edge, and he fell fainting just outside the shade.

My wits and common-sense came back to me with my bodily strength. I got my friend on my back, and staggered with him towards the house. I was afraid in real earnest now, and what frightened me most was the thought that I had not been afraid sooner. I had come very near the "abomination of the Zidonians".

At the door I found the scared valet waiting. He had apparently done this sort of thing before.

"Your master has been sleep-walking, and has had a fall," I said. "We must get him to bed at once."

We bathed the wounds as he lay in a deep stupor, and I dressed them as well as I could. The only danger lay in his utter exhaustion, for happily the gashes were not serious, and no artery had been touched. Sleep and rest would make him well, for he had the constitution of a strong man. I was leaving the room when he opened his eyes and spoke. He did not recognize me, but I noticed that his face had lost its strangeness, and was once more that of the friend I had known. Then I suddenly bethought me of an old hunting remedy which he and I always carried on our expeditions. It is a pill made up from an ancient Portuguese prescription. One is an excellent specific for fever. Two are invaluable if you are lost in the bush, for they send a man for many hours into a deep sleep, which prevents suffering and madness, till help comes. Three give a painless death. I went to my room and found the little box in my jewel-case. Lawson swallowed two, and turned wearily on his side. I bade his man let him sleep till he woke, and went off in search of food.

I had business on hand which would not wait. By seven, Jobson, who had been sent for, was waiting for me in the library. I knew by his grim face that here I had a very good substitute for a prophet of the Lord.

"You were right," I said. "I have read the 11th chapter of 1st Kings, and I have spent such a night as I pray God I shall never spend again."

"I thought you would," he replied. "I've had the same experience myself."

"The Grove?" I said.

"Ay, the wud," was the answer in broad Scots.

I wanted to see how much he understood.

"Mr Lawson's family is from the Scottish Border?"

"Ay. I understand they come off Borthwick Water side," he replied, but I saw by his eyes that he knew what I meant.

"Mr Lawson is my oldest friend," I went on, "and I am going to take measures to cure him. For what I am going to do I take the sole responsibility. I will make that plain to your master. But if I am to succeed I want your help. Will you give it to me? It sounds like madness, and you are a sensible man and may like to keep out of it. I leave it to your discretion."

Jobson looked me straight in the face. "Have no fear for me," he said; "there is an unholy thing in that place, and if I have the strength in me I will destroy it. He has been a good master to me, and forbye, I am a believing Christian. So say on, sir."

There was no mistaking the air. I had found my Tishbite.

"I want men," I said, – "as many as we can get."

Jobson mused. "The Kaffirs will no' gang near the place, but there's some thirty white men on the tobacco farm. They'll do your will, if you give them an indemnity in writing."

"Good," said I. "Then we will take our instructions from the only authority which meets the case. We will follow the example of King Josiah." I turned up the 23rd Chapter of 2nd Kings, and read:

And the high places that were before Jerusalem, which were on the right hand of the Mount of Corruption, which Solomon the king of Israel had builded for Ashtaroth the abomination of the Zidonians . . . did the king defile.

> And he brake in pieces the images, and cut down the groves, and filled their places with the bones of men.
>
> Moreover the altar that was at Beth-el, and the high place which Jeroboam the son of Nebat, who made Israel to sin, had made, both that altar and the high place he brake down, and burned the high place, and stamped it small to powder, and burned the grove.

Jobson nodded. "It'll need dinnymite. But I've plenty of yon down at the workshops. I'll be off to collect the lads."

Before nine the men had assembled at Jobson's house. They were a hardy lot of young farmers from home, who took their instructions docilely from the masterful factor. On my orders they had brought their shot-guns. We armed them with spades and woodmen's axes, and one man wheeled some coils of rope in a hand-cart.

In the clear, windless air of morning the Grove, set amid its lawns, looked too innocent and exquisite for ill. I had a pang of regret that a thing so fair should suffer; nay, if I had come alone, I think I might have repented. But the men were there, and the grim-faced Jobson was waiting for orders. I placed the guns, and sent beaters to the far side. I told them that every dove must be shot.

It was only a small flock, and we killed fifteen at the first drive. The poor birds flew over the glen to another spinney, but we brought them back over the guns and seven fell. Four more were got in the trees, and the last I killed myself with a long shot. In half an hour there was a pile of little green bodies on the sward.

Then we went to work to cut down the trees. The slim stems were an easy task to a good woodman, and one after another they toppled to the ground. And meantime, as I watched, I became conscious of a strange emotion.

It was as if someone were pleading with me. A gentle voice, not threatening, but pleading – something too fine for the sensual ear, but touching inner chords of the spirit. So tenuous it was and distant that I could think of no personality behind it. Rather it was the viewless, bodiless grace of this delectable vale, some old exquisite divinity of the groves. There was the heart of all sorrow in it, and the soul of all loveliness. It seemed a woman's voice, some lost lady who had brought nothing but goodness unrepaid to the world. And what the voice told me was that I was destroying her last shelter.

That was the pathos of it – the voice was homeless. As the axes flashed in the sunlight and the wood grew thin, that gentle spirit was pleading with me for mercy and a brief respite. It seemed to be telling of a world for centuries grown coarse and pitiless, of long sad wanderings, of hardly won shelter, and a peace which was the little all she sought from men. There was nothing terrible in it, no thought of wrongdoing. The spell which to Semitic blood held the mystery of evil, was to me, of the Northern race, only delicate and rare and beautiful. Jobson and the rest did not feel it, I with my finer senses caught nothing but the hopeless sadness of it. That which had stirred the passion in Lawson was only wringing my heart. It was almost too pitiful to bear. As the trees crashed down and the men wiped the sweat from their brows, I seemed to myself like the murderer of fair women and innocent children. I remember that the tears were running over my cheeks. More than once I opened my mouth to countermand the work, but the face of Jobson, that grim Tishbite, held me back. I knew now what gave the Prophets of the Lord their mastery, and I knew also why the people sometimes stoned them.

The last tree fell, and the little tower stood like a ravished shrine, stripped of all defence against the world. I heard Jobson's voice speaking. "We'd better blast that stane thing now. We'll trench on four sides and lay the dinnymite. Ye're no' looking weel, sir. Ye'd better go and sit down on the brae-face."

I went up the hillside and lay down. Below me, in the waste of shorn trunks, men were running about, and I saw the mining begin. It all seemed like an aimless dream in which I had no part. The voice of that homeless goddess was still pleading. It was the innocence of it that tortured me. Even so must a merciful Inquisitor have suffered from the plea of some fair girl with the aureole of death on her hair. I knew I was killing rare and unrecoverable beauty. As I sat dazed and heartsick, the whole loveliness of Nature seemed to plead for its divinity. The sun in the heavens, the mellow lines of upland, the blue mystery of the far plains, were all part of that soft voice. I felt bitter scorn for myself. I was guilty of blood; nay, I was guilty of the sin against light which knows no forgiveness. I was murdering innocent gentleness, and there would be no peace on earth for me. Yet I sat helpless. The power of a sterner will constrained me. And all the while the voice was growing fainter and dying away into unutterable sorrow.

Suddenly a great flame sprang to heaven, and a pall of smoke. I heard men crying out, and fragments of stone fell around the ruins of the grove. When the air cleared, the little tower had gone out of sight.

The voice had ceased and there seemed to me to be a bereaved silence in the world. The shock moved me to my feet, and I ran down the slope to where Jobson stood rubbing his eyes.

"That's done the job. Now we maun get up the tree-roots. We've no time to howk. We'll just dinnymite the feck o' them."

The work of destruction went on, but I was coming back to my senses. I forced myself to be practical and reasonable. I thought of the night's experience and Lawson's haggard eyes, and I screwed myself into a determination to see the thing through. I had done the deed; it was my business to make it complete. A text in Jeremiah came into my head: "*Their children remember their altars and their groves by the green trees upon the high hills.*" I would see to it that this grove should be utterly forgotten.

We blasted the tree roots, and, yoking oxen, dragged the *débris* into a great heap. Then the men set to work with their spades, and roughly levelled the ground. I was getting back to my old self, and Jobson's spirit was becoming mine.

"There is one thing more," I told him. "Get ready a couple of ploughs. We will improve upon King Josiah." My brain was a medley of Scripture precedents, and I was determined that no safeguard should be wanting.

We yoked the oxen again and drove the ploughs over the site of the grove. It was rough ploughing, for the place was thick with bits of stone from the tower, but the slow Afrikander oxen plodded on, and sometime in the afternoon the work was finished. Then I sent down to the farm for bags of rock-salt, such as they use for cattle. Jobson and I took a sack apiece, and walked up and down the furrows, sowing them with salt.

The last act was to set fire to the pile of tree-trunks. They burned well, and on the top we flung the bodies of the green doves. The birds of Ashtaroth had an honourable pyre.

Then I dismissed the much-perplexed men, and gravely shook hands with Jobson. Black with dust and smoke I went back to the house, where I bade Travers pack my bags and order the motor. I found Lawson's servant, and heard from him that his master was sleeping peacefully. I gave some directions, and then went to wash and change.

Before I left I wrote a line to Lawson. I began by transcribing the verses from the 23rd Chapter of 2nd Kings. I told him what I had done, and my reason. "I take the whole responsibility upon myself," I wrote. "No man in the place had anything to do with it but me. I acted as I did for the sake of our old friendship, and you will believe it was no easy task for me. I hope you will understand. Whenever you are able to see me send me word, and I will come back and settle with you. But I think you will realize that I have saved your soul."

* * *

The afternoon was merging into twilight as I left the house on the road to Taqui. The great fire, where the grove had been, was still blazing fiercely, and the smoke made a cloud over the upper glen, and filled all the air with a soft violet haze. I knew that I had done well for my friend, and that he would come to his senses and be grateful. My mind was at ease on that score, and in something like comfort I faced the future. But as the car reached the ridge I looked back to the vale I had outraged. The moon was rising and silvering the smoke, and through the gaps I could see the tongues of fire. Somehow, I know not why, the lake, the stream, the garden-coverts, even the green slopes of hill, wore an air of loneliness and desecration.

And then my heartache returned, and I knew that I had driven something lovely and adorable from its last refuge on earth.

A Man From Glasgow

Somerset Maugham

Location: Ecija, near Seville, Spain.

Time: May, 1925.

Eyewitness Description: *"I jumped out of bed and went to the window. My legs began to tremble. It was horrible to stand there and listen to the shouts of laughter that rang through the night. Then there was a pause, and after that a shriek of pain and that ghastly sobbing. It didn't sound human . . ."*

Author: William Somerset Maugham (1874–1965) was a multi-talented man as befitted someone born in Paris of Irish origin, read philosophy and literature at Heidelberg and qualified as a surgeon in London. Instead of a medical profession, though, he turned to writing and enjoyed a huge success with his magnificent autobiographical *Of Human Bondage* published in 1915. The First World War saw him serving as a secret agent in Geneva followed by a time in Russia attempting to prevent the outbreak of the Bolshevik revolution. Travels in France, Spain, the Far East and the South Seas provided the themes for some of Maugham's greatest books including *Moon and Sixpence* (1919), *Ashenden* (1928) and *Cakes and Ale* (1930). He never discussed his conviction about ghosts, however, but his evident fascination with the supernatural and the occult is evident in *The Magician* (1908), a thinly disguised portrait of the Black Magician, Aleister Crowley, and three brilliant short stories, "The Taipan", "The End of the Flight" and, especially, "A Man From Glasgow" which is an exercise in mounting terror and enough to make any reader dread the full moon.

It is not often that anyone entering a great city for the first time has the luck to witness such an incident as engaged the poet Shelley's attention when he drove into Naples. A youth ran out of a shop pursued by a man armed with a knife. The man overtook him and with one blow in the neck laid him dead on the road. Shelley had a tender heart. He didn't look upon it as a bit of local colour; he was seized with horror and indignation. But when he expressed his emotions to a Calabrian priest who was travelling with him, a fellow of gigantic strength and stature, the priest laughed heartily and attempted to quiz him. Shelley says he never felt such an inclination to beat anyone.

I have never seen anything so exciting as that, but the first time I went to Algeciras I had an experience that seemed to me far from ordinary. Algeciras was then an untidy, neglected town. I arrived somewhat late at night and went to an inn on the quay. It was rather shabby, but it had a fine view of Gibraltar, solid and matter of fact, across the bay. The moon was full. The office was on the first floor, and a slatternly maid, when I asked for a room, took me upstairs. The landlord was playing cards. He seemed little pleased to see me. He looked me up and down, curtly gave me a number, and then, taking no further notice of me, went on with his game.

When the maid had shown me to my room I asked her what I could have to eat.

"What you like," she answered.

I knew well enough the unreality of the seeming profusion.

"What have you got in the house?"

"You can have eggs and ham."

The look of the hotel had led me to guess that I should get little else. The maid led me to a narrow room with whitewashed walls and a low ceiling in which was a long table laid already for the next day's luncheon. With his back to the door sat a tall man, huddled over a *brasero*, the round brass dish of hot ashes which is erroneously supposed to give sufficient warmth for the temperate winter of Andalusia. I sat down at the table and waited for my scanty meal. I gave the stranger an idle glance. He was looking at me, but meeting my eyes he quickly turned away. I waited for my eggs. When at last the maid brought them he looked up again.

"I want you to wake me in time for the first boat," he said.

"*Si, señor.*"

His accent told me that English was his native tongue, and the breadth of his build, his strongly marked features, led me to suppose him a northerner. The hardy Scot is far more often found in Spain than the Englishman. Whether you go to the rich mines of Rio Tinto, or to the bodegas of Jerez, to Seville or to Cadiz, it is the leisurely speech of beyond the Tweed that you hear. You will meet Scotsmen in the olive groves of Carmona, on the railway between Algeciras and Bobadilla, and even in the remote cork woods of Merida.

I finished eating and went over to the dish of burning ashes. It was midwinter and the windy passage across the bay had chilled my blood. The man pushed his chair away as I drew mine forwards.

"Don't move," I said. "There's heaps of room for two."

I lit a cigar and offered one to him. In Spain the Havana from Gib is never unwelcome.

"I don't mind if I do," he said, stretching out his hand.

I recognised the singing speech of Glasgow. But the stranger was not talkative, and my efforts at conversation broke down before his monosyllables. We smoked in silence. He was even bigger than I had thought, with great broad shoulders and ungainly limbs; his face was sunburned, his hair short and grizzled. His features were hard; mouth, ears and nose were large and heavy and his skin much wrinkled. His blue eyes were pale. He was constantly pulling his ragged, grey moustache. It was a nervous gesture that I found faintly irritating. Presently I felt that he was looking at me, and the intensity of his stare grew so irksome that I glanced up expecting him, as before, to drop his eyes. He did, indeed, for a moment, but then raised them again. He inspected me from under his long, bushy eyebrows.

"Just come from Gib?" he asked suddenly.

"Yes."

"I'm going back tomorrow – on my way home. Thank God."

He said the last two words so fiercely that I smiled.

"Don't you like Spain?"

"Oh, Spain's all right."

"Have you been here long?"

"Too long. Too long."

He spoke with a kind of gasp. I was surprised at the emotion my casual inquiry seemed to excite in him. He sprang to his feet and walked backwards and forwards. He stamped to and fro like a caged beast, pushing aside a chair that stood in his way, and now and again repeated the words in a groan. "Too long. Too long." I sat still. I was embarrassed. To give myself countenance I stirred the *brasero* to bring the hotter ashes to the top, and he stood suddenly still, towering over me, as though my movement had brought back my existence to his notice. Then he sat down heavily in his chair.

"Do you think I'm queer?" he asked.

"Not more than most people," I smiled.

"You don't see anything strange in me?"

He leant forward as he spoke so that I might see him well.

"No."

"You'd say so if you did, wouldn't you?"

"I would."

I couldn't quite understand what all this meant. I wondered if he was drunk. For two or three minutes he didn't say anything and I had no wish to interrupt the silence.

"What's your name?" he asked suddenly. I told him.

"Mine's Robert Morrison."

"Scotch?"

"Glasgow. I've been in this blasted country for years. Got any baccy?"

I gave him my pouch and he filled his pipe. He lit it from a piece of burning charcoal.

"I can't stay any longer. I've stayed too long. Too long."

He had an impulse to jump up again and walk up and down, but he resisted it, clinging to his chair. I saw on his face the effort he was making. I judged that his restlessness was due to chronic alcoholism. I find drunks very boring, and I made up my mind to take an early opportunity of slipping off to bed.

"I've been managing some olive groves," he went on. "I'm here working for the Glasgow and South of Spain Olive Oil Company Limited."

"Oh, yes."

"We've got a new process for refining oil, you know. Properly treated, Spanish oil is every bit as good as Lucca. And we can sell it cheaper."

He spoke in a dry, matter-of-fact, business-like way. He chose his words with Scotch precision. He seemed perfectly sober.

"You know, Ecija is more or less the centre of the olive trade, and we had a Spaniard there to look after the business. But I found he was robbing us right and left, so I had to turn him out. I used to live in Seville; it was more convenient for shipping the oil. However, I found I couldn't get a trustworthy man to be at Ecija, so last year I went there myself. D'you know it?"

"No."

"The firm has got a big estate two miles from the town, just outside the village of San Lorenzo, and it's got a fine house on it. It's on the crest of a hill, rather pretty to look at, all white, you know, and straggling, with a couple of storks perched on the roof. No one lived there, and I thought it would save the rent of a place in town if I did."

"It must have been a bit lonely," I remarked.

"It was."

Robert Morrison smoked on for a minute or two in silence. I wondered whether there was any point in what he was telling me. I looked at my watch.

"In a hurry?" he asked sharply.

"Not particularly. It's getting late."

"Well, what of it?"

"I suppose you didn't see many people?" I said, going back.

"Not many. I lived there with an old man and his wife who looked after me, and sometimes I used to go down to the village and play *tresillo* with Fernandez, the chemist, and one or two men who met at his shop. I used to shoot a bit and ride."

"It doesn't sound such a bad life to me."

"I'd been there two years last spring. By God, I've never known such heat as we had in May. No one could do a thing. The labourers just lay about in the shade and slept. Sheep died and some of the animals went mad. Even the oxen couldn't work. They stood around with their backs all humped up and gasped for breath. That blasted sun beat down and the glare was so awful, you felt your eyes would shoot out of your head. The earth cracked and crumbled, and the crops frizzled. The olives went to rack and ruin. It was simply hell. One couldn't get a wink of sleep. I went from room to room, trying to get a breath of air. Of course I kept the windows shut and had the floors watered, but that didn't do any good. The nights were just as hot as the days. It was like living in an oven.

"At last I thought I'd have a bed made up for me downstairs on the north side of the house in a room that was never used because in ordinary weather it was damp. I had an idea that I might get a few hours' sleep there at all events. Anyhow it was worth trying. But it was no damned good; it was a washout. I turned and tossed and my bed was so hot that I couldn't stand it. I got up and opened the doors that led to the veranda and walked out. It was a glorious night. The moon was so bright that I swear you could read a book by it. Did I tell you the house was on the crest of a hill? I leant against the parapet and looked at the olive-trees. It was like the sea. I suppose that's what made me think of home. I thought of the cool breeze in the fir-trees and the racket of the streets in Glasgow. Believe it or not, I could smell them, and I could smell the sea. By God, I'd have given every bob I had in the world for an hour of that air. They say it's a foul climate in Glasgow. Don't you believe it. I like the rain and the grey sky and that yellow sea and the waves. I forgot that I was in Spain, in the middle of the olive country, and I opened my mouth and took a long breath as though I were breathing in the sea-fog.

"And then all of a sudden I heard a sound. It was a man's voice. Not loud, you know, low. It seemed to creep through the silence like – well, I don't know what it was like. It surprised me. I couldn't think who could be down there in the olives at that hour. It was past midnight. It was a chap laughing. A funny sort of laugh. I suppose you'd call it a chuckle. It seemed to crawl up the hill – disjointedly."

Morrison looked at me to see how I took the odd word he used to express a sensation that he didn't know how to describe.

"I mean, it seemed to shoot up in little jerks, something like shooting stones out of a pail. I leant forward and stared. With the full moon it was almost as light as day, but I'm dashed if I could see a thing. The sound stopped, but I kept on looking at where it had come from in case somebody moved. And in a minute it started off again, but louder. You couldn't have called it a chuckle any more, it was a real belly laugh. It just rang through the night. I wondered it didn't wake my servants. It sounded like someone who was roaring drunk.

"'Who's there?'" I shouted.

"The only answer I got was a roar of laughter. I don't mind telling you I was getting a bit annoyed. I had half a mind to go down and see what it was all about. I wasn't going to let some drunken swine kick up a row like that on my place in the middle of the night. And then suddenly there was a yell. By God, I was startled. Then cries. The man had laughed with a deep bass voice, but his cries were – shrill, like a pig having his throat cut.

"'My God,' I cried.

"I jumped over the parapet and ran down towards the sound. I thought somebody was being killed. There was silence and then one piercing shriek. After that sobbing and moaning. I'll tell you what it sounded like, it sounded like someone at the point of death. There was a long groan and then nothing. Silence. I ran from place to place. I couldn't find anyone. At last I climbed the hill again and went back to my room.

"You can imagine how much sleep I got that night. As soon as it was light, I looked out of the window in the direction from which the row had come and I was surprised to see a little white house in a sort of dale among the olives. The ground on that side didn't belong to us and I'd never been through it. I hardly ever went to that part of the house and so I'd never seen the house before. I asked Josè who lived there. He told me that a madman had inhabited it, with his brother and a servant."

"Oh, was that the explanation?" I said. "Not a very nice neighbour."

The Scot bent over quickly and seized my wrist. He thrust his face into mine and his eyes were staring out of his head with terror.

"The madman had been dead for twenty years," he whispered.

He let go my wrist and leant back in his chair panting.

"I went down to the house and walked all round it. The windows were barred and shuttered and the door was locked. I knocked. I shook the handle and rang the bell. I heard it tinkle, but no one came. It was a two-storey house and I looked up. The shutters were tight closed, and there wasn't a sign of life anywhere."

"Well, what sort of condition was the house in?" I asked.

"Oh, rotten. The whitewash had worn off the walls and there was practically no paint left on the door or the shutters. Some of the tiles off the rooff were lying on the ground. They looked as though they'd been blown away in a gale."

"Queer," I said.

"I went to my friend Fernandez, the chemist, and he told me the same story as Josè. I asked about the madman and Fernandez said that no one ever saw him. He was more or less comatose ordinarily, but now and then he had an attack of acute mania and then he could be heard from ever so far laughing his head off and then crying. It used to scare people. He died in one of his attacks and his keepers cleared out at once. No one had ever dared to live in the house since.

"I didn't tell Fernandez what I'd heard. I thought he'd only laugh at me. I stayed up that night and kept watch. But nothing happened. There wasn't a sound. I waited about till dawn and then I went to bed."

"And you never heard anything more?"

"Not for a month. The drought continued and I went on sleeping in the lumber-room at the back. One night I was fast asleep, when something seemed to happen to me; I don't exactly know how to describe it, it was a funny feeling as though someone had given me a little nudge, to warn me, and suddenly I was wide awake. I lay there in my bed and then in the same way as before I heard a long, low gurgle, like a man enjoying an old joke. It came from away down in the valley and it got louder. It was a great bellow of laughter. I jumped out of bed and went to the window. My legs began to tremble. It was horrible to stand there and listen to the shouts of laughter that rang through the night. Then there was the pause, and after that a shriek of pain and that ghastly sobbing. It didn't sound human. I mean, you might have thought it was an animal being tortured. I don't mind telling you I was scared stiff. I couldn't have moved if I'd wanted to. After a time the sounds stopped, not suddenly, but dying away little by little. I strained my ears, but I couldn't hear a thing. I crept back to bed and hid my face.

"I remembered then that Fernandez had told me that the madman's attacks only came at intervals. The rest of the time he was quite quiet. Apathetic, Fernandez said. I wondered if the fits of mania came regularly. I reckoned out how long it had been between the two attacks I'd heard. Twenty-eight days. It didn't take me long to put two and two together; it was quite obvious that it was the full moon that set him off. I'm not a nervous man really and I made up my mind to get to the bottom of it, so I looked out in the calendar which day the moon would be full next and that night I didn't go to bed. I cleaned my revolver and loaded it. I prepared a lantern and sat down on the parapet of my house to wait. I felt perfectly cool. To tell you the truth, I was rather pleased with myself because I didn't feel scared. There was a bit of a wind, and it whistled about the roof. It rustled over the leaves of the olive trees like waves shishing on the pebbles of the beach. The moon shone on the white walls of the house in the hollow. I felt particularly cheery.

"At last I heard a little sound, the sound I knew, and I almost laughed. I was right; it was the full moon and the attacks came as regular as clockwork That was all to the good. I threw myself over the wall into the olive grove and ran straight to the house. The chuckling grew louder as I came near. I got to the house and looked up. There was no light anywhere. I put my ears to the door and listened. I heard the madman simply laughing his bloody head off. I beat on the door with my fist and I pulled the bell. The sound of it seemed to amuse him. He roared with laughter. I knocked again, louder and louder, and the more I knocked the more he laughed. Then I shouted at the top of my voice.

'Open the blasted door, or I'll break it down.'

"I stepped back and kicked at the latch with all my might. I flung myself at the door with the whole weight of my body. It cracked. Then I put all my strength into it and the damned thing smashed open.

"I took the revolver out of my pocket and held my lantern in the other hand. The laughter sounded louder now that the door was opened. I stepped in. The stink nearly knocked me down. I mean, just think, the windows hadn't been opened for twenty years. The row was enough to raise the dead, but for a moment I didn't know where it was coming from. The walls seemed to throw the sound backwards and forwards. I pushed open a door by my side and went into a room. It was bare and white and there wasn't a stick of furniture in it. The sound was louder and I followed it. I went into another room, but there was nothing there. I opened a door and found myself at the foot of a staircase. The madman was laughing just over my head. I walked up, cautiously, you know, I wasn't taking any risks, and at the top of the stairs there was a passage. I walked along it, throwing my light ahead of me, and I came to a room at the end. I stopped. He was in there. I was only separated from the sound by a thin door.

"It was awful to hear it. A shiver passed through me and I cursed myself because I began to tremble. It wasn't like a human being at all. By Jove, I very nearly took to my heels and ran. I had to clench my teeth to force myself to stay. But I simply couldn't bring myself to turn the handle. And then the laughter was cut, cut with a knife you'd have said, and I heard a hiss of pain. I hadn't heard that before, it was too low to carry to my place, and then a gasp.

" 'Ay!' I heard the man speak in Spanish. 'You're killing me. Take it away. O God, help me!'

"He screamed. The brutes were torturing him. I flung open the door and burst in. The draught blew a shutter back and the moon streamed in so bright that it dimmed my lantern. In my ears, as clearly as I hear you speak and as close, I heard the wretched chap's groans. It was awful, moaning and sobbing, and frightful gasps. No one could survive that. He was at the point of death. I tell you I heard his broken, choking cries right in my ears. And the room was empty."

Robert Morrison sank back in his chair. That huge solid man had strangely the look of a lay figure in a studio. You felt that if you pushed him he would fall over in a heap on to the floor.

"And then?" I asked.

He took a rather dirty handkerchief out of his pocket and wiped his forehead.

"I felt I didn't want to sleep in that room on the north side so, heat or no heat, I moved back to my own quarters. Well, exactly four weeks later, about two in the morning, I was waked up by the madman's chuckle. It was almost at my elbow. I don't mind telling you that my nerve was a bit shaken by then, so next time the blighter was due to have an attack, next time the moon was full, I mean, I got Fernandez to come and spend the night with me. I didn't tell him anything. I kept him up playing cards till two in the morning, and then I heard it again. I asked him if he heard anything. 'Nothing,' he said. 'There's somebody laughing,' I said. 'You're drunk, man,' he said, and he began laughing too. That was too much. 'Shut up, you fool,' I said. The laughter grew louder and louder. I cried out. I tried to shut it out by putting my hands to my ears, but it wasn't a damned bit of good. I heard it and I heard the scream of pain. Fernandez thought I was mad. He didn't dare say so, because he knew I'd have killed him. He said he'd go to bed, and in the morning I found he'd slunk away. His bed hadn't been slept in. He'd taken himself off when he left me.

"After that I couldn't stop in Ecija. I put a factor there and went back to Seville. I felt myself pretty safe there, but as the time came near I began to get scared. Of course I told myself not to be a damned fool, but you know, I damned well couldn't help myself. The fact is, I was afraid the sounds had followed me, and I knew if I heard them in Seville I'd go on hearing them all my life. I've got as much courage as any man, but damn it all, there are limits to everything. Flesh and blood couldn't stand it. I knew I'd go stark staring mad. I got in such a state that I began drinking, the suspense was so awful, and I used to lie awake counting the days. And at last I knew it'd come. And it came. I heard those sounds in Seville – sixty miles away from Ecija."

I didn't know what to say. I was silent for a while.

"When did you hear the sounds last?" I asked.

"Four weeks ago."

I looked up quickly. I was startled.

"What d'you mean by that? It's not full moon tonight?"

He gave me a dark, angry look. He opened his mouth to speak and then stopped as though he couldn't. You would have said his vocal cords were paralysed, and it was with a strange croak that at last he answered.

"Yes, it is."

He stared at me and his pale blue eyes seemed to shine red. I have never seen in a man's face a look of such terror. He got up quickly and stalked out of the room, slamming the door behind him.

I must admit that I didn't sleep any too well that night myself.

The Last Laugh

D. H. Lawrence

Location: Hampstead, London.
Time: December, 1927.
Eyewitness Description: *"The whirling, snowy air seemed full of presences, full of strange unheard voices. She was used to the sensation of noises taking place which she could not hear. The sensation became very strong. She felt something was happening in the wild air."*
Author: David Herbert Lawrence (1885–1930), the frail son of a Nottinghamshire miner and former schoolteacher turned writer, is forever associated with *Lady Chatterley's Lover*, first published in Florence in 1928. In this he attempted to interpret human emotions on a deeper level of consciousness than his contemporaries and found himself prosecuted for obscenity on the one hand, but becoming a massive influence on the young intellectuals of his time on the other. Like Somerset Maugham, he lived in various parts of the world including Germany, Austria, Italy and Capri before settling in Mexico for the sake of his health. Although often attacked for his eroticism, Lawrence was capable of brilliantly descriptive short stories and three of these demonstrate a typically challenging approach to the supernatural: "The Rocking Horse Winner" featuring a boy who can predict winning horses; "The Woman Who Rode Away" about Native American supernaturalism; and "The Last Laugh" which, with its chilling setting, wild pagan mood and unexpected finale, is undoubtedly one of the finest *conte cruel* tales of the "Golden Era".

There was a little snow on the ground, and the church clock had just struck midnight. Hampstead in the night of winter for once was looking pretty, with clean white earth and lamps for moon, and dark sky above the lamps.

A confused little sound of voices, a gleam of hidden yellow light. And then the garden door of a tall, dark Georgian house suddenly opened, and three people confusedly emerged. A girl in a dark blue coat and fur turban, very erect: a fellow with a little dispatch-case, slouching: a thin man with a red beard, bareheaded, peering out of the gateway down the hill that swung in a curve downwards towards London.

"Look at it! A new world!" cried the man in the beard, ironically, as he stood on the step and peered out.

"No, Lorenzo! It's only whitewash!" cried the young man in the overcoat. His voice was handsome, resonant, plangent, with a weary sardonic touch. As he turned back his face was dark in shadow.

The girl with the erect, alert head, like a bird, turned back to the two men.

"What was that?" she asked, in her quick, quiet voice.

"Lorenzo says it's a new world. I say it's only whitewash," cried the man in the street.

She stood still and lifted her woolly, gloved finger. She was deaf and was taking it in.

Yes, she had got it. She gave a quick, chuckling laugh, glanced very quickly at the man in the bowler hat, then back at the man in the stucco gateway, who was grinning like a satyr and waving good-bye.

"Good-bye, Lorenzo!" came the resonant, weary cry of the man in the bowler hat.

"Good-bye!" came the sharp, night-bird call of the girl.

The green gate slammed, then the inner door. The two were alone in the street, save for the policeman at the corner. The road curved steeply downhill.

"You'd better mind how you *step!*" shouted the man in the bowler hat, leaning near the erect, sharp girl, and slouching in his walk. She paused a moment, to make sure what he had said.

"Don't mind me, I'm quite all right. Mind yourself!" she said quickly. At that very moment he gave a wild lurch on the slippery snow, but managed to save himself from falling. She watched him, on tiptoes of alertness. His bowler hat bounced away in the thin snow. They were under a lamp near the curve. As he ducked for his hat he showed a bald spot, just like a tonsure, among his dark, thin, rather curly hair. And when he looked up at her, with his thick black brows sardonically arched, and his rather hooked nose self-derisive, jamming his hat on again, he seemed like a satanic young priest. His face had beautiful lines, like a faun, and a doubtful martyred expression. A sort of faun on the Cross, with all the malice of the complication.

"Did you hurt yourself?" she asked, in her quick, cool, unemotional way.

"No!" he shouted derisively.

"Give me the machine, won't you?" she said, holding out her woolly hand. "I believe I'm safer."

"Do you *want* it?" he shouted.

"Yes, I'm sure I'm safer."

He handed her the little brown dispatch-case, which was really a Marconi listening machine for her deafness. She marched erect as ever. He shoved his hands deep in his overcoat pockets and slouched along beside her, as if he wouldn't make his legs firm. The road curved down in front of them, clean and pale with snow under the lamps. A motor-car came churning up. A few dark figures slipped away into the dark recesses of the houses, like fishes among rocks above a sea-bed of white sand. On the left was a tuft of trees sloping upwards into the dark.

He kept looking around, pushing out his finely shaped chin and his hooked nose as if he were listening for something. He could still hear the motor-car climbing on to the Heath. Below was the yellow, foul-smelling glare of the Hampstead Tube station. On the right the trees.

The girl, with her alert pink-and-white face looked at him sharply, inquisitively. She had an odd nymph-like inquisitiveness, sometimes like a bird, sometimes a squirrel, sometimes a rabbit: never quite like a woman. At last he stood still, as if he would go no farther. There was a curious, baffled grin on his smooth, cream-coloured face.

"James," he said loudly to her, leaning towards her ear. "Do you hear somebody *laughing*?"

"Laughing?" she retorted quickly. "Who's laughing?"

"I don't know. *Somebody!*" he shouted, showing his teeth at her in a very odd way.

"No, I hear nobody," she announced.

"But it's most *extraordinary!*" he cried, his voice slurring up and down. "Put on your machine."

"Put it on?" she retorted. "What for?"

"To see if you can *hear* it," he cried.

"Hear what?"

"The *laughing*. Somebody laughing. It's most *extraordinary*."

She gave her odd little chuckle and handed him her machine. He held it while she opened the lid and attached the wires, putting the band over her head and the receivers at her ears, like a wireless operator. Crumbs of snow fell down the cold darkness. She switched on: little yellow lights in glass tubes shone in the machine. She was connected, she was listening. He stood with his head ducked, his hands shoved down in his overcoat pockets.

Suddenly he lifted his face and gave the weirdest, slightly neighing laugh, uncovering his strong, spaced teeth and arching his black brows, and watching her with queer, gleaming, goat-like eyes.

She seemed a little dismayed.

"There!" he said. "Didn't you hear it?"

"I heard *you!*" she said, in a tone which conveyed that *that* was enough.

"But didn't you hear *it?*" he cried, unfurling his lips oddly again.

"No!" she said.

He looked at her vindictively, and stood again with ducked head. She remained erect, her fur hat in her hand, her fine bobbed hair banded with the machine-band and catching crumbs of snow, her odd, bright-eyed, deaf nymph's face lifted with blank listening.

"There!" he cried, suddenly jerking up his gleaming face. "You mean to tell me you can't –" He was looking at her almost diabolically. But something else was too strong for him. His face wreathed with a startling, peculiar smile, seeming to gleam, and suddenly the most extraordinary laugh came bursting out of him, like an animal laughing. It was a strange, neighing sound, amazing in her ears. She was startled, and switched her machine quieter.

A large form loomed up: a tall, clean-shaven young policeman.

"A radio?" he asked laconically.

"No, it's my machine. I'm deaf!" said Miss James quickly and distinctly. She was not the daughter of a peer for nothing.

The man in the bowler hat lifted his face and glared at the fresh-faced young policeman with a peculiar white glare in his eyes.

"Look here!" he said distinctly. "Did you hear someone laughing?"

"Laughing? I heard you, sir."

"No, *not* me." He gave an impatient jerk of his arm, and lifted his face again. His smooth, creamy face seemed to gleam, there were subtle curves of derisive triumph in all its lines. He was careful not to look directly at the young policeman. "The morst extraordinary laughter I ever heard," he added, and the same touch of derisive exultation sounded in his tones.

The policeman looked down on him cogitatingly.

"It's perfectly all right," said Miss James coolly. "He's not drunk. He just hears something that we don't hear."

"Drunk!" echoed the man in the bowler hat, in profoundly amused derision. "If I were merely drunk –" And off he went again in the wild, neighing, animal laughter, while his averted face seemed to flash.

At the sound of the laughter something roused in the blood of the girl and of the policeman. They stood nearer to one another, so that their sleeves touched and they looked wonderingly across at the man in the bowler hat. He lifted his black brows at them.

"Do you mean to say you heard nothing?" he asked.

"Only you," said Miss James.

"Only you, sir!" echoed the policeman.

"What was it like?" asked Miss James.

"Ask me to *describe* it!" retorted the young man, in extreme contempt. "It's the most marvellous sound in the world."

And truly he seemed wrapped up in a new mystery.

"Where does it come from?" asked Miss James, very practical.

"*Apparently,*" he answered in contempt, "from over there." And he pointed to the trees and bushes inside the railings over the road.

"Well, let's go and see!" she said. "I can carry my machine and go on listening."

The man seemed relieved to get rid of the burden. He shoved his hands in his pockets again and sloped off across the road. The policeman, a queer look flickering on his fresh young face, put his hand round the girl's arm carefully and subtly, to help her. She did not lean at all on the support of the big hand, but she was interested, so she did not resent it. Having held herself all her life intensely aloof from physical contact, and never having let any man touch her, she now, with a certain nymph-like voluptuousness, allowed the large hand of the young policeman to support her as they followed the quick wolf-like figure of the other man across the road uphill. And she could feel the presence of the young policeman, through all the thickness of his dark-blue uniform, as something young and alert and bright.

When they came up to the man in the bowler hat, he was standing with his head ducked, his ears pricked, listening beside the iron rail inside which grew big black holly-trees tufted with snow, and old, ribbed, silent English elms.

The policeman and the girl stood waiting. She was peering into the bushes with the sharp eyes of a deaf nymph, deaf to the world's noises. The man in the bowler hat listened intensely. A lorry rolled downhill, making the earth tremble.

"There!" cried the girl, as the lorry rumbled darkly past. And she glanced round with flashing eyes at her policeman, her fresh soft face gleaming with startled life. She glanced straight into the puzzled, amused eyes of the young policeman. He was just enjoying himself.

"Don't you see?" she said, rather imperiously.

"What is it, Miss?" answered the policeman.

"I mustn't point," she said. "Look where I look."

And she looked away with brilliant eyes, into the dark holly bushes. She must see something, for she smiled faintly, with subtle satisfaction, and she tossed her erect head in all the pride of vindication. The policeman looked at her instead of into the bushes. There was a certain brilliance of triumph and vindication in all the poise of her slim body.

"I always knew I should see him," she said triumphantly to herself.

"Whom do you see?" shouted the man in the bowler hat.

"Don't you see him too?" she asked, turning round her soft, arch, nymph-like face anxiously. She was anxious for the little man to see.

"No, I see nothing. What do you see, James?" cried the man in the bowler hat, insisting.

"A man."

"Where?"

"There. Among the holly bushes."

"Is he there now?"

"No! He's gone."

"What sort of a man?"

"I don't know."

"What did he look like?"

"I can't tell you."

But at that instant the man in the bowler hat turned suddenly, and the arch, triumphant look flew to his face.

"Why he must be *there!*" he cried, pointing up the grove. "Don't you hear him laughing? He must be behind those trees."

And his voice, with curious delight, broke into a laugh again, as he stood and stamped his feet on the snow, and danced to his own laughter, ducking his head. Then he turned away and ran swiftly up the avenue lined with old trees.

He slowed down as a door at the end of a garden path, white with untouched snow, suddenly opened, and a woman in a long-fringed black shawl stood in the light. She peered out into the night. Then she came down to the low garden gate. Crumbs of snow still fell. She had dark hair and a tall dark comb.

"Did you knock at my door?" she asked of the man in the bowler hat.

"I? No!"

"Somebody knocked at my door."

"Did they? Are you sure? They can't have done. There are no footmarks in the snow."

"Nor are there!" she said. "But somebody knocked and called something."

"That's very curious," said the man. "Were you expecting someone?"

"No. Not exactly expecting anyone. Except that one is always expecting Somebody, you know." In the dimness of the snow-lit night he could see her making big, dark eyes at him.

"Was it someone laughing?" he said.

"No. It was no one laughing, exactly. Some one knocked, and I ran to open, hoping as one always hopes, you know—"

"What?"

"Oh— that something wonderful is going to happen."

He was standing close to the low gate. She stood on the opposite side. Her hair was dark, her face seemed dusky, as she looked up at him with her dark, meaningful eyes.

"Did you wish someone would come?" he asked.

"Very much," she replied, in her plangent Jewish voice. She must be a Jewess.

"No matter who?" he said, laughing.

"So long as it was a man I could like," she said in a low, meaningful, falsely shy voice.

"Really!" he said. "Perhaps after all it was I who knocked – without knowing."

"I think it was," she said. "It must have been."

"Shall I come in?" he asked, putting his hand on the little gate.

"Don't you think you'd better?" she replied.

He bent down, unlatching the gate. As he did so the woman in the black shawl turned, and, glancing over her shoulder, hurried back to the house, walking unevenly in the snow, on her high-heeled shoes. The man hurried after her, hastening like a hound to catch up.

Meanwhile the girl and the policeman had come up. The girl stood still when she saw the man in the bowler hat going up the garden walk after the woman in the black shawl with the fringe.

"Is he going in?" she asked quickly.

"Looks like it, doesn't it?" said the policeman.

"Does he know that woman?"

"I can't say. I should say he soon will," replied the policeman.

"But who is she?"

"I couldn't say who she is."

The two dark, confused figures entered the lighted doorway, then the door closed on them.

"He's gone," said the girl outside on the snow. She hastily began to pull off the band of her telephone-receiver, and switched off her machine. The tubes of secret light disappeared, she packed up the little leather case. Then, pulling on her soft fur cap, she stood once more ready.

The slightly martial look which her long, dark-blue, military-seeming coat gave her was intensified, while the slightly anxious, bewildered look of her face had gone. She seemed to stretch herself, to stretch her limbs free. And the inert look had left her full soft cheeks. Her cheeks were alive with the glimmer of pride and a new dangerous surety.

She looked quickly at the tall young policeman. He was clean-shaven, fresh-faced, smiling oddly under his helmet, waiting in subtle patience a few yards away. She saw that he was a decent young man, one of the waiting sort.

The second of ancient fear was followed at once in her by a blithe, unaccustomed sense of power.

"Well!" she said. "I should say it's no use waiting." She spoke decisively.

"You don't have to wait for him, do you?" asked the policeman.

"Not at all. He's much better where he is." She laughed an odd, brief laugh. Then, glancing over her shoulder, she set off down the hill, carrying her little case. Her feet felt light, her legs felt long and strong. She glanced over her shoulder again. The young policeman was following her, and she laughed to herself. Her limbs felt so lithe and so strong, if she wished she could easily run faster than he. If she wished she could easily kill him, even with her hands.

So it seemed to her. But why kill him? He was a decent young fellow. She had in front of her eyes the dark face among the holly bushes, with the brilliant, mocking eyes. Her breast felt full of power, and her legs felt long and strong and wild. She was surprised herself at the strong, bright, throbbing sensation beneath her breasts, a sensation of triumph and of rosy anger. Her hands felt keen on her wrists. She who had always declared she had not a muscle in her body! Even now, it was not muscle, it was a sort of flame.

Suddenly it began to snow heavily, with fierce frozen puffs of wind. The snow was small, in frozen grains, and hit sharp on her face. It seemed to whirl round her as if she herself were whirling in a cloud. But she did not mind. There was a flame in her, her limbs felt flamey and strong, amid the whirl.

And the whirling, snowy air seemed full of presences, full of strange unheard voices. She was used to the sensation of noises taking place which she could not hear. This sensation became very strong. She felt something was happening in the wild air.

The London air was no longer heavy and clammy, saturated with ghosts of the unwilling dead. A new, clean tempest swept down from the Pole, and there were noises.

Voices were calling. In spite of her deafness she could hear someone, several voices, calling and whistling, as if many people were hallooing through the air:

"He's come back! Aha! He's come back!"

There was a wild, whistling, jubilant sound of voices in the storm of snow. Then obscured lightning winked through the snow in the air.

"Is that thunder and lightning?" she asked of the young policeman, as she stood still, waiting for his form to emerge through the veil of whirling snow.

"Seems like it to me," he said.

And at that very moment the lightning blinked again, and the dark, laughing face was near her face, it almost touched her cheek.

She started back, but a flame of delight went over her.

"There!" she said. "Did you see that?"

"It lightened," said the policeman.

She was looking at him almost angrily. But then the clean, fresh animal look of his skin and the tame-animal look in his frightened eyes amused her, she laughed her low, triumphant laugh. He was obviously afraid, like a frightened dog that sees something uncanny.

The storm suddenly whistled louder, more violently, and, with a strange noise like castanets, she seemed to hear voices clapping and crying:

"He is here! He's come back!"

She nodded her head gravely.

The policeman and she moved on side by side. She lived alone in a little stucco house in a side street down the hill. There was a church and a grove of trees and then the little old row of houses. The wind blew fiercely, thick with snow. Now and again a taxi went by, with its lights showing weirdly. But the world seemed empty, uninhabited save by snow and voices.

As the girl and the policeman turned past the grove of trees near the church, a great whirl of wind and snow made them stand still, and in the wild confusion they heard a whirling of sharp, delighted voices, something like seagulls, crying:

"He's here! He's here!"

"Well, I'm jolly glad he's back," said the girl calmly.

"What's that?" said the nervous policeman, hovering near the girl.

The wind let them move forward. As they passed along the railings it seemed to them the doors of the church were open, and the windows were out, and the snow and the voices were blowing in a wild career all through the church.

"How extraordinary that they left the church open!" said the girl. The policeman stood still. He could not reply.

And as they stood they listened to the wind and the church full of whirling voices all calling confusedly.

"*Now* I hear the laughing," she said suddenly.

It came from the church: a sound of low, subtle, endless laughter, a strange, naked sound.

"Now I hear it!" she said.

But the policeman did not speak. He stood cowed, with his tail between his legs, listening to the strange noises in the church.

The wind must have blown out one of the windows, for they could see the snow whirling in volleys through the black gap, and whirling inside the church like a dim light. There came a sudden crash, followed by a burst of chuckling, naked laughter. The snow seemed to make a queer light inside the building, like ghosts moving, big and tall.

There was more laughter, and a tearing sound. On the wind, pieces of paper, leaves of books, came whirling among the snow through the dark window. Then a white thing, soaring like a crazy bird, rose up on the wind as if it had wings, and lodged on a black tree outside, struggling. It was the altar-cloth.

There came a bit of gay, trilling music. The wind was running over the organ-pipes like pan-pipes, quickly up and down. Snatches of wild, gay, trilling music, and bursts of the naked low laughter.

"Really!" said the girl. "This is most extraordinary. Do you hear the music and the people laughing?"

"Yes, I hear somebody on the organ!" said the policeman.

"And do you get the puff of warm wind? Smelling of spring. Almond blossom, that's what it is! A most marvellous scent of almond blossom. *Isn't* it an extraordinary thing!"

She went on triumphantly past the church, and came to the row of little old houses. She entered her own gate in the little railed entrance.

"Here I am!" she said finally. "I'm home now. Thank you very much for coming with me."

She looked at the young policeman. His whole body was white as a wall with snow, and in the vague light of the arc-lamp from the street his face was humble and frightened.

"Can I come in and warm myself a bit?" he asked humbly. She knew it was fear rather than cold that froze him. He was in mortal fear.

"Well!" she said. "Stay down in the sitting-room if you like. But don't come upstairs, because I am alone in the house. You can make up the fire in the sitting-room, and you can go when you are warm."

She left him on the big, low couch before the fire, his face bluish and blank with fear. He rolled his blue eyes after her as she left the room. But she went up to her bedroom, and fastened her door.

In the morning she was in her studio upstairs in her little house, looking at her own paintings and laughing to herself. Her canaries were talking and shrilly whistling in the sunshine that followed the storm. The cold snow outside was still clean, and the white glare in the air gave the effect of much stronger sunshine than actually existed.

She was looking at her own paintings, and chuckling to herself over their comicalness. Suddenly they struck her as absolutely absurd. She quite enjoyed looking at them, they seemed to her so grotesque. Especially her self-portrait, with its nice brown hair and its slightly opened rabbit-mouth and its baffled, uncertain rabbit eyes. She looked at the painted face and laughed in a long, rippling laugh, till the yellow canaries like faded daffodils almost went mad in an effort to sing louder. The girl's long, rippling laugh sounded through the house uncannily.

The housekeeper, a rather sad-faced young woman of a superior sort – nearly all people in England are of the superior sort, superiority being an English ailment – came in with an inquiring and rather disapproving look.

"Did you call, Miss James?" she asked loudly.

"No. No, I didn't call. Don't shout, I can hear quite well," replied the girl.

The housekeeper looked at her again.

"You knew there was a young man in the sitting-room?" she said.

"No. Really!" cried the girl. "What, the young policeman? I'd forgotten all about him. He came in the storm to warm himself. Hasn't he gone?"

"No, Miss James."

"How extraordinary of him! What time is it? Quarter to nine?

Why didn't he go when he was warm? I must go and see him, I suppose."

"He says he's lame," said the housekeeper censoriously and loudly.

"Lame! That's extraordinary. He certainly wasn't last night. But don't shout. I can hear quite well."

"Is Mr Marchbanks coming in to breakfast, Miss James?" said the housekeeper, more and more censorious.

"I couldn't say. But I'll come down as soon as mine is ready. I'll be down in a minute, anyhow, to see the policeman. Extraordinary that he is still here."

She sat down before her window, in the sun, to think a while. She could see the snow outside, the bare, purplish trees. The air all seemed rare and different. Suddenly the world had become quite different: as if some skin or integument had broken, as if the old, mouldering London sky had crackled and rolled back, like an old skin, shrivelled, leaving an absolutely new blue heaven.

"It really is extraordinary!" she said to herself. "I certainly saw that man's face. What a wonderful face it was! I shall never forget it. Such laughter! He laughs longest who laughs last. He certainly will have the last laugh. I like him for that: he will laugh last. Must be someone really extraordinary! How very nice to be the one to laugh last. He certainly will. What a wonderful being! I suppose I must call him a being. He's not a person exactly.

"But how wonderful of him to come back and alter all the world immediately! *Isn't* that extraordinary. I wonder if he'll have altered Marchbanks. Of course Marchbanks never *saw* him. But he heard him. Wouldn't that do as well, I wonder! – I *wonder!*"

She went off into a muse about Marchbanks. She and he were *such* friends. They had been friends like that for almost two years. Never lovers. Never that at all. But *friends*.

And after all, she had been in love with him: in her head. This seemed now so funny to her: that she had been, in her head, so much in love with him. After all, life was too absurd.

Because now she saw herself and him as such a funny pair. He so funnily taking life terribly seriously, especially his own life. And she so ridiculously *determined* to save him from himself. Oh, how absurd! *Determined* to save him from himself, and wildly in love with him in the effort. The determination to save him from himself.

Absurd! Absurd! Absurd! Since she had seen the man laughing among the holly-bushes – *such* extraordinary, wonderful laughter – she had seen her own ridiculousness. Really, what fantastic silliness, saving a man from himself! Save anybody. What fantastic silliness! How much more amusing and lively to let a man go to perdition in his own way. Perdition was more amusing than salvation anyhow, and a much better place for most men to go to.

She had never been in love with any man, and only spuriously in love with Marchbanks. She saw it quite plainly now. After all, what nonsense it all was, this being-in-love business. Thank goodness she had never made the humiliating mistake.

No, the man among the holly-bushes had made her see it all so plainly: the ridiculousness of being in love, the *infra dig.* business of chasing a man or being chased by a man.

"Is love *really* so absurd and *infra dig?*" she said aloud to herself.

"Why, of course!" came a deep, laughing voice.

She started round, but nobody was to be seen.

"I expect it's that man again!" she said to herself. "It really *is* remarkable, you know. I consider it's a remarkable thing that I never really wanted a man, *any* man. And there I am over thirty. It *is* curious. Whether it's something wrong with me, or right with me, I can't say. I don't know till I've proved it. But I believe, if that man kept on laughing something would happen to me."

She smelt the curious smell of almond blossom in the room, and heard the distant laugh again.

"I do wonder why Marchbanks went with that woman last night – that Jewish-looking woman. Whatever could he want of her? – or she him? So strange, as if they both had made up their minds to something! How extraordinarily puzzling life is! So messy, it all seems.

"Why does nobody ever laugh in life like that man. He *did* seem so wonderful. So scornful! And so proud! And so real! With those laughing, scornful, amazing eyes, just laughing and disappearing again. I can't imagine him chasing a Jewish-looking woman. Or chasing any woman, thank goodness. It's all *so* messy. My policeman would be messy if one would let him: like a dog. I do dislike dogs, really I do. And men do seem so doggy!—"

But even while she mused, she began to laugh again to herself with a long, low chuckle. How wonderful of that man to come and laugh like that and make the sky crack and shrivel like an old skin! Wasn't he wonderful! Wouldn't it be wonderful if he just touched her. Even touched her. She felt, if he touched her, she herself would emerge new and tender out of an old, hard skin. She was gazing abstractedly out of the window.

"There he comes, just now," she said abruptly. But she meant Marchbanks, not the laughing man.

There he came, his hands still shoved down in his overcoat pockets, his head still rather furtively ducked, in the bowler hat, and his legs still rather shambling. He came hurrying across the road, not looking up, deep in thought, no doubt. Thinking profoundly, with agonies of agitation, no doubt about his last night's experience. It made her laugh.

She, watching from the window above, burst into a long laugh, and the canaries went off their heads again.

He was in the hall below. His resonant voice was calling, rather imperiously:

"James! Are you coming down?"

"No," she called. "You come up."

He came up two at a time, as if his feet were a bit savage with the stairs for obstructing him.

In the doorway he stood staring at her with a vacant, sardonic look, his grey eyes moving with a queer light. And she looked back at him with a curious, rather haughty carelessness.

"Don't you want your breakfast?" she asked. It was his custom to come and take breakfast with her each morning.

"No," he answered loudly. "I went to a tea-shop."

"Don't shout," she said. "I can hear you quite well."

He looked at her with mockery and a touch of malice.

"I believe you always could," he said, still loudly.

"Well, anyway, I can now, so you needn't shout," she replied.

And again his grey eyes, with the queer, greyish phosphorescent gleam in them, lingered malignantly on her face.

"Don't look at me," she said calmly. "I know all about everything."

He burst into a pouf of malicious laughter.

"Who taught you – the policeman?" he cried.

"Oh, by the way, he must be downstairs! No, he was only incidental. So, I suppose, was the woman in the shawl. Did you stay all night?"

"Not entirely. I came away before dawn. What did you do?"

"Don't shout. I came home long before dawn." And she seemed to hear the long, low laughter.

"Why, what's the matter!" he said curiously. "What have you been doing?"

"I don't quite know. Why? – are you going to call me to account?"

"Did you hear that laughing?"

"Oh, yes. And many more things. And saw things too."

"Have you seen the paper?"

"No. Don't shout, I can hear."

"There's been a great storm, blew out the windows and doors of the church outside here, and pretty well wrecked the place."

"I saw it. A leaf of the church Bible blew right in my face: from the Book of Job —" she gave a low laugh.

"But what else did you see?" he cried loudly.

"I saw *him*."

"Who?"

"Ah, that I can't say."

"But what was he like?"

"That I can't tell you. I don't really know."

"But you must know. Did your policeman see him too?"

"No, I don't suppose he did. My policeman!" And she went off into a long ripple of laughter. "He is by no means mine. But I *must* go downstairs and see him."

"It's certainly made you very strange," Marchbanks said. "You've got no *soul*, you know."

"Oh, thank goodness for that!" she cried. "My policeman has one, I'm sure. *My policeman!*" And she went off again into a long peal of laughter, the canaries pealing shrill accompaniment.

"What's the matter with you?" he said.

"Having no soul. I never had one really. It was always fobbed off on me. Soul was the only thing there was between you and me. Thank goodness it's gone. Haven't you lost yours? The one that seemed to worry you, like a decayed tooth?"

"But what are you *talking* about?" he cried.

"I don't know," she said. "It's all so extraordinary. But look here, I *must* go down and see my policeman. He's downstairs in the sitting-room. You'd better come with me."

They went down together. The policeman, in his waistcoat and shirt-sleeves, was lying on the sofa, with a very long face.

"Look here!" said Miss James to him. "Is it true you're lame?"

"It is true. That's why I'm here. I can't walk," said the fair-haired young man as tears came to his eyes.

"But how did it happen? You weren't lame last night," she said.

"I don't know how it happened — but when I woke up and tried to stand up, I couldn't do it." The tears ran down his distressed face.

"How very extraordinary!" she said. "What can we do about it?"

"Which foot is it?" asked Marchbanks. "Let us have a look at it."

"I don't like to," said the poor devil.

"You'd better," said Miss James.

He slowly pulled off his stocking, and showed his white left foot curiously clubbed, like the weird paw of some animal. When he looked at it himself, he sobbed.

And as he sobbed, the girl heard again the low, exulting laughter. But she paid no heed to it, gazing curiously at the weeping young policeman.

"Does it hurt?" she asked.

"It does if I try to walk on it," wept the young man.

"I'll tell you what," she said. "We'll telephone for a doctor, and he can take you home in a taxi."

The young fellow shamefacedly wiped his eyes.

"But have you no idea how it happened?" asked Marchbanks anxiously.

"I haven't myself," said the young fellow.

At that moment the girl heard the low, eternal laugh right in her ear. She started, but could see nothing.

She started round again as Marchbanks gave a strange, yelping cry, like a shot animal. His white face was drawn, distorted in a curious grin, that was chiefly agony but partly wild recognition. He was staring with fixed eyes at something. And in the rolling agony of his eyes was the horrible grin of a man who realizes he has made a final, and this time fatal, fool of himself.

"Why," he yelped in a high voice, "I knew it was he!" And with a queer shuddering laugh he pitched forward on the carpet and lay writhing for a moment on the floor. Then he lay still, in a weird, distorted position, like a man struck by lightning.

Miss James stared with round, staring brown eyes.

"Is he dead?" she asked quickly.

The young policeman was trembling so that he could hardly speak. She could hear his teeth chattering.

"Seems like it," he stammered.

There was a faint smell of almond blossom in the air.

The Visit to the Museum

Vladimir Nabokov

Location: Montisert, France.
Time: November, 1939.
Eyewitness Description: *"Then I found myself in darkness and kept bumping into unknown furniture until I finally saw a red light and walked out onto a platform that clanged under me – and, suddenly, beyond it, there was a bright parlour, tastefully furnished in Empire style, but not a living soul, not a living soul."*

Author: Vladimir Nabokov (1899–1977) the Russian-born author and academic is best known for his notorious novel, *Lolita* (1955) which records the obsession of a middle aged intellectual for a twelve-year-old girl and coined the term, "nymphet". Nabokov studied at Trinity College, Cambridge in the late Thirties where he became aware of the work of M. R. James and wrote several fantasy stories. Among his relevant books from this time are *The Enchanter* (1928), *The Eye* (1930) and *The Waltz Invention* (1938), all written in Russian and not translated until Nabokov moved to America in 1940. Here he worked as a research fellow in entomology at Harvard before becoming professor of Russian literature at Cornell in 1948. Among Nabokov's excellent fantasy stories must be mentioned "The Vane Sisters", "Signs and Symbols" and "Scenes from the Life of a Double Monster," with the nearest to a traditional ghost story being "The Visit to the Museum". It can, though, be regarded as a significant step in the development of the genre and an outstanding contribution to the "Golden Era". In praise of the story, Robert Aickman wrote in 1971, "Mr Nabokov's genius unites the searchlight with the microscope."

S everal years ago a friend of mine in Paris – a person with oddities, to put it mildly – learning that I was going to spend two or three days at Montisert, asked me to drop in at the local museum where there hung, he was told, a portrait of his grandfather by Leroy. Smiling and spreading out his hands, he related a rather vague story to which I confess I paid little attention, partly because I do not like other people's obtrusive affairs, but chiefly because I had always had doubts about my friend's capacity to remain this side of fantasy. It went more or less as follows: after the grandfather died in their St Petersburg house back at the time of the Russo-Japanese War, the contents of his apartment in Paris were sold at auction. The portrait, after some obscure peregrinations, was acquired by the museum of Leroy's native town. My friend wished to know if the portrait was really there; if there, if it could be ransomed; and if it could, for what price. When I asked why he did not get in touch with the museum, he replied that he had written several times, but had never received an answer.

I made an inward resolution not to carry out the request – I could always tell him I had fallen ill or changed my itinerary. The very notion of seeing sights, whether they be museums or ancient buildings, is loathsome to me; besides, the good freak's commission seemed absolute nonsense. It so happened, however, that, while wandering about Montisert's empty streets in search of a stationery store, and cursing the spire of a long-necked cathedral, always the same one, that kept popping up at the end of every street, I was caught in a violent downpour which immediately went about accelerating the fall of the maple leaves, for the fair weather of a southern October was holding on by a mere thread. I dashed for cover and found myself on the steps of the museum.

It was a building of modest proportions, constructed of many-coloured stones, with columns, a gilt inscription over the frescoes of the pediment, and a lion-legged stone bench on either side of the bronze door. One of its leaves stood open, and the interior seemed dark against the shimmer of the shower. I stood for a while on the steps, but, despite the overhanging roof, they were gradually growing speckled. I saw that the rain had set in for good, and so, having nothing better to do, I decided to go inside. No sooner had I trod on the smooth, resonant flagstones of the vestibule than the clatter of a moved stool came from a distant corner, and the custodian – a banal pensioner with an empty sleeve – rose to meet me, laying aside his newspaper and peering at me over his spectacles. I paid my franc and, trying not to look at some statues at the entrance (which were as traditional and as insignificant as the first number in a circus programme), I entered the main hall.

Everything was as it should be: grey tints, the sleep of substance, matter dematerialized. There was the usual case of old, worn coins resting in the inclined velvet of their compartments. There was, on top of the case, a pair of owls, Eagle Owl and Long-eared, with their French names reading "Grand Duke" and "Middle Duke" if translated. Venerable minerals lay in their open graves of dusty papier-mâché; a photograph of an astonished gentleman with a pointed beard dominated an assortment of strange black lumps of various sizes. They bore a great resemblance to frozen frass, and I paused involuntarily over them for I was quite at a loss to guess their nature, composition and function. The custodian had been following me with felted steps, always keeping a respectful distance; now, however, he came up, with one hand behind his back and the ghost of the other in his pocket, and gulping, if one judged by his Adam's apple.

"What are they?" I asked.

"Science has not yet determined," he replied, undoubtedly having learned the phrase by rote. "They were found," he continued in the same phony tone, "in 1895, by Louis Pradier, Municipal Councillor and Knight of the Legion of Honour," and his trembling finger indicated the photograph.

"Well and good," I said, "but who decided, and why, that they merited a place in the museum?"

"And now I call your attention to this skull!" the old man cried energetically, obviously changing the subject.

"Still, I would be interested to know what they are made of," I interrupted.

"Science . . ." he began anew, but stopped short and looked crossly at his fingers, which were soiled with dust from the glass.

I proceeded to examine a Chinese vase, probably brought back by a naval officer; a group of porous fossils; a pale worm in clouded alcohol; a red-and-green map of Montisert in the seventeenth century; and a trio of rusted tools bound by a funereal ribbon – a spade, a mattock and a pick. "To dig in the past," I thought absentmindedly, but this time did not seek clarification from the custodian, who was following me noiselessly and meekly, weaving in and out among the display cases. Beyond the first hall there was another, apparently the last, and in its centre a large sarcophagus stood like a dirty bathtub, while the walls were hung with paintings.

At once my eye was caught by the portrait of a man between two abominable landscapes (with cattle and "atmosphere"). I moved closer and, to my considerable amazement, found the very object whose existence had hitherto seemed to me but the figment of an unstable mind. The man, depicted in wretched oils, wore a frock coat, whiskers and a large pince-nez on a cord; he bore a likeness to Offenbach, but, in spite of the work's vile conventionality, I had the feeling one could make out in his features the horizon of a resemblance, as it were, to my friend. In one corner, meticulously traced in carmine against a black background, was the signature *Leroy* in a hand as commonplace as the work itself.

I felt a vinegarish breath near my shoulder, and turned to meet the custodian's kindly gaze. "Tell me," I asked, "supposing someone wished to buy one of these paintings, whom should he see?"

"The treasures of the museum are the pride of the city," replied the old man, "and pride is not for sale."

Fearing his eloquence, I hastily concurred, but nevertheless asked for the name of the museum's director. He tried to distract me with the story of the sarcophagus, but I insisted. Finally he gave me the name of one M. Godard and explained where I could find him.

Frankly, I enjoyed the thought that the portrait existed. It is fun to be present at the coming true of a dream, even if it is not one's own. I decided to settle the matter without delay. When I get in the spirit, no one can hold me back. I left the museum with a brisk, resonant step, and found that the rain had stopped, blueness had spread across the sky, a woman in besplattered stockings was spinning along on a silver-shining bicycle, and only over the surrounding hills did clouds still hang. Once again the cathedral began playing hide-and-seek with me, but I outwitted it. Barely escaping the onrushing tyres of a furious red bus packed with singing youths, I crossed the asphalt thoroughfare and a minute later was ringing at the garden gate of M. Godard. He turned out to be a thin, middle-aged gentleman in high collar and dickey, with a pearl in the knot of his tie, and a face very much resembling a Russian wolfhound; as if that were not enough, he was licking his chops in a most doglike manner, while sticking a stamp on an envelope, when I entered his small but lavishly furnished room with its malachite inkstand on the desk and a strangely familiar Chinese vase on the mantel. A pair of fencing foils hung crossed over the mirror, which reflected the narrow grey back of his head. Here and there photographs of a warship pleasantly broke up the blue flora of the wallpaper.

"What can I do for you?" he asked, throwing the letter he had just sealed into the wastebasket. This act seemed unusual to me; however,

I did not see fit to interfere. I explained in brief my reason for coming, even naming the substantial sum with which my friend was willing to part, though he had asked me not to mention it, but wait instead for the museum's terms.

"All this is delightful," said M. Godard. "The only thing is, you are mistaken – there is no such picture in our museum."

"What do you mean there is no such picture? I have just seen it! Portrait of a Russian nobleman, by Gustave Leroy."

"We do have one Leroy," said M. Godard when he had leafed through an oilcloth notebook and his black fingernail had stopped at the entry in question. "However, it is not a portrait but a rural landscape: The Return of the Herd."

I repeated that I had seen the picture with my own eyes five minutes before and that no power on earth could make me doubt its existence.

"Agreed," said M. Godard, "but I am not crazy either. I have been curator of our museum for almost twenty years now and know this catalogue as well as I know the Lord's Prayer. It says here Return of the Herd and that means the herd is returning, and, unless perhaps your friend's grandfather is depicted as a shepherd, I cannot conceive of his portrait's existence in our museum."

"He is wearing a frock coat," I cried. "I swear he is wearing a frock coat!"

"And how did you like our museum in general?" M. Godard asked suspiciously. "Did you appreciate the sarcophagus?"

"Listen," I said (and I think there was already a tremor in my voice), "do me a favour – let's go there this minute, and let's make an agreement that if the portrait is there, you will sell it."

"And if not?" inquired M. Godard.

"I shall pay you the sum anyway."

"All right," he said. "Here, take this red-and-blue pencil and using the red – the red, please – put it in writing for me."

In my excitement I carried out his demand. Upon glancing at my signature, he deplored the difficult pronunciation of Russian names. Then he appended his own signature and, quickly folding the sheet, thrust it into his waistcoat pocket.

"Let's go," he said, freeing a cuff.

On the way he stepped into a shop and bought a bag of sticky looking caramels which he began offering me insistently; when I flatly refused, he tried to shake out a couple of them into my hand. I pulled my hand away. Several caramels fell on the sidewalk; he stopped to pick them up and then overtook me at a trot. When we drew near the museum we saw the red tourist bus (now empty) parked outside.

"Aha," said M. Godard, pleased. "I see we have many visitors today."

He doffed his hat and, holding it in front of him, walked decorously up the steps.

All was not well at the museum. From within issued rowdy cries, lewd laughter, and even what seemed like the sound of a scuffle. We entered the first hall; there the elderly custodian was restraining two sacrilegists who wore some kind of festive emblems in their lapels and were altogether very purple-faced and full of pep as they tried to extract the municipal councillor's merds from beneath the glass. The rest of the youths, members of some rural athletic organization, were making noisy fun, some of the worm in alcohol, others of the skull. One joker was in rapture over the pipes of the steam radiator, which he pretended was an exhibit; another was taking aim at an owl with his fist and forefinger. There were about thirty of them in all, and their motion and voices created a condition of crush and thick noise.

M. Godard clapped his hands and pointed at a sign reading "Visitors to the Museum must be decently attired." Then he pushed his way, with me following, into the second hall. The whole company immediately swarmed after us. I steered Godard to the portrait; he froze before it, chest inflated, and then stepped back a bit, as if admiring it, and his feminine heel trod on somebody's foot.

"Splendid picture," he exclaimed with genuine sincerity. "Well, let's not be petty about this. You were right, and there must be an error in the catalogue."

As he spoke, his fingers, moving as it were on their own, tore up our agreement into little bits which fell like snowflakes into a massive spittoon.

"Who's the old ape?" asked an individual in a striped jersey, and, as my friend's grandfather was depicted holding a glowing cigar, another funster took out a cigarette and prepared to borrow a light from the portrait.

"All right, let us settle on the price," I said, "and, in any case, let's get out of here."

"Make way, please!" shouted M. Godard, pushing aside the curious.

There was an exit, which I had not noticed previously, at the end of the hall and we thrust our way through to it.

"I can make no decision," M. Godard was shouting above the din. "Decisiveness is a good thing only when supported by law. I must first discuss the matter with the mayor, who has just died and has not yet been elected. I doubt that you will be able to purchase the portrait but nonetheless I would like to show you still other treasures of ours."

We found ourselves in a hall of considerable dimensions. Brown books, with a half-baked look and coarse, foxed pages, lay open under glass on a long table. Along the walls stood dummy soldiers in jack-boots with flared tops.

"Come, let's talk it over," I cried out in desperation, trying to direct M. Godard's evolutions to a plush-covered sofa in a corner. But in this I was prevented by the custodian. Flailing his one arm, he came running after us, pursued by a merry crowd of youths, one of whom had put on his head a copper helmet with a Rembrandtesque gleam.

"Take it off, take it off!" shouted M. Godard, and someone's shove made the helmet fly off the hooligan's head with a clatter.

"Let us move on," said M. Godard, tugging at my sleeve, and we passed into the section of Ancient Sculpture.

I lost my way for a moment among some enormous marble legs, and twice ran around a giant knee before I again caught sight of M. Godard, who was looking for me behind the white ankle of a neighbouring giantess. Here a person in a bowler, who must have clambered up her, suddenly fell from a great height to the stone floor. One of his companions began helping him up, but they were both drunk, and, dismissing them with a wave of the hand, M. Godard rushed on to the next room, radiant with Oriental fabrics; there hounds raced across azure carpets, and a bow and quiver lay on a tiger skin.

Strangely, though, the expanse and motley only gave me a feeling of oppressiveness and imprecision, and, perhaps because new visitors kept dashing by or perhaps because I was impatient to leave the unnecessarily spreading museum and amid calm and freedom conclude my business negotiations with M. Godard, I began to experience a vague sense of alarm. Meanwhile we had transported ourselves into yet another hall, which must have been really enormous, judging by the fact that it housed the entire skeleton of a whale, resembling a frigate's frame; beyond were visible still other halls, with the oblique sheen of large paintings, full of storm clouds, among which floated the delicate idols of religious art in blue and pink vestments; and all this resolved itself in an abrupt turbulence of misty draperies, and chandeliers came aglitter and fish with translucent frills meandered through illuminated aquariums. Racing up a staircase, we saw, from the gallery above, a crowd of grey-haired people with umbrellas examining a gigantic mock-up of the universe.

At last, in a sombre but magnificent room dedicated to the history of steam machines, I managed to halt my carefree guide for an instant.

"Enough!" I shouted. "I'm leaving. We'll talk tomorrow."

He had already vanished. I turned and saw, scarcely an inch from me, the lofty wheels of a sweaty locomotive. For a long time I tried to find the way back among models of railroad stations. How strangely glowed the violet signals in the gloom beyond the fan of wet tracks, and what spasms shook my poor heart! Suddenly everything changed again: in front of me stretched an infinitely long passage, containing numerous office cabinets and elusive, scurrying people. Taking a sharp turn, I found myself amid a thousand musical instruments; the walls, all mirror, reflected an enfilade of grand pianos, while in the centre there was a pool with a bronze Orpheus atop a green rock. The aquatic theme did not end here as, racing back, I ended up in the Section of Fountains and Brooks, and it was difficult to walk along the winding, slimy edges of those waters.

Now and then, on one side or the other, stone stairs, with puddles on the steps, which gave me a strange sensation of fear, would descend into misty abysses, whence issued whistles, the rattle of dishes, the clatter of typewriters, the ring of hammers and many other sounds, as if, down there, were exposition halls of some kind or other, already closing or not yet completed. Then I found myself in darkness and kept bumping into unknown furniture until I finally saw a red light and walked out onto a platform that clanged under me – and suddenly, beyond it, there was a bright parlour, tastefully furnished in Empire style, but not a living soul, not a living soul. . . . By now I was indescribably terrified, but every time I turned and tried to retrace my steps along the passages, I found myself in hitherto unseen places – a greenhouse with hydrangeas and broken window-panes with the darkness of artificial night showing through beyond; or a deserted laboratory with dusty alembics on its tables. Finally I ran into a room of some sort with coat-racks monstrously loaded down with black coats and astrakhan furs; from beyond a door came a burst of applause, but when I flung the door open, there was no theatre, but only a soft opacity and splendidly counterfeited fog with the perfectly convincing blotches of indistinct street-lights. More than convincing! I advanced, and immediately a joyous and unmistakable sensation of reality at last replaced all the unreal trash amid which I had just been dashing to and fro. The stone beneath my feet was real sidewalk, powdered with wonderfully fragrant, newly fallen snow in which the infrequent pedestrians had already left fresh black tracks. At first the quiet and the snowy coolness of the night, somehow strikingly familiar, gave me a pleasant feeling after my feverish wanderings. Trustfully, I started to conjecture just where I had come out, and why the snow, and what were those lights exaggeratedly but indistinctly beaming here and there in the brown darkness. I examined and, stooping, even touched a round spur stone on the curb, then glanced at the palm of my hand, full of wet granular cold, as if hoping to read an explanation there. I felt how lightly, how naïvely I was clothed, but the distinct realization that I had escaped from the museum's maze was still so strong that, for the first two or three minutes, I experienced neither surprise nor fear. Continuing my leisurely examination, I looked up at the house beside which I was standing and was immediately struck by the sight of iron steps and railings that descended into the snow on their way to the cellar. There was a twinge in my heart, and it was with a new, alarmed curiosity that I glanced at the pavement, at its white cover along which stretched black lines, at the brown sky across which there kept sweeping a mysterious light, and at the massive parapet some distance away. I sensed that there was a drop beyond it; something was creaking and gurgling down there. Further on, beyond the murky cavity, stretched a chain of fuzzy lights. Scuffling along the snow in my soaked shoes, I walked a few paces, all the time glancing at the dark house on my right; only in a single window did a lamp glow softly under its green-glass shade. Here, a locked wooden gate. . . . There, what must be the shutters of a sleeping shop. . . . And by the light of a streetlamp whose shape had long been shouting to me its impossible message, I made out the ending of a sign – ". . . *inka Sapog'* (. . . *oe Repair*") – but no, it was not the snow that had obliterated the "hard sign" at the end. "No, no, in a minute I shall wake up," I said aloud, and, trembling, my heart pounding, I turned, walked on, stopped again. From somewhere came the receding sound of hooves, the snow sat like a skullcap on a slightly leaning spur stone, and indistinctly showed white on the woodpile on the other side of the fence, and already I knew, irrevocably, where I was. Alas, it was not the Russia I remembered, but the factual Russia of today, forbidden to me, hopelessly slavish, and hopelessly my own native land. A semi-phantom in a light foreign suit, I stood on the impassive snow of an October night, somewhere on the Moyka or the Fontanka Canal, or perhaps on the Obvodny, and I had to do something, go somewhere, run, desperately protect my fragile, illegal life. Oh, how many times in my sleep I had experienced a similar sensation! Now, though, it was reality. Everything was real – the air that seemed to mingle with scattered snowflakes, the still unfrozen canal, the floating fish house, and that peculiar squareness of the darkened and the yellow windows. A man in a fur cap, with a briefcase under his arm, came toward me out of the fog, gave me a startled glance, and turned to look again when he had passed me. I waited for him to disappear and then, with a tremendous haste, began pulling out everything I had in my pockets, ripping up papers, throwing them into the snow and stamping them down. There were some documents, a letter from my sister in Paris, five-hundred francs, a handkerchief, cigarettes; however, in order to shed all the integument of exile, I would have to tear off and destroy my clothes, my linen, my shoes, everything, and remain ideally naked; and, even though I was already shivering from my anguish and from the cold, I did what I could.

But enough. I shall not recount how I was arrested, nor tell of my subsequent ordeals. Suffice it to say that it cost me incredible patience and effort to get back abroad, and that, ever since, I have foresworn carrying out commissions entrusted one by the insanity of others.

NOTE: The unfortunate narrator notices a shop sign and realizes he is not in the Russia of his past but in the Russia of the Soviets: what gives it away is the absence of one letter which used to decorate the end of words after consonants but is now omitted in the reformed orthography.   *Vladimir Nabokov*

3

Phantom Ranks

Supernatural at War

The Bowmen

Arthur Machen

Location: Mons, France.

Time: August, 1914.

Eyewitness Description: *"He saw before him, beyond the trench, a long line of shapes, with a shining about them. They were like men who drew the bow, and with another shout their cloud of arrows flew singing and tingling through the air towards the German hosts . . ."*

Author: Arthur Machen (1863–1947), born Arthur Llewellyn Jones in Caerleon, Wales, fell in love with London as a young man and moved to the capital to try and earn his living as a writer. For years he lived in a shabby rented room, existing on "dry bread, green tea and tobacco", churning out journalism and short stories until he accidentally found fame with this story about cut-off British troops being rescued from the Germans by a ghostly St George and his archers from Agincourt. The story was published in the London *Evening News* and, despite Machen's insistence that it was purely imaginary, rapidly became regarded as true and the centre of a legend that has persisted to this day. So entrenched did belief in the "account" become, that claims were even made that the corpses of dead Prussian soldiers had actually been found at Mons, their bodies pierced by arrow wounds. "The Bowmen" has subsequently often been cited as fact in histories of the supernatural as well as inspiring a virtual library of "faction" ghost stories set during wartime.

It was during the Retreat of the Eighty Thousand, and the authority of the Censorship is sufficient excuse for not being more explicit. But it was on the most awful day of that awful time, on the day when ruin and disaster came so near that their shadow fell over London far away; and, without any certain news, the hearts of men failed within them and grew faint; as if the agony of the army in the battlefield had entered into their souls.

On this dreadful day, then, when three hundred thousand men in arms with all their artillery swelled like a flood against the little English company, there was one point above all other points in our battle line that was for a time in awful danger, not merely of defeat, but of utter annihilation. With the permission of the Censorship and of the military expert, this corner may, perhaps, be described as a salient, and if this angle were crushed and broken, then the English force as a whole would be shattered, the Allied left would be turned, and Sedan would inevitably follow.

All the morning the German guns had thundered and shrieked against this corner, and against the thousand or so of men who held it. The men joked at the shells, and found funny names for them, and had bets about them, and greeted them with scraps of music-hall songs. But the shells came on and burst, and tore good Englishmen limb from limb, and tore brother from brother, and as the heat of the day increased so did the fury of that terrific cannonade. There was no help, it seemed. The English artillery was good, but there was not nearly enough of it; it was being steadily battered into scrap iron.

There comes a moment in a storm at sea when people say to one another, "It is at its worst; it can blow no harder," and then there is a blast ten times more fierce than any before it. So it was in these British trenches.

There were no stouter hearts in the whole world than the hearts of these men; but even they were appalled as this seven-times-heated hell of the German cannonade fell upon them and overwhelmed them and destroyed them. And at this very moment they saw from their trenches that a tremendous host was moving against their lines. Five hundred of the thousand remained, and as far as they could see the German infantry was pressing on against them, column upon column, a grey world of men, ten thousand of them, as it appeared afterwards.

There was no hope at all. They shook hands, some of them. One man improvised a new version of the battlesong, "Good-bye, good-bye to Tipperary," ending with "And we shan't get there." And they all went on firing steadily. The officers pointed out that such an opportunity for high-class, fancy shooting might never occur again; the Germans dropped line after line; the Tipperary humorist asked, "What price Sidney Street?" And the few machine guns did their best.

But everybody knew it was of no use. The dead grey bodies lay in companies and battalions, as others came on and on and on, and they swarmed and stirred and advanced from beyond and beyond.

"World without end. Amen," said one of the British soldiers with some irrelevance as he took aim and fired. And then he remembered – he says he cannot think why or wherefore – a queer vegetarian restaurant in London where he had once or twice eaten eccentric dishes of cutlets made of lentils and nuts that pretended to be steak. On all the plates in this restaurant there was printed a figure of St George in blue, with the motto, *Adsit Anglis Sanctus Georgius* – May St George be a present help to the English. This soldier happened to know Latin and other useless things, and now, as he fired at his man in the grey advancing mass – 300 yards away – he uttered the pious vegetarian motto. He went on firing to the end, and at last Bill on his right had to clout him cheerfully over the head to make him stop, pointing out as he did so that the King's ammunition cost money and was not lightly to be wasted in drilling funny patterns into dead Germans.

For as the Latin scholar uttered his invocation he felt something between a shudder and an electric shock pass through his body. The roar of the battle died down in his ears to a gentle murmur; instead of it, he says, he heard a great voice and a shout louder than a thunder-peal crying, "Array, array, array!"

His heart grew hot as a burning coal, it grew cold as ice within him, as it seemed to him that a tumult of voices answered to his summons. He heard, or seemed to hear, thousands shouting: "St George! St George!"

"Ha! messire; ha! sweet Saint, grant us good deliverance!"

"St George for merry England!"

"Harow! Harow! Monseigneur St George, succour us."

"Ha! St George! Ha! St George! a long bow and a strong bow."

"Heaven's Knight, aid us!"

And as the soldier heard these voices he saw before him, beyond the trench, a long line of shapes, with a shining about them. They were like men who drew the bow, and with another shout their cloud of arrows flew singing and tingling through the air towards the German hosts.

The other men in the trench were firing all the while. They had no hope; but they aimed just as if they had been shooting at Bisley.

Suddenly one of them lifted up his voice in the plainest English.

"Gawd help us!" he bellowed to the man next to him, "but we're blooming marvels! Look at those grey . . . gentlemen, look at them! D'ye see them? They're not going down in dozens, nor in 'undreds; it's thousands, it is. Look! look! there's a regiment gone while I'm talking to ye."

"Shut it!" the other soldier bellowed, taking aim, "what are ye gassing about?"

But he gulped with astonishment even as he spoke, for, indeed, the grey men were falling by the thousands. The English could hear the guttural scream of the German officers, the crackle of their revolvers as they shot the reluctant; and still line after line crashed to the earth.

All the while the Latin-bred soldier heard the cry:

"Harow! Harow! Monseigneur, dear saint, quick to our aid! St George help us!"

"High Chevalier, defend us!"

The singing arrows fled so swift and thick that they darkened the air; the heathen horde melted from before them.

"More machine guns!" Bill yelled to Tom.

"Don't hear them," Tom yelled back. "But, thank God, anyway; they've got it in the neck."

In fact, there were ten thousand dead German soldiers left before that salient of the English army, and consequently there was no Sedan. In Germany, a country ruled by scientific principles, the Great General Staff decided that the contemptible English must have employed shells containing an unknown gas of a poisonous nature, as no wounds were discernible on the bodies of the dead German soldiers. But the man who knew what nuts tasted like when they called themselves steak knew also that St George had brought his Agincourt Bowmen to help the English.

The Ghost of *U65*

George Minto

Location: Wilhelmshaven, Germany.
Time: Spring, 1917.
Eyewitness Description: *"At 4.30 exactly the
starboard look-out was amazed to see a
figure in officer's uniform, without coat or
oilskins, standing right in the bows,*
*apparently impervious to the seas that burst round him. Then
the apparition turned, and, even in the failing light, the
stupefied sailor was able to recognize the features of the officer
whose pitiful remains lay buried in the naval cemetery . . ."*
Author: George Minto (1901–79) was a Scottish writer and
naval historian who became fascinated with the "supernatural
at war" after reading Arthur Machen's story and was made
aware of the furore that surrounded it in the aftermath of the
conflict. He spent much of his working life as a civil servant,
although he did see action in the Royal Navy during the
Second World War. While at sea, Minto devoted his spare time
to researching the "curious and fascinating facts" to be found
in the annals of the world's navies and later began contributing
articles to the leading Scottish periodical, *Blackwood's
Magazine*. He was particularly fascinated by stories that had
occurred during the First World War while he was growing up
in Glasgow, and when consulting German records came across
the following story of a haunted U-Boat. A bit like Machen's
legendary tale of phantom bowmen – though having none of its
notoriety – "The Ghost of *U65*" is an excellent combination of
some curious facts and the beguiling art of the storyteller.

I have been a servant of the State for most of my working life and,
up till very recently, believed that no Governmental activity,

however exotic, could surprise me. The complexity of modern life being what it is, there are few pies untouched by official fingers, and the process, for good and evil, continues apace. Nevertheless, when I learned from cold clear print that the German Admiralty had, within living memory, officially laid a ghost on board, of all things, a brand-new submarine, I confess that I blinked incredulously. Church and State throughout the ages have been closely interwoven, but it is surely unique, certainly in the twentieth century, for the High Command of a great armed service to call upon the clergy to exorcise an unquiet spirit. This actually happened in the spring of 1917, and I have been at some pains, so far as is now possible, to trace and verify this strangest of stories. It must be exceedingly rare for reports of such a nature to be submitted by responsible officers to their superiors, and the Naval Staff in Berlin were, no doubt, puzzled and intrigued. There must have been eager competition in the Marineamt for the papers; for to my mind the haunting of *U65* ranks as one of the best authenticated ghost stories of the sea.

In 1915 the naval policy of the Imperial Government had at last been formulated. Briefly, among other weighty matters, it called for a large expansion of submarine construction; for the High Command were gradually coming round to the idea, energetically and perpetually expounded by Grand Admiral von Tirpitz, that the war might well be won by the U-boats. This strategy was particularly congenial to the Kaiser, who was most reluctant to risk his surface ships in an all-out clash with Jellicoe's Grand Fleet. Accordingly, large contracts were placed with State and private shipyards for submarines, and soon they were sliding down the ways in ever-increasing numbers.

U65, the subject of our story, was one of a class of twenty-four vessels especially designed to operate from the ports of the occupied coast of Flanders. Fully loaded, she displaced five hundred and twelve tons and her diesel engines gave her a surface speed of just under fourteen knots. In commission she was manned by three officers and thirty-one petty officers and men.

Her keel had been laid in the great naval dockyard of Wilhelmshaven in June 1916, and, almost from the first, ill-luck had dogged her construction. A few days after work on her had started she claimed her first victims. A heavy steel girder was being lowered into position when it slipped from the crane tackle and, crashing down on the embryo boat, killed one workman outright and mortally injured another. Accidents are, of course, unhappily frequent in all places of heavy labour, but it was a bad beginning for a new ship. Her reputation as unlucky was luridly enhanced a few months later when three men were suffocated in her engine-room by poisonous fumes. U65 had cost five men their lives even before she put to sea.

Her trial trip was equally marked by tragedy. Meeting very heavy weather in the Heligoland Bight, she lost one seaman overboard, and only chance prevented the loss of two more. Nor was that the whole tale of the trials (in both senses); for U65 came near to killing her entire complement when she submerged for diving tests a few hours later. A serious leak developed in one of the forward ballast-tanks, and it was over half a day before she could be persuaded to surface again. Meanwhile the flood water had reached the giant batteries and, releasing deadly gases, almost asphyxiated every man aboard. When, at last, she emerged on to the surface, two-thirds of the technicians and crew were unconscious and the remainder violently sick and ill. Two died in hospital soon after getting ashore. Eight lives was now U65's melancholy score.

However, the necessary repairs were made and a second series of trials passed off without any noteworthy incident. Early in February 1917 she was officially accepted for the Imperial Navy and Ober-leutnant Karl Honig was appointed in command. He was a Regular officer of experience and high reputation in the submarine service, and one marked out for accelerated promotion in the future. He appears to have been quite satisfied with his command, and his Letter of Proceedings after the first operational cruise makes no mention of any constructional defects.

Unhappily, though the word gremlin was unknown in the First World War, there was a very evil one lurking in the shapely grey hull of U65. A few days after her return to Wilhelmshaven she was hoisting in torpedoes when a war-head exploded, blowing five men, including the Second Officer, into fragments of humanity. Nine others received serious injuries. A court of enquiry was unable to discover the cause of the disaster, and returned the German version of the verdict "Act of God".

A few weeks later, while still in port, the post-luncheon calm of the wardroom was rudely disturbed when a white-faced seaman dashed in shouting, "Herr Kapitan, the dead Second Officer has come aboard!" Such a breach of the iron Prussian discipline must have, thought the shocked Captain Honig, some rational explanation, and, selecting the most obvious, he taxed the sailor sternly with being drunk. But the man seemed perfectly sober, albeit terrified, and repeated the story that he had seen the dead officer mount the gang-plank to board the ship. Deeply puzzled but thoroughly sceptical, the Commanding Officer picked up his cap, and, followed by his subordinates, climbed on deck. It was a perfect spring afternoon, and a less likely time to see ghosts could hardly be imagined. Nevertheless he was amazed to find another seaman called Petersen crouching behind the conning-tower in an extremity of terror. In response to a barked order this man pulled himself together sufficiently to stammer that he, too, had seen the dead officer come aboard, salute and walk forward to the bows, there to vanish into thin air.

Like a good officer, Honig was determined to get to the bottom of an incident so obviously dangerous to the morale of his crew. A doctor was called, and certified that both men were sane and sober; then Honig interrogated them strictly about what they had seen. They were unshaken in their separate yet similar accounts, and since they both bore excellent characters, their puzzled captain had to accept the fact that they had at any rate seen someone or something. For a little he toyed with the idea that some misguided humorist had perpetrated a practical joke in the worst possible taste, and vowed grimly that the joker, if detected, would be sorry. He decided to seek the discreet help of the Chief of the Dockyard Police, and that officer, sworn to secrecy, made very thorough enquiries. They all led to nothing, and it seemed clear that practical joking could be ruled out. More puzzled and more than a little worried, Honig reported the strange incident to his Flotilla Captain, who put the matter down to the over-strained nerves of tired men. The incident, however, had, as Honig had feared, made a serious and distressing impression on his crew, who were now convinced that the submarine and her company were doomed. The day before she sailed on her next cruise Seaman Petersen deserted, and, so far as is known, was never apprehended by the naval authorities.

In due course *U65* left her home port, and her next two forays against Allied shipping were moderately successful. Seven ships were sunk, and Captain Honig may well have thought that his superior's explanation had been correct. His subordinates were not so cheerful, for they were uneasy and depressed. The story of the ghost at Wilhelmshaven had lost nothing in the telling, and a number of the men swore that the boat was haunted. At least three officially reported that they had seen an unknown officer walk into the torpedo-room, from which he did not emerge.

Captain Honig, like the good commanding officer he was, did his best to treat the whole matter with sceptical contempt, but he was soon to have a rude awakening.

Leaving Heligoland on New Year's Day, 1918, *U65* called at Zeebrugge *en route* to her war station in the English Channel. During her stay in port three men reported that they had seen the ghost. All three had only that day joined the ship, and, so far as could be ascertained, had no previous knowledge of the haunting.

Towards dusk of 21 January, the U-boat was in a position about fifteen miles due south of Portland Bill. The weather was rapidly worsening, with fierce gusts and a rising sea which threw sheets of spray over the bridge. Captain Honig and two look-outs, one on either side, were on watch, crouching behind the meagre shelter of the canvas screens on which the spindrift rattled like rifle-fire. At 4.30 exactly the starboard look-out was amazed to see a figure in officer's uniform, without coat or oilskins, standing right in the bows, apparently impervious to the seas that burst around him. Then the apparition turned, and, even in the failing light, the stupefied sailor was able to recognize the features of the officer whose pitiful remains lay buried in the naval cemetery at Wilhelmshaven. "Lord God, it's the ghost!" he shrieked, and, staggering back with out-stretched hands, bumped violently into the captain at the after end of the narrow bridge. That officer, cursing roundly, peered forward in his turn, and what he saw struck him, in the words of his official report, "*sprachlos*" – speechless. But training and discipline always tell, and automatically he shouted for the reserve watch below. As they tumbled up the hatch they found the captain and the look-outs pointing excitedly to the deserted foredeck, which showed only the white foam of the breaking seas. To the new arrivals Honig lamely explained that he had simply been testing their alertness.

Thenceforward a cloud of depression enfolded *U65*. Men were disinclined to be alone, and none would venture unaccompanied into the forward torpedo-room. Possibly due to suggestion, more men than ever swore they saw the ghost, and one, at least, said that it greeted him in passing. Fear gripped the vessel in those winter days amidst the grey seas of the Channel.

Nevertheless she completed her patrol and returned safely to Bruges, her new operational base, early in February. No doubt eager for relaxation after his many worries, Captain Honig went ashore on the first night in port to visit the Officers' Club, but on his way there the air-raid sirens sounded. He was about to enter a shelter when a shell-splinter decapitated him before the eyes of several members of his crew. The headless body was carried aboard *U65*, and that night one officer and eight men saw the ghost standing mournfully beside the canvas-shrouded corpse.

The matter was now far beyond a joke and Higher Authority intervened. No less a personage than the Admiral of Submarines visited *U65* and personally questioned each of the crew. Officially sceptical he was nevertheless impressed by what he heard, especially when he received a unanimous request from the ship's company for transfer to another boat. In theory this request was ignored, but in practice almost every man was drafted on one pretext or another over the next few weeks, and *U65* was ordered into reserve at Bruges.

It was at this point that unorthodox methods were adopted by the Admiral to raise the morale of the new crew. A Lutheran chaplain, Pastor Franz Weber, then serving at the base, was summoned by the Senior Officer of Submarines and told the whole weird story. In response, the reverend gentleman suggested that he might conduct a service of exorcism to lay the unquiet spirit of *U65*. It could do no harm, he thought, and might possibly do a lot of good. To this the Admiral agreed, reporting his decision to the Naval Staff in Berlin. Pastor Weber duly held the service, but, unfortunately, it had unexpected results. For the new crew, already despondent and nervous, were gravely upset by this official recognition of the ghost. As one man they applied for transfer from the boat, but this time the request was brusquely refused.

Early in May a new Commanding Officer was appointed, Lieu-tenant-Commander Schelle. A strict disciplinarian, he refused to tolerate "any damned nonsense about ghosts", and made it clear that any man who so much as mentioned the word would have cause to regret it. As if in justification of his uncompromising attitude the fearsome tales died down, and the next two operational cruises were without incident. In June, however, the ghost reappeared, and two men deserted rather than sail in that haunted ship. They were arrested and tried by court-martial, but they sturdily maintained that nothing would induce them to return to *U65*. Sentenced to death, both were reprieved and drafted to a penal battalion on the Western Front. (One, at least, survived the war, and wrote an excellent account of his experiences in the submarine in a journal devoted to psychical research.)

On 30 June, *U65* sailed on what was to be her last voyage. True to form, her death was to be as mysterious as her life, for no real explanation of her loss was ever found. The main facts, however, are well authenticated.

Early in the morning of 10 July the US submarine *L2* was patrolling at periscope depth nine miles off Cape Clear on the southern Irish coast. Suddenly she sighted a German U-boat on the surface, cruising slowly as she charged her batteries. She was

U65. Conditions were ideal and the American captain manœuvred his vessel into the attacking position. He was about to give the order to fire when there was a tremendous explosion. As soon as the mountain of water had subsided the startled officer saw that his prospective victim had vanished, leaving masses of wreckage and oil-slick on the calm surface.

There have, of course, been a number of theories to explain her destruction. She may have been torpedoed by another German submarine in mistake, for there were a number of these operating in the vicinity at the time, but I have been unable to trace any official report to that effect. It is also possible that yet another defective war-head (as had happened at the outset of her career) had exploded, setting off a chain reaction among the others. That would account for the tremendous violence of the explosion which *L2* had noted.

The explanation of this strange story? There is none that I can see. In 1921, Professor Dr Hecht, a very distinguished psychologist, conducted a profound investigation into the whole matter, seeking out and questioning as many witnesses as he could trace. He had access to the archives of the German Admiralty, but even with these facilities he could produce no satisfactory explanation of the haunting of *U65*. As a man of science he naturally deprecated any suggestion of the supernatural, but in his conclusion he rather ruefully, as it seems to me, refers to Hamlet's dictum to the sadly puzzled Horatio.

There are also more things in the sea than our philosophy can yet compass.

"Vengeance Is Mine"

Algernon Blackwood

Location: Louvain, France.
Time: March, 1918.
Eyewitness Description: *"The spell of this woman's strange enchantment poured over him, seeking the reconciliation he himself could not achieve. Yet the reconciliation she sought meant victory or defeat; no compromise lay in it . . ."*

Author: Algernon Blackwood (1869–1951), like Arthur Machen, was a rebel against conformity and turned his back on a strict religious upbringing to travel across North America and make his living as a reporter and short story writer. One of his earliest successes was "A Haunted Island" (1899), a narrative in the first person set on a remote Canadian island haunted by a murderous Indian, which bears the hallmarks of personal experience. Later stories were to contain similar ingredients of supernatural insight and after Blackwood had become a familiar figure broadcasting on UK radio and television, he was labelled, "The Ghost Man". During the First World War, he was initially a Red Cross worker and then recruited for "secret service" work, following in the footsteps of Somerset Maugham to operate a network of agents in France and Switzerland. From his war experiences came several short stories including, "Wireless Confusion", "The World-Dream of McCallister" and particularly "Vengeance is Mine", which has echoes of Arthur Machen's classic. Here, the narrator is pondering if the ancient gods are favouring *not* the British, but the Germans, and finds himself thrust into a horrifying situation when the soul of a terribly wronged young woman demands the sacrifice of an enemy POW.

1

An active, vigorous man in Holy Orders, yet compelled by heart trouble to resign a living in Kent before full middle age, he had found suitable work with the Red Cross in France; and it rather pleased a strain of innocent vanity in him that Rouen, whence he derived his Norman blood, should be the scene of his activities.

He was a gentle-minded soul, a man deeply read and thoughtful, but goodness perhaps his out-standing quality, believing no evil of others. He had been slow, for instance, at first to credit the German atrocities, until the evidence had compelled him to face the appalling facts. With acceptance, then, he had experienced a revulsion which other gentle minds have probably also experienced – a burning desire, namely, that the perpetrators should be fitly punished.

This primitive instinct of revenge – he called it a lust – he sternly repressed; it involved a descent to lower levels of conduct irreconcilable with the progress of the race he so passionately believed in. Revenge pertained to savage days. But, though he hid away the instinct in his heart, afraid of its clamour and persistency, it revived from time to time, as fresh horrors made it bleed anew. It remained alive, unsatisfied; while, with its analysis, his mind strove unconsciously. That an intellectual nation should deliberately include frightfulness as a chief item in its creed perplexed him horribly; it seemed to him conscious spiritual evil openly affirmed. Some genuine worship of Odin, Wotan, Moloch lay still embedded in the German outlook, and beneath the veneer of their pretentious culture. He often wondered, too, what effect the recognition of these horrors must have upon gentle minds in other men, and especially upon imaginative minds. How did they deal with the fact that this appalling thing existed in human nature in the twentieth century? Its survival, indeed, caused his belief in civilization as a whole to waver. Was progress, his pet ideal and cherished faith, after all a mockery? Had human nature not advanced . . .?

His work in the great hospitals and convalescent camps beyond the town was tiring; he found little time for recreation, much less for rest; a light dinner and bed by ten o'clock was the usual way of spending his evenings. He had no social intercourse, for everyone else was as busy as himself. The enforced solitude, not quite wholesome, was unavoidable. He found no outlet for his thoughts. First-hand acquaintance with suffering, physical and mental, was no new thing to him, but this close familiarity, day by day, with maimed and broken humanity preyed considerably on his mind, while the fortitude and cheerfulness shown by the victims deepened the impression of respectful, yearning wonder made upon him. They were so young, so fine and careless, these lads whom the German lust for power had robbed of limbs, and eyes, of mind, of life itself. The sense of horror grew in him with cumulative but unrelieved effect.

With the lengthening of the days in February, and especially when March saw the welcome change to summer time, the natural desire for open air asserted itself. Instead of retiring early to his dingy bedroom, he would stroll out after dinner through the ancient streets. When the air was not too chilly, he would prolong these outings, starting at sunset and coming home beneath the bright mysterious stars. He knew at length every turn and winding of the old-world alleys, every gable, every tower and spire, from the *Vieux Marché*, where Joan of Arc was burnt, to the busy quays, thronged now with soldiers from half a dozen countries. He wandered on past grey gateways of crumbling stone that marked the former banks of the old tidal river. An English army, five centuries ago, had camped here among reeds and swamps, besieging the Norman capital, where now they brought in supplies of men and material upon modern docks, a mighty invasion of a very different kind. Imaginative reflection was his constant mood.

But it was the haunted streets that touched him most, stirring some chord his ancestry had planted in him. The forest of spires thronged the air with strange stone flowers, silvered by moonlight as though white fire streamed from branch and petal; the old church towers soared; the cathedral touched the stars. After dark the modern note, paramount in the daylight, seemed hushed; with sunset it underwent a definite night-change. Although the darkened streets kept alive in him the menace of fire and death, the crowding soldiers, dipped to the face in shadow, seemed somehow negligible; the leaning roofs and gables hid them in a purple sea of mist that blurred their modern garb, steel weapons, and the like. Shadows themselves, they entered the being of the town; their feet moved silently; there was a hush and murmur; the brooding buildings absorbed them easily.

Ancient and modern, that is, unable successfully to mingle, let fall grotesque, incongruous shadows on his thoughts. The spirit of mediæval days stole over him, exercising its inevitable sway upon a temperament already predisposed to welcome it. Witchcraft and wonder, pagan superstition and speculation, combined with an ancestral tendency to weave a spell, half of acceptance, half of shrinking, about his imaginative soul in which poetry and logic seemed otherwise fairly balanced. Too weary for critical judgment to discern clear outlines, his mind, during these magical twilight walks, became the playground of opposing forces, some power of dreaming, it seems, too easily in the ascendant. The soul of ancient Rouen, stealing beside his footsteps in the dusk, put forth a shadowy hand and touched him.

This shadowy spell he denied as far as in him lay, though the resistance offered by reason to instinct lacked true driving power. The dice were loaded otherwise in such a soul. His own blood harked back unconsciously to the days when men were tortured, broken on the wheel, walled up alive, and burnt for small offences. This shadowy hand stirred faint ancestral memories in him, part instinct, part desire. The next step, by which he saw a similar attitude flowering full blown in the German frightfulness, was too easily made to be rejected. The German horrors made him believe that this ignorant cruelty of olden days threatened the world now in a modern, organized shape that proved its survival in the human heart. Shuddering, he fought against the natural desire for adequate punishment, but forgot that repressed emotions sooner or later must assert themselves. Essentially irrepressible, they may force an outlet in distorted fashion. He hardly recognized, perhaps, their actual claim, yet it was audible occasionally. For, owing to his loneliness, the natural outlet, in talk and intercourse, was denied.

Then, with the softer winds, he yearned for country air. The sweet spring days had come; morning and evening were divine; above the town the orchards were in bloom. Birds blew their tiny bugles on the hills. The midday sun began to burn.

It was the time of the final violence, when the German hordes flung like driven cattle against the Western line where free men fought for liberty. Fate hovered dreadfully in the balance that spring of 1918; Amiens was threatened, and if Amiens fell, Rouen must be evacuated. The town, already full, became now over-full. On his way home one evening he passed the station, crowded with homeless new arrivals. "Got the wind up, it seems, in Amiens!" cried a cheery voice, as an officer he knew went by him hurriedly. And as he heard it the mood of the spring became of a sudden uppermost. He reached a decision. The German horror came abruptly closer. This further overcrowding of the narrow streets was more than he could face.

It was a small, personal decision merely, but he *must* get out among woods and fields, among flowers and wholesome, growing things, taste simple, innocent life again. The following evening he would pack his haversack with food and tramp the four miles to the great *Forêt Verte* – delicious name! – and spend the night with trees and stars, breathing his full of sweetness, calm and peace. He was too accustomed to the thunder of the guns to be disturbed by it. The song of a thrush, the whistle of a blackbird, would easily drown that. He made his plan accordingly.

The next two nights, however, a warm soft rain was falling; only on the third evening could he put his little plan into execution. Anticipatory enjoyment, meanwhile, lightened his heart; he did his daily work more competently, the spell of the ancient city weakened somewhat. The shadowy hand withdrew.

2

Meanwhile, a curious adventure intervened.

His good and simple heart, disciplined these many years in the way a man should walk, received, upon its imaginative side, a stimulus that, in his case, amounted to a shock. That a strange and comely woman should make eyes at him disturbed his equilibrium considerably; that he should enjoy the attack, though without at first responding openly – even without full comprehension of its meaning – disturbed it even more. It was, moreover, no ordinary attack.

He saw her first the night after his decision when, in a mood of disappointment due to the rain, he came down to his lonely dinner. The room, he saw, was crowded with new arrivals, from Amiens, doubtless, where they had "the wind up." The wealthier civilians had fled for safety to Rouen. These interested and, in a measure, stimulated him. He looked at them sympathetically, wondering what dear home-life they had so hurriedly relinquished at the near thunder of the enemy guns, and, in so doing, he noticed, sitting alone at a small table just in front of his own – yet with her back to him – a woman.

She drew his attention instantly. The first glance told him that she was young and well-to-do; the second, that she was unusual. What precisely made her unusual he could not say, although he at once began to study her intently. Dignity, atmosphere, personality, he perceived beyond all question. She sat there with an air. The becoming little hat with its challenging feather slightly tilted, the set of the shoulders, the neat waist and slender outline; possibly, too, the hair about the neck, and the faint perfume that was wafted towards him as the serving girl swept past, combined in the persuasion. Yet he felt it as more than a persuasion. She attracted him with a subtle vehemence he had never felt before. The instant he set eyes upon her his blood ran faster. The thought rose passionately in him, almost the words that phrased it: "I wish I knew her."

This sudden flash of response his whole being certainly gave – to the back of an unknown woman. It was both vehement and instinctive. He lay stress upon its instinctive character: he was aware of it before reason told him why. That it was "in response" he also noted, for although he had not seen her face and she assuredly had made no sign, he felt that attraction which involves also invitation. So vehement, moreover, was this response in him that he felt shy and ashamed the same instant, for it almost seemed he had expressed his thought in audible words. He flushed, and the flush ran through his body; he was conscious of heated blood as in a youth of twenty-five, and when a man past forty knows this touch of fever he may also know, though he may not recognize it, that the danger signal which means possible abandon has been lit. Moreover, as though to prove his instinct justified, it was at this very instant that the woman turned and stared at him deliberately. She looked into his eyes, and he looked into hers. He knew a moment's keen distress, a sharpest possible discomfort, that after all he *had* expressed his desire audibly. Yet, though he blushed, he did not lower his eyes. The embarrassment passed instantly, replaced by a thrill of strangest pleasure and satisfaction. He knew a tinge of inexplicable dismay as well. He felt for a second helpless before what seemed a challenge in her eyes. The eyes were too compelling. They mastered him.

In order to meet his gaze she had to make a full turn in her chair, for her table was placed directly in front of his own. She did so without concealment. It was no mere attempt to see what lay behind by making a half-turn and pretending to look elsewhere; no corner of the eye business; but a full, straight, direct, significant stare. She looked into his soul as though she called him, he looked into hers as though he answered. Sitting there like a statue, motionless, without a bow, without a smile, he returned her intense regard unflinchingly and yet unwillingly. He made no sign. He shivered again. . . . It was perhaps ten seconds before she turned away with an air as if she had delivered her message and received his answer, but in those ten seconds a series of singular ideas crowded his mind, leaving an impression that ten years could never efface. The face and eyes produced a kind of intoxication in him. There was almost recognition, as though she said: "Ah, there you are! I was waiting; you'll have to come, of course. You must!" And just before she turned away she smiled.

He felt confused and helpless.

The face he described as unusual; familiar, too, as with the atmosphere of some long forgotten dream, and if beauty perhaps was absent, character and individuality were supreme. Implacable resolution was stamped upon the features, which yet were sweet and womanly, stirring an emotion in him that he could not name and certainly did not recognize. The eyes, slanting a little upwards, were full of fire, the mouth voluptuous but very firm, the chin and jaw most delicately modelled, yet with a masculine strength that told of inflexible resolve. The resolution, as a whole, was the most relentless he had ever seen upon a human countenance. It dominated him. "How vain to resist the will," he thought, "that lies behind!" He was conscious of enslavement; she conveyed a message that he must obey, admitting compliance with her unknown purpose.

That some extraordinary wordless exchange was registered thus between them seemed very clear; and it was just at this moment, as if to signify her satisfaction, that she smiled. At his feeling of willing compliance with some purpose in her mind, the smile appeared. It was faint, so faint indeed that the eyes betrayed it rather than the mouth and lips; but it was there; he saw it, and he thrilled again to this added touch of wonder and enchantment. Yet, strangest of all, he maintains that with the smile there fluttered over the resolute face a sudden arresting tenderness, as though some wild flower lit a granite surface with its melting loveliness. He was aware in the clear strong eyes of unshed tears, of sympathy, of self-sacrifice he called maternal, of clinging love. It was this tenderness, as of a soft and gracious mother, and this implacable resolution, as of a stern, relentless man, that left upon his receptive soul the strange impression of sweetness yet of domination.

The brief ten seconds were over. She turned away as deliberately as she had turned to look. He found himself trembling with confused emotions he could not disentangle, could not even name; for, with the subtle intoxication of compliance in his soul lay also a vigorous protest that included refusal, even a violent refusal given with horror. This unknown woman, without actual speech or definite gesture, had lit a flame in him that linked on far away and out of sight with the magic of the ancient city's mediæval spell. Both, he decided, were undesirable, both to be resisted.

He was quite decided about this. She pertained to forgotten yet unburied things, her modern aspect a mere disguise, a disguise that some deep unsatisfied instinct in him pierced with ease.

He found himself equally decided, too, upon another thing which, in spite of his momentary confusion, stood out clearly: the magic of the city, the enchantment of the woman, both attacked a constitutional weakness in his blood, a line of least resistance. It wore no physical aspect, breathed no hint of ordinary romance; the mere male and female, moral or immoral touch was wholly absent; yet passion lurked there, tumultuous if hidden, and a tract of consciousness, long untravelled, was lit by sudden ominous flares. His character, his temperament, his calling in life as a former clergyman and now a Red Cross worker, being what they were, he stood on the brink of an adventure not dangerous alone but containing a challenge of fundamental kind that involved his very soul.

No further thrill, however, awaited him immediately. He left his table before she did, having intercepted no slightest hint of desired acquaintanceship or intercourse. He, naturally, made no advances; she, equally, made no smallest sign. Her face remained hidden, he caught no flash of eyes, no gesture, no hint of possible invitation. He went upstairs to his dingy room, and in due course fell asleep. The next day he saw her not, her place in the dining-room was empty; but in the late evening of the following day, as the soft spring sunshine found him prepared for his postponed expedition, he met her suddenly on the stairs. He was going down with haversack and in walking kit to an early dinner, when he saw her coming up; she was perhaps a dozen steps below him; they must meet. A wave of confused, embarrassed pleasure swept him. He realized that this was no chance meeting. She meant to speak to him.

Violent attraction and an equally violent repulsion seized him. There was no escape, nor, had escape been possible, would he have attempted it. He went down four steps, she mounted four towards him; then he took one and she took one. They met. For a moment they stood level, while he shrank against the wall to let her pass. He had the feeling that but for the support of that wall he must have lost his balance and fallen into her, for the sunlight from the landing window caught her face and lit it, and she was younger, he saw, than he had thought, and far more comely. Her atmosphere enveloped him, the sense of attraction and repulsion became intense. She moved past him with the slightest possible bow of recognition; then, having passed, she turned.

She stood a little higher than himself, a step at most, and she thus looked down at him. Her eyes blazed into his. She smiled, and he was aware again of the domination and the sweetness. The perfume of her near presence drowned him; his head swam. "We count upon you," she said in a low firm voice, as though giving a command; "I know . . . we may. We do." And, before he knew what he was saying, trembling a little between deep pleasure and a contrary impulse that sought to choke the utterance, he heard his own voice answering. "You can count upon me. . . ." And she was already halfway up the next flight of stairs ere he could move a muscle, or attempt to thread a meaning into the singular exchange.

Yet meaning, he well knew, there was.

She was gone; her footsteps overhead had died away. He stood there trembling like a boy of twenty, yet also like a man of forty in whom fires, long dreaded, now blazed sullenly. She had opened the furnace door, the draught rushed through. He felt again the old unwelcome spell; he saw the twisted streets 'mid leaning gables and shadowy towers of a day forgotten; he heard the ominous murmurs of a crowd that thirsted for wheel and scaffold and fire; and, aware of vengeance, sweet and terrible, aware, too, that he welcomed it, his heart was troubled and afraid.

In a brief second the impression came and went; following it swiftly, the sweetness of the woman swept him: he forgot his shrinking in a rush of wild delicious pleasure. The intoxication in him deepened. She had recognized him! She had bowed and even smiled; she had spoken, assuming familiarity, intimacy, including him in her secret purposes! It was this sweet intimacy, cleverly injected, that overcame the repulsion he acknowledged, winning complete obedience to the unknown meaning of her words. This meaning, for the moment, lay in darkness; yet it was a portion of his own self, he felt, that concealed it of set purpose. He kept it hid, he looked deliberately another way; for, if he faced it with full recognition, he knew that he must resist it to the death. He allowed himself to ask vague questions – then let her dominating spell confuse the answers so that he did not hear them. The challenge to his soul, that is, he evaded.

What is commonly called sex lay only slightly in his troubled emotions; her purpose had nothing that kept step with chance acquaintanceship. There lay meaning, indeed, in her smile and voice, but these were no handmaids to a vulgar intrigue in a foreign hotel. Her will breathed cleaner air; her purpose aimed at some graver, mightier climax than the mere subjection of an elderly victim like himself. That will, that purpose, he felt certain, were implacable as death, the resolve in those bold eyes was not a common one. For, in some strange way, he divined the strong maternity in her; the maternal instinct was deeply, even predominantly, involved; he felt positive that a divine tenderness, deeply outraged, was a chief ingredient too. In some way, then, she needed him, yet not she alone, for the pronoun "we" was used, and there were others with her; in some way, equally, a part of him was already her and their accomplice, an unresisting slave, a willing co-conspirator.

He knew one other thing, and it was this that he kept concealed so carefully from himself. His recognition of it was sub-conscious possibly, but for that very reason true: her purpose was consistent with the satisfaction at last of a deep instinct in him that clamoured to know gratification. It was for these odd, mingled reasons that he stood trembling when she left him on the stairs, and finally went down to his hurried meal with a heart that knew wonder, anticipation, and delight, but also dread.

3

The table in front of him remained unoccupied; his dinner finished, he went out hastily.

As he passed through the crowded streets, his chief desire was to be quickly free of the old muffled buildings and airless alleys with their clinging atmosphere of other days. He longed for the sweet taste of the heights, the smells of the forest whither he was bound. This *Forêt Verte*, he knew, rolled for leagues towards the north, empty of houses as of human beings; it was the home of deer and birds and rabbits, of wild boar too. There would be spring flowers among the brushwood, anemones, celandine, oxslip, daffodils. The vapours of the town oppressed him, the warm and heavy moisture stifled; he wanted space and the sight of clean simple things that would stimulate his mind with lighter thoughts.

He soon passed the *Rampe*, skirted the ugly villas of modern Bihorel and, rising now with every step, entered the *Route Neuve*. He went unduly fast; he was already above the Cathedral spire; below him the Seine meandered round the chalky hills, laden with warbarges, and across a dip, still pink in the afterglow, rose the blunt Down of Bonsecours with its anti-aircraft batteries. Poetry and violent fact crashed everywhere; he longed to top the hill and leave these unhappy reminders of death behind him. In front the sweet woods already beckoned through the twilight. He hastened. Yet while he deliberately fixed his imagination on promised peace and beauty, an undercurrent ran sullenly in his mind, busy with quite other thoughts. The unknown woman and her singular words, the following mystery of the ancient city, the soft beating wonder of the two together, these worked their incalculable magic persistently about him. Repression merely added to their power. His mind was a prey to some shadowy, remote anxiety that, intangible, invisible, yet knocked with ghostly fingers upon some door of ancient memory. . . . He watched the moon rise above the eastern ridge, in the west the afterglow of sunset still hung red. But these did not hold his attention as they normally must have done. Attention seemed elsewhere. The undercurrent bore him down a siding, into a back-water, as it were, that clamoured for discharge.

He thought suddenly, then, of weather, what he called "German weather" – that combination of natural conditions which so oddly favoured the enemy always. It had often occurred to him as strange; on sea and land, mist, rain and wind, the fog and drying sun worked ever on *their* side. The coincidence was odd, to say the least. And now this glimpse of rising moon and sunset sky reminded him unpleasantly of the subject. Legends of pagan weather-gods passed through his mind like hurrying shadows. These shadows multiplied, changed form, vanished and returned. They came and went with incoherence, a straggling stream, rushing from one point to another, manœuvring for position, but all unled, unguided by his will. The physical exercise filled his brain with blood, and thought danced undirected, picture upon picture driving by, so that soon he slipped from German weather and pagan gods to the witchcraft of past centuries, of its alleged association with the natural powers of the elements, and thus, eventually, to his cherished beliefs that humanity had advanced.

Such remnants of primitive days were grotesque superstition, of course. But had humanity advanced? Had the individual progressed after all? Civilization, was it not the merest artificial growth? And the old perplexity rushed through his mind again – the German barbarity and blood-lust, the savagery, the undoubted sadic impulses, the frightfulness taught with cool calculation by their highest minds, approved by their professors, endorsed by their clergy, applauded by their women even – all the unwelcome, undesired thoughts came flocking back upon him, escorted by the trooping shadows. They lay, these questions, still unsolved within him; it was the undercurrent, flowing more swiftly now, that bore them to the surface. It had acquired momentum; it was leading somewhere.

They were a thoughtful, intellectual race, these Germans; their music, literature, philosophy, their science – how reconcile the opposing qualities? He had read that their herd-instinct was unu-sually developed, though betraying the characteristics of a low wild savage type – the lupine. It might be true. Fear and danger wakened this collective instinct into terrific activity, making them blind and humourless; they fought best, like wolves, in contact; they howled and whined and boasted loudly all together to inspire terror; their Hymn of Hate was but an elaboration of the wolf's fierce bark, giving them herd-courage; and a savage discipline was necessary to their lupine type.

These reflections thronged his mind as the blood coursed in his veins with the rapid climbing; yet one and all, the beauty of the evening, the magic of the hidden town, the thoughts of German horror, German weather, German gods, all these, even the odd detail that they revived a pagan practice by hammering nails into effigies and idols – all led finally to one blazing centre that nothing could dislodge nor anything conceal: a woman's voice and eyes. To these, he knew quite well, was due the undesired intensification of the very mood, the very emotions, the very thoughts he had come out on purpose to escape.

"It is the night of the vernal equinox," occurred to him suddenly, sharp as a whispered voice beside him. He had no notion whence the idea was born. It had no particular meaning, so far as he remembered.

"It had *then* . . ." said the voice imperiously, rising, it seemed, directly out of the under-current in his soul.

It startled him. He increased his pace. He walked very quickly, whistling softly as he went.

The dusk had fallen when at length he topped the long, slow hill, and left the last of the atrocious straggling villas well behind him. The ancient city lay far below in murky haze and smoke, but tinged now with the silver of the growing moon.

4

He stood now on the open plateau. He was on the heights at last.

The night air met him freshly in the face, so that he forgot the fatigue of the long climb uphill, taken too fast somewhat for his years. He drew a deep draught into his lungs and stepped out briskly.

Far in the upper sky light flaky clouds raced through the reddened air, but the wind kept to these higher strata, and the world about him lay very still. Few lights showed in the farms and cottages, for this was the direct route of the Gothas, and nothing that could help the German hawks to find the river was visible.

His mind cleared pleasantly; this keen sweet air held no mystery; he put his best foot foremost, whistling still, but a little more loudly than before. Among the orchards he saw the daisies glimmer. Also, he heard the guns, a thudding concussion in the direction of the coveted Amiens, where, some sixty miles as the crow flies, they roared their terror into the calm evening skies. He cursed the sound, in the town below it was not audible. Thought jumped then to the men who fired them, and so to the prisoners who worked on the roads outside the hospitals and camps he visited daily. He passed them every morning and night, and the N.C.O. invariably saluted his Red Cross uniform, a salute he returned, when he could not avoid it, with embarrassment.

One man in particular stood out clearly in this memory; he had exchanged glances with him, noted the expression of his face, the number of his gang printed on coat and trousers – "82." The fellow had somehow managed to establish a relationship; he would look up and smile or frown; if the news, from his point of view, was good, he smiled; if it was bad, he scowled; once, insolently enough – when the Germans had taken Albert, Péronne, Bapaume – he grinned.

Something about the sullen, close-cropped face, typically Prussian, made the other shudder. It was the visage of an animal, neither evil nor malignant, even good-natured sometimes when it smiled, yet of an animal that could be fierce with the lust of happiness, ferocious with delight. The sullen savagery of a human wolf lay in it somewhere. He pictured its owner impervious to shame, to normal human instinct as civilized people know these. Doubtless he read his own feelings into it. He could imagine the man doing anything and everything, regarding chivalry and sporting instinct as proof of fear or weakness. He could picture this member of the wolf-pack killing a woman or a child, mutilating, cutting off little hands even, with the conscientious conviction that it was right and sensible to destroy *any* individual of an enemy tribe. It was, to him, an atrocious and inhuman face.

It now cropped up with unpleasant vividness, as he listened to the distant guns and thought of Amiens with its back against the wall, its inhabitants flying—

Ah! Amiens . . .! He again saw the woman staring into his obedient eyes across the narrow space between the tables. He smelt the delicious perfume of her dress and person on the stairs. He heard her commanding voice, her very words: "We count on you. . . . I know we can . . . we do." And her background was of twisted streets, dark alley-ways and leaning gables. . . .

He hurried, whistling loudly an air that he invented suddenly, using his stick like a golf club at every loose stone his feet encountered, making as much noise as possible. He told himself he was a parson and a Red Cross worker. He looked up and saw that the stars were out. The pace made him warm, and he shifted his haversack to the other shoulder. The moon, he observed, now cast his shadow for a long distance on the sandy road.

After another mile, while the air grew sharper and twilight surrendered finally to the moon, the road began to curve and dip, the cottages lay farther out in the dim fields, the farms and barns occurred at longer intervals. A dog barked now and again; he saw cows lying down for the night beneath shadowy fruit-trees. And then the scent in the air changed slightly, and a darkening of the near horizon warned him that the forest had come close.

This was an event. Its influence breathed already a new perfume; the shadows from its myriad trees stole out and touched him. Ten minutes later he reached its actual frontier cutting across the plateau like a line of sentries at attention. He slowed down a little. Here, within sight and touch of his long-desired objective, he hesitated. It stretched, he knew from the map, for many leagues to the north, uninhabited, lonely, the home of peace and silence; there were flowers there, and cool sweet spaces where the moonlight fell. Yet here, within scent and touch of it, he slowed down a moment to draw breath. A forest on the map is one thing; visible before the eyes when night has fallen, it is another. It is real.

The wind, not noticeable hitherto, now murmured towards him from the serried trees that seemed to manufacture darkness out of nothing. This murmur hummed about him. It enveloped him. Piercing it, another sound that was not the guns just reached him, but so distant that he hardly noticed it. He looked back. Dusk suddenly merged in night. He stopped.

"How practical the French are," he said to himself – aloud – as he looked at the road running straight as a ruled line into the heart of the trees. "They waste no energy, no space, no time. Admirable!"

It pierced the forest like a lance, tapering to a faint point in the misty distance. The trees ate its undeviating straightness as though they would smother it from sight, as though its rigid outline marred their mystery. He admired the practical makers of the road, yet sided, too, with the poetry of the trees. He stood there staring, waiting, dawdling. . . . About him, save for this murmur of the wind, was silence. Nothing living stirred. The world lay extraordinarily still. That other distant sound had died away.

He lit his pipe, glad that the match blew out and the damp tobacco needed several matches before the pipe drew properly. His puttees hurt him a little, he stooped to loosen them. His haversack swung round in front as he straightened up again, he shifted it laboriously to the other shoulder. A tiny stone in his right boot caused irritation. Its removal took a considerable time, for he had to sit down, and a log was not at once forthcoming. Moreover, the laces gave him trouble, and his fingers had grown thick with heat and the knots were difficult to tie. . . .

"There!" He said it aloud, standing up again. "Now, at last, I'm ready!" Then added a mild imprecation, for his pipe had gone out while he stooped over the recalcitrant boot, and it had to be lighted once again. "Ah!" he gasped finally with a sigh as, facing the forest for the third time, he shuffled his tunic straight, altered his haversack once more, changed his stick from the right hand to the left – and faced the foolish truth without further pretence.

He mopped his forehead carefully, as though at the same time trying to mop away from his mind a faint anxiety, a very faint uneasiness, that gathered there. Was someone standing near him? Had somebody come close? He listened intently. It was the blood singing in his ears, of course, that curious distant noise. For, truth to tell, the loneliness bit just below the surface of what he found enjoyable. It seemed to him that somebody was coming, someone he could not see, so that he looked back over his shoulder once again, glanced quickly right and left, then peered down the long opening cut through the woods in front – when there came suddenly a roar and a blaze of dazzling light from behind, so instantaneously that he barely had time to obey the instinct of self-preservation and step aside. He actually leapt. Pressed against the hedge, he saw a motor-car rush past him like a whirlwind, flooding the sandy road with fire; a second followed it; and, to his complete amazement, then, a third.

They were powerful, private cars, so-called. This struck him instantly. Two other things he noticed, as they dived down the throat of the long white road – they showed no tail-lights. This made him wonder. And, secondly, the drivers, clearly seen, were women. They were not even in uniform – which made him wonder even more. The occupants, too, were women. He caught the outline of toque and feather – or was it flowers? – against the closed windows in the moonlight as the procession rushed past him.

He felt bewildered and astonished. Private motors were rare, and military regulations exceedingly strict; the danger of spies dressed in French uniform was constant; cars armed with machine guns, he knew, patrolled the countryside in all directions. Shaken and alarmed, he thought of favoured persons fleeing stealthily by night, of treachery, disguise and swift surprise; he thought of various things as he stood peering down the road for ten minutes after all sight and sound of the cars had died away. But no solution of the mystery occurred to him. Down the white throat the motors vanished. His pipe had gone out; he lit it, and puffed furiously.

His thoughts, at any rate, took temporarily a new direction now. The road was not as lonely as he had imagined. A natural reaction set in at once, and this proof of practical, modern life banished the shadows from his mind effectually. He started off once more, oblivious of his former hesitation. He even felt a trifle shamed and foolish, pretending that the vanished mood had not existed. The tobacco had been damp. His boot had really hurt him. . . .

Yet bewilderment and surprise stayed with him. The swiftness of the incident was disconcerting; the cars arrived and vanished with such extraordinary rapidity; their noisy irruption into this peaceful spot seemed incongruous; they roared, blazed, rushed and disappeared; silence resumed its former sway.

But the silence persisted, whereas the noise was gone.

This touch of the incongruous remained with him as he now went ever deeper into the heart of the quiet forest. This odd incongruity of dreams remained.

5

The keen air stole from the woods, cooling his body and his mind; anemones gleamed faintly among the brushwood, lit by the pallid moonlight. There were beauty, calm and silence, the slow breathing of the earth beneath the comforting sweet stars. War, in this haunt of ancient peace, seemed an incredible anachronism. His thoughts turned to gentle happy hopes of a day when the lion and the lamb would yet lie down together, and a little child would lead them without fear. His soul dwelt with peaceful longings and calm desires.

He walked on steadily, until the inflexible straightness of the endless road began to afflict him, and he longed for a turning to the right or left. He looked eagerly about him for a woodland path. Time mattered little; he could wait for the sunrise and walk home "beneath the young grey dawn"; he had food and matches, he could light a fire, and sleep— No! – after all, he would not light a fire, perhaps; he might be accused of signalling to hostile aircraft, or a *garde forestière* might catch him. He would not bother with a fire. The night was warm, he could enjoy himself and pass the time quite happily without artificial heat; probably he would need no sleep at all. . . . And just then he noticed an opening on his right, where a seductive pathway led in among the trees. The moon, now higher in the sky, lit this woodland trail enticingly; it seemed the very opening he had looked for, and with a thrill of pleasure he at once turned down it, leaving the ugly road behind him with relief.

The sound of his footsteps hushed instantly on the leaves and moss; the silence became noticeable; an unusual stillness followed; it seemed that something in his mind was also hushed. His feet moved stealthily, as though anxious to conceal his presence from surprise. His steps dragged purposely; their rustling through the thick dead leaves, perhaps, was pleasant to him. He was not sure.

The path opened presently into a clearing where the moonlight made a pool of silver, the surrounding brushwood fell away; and in the centre a gigantic outline rose. It was, he saw, a beech tree that dwarfed the surrounding forest by its grandeur. Its bulk loomed very splendid against the sky, a faint rustle just audible in its myriad tiny leaves. Dipped in the moonlight, it had such majesty of proportion, such symmetry, that he stopped in admiration. It was, he saw, a multiple tree, five stems springing with attempted spirals out of an enormous trunk; it was immense; it had a presence, the space framed it to perfection. The clearing, evidently, was a favourite resting-place for summer picnickers, a playground, probably, for city children on holiday afternoons; woodcutters, too, had been here recently, for he noticed piled brushwood ready to be carted. It indicated admirably, he felt, the limits of his night expedition. Here he would rest awhile, eat his late supper, sleep perhaps round a small— No! again – a fire he need *not* make; a spark might easily set the woods ablaze, it was against both forest and military regulations. This idea of a fire, otherwise so natural, was distasteful, even repugnant, to him. He wondered a little why it recurred. He noticed this time, moreover, something unpleasant connected with the suggestion of a fire, something that made him shrink; almost a ghostly dread lay hidden in it.

This startled him. A dozen excellent reasons, supplied by his brain, warned him that a fire was unwise; but the true reason, supplied by another part of him, concealed itself with care, as though afraid that reason might detect its nature and fix the label on. Disliking this reminder of his earlier mood, he moved forward into the clearing, swinging his stick aggressively and whistling. He approached the tree, where a dozen thick roots dipped into the earth. Admiring, looking up and down, he paced slowly round its prodigious girth, then stood absolutely still. His heart stopped abruptly, his blood became congealed. He saw something that filled him with a sudden emptiness of terror. On this western side the shadow lay very black; it was between the thick limbs, half stem, half root, where the dark hollows gave easy hiding-places, that he was positive he detected movement. A portion of the trunk had moved.

He stood stock still and stared – not three feet from the trunk – when there came a second movement. Concealed in the shadows there crouched a living form. The movement defined itself immediately. Half reclining, half standing, a living being pressed itself close against the tree, yet fitting so neatly into the wide scooped hollows, that it was scarcely distinguishable from its ebony background. But for the chance movement he must have passed it undetected. Equally, his outstretched fingers might have touched it. The blood rushed from his heart, as he saw this second movement.

Detaching itself from the obscure background, the figure rose and stood before him. It swayed a little, then stepped out into the patch of moonlight on his left. Three feet lay between them. The figure then bent over. A pallid face with burning eyes thrust forward and peered straight into his own.

The human being was a woman. The same instant he recognized the eyes that had stared him out of countenance in the dining-room two nights ago. He was petrified. She stared him out of countenance now.

And, as she did so, the under-current he had tried to ignore so long swept to the surface in a tumultuous flood, obliterating his normal self. Something elaborately built up in his soul by years of artificial training collapsed like a house of cards, and he knew himself undone.

"They've got me . . .!" flashed dreadfully through his mind. It was, again, like a message delivered in a dream where the significance of acts performed and language uttered, concealed at the moment, is revealed much later only.

"After all – they've got me . . .!"

6

The dialogue that followed seemed strange to him only when looking back upon it. The element of surprise again was negligible if not wholly absent, but the incongruity of dreams, almost of nightmare, became more marked. Though the affair was unlikely, it was far from incredible. So completely were this man and woman involved in some purpose common to them both that their talk, their meeting, their instinctive sympathy at the time seemed natural. The same stream bore them irresistibly towards the same far sea. Only, as yet, this common purpose remained concealed. Nor could he define the violent emotions that troubled him. Their exact description was in him, but so deep that he could not draw it up. Moonlight lay upon his thought, merging clear outlines.

Divided against himself, the cleavage left no authoritative self in control; his desire to take an immediate decision resulted in a confused struggle, where shame and pleasure, attraction and revulsion mingled painfully. Incongruous details tumbled helter-skelter about his mind: for no obvious reason, he remembered again his Red Cross uniform, his former holy calling, his nationality too; he was a servant of mercy, a teacher of the love of God; he was an English gentleman. Against which rose other details, as in opposition, holding just beyond the reach of words, yet rising, he recognized well enough, from the bed-rock of the human animal, whereon a few centuries have imposed the thin crust of refinement men call civilization. He was aware of joy and loathing.

In the first few seconds he knew the clash of a dreadful fundamental struggle, while the spell of this woman's strange enchantment poured over him, seeking the reconciliation he himself could not achieve. Yet the reconciliation *she* sought meant victory or defeat; no compromise lay in it. Something imperious emanating from her already dominated the warring elements towards a coherent whole. He stood before her, quivering with emotions he dared not name. Her great womanhood he recognized, acknowledging obedience to her undisclosed intentions. And this idea of coming surrender terrified him. Whence came, too, that queenly touch about her that made him feel he should have sunk upon his knees?

The conflict resulted in a curious compromise. He raised his hand; he saluted; he found very ordinary words.

"You passed me only a short time ago," he stammered, "in the motors. There were others with you—"

"Knowing that you would find us and come after. We count on your presence and your willing help." Her voice was firm as with unalterable conviction. It was persuasive too. He nodded, as though acquiescence seemed the only course.

"We need your sympathy; we must have your power too."

He bowed again. "My power!" Something exulted in him. But he murmured only. It was natural, he felt; he gave consent without a question.

Strange words he both understood and did not understand. Her voice, low and silvery, was that of a gentle, cultured woman, but command rang through it with a clang of metal, terrible behind the sweetness. She moved a little closer, standing erect before him in the moonlight, her figure borrowing something of the great tree's majesty behind her. It was incongruous, this gentle and yet sinister air she wore. Whence came, in this calm peaceful spot, the suggestion of a wild and savage background to her? Why were there tumult and oppression in his heart, pain, horror, tenderness and mercy, mixed beyond disentanglement? Why did he think already, but helplessly, of escape, yet at the same time burn to stay? Whence came again, too, a certain queenly touch he felt in her?

"The gods have brought you," broke across his turmoil in a half whisper whose breath almost touched his face. "You belong to us."

The deeps rose in him. Seduced by the sweetness and the power, the warring divisions in his being drew together. His under-self more and more obtained the mastery she willed. Then something in the French she used flickered across his mind with a faint reminder of normal things again.

"Belgian—" he began, and then stopped short, as her instant rejoinder broke in upon his halting speech and petrified him. In her voice sang that triumphant tenderness that only the feminine powers of the Universe may compass: it seemed the sky sang with her, the mating birds, wild flowers, the south wind and the running streams. All these, even the silver birches, lent their fluid, feminine undertones to the two pregnant words with which she interrupted him and completed his own unfinished sentence:

"— and mother."

With the dreadful calm of an absolute assurance, she stood and watched him.

His understanding already showed signs of clearing. She stretched her hands out with a passionate appeal, a yearning gesture, the eloquence of which should explain all that remained unspoken. He saw their grace and symmetry, exquisite in the moonlight, then watched them fold together in an attitude of prayer. Beautiful mother hands they were; hands made to smooth the pillows of the world, to comfort, bless, caress, hands that little children everywhere must lean upon and love – perfect symbol of protective, self-forgetful mother-hood.

This tenderness he noted; he noted next – the strength. In the folded hands he divined the expression of another great world-power, fulfilling the implacable resolution of the mouth and eyes. He was aware of relentless purpose, more – of merciless revenge, as by a protective motherhood outraged beyond endurance. Moreover, the gesture held appeal; these hands, so close that their actual perfume reached him, sought his own in help. The power in himself as man, as male, as father – this was required of him in the fulfilment of the unknown purpose to which this woman summoned him. His understanding cleared still more.

The couple faced one another, staring fixedly beneath the giant beech that overarched them. In the dark of his eyes, he knew, lay growing terror. He shivered, and the shiver passed down his spine, making his whole body tremble. There stirred in him an excitement he loathed, yet welcomed, as the primitive male in him, answering the summons, reared up with instinctive, dreadful glee to shatter the bars that civilization had so confidently set upon its freedom. A primal emotion of his under-being, ancient lust that had too long gone hungry and unfed, leaped towards some possible satisfaction. It was incredible; it was, of course, a dream. But judgment wavered; increasing terror ate his will away. Violence and sweetness, relief and degradation, fought in his soul, as he trembled before a power that now slowly mastered him. This glee and loathing formed their ghastly partnership. He could have strangled the woman where she stood. Equally, he could have knelt and kissed her feet.

The vehemence of the conflict paralysed him.

"A mother's hands . . ." he murmured at length, the words escaping like bubbles that rose to the surface of a seething cauldron and then burst.

And the woman smiled as though she read his mind and saw his little trembling. The smile crept down from the eyes towards the mouth; he saw her lips part slightly; he saw her teeth.

But her reply once more transfixed him. Two syllables she uttered in a voice of iron:

"Louvain."

The sound acted upon him like a Word of Power in some Eastern fairy tale. It knit the present to a past that he now recognized could never die. Humanity had *not* advanced. The hidden source of his secret joy began to glow. For this woman focused in him passions that life had hitherto denied, pretending they were atrophied, and the primitive male, the naked savage rose up, with glee in its lustful eyes and blood upon its lips. Acquired civilization, a pitiful mockery, split through its thin veneer and fled.

"Belgian . . . Louvain . . . Mother . . ." he whispered, yet astonished at the volume of sound that now left his mouth. His voice had a sudden fullness. It seemed a cave-man roared the words.

She touched his hand, and he knew a sudden intensification of life within him; immense energy poured through his veins; a mediæval spirit used his eyes; great pagan instincts strained and urged against his heart, against his very muscles. He longed for action.

And he cried aloud: "I am with you, with you to the end!"

Her spell had vivified beyond all possible resistance that primitive consciousness which is ever the bed-rock of the human animal.

A racial memory, inset against the forest scenery, flashed suddenly through the depths laid bare. Below a sinking moon dark figures flew in streaming lines and groups; tormented cries went down the wind; he saw torn, blasted trees that swayed and rocked; there was a leaping fire, a gleaming knife, an altar. He saw a sacrifice.

It flashed away and vanished. In its place the woman stood, with shining eyes fixed on his face, one arm outstretched, one hand upon his flesh. She shifted slightly, and her cloak swung open. He saw clinging skins wound closely about her figure; leaves, flowers and trailing green hung from her shoulders, fluttering down the lines of her triumphant physical beauty. There was a perfume of wild roses, incense, ivy bloom, whose subtle intoxication drowned his senses. He saw a sparkling girdle round the waist, a knife thrust through it tight against the hip. And his secret joy, the glee, the pleasure of some unlawful and unholy lust leaped through his blood towards the abandonment of satisfaction.

The moon revealed a glimpse, no more. An instant he saw her thus, half savage and half sweet, symbol of primitive justice entering the present through the door of vanished centuries.

The cloak swung back again, the outstretched hand withdrew, but from a world he knew had altered.

Today sank out of sight. The moon shone pale with terror and delight on Yesterday.

7

Across this altered world a faint new sound now reached his ears, as though a human wail of anguished terror trembled and changed into the cry of some captured helpless animal. He thought of a wolf apart from the comfort of its pack, savage yet abject. The despair of a last appeal was in the sound. It floated past, it died away. The woman moved closer suddenly.

"All is prepared," she said, in the same low, silvery voice; "we must not tarry. The equinox is come, the tide of power flows. The sacrifice is here; we hold him fast. We only awaited you." Her shining eyes were raised to his. "Your soul is with us now?" she whispered.

"My soul is with you."

"And midnight," she continued, "is at hand. We use, of course, their methods. Henceforth the gods – their old-world gods – shall work on our side. They demand a sacrifice, and justice has provided one."

His understanding cleared still more then; the last veil of confusion was drawing from his mind. The old, old names went thundering through his consciousness – Odin, Wotan, Moloch – accessible ever to invocation and worship of the rightful kind. It seemed as natural as though he read in his pulpit the prayer for rain, or gave out the hymn for those at sea. That was merely an empty form, whereas this was real. Sea, storm and earthquake, all natural activities, lay under the direction of those elemental powers called the gods. Names changed, the principle remained.

"Their weather shall be ours," he cried, with sudden passion, as a memory of unhallowed usages he had thought erased from life burned in him; while, stranger still, resentment stirred – revolt – against the system, against the very deity he had worshipped hitherto. For these had never once interfered to help the cause of right; their feebleness was now laid bare before his eyes. And a twofold lust rose in him. "Vengeance is ours!" he cried in a louder voice, through which this sudden loathing of the cross poured hatred. "Vengeance and justice! Now bind the victim! Bring on the sacrifice!"

"He is already bound." And as the woman moved a little, the curious erection behind her caught his eye – the piled brushwood he had imagined was the work of woodmen, picnickers, or playing children. He realized its true meaning.

It now delighted and appalled him. Awe deepened in him, a wind of ice passed over him. Civilization made one more fluttering effort. He gasped, he shivered; he tried to speak. But no words came. A thin cry, as of a frightened child, escaped him.

"It is the only way," the woman whispered softly. "We steal from them the power of their own deities." Her head flung back with a marvellous gesture of grace and power; she stood before him a figure of perfect womanhood, gentle and tender, yet at the same time alive and cruel with the passions of an ignorant and savage past. Her folded hands were clasped, her face turned heavenwards. "I am a mother," she added, with amazing passion, her eyes glistening in the moonlight with unshed tears. "We all" – she glanced towards the forest, her voice rising to a wild and poignant cry – "all, all of us are mothers!"

It was then the final clearing of his understanding happened, and he realized his own part in what would follow. Yet before the realization he felt himself not merely ineffective, but powerless. The struggling forces in him were so evenly matched that paralysis of the will resulted. His dry lips contrived merely a few words of confused and feeble protest.

"Me!" he faltered. "My help—?"

"Justice," she answered; and though softly uttered, it was as though the mediæval towers clanged their bells. That secret, ghastly joy again rose in him; admiration, wonder, desire followed instantly. A fugitive memory of Joan of Arc flashed by, as with armoured wings, upon the moonlight. Some power similarly heroic, some purpose similarly inflexible, emanated from this woman, the savour of whose physical enchantment, whose very breath, rose to his brain like incense. Again he shuddered. The spasm of secret pleasure shocked him. He sighed. He felt alert, yet stunned.

Her words went down the wind between them:

"You are so weak, you English," he heard her terrible whisper, "so nobly forgiving, so fine, yet so forgetful. You refuse the weapon *they* place within your hands." Her face thrust closer, the great eyes blazed upon him. "If we would save the children" – the voice rose and fell like wind – "we must worship where they worship, we must sacrifice to their savage deities. . . ."

The stream of her words flowed over him with this nightmare magic that seemed natural, without surprise. He listened, he trembled, and again he sighed. Yet in his blood there was sudden roaring.

" . . .Louvain . . . the hands of little children . . . we have the proof," he heard, oddly intermingled with another set of words that clamoured vainly in his brain for utterance; "the diary in his own handwriting, his gloating pleasure . . . the little, innocent hands. . . ."

"Justice is mine!" rang through some fading region of his now fainting soul, but found no audible utterance.

". . . Mist, rain and wind . . . the gods of German Weather. . . . We all . . . are mothers. . . ."

"I will repay," came forth in actual words, yet so low he hardly heard the sound. But the woman heard.

"*We!*" she cried fiercely, "*we* will repay!"

"God!" The voice seemed torn from his throat. "Oh God – *my* God!"

"*Our* gods," she said steadily in that tone of iron, "are near. The sacrifice is ready. And *you* – servant of mercy, priest of a younger deity, and English – you bring the power that makes it effectual. The circuit is complete."

It was perhaps the tears in her appealing eyes, perhaps it was her words, her voice, the wonder of her presence; all combined possibly in the spell that finally then struck down his will as with a single blow that paralysed his last resistance. The monstrous, half-legendary spirit of a primitive day recaptured him completely; he yielded to the spell of this tender, cruel woman, mother and avenging angel, whom horror and suffering had flung back upon the practices of uncivilized centuries. A common desire, a common lust and purpose, degraded both of them. They understood one another. Dropping back into a gulf of savage worship that set up idols in the place of God, they prayed to Odin and his awful crew. . . .

It was again the touch of her hand that galvanized him. She raised him; he had been kneeling in slavish wonder and admiration at her feet. He leaped to do the bidding, however terrible, of this woman who was priestess, queen indeed, of a long-forgotten orgy.

"Vengeance at last!" he cried, in an exultant voice that no longer frightened him. "Now light the fire! Bring on the sacrifice!"

There was a rustling among the nearer branches, the forest stirred; the leaves of last year brushed against advancing feet. Yet before he could turn to see, before even the last words had wholly left his lips, the woman, whose hand still touched his fingers, suddenly tossed her cloak aside, and flinging her bare arms about his neck, drew him with impetuous passion towards her face and kissed him, as with delighted fury of exultant passion, full upon the mouth. Her body, in its clinging skins, pressed close against his own; her heat poured into him. She held him fiercely, savagely, and her burning kiss consumed his modern soul away with the fire of a primal day.

"The gods have given you to us," she cried, releasing him. "Your soul is ours!"

She turned – they turned together – to look for one upon whose last hour the moon now shed her horrid silver.

8

This silvery moonlight fell upon the scene.

Incongruously he remembered the flowers that soon would know the cuckoo's call; the soft mysterious stars shone down; the woods lay silent underneath the sky.

An amazing fantasy of dream shot here and there. "I am a man, an Englishman, a padre!" ran twisting through his mind, as though *she* whispered them to emphasize the ghastly contrast of reality. A memory of his own Kentish village with its Sunday school fled past, his dream of the Lion and the Lamb close after it. He saw children playing on the green . . . He saw their happy little hands . . .

Justice, punishment, revenge – he could not disentangle them. No longer did he wish to. The tide of violence was at his lips, quenching an ancient thirst. He drank. It seemed he could drink for ever. These tender pictures only sweetened horror. That kiss had burned his modern soul away.

The woman waved her hand; there swept from the underbrush a score of figures dressed like herself in skins, with leaves and flowers entwined among their flying hair. He was surrounded in a moment. Upon each face he noted the same tenderness and terrible resolve that their commander wore. They pressed about him, dancing with enchanting grace, yet with full-blooded abandon, across the chequered light and shadow. It was the brimming energy of their movements that swept him off his feet, waking the desire for fierce rhythmical expression. His own muscles leaped and ached; for this energy, it seemed, poured into him from the tossing arms and legs, the shimmering bodies whence hair and skins flung loose, setting the very air awhirl. It flowed over into inanimate objects even, so that the trees waved their branches although no wind stirred – hair, skins and hands, rushing leaves and flying fingers touched his face, his neck, his arms and shoulders, catching him away into this orgy of an ancient, sacrificial ritual. Faces with shining eyes peered into his, then sped away; grew in a cloud upon the moonlight; sank back in shadow; reappeared, touched him, whispered, vanished. Silvery limbs gleamed everywhere. Chanting rose in a wave, to fall away again into forest rustlings; there were smiles that flashed, then fainted into moonlight, red lips and gleaming teeth that shone, then faded out. The secret glade, picked from the heart of the forest by the moon, became a torrent of tumultuous life, a whirlpool of passionate emotions Time had not killed.

But it was the eyes that mastered him, for in their yearning, mating so incongruously with the savage grace – in the eyes shone ever tears. He was aware of gentle women, of womanhood, of accumulated feminine power that nothing could withstand, but of feminine power in majesty, its essential protective tenderness roused, as by tribal instinct, into a collective fury of implacable revenge. He was, above all, aware of motherhood – of mothers. And the man, the male, the father in him rose like a storm to meet it.

From the torrent of voices certain sentences emerged; sometimes chanted, sometimes driven into his whirling mind as though big whispers thrust them down his ears. "You are with us to the end," he caught. "We have the proof. And punishment is ours!"

It merged in wind, others took its place:

"We hold him fast. The old gods wait and listen."

The body of rushing whispers flowed like a stormwind past.

A lovely face, fluttering close against his own, paused an instant, and starry eyes gazed into his with a passion of gratitude, dimming a moment their stern fury with a mother's tenderness: "For the little ones . . . it is necessary, it is the only way. . . . Our own children. . . ." The face went out in a gust of blackness, as the chorus rose with a new note of awe and reverence, and a score of throats uttered in unison a single cry: "The raven! The White Horses! His signs! Great Odin hears!"

He saw the great dark bird flap slowly across the clearing, and melt against the shadow of the giant beech; he heard its hoarse, croaking note; the crowds of heads bowed low before its passage. The White Horses he did not see; only a sound as of considerable masses of air regularly displaced was audible far overhead. But the veiled light, as though great thunder-clouds had risen, he saw distinctly. The sky above the clearing where he stood, panting and dishevelled, was blocked by a mass that owned unusual outline. These clouds now topped the forest, hiding the moon and stars. The flowers went out like nightlights blown. The wind rose slowly, then with sudden violence. There was a roaring in the tree-tops. The branches tossed and shook.

"The White Horses!" cried the voices, in a frenzy of adoration. "He is here!"

It came swiftly, this collective mass; it was both apt and terrible. There was an immense footstep. It was there.

Then panic seized him, he felt an answering tumult in himself, the Past surged through him like a sea at flood. Some inner sight, peering across the wreckage of Today, perceived an outline that in its size dwarfed mountains, a pair of monstrous shoulders, a face that rolled through a full quarter of the heavens. Above the ruin of civilization, now fulfilled in the microcosm of his own being, the menacing shadow of a forgotten deity peered down upon the earth, yet upon one detail of it chiefly – the human group that had been wildly dancing, but that now chanted in solemn conclave about a forest altar.

For some minutes a dead silence reigned; the pouring winds left emptiness in which no leaf stirred; there was a hush, a stillness that could be felt. The kneeling figures stretched forth a level sea of arms towards the altar; from the lowered heads the hair hung down in torrents, against which the naked flesh shone white; the skins upon the rows of backs gleamed yellow. The obscurity deepened overhead. It was the time of adoration. He knelt as well, arms similarly outstretched, while the lust of vengeance burned within him.

Then came, across the stillness, the stirring of big wings, a rustling as the great bird settled in the higher branches of the beech. The ominous note broke through the silence; and with one accord the shining backs were straightened. The company rose, swayed, parting into groups and lines. Two score voices resumed the solemn chant. The throng of pallid faces passed to and fro like great fire-flies that shone and vanished. He, too, heard his own voice in unison, while his feet, as with instinctive knowledge; trod the same measure that the others trod.

Cut of this tumult and clearly audible above the chorus and the rustling feet rang out suddenly, in a sweetly fluting tone, the leader's voice:

"The Fire! But first the hands!"

A rush of figures set instantly towards a thicket where the underbrush stood densest. Skins, trailing flowers, bare waving arms and tossing hair swept past on a burst of perfume. It was as though the trees themselves sped by. And the torrent of voices shook the very air in answer:

"The Fire! But first – the hands!"

Across this roaring volume pierced then, once again, that wailing sound which seemed both human and nonhuman – the anguished cry as of some lonely wolf in metamorphosis, apart from the collective safety of the pack, abjectly terrified, feeling the teeth of the final trap, and knowing the helpless feet within the steel. There was a crash of rending boughs and tearing branches. There was a tumult in the thicket, though of brief duration – then silence.

He stood watching, listening, overmastered by a diabolical sensation of expectancy he knew to be atrocious. Turning in the direction of the cry, his straining eyes seemed filled with blood; in his temples the pulses throbbed and hammered audibly. The next second he stiffened into a stone-like rigidity, as a figure, struggling violently yet half collapsed, was borne hurriedly past by a score of eager arms that swept it towards the beech tree, and then proceeded to fasten it in an upright position against the trunk. It was a man bound tight with thongs, adorned with leaves and flowers and trailing green. The face was hidden, for the head sagged forward on the breast, but he saw the arms forced flat against the giant trunk, held helpless beyond all possible escape; he saw the knife, poised and aimed by slender, graceful fingers above the victim's wrists laid bare; he saw the – hands.

"An eye for an eye," he heard, "a tooth for a tooth!" It rose in awful chorus. Yet this time, although the words roared close about him, they seemed farther away, as if wind brought them through the crowding trees from far off.

"Light the fire! Prepare the sacrifice!" came on a following wind; and, while strange distance held the voices as before, a new faint sound now audible was very close. There was a crackling. Some ten feet beyond the tree a column of thick smoke rose in the air; he was aware of heat not meant for modern purposes; of yellow light that was not the light of stars.

The figure writhed, and the face swung suddenly sideways. Glaring with panic hopelessness past the judge and past the hanging knife, the eyes found his own. There was a pause of perhaps five seconds, but in these five seconds centuries rolled by. The priest of Today looked down into the well of time. For five hundred years he gazed into those twin eyeballs, glazed with the abject terror of a last appeal. They recognized one another.

The centuries dragged appallingly. The drama of civilization, in a sluggish stream, went slowly by, halting, meandering, losing itself, then reappearing. Sharpest pains, as of a thousand knives, accompanied its dreadful, endless lethargy. Its million hesitations made him suffer a million deaths of agony. Terror, despair and anger, all futile and without effect upon its progress, destroyed a thousand times his soul, which yet some hope – a towering, indestructible hope – a thousand times renewed. This despair and hope alternately broke his being, ever to fashion it anew. His torture seemed not of this world. Yet hope survived. The sluggish stream moved onward, forward . . .

There came an instant of sharpest, dislocating torture. The yellow light grew slightly brighter. He saw the eyelids flicker.

It was at this moment he realized abruptly that he stood alone, apart from the others, unnoticed apparently, perhaps forgotten; his feet held steady; his voice no longer sang. And at this discovery a quivering shock ran through his being, as though the will were suddenly loosened into a new activity, yet an activity that halted between two terrifying alternatives.

It was as though the flicker of those eyelids loosed a spring.

Two instincts, clashing in his being, fought furiously for the mastery. One, ancient as this sacrifice, savage as the legendary figure brooding in the heavens above him, battled fiercely with another, acquired more recently in human evolution, that had not yet crystallized into permanence. He saw a child, playing in a Kentish orchard with toys and flowers the little innocent hands made living . . . he saw a lowly manger, figures kneeling round it, and one star shining overhead in piercing and prophetic beauty.

Thought was impossible; he saw these symbols only, as the two contrary instincts, alternately hidden and revealed, fought for permanent possession of his soul. Each strove to dominate him; it seemed that violent blows were struck that wounded physically; he was bruised, he ached, he gasped for breath; his body swayed, held upright only, it seemed, by the awful appeal in the fixed and staring eyes.

The challenge had come at last to final action; the conqueror, he well knew, would remain an integral portion of his character, his soul.

It was the old, old battle, waged eternally in every human heart, in every tribe, in every race, in every period, the essential principle indeed, behind the great world-war. In the stress and confusion of the fight, as the eyes of the victim, savage in victory, abject in defeat – the appealing eyes of that animal face against the tree stared with their awful blaze into his own, this flashed clearly over him. It was the battle between might and right, between love and hate, forgiveness and vengeance, Christ and the Devil. He heard the menacing thunder of "an eye for an eye, a tooth for a tooth", then above its angry volume rose suddenly another small silvery voice that pierced with sweetness: – "Vengeance is mine, I will repay . . ." sang through him as with unimaginable hope.

Something became incandescent in him then. He realized a singular merging of powers in absolute opposition to each other. It was as though they harmonized. Yet it was through this small, silvery voice the apparent magic came. The words, of course, were his own in memory, but they rose from his modern soul, now re-awakening. . . . He started painfully. He noted again that he stood apart, alone, perhaps forgotten of the others. The woman, leading a dancing throng about the blazing brushwood, was far from him. Her mind, too sure of his compliance, had momentarily left him. The chain was weakened. The circuit knew a break.

But this sudden realization was not of spontaneous origin. His heart had not produced it of its own accord. The unholy tumult of the orgy held him too slavishly in its awful sway for the tiny point of his modern soul to have pierced it thus unaided. The light flashed to him from an outside, natural source of simple loveliness – the singing of a bird. From the distance, faint and exquisite, there had reached him the silvery notes of a happy thrush, awake in the night, and telling its joy over and over again to itself. The innocent beauty of its song came through the forest and fell into his soul. . . .

The eyes, he became aware, had shifted, focusing now upon an object nearer to them. The knife was moving. There was a convulsive wriggle of the body, the head dropped loosely forward, no cry was audible. But, at the same moment, the inner battle ceased and an unexpected climax came. Did the soul of the bully faint with fear? Did his spirit leave him at the actual touch of earthly vengeance? The watcher never knew. In that appalling moment when the knife was about to begin the mission that the fire would complete, the roar of inner battle ended abruptly, and that small silvery voice drew the words of invincible power from his reawakening soul. "Ye do it also unto me . . ." pealed o'er the forest.

He reeled. He acted instantaneously. Yet before he had dashed the knife from the hand of the executioner, scattered the pile of blazing wood, plunged through the astonished worshippers with a violence of strength that amazed even himself; before he had torn the thongs apart and loosened the fainting victim from the tree; before he had uttered a single word or cry, though it seemed to him he roared with a voice of thousands – he witnessed a sight that came surely from the Heaven of his earliest childhood days, from that Heaven whose God is love and whose forgiveness was taught him at his mother's knee.

With superhuman rapidity it passed before him and was gone. Yet it was no earthly figure that emerged from the forest, ran with this incredible swiftness past the startled throng, and reached the tree. He saw the shape; the same instant it was there; wrapped in light, as though a flame from the sacrificial fire flashed past him over the ground. It was of an incandescent brightness, yet brightest of all were the little outstretched hands. These were of purest gold, of a brilliance incredibly shining.

It was no earthly child that stretched forth these arms of generous forgiveness and took the bewildered prisoner by the hand just as the knife descended and touched the helpless wrists. The thongs were already loosened, and the victim, fallen to his knees, looked wildly this way and that for a way of possible escape, when the shining hands were laid upon his own. The murderer rose. Another instant and the throng must have been upon him, tearing him limb from limb. But the radiant little face looked down into his own; she raised him to his feet; with superhuman swiftness she led him through the infuriated concourse as though he had become invisible, guiding him safely past the furies into the cover of the trees. Close before his eyes, this happened; he saw the waft of golden brilliance, he heard the final gulp of it, as wind took the dazzling of its fiery appearance into space. They were gone . . .

9

He stood, watching the disappearing motor-cars, wondering uneasily who the occupants were and what their business, whither and why did they hurry so swiftly through the night? He was still trying to light his pipe, but the damp tobacco would not burn.

The air stole out of the forest, cooling his body and his mind; he saw the anemones gleam; there was only peace and calm about him, the earth lay waiting for the sweet, mysterious stars. The moon was higher; he looked up; a late bird sang. Three strips of cloud, spaced far apart, were the footsteps of the South Wind, as she flew to bring more birds from Africa. His thoughts turned to gentle, happy hopes of a day when the lion and the lamb should lie down together, and a little child should lead them. War, in this haunt of ancient peace, seemed an incredible anachronism.

He did not go farther; he did not enter the forest; he turned back along the quiet road he had come, ate his food on a farmer's gate, and over a pipe sat dreaming of his sure belief that humanity had advanced. He went home to his hotel soon after midnight. He slept well, and next day walked back the four miles from the hospitals, instead of using the car. Another hospital searcher walked with him. They discussed the news.

"The weather's better anyhow," said his companion. "In our favour at last!"

"That's something," he agreed, as they passed a gang of prisoners and crossed the road to avoid saluting.

"Been another escape, I hear," the other mentioned. "He won't get far. How on earth do they manage it? The M.O. had a yarn that he was helped by a motor-car. I wonder what they'll do to him."

"Oh, nothing much. Bread and water and extra work, I suppose?"

The other laughed. "I'm not so sure," he said lightly. "Humanity hasn't advanced very much in that kind of thing."

A fugitive memory flashed for an instant through the other's brain as he listened. He had an odd feeling for a second that he had heard this conversation before somewhere. A ghostly sense of familiarity brushed his mind, then vanished. At dinner that night the table in front of him was unoccupied. He did not, however, notice that it was unoccupied.

The Punishment

Lord Dunsany

Location: Potsdam, Germany.
Time: October, 1918.
Eyewitness Description: *"Had you been out that night in Germany, and able to see visions, you would have seen an imperious figure passing from place to place looking on many scenes. He looked on them, and families withered away, and happy scenes faded, and the phantom said to him, 'Come!' . . ."*

Author: Edward John Moreton Drax Plunkett, 18th Baron Dunsany, (1878–1957) was a larger-than-life Irish nobleman, big-game hunter and chess champion, who became a major writer of fantasy fiction, often ranked with J. R. R. Tolkien and Mervyn Peake. The military traditions of his ancient family naturally enough saw Dunsany fight in the Boer War, take up arms in the Irish Easter Rising in 1916, when he was hit by a bullet in the head, and then see service in France during the First World War. His outlook on life was, though, deeply soured by what he experienced in the trenches and this is very evident in his subsequent collections of short stories, *Tales of War* (1918), *Unhappy Far-Off Things* (1919) and *Tales of Three Hemispheres* (1919). Among these tales, "The Punishment" is significant for two reasons. Firstly, because it is reminiscent of one of Charles Dickens' classic stories, *A Christmas Carol*. Secondly, because it was first published – prophetically – in October 1918 when revolutionary feeling against the war was growing in Germany. Indeed, a month later, on 9 November, the Kaiser abdicated, and two days later, the Armistice was signed between the warring nations.

An exhalation arose, drawn up by the moon, from an old battle-field after the passing of years. It came out of very old craters and gathered from trenches, smoked up from Noman's Land and the ruins of farms; it rose from the rottenness of dead brigades, and lay for half the night over two armies, but at midnight the moon drew it up all into one phantom, and it rose and trailed away eastwards.

It passed over men in grey that were weary of war, it passed over a land once prosperous, happy and mighty, in which were a people that were gradually starving, it passed by ancient belfries in which there were no bells now, it passed over fear and misery and weeping, and so came to the Palace at Potsdam. It was the dead of the night, between midnight and dawn, and the Palace was very still that the emperor might sleep, and sentries guarded it who made no noise and relieved others in silence. Yet it was not so easy to sleep. Picture yourself a murderer who had killed a man. Would you sleep? Picture yourself the man who made this war. Yes, you sleep, but nightmares come.

The phantom entered the chamber. "Come," it said.

The Kaiser leaped up at once as obediently as when he came to attention on parade, years ago, as a subaltern in the Prussian Guard, a man whom no woman or child as yet had ever cursed; he leaped up and followed. They passed the silent sentries, none challenged and none saluted; they were moving swiftly over the town as the felon Gothas go; they came to a cottage in the country. They drifted over a little garden gate, and there in a neat little garden the phantom halted, like a wind that has suddenly ceased. "Look," it said.

Should he look? Yet he must look. The Kaiser looked, and saw a window shining and a neat room in the cottage: there was nothing dreadful there: thank the good German God for that; it was all right, after all. The Kaiser had had a fright, but it was all right, there was only a woman with a baby sitting before the fire; and two small children and a man. And it was quite a jolly room. And the man was a young soldier; and, why, he was a Prussian Guardsman; there was his helmet hanging on the wall; so everything was all right. They were jolly German children, that was well. How nice and homely the room was. There shone before him, and showed far off in the night, the visible reward of German thrift and industry. It was all so tidy and neat, and yet they were quite poor people. The man had done his work for the Fatherland and yet beyond all that had been able to afford all those little knick-knacks that make a home so pleasant and that in their humble little way were luxury. And while the Kaiser looked the two young children laughed as they played on the floor, not seeing that face at the window.

Why! look at the helmet. That was lucky. A bullet-hole right through the front of it. That must have gone very close to the man's head. How ever did it get through? It must have glanced upwards, as bullets sometimes do. The hole was quite low in the helmet. It would be dreadful to have bullets coming by close like that.

The firelight flickered, and the lamp shone on, and the children played on the floor, and the man was smoking out of a china pipe; he was strong and able and young, one of the wealth-winners of Germany.

"Have you seen?" said the phantom.

"Yes," said the Kaiser. It was well, he thought, that a Kaiser should see how his people lived.

At once the fire went out and the lamp faded away, the room fell sombrely into neglect and squalor, and the soldier and the children faded away with the room; all disappeared phantasmally, and nothing remained but the helmet in a kind of glow on the wall, and the woman sitting all by herself in the darkness.

"It has all gone," said the Kaiser.

"It has never been," said the phantom.

The Kaiser looked again. Yes, there was nothing there, it was just a vision. There were the grey walls all damp and uncared for, and that helmet standing out solid and round, like the only real thing among fancies. No, it had never been. It was just a vision.

"It might have been," said the phantom.

Might have been? How might it have been?

"Come," said the phantom.

They drifted away down a little lane that in summer would have had roses, and came to an Uhlan's house, in times of peace a small farmer. Farm buildings in good repair showed even in the night, and the black shapes of haystacks: again a well-kept garden lay by the house. The phantom and the Kaiser stood in the garden; before them a window glowed in a lamp-lit room.

"Look," said the phantom.

The Kaiser looked again and saw a young couple, the woman played with a baby, and all was prosperous in the merry room. Again the hard-won wealth of Germany shone out for all to see; the cosy, comfortable furniture spoke of acres well cared for, spoke of victory in the struggle with the seasons, on which wealth of nations depends.

"It might have been," said the phantom.

Again the fire died out and the merry scene faded away, leaving a melancholy ill-kept room with poverty and mourning haunting dusty corners and the woman sitting alone.

"Why do you show me this?" said the Kaiser. "Why do you show me these visions?"

"Come," said the phantom.

"What is it?" said the Kaiser. "Where are you bringing me?"

"Come," said the phantom.

They went from window to window, from land to land. You had seen, had you been out that night in Germany, and able to see visions, an imperious figure passing from place to place looking on many scenes. He looked on them, and families withered away, and happy scenes faded; and the phantom said to him: "Come." He expostulated, but obeyed; and so they went from window to window of hundreds of farms in Prussia, till they came to the Prussian border and went on into Saxony; and always you would have heard, could you hear spirits speak, "It might have been," "It might have been," repeated from window to window.

They went down through Saxony heading for Austria.

And for long the Kaiser kept that callous imperious look. But at last he, even he, at last he nearly wept. And the phantom turned then and swept him back over Saxony, and into Prussia again and over the sentries' heads, back to his comfortable bed where it was so hard to sleep. And though they had seen thousands of merry homes, homes that can never be merry now, shrines of perpetual mourning; though they had seen thousands of smiling German children, who will never be born now, but were only the visions of hopes blasted by him; for all the leagues over which he had been so ruthlessly hurried, dawn was yet barely breaking.

He had looked on the first few thousand homes of which he had robbed all time, and which he must see with his eyes before he may go hence. The first night of the Kaiser's punishment was accomplished.

The Haunted Chateau

Dennis Wheatley

Location: Cheterau, Eastern France.
Time: Spring, 1940.
Eyewitness Description: *"The Thing was in the pentacle!* Inside it! *There* with *them; at their elbows, instead of beyond the barrier which should have kept it out. Why had he felt no warning – no indication of evil . . .?"*

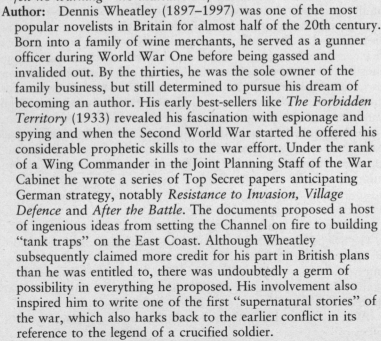

Author: Dennis Wheatley (1897–1997) was one of the most popular novelists in Britain for almost half of the 20th century. Born into a family of wine merchants, he served as a gunner officer during World War One before being gassed and invalided out. By the thirties, he was the sole owner of the family business, but still determined to pursue his dream of becoming an author. His early best-sellers like *The Forbidden Territory* (1933) revealed his fascination with espionage and spying and when the Second World War started he offered his considerable prophetic skills to the war effort. Under the rank of a Wing Commander in the Joint Planning Staff of the War Cabinet he wrote a series of Top Secret papers anticipating German strategy, notably *Resistance to Invasion, Village Defence* and *After the Battle*. The documents proposed a host of ingenious ideas from setting the Channel on fire to building "tank traps" on the East Coast. Although Wheatley subsequently claimed more credit for his part in British plans than he was entitled to, there was undoubtedly a germ of possibility in everything he proposed. His involvement also inspired him to write one of the first "supernatural stories" of the war, which also harks back to the earlier conflict in its reference to the legend of a crucified soldier.

"France!" Bruce Hemmingway raised his eyebrows and looked inquiringly across the table at his curious little host. "Would I like to go on a visit to the front? I'll say I would; but as an American and a neutral, I'd never get a pass."

Neils Orsen smiled and scrutinized one of his long slender hands. "I'm a neutral, too, but I've been invited to go over there to investigate a little matter. It won't actually be the Maginot Line, but it's in the *Zone des Armées* and I have permission to take an assistant, so I'm sure a pass for you could be arranged."

"My dear Neils, I'd love to go," the young international lawyer declared with rising excitement. "Tell me all about it."

"Two days ago General Hayes, who is an old friend of mine, came to see me," Orsen began, his cool voice only slightly tinged with a Swedish accent. "He has always been interested in psychical research and is now on leave from France. It seems that an old château which had been taken over by the British had to be abandoned as a billet because it is so badly haunted that even the officers refuse to stay in it."

The big American lit a cigarette. "Then it must be the grandfather of all hauntings. What form does it take?"

"As usual, it does not affect everyone, but at least one or two out of each group of men that has been stationed there have felt its influence, and the manifestations always occur at night. The wretched victim is apparently always taken by surprise, lets out a piercing yell, and throws some sort of fit. Afterwards they state that they heard nothing, saw nothing, but were stabbed through the hands or feet and paralysed, rooted to the spot, transfixed by an agonizing pain which racked their whole bodies. The curious thing is that these attacks have taken place in nearly every room in the house. However, the worst cases have occurred in the one and only bathroom and it was there, about ten days ago, that one victim died – presumably as the result of a heart attack. It was that which finally decided the authorities to evacuate the château."

"How long has the haunting been going on?"

The Swede blinked his large pale-blue eyes, so curiously like those of his Siamese cat, Past. "I'm not sure. You see, the château was empty and in a very dilapidated condition when the Army took over. I gather that it was untenanted for some considerable time before war started."

"Was your friend able to find out the history of the place from the villagers?"

"Yes, and a most unpleasant story it is. But they seemed vague as to when the haunting began."

"What was the story?"

"Before the French Revolution the château was owned by a really bad example of the French aristocracy of that time. Cruel, avaricious, and inordinately proud, the Vicomte de Cheterau treated his serfs worse than animals, beating, imprisoning, and torturing them at his pleasure. One day he devised the sadistic idea of adding yet another thong to his whip by placing a local tax on nails. As you know, it's practically impossible to build anything without them, so the poorest peasants had to revert to the ancient, laborious practice of carving their own from the odd pieces of wood they could gather from the hedge-rows."

"He must have been a swine."

"Perhaps," Neils agreed. "But no man, however cruel, deserved such a frightful death."

"How did he die?"

Orsen stared at his reflection in the polished table. "One dark night, soon after the Revolution broke loose, his serfs crept into the château and pulled him out of bed. They dragged him to his business room and there they crucified him with their wooden nails. It took him three days to die; and they came each night to mock him in his agony with tantalizing jars of water and bowls of food."

Bruce shuddered. "Horrible – did anyone ever live in the château again?"

"I believe so; but no tenant has ever stayed for long in recent years. Of course, the villagers won't go near it. They are convinced that it's haunted, as the story of the Vicomte de Cheterau has been handed down from father to son for generations."

Hemmingway leaned forward. "Do you think these stabs the victims feel in their hands and feet are some sort of psychic repetition of the pains the Vicomte felt when the mob drove their wooden nails through his palms and insteps?"

"Quite possibly," replied Orsen slowly. "There are many well-authenticated cases of monks and nuns who have developed stigmata from too intensive a contemplation of the agony suffered by Jesus Christ at His crucifixion."

"It sounds a pretty tough proposition, then. When do we leave?"

"The day after tomorrow." Neils gently stroked the back of his Siamese cat and his big pale eyes were glowing. "I may be able to show you a real Saati manifestation this time, Bruce; but we must take nothing for granted. You can leave all arrangements to me."

*   *   *

A watery sun was shining through the avenue of lime trees, throwing chequered patterns on the wet gravel below, as the two friends were driven towards the château by a cheerful young captain into whose charge they had been given at the local H.Q.

"General Hayes told me about you, Mr Orsen," he was saying. "I find it difficult to believe in spooks myself, but there's certainly something devilish going on in the old place, and we shall be jolly grateful if you can find it for us. Those cottages in the village are damned uncomfortable."

Neils leaned forwards to peer through the window at the rearing pile of grey stone just ahead of them, and the captain added: "Gloomy sort of place, isn't it?"

As Bruce stepped out of the car he thoroughly agreed. The silence was eerie, broken only by a monotonous sound of water dripping from the rain-sodden trees that surrounded the château and almost shut out the sky. A dank, musty smell greeted them as they entered; a rat scurried away into the dark shadows of the hall.

"Well, Neils, old man," he said with a wry grin. "This place certainly seems to have the right atmosphere."

The little Swede did not appear to hear him. He was standing quite still, his large head thrown back and his eyes closed as if he were listening. Their guide gave an embarrassed cough, Unlike Bruce, he was not accustomed to Orsen's peculiarities, and he felt that ghost-hunting was at the best an unhealthy form of amusement.

"Shall we get a move on?" he asked abruptly. "I mean, if you want me to show you round; it's quite a big place, and the light will be gone in less than an hour."

Neils blinked, then fluttered one slender hand apologetically. "Forgive me; please lead the way."

They mounted the twisting stairs and as they passed the windows the evening light threw their shadows, elongated and grotesque, against the damp-sodden walls; no one spoke and the emptiness seemed to close in on them like a fog. As they wandered from room to room Neils followed behind the other two men humming a quaint old-fashioned tune to himself.

After an hour they made their way back to the hall and as they walked out towards the car their guide turned towards Orsen. "Well, now you've seen it. Are you really going to spend the night here?"

The little man smiled. "Certainly we are."

Mentally shrugging his shoulders the captain helped Bruce to carry the luggage upstairs, then ironically wished them good night. When the sound of the car was lost in the distance Bruce returned to the ballroom and found Neils standing by one of the long bow-windows.

"Can you hear the sh-sh-sh of panniered dresses, the brittle laughter of powdered ladies with their gallants, and the tapping of their heels as they dance a minuet to the tinkle of the harpsichord?" he said softly. His eyes stared blindly, and their pupils contracted. "Or do you hear the hoarse cries of those ragged, half-starved creatures as they stumble through these rooms smashing everything in sight, their mouths slobbering with frantic desire for revenge? Can you hear the shrieks, hardly human in their terror, of the wretched Vicomte as he is dragged to his death by those who were once his slaves?"

"No," said Bruce uneasily, "but I'll believe you that these walls would have a tale to tell if they could only talk."

"My friend, they have no need when the seventh child of a seventh child is listening."

Bruce shivered, as an icy chill seemed to rise up from the bare floor. "I'm hungry," he said as brightly as he could. "What about unpacking and having a little light on the scene?"

Neils smiled. "Yes, we will eat and sleep here. We shall have to shade the candles though, as there aren't any black-out precautions. I suppose the Army thought this room too big to bother about. I see they've done the bedrooms and everywhere else downstairs."

"What made you choose the ballroom?"

"Because Hayes told that it is one of the few rooms in which no one has yet been attacked; so we shall be able to see if the Force possesses harmful powers against humans anywhere in the house, or whether it can only become an evil manifestation in certain spots."

While Bruce set out an appetizing array of food from the hamper on the floor, Neils unpacked his cameras. The American had seen them keep him company on more than one thrilling adventure, but their process, Orsen's invention, was a mystery to him. Neils explained them only by saying that their plates were abnormally sensitive. He said the same thing of his sound-recorder, an instrument like a miniature dictaphone.

Having finished their dinner with some excellent coffee, cooked on a primus stove, they went along to the big, old-fashioned bathroom to fix Orsen's first camera and his sound machine. As they entered the room Bruce wrinkled his nose. "What a filthy smell! The drainage must be terrible."

Neils agreed as he placed one instrument on the window-sill and one on the broad mahogany ledge that surrounded the old-fashioned bath. He sealed the windows with fine silken threads and did the same to the door. Then, with their footsteps echoing behind them, they made a tour of the silent château, leaving the Swede's cameras in carefully selected places, till they came to the front hall, where Orsen left his last camera, and sealed the door leading to the back stairs with the remains of the reel of silk. Their job done they returned to the ballroom, and having made themselves as comfortable as possible with the rugs and cushions, settled down for the night.

Bruce could not sleep. They had lit a fire with some dry logs found in the kitchen and its dying flames sent a cavalcade of writhing shapes racing across the walls and ceiling.

Presently a moon shone through the uncurtained windows; propping himself on his elbow Bruce started at the unfamiliar lines it etched on Neils's face as he lay on his back, breathing gently. Orsen's enormous domed forehead shone like some beautiful Chinese ivory as the cold white light glanced across it, and his heavy blue-veined lids and sensitive mouth were curiously like those of a woman. He was sound asleep, yet Bruce knew that if there were the slightest sound or if an evil presence approached, he would be alert and fully in command of all his faculties in a fraction of a second.

Bruce lay back reassured. He could hear the muffled scuffling of rats behind the wainscoting. At length he dozed off.

Suddenly a shrill scream rent the silence, tearing it apart with devastating hands of terror. Bruce sprang to his feet and rushed to the window. The driveway was brilliantly illuminated by the glare of the moon, but he could see nothing. Orsen sat up slowly. "It's all right," he murmured; "only an owl."

Nodding dumbly, Bruce returned to his couch, his heart thudding against his ribs.

Morning came at last, and after breakfast Orsen went off to examine his cameras. He found their plates negative and his seals all undisturbed, whilst the sound-machine recorded only the scrambling noise of rats. Re-setting his apparatus, he returned to the ballroom. Bruce was staring gloomily out of the window at the steady downpour of rain now falling from a leaden sky. He wheeled round as Neils came in. "Well?"

"Nothing. I think we'll go down to the village now. We might get a hot bath and you can have a drink. You look pretty done in."

"Yes," Bruce agreed laconically.

After lunch in the officers' mess, Neils arranged with his friend to bring their provisions up to the château before dark and left him in the genial company of the officers. As the rain had ceased he had decided to go for a walk and wandered off, a queer little figure in the misty yellow light of the afternoon.

The woods that almost covered the estate were full of a quiet beauty as the dusty sunlight filtered through their branches on to the sharply scented earth below and their calm, ageless indifference to the travails of men filled Orsen with a delightful sense of being in another world.

The evening passed slowly. Bruce played patience, whilst Orsen paced up and down like a small caged animal. He would never have admitted it, but his nerves were badly on edge, for, although they had lit a fire, the cold was intense, a thing that always made him feel ill. After dinner, having made a final inspection of his cameras, he boiled some water on the primus for a hot-water-bottle, and settled down in his improvised bed. Bruce followed suit.

The black moonless night dragged by on crippled feet, its silence disturbed only by the rats and the faint boom of gun-fire in the distance. Morning found the two men pale and haggard. They fried themselves eggs and bacon, then went along to the bathroom, where the stench was now so appalling that they had to hold their noses.

Once again the camera plates proved negative and the seals were untouched; but on the record of the sound-machine there was a new noise. It came at intervals above the scuffling of the rats and was like that of someone beating with his fingernails irregularly against a pane of glass.

"What do you think it is?" Bruce asked excitedly.

Neils went over to the window and peered out. "It's possible that it was caused by this branch of creeper," he said, opening the window and breaking off the branch. "If it was, the noise won't recur tonight."

The day passed uneventfully and both men were curiously relieved when darkness fell once more.

Close on midnight Orsen slid out of bed noiselessly and crept along to the bathroom. On reaching it he stood motionless for a second. In the queer half-green light of his torch he resembled a ghost himself.

Not a sound disturbed the silence; even the rats seemed to have disappeared. Putting his ear to the keyhole he listened, but could hear nothing. He hesitated, then, grasping the door-handle, he twisted it sharply and with a vicious kick sent the door flying open, at the same instant flattening himself back against the wall.

Breathlessly, he waited, the unearthly quiet singing in his head. Still nothing happened. Making the sign of the Cross he muttered four words of power and, easing himself forward, peered into the bathroom. Only the horrible stench of decaying life and the heavy tomb-like atmosphere greeted him. He flashed his torch across the ceiling and sent its beams piercing into every corner, but his cameras were all unviolated. With a sigh of disappointment he closed the door softly behind him and retraced his steps.

After breakfast the next morning they developed the plates from those in the bathroom last, having found all the others blank. Those of the one on the window-sill showed the door open and Neils's head and shoulders. On the other was only the flash of his torch. They tried the sound-machine and a puzzled frown crossed Orsen's brow as once again they heard the faint noise like fingernails beating against the window.

"This is most peculiar," he murmured, as the record ceased. "I tore off that branch and I'll swear there was no sound perceptible to human ears when I was in the room ten hours ago."

"Perhaps it had started before – or afterwards," Bruce hazarded.

"No; the sound-machine does not start recording until the cameras operate. On our first night I set them to function automatically at midnight; but last night I fixed them so that they should not operate at all unless someone or something broke the threads across the window or the door. I set them off myself by entering the room, so that noise must have been going on." He paused. "I shall spend the coming night there myself."

"Not on your own!" Bruce declared quickly. "Remember, a man died in that room from – well, from unknown causes little more than a fortnight ago."

A gentle smile illuminated Neils's face. "I was hoping you would offer to keep me company; but I wouldn't agree to you doing so unless I felt confident I could protect you. I intend to make a pentacle; one of the oldest forms of protection against evil manifestations, and, fortunately, I brought all the things necessary for it in my luggage. But we must get a change of clothes in the village."

That afternoon they began their preparations with handkerchiefs soaked in eau-de-Cologne tied over the lower part of their faces to counteract the appalling smell. First, they spring-cleaned the whole room with infinite care, Bruce scrubbing the floor and bath with carbolic soap, whilst Orsen went over the walls and ceiling with a mop which he dipped constantly in a pail of disinfected water.

"There must not be a speck of dust anywhere, particularly on the floor," the Swede explained, "since evil entities can fasten on any form of dirt to assist their materialization. That is why I asked the captain to lend us blankets, battle-dresses, and issue underclothes straight from new stocks in the quarter-master's stores. And now," he went on, "I want two glasses and a jug of water, also fruit and biscuits. We must have no material needs to tempt us from our astral stronghold should any dark force try to corrupt our will-power through our sub-conscious minds."

When Bruce returned, Neils had opened a suit-case and taken from it a piece of chalk, a length of string, and a foot-rule. Marking a spot approximately in the centre of the room, he asked Bruce to hold the end of the string to it and, using him as a pivot, drew a large circle in chalk.

Next the string was lengthened and an outer circle drawn. Then the most difficult part of the operation began. A five-rayed star had to be made with its points touching the outer circle and its valleys resting upon the inner. But, as Neils pointed out, while such a defence could be highly potent if constructed with geometrical accuracy, should any of the angles vary to any marked degree or the distance of the apexes from the central point differ more than a fraction, the pentacle would prove not only useless, but even dangerous. "This may all be completely unnecessary," he added. "We have no actual proof yet that an evil power is active here, but I have always thought that it was better not to spill the milk than to have to cry when it was done."

Bruce smiled at the Swede's slightly muddled version of the old English proverb, but at the same time he heartily concurred with his friend's sentiments.

For an hour they measured and checked till eventually the broad white lines were drawn to Neils's satisfaction, forming the magical star in which it was his intention they should remain while darkness lasted. He then drew certain ancient symbols in its valleys and mounts, and when he had finished Bruce laid the blankets, glasses, water jug, and food in its centre. Meanwhile, Orsen was producing further impedimenta from his case. With lengths of asafœtida grass and blue wax he sealed the windows and bath-waste, making the Sign of the Cross over each seal as he completed it.

"That'll do for now. I must leave the door till we're settled in," he said. "I think we might as well go out and get some fresh air while we can."

It was then nearly six o'clock. An hour later they returned to the château for an early supper. Almost before they had finished eating, dusk began to fall and Orsen glanced anxiously at the lengthening shadows. "We'd better go now," he said, gulping down the remains of his coffee.

Shivering with cold they undressed and reclothed themselves outside the bathroom. Once inside, the Swede sealed the door; then turning to Bruce gave him a long wreath of garlic flowers and a gold crucifix on a chain which he told him to hang round his neck. Unquestioningly the American obeyed and watched the little man follow suit. As they stepped into the pentacle, Neils gripped his friend by the hand, and said urgently:

"Now, whatever happens and whatever ideas you get about all this being nonsense, you must on no account leave the circle. The evil force, if there is one, is almost certain to try to undermine our defences through you, owing to your spiritual inexperience. *Please* remember what I've said."

Having huddled into their blankets and tied the handkerchiefs newly soaked in eau-de-Cologne over their faces, they settled down to wait.

Time plodded wearily by and as they had left their watches outside with their clothes they had no means of checking it. Conversation soon flagged owing to the difficulty of speaking through the wet masks, so the two men crouched in silence, each longing desperately for the coming of dawn. Outside, the trees sighed quietly and darkness held the château in its thrall.

"It's very odd, I can't sense any evil presence here; and if there were one I should have by now," Orsen whispered after a long silence.

Bruce stiffened and peered through the darkness at the white blob that was Neils's face. "Now don't *you* start talking like that. Remember what you told *me*. It looks as though those things you mentioned a while ago are having a dig at you."

"No," Orsen muttered after a moment, "no, it's not that. Will you give me some water, please, it's over on your side."

Bruce put out his hand to feel for the jug. Without the least warning his strangled yell shattered the deep quiet of the night and he collapsed in a limp tangle over the Swede's legs.

Orsen stumbled to his feet, his mind reeling – the Thing was in the pentacle. *Inside it!* There, *with* them; at their elbows, instead of beyond the barrier which should have kept it out. Why had he felt no warning – no indication of evil?

Shouting aloud a Latin exorcism which would keep the evil at bay for a space of eleven human heart-beats, he stooped, grabbed Bruce under the armpits, and dragged him from the circle.

Once outside it he allowed himself a pause to get back his breath; knowing that since the Thing was *in* the pentacle the magic barrier would act like the bars of a cage and keep it from getting *out*. But would it? Even Neils was scared by such an unusual and extra-ordinarily potent phenomenon.

Wrenching the door open he seized Bruce's unconscious form again and, exerting all his frail physical strength, hauled it along the passage. When at last he reached the ballroom sweat was pouring down his face and he was gasping as though his lungs would burst. Feverishly he searched for his torch and finding it threw its beams on Bruce's face. It was deathly pale, but with a sob of relief Neils felt the faintly beating heart beneath his hand.

A few minutes later Bruce came out of his faint, but he could remember nothing, save that when he had put out his hand for the water-jug it seemed as though a thousand knives had pierced his body; then everything had gone black.

Neils nodded as his friend finished. "It's a good thing we left our blankets here. We'll try and get some sleep!" But he himself did not attempt to sleep. Puzzled and anxious, he remained on watch all night, and as the first rays of dawn crept through the windows he returned to the bathroom.

Two hours later he told Bruce: "I think I've found the root of the evil, and I'm going down the village to borrow the largest electric battery I can find."

"Whatever for?"

"Electric force can be used for many purposes," was all Neils would say.

It was not until they had completed their evening meal that Neils undid a parcel and produced four bottles of champagne.

"Hullo! What's this?" Bruce exclaimed.

"I got them from the local *estaminet* this morning as I thought it was time we returned hospitality to some of the officers in the mess. They're coming in about ten o'clock."

"That's fine," Bruce grinned. "I reckon I deserve a party after last night."

Soon after ten their friend the captain, a colonel, and three other officers arrived and they immediately began to make half-humorous inquiries about the ghost.

"Gentlemen," replied Neils, "I asked you up here because I hope to lay the ghost tonight; but we can't start work for an hour or two, and in the meantime, as I am a teetotaller, I hope you'll join Bruce Hemmingway in a glass of wine."

For two hours Neils kept them enthralled with stories of Saati manifestations he had encountered, so that even the most sceptical was secretly glad that the party numbered seven resolute men; but he would say nothing of his discoveries in the château until, glancing at his watch, he saw that it was half-past twelve. Then he began to recount the experiences of Bruce and himself since their arrival.

Turning to Bruce, he went on: "My suspicions were aroused last night when you were attacked in the pentacle. Mentally you were unharmed, but your hand was red and inflamed, as though it had been burnt. Early this morning I returned to the bathroom and pulled up the boards upon which the water-jug was resting, taking care not to touch the floor anywhere near it. Underneath there were the decaying bodies of two rats and three electric wires, the naked leads of which were inserted in the plank to look from above like nails. You remember that curious sound of tapping fingers on the recording machine, which is so much more sensitive than our ears. When I saw those wires I suddenly realized what it meant. Somewhere in the château a person was working a morse transmitter."

"By Jove!" The Colonel jumped to his feet. "A spy!"

Neils nodded. "Yes. Long before the war, no doubt, the Germans laid a secret cable from their own lines to the château, reckoning that their agent here would be able to work undisturbed because no one would come to the place on account of its sinister reputation. But to make quite certain of being able to scare away any intruders they ran electric wires to a dozen different points in the building, mainly to door-knobs; but the lavatory seats and bathroom also particularly lent themselves to such a purpose."

"But we've searched every room in the place," Bruce exclaimed, "so where does the spy conceal himself?"

The officers were now all on their feet. "Grand work, Mr Orsen!" cried the Colonel. "He may even be sending a message now. Let's go and get him."

It was after one o'clock when Orsen led the way out of the château. They stumbled through tangled undergrowth, barking their shins on unseen obstacles for nearly twenty minutes until Neils halted in a clearing among the trees which was almost filled by a large grassy mound.

"What's this?" the captain asked, flashing his torch.

"It's an ice-house," the little man replied as he pulled open a thick, slanting wooden trap almost hidden by moss and ivy. "In the old days, before refrigerators were invented, people used to cut blocks of ice out of their lakes when they were frozen in the winter and store them in these places. The temperature remained constant owing to the fact that they were underground and invariably in woods, which always retain moisture, so the ice was preserved right through the summer."

A dank musty smell filled their nostrils as, almost bent double, they followed Neils inside. Ahead of them in the far corner of the cellar loomed a dark cavity. "This is the way the ghost comes," Orsen murmured. "Mind how you go; there'll be one or two holes, I expect."

The silence seemed to bear down on them as they crept forward through a dark tunnel and the deathly chill penetrated their thick overcoats. No one spoke. On and on they went. The passage seemed to wind interminably before them; occasionally a rat scurried across their path. Suddenly, as they rounded a bend, a bright shaft of light struck their eyes. For a second they stood practically blinded and two of the officers produced revolvers.

Neils let them precede him into the secret cellar, but they did not need their weapons. At its far end, sprawled over the table which held a big telegraphic transmitting-set, was the body of a man.

"There, gentlemen, is your ghost," Orsen announced quietly. "No, don't touch him, you fool!" he snapped, as the captain stretched out a hand towards the corpse. "He's been electrocuted and the current isn't switched off yet."

"Electrocuted?" the captain gasped. "But how did that happen?"

"The powerful battery you borrowed for me this morning from the Air Force people," Neils said. "I attached it to the leads in the bathroom, then came down here and fixed the other end of the wires to the side of the transmitter key."

"Good God!" exclaimed the colonel. "But this is most irregular."

"Quite," Neils agreed, "and, of course, I'm neutral in this war, but I'm not neutral in the greater war that is always going on between good and evil. This man murdered that poor fellow who died in the bathroom. So I decided to save you a shooting party."

Pink May

Elizabeth Bowen

Location: Aldershot, Hampshire.
Time: May, 1942.
Eyewitness Description: *"She was there. And she aimed at encircling me. I think maybe she had a poltergeist that she brought along with her. The little things that happened to my belongings . . ."*

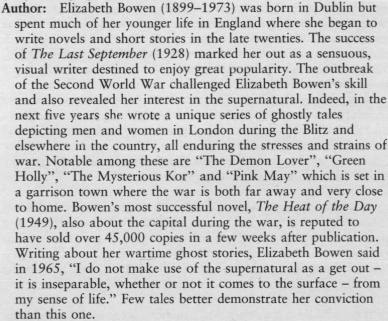

Author: Elizabeth Bowen (1899–1973) was born in Dublin but spent much of her younger life in England where she began to write novels and short stories in the late twenties. The success of *The Last September* (1928) marked her out as a sensuous, visual writer destined to enjoy great popularity. The outbreak of the Second World War challenged Elizabeth Bowen's skill and also revealed her interest in the supernatural. Indeed, in the next five years she wrote a unique series of ghostly tales depicting men and women in London during the Blitz and elsewhere in the country, all enduring the stresses and strains of war. Notable among these are "The Demon Lover", "Green Holly", "The Mysterious Kor" and "Pink May" which is set in a garrison town where the war is both far away and very close to home. Bowen's most successful novel, *The Heat of the Day* (1949), also about the capital during the war, is reputed to have sold over 45,000 copies in a few weeks after publication. Writing about her wartime ghost stories, Elizabeth Bowen said in 1965, "I do not make use of the supernatural as a get out – it is inseparable, whether or not it comes to the surface – from my sense of life." Few tales better demonstrate her conviction than this one.

"Yes, it was funny," she said, "about the ghost. It used to come into my bedroom when I was dressing for dinner – when I was dressing to go out."

"*You were frightened?*"

"I was in such a hurry; there never was any time. When you have to get dressed in such a hell of a hurry any extra thing is just one thing more. And the room at the times I'm talking about used to be full of daylight – sunset. It had two french windows, and they were on a level with the tops of may trees out in the square. The may was in flower that month, and it was pink. In that sticky sunshine you have in the evenings the may looked sort of theatrical. It used to be part of my feeling of going out." She paused, then said, "That was the month of my life."

"*What month?*"

"The month we were in that house. I told you, it was a furnished house that we took. With rents the way they are now, it cost less than a flat. They say a house is more trouble, but this was no trouble, because we treated it like a flat, you see. I mean, we were practically never in. I didn't try for a servant because I know there aren't any. When Neville got up in the mornings he percolated the coffee; a char came in to do cleaning when I'd left for the depot, and we fixed with the caretaker next door to look after the boiler, so the baths were hot. And the beds were comfortable, too. The people who really lived there did themselves well."

"*You never met them?*"

"No, never – why should we? We'd fixed everything through an agent, the way one does. I've an idea the man was soldiering somewhere, and she'd gone off to be near him somewhere in the country. They can't have had any children, any more than we have – it was one of those small houses, just for two."

"*Pretty?*"

"Y-yes," she said. "It was chintzy. It was one of those oldish houses made over new inside. But you know how it is about other people's belongings – you can't ever quite use them, and they seem to watch you the whole time. Not that there was any question of settling down – how could we, when we were both out all day? And at the beginning of June we moved out again."

"*Because of the . . .?*"

"Oh no," she said quickly. "Not that reason, at all." She lighted a cigarette, took two puffs and appeared to deliberate. "But what I'm telling you *now* is about the ghost."

"*Go on.*"

"I was going on. As I say, it used to be funny, dressing away at top speed at the top of an empty house, with the sunset blazing away outside. It seems to me that all those evenings were fine. I used to take taxis back from the depot: you must pay money these days if you want time, and a bath and a change from the skin up was essential – you don't know how one feels after packing parcels all day! I couldn't do like some of the girls I worked with and go straight from the depot on to a date. I can't go and meet someone unless I'm feeling special. So I used to hare home. Neville was never in."

"*I'd been going to say . . .*"

"No, Neville worked till all hours, or at least he had to hang round in case something else should come in. So he used to dine at his club on the way back. Most of the food would be off by the time he got there. It was partly that made him nervy, I dare say."

"But you weren't nervy?"

"I tell you," she said, "I was happy. Madly happy – perhaps in rather a nervy way. Whatever you are these days, you are rather more so. That's one thing I've discovered about this war."

"*You were happy . . .*"

"I had my reasons – which don't come into the story."

After two or three minutes of rapid smoking she leaned forward to stub out her cigarette. "Where was I?" she said, in a different tone. "*Dressing . . .*"

"Well, first thing when I got in I always went across and opened my bedroom windows, because it seemed to me the room smelled of the char. So I always did that before I turned on my bath. The glare on the trees used to make me blink, and the thick sort of throaty smell of the may came in. I was never certain if I liked it or not, but it somehow made me feel like after a drink. Whatever happens tomorrow, I've got tonight. You know the feeling? Then I turned on my bath. The bathroom was the other room on that floor, and a door led through to it from one side of the bed. I used to have my bath with that door ajar, to let light in. The bathroom black-out took so long to undo.

"While the bath ran in I used to potter about and begin to put out what I meant to wear, and cold-cream off my old make-up, and so on. I say 'potter' because you cannot hurry a bath. I also don't mind telling you that I whistled. Well, what's the harm in *somebody's* being happy? Simply thinking things over won't win this war. Looking back at that month, I whistled most of the time. The way they used to look at me, at the depot! The queer thing is, though, I remember whistling but I can't remember when I happened to stop. But I must *have* stopped, because it was then I heard."

"*Heard?*"

She lit up again, with a slight frown. "What was it I heard first, that first time? I suppose, the silence. So I must have stopped whistling, mustn't I? I was lying there in my bath, with the door open behind me, when the silence suddenly made me sit right up. Then I said to myself, 'My girl, there's nothing queer about *that*. What else would you expect to hear, in an empty house?' All the same, it made me heave the other way round in my bath, in order to keep one eye on the door. After a minute I heard what wasn't a silence – which immediately made me think that Neville had come in early, and I don't mind telling you I said 'Damn'."

"*Oh?*"

"It's a bore being asked where one is going, though it's no bother to say where one has been. If Neville *was* in he'd be certain to search the house, so I put a good face on things and yelled 'Hoi'. But he didn't answer, because it wasn't him."

"No?"

"No, it wasn't. And whatever was in my bedroom must have been in my bedroom for some time. I thought, 'A wind has come up and got into that damned chintz!' Any draught always fidgets me; somehow it gets me down. So I got out of my bath and wrapped the big towel round me and went through to shut the windows in my room. But I was surprised when I caught sight of the may trees – all their branches were standing perfectly still. That seemed queer. At the same time, the door I'd come through from the bathroom blew shut, and the lid fell off one of my jars of face cream on to the dressing-table, which had a glass top.

"No, I didn't see what it was. The point was, whatever it was saw me.

"That first time, the whole thing was so slight. If it had been only that one evening, I dare say I shouldn't have thought of it again. Things only get a hold on you when they go on happening. But I always have been funny in one way – I especially don't like being watched. You might not think so from my demeanour, but I don't really like being criticized. I don't think I get my knife into other people: why should they get their knife into me? I don't like it when my ear begins to burn.

"I went to put the lid back on the jar of cream and switch the lights on into the mirror, which being between the two windows never got the sort of light you would want. I thought I looked odd in the mirror – rattled. I said to myself, 'Now what have I done to *someone?*' but except for Neville I literally couldn't think. Anyway, there was no time – when I picked up my wrist-watch I said, 'God!' So I flew round, dressing. Or rather, I flew round as much as one could with something or somebody getting in the way. That's all I remember about that *first* time, I think. Oh yes, I did notice that the veil on my white hat wasn't all that it ought to be. When I had put that hat out before my bath the whole affair had looked as crisp as a marguerite – a marguerite that has only opened today.

"You know how it is when a good deal hangs on an evening – you simply can't afford to be not in form. So I gave myself a good shake on the way downstairs. 'Snap out of that!' I said. 'You've got personality. You can carry a speck or two on the veil.'

"Once I got to the restaurant – once I'd met him – the whole thing went out of my mind. I was in twice as good form as I'd ever been. And the turn events took . . .

"It was about a week later that I had to face it. I was up against something. The more the rest of my life got better and better, the more that one time of each evening got worse and worse. Or rather, it wanted to. But I wasn't going to let it. With everything else quite perfect – well, would *you* have? There's something exciting, I mean, some sort of a challenge about knowing someone's *trying* to get you down. And when that someone's another woman you soon get a line on her technique. She was jealous, that was what was the matter with her.

"Because, at all other times the room was simply a room. There wasn't any objection to me and Neville. When I used to slip home he was always asleep. I could switch all the lights on and kick my shoes off and open and shut the cupboards – he lay like the dead. He *was* abnormally done in, I suppose. And the room was simply a room in somebody else's house. And the mornings, when he used to roll out of bed and slip-slop down to make the coffee, without speaking, exactly like someone walking in his sleep, the room was no more than a room in which you've just woken up. The may outside looked pink-pearl in the early sunshine, and there were some regular birds who sang. Nice. While I waited for Neville to bring the coffee I used to like to lie there and think my thoughts.

"If he was awake at all before he had left the house, he and I exchanged a few perfectly friendly words. I had *no* feeling of anything blowing up. If I let him form the impression that I'd been spending the evenings at movies with girl friends I'd begun to make at the depot, then going back to their flats to mix Ovaltine – well, that seemed to me the considerate thing to do. If he'd even been more *interested* in my life – but he wasn't interested in anything but his work. I never picked on him about that – I must say, I do know when a war's a war. Only, men are so different. You see, this other man worked just as hard but *was* interested in me. He said he found me so restful. Neville never said that. In fact, all the month we were in that house, I can't remember anything Neville said at all.

"No, what *she* couldn't bear was my going out, like I did. She was either a puritan, with some chip on her shoulder, or else she'd once taken a knock. I incline to that last idea – though I can't say why.

"No, I can't say why. I have never at all been a subtle person. I don't know whether that's a pity or not. I must say I don't care for subtle people – my instinct would be to give a person like that a miss. And on the whole I should say I'd succeeded in doing so. But that, you see, was where her advantage came in. You can't give a . . . well, I couldn't give *her* a miss. She was there. And she aimed at encircling me.

"I think maybe she had a poltergeist that she brought along with her. The little things that happened to my belongings . . . Each evening I dressed in that room I lost five minutes – I mean, each evening it took me five minutes longer to dress. But all that was really below her plane. That was just one start at getting me down before she opened up with her real technique. The really subtle thing was the way her attitude changed. That first time (as I've told you) I felt her disliking me – well, really 'dislike' was to put it mildly. But after an evening or two she was through with that. She conveyed the impression that she had got me taped and was simply so damned sorry for me. She was sorry about every garment I put on, and my hats were more than she was able to bear. She was sorry about the way I did up my face – she used to be right at my elbow when I got out my make-up, absolutely silent with despair. She was sorry I should never again see thirty, and sorry I should kid myself about that . . . I mean to say, she started pitying me.

"Do you see what I mean when I say her attitude could have been quite infectious?

"And that wasn't all she was sorry for me about. I mean, there are certain things that a woman who's being happy keeps putting out of her mind. (I mean, when she's being happy about a man.) And other things you keep putting out of your mind if your husband is *not* the man you are being happy about. There's a certain amount you don't ask yourself, and a certain amount that you might as well not remember. Now those were exactly the things she kept bringing up. She liked to bring those up better than anything.

"What I don't know is, and what I still don't know – *why* do all that to a person who's being happy? To a person who's living the top month of her life, with the may in flower and everything? What had I ever done to her? She was dead – I suppose? . . . Yes, I see now, she must have taken a knock."

"*What makes you think that?*"

"I know now how a knock feels."

"*Oh . . .?*"

"Don't look at me such a funny way. I haven't changed, have I? You wouldn't have noticed anything? . . . I expect it's simply this time of year: August's rather a tiring month. And things end without warning, before you know where you are. I hope the war will be over by next spring; I do want to be abroad, if I'm able to. Somewhere where there's nothing but pines or palms. I don't want to see London pink may in flower again – *ever.*"

"*Won't Neville . . .?*"

"Neville? Oh, didn't you really realize? Didn't I . . .? He, I, we've – I mean, we're living apart." She rose and took the full, fuming ash-tray across to another table, and hesitated, then brought an empty tray back. "Since we left that house," she said. "I told you we left that house. That was why. We broke up.

"It was the *other* thing that went wrong," she said. "If I'd still kept my head with Neville, he and I needn't ever – I mean, one's marriage *is* something. . . . I'd thought I'd always be married, whatever else happened. I ought to have realized Neville was in a nervy state. Like a fool I spilled over to Neville; I lost my head. But by that time I hadn't any control left. When the one thing you've lived for has crashed to bits . . .

"Crashed was the word. And yet I see now, really, that things had been weakening for some time. At the time I didn't see, any more than I noticed the may was fading out in the square – till one morning the weather changed and I noticed the may was brown. All the happiness stopped like my stopping whistling – but at what particular moment I'm never sure.

"The beginnings of the end of it were so small. Like my being a bit more unpunctual every evening we met. That made us keep losing our table at restaurants – you know how the restaurants are these days. Then I somehow got the idea that none of my clothes were becoming; I began to think he was eyeing my hats unkindly, and that made me fidget and look my worst. Then I got an idiot thing about any girl that he spoke of – I didn't like anyone being younger than me. Then, at what had once been our most perfect moments, I began to ask myself if I *was* really happy, till I said to him – which was fatal

– 'Is there so much in this?' . . . I should have seen more red lights – when, for instance, he said, 'You know, *you're* getting nervy.' And he quite often used to say 'Tired?' in rather a tired way. I used to say, it was just getting dressed in a rush. But the fact is, a man hates the idea of a woman rushing. One night I know I did crack: I said, 'Hell, I've got a ghost in my room!' He put me straight into a taxi and sent me – not took me – home.

"I did see him several times after that. So his letter – his letter was a complete surprise. . . . The joke was, I really had been out with a girl that evening I came in, late, to find his letter.

"If Neville had not been there when I got the letter, Neville and I might still – I suppose – be married. On the other hand – there are always two ways to see things – if Neville had *not* been there I should have gone mad . . . So now," she said, with a change of tone, "I'm living in an hotel. Till I see how things turn out. Till the war is over, or something. It isn't really so bad, and I'm out all day. Look, I'll give you my address and telephone number. It's been wonderful seeing you, darling. You promise we'll meet again? I do really need to keep in touch with my friends. And *you* don't so often meet someone who's seen a ghost!"

"*But look, did you ever* see *it?*"

"Well, not exactly. No, I can't say I *saw* it."

"*You mean, you simply heard it?*"

"Well, not exactly that . . ."

"*You saw things move?*"

"Well, I never turned round in time. I . . .

"If you don't understand – I'm sorry I ever told you the story! Not a ghost – when it ruined my whole life! Don't you see, can't you see there must have been *something*? Left to oneself, one doesn't ruin one's life!"

A Gremlin in the Beer

Derek Barnes

Location: RAF North Coates, Lincolnshire.
Time: January, 1942.
Eyewitness Description: *"The crew came shuffling in, in their soft flying-boots, they were red-eyed and stiff with cold, and their normally pink and fresh young faces looked drawn and stubble-marked under the office lights. It appeared, to my not inexperienced eye, that the Gremlin was still aboard the Beaufort."*
Author: Derek Barnes (1904–78) grew up on the outskirts of London and in his teens developed a passion for flying. After working for several years as a journalist, he became a PR in London. In his spare time he trained to fly a Tiger Moth and had almost a hundred hours in his logbook when war was declared. Barnes was called up into the RAF, but instead of being allowed to fly was trained as an Intelligence Officer to debrief crews after operations. He was stationed in Lincolnshire with a squadron of Beauforts when he first heard stories about Gremlins, mysterious and malicious spirits apparently set on causing as many mishaps as possible to pilots. According to some accounts, the phantoms had first been detected in 1918 by the newly constituted RAF, but were now back with a vengeance. Barnes' account for *The Spectator* was written at the same time as a certain Flight Lieutenant Roald Dahl was creating his first children's story, "The Gremlins" for *Collier's* magazine in America in May 1942. Unfortunately for Barnes, of course, it was to be Dahl's account that would lead the writer to fame and fortune.

It has never been my way to take any part in the flying talk which, of a winter evening, takes place around the anteroom fire. Such talk is for flying men only, and not for earth-bound Intelligence Officers like me. Should the conversation turn to aircraft recognition, the flak positions down the enemy's coastlines or the location of targets in German-occupied territory, then I speak my piece in my due turn. But flying "shop" – no! My modest thirty hours in a "Moth", in peace-time, do not entitle me to swap yarns with boys who have flown their fifty, sixty or hundred sorties against the enemy. No, sir!

But, though I lie low, I keep an ear cocked when the chaps are talking shop, for it is often helpful when I have to interrogate the crews on their return. By quietly listening one gains an insight into a pilot's reactions at awkward moments; one gleans a few more words of technical jargon and a scrap or two of flying "gen". And these things go to make the interrogator sound less of an amateur and gain for him acceptance as a well-informed, professional collaborator from the flying personnel.

Sometimes the talk is not so technical. As, for instance, that night a year ago when there arose a lively argument upon the subject of Gremlins. Once again I said little, but listened with interest as well as amusement, for even these wild speculations enhanced my knowledge of the men who made them.

The existence of Gremlins is tacitly admitted by all R.A.F. air crews. Nobody has seen one, though many have felt their influence. It has fallen to my lot to paint their portraits upon the aircraft of superstitious pilots – in propitiation of the imps believed to haunt them.

A Gremlin, then, is an imp or sprite whom pilots blame when things go wrong. One type, for example, lives at the aircraft's centre of gravity and only hurls himself forward when the machine is about to land, thus making it nose-heavy at an unfortunate moment. Others stiffen the controls, jam rudder, undercart or ailerons, dispel cloud cover when most urgently needed, or spread it plentifully between aircraft and target, thus foxing the bomb-aimer at a vital time. Yet another type – "with a long nose and wings like a bat" – as the experts assure me, spins the compass like a teetotum the moment it becomes the aircraft's sole navigational aid.

"Old Moaner" set the ball rolling. For weeks he had been suffering from the filthiest luck which defied even his exceptional skill. And he had long adopted a comical "defeatist" line of talk to cover his disappointment. Hence his nickname. That night, by the fire, he startled us by declaring that a super-Gremlin had taken up its abode in his Beaufort within the last few days and that this was not to be confused with any common-or-garden Gremlin "such as other types have". It was, if you please, a Universal Gremlin! It put all others in the shade, for it mucked up everything – compass, maps, ailerons, rudder, the "R.T." undercart, oxygen, and even Moaner's own thermos flask – all at the same time.

There was a silence while his friends absorbed this extreme claim. Somebody at last was moved to speak.

"If it did even half what you say," he remarked gently, "you wouldn't be here to say it. You'd have hit the deck so hard that you'd come up in Australia – like a ruddy bulb!"

And Moaner sat there, looking at us all with a provocative eye. The scar on his cheek twitched as an impish grin stirred his sallow features. A lock of dark hair hung down over his forehead. A can of beer dangled by its handle from his thumb.

His bitter disappointment egged him on to shoot a yet bigger line about his Gremlin. Fortified by another pint, he proceeded to justify his stupendous claim.

"Even though you chaps are pretty ham-handed," he said, amidst cries of "Oh!" "you can most of you recognize genius when you see it! So you'll know that I *never* make a floater! Yet, the last week or two, every bit of dirt that's flying about has stuck to *ME*!"

"Course it has, you line-shooting bus-driver!" said somebody. But Moaner would not have his "patron saint" denied.

" 'S a Gremlin!" he mumbled into his tankard. "One colossal, stinking, evil-minded, all-powerful Gremlin!" And he eyed the lot of us, under that lock of hair, deliberately provoking somebody to argue the point.

Somebody did. Moaner's chair, Moaner's beer and Moaner himself went over backwards and, in a split second, a rough-and-tumble was on – in which six "attached" pilots of the Fleet Air Arm instantly joined. I saved the radiogram and a table full of cups and beer-mugs and withdrew out of range before my glasses got smashed. Moaner fought gallantly but was much outnumbered, and soon succumbed.

As we laughed and righted the chairs, tables, rugs, cushions, and tankards, Moaner – still panting from his exertions – said, "*Must* be a super-Gremlin! Isn't room in a 'Beau' for all the departmental Gremlins that have been playing ME up!" And he added "Ouch! Blast you!" as another cushion caught him in the tummy.

But peace finally returned. The tankards were refuelled at Moaner's expense – in expiation of his line-shooting. And he grinned sourly, yet amiably, and fell asleep.

An hour later he woke, yawned, and set off to bed, pausing at the door.

"If I've been shooting a bit of a line, chaps," he said, "don't blame *me*! Blame the beer! Must've been a Gremlin in it!" And off he went.

A foolish, pointless evening? Not a bit of it. A good time was had by all – and I had learned a little more of what lay behind Old Moaner's wry humour. I was to need it. And soon.

Upon the following day Moaner and his crew set forth to dare the Gremlin again, not to mention their intention to disturb an enemy convoy which reconnaissance had located off the Dutch coast. I remember faintly dreading the job of interrogating him later. He was a touchy, strange, awkward sort of a customer to question when the exhaustion of a long and difficult operation combined with his cussed brand of humour to make things difficult for the questioner.

At such times, when a pilot and his crew are weary and suffering the inevitable reaction after prolonged strain, even the most placid of men needs and deserves the most delicate handling, and the Intelligence Officer can make use of everything he knows about each airman's way of looking at things. They are always courteous and eager to help; but there are men who, under such stress, cannot at once recall some of the minute details which, though maybe seen only for an instant, are the stuff of which "Intelligence" is built up.

When "Moaner" and his crew came shuffling in, in their soft flying-boots, they were red-eyed and stiff with cold, and their normally pink and fresh young faces looked drawn and stubble-marked under the office lights. It appeared, to my not inexperienced eye, that the Super-Gremlin was still aboard that Beaufort.

They had been roaming the inhospitable airs over the North Sea, ploughing through the dirtiest conditions, and sampling an unseemly warmth of welcome from the enemy coasts, not to mention a bit of trouble flung at them from the skulking convoy which, even in that mucky weather, they had duly found and attacked.

"Moaner" had seen a couple of his formation go "in the drink" – and it was no time or place for bathing. His own aircraft had been shot up, and he had limped it home for the last hundred miles upon one labouring engine and with one eye on the temperature gauges all the way. But he had put a torpedo, sweet and pretty, into "a large motor-vessel strongly escorted by flak ships" – as the wireless news expressed it later on.

He was in the hell of a mood, elated by his success and yet

depressed by his ordeal. He stumbled into a chair and gave me the outline of his adventures, with which his crew agreed. But, at the end of it all, I somehow sensed that there was something more. Some little point which he or they had spotted, momentarily, out there in the flak and the mucky weather, and which would not now be brought to mind. One learns to sense such things.

But neither he nor his crew could recall it, though the navigator gave me my first real clue. "There *was* something, sir!" said he to "Moaner"; "you called out something to me just as we jinked to avoid the flak from the little ship. I couldn't get it . . . but you called out something!"

No answering recollection lit Moaner's tired eyes. He shook his head wearily, slumped in his chair and then, pulling himself together, treated me to a tirade about his Gremlin.

It had summoned clouds when visibility was wanted, dispersing them when cover was the urgent need. It had fiddled with his controls so that the ruddy kite wouldn't go where he put it. Passing lightly from the compass to the undercart control, it had jammed the wheels in the "up" position so that, to cap all, Moaner had just had the nasty job of making a belly landing on a misty evening after seven hours of the most exhausting strain, though he didn't put it that way. "Ruined a hundred yards of perfectly good turf" was his version. The Gremlin had been having a field-day.

The crew shuffled and coughed, as though a drop of shut-eye would be welcome. I could feel their hunger in my own stomach. Their fatigue made my own eyelids ache. But still I probed to evoke that fleeting, forgotten memory which I felt sure was there.

But Moaner was getting obstinate now – due to fatigue and strain. The fact that he could not remember now strengthened his conviction that there was nothing to recall. His mind was set in the bitterness of reaction.

"I tell you, there was nothing else . . . nothing of importance. If there had been I'd have remembered it, or one of the boys would." He rose to his feet and stifled a soul-deep yawn. "We're going to beat it . . . we're all-in. See me to-morrow if you must go on yapping!" And he headed for the door towards which, after an instant's hesitation, his crew began to follow him.

My last chance was going. By to-morrow, maybe, sleep would have cleaned the slate of his mind from every trace of the incident I sought. Would a change of subject release his brain from the worn channels of fatigue?

"O.K.," said I. "I reckon you had some beer on board!"

He stopped dead, his brow creasing irritably as he sought some connection between my idiotic remark and our previous conversation.

"Beer?" he said. "What the hell are you suggesting?"

"Beer!" I said. "With a Gremlin in it, to make you talk like that!" And the trick was done.

His tired mind was jerked backward to the previous night, to the warm fireside, to the chaffing of his friends, to that comradeship which linked even my plodding duties with his valiant adventure. The strain was relaxed and I ceased to be a pestilential official who sat safely on his bottom while better men went a-flying. I became, instead, to his refreshed outlook, a cog – small but vital – in the pattern of service of the R.A.F. A bloke, in short, who was trying to do his job.

Moaner raised a smile . . . wan and weary . . . but still a smile. "Sorry, old boy," he said, "but there really isn't anything else . . . not a thing! You don't mind if we push off? We've had quite a party out there!"

"I'm sure you have," I answered, "and thanks for being so patient – all of you. Good night!"

But, even as the sergeants chorused "Good night, sir," the shutter clicked in Moaner's brain.

"Gosh!" he cried. "There *was* something. . . . Ginger! Bradley! Jones! Didn't any of you chaps spot it, too? I yelled out on the intercom . . . and a moment later that flak burst turned us bottom up'ards. Damn nearly slipped my memory . . ."

And out it came.

It was flashed to Group, to Command, to the Air Ministry, Admiralty and War Office. A mere scrap of "gen", photographed on to Moaner's mind in that perilous instant while he fought for control of his machine over the enemy ships. Yet it fitted, like a lost piece of a jig-saw, into a picture which "Intelligence" had been struggling to complete for months. A night's intervening sleep might have lost it for ever.

At the first opportunity I stood Moaner a pint of beer – Gremlin or no Gremlin. And he winked over the tankard's edge as he said "Cheers" in the accepted style.

Money for Jam

Sir Alec Guinness

Location: Vis island, Yugoslavia.

Time: December, 1943.

Eyewitness Description: *"I woke up with a start, the sweat pouring off me. I trembled. The cabin was filled with an evil presence and it was concentrated twelve to eighteen inches from my left ear. Fully awake, I heard with my ear, so it seemed to me, the word, 'TOMORROW' . . ."*

Author: Sir Alec Guinness (1914–2000), like Derek Barnes, began his working life as an advertising copywriter before he discovered his real metier as an actor and made his stage debut in 1934. After several years at the Old Vic, he joined the Royal Navy in 1941 as an ordinary seaman and the following year was commissioned, experiencing action off Malta, Sicily and Yugoslavia. Returned to his profession, Guinness broke into films and became an international star as Fagin in *Oliver Twist* in 1948. Other great character roles ensured his reputation, while his autobiography, *Blessings in Disguise* (1985), also revealed a striking literary talent. Sir Alec never forget a ghostly experience he had in 1943 while commanding a Landing Craft off Yugoslavia under orders to evacuate 400 women and children in advance of an anticipated German invasion. The day proved to be one filled with surprises and shocks: the boat was hit by a hurricane, lit up by the weird St Elmo's fire and a sinister voice whispered a warning to him. Afterwards he wrote a chilling ghost story around the events for John Lehmann's *New Writing* (1945), which is now reprinted here for the first time in over 60 years.

The sun was hot and the foreign sea like plate-glass, the colour of peacocks' tails. Little breezes played around a salt, low, bare, rocky Arcadia, and at noon, when we sailed, the day sang with prettiness. It was like the sound of a flute. Or an oboe. Or was that the wind? The wind? No, little breezes, pirouetting down from the north, a trifle cold, for they came from high, snow-covered mountains. Even in retrospect the day held nothing sinister, not until the sun went down. There was nothing that wasn't quite as it ought to be. Yet this was the day dated 31 December, 1943. Curiously enough, I still have my diary for that time, somewhat battered and stained, but legible, and a proof to myself what life was like before the storm and what I was after it. There is no entry under 31 December except a jotting in pencil, "St. Luke 12. And if he shall come in the second watch, or come in the third watch, and find them so, blessed are those servants." Why does this fascinate? Then it is blank for three days. Finally in ink, with a strange borrowed pen and writing mine, but not like my own, are the words, "January 2. Not the second or third watches. Unprepared in the morning, but resigned in the Dogs." For January 3 there is entered up, "We took the rings off Broadstairs' hand." After that I didn't bother to keep a diary.

This was the situation. The enemy, thirty miles up the coast, also held all the opposite shore except the island of K. During the week ending 28 December they had attacked and overrun the three large islands that are grouped round K. It was apparent they would land on K. at any moment. They had complete air superiority in that part of the world, and no Allied craft could sail in those waters except under cover of darkness. The idea was that the ninety-foot schooner, of which I was captain, should run fifty tons of ammunition to the resistance group on K. and take off as many women and children as possible. K., being the last link on the opposite coast, must be saved at best, or turned into a battlefield at worst. Losing it was out of the question. It meant a trip of two hundred and twenty miles for us, there and back. The plans were hurried, but reasonably good and simple. We were to arrive at midnight and leave not later than 2 a.m. That would give us six hours of darkness at ten knots to get away from enemy reconnaissance planes. Everything had to be done in the dark, and if, by some misfortune, such as a breakdown or encountering an enemy vessel off the island, it would be imprudent for us to get away at the prescribed time, we were to find a small creek, run the schooner alongside rocks, disguise her with branches and camouflage netting and try our luck the following night. That is if we weren't spotted during the day. When loaded with the "ammo" the *Peter* – for that was her name – sat down squarely in the water.

"You know what to look for, don't you?" said the wiry little naval officer who brought me my sailing orders. "There's no moon, but if it's a clear night you should see the mountains of B. fine on your port bow by 22.00. Z. island is very low, but, as you can see on the chart, there's plenty of water round it. Keep as close inshore as possible in case of mines. When you come into the bay keep the guns closed up and slow down. And for God's sake tell the crew to keep their mouths shut. Silence is vital. When the chaps on K. spot you they will light a bonfire for ten minutes. If they light two bonfires or no bonfire, buzz off – it means we are too late. If it's all O.K. and they are ready for you, they'll swing a red lantern at the end of the jetty. There's a Major Backslide there, a drunken old so-and-so, but he knows his onions. He'll give you the latest dope which, incidentally, we'd like in the office when you get back. So long! It's money for jam."

"One moment," I said. "What other craft are out tonight?"

"Well, there's the usual patrol, but they won't touch you. Anything you see will be enemy. Except for twelve schooners, including *Mother of God, Topaz* and *Helena*, which are leaving here a few hours after you and working their way up the coast. Secret job. But you won't see them on the outward passage. Possibly coming back, though."

He went as briskly as he came, leaving my first lieutenant muttering "Money for jam!" Jimmy had an instinctive, and often unreasonable, dislike of the people who issued orders from offices. But really it wasn't a bad-looking little job, so long as the weather lasted. Never cared for the *Peter* when the sea got up. Always considered her top heavy.

So we sailed at noon on this cloudless day, hardly apprehensive, pleased to think we were on a mission of some small importance, but grumbling that it was going to mean New Year's Eve at sea. This annoyed the Scots lads in particular, but Taffey said "Think of the WOMEN we will be bringing back"; and the coxswain said, "Got a tin of turkey and two of ham. Big eats!" Able Seaman Broadstairs went down to the mess-deck, stripped, and vigorously applied hair-oil to his chest. "You'll never get it to grow by to-morrow night, son," grunted Stoker White, the oldest member of the crew. Broadstairs had a fine figure, and was a decent living kid, but he had no hair on his chest, which distressed him deeply. Whenever women were mentioned out came the violently-smelling hair-oil. Now he put it away and took to cleaning his silver signet rings with metal polish. He wore five of them and had a ring tattooed on the little finger of his left hand.

"Money for jam!" said Jimmy. "I could kick the tight little arse of that office boy!"

We sailed up the coast for ten miles, then pushed out to sea. I came off watch at tea-time and Jimmy took over. The crew consisted of the two of us and fourteen ratings, and we worked it watch and watch about, which is easy going on these short trips. Off watch in the daytime I usually sat in the cabin reading. Thinking to myself, I'm bound to be up all night, I turned in to get some early sleep after tea. The sun had grown dim, the bright blue sky was overcast with pale grey, and the sea was oily looking, shot with patches of dark satin-like water. No stars, tonight, I thought, and turned away from the scuttle and the light. A minute later Broadstairs entered the cabin to "darken ship." Very easily and swiftly I fell asleep. No dreams that I can remember. I slept for nearly two hours. When I woke it was with the strangest notion I have ever had in my life.

I am not a deeply religious man, and before the war was avowedly irreligious. I did not have convictions that could be called atheistic, but they were certainly agnostic. The war brought me back to an acceptance of the doctrines of the Church of England. I suppose I believe in ghosts. Certainly in good and evil spirits. But all that speculation had always seemed unimportant – chit-chat for a winter's evening at home, by a log fire, in the good old days of indifference. All thoughts of religious subjects, angelology, demons and what not were far from my mind that evening. I had no worries, other than the navigational one of successfully finding the island K.; and there was no obvious difficulty about that; I only call it "worry", because I have never sailed anywhere without wondering whether I would find the place. It is difficult to describe what happened to me at six o'clock that evening, yet I must attempt it, for on it hangs the whole significance of this experience from a personal point of view. It was as if—. It is impossible to state it simply enough and sound credible. It was as if—. I woke up with a start, the sweat pouring off me. I trembled. The cabin was filled with an evil presence and it was concentrated twelve or eighteen inches from my left ear. Fully awake, I heard with my ear, so it seemed to me, the word "TOMORROW." It was spoken clearly and quite loudly. Then the evil thing withdrew. Never have I felt so relieved at the departure of an unwanted guest as

I was by that one. The electric light on the table, throwing its warm, yellow circle of light on the dark blue cloth, the books on the shelves, the luminous clock, the barometer, the coffee percolator, the chairs, a pair of sea-boots, an old sweater, an etching of New York on the bulkhead, all these things seemed so friendly and clinging, as if they had resented the intruder as much as myself. For there was no doubt of the meaning conveyed in that one word "Tomorrow". A whole sentence had been condensed, with evil intent, into that word. It had said, in fact, "Tomorrow you will die an unpleasant death." Now, death is a fearful thing, and often terrible, and much has been thought and written on the subject, but it has never preoccupied my mind. We are hedged in with platitudes about death . . . we must all die – that makes death seem easier and less important. The poems of Beddoes I have always found funny. Death held no special terrors for me, I'm convinced. But there was something in that evil experience which shook me. Not so much the personal, unpleasant message as the feeling that swept through me that this had been a devil's voice, and if the workings of this curious world were controlled by devils, then life was the most wretched affair, human kind the saddest creation, children merely sent into the world to mock a man with. This was diametrically opposed to what I had always believed to be true. To have trusted such a voice would have been to banish God and render Christ ridiculous. "If I am to die tomorrow," I said to myself, "why can I not be informed by an angel, or one of the fates, or the ghost of an angry saint, if I *must* be told supernaturally? Why must I be told by this evil, sneaking, contemptible thing?" That gave me hope, for there was something gossipy, hearsay and underhand about that voice. I went on to the bridge.

"Hullo," I said.

"Hullo," said Jimmy.

"What's the matter?" I asked. "You look white."

"Do I?" Jimmy gave a direction down the voice-pipe. "If I do it's because I feel a bit sick. Just had a bit of a scare. Don't know what it was. Got the creeps. But it's O.K. now."

I was silent for a moment and looked round the horizon. It was getting dark, and all land had disappeared.

"How's the barometer?" I asked.

"Steady."

The *Peter* was beginning to roll a little – not an unusual occurrence even in a calm sea. But I didn't like the soft sighing sound in the rigging. I do not think there is a more melancholy lonely sound in the world than that whine of wind on wires and ropes. Curious, but sometimes you hear it, and it makes you shiver, when you can hardly feel a breath of wind on your face. The air round the ship seemed quite gentle, but the sighing was there unmistakably. Then suddenly a hard, bleak puff of wind screamed down, turning the small black waves white, tugging at one's hair, the flag, sending doors banging, lifting the heavy canvas lashed over the hold, raising the sadness in the rigging to a screech, and passing as swiftly as it had come. Oh, that depressing sound, and the cold, leaden splash of the bow wave breaking on the night sea! I sent for a duffel coat and remained on the bridge.

At 20.30 the wind, such as it was, came from a north-westerly direction. Six minutes later it changed abruptly and increased. By a quarter to nine it was blowing gale force from the south. In this part of the world the dangerous winds are reputed to be the northerly ones, so I thought little of it. It was a nuisance and was going to mean a bad night unless it slackened. Almost perceptibly the waves increased in height from four or five feet to twelve. Within another half hour they were fifteen feet; that is, as high as the bridge. Coming right on the starboard beam, we rolled heavily.

"How's the barometer?"

"Dropped two points since six o'clock."

We altered course five degrees to starboard to make allowance for the beam sea. Jimmy turned in to get some sleep, but within half an hour was up again.

"It's a bastard, isn't it!" he said. He stood by me, and then added, "They are getting bigger, aren't they?" They certainly were getting bigger, and also increasingly difficult to see in the darkness. As he said it the signalman, whose cap had gone in the wind, but who continued to hold a hand to his head, as if to keep that in place, cried out, "Look at this one, sir! Bet it's twenty foot or more." The monster of a wave looked as if it might crush us, but the *Peter* lifted herself, swayed to an alarming angle, and rode lightly over. A motor mechanic, an ill-shaped little fellow from Glasgow, put his face up the companion-way. " 'Scuse me, sir, we going on?" "Yes, Mickey Mouse." Mickey Mouse whistled and slid down the steps.

At 23.00 we saw the black, low shape of Z. We were much closer than I had expected, and on the wrong side. So we altered course for a while and rode more easily with the sea astern. Z. having been put in its right place, we continued on our way. The spray, which was being whipped off the water, was getting hellish. Shortly before midnight we were in the narrow waters that divide K. from Z. Here, considering we were almost hemmed in by islands, we expected to find some abatement. There was none. The lightning broke out in a vivid pink flash and we saw clearly, for the first time, exactly how enormous the waves were. It seemed odd that they should race at this size into this almost protected area. What I had not realised was the deterioration of the weather outside the islands. Within the past half hour, on the weather side of Z., which was in fact offering us stout protection, had begun the greatest storm in living memory in these stormy parts. The *Peter* was increasingly difficult to handle, her bow continuously swinging away from the wind, and she wouldn't answer to the helm even when hard over. To turn her into those giant waves and that roaring wind we had to go full ahead on the engines, which nearly shook her to pieces, or play one engine off against the other, putting the outboard full ahead and the inboard half astern. The spray took the form of a rushing mist, which, seen in the lightning, had all the qualities of a nightmare. We wallowed down past K. bay. No bonfires. No red lanterns – though if they had lit twenty we should never have seen them. In any case, we could never have reached the jetty. The sea was tumbling from all sides, and I heard later the jetty had been carried away. Mercilessly our stern was lifted thirty feet in the air and then our bows, thirty feet in the air into this pink, hail-like mist, and then we were dropped with a sickening thud. To have used oil would have been sensible, but the movement of the ship was so violent it was impossible for a man to shift his position. To have gone on deck was certain death; where you were you stayed, holding on for very life.

We turned back. So far as any direction was possible we headed towards the south-west. I had no desire on arriving back at the far coast, to find myself on the wrong side of the front line of battle. The ship could not be steered in any sense of the word. All we could do was to try keep the heavy seas on the port bow. I must say the *Peter* rode them magnificently.

A few minutes after midnight there was a sound like a muffled pistol-shot heard above the deafening roar. I didn't see it go, but it was the wireless mast.

At about 2 A.M. there began a curious phenomenon. There were four of us on the bridge – Jimmy, the signalman Douglas, a lookout nicknamed Hopeless, and myself. We were all drenched to the skin and exhausted by the violence of our beating from the wind. We huddled together, clutching at the sides of the bridge. It was impossible to speak, for even if we bawled the wind, now tearing past us at a hundred miles an hour, laden with stinging salt water, wrenched the sound away from our lips and drowned it in a howl. But Hopeless managed, after a couple of attempts, to make some words heard. "CAN YOU SEE? IS – IT – SPIRITS?" He was obviously upset about something. He couldn't let go to point, but it wasn't necessary, for we saw for ourselves. Creeping along the gunwale, starting from the bows, were ripples of bright blue light. In a minute they reached the bridge and crept under our fingers. Then the stump of the mast was ringed with blue – then every wire, every rope, all the edges of everything, including the hoods of our duffel coats, our finger-nails, the tops of our sea-boots. The light varied in thickness from the tenth of an inch to the breadth of a thumb, but all was of equal brilliance, a vivid blue, and seemed to move to and fro as if alive. For two hours we battled on, bristling with blue light, fascinated, entranced by its prettiness, and each of us hardly daring to wonder how the night would end. Before dawn the light receded.

The dawn came very late that morning. Jimmy managed to say "Happy New Year!" in my ear. The dawn was more terrible than the night, for the waves were thirty feet and over, and we could see each one completely and calculate its danger. They were a dirty yellow in colour, where they weren't white, as if they were scooping up the sea-bed. Some of them assumed fantastic toppling shapes, tapering up to narrow ribands of water through which we could see the wave behind; then the tops would be blown clean off, like eggs cut with a knife, and a solid mass of water would disappear in streaks in the air. Part of the port gunwale was smashed and washed away. At ten to eight we sighted a rocky island, tow hundred yards ahead. We saw it for the second we were balanced on top of a wave. We didn't get another opportunity, for it was hidden by walls of water. That island rises to twenty feet above sea level. It is about a quarter of a mile in circumference and uninhabited. From our perch on the top of the wave we saw the whole island was awash and at the northern end submerged. From that glimpse I was able to ascertain our position. We had been blown twenty-six miles north of our rough course during the night. I turned the ship head on into the sea. On a calm day the *Peter* could knock up fourteen knots. Her speed of advance into this sea, flat out, was half a knot.

Throughout the day we maintained the same speed – half a knot. The four of us clung together, in the same position we had been in all the time. I bawled down the voice-pipe to the coxswain, asking him if he was all right. "Fine!" came the reply, and I think I heard whistling. We all longed for something to drink, but it was out of the question.

Every man in the ship was pinned to his position. How the lads in the engine-room, in that sickly smell of hot oil, stood it out I shall never know.

I cannot remember when we began to pray. When we realised, I think, that at this speed we had no hope of shelter that night, and a very good chance three or four times a minute of capsizing or being pounded to pieces. When we saw the rocky island awash, I was aware that Douglas, crouched against me, had released his hand for a moment to cross himself. That, I think, set us all – anyway, those of us on the bridge – saying the Our Father. We mingled our muttered prayers with attempts at rather bawdy music-hall songs, not in defiance of God, but to relieve our minds of the strain. By the afternoon our faces were sodden with water, puffy and raw. Our eyes were ghastly to look at and painful to keep open. One at a time we probably dropped asleep, to awake thirty seconds later wondering how many hours had gone by. So we stayed there, having no alternative. At six o'clock I tried to sing "For those in peril on the sea" – and then it occurred to me to exorcise the ship. How silly and inexplicable that sounds! I am almost ashamed to write it. I wriggled round to face the after part of the ship, which included the cabin where I had experienced that evil thing. Jimmy and Douglas clasped me round the chest while I raised my right hand, making the sign of the cross. "In the name of Jesus Christ, leave us!" I said. Poor Hopeless! That depressed him more than anything. He began to cry.

The next morning we were weak and bitterly cold. The waves were of the same menacing height and ferocity, but the wind had dropped, probably to about eighty miles an hour. And we had lost our fear. We were all convinced we would die during the day. Shortly after noon we passed very close to the battered overturned hulk of a schooner. We could make out the name, *Topaz*. Subsequently we learnt that every one of those twelve that had sailed up the coast had been lost with all hands. On shore aircraft had been overturned by the wind on the airfields, gun emplacements on harbour walls had been washed away, with their gun crews, and in one well-protected harbour six sailors had been drowned. Giant waves rolled up the coast, in some cases running inland for two or three hundred yards.

Visibility was as bad as ever, but something about the sea suggested we were close to land. At 15.30 the engines, overheated, failed. We were drifting hopelessly. We were all resigned. The only anxiety of which I was conscious was the fact that Able Seaman

Broadstairs couldn't swim. We all knew swimming would be of no help, but it seemed bad that he had never learnt to swim. I remember thinking, "I wish I couldn't swim, because that will make it worse. I shall struggle for life." It was on such lines that I tried to comfort myself about Broadstairs.

It began to get dusk. Jimmy said, "Christ! Not another night! I couldn't!" The waves were now of a tumbling, clumsy, falling-on-top-of-each-other nature. At 17.15 we grounded, twenty yards from a rocky beach. The sea was on the beam. "Abandon ship!" I yelled. One carley float was loosed by Hopeless. It somersaulted towards the shore before anyone could grab the line that held it. Then a gigantic wave, which made the others appear ripples, picked us up and carried us right inshore, flinging us on the rocks. We heard a splitting sound. The four of us on the bridge clambered down. The *Peter* was lying on her side, at an angle of thirty degrees, precariously balanced. She was still surrounded by heavy surf. It was then that Stoker White came out in his true colours. He girded himself with a rope and flung himself into the filthy yellow water. It looked suicidal – but he reached the shore and lay there – a large, fat, exhausted, panting creature – a link between us and safety. "Come on, you sons of she-devils!" he croaked. "Come on, sonny!". This last to Broadstairs. Broadstairs, grinning, caught hold of the rope and sprang from the ship's side. He slipped, fell, cracked his skull and broke his back. He didn't make any noise. The surf washed him away. The others wasted no time. One by one, orderly, silently, they got ashore. Jimmy was next to last. Then my turn came. I was scared, and put off the moment, though I knew to do so was taking a far greater risk than swinging on the rope. I crawled along to the cabin. Everything was broken, upside down, ruined – as if that evil presence had sought revenge on harmless, inanimate objects, the friendly possessions of a man. I have always had some decent books on board. I couldn't resist snatching one up from the deck, where it had fallen, splayed out. In drawing-room games of Desert Island Books I had always chosen the most rewarding to spend the rest of my life with – the Bible, Shakespeare, Dickens, Milton, and so on. I rejected them all at this moment and took a cheap thriller I hadn't read. That, and my diary. I stepped out on deck. The crew were all halloaing me. Managed the rope easily. So there we all were. That is, all of us except Broadstairs. We recovered his body next day, terribly battered. It was difficult getting the rings off his fingers. We sent them to his mother.

The *Peter* slipped on her side, rolled over, and split in two. We were five miles behind the Allied lines. Good.

One thing we all understood, each in his different way. Everyone of us had been purged of a pet vice or special fear.

4

The Ghost-Feelers

Modern Gothic Tales

The Lady's Maid's Bell

Edith Wharton

Location: Brympton Place, Hudson, USA.
Time: Autumn, 1902.
Eyewitness Description: *"The silence began to be more dreadful to me than the most mysterious sounds. I felt that* someone *was cowering there, behind the locked door, watching and listening as I watched and listened . . ."*

Author: Edith Wharton (1862–1937) is another writer whose ghost stories are acknowledged as "landmarks in supernatural fiction". She was a central practitioner of the genre in the Twentieth century, redefining the old Gothic melodrama into a new form combining supernatural dread with sexual tension and founding a school of female "Ghost-Feelers" who *sensed* rather than saw spirits. Growing up in a haunted house in New York that instilled in her a "chronic state of fear", Wharton later confessed that she could not bear to even sleep in the same room as a book of ghost stories until she was 28. A loveless and repressed marriage made her seek escape in writing, creating novels about the morals and private passions of American society and ghost stories that described dark and mysterious events in unstable households. These began with "The Lady's Maid's Bell", written in 1904, which deeply moved readers in recounting a story of adultery and supernatural protection. There can be little doubt that Wharton drew on her own experiences for this groundbreaking tale, in particular the narrator, the maid Alice Hartley's near-fatal attack of typhoid, which she had herself survived.

I

It was the autumn after I had the typhoid. I'd been three months in hospital, and when I came out I looked so weak and tottery that the two or three ladies I applied to were afraid to engage me. Most of my money was gone, and after I'd boarded for two months, hanging about the employment-agencies, and answering any advertisement that looked any way respectable, I pretty nearly lost heart, for fretting hadn't made me fatter, and I didn't see why my luck should ever turn. It did though – or I thought so at the time. A Mrs Railton, a friend of the lady that first brought me out to the States, met me one day and stopped to speak to me: she was one that had always a friendly way with her. She asked me what ailed me to look so white, and when I told her, "Why, Hartley," says she, "I believe I've got the very place for you. Come in tomorrow and we'll talk about it."

The next day, when I called, she told me the lady she'd in mind was a niece of hers, a Mrs Brympton, a youngish lady, but something of an invalid, who lived all the year round at her country-place on the Hudson, owing to not being able to stand the fatigue of town life.

"Now, Hartley," Mrs Railton said, in that cheery way that always made me feel things must be going to take a turn for the better – "now understand me; it's not a cheerful place I'm sending you to. The house is big and gloomy; my niece is nervous, vapourish; her husband – well, he's generally away; and the two children are dead. A year ago I would as soon have thought of shutting a rosy active girl like you into a vault; but you're not particularly brisk yourself just now, are you? and a quiet place, with country air and wholesome food and early hours, ought to be the very thing for you. Don't mistake me," she added, for I suppose I looked a trifle downcast; "you may find it dull, but you won't be unhappy. My niece is an angel. Her former maid, who died last spring, had been with her twenty years and worshipped the ground she walked on. She's a kind mistress to all, and where the mistress is kind, as you know, the servants are generally good-humoured, so you'll probably get on well enough with the rest of the household. And you're the very woman I want for my niece: quiet, well-mannered, and educated above your station. You read aloud well, I think? That's a good thing; my niece likes to be read to. She wants a maid that can be something of a companion: her last was, and I can't say how she misses her. It's a lonely life . . . Well, have you decided?"

"Why, ma'am," I said, "I'm not afraid of solitude."

"Well, then, go; my niece will take you on my recommendation. I'll telegraph her at once and you can take the afternoon train. She has no one to wait on her at present, and I don't want you to lose any time."

I was ready enough to start, yet something in me hung back; and to gain time I asked, "And the gentleman, ma'am?"

"The gentleman's almost always away, I tell you," said Mrs Railton, quick-like — "and when he's there," says she suddenly, "you've only to keep out of his way."

I took the afternoon train and got out at D——station at about four o'clock. A groom in a dogcart was waiting, and we drove off at a smart pace. It was a dull October day, with rain hanging close overhead, and by the time we turned into Brympton Place woods the daylight was almost gone. The drive wound through the woods for a mile or two, and came out on a gravel court shut in with thickets of tall black-looking shrubs. There were no lights in the windows and the house *did* look a bit gloomy.

I had asked no questions of the groom, for I never was one to get my notion of new masters from their other servants: I prefer to wait and see for myself. But I could tell by the look of everything that I had got into the right kind of house, and that things were done handsomely. A pleasant-faced cook met me at the back door and called the house-maid to show me up to my room. "You'll see madam later," she said. "Mrs Brympton has a visitor."

I hadn't fancied Mrs Brympton was a lady to have many visitors, and somehow the words cheered me. I followed the house-maid upstairs, and saw, through a door on the upper landing, that the main part of the house seemed well furnished, with dark panelling and a number of old portraits. Another flight of stairs led us up to the servants' wing. It was almost dark now, and the housemaid excused herself for not having brought a light. "But there's matches in your room," she said, "and if you go careful you'll be all right. Mind the step at the end of the passage. Your room is just beyond."

I looked ahead as she spoke, and half-way down the passage I saw a woman standing. She drew back into a doorway as we passed and the housemaid didn't appear to notice her. She was a thin woman with a white face, and a darkish stuff gown and apron. I took her for the housekeeper and thought it odd that she didn't speak, but just gave me a long look as she went by. My room opened into a square hall at the end of the passage. Facing my door was another which stood open; the housemaid exclaimed when she saw it:

"There – Mrs Blinder's left that door open again!" said she, closing it.

"Is Mrs Blinder the housekeeper?"

"There's no housekeeper: Mrs Blinder's the cook."

"And is that her room?"

"Laws, no," said the house-maid, cross-like. "That's nobody's room. It's empty, I mean, and the door hadn't ought to be open. Mrs Brympton wants it kept locked."

She opened my door and led me into a neat room, nicely furnished, with a picture or two on the walls; and having lit a candle she took leave, telling me that the scrvants'-hall tea was at six, and that Mrs Brympton would see me afterward.

I found them a pleasant-spoken set in the servants' hall, and by what they let fall I gathered that, as Mrs Railton had said, Mrs Brympton was the kindest of ladies; but I didn't take much notice of their talk, for I was watching to see the pale woman in the dark gown come in. She didn't show herself, however, and I wondered if she ate apart; but if she wasn't the housekeeper, why should she? Suddenly it struck me that she might be a trained nurse, and in that case her meals would of course be served in her room. If Mrs Brympton was an invalid it was likely enough she had a nurse. The idea annoyed me, I own, for they're not always the easiest to get on with, and if I'd known I shouldn't have taken the place. But there I was and there was no use pulling a long face over it; and not being one to ask questions I waited to see what would turn up.

When tea was over the house-maid said to the footman: "Has Mr Ranford gone?" and when he said yes, she told me to come up with her to Mrs Brympton.

Mrs Brympton was lying down in her bedroom. Her lounge stood near the fire and beside it was a shaded lamp. She was a delicate-looking lady, but when she smiled I felt there was nothing I wouldn't do for her. She spoke very pleasantly, in a low voice, asking me my name and age and so on, and if I had everything I wanted, and if I wasn't afraid of feeling lonely in the country.

"Not with you I wouldn't be, madam," I said, and the words surprised me when I'd spoken them, for I'm not an impulsive person; but it was just as if I'd thought aloud.

She seemed pleased at that, and said she hoped I'd continue in the same mind; then she gave me a few directions about her toilet, and said Agnes the house-maid would show me next morning where things were kept.

"I am tired tonight, and shall dine upstairs," she said. "Agnes will bring me my tray, that you may have time to unpack and settle yourself; and later you may come and undress me."

"Very well, ma'am," I said. "You'll ring, I suppose?"

I thought she looked odd.

"No – Agnes will fetch you," says she quickly, and took up her book again.

Well – that was certainly strange: a lady's maid having to be fetched by the house-maid whenever her lady wanted her! I wondered if there were no bells in the house; but the next day I satisfied myself that there was one in every room, and a special one ringing from my mistress's room to mine; and after that it did strike me as queer that, whenever Mrs Brympton wanted anything, she rang for Agnes, who had to walk the whole length of the servants' wing to call me.

But that wasn't the only queer thing in the house. The very next day I found out that Mrs Brympton had no nurse; and then I asked Agnes about the woman I had seen in the passage the afternoon before. Agnes said she had seen no one, and I saw that she thought I was dreaming. To be sure, it was dusk when we went down the passage, and she had excused herself for not bringing a light; but I had seen the woman plain enough to know her again if we should meet. I decided that she must have been a friend of the cook's, or of one of the other women servants; perhaps she had come down from town for a night's visit, and the servants wanted it kept secret. Some ladies are very stiff about having their servants' friends in the house overnight. At any rate, I made up my mind to ask no more questions.

In a day or two another odd thing happened. I was chatting one afternoon with Mrs Blinder, who was a friendly-disposed woman, and had been longer in the house than the other servants, and she asked me if I was quite comfortable and had everything I needed. I said I had no fault to find with my place or with my mistress, but I thought it odd that in so large a house there was no sewing-room for the lady's maid.

"Why," says she, "there *is* one: the room you're in is the old sewing-room."

"Oh," said I; "and where did the other lady's maid sleep?"

At that she grew confused, and said hurriedly that the servants' rooms had all been changed last year, and she didn't rightly remember.

That struck me as peculiar, but I went on as if I hadn't noticed: "Well, there's a vacant room opposite mine, and I mean to ask Mrs Brympton if I mayn't use that as a sewing-room."

To my astonishment, Mrs Blinder went white and gave my hand a kind of squeeze. "Don't do that, my dear," said she, trembling-like. "To tell you the truth, that was Emma Saxon's room, and my mistress has kept it closed ever since her death."

"And who was Emma Saxon?"

"Mrs Brympton's former maid."

"The one that was with her so many years?" said I, remembering what Mrs Railton had told me.

Mrs Blinder nodded.

"What sort of woman was she?"

"No better walked the earth," said Mrs Blinder. "My mistress loved her like a sister."

"But I mean – what did she look like?"

Mrs Blinder got up and gave me a kind of angry stare. "I'm no great hand at describing," she said; "and I believe my pastry's rising." And she walked off into the kitchen and shut the door after her.

II

I had been near a week at Brympton before I saw my master. Word came that he was arriving one afternoon, and a change passed over the whole household. It was plain that nobody loved him below stairs. Mrs Blinder took uncommon care with the dinner that night, but she snapped at the kitchen-maid in a way quite unusual with her; and Mr Wace, the butler, a serious slow-spoken man, went about his duties as if he'd been getting ready for a funeral. He was a great Bible-reader, Mr Wace was, and had a beautiful assortment of texts at his command; but that day he used such dreadful language that I was about to leave the table, when he assured me it was all out of Isaiah; and I noticed that whenever the master came Mr Wace took to the prophets.

About seven, Agnes called me to my mistress's room; and there I found Mr Brympton. He was standing on the hearth; a big, fair, bull-necked man, with a red face and little bad-tempered blue eyes: the kind of man a young simpleton might have thought handsome, and would have been like to pay dear for thinking it.

He swung about when I came in, and looked me over in a trice. I knew what the look meant, from having experienced it once or twice in my former places. Then he turned his back on me, and went on talking to his wife; and I knew what *that* meant, too. I was not the kind of morsel he was after. The typhoid had served me well enough in one way: it kept that kind of gentleman at arm's-length.

"This is my new maid, Hartley," says Mrs Brympton in her kind voice; and he nodded and went on with what he was saying.

In a minute or two he went off, and left my mistress to dress for dinner, and I noticed as I waited on her that she was white, and chill to the touch.

Mr Brympton took himself off the next morning, and the whole house drew a long breath when he drove away. As for my mistress, she put on her hat and furs (for it was a fine winter morning) and went out for a walk in the gardens, coming back quite fresh and rosy, so that for a minute, before her colour faded, I could guess what a pretty young lady she must have been, and not so long ago, either.

She had met Mr Ranford in the grounds, and the two came back together, I remember, smiling and talking as they walked along the terrace under my window. That was the first time I saw Mr Ranford, though I had often heard his name mentioned in the hall. He was a neighbour, it appeared, living a mile or two beyond Brympton, at the end of the village; and as he was in the habit of spending his winters in the country he was almost the only company my mistress had at that season. He was a slight tall gentleman of about thirty, and I thought him rather melancholy-looking till I saw his smile, which had a kind of surprise in it, like the first warm day in spring. He was a great reader, I heard, like my mistress, and the two were for ever borrowing books of one another, and sometimes (Mr Wace told me) he would read aloud to Mrs Brympton by the hour, in the big dark library where she sat in the winter afternoons. The servants all liked him, and perhaps that's more of a compliment than the masters suspect. He had a friendly word for every one of us, and we were all glad to think that Mrs Brympton had a pleasant companionable gentleman like that to keep her company when the master was away. Mr Ranford seemed on excellent terms with Mr Brympton too; though I couldn't but wonder that two gentlemen so unlike each other should be so friendly. But then I knew how the real quality can keep their feelings to themselves.

As for Mr Brympton, he came and went, never staying more than a day or two, cursing the dullness and the solitude, grumbling at everything, and (as I soon found out) drinking a deal more than was good for him. After Mrs Brympton left the table he would sit half the night over the old Brympton port and madeira, and once, as I was leaving my mistress's room rather later than usual, I met him coming up the stairs in such a state that I turned sick to think of what some ladies have to endure and hold their tongues about.

The servants said very little about their master; but from what they let drop I could see it had been an unhappy match from the beginning. Mr Brympton was coarse, loud, and pleasure-loving; my mistress quiet, retiring, and perhaps a trifle cold. Not that she was not always pleasant-spoken to him: I thought her wonderfully forbearing; but to a gentleman as free as Mr Brympton I dare say she seemed a little offish.

Well, things went on quietly for several weeks. My mistress was kind, my duties were light, and I got on well with the other servants. In short, I had nothing to complain of; yet there was always a weight on me. I can't say why it was so, but I know it was not the loneliness that I felt. I soon got used to that; and being still languid from the fever I was thankful for the quiet and the good country air. Nevertheless, I was never quite easy in my mind. My mistress, knowing I had been ill, insisted that I should take my walk regular, and often invented errands for me – a yard of ribbon to be fetched from the village, a letter posted, or a book returned to Mr Ranford. As soon as I was out of doors my spirits rose, and I looked forward to my walks through the bare moist-smelling woods; but the moment I caught sight of the house again my heart dropped down like a stone in a well. It was not a gloomy house exactly, yet I never entered it but a feeling of gloom came over me.

Mrs Brympton seldom went out in winter; only on the finest days did she walk an hour at noon on the south terrace. Excepting Mr Ranford, we had no visitors but the doctor, who drove over from D—about once a week. He sent for me once or twice to give me some trifling direction about my mistress, and though he never told me what her illness was, I thought, from a waxy look she had now and then of a morning, that it might be the heart that ailed her. The season was soft and unwholesome, and in January we had a long spell of rain. That was a sore trial to me, I own, for I couldn't go out, and sitting over my sewing all day, listening to the drip, drip of the eaves, I grew so nervous that the least sound made me jump. Somehow, the thought of that locked room across the passage began to weigh on me. Once or twice, in the long rainy nights, I fancied I heard noises there; but that was nonsense, of course, and the daylight drove such notions out of my head. Well, one morning Mrs Brympton gave me quite a start of pleasure by telling me she wished me to go to town for some shopping. I hadn't known till then how low my spirits had fallen. I set off in high glee, and my first sight of the crowded streets and the cheerful-looking shops quite took me out of myself. Toward afternoon, however, the noise and confusion began to tire me, and I was actually looking forward to the quiet of Brympton, and thinking how I should enjoy the drive home through the dark woods, when I ran across an old acquaintance, a maid I had once been in service with. We had lost sight of each other for a number of years, and I had to stop and tell her what had happened to me in the interval. When I mentioned where I was living she rolled up her eyes and pulled a long face.

"What! The Mrs Brympton that lives all the year at her place on the Hudson? My dear, you won't stay there three months."

"Oh, but I don't mind the country," says I, offended somehow at her tone. "Since the fever I'm glad to be quiet."

She shook her head. "It's not the country I'm thinking of. All I know is she's had four maids in the last six months, and the last one, who was a friend of mine, told me nobody could stay in the house."

"Did she say why?" I asked.

"No – she wouldn't give me her reason. But she says to me, *Mrs Ansey*, she says, *if ever a young woman as you know of thinks of going there, you tell her it's not worth while to unpack her boxes*."

"Is she young and handsome?" said I, thinking of Mr Brympton.

"Not her! She's the kind that mothers engage when they've gay young gentlemen at college."

Well, though I knew the woman was an idle gossip, the words stuck in my head, and my heart sank lower than ever as I drove up to Brympton in the dusk. There *was* something about the house – I was sure of it now. . . .

When I went in to tea I heard that Mr Brympton had arrived, and I saw at a glance that there had been a disturbance of some kind. Mrs Blinder's hand shook so that she could hardly pour the tea, and Mr Wace quoted the most dreadful texts full of brimstone. Nobody said a word to me then, but when I went up to my room, Mrs Blinder followed me.

"Oh, my dear," says she, taking my hand, "I'm so glad and thankful you've come back to us!"

That struck me, as you may imagine. "Why," said I, "did you think I was leaving for good?"

"No, no, to be sure," said she, a little confused, "but I can't a-bear to have madam left alone for a day even." She pressed my hand hard, and, "Oh, Miss Hartley," says she, "be good to your mistress, as you're a Christian woman." And with that she hurried away, and left me staring.

A moment later Agnes called me to Mrs Brympton. Hearing Mr Brympton's voice in her room, I went round by the dressing-room, thinking I would lay out her dinner-gown before going in. The dressing-room is a large room with a window over the portico that looks toward the gardens. Mr Brympton's apartments are beyond. When I went in, the door into the bedroom was ajar, and I heard Mr Brympton saying angrily: "One would suppose he was the only person fit for you to talk to."

"I don't have many visitors in winter," Mrs Brympton answered quietly.

"You have *me*!" he flung at her, sneeringly.

"You are here so seldom," said she.

"Well – whose fault is that? You make the place about as lively as the family vault—"

With that I rattled the toilet-things, to give my mistress warning, and she rose and called me in.

The two dined alone, as usual, and I knew by Mr Wace's manner at supper that things must be going badly. He quoted the prophets something terrible, and worked on the kitchen-maid so that she declared she wouldn't go down alone to put the cold meat in the ice-box. I felt nervous myself, and after I had put my mistress to bed I was half-tempted to go down again and persuade Mrs Blinder to sit up a while over a game of cards. But I heard her door closing for the night and so I went on to my own room. The rain had begun again, and the drip, drip, drip seemed to be dropping into my brain. I lay awake listening to it, and turning over what my friend in town had said. What puzzled me was that it was always the maids who left . . .

After a while I slept; but suddenly a loud noise wakened me. My bell had rung. I sat up, terrified by the unusual sound, which seemed to go on jangling through the darkness. My hands shook so that I couldn't find the matches. At length I struck a light and jumped out of bed. I began to think I must have been dreaming; but I looked at the bell against the wall, and there was the little hammer still quivering.

I was just beginning to huddle on my clothes when I heard another sound. This time it was the door of the locked room opposite mine softly opening and closing. I heard the sound distinctly, and it frightened me so that I stood stock-still. Then I heard a footstep hurrying down the passage toward the main house. The floor being carpeted, the sound was very faint, but I was quite sure it was a woman's step. I turned cold with the thought of it, and for a minute or two I dursn't breathe or move. Then I came to my senses.

"Alice Hartley," says I to myself, "someone left that room just now and ran down the passage ahead of you. The idea isn't pleasant, but you may as well face it. Your mistress has rung for you, and to answer her bell you've got to go the way that other woman has gone."

Well – I did it. I never walked faster in my life, yet I thought I should never get to the end of the passage or reach Mrs Brympton's room. On the way I heard nothing and saw nothing: all was dark and quiet as the grave. When I reached my mistress's door the silence was so deep that I began to think I must be dreaming, and was half-minded to turn back. Then a panic seized me, and I knocked.

There was no answer, and I knocked again, loudly. To my astonishment the door was opened by Mr Brympton. He started back when he saw me, and in the light of my candle his face looked red and savage.

"*You?*" he said, in a queer voice. "*How many of you are there, in God's name?*"

At that I felt the ground give under me; but I said to myself that he had been drinking, and answered as steadily as I could: "May I go in, sir? Mrs Brympton has rung for me."

"You may all go in, for what I care," says he, and, pushing by me, walked down the hall to his own bedroom. I looked after him as he went, and to my surprise I saw that he walked as straight as a sober man.

I found my mistress lying very weak and still but she forced a smile when she saw me, and signed to me to pour out some drops for her. After that she lay without speaking, her breath coming quick, and her eyes closed. Suddenly she groped out with her hand, and "*Emma,*" says she, faintly.

"It's Hartley, madam," I said. "Do you want anything?"

She opened her eyes wide and gave me a startled look.

"I was dreaming," she said. "You may go now, Hartley, and thank you kindly. I'm quite well again, you see." And she turned her face away from me.

III

There was no more sleep for me that night, and I was thankful when daylight came.

Soon afterward, Agnes called me to Mrs Brympton. I was afraid she was ill again, for she seldom sent for me before nine, but I found her sitting up in bed, pale and drawn-looking, but quite herself.

"Hartley," says she quickly, "will you put on your things at once and go down to the village for me? I want this prescription made up" – here she hesitated a minute and blushed – "and I should like you to be back again before Mr Brympton is up."

"Certainly, madam," I said.

"And – stay a moment" – she called me back as if an idea had just struck her – "while you're waiting for the mixture, you'll have time to go on to Mr Ranford's with this note."

It was a two-mile walk to the village, and on my way I had time to turn things over in my mind. It struck me as peculiar that my mistress should wish the prescription made up without Mr Brympton's knowledge; and, putting this together with the scene of the night before, and with much else that I had noticed and suspected, I began to wonder if the poor lady was weary of her life, and had come to the mad resolve of ending it. The idea took such hold on me that I reached the village on a run, and dropped breathless into a chair before the chemist's counter. The good man, who was just taking down his shutters, stared at me so hard that it brought me to myself.

"Mr Limmel," I says, trying to speak indifferent, "will you run your eye over this, and tell me if it's quite right?"

He put on his spectacles and studied the prescription.

"Why, it's one of Dr Walton's," says he. "What should be wrong with it?"

"Well – is it dangerous to take?"

"Dangerous – how do you mean?"

I could have shaken the man for his stupidity.

"I mean – if a person was to take too much of it – by mistake of course—" says I, my heart in my throat.

"Lord bless you, no. It's only lime-water. You might feed it to a baby by the bottleful."

I gave a great sigh of relief and hurried on to Mr Ranford's. But on the way another thought struck me. If there was nothing to conceal about my visit to the chemist's, was it my other errand that Mrs Brympton wished me to keep private? Somehow, that thought frightened me worse than the other. Yet the two gentlemen seemed fast friends, and I would have staked my head on my mistress's goodness. I felt ashamed of my suspicions, and concluded that I was still disturbed by the strange events of the night. I left the note at Mr Ranford's, and hurrying back to Brympton, slipped in by a side door without being seen, as I thought.

An hour later, however, as I was carrying in my mistress's breakfast, I was stopped in the hall by Mr Brympton.

"What were you doing out so early?" he says, looking hard at me.

"Early – me, sir?" I said, in a tremble.

"Come, come," he says, an angry red spot coming out on his forehead, "didn't I see you scuttling home through the shrubbery an hour or more ago?"

I'm a truthful woman by nature, but at that a lie popped out ready-made. "No, sir, you didn't," said I, and looked straight back at him.

He shrugged his shoulders and gave a sullen laugh. "I suppose you think I was drunk last night?" he asked suddenly.

"No, sir, I don't," I answered, this time truthfully enough.

He turned away with another shrug. "A pretty notion my servants have of me!" I heard him mutter as he walked off.

Not till I had settled down to my afternoon's sewing did I realize how the events of the night had shaken me. I couldn't pass that locked door without a shiver. I knew I had heard someone come out of it, and walk down the passage ahead of me. I thought of speaking to Mrs Blinder or to Mr Wace, the only two in the house who appeared to have an inkling of what was going on, but I had a feeling that if I questioned them they would deny everything, and that I might learn more by holding my tongue and keeping my eyes open. The idea of spending another night opposite the locked room sickened me, and once I was seized with the notion of packing my trunk and taking the first train to town; but it wasn't in me to throw over a kind mistress in that manner, and I tried to go on with my sewing as if nothing had happened. I hadn't worked ten minutes before the sewing machine broke down. It was one I had found in the house, a good machine but a trifle out of order: Mrs Blinder said it had never been used since Emma Saxon's death. I stopped to see what was wrong, and as I was working at the machine a drawer which I had never been able to open slid forward, and a photograph fell out. I picked it up and sat looking at it in a maze. It was a woman's likeness, and I knew I had seen the face somewhere – the eyes had an asking look that I had felt on me before. And suddenly I remembered the pale woman in the passage.

I stood up, cold all over, and ran out of the room. My heart seemed to be thumping in the top of my head, and I felt as if I should never get away from the look in those eyes. I went straight to Mrs Blinder. She was taking her afternoon nap, and sat up with a jump when I came in.

"Mrs Blinder," said I, "who is that?" And I held out the photograph.

She rubbed her eyes and stared.

"Why, Emma Saxon," says she. "Where did you find it?"

I looked hard at her for a minute. "Mrs Blinder," I said, "I've seen that face before."

Mrs Blinder got up and walked over to the looking-glass. "Dear me! I must have been asleep," she says. "My front is all over one ear. And now do run along, Miss Hartley, dear, for I hear the clock striking four, and I must go down this very minute and put on the Virginia ham for Mr Brympton's dinner."

IV

To all appearances, things went on as usual for a week or two. The only difference was that Mr Brympton stayed on, instead of going off as he usually did, and that Mr Ranford never showed himself. I heard Mr Brympton remark on this one afternoon when he was sitting in my mistress's room before dinner.

"Where's Ranford?" says he. "He hasn't been near the house for a week. Does he keep away because I'm here?"

Mrs Brympton spoke so low that I couldn't catch her answer.

"Well," he went on, "two's company and three's trumpery; I'm sorry to be in Ranford's way, and I suppose I shall have to take myself off again in a day or two and give him a show." And he laughed at his own joke.

The very next day, as it happened, Mr Ranford called. The footman said the three were very merry over their tea in the library, and Mr Brympton strolled down to the gate with Mr Ranford when he left.

I have said that things went on as usual; and so they did with the rest of the household; but as for myself, I had never been the same since the night my bell had rung. Night after night I used to lie awake, listening for it to ring again, and for the door of the locked room to open stealthily. But the bell never rang, and I heard no sound across the passage. At last the silence began to be more dreadful to me than the most mysterious sounds. I felt that *someone* was cowering there, behind the locked door, watching and listening as I watched and listened, and I could almost have cried out, "Whoever you are, come out and let me see you face to face, but don't lurk there and spy on me in the darkness!"

Feeling as I did, you may wonder I didn't give warning. Once I very nearly did so; but at the last moment something held me back. Whether it was compassion for my mistress, who had grown more and more dependent on me, or unwillingness to try a new place, or some other feeling that I couldn't put a name to, I lingered on as if spellbound, though every night was dreadful to me, and the days but little better.

For one thing, I didn't like Mrs Brympton's looks. She had never been the same since that night, no more than I had. I thought she would brighten up after Mr Brympton left, but though she seemed easier in her mind, her spirits didn't revive, nor her strength either. She had grown attached to me and seemed to like to have me about; and Agnes told me one day that, since Emma Saxon's death, I was the only maid her mistress had taken to. This gave me a warm feeling for the poor lady, though after all there was little I could do to help her.

After Mr Brympton's departure Mr Ranford took to coming again, though less often than formerly. I met him once or twice in the grounds, or in the village, and I couldn't but think there was a change in him too; but I set it down to my disordered fancy.

The weeks passed, and Mr Brympton had now been a month absent. We heard he was cruising with a friend in the West Indies, and Mr Wace said that was a long way off, but though you had the wings of a dove and went to the uttermost parts of the earth, you couldn't get away from the Almighty. Agnes said that as long as he stayed away from Brympton the Almighty might have him and welcome; and this raised a laugh, though Mrs Blinder tried to look shocked, and Mr Wace said the bears would eat us.

We were all glad to hear that the West Indies were a long way off, and I remember that, in spite of Mr Wace's solemn looks, we had a very merry dinner that day in the hall. I don't know if it was because of my being in better spirits, but I fancied Mrs Brympton looked better too, and seemed more cheerful in her manner. She had been for a walk in the morning, and after luncheon she lay down in her room, and I read aloud to her. When she dismissed me I went to my own room feeling quite bright and happy, and for the first time in weeks walked past the locked door without thinking of it. As I sat down to my work I looked out and saw a few snowflakes falling. The sight was pleasanter than the eternal rain, and I pictured to myself how pretty the bare gardens would look in their white mantle. It seemed to me as if the snow would cover up all the dreariness, indoors as well as out.

The fancy had hardly crossed my mind when I heard a step at my side. I looked up, thinking it was Agnes.

"Well, Agnes—" said I, and the words froze on my tongue; for there, in the door, stood Emma Saxon.

I don't know how long she stood there. I only know I couldn't stir or take my eyes from her. Afterward I was terribly frightened, but at the time it wasn't fear I felt, but something deeper and quieter. She looked at me long and long, and her face was just one dumb prayer to me – but how in the world was I to help her? Suddenly she turned, and I heard her walk down the passage. This time I wasn't afraid to follow – I felt that I must know what she wanted. I sprang up and ran out. She was at the other end of the passage, and I expected her to take the turn toward my mistress's room; but instead of that she pushed open the door that led to the back stairs. I followed her down the stairs, and across the passage-way to the back door. The kitchen and hall were empty at that hour, the servants being off duty, except for the footman, who was in the pantry. At the door she stood still a moment, with another look at me; then she turned the handle, and stepped out. For a minute I hesitated. Where was she leading me to? The door had closed softly after her, and I opened it and looked out, half-expecting to find that she had disappeared. But I saw her a few yards off hurrying across the court-yard to the path through the woods. Her figure looked black and lonely in the snow, and for a second my heart failed me and I thought of turning back. But all the while she was drawing me after her; and catching up an old shawl of Mrs Blinder's I ran out into the open.

Emma Saxon was in the wood-path now. She walked on steadily, and I followed at the same pace till we passed out of the gates and reached the highroad. Then she struck across the open fields to the village. By this time the ground was white, and as she climbed the slope of a bare hill ahead of me I noticed that she left no footprints behind her. At sight of that my heart shrivelled up within me and my knees were water. Somehow it was worse here than indoors. She made the whole countryside seem lonely as the grave, with none but us two in it, and no help in the wide world.

Once I tried to go back; but she turned and looked at me, and it was as if she had dragged me with ropes. After that I followed her like a dog. We came to the village and she led me through it, past the church and the blacksmith's shop, and down the lane to Mr Ranford's. Mr Ranford's house stands close to the road: a plain old-fashioned building, with a flagged path leading to the door between box-borders. The lane was deserted, and as I turned into it I saw Emma Saxon pause under the old elm by the gate. And now another fear came over me. I saw that we had reached the end of our journey, and that it was my turn to act. All the way from Brympton I had been asking myself what she wanted of me, but I had followed in a trance, as it were, and not till I saw her stop at Mr Ranford's gate did my brain begin to clear itself. I stood a little way off in the snow, my heart beating fit to strangle me, and my feet frozen to the ground; and she stood under the elm and watched me.

I knew well enough that she hadn't led me there for nothing. I felt there was something I ought to say or do – but how was I to guess what it was? I had never thought harm of my mistress and Mr Ranford, but I was sure now that, from one cause or another, some dreadful thing hung over them. *She* knew what it was; she would tell me if she could; perhaps she would answer if I questioned her.

It turned me faint to think of speaking to her; but I plucked up heart and dragged myself across the few yards between us. As I did so, I heard the house door open and saw Mr Ranford approaching. He looked handsome and cheerful, as my mistress had looked that morning, and at sight of him the blood began to flow again in my veins.

"Why, Hartley," said he, "what's the matter? I saw you coming down the lane just now, and came out to see if you had taken root in the snow." He stopped and stared at me. "What are you looking at?" he says.

I turned toward the elm as he spoke, and his eyes followed me; but there was no one there. The lane was empty as far as the eye could reach.

A sense of helplessness came over me. She was gone, and I had not been able to guess what she wanted. Her last look had pierced me to the marrow; and yet it had not told me! All at once, I felt more desolate than when she had stood there watching me. It seemed as if she had left me all alone to carry the weight of the secret I couldn't guess. The snow went round me in great circles, and the ground fell away from me. . . .

A drop of brandy and the warmth of Mr Ranford's fire soon brought me to, and I insisted on being driven back at once to Brympton. It was nearly dark, and I was afraid my mistress might be wanting me. I explained to Mr Ranford that I had been out for a walk and had been taken with a fit of giddiness as I passed his gate. This was true enough; yet I never felt more like a liar than when I said it.

When I dressed Mrs Brympton for dinner she remarked on my pale looks and asked what ailed me. I told her I had a headache, and she said she would not require me again that evening, and advised me to go to bed.

It was a fact that I could scarcely keep on my feet; yet I had no fancy to spend a solitary evening in my room. I sat downstairs in the hall as long as I could hold my head up; but by nine I crept upstairs, too weary to care what happened if I could but get my head on a pillow. The rest of the household went to bed soon afterward; they kept early hours when the master was away, and before ten I heard Mrs Blinder's door close, and Mr Wace's soon after.

It was a very still night, earth and air all muffled in snow. Once in bed I felt easier, and lay quiet, listening to the strange noises that come out in a house after dark. Once I thought I heard a door open and close again below: it might have been the glass door that led to the gardens. I got up and peered out of the window; but it was in the dark of the moon, and nothing visible outside but the streaking of snow against the panes.

I went back to bed and must have dozed, for I jumped awake to the furious ringing of my bell. Before my head was clear I had sprung out of bed and was dragging on my clothes. *It is going to happen now*, I heard myself saying; but what I meant I had no notion. My hands seemed to be covered with glue – I thought I should never get into my clothes. At last I opened my door and peered down the passage. As far as my candle-flame carried, I could see nothing unusual ahead of me. I hurried on, breathless; but as I pushed open the baize door leading to the main hall my heart stood still, for there at the head of the stairs was Emma Saxon, peering dreadfully down into the darkness.

For a second I couldn't stir; but my hand slipped from the door, and as it swung shut the figure vanished. At the same instant there came another sound from below stairs – a stealthy mysterious sound, as of a latch-key turning in the house door. I ran to Mrs Brympton's room and knocked.

There was no answer, and I knocked again. This time I heard someone moving in the room; the bolt slipped back and my mistress stood before me. To my surprise I saw that she had not undressed for the night. She gave me a startled look.

"What is this, Hartley?" she says in a whisper. "Are you ill? What are you doing here at this hour?"

"I am not ill, madam; but my bell rang."

At that she turned pale, and seemed about to fall.

"You are mistaken," she said harshly; "I didn't ring. You must have been dreaming." I had never heard her speak in such a tone. "Go back to bed," she said, closing the door on me.

But as she spoke I heard sounds again in the hall below; a man's step this time; and the truth leaped out on me.

"Madam," I said, pushing past her, "there is someone in the house—"

"Someone—?"

"Mr Brympton, I think – I hear his step below—"

A dreadful look came over her, and without a word, she dropped flat at my feet. I fell on my knees and tried to lift her: by the way she breathed I saw it was no common faint. But as I raised her head there came quick steps on the stairs and across the hall: the door was flung open, and there stood Mr Brympton, in his travelling-clothes, the snow dripping from him. He drew back with a start as he saw me kneeling by my mistress.

"What the devil is this?" he shouted. He was less high-coloured than usual, and the red spot came out on his forehead.

"Mrs Brympton has fainted, sir," said I.

He laughed unsteadily and pushed by me. "It's a pity she didn't choose a more convenient moment. I'm sorry to disturb her, but—"

I raised myself up, aghast at the man's action.

"Sir," said I, "are you mad? What are you doing?"

"Going to meet a friend," said he, and seemed to make for the dressing-room.

At that my heart turned over. I don't know what I thought or feared; but I sprang up and caught him by the sleeve.

"Sir, sir," said I, "for pity's sake look to your wife!"

He shook me off furiously.

"It seems that's done for me," says he, and caught hold of the dressing-room door.

At that moment I heard a slight noise inside. Slight as it was, he heard it too, and tore the door open; but as he did so he dropped back. On the threshold stood Emma Saxon. All was dark behind her, but I saw her plainly, and so did he. He threw up his hands as if to hide his face from her; and when I looked again she was gone.

He stood motionless, as if the strength had run out of him; and in the stillness my mistress suddenly raised herself, and opening her eyes fixed a look on him. Then she fell back, and I saw the death-flutter pass over her. . . .

We buried her on the third day, in a driving snow-storm. There were few people in the church, for it was bad weather to come from town, and I've a notion my mistress was one that hadn't many near friends. Mr Ranford was among the last to come, just before they carried her up the aisle. He was in black, of course, being such a friend of the family, and I never saw a gentleman so pale. As he passed me I noticed that he leaned a trifle on a stick he carried; and I fancy Mr Brympton noticed it too, for the red spot came out sharp on his forehead, and all through the service he kept staring across the church at Mr Ranford, instead of following the prayers as a mourner should.

When it was over and we went out to the graveyard, Mr Ranford had disappeared, and as soon as my poor mistress's body was underground, Mr Brympton jumped into the carriage nearest the gate and drove off without a word to any of us. I heard him call out, "To the station," and we servants went back alone to the house.

The Duenna

Marie Belloc Lowndes

Location: Treville Place, Yorkshire.

Time: January, 1925.

Eyewitness Description: *"She found with delight that Mrs Doray spoke excellent French and told her that if she heard strange sounds, or maybe a stifled sob, she was not to feel afraid, as it would only be the wraith of* La Belle Julie *expiating her sin where that sin had not only been committed but exulted in . . ."*

Author: Marie Belloc Lowndes (1868–1947) was as challenging and forward-looking in her fiction as her American contemporary Edith Wharton. The daughter of a radical mother and French barrister father, and sister of Hilaire Belloc, she grew up in a free-speaking household and had her first story published when she was just 16. An early champion of feminism and women's rights, she became famous in 1913 with *The Lodger*, a fictionalized version of the Jack the Ripper murders which sold over a million copies. In 1919 she published a novel, *The Lonely House*, and several short stories about a short, stout, very vain former Paris *Sûreté* policeman turned private detective, Hercules Popeau. This rather pompous little man with his intense curiosity and keen insight into human nature has been suggested as a source of inspiration for Agatha Christie's more famous Hercule Poirot, who made his debut in 1920. Be that as it may, Lowndes also wrote some very significant stories of "ghost feelers" like this tale of beautiful, neglected Laura Delacourt who finds her temptation to commit adultery tested by an unseen force that both entices and frightens her.

"Que vous me coutez cher, O, mon cœur, pour vos plaisirs."

1

Laura Delacourt, after a long and gallant defence of what those who formed the old-fashioned world to which she belonged would have called her virtue, had capitulated to the entreaties of Julian Treville. They had been friends – from tomorrow they would be lovers.

As she lay enfolded in his arms, her head resting on his breast, while now and again their lips met in a trembling, clinging kiss, the strangest and, in some ways, the most incongruous thoughts flitted shadow-wise through her mind, mingled with terror at the possible, though not the probable, consequences of her surrender.

Her husband, Roger Delacourt, was thirty years older than herself. Though still a vigorous man, he had come to a time of life when even a vigorous man longs instinctively for warmth; so he had left London the day after Christmas Day to join a friend's yacht for a month's cruise in the Mediterranean. And now, just a week later, the wife whom he considered a negligible quantity in his self-indulgent, still agreeable existence, had consented to embark on what she knew must be a perilous adventure in a one-storied stone house, well named The Folly, built by Julian Treville's great-grandfather.

Long, low, fantastic – it stood at the narrow end of a wide lake on the confines of his property; and a French dancer, known in the Paris of her day as *La Belle Julie*, had spent there a lifetime in exile.

Though Laura in her lover's arms felt strangely at peace, her homing joy was threaded with terror. Constantly her thoughts reverted to her child, David, who, till the man who now held her so closely to him had come into her life, had been the only thing that made that then mournful life worth living.

The boy was spending the New Year with his mother's one close woman friend and her houseful of happy children, so Laura hoped her little son did not miss her. At any other time the thought that this might be so would have stabbed her with unreasonable pain, but what now filled her heart with shrinking fear was the dread thought of David's father, and of the punishment he would exact if he found her out.

Like so many men of his type and generation Roger Delacourt had a poor opinion of women. He believed that the woman tempted always falls. But, again true to type, he made, in this one matter, an exception as to his own wife. That Laura might be tempted was a possibility which never entered his shrewd and cynical mind; and had he been compelled to admit the temptation, he would have felt confident as to her power of resistance. So it was that she faced the awful certainty that were she ever "found out", immediate separation from her son, followed by a divorce, would be her punishment.

She had been a child of seventeen when her mother had elected to sell her into the slavery of marriage with the voluptuary to whom she had now been married ten years. For three years she had been her husband's plaything, and then, suddenly, when their boy was about two years old, he had tired of her. Even so, they lived, both in London and in the country, under the same roof, and many of the people about them thought the Delacourts got on better than do most modern couples. They were, however, often apart for weeks at a time, for Roger Delacourt still hunted, still shot, still fished, with unabated zest, and his wife did none of these things.

As time went on, Laura's joyless life was at once illumined and shadowed by her passionate love for her child, for all great love brings with it fear. A year ago, by his father's decree, David had been sent to a noted preparatory school, leaving his young mother forlornly lonely. It was then that she had met Julian Treville.

By one of those odd accidents of which human life is full, he and she had been the only two guests of an aged brother and sister, distant connections of Laura's own, in a Yorkshire country house. Cousin John and Cousin Mary had watched the sudden friendship with approval. "Dear Laura Delacourt is just the friend for Julian Treville," said old Mary to old John. She had added, pensively, "It is so very nice for a nice young man to have a nice married woman as a nice friend."

That had been eight months ago, and since then Treville had altered the whole of his life for Laura's sake, she, till to-day, taking everything and giving nothing, as is so often the way with a woman who believes herself to be good . . .

During their long drive the lovers scarcely spoke; to be alone together, as they were now, was sufficient bliss.

Treville had met her at a distant railway junction where a motor had been hired in the name of "Mrs Darcy." This was part of the plan which was to make the few who must perforce know of her presence at The Folly believe her there as the guest of Treville's stepmother, who was now abroad.

Darcy had been Laura's maiden name, and it was the only name she felt she had the right to call herself. She and her lover were both amateurs in the most dangerous and most exciting drama for which a man and woman can be cast.

The hireling motor had brought them across wide stretches of solitary downland, but now they were speeding through one of the long avenues of Treville Place, their journey nearly at an end.

His neighbours would have told you that Julian Treville was a reserved, queer kind of chap. Laura Delacourt was the first woman he had ever loved; and even now, in this hour of unexpected, craved-for joy, he was asking himself if even his great love gave him the right to make her run what seemed an exceedingly slight risk of detection and consequent disgrace.

Each felt a sense of foreboding, though Laura's reason told her that her terrors were vain, and that it was conscience alone that made her feel afraid. Every possible danger had been countered by her companion. Her pride, her delicacy, her sense of shame – was it false shame? – had been studied by him with a selfless devotion which had deeply moved her. Thus he was leaving her to spend a lonely evening, tended by the old Frenchwoman, who, together with her husband, waited on The Folly's infrequent occupants.

The now aged couple in their hot youth had been on the losing side in the Paris Commune of 1871. They had been saved from imprisonment, possibly worse, by Julian Treville's grandmother, a lawless, high-minded Scotchwoman who called herself a Liberal. She had brought them to England, and for fifty odd years they had lived in a cottage a quarter of a mile from The Folly. There was small reason, as Treville could have argued with perfect truth, to be afraid of this old pair. But Laura did feel afraid, and so it had been arranged between the lovers that only to-morrow, after she had spent at The Folly a solitary night and day, would he, at the close of a day's hunting, share "Mrs Darcy's" simple dinner . . .

The motor stopped, and the man and woman, who had been clasped in each other's arms, drew quickly apart.

"We have to get out here," muttered Treville, "for there is no carriage-way down to The Folly. I'll carry your bag."

Keeping up the sorry comedy she paid off and dismissed the chauffeur.

In the now fading daylight Laura saw that to her left the ground sloped steeply down to the shores of a lake whose now grey waters narrowed to a point beyond which there stood a low, pillared building. It was more like an eighteenth-century orangery than a house meant for human habitation. Eerily beautiful, and yet exceedingly desolate, to Laura The Folly appeared unreal – a fairy dwelling in that Kingdom of Romance whither her feet had never strayed, rather than a place where men and women had joyed and sorrowed, lived and died.

"If only I could feel that you will never regret that you came here," Treville whispered.

She answered quickly, "I shall always be glad, not sorry, Julian."

He took her hand and raised it to his lips. Then he said: "Old Célestine will have it that The Folly is haunted by *La Belle Julie*. You're not afraid of ghosts, my dearest?"

Laura smiled a little wanly in the twilight. "Far more afraid of flesh and blood than ghosts," she murmured. "Where do Célestine and her husband live, Julian?"

"We can't see their cottage from here; but it's quite close by." His voice sank: "I've told them that you're not afraid of being in the house alone at night."

They went down a winding footpath, she clinging to him for very joy in his nearness, till they reached the stone-paved space which lay between the shore of the lake and the low grey building. And then, suddenly, while they were walking towards the high front door, Laura gave a stifled cry, for a gnome-like figure had sprung, as if from nowhere, across their path.

"Here's old Jacques," exclaimed Treville vexedly. "He always shows an excess of zeal!"

The little Frenchman was gesticulating and talking eagerly, explaining that fires had been burning all day in the three rooms which were to be occupied by the visitor. He further told, at unnerving length, that Célestine would be at The Folly herself very shortly to install "Madame."

When the old chap had shuffled off, Julian Treville put a key in the lock of the heavy old door; taking Laura's slight figure up into his strong arms, he lifted her over the threshold straight into an enchanting living-room where nothing had been altered for over a hundred years.

She gave a cry of delight. "What a delicious place, Julian! I never thought it would be like this—"

A log fire threw up high flames in the deep fire-place, and a lighted lamp stood on a round, gilt-rimmed, marble table close to a low and roomy, if rather stiff, square arm-chair. The few pieces of fine Empire furniture were covered with faded yellow satin which had been brought from Paris when Napoleon was ironing out the frontiers of Europe, for the Treville of that day had furnished The Folly to please the Frenchwoman he loved. The walls of the room were hung with turquoise silk. There was a carved-wood gilt mirror over the mantelpiece, and on the right-hand wall there hung an oval pastel of *La Belle Julie*.

Hand in hand they stood, looking up at the lovely smiling face.

"According to tradition," said Treville, "that picture was the only thing the poor soul brought with her when she left France. The powdered hair proves it must have been done when Julie was in her teens, before the Revolution. My great-great-grandfather fell in love with her when she must have been well over thirty—"

Then, dropping the mask he had worn since they had left the motor, "Laura!" he exclaimed; "Beloved! At last – at last!"

For him, and for her, too, the world sank away, though, even so, that which is now called her subconscious self was listening, full of shrinking fear, for the sound of a key in the lock . . .

He said at last in a low, shaken voice, "And now I suppose that I must leave you? . . ."

Her lips formed the words telling him that he had been over-scrupulous in his care for her, that they might as well brave the curious eyes of old Célestine tonight as tomorrow. And then, before she could utter them, there came the sound of steps on the stone path outside.

"It's Célestine, come before her time," muttered Treville.

The front door opened and Laura, turning round quickly, saw a tall, thin, old woman, clad in a black stuff dress; a white muslin cap lay on her white hair, and over her shoulders a fur cape.

Standing just within the door, which she had shut behind her, she cast a long, measuring glance at her master, and at the lady who had come to spend a week at The Folly at this untoward time of the year.

It was a kindly, even an indulgent, glance, but it made Laura feel suddenly afraid.

"I come to ask," exclaimed Célestine in very fair English, "if Madame is comfortable? Is there anything I can do for Madame besides laying the table and cooking Madame's dinner?"

"I don't think so – everything is delightful," murmured Laura.

The old woman, taking a few steps forward, vanished into what the newcomer was soon to learn was the dining-room.

Treville said wistfully, "And now I must leave you—"

Laura whispered faintly, "I am a coward, Julian."

He answered eagerly, "I would not have you other than you are."

She took his hand in hers, and laid it against her cheek. "It's because of David – only because of David – that I feel afraid."

And as she said the word "afraid", the old Frenchwoman came

back into the room. "Would Madame like me to come in to sleep each night?" she asked.

Treville answered for Laura. "Mrs Darcy prefers being here alone. She will live as does my stepmother, when she is staying at The Folly."

He turned to Laura. "I will say good night now, but after I come in from hunting to-morrow I'll come down, as you have kindly asked me to do, to dinner."

She answered in a low voice, "I shall be so glad to see you to-morrow evening."

"By the way—" he waited a moment.

Why did Célestine stand there, looking at them? Why didn't she go away, as she would have hastened to do if his companion had been his stepmother?

But at last he ended his sentence with "—there's a private telephone from The Folly to my study, if you have occasion to speak to me."

After her lover had left her with a quiet clasp of the hand, and after old Célestine had gone off, at last, to her own quarters, Laura sat down and covered her face with her hands; she felt both happy and miserable, exultant and afraid.

At last she threw a tender thought to *La Belle Julie*, who had given up everything that to her should have seemed worth living for, in a material sense, to follow the man she loved into what must have been a piteous exile. And yet Laura felt tonight that she too would have had that cruel courage, had she not been the mother of a child.

She got up at last, and walked across the room, wondering how lovely Julie had fared during the long, weary hours she must have waited here for her lover.

Would the Treville of that day have done for his Julie what Julian had done for his Laura to-night? Would he have respected her cowardly fears? She felt sure not. Julie's Treville might have gone away, but Julie's Treville would have come back. Well, she knew that Laura's Treville would not return to-night.

And then she turned round quickly, for across the still air of the room had fallen the sound of a deep sigh.

Swiftly Laura went across to the door, masked by a stiff curtain of tapestry, which led into the corridor linking the various rooms of The Folly.

She lifted the curtain, and slipped out into the dimly lit corridor, but there was no one there.

Coming back into the sitting-room she sat down again by the fire, convinced that her nerves had played her a trick, and once more she found herself thinking of *La Belle Julie*. She felt as if there was a bond between herself and the long dead dancer; the bond which links all poor women who embark on the danger-fraught adventure of secret, illicit love.

2

That evening Célestine proved that her hand had not lost its French cunning. But Laura was too excited, as well as too tired, to eat. The old woman made no comment as to that, but when at last she found with delight that "Mrs Darcy" spoke excellent French, she did tell her that if she heard strange signs, or maybe a stifled sob, she was not to feel afraid, as it would only be the wraith of *La Belle Julie* expatiating her sin where that sin had not only been committed but exulted in.

But it was not the ghost of Julie of whom Laura was afraid – it was Célestine, with her gleaming brown eyes and shrewd face, whom she feared. She breathed more easily when the old Frenchwoman was gone. . . .

The bedchamber where she was to sleep had also been left unaltered for a hundred years and more. It was hung with faded lavender silk, and on the floor lay an Aubusson carpet, while at the farther end of the room was the wide, low, Directoire bed which had been brought from the Paris of the young Napoleon.

The telephone of which Treville had told her stood on a table close to her pillow. How amazed would Julie have been to hear that a day would come when a woman lying in what had been her bed would be able to speak from there to her lover – the man who, like Julie's own lover, was master of the great house which stood over a mile away from The Folly.

Célestine had forgotten to draw the heavy embroidered yellow silk curtains, and Laura walked to the nearest window and looked out on to the gleaming waters of the lake.

Across to the right rose dense clumps of dark ilexes; to the left tall trees, now stripped of leaves, stood black and drear against the winter sky.

The telephone bell tinkled. She turned and ran across the room, and then she heard Julian Treville's voice as strong, as clear, as love-laden, as if he were with her here, tonight.

*   *   *

The next day's sun illumined a beautiful soft winter morning, and Laura felt not only tremblingly happy, but also what she had not thought to feel – at peace. She went for a walk round the lake, then enjoyed the luncheon Célestine had prepared for her. Célestine, so much was clear, was set on waiting on her far more assiduously than she did on her own mistress, old Mrs Treville.

About three o'clock Laura went again out of doors, to come in, an hour later, to find the lamp in the drawing-room lit, though it was not yet dark.

She went through into her bedroom, and then she heard the telephone ring – not loudly, insistently, as it had rung last night, but with a thin, tenuous sound.

Eagerly she went over to the side of the bed and took off the receiver, and then, as if coming from infinitely far away, she heard Julian Treville's voice.

"Are you there, my darling? I am in darkness, but our love is my beacon, and my heart is full of you," and his voice, his dear voice, sank away . . .

Then he was home from hunting far sooner than he had thought to be? This surely meant that very soon he would be here.

She took off her hat and coat, put on a frock Julian had once said he loved to see her wear, and then went back to wait for his coming in the sitting-room. But the moments became minutes, and the minutes quarters of an hour, and the time went by very slowly.

At last a key turned in the lock of the front door, and she stood up – then felt a pang of bitter disappointment, for it was only the old Frenchwoman who passed through into the room.

Célestine shut the door behind her, and then she came close up to where Laura had sat down again, wearily, by the fire.

"Madame!" she exclaimed. And then she stopped short, a tragic look on her pale withered face.

Laura's thoughts flew to her child. She leapt up from her chair. "What is it, Célestine? A message for me?"

Very solemnly Célestine said the fearful words: "Prepare for ill news."

"Ill news?" Oh! how could she have left her child? "What do you mean?" cried Laura violently.

"There is no message come for you. But – but – our good kind master, Mr Treville, is dead. He was killed out hunting today. I was in the village when the news was brought." She went on, speaking in quick gasps: "His horse – how say you?—" she waited, and then, finding the word she sought, "stumbled," she sobbed.

Laura for a moment stood still, as if she had not heard, or did not understand the purport of, the other's words, and then she gave a strangled cry, as Célestine, gathering her to her gaunt breast, said quickly in French, "My poor, poor lady! Well did I see that my master loved you – and that you loved him. You must leave The Folly tonight, at once. They have already telegraphed for old Mrs Treville."

3

An hour later Laura was dressed, ready for departure. In a few minutes from now Célestine would be here to carry her bag to the car which the old Frenchwoman had procured to take her to the distant station where Julian Treville had met her yesterday. Yesterday? It seemed æons of time ago.

Suddenly there came a loud knock on the heavy door, and at once she walked across the room and opened it wide.

Nothing mattered to her now; and when Roger Delacourt strode into the room she felt scarce any surprise, and that though she had believed him a thousand miles away.

"Are you alone, Laura?" he asked harshly.

There was a look of savage anger in his face. His vanity – the vanity of a man no longer young who has had a strong allure for women – felt bruised in its tenderest part.

As she said nothing, only looked at him with an air of tragic pain and defiance, he went on, jeeringly, "No doubt you are asking yourself how I found out where you were, and on what pretty business you were engaged? I will give you a clue, and you can guess the rest for yourself. I had to come back unexpectedly to England, and the one person to whom you gave this address – I presume so you might have news of the boy – unwittingly gave you away!"

She still said nothing, and he went on bitterly: "I thought you – fool that I was – a good woman. But from what I hear I now know that your lover, Julian Treville, is no new friend. But I do not care, I do not enquire, how often you have been here—"

"This is the first time," she said dully, "that I have been here."

And then it was as if something outside herself impelled her to add the untrue words, "I am not, as you seem to think, Roger, alone—" for with a sharp thrill of intense fear she had remembered her child.

"Not alone?" he repeated incredulously. And then he saw the tapestried curtain which hung over the door, opposite to where he stood, move, and he realized that someone was behind it, listening.

He took a few steps forward, and pulled the curtain roughly back. But the dimly illumined corridor was empty; whoever had been there eavesdropping had scurried away into shelter.

He came back to the spot where he had been standing before. Baffled, angry, still full of doubt, and yet, deep in his heart, unutterably relieved. Already a half-suspicion that Laura was sheltering some woman friend engaged in an intrigue had flashed into his mind, and the suspicion crystallised into certainty as he looked loweringly into her pale, set face. She did not look as more than once, in the days of his good fortunes, he had seen a guilty wife look.

Yes, that must be the solution of this queer secret escapade! Laura, poor fool! had been the screen behind which hid a pair of guilty lovers. Thirty years ago a woman had played the same thankless part in an intrigue of his own.

"Who is your friend?" he asked roughly.

Her lips did not move, and he told himself, with a certain satisfaction, that she was paralysed with fear.

"How long have you and your friend been here? That, at least, you can tell me."

At last she whispered what sounded like the absurd answer, "Just a hundred years."

Then, turning quickly, she went through the door which gave into the dining-room, and shut it behind her.

Roger Delacourt began pacing about the room; he felt what he had very seldom come to feel in his long, hard, if till now fortunate, life, just a little foolish, but relieved – unutterably relieved – and glad.

The Folly? Well named indeed! The very setting for a secret love-affair. Beautiful, too, in its strange and romantic aloofness from everyday life.

He went and gazed up at the pastel, which was the only picture in the room. What an exquisite, flower-like face! It reminded him of a French girl he had known when he was a very young man. Her name had been Zélie Mignard, and she had been reader-companion to an old marquise with whose son he had spent a long summer and autumn on the Loire. From the first moment he had seen Zélie she had attracted him violently, and though little more than a boy, he had made up his mind to seduce her. But she had resisted him, and then, in spite of himself, he had come to love her with that ardent first love which returns no more.

Suddenly there fell on the air of the still room the sound of a long, deep sigh. He wheeled sharply round to see that between himself and the still uncurtained window there stood a slender young woman – Laura's peccant friend, without a doubt!

He could not see her very clearly, yet of that he was not sorry, for he was not and he had never been – he told himself with an inward chuckle – the man to spoil sport.

Secretly he could afford to smile at the thought of his cold, passionless wife acting as duenna. Hard man as he was, his old heart warmed to the erring stranger, the more so that her sudden apparition had removed a last lingering doubt from his mind.

She threw out her slender hands with a gesture that again seemed to fill his mind with memories of his vanished youth, and there floated across the dark room the whispered words, "Be not unkind." And then – did she say "Remember Zélie?"

No, no – it was his heart, less atrophied than he had thought it to be, which had evoked, quickened into life, the name of his first love, the French girl who, if alive, must be – hateful, disturbing thought – an old woman today.

Then, as he gazed at her, the shadowy figure swiftly walked across the room, and so through the tapestry curtain.

He waited a moment, then slowly passed through the dining-room, and so into the firelit bedroom beyond.

His wife was standing by the window, looking as wraith-like as had done, just now, her friend. She was staring out into the darkness, her arms hanging by her side. She had not turned round when she had heard the door of the room open.

"Laura!" said her husband gruffly. And then she turned and cast on him a suffering alien glance.

"I accept your explanation of your presence here. And, well, I apologize for my foolish suspicions. Still, you're not a child! The part you're playing is not one any man would wish his wife to play. How long do you – and your friend – intend to stay here?"

"We meant to stay ten days," she said listlessly, "but as you're home, Roger, I'll leave now, if you like."

"And your friend, Laura, what of her?"

"I think she has already left The Folly."

She waited a moment, then forced herself to add, "Julian Treville was killed today out hunting – as I suppose you know."

"Good God! How awful! Believe me, I did not know—"

Roger Delacourt was sincerely affected, as well he might be, for already he had arranged, in his own mind, to go to Leicestershire next week.

And, strange to say, as the two travelled up to town together, he was more considerate in his manner to his wife than he had been for many years. For one thing, he felt that this curious episode proved Laura to have more heart than he had given her credit for. But, being the manner of man and of husband he happened to be, he naturally did not approve of her having risked her spotless reputation in playing the part of duenna to a friend who had loved not wisely but too well. He trusted that what had just happened would prove a lesson to his wife and, for the matter of that, to himself.

Clytie

Eudora Welty

Location: Farr's Gin, Jackson, Mississippi.

Time: June, 1941.

Eyewitness Description: *"This face had been very close to hers; almost familiar, almost accessible. And then the face of Octavia was thrust between, and at other times the apoplectic face of her father, the face of her brother Henry with the bullet hole through the forehead . . ."*

Author: Eudora Welty (1909–2001) has been described as the "Queen of Southern Gothic", a story tradition evolved from the original European version set in the southern states of the USA and including tales by the likes of William Faulkner ("A Rose for Emily", 1930) and Flannery O'Connor ("Judgement Day" 1956). Growing up in Jackson, Mississippi, Welty worked for a local radio station and as a journalist for the *Commercial Appeal* writing and photographing the local area. During her later career she lectured on writing and for a time had an extended residence at Cambridge University where she became the first woman to enter Peterhouse College. Her fascination with the gothic was evident in her early short stories and particularly a novel, *The Robber Bridegroom* (1946), set in Natchez about a highwayman masquerading as a part-time gentleman, which earned laudatory reviews for its "mystery, sense of the inexplicable and gothic horror". Among her stories cast in the same mould are "A Still Moment" (1943), "Moon Lake" (1949) and the earlier "Clytie" which she wrote for *The Southern Review* in 1941 and is the account of another "ghost feeler", the enigmatic, mysterious Clytie Farr, as well as a landmark in 20th century Gothic fiction.

I t was late afternoon, with heavy silver clouds which looked bigger and wider than cotton-fields, and presently it began to rain. Big round drops fell, still in the sunlight, on the hot tin sheds, and stained the white false fronts of the row of stores in the little town of Farr's Gin. A hen and her string of yellow chickens ran in great alarm across the road, the dust turned river-brown, and the birds flew down into it immediately, seeking out little pockets in which to take baths. The bird dogs got up from the doorways of the stores, shook themselves down to the tail, and went to lie inside. The few people standing with long shadows on the level road moved over into the post office. A little boy kicked his bare heels into the sides of his mule, which proceeded slowly through the town toward the country.

After everyone else had gone under cover, Miss Clytie Farr stood still in the road, peering ahead in her near-sighted way, and as wet as the little birds.

She usually came out of the old big house about this time in the afternoon, and hurried through the town. It used to be that she ran about on some pretext or other, and for a while she made soft-voiced explanations that nobody could hear, and after that she began to charge up bills, which the postmistress declared would never be paid any more than anyone else's, even if the Farrs were too good to associate with other people. But now Clytie came for nothing. She came every day, and no one spoke to her any more: she would be in such a hurry, and couldn't see who it was. And every Saturday they expected her to be run over, the way she darted out into the road with all the horses and trucks.

It might be simply that Miss Clytie's wits were all leaving her, said the ladies standing in the door to feel the cool, the way her sisters had left her; and she would just wait there to be told to go home. She would have to wring out everything she had on – the waist and the jumper skirt, and the long black stockings. On her head was one of the straw hats from the furnishing store, with an old black satin ribbon pinned to it to make it a better hat, and tied under the chin. Now, under the force of the rain, while the ladies watched, the hat slowly began to sag down on each side until it looked even more absurd and done for, like an old bonnet on a horse. And indeed it was with the patience almost of a beast that Miss Clytie stood there in the rain and stuck her long empty arms out a little from her sides, as if she were waiting for something to come along the road and drive her to shelter.

In a little while there was a clap of thunder.

"Miss Clytie! Go in out of the rain, Miss Clytie!" someone called.

The old maid did not look around, but clenched her hands and drew them up under her armpits, and sticking out her elbows like hen wings, she ran out of the street, her poor hat creaking and beating about her ears.

"Well, there goes Miss Clytie," the ladies said, and one of them had a premonition about her.

Through the rushing water in the sunken path under the four wet black cedars, which smelled bitter as smoke, she ran to the house.

"Where the devil have you been?" called the older sister, Octavia, from an upper window.

Clytie looked up in time to see the curtain fall back.

She went inside, into the hall, and waited, shivering. It was very dark and bare. The only light was falling on the white sheet which covered the solitary piece of furniture, an organ. The red curtains over the parlour door, held back by ivory hands, were still as tree trunks in the airless house. Every window was closed, and every shade was down, though behind them the rain could still be heard.

Clytie took a match and advanced to the stair-post, where the bronze cast of Hermes was holding up a gas fixture; and at once above this, lighted up, but quite still, like one of the unmovable relics of the house, Octavia stood waiting on the stairs.

She stood solidly before the violet-and-lemon-coloured glass of the window on the landing, and her wrinkled, unresting fingers took hold of the diamond cornucopia she always wore in the bosom of her long black dress. It was an unwithered grand gesture of hers, fondling the cornucopia.

"It is not enough that we are waiting here – hungry," Octavia was saying, while Clytie waited below. "But you must sneak away and not answer when I call you. Go off and wander about the streets. Common – common—!"

"Never mind, Sister," Clytie managed to say.

"But you always return."

"Of course. . . ."

"Gerald is awake now, and so is Papa," said Octavia, in the same vindictive voice – a loud voice, for she was usually calling.

Clytie went to the kitchen and lighted the kindling in the wood stove. As if she were freezing cold in June, she stood before its open door, and soon a look of interest and pleasure lighted her face, which had in the last years grown weather-beaten in spite of the straw hat. Now some dream was resumed. In the street she had been thinking about the face of a child she had just seen. The child, playing with another of the same age, chasing it with a toy pistol, had looked at her with such an open, serene, trusting expression as she passed by! With this small, peaceful face still in her mind, rosy like these flames, like an inspiration which drives all other thoughts away, Clytie had forgotten herself and had been obliged to stand where she was in the middle of the road. But the rain had come down, and someone had shouted at her, and she had not been able to reach the end of her meditations.

It had been a long time now, since Clytie had first begun to watch faces, and to think about them.

Anyone could have told you that there were not more than 150 people in Farr's Gin, counting Negroes. Yet the number of faces seemed to Clytie almost infinite. She knew now to look slowly and carefully at a face; she was convinced that it was impossible to see it all at once. The first thing she discovered about a face was always that she had never seen it before. When she began to look at people's actual countenances there was no more familiarity in the world for her. The most profound, the most moving sight in the whole world must be a face. Was it possible to comprehend the eyes and the mouths of other people, which concealed she knew not what, and secretly asked for still another unknown thing? The mysterious smile of the old man who sold peanuts by the church gate returned to her; his face seemed for a moment to rest upon the iron door of the stove, set into the lion's mane. Other people said Mr Tom Bate's Boy, as he called himself, stared away with a face as clean-blank as a water-melon seed, but to Clytie, who observed grains of sand in his eyes and in his old yellow lashes, he might have come out of a desert, like an Egyptian.

But while she was thinking of Mr Tom Bate's Boy, there was a terrible gust of wind which struck her back, and she turned around. The long green window-shade billowed and plunged. The kitchen window was wide open – she had done it herself. She closed it gently. Octavia, who never came all the way downstairs for any reason, would never have forgiven her for an open window, if she knew. Rain and sun signified ruin, in Octavia's mind. Going over the whole house, Clytie made sure that everything was safe. It was not that ruin in itself could distress Octavia. Ruin or encroachment, even upon priceless treasures and even in poverty, held no terror for her; it was simply some form of prying from without, and this she would not forgive. All of that was to be seen in her face.

Clytie cooked the three meals on the stove, for they all ate different things, and set the three trays. She had to carry them in proper order up the stairs. She frowned in concentration, for it was hard to keep all the dishes straight, to make them come out right in the end, as Old Lethy could have done. They had had to give up the cook long ago when their father suffered the first stroke. Their father had been fond of Old Lethy, she had been his nurse in childhood, and she had come back out of the country to see him when she heard he was dying. Old Lethy had come and knocked at the back door. And as usual, at the first disturbance, front or back, Octavia had peered down from behind the curtain and cried, "Go away! Go away! What the devil have you come *here* for?" And although Old Lethy and their father had both pleaded that they might be allowed to see each other, Octavia had shouted as she always did, and sent the intruder away. Clytie had stood as usual, speechless in the kitchen, until finally she had repeated after her sister, "Lethy, go away." But their father had not died. He was, instead, paralyzed, blind, and able only to call out in unintelligible sounds and to swallow liquids. Lethy still would come to the back door now and then, but they never let her in, and the old man no longer heard or knew enough to beg to see her. There was only one caller admitted to his room. Once a week the barber came by appointment to shave him. On this occasion not a word was spoken by anyone.

Clytie went up to her father's room first and set the tray down on a little marble table they kept by his bed.

"I want to feed Papa," said Octavia, taking the bowl from her hands.

"You fed him last time," said Clytie.

Relinquishing the bowl, she looked down at the pointed face on the pillow. To-morrow was the barber's day, and the sharp black points, at their longest, stuck out like needles all over the wasted cheeks. The old man's eyes were half closed. It was impossible to know what he felt. He looked as though he were really far away, neglected, free. . . . Octavia began to feed him.

Without taking her eyes from her father's face, Clytie suddenly began to speak in rapid, bitter words to her sister, the wildest words that came to her head. But soon she began to cry and gasp, like a small child who has been pushed by the big boys into the water.

"That is enough," said Octavia.

But Clytie could not take her eyes from her father's unshaven face and his still-open mouth.

"And I'll feed him tomorrow if I want to," said Octavia. She stood up. The thick hair, growing back after an illness and dyed almost purple, fell over her forehead. Beginning at her throat, the long accordion pleats which fell the length of her gown opened and closed over her breasts as she breathed. "Have you forgotten Gerald?" she said. "And I am hungry too."

Clytie went back to the kitchen and brought her sister's supper. Then she brought her brother's.

Gerald's room was dark, and she had to push through the usual barricade. The smell of whisky was everywhere; it even flew up in the striking of the match when she lighted the jet.

"It's night," said Clytie presently.

Gerald lay on his bed looking at her. In the bad light he resembled his father.

"There's some more coffee down in the kitchen," said Clytie.

"Would you bring it to me?" Gerald asked. He stared at her in an exhausted, serious way.

She stooped and held him up. He drank the coffee while she bent over him with her eyes closed, resting.

Presently he pushed her away and fell back on the bed, and began to describe how nice it was when he had a little house of his own down the street, all new, with all conveniences, gas stove, electric lights, when he was married to Rosemary. Rosemary – she had given up a job in the next town, just to marry him. How had it happened that she had left him so soon? It meant nothing that he had threatened time and again to shoot her, it was nothing at all that he had pointed the gun against her breast. She had not understood. It was only that he had relished his contentment. He had only wanted to play with her. In a way he had wanted to show her that he loved her above life and death.

"Above life and death," he repeated, closing his eyes.

Clytie did not make an answer, as Octavia always did during these scenes, which were bound to end in Gerald's tears.

Outside the closed window a mocking-bird began to sing. Clytie held back the curtain and pressed her ear against the glass. The rain had dropped. The bird's song sounded in liquid drops down through the pitch-black trees and the night.

"Go to hell," Gerald said. His head was under the pillow.

She took up the tray, and left Gerald with his face hidden. It was not necessary for her to look at any of their faces. It was their faces which came between.

Hurrying, she went down to the kitchen and began to eat her own supper.

Their faces came between her face and another. It was their faces which had come pushing in between, long ago, to hide some face that had looked back at her. And now it was hard to remember the way it looked, or the time when she had seen it first. It must have been when she was young. Yes, in a sort of arbour, hadn't she laughed, leaned forward . . . and that vision of a face – which was a little like all the other faces, the trusting child's, the innocent old traveller's, even the greedy barber's and Lethy's and the wandering peddlers' who one by one knocked and went unanswered at the door – and yet different, yet far more – this face had been very close to hers, almost familiar, almost accessible. And then the face of Octavia was thrust between, and at other times the apoplectic face of her father, the face of her brother Gerald and the face of her brother Henry with the bullet hole through the forehead. . . . It was purely for a resemblance to a vision that she examined the secret, mysterious, unrepeated faces she met in the street of Farr's Gin.

But there was always an interruption. If anyone spoke to her, she fled. If she saw she was going to meet someone on the street, she had been known to dart behind a bush and hold a small branch in front of her face until the person had gone by. When anyone called her by name, she turned first red, then white, and looked somehow, as one of the ladies in the store remarked, *disappointed*.

She was becoming more frightened all the time, too. People could tell because she never dressed up any more. For years, every once in a while, she would come out in what was called an "outfit," all in a hunter's green, a hat that came down around her face like a bucket, a green silk dress, even green shoes with pointed toes. She would wear the outfit all one day, if it was a pretty day, and then next morning she would be back in the faded jumper with her old hat tied under the chin, as if the outfit had been a dream. It had been a long time now since Clytie had dressed up so that you could see her coming.

Once in a while when a neighbour, trying to be kind or only being curious, would ask her opinion about anything – such as a pattern of crochet – she would not run away; but, giving a thin trapped smile, she would say in a childish voice, "It's nice." But, the ladies always added, nothing that came anywhere close to the Farrs' house was nice for long.

"It's nice," said Clytie when the old lady next door showed her the new rosebush she had planted, all in bloom.

But before an hour was gone, she came running out of her house screaming, "My sister Octavia says you take that rosebush up! My sister Octavia says you take that rosebush up and move it away from our fence! If you don't I'll kill you! You take it away."

And on the other side of the Farrs lived a family with a little boy who was always playing in his yard. Octavia's cat would go under the fence, and he would take it and hold it in his arms. He had a song he sang to the Farrs' cat. Clytie would come running straight out of the house, flaming with her message from Octavia. "Don't you do that! Don't you do that!" she would cry in anguish. "If you do that again, I'll have to kill you!"

And she would run back to the vegetable patch and begin to curse.

The cursing was new, and she cursed softly, like a singer going over a song for the first time. But it was something she could not stop. Words which at first horrified Clytie poured in a full, light stream from her throat, which soon, nevertheless, felt strangely relaxed and rested. She cursed all alone in the peace of the vegetable garden. Everybody said, in something like deprecation, that she was only imitating her older sister, who used to go out to that same garden and curse in that same way, years ago, but in a remarkably loud, commanding voice that could be heard in the post office.

Sometimes in the middle of her words Clytie glanced up to where Octavia, at her window, looked down at her. When she let the curtain drop at last, Clytie would be left there speechless.

Finally, in a gentleness compounded of fright and exhaustion and love, an overwhelming love, she would wander through the gate and out through the town, gradually beginning to move faster, until her long legs gathered a ridiculous, rushing speed. No one in town could have kept up with Miss Clytie, they said, giving them an even start.

She always ate rapidly, too, all alone in the kitchen, as she was eating now. She bit the meat savagely from the heavy silver fork and gnawed the little chicken bone until it was naked and clean.

Half-way upstairs, she remembered Gerald's second pot of coffee, and went back for it. After she had carried the other trays down again and washed the dishes, she did not forget to try all the doors and windows to make sure that everything was locked up absolutely tight.

The next morning, Clytie bit into smiling lips as she cooked breakfast. Far out past the secretly opened window a freight train was crossing the bridge in the sunlight. Some Negroes filed down the road going fishing, and Mr Tom Bate's Boy, who was going along, turned and looked at her through the window.

Gerald had appeared dressed and wearing his spectacles, and announced that he was going to the store to-day. The old Farr furnishing store did little business now, and people hardly missed

Gerald when he did not come; in fact, they could hardly tell when he did because of the big boots strung on a wire, which almost hid the cagelike office. A little high-school girl could wait on anybody who came in.

Now Gerald entered the dining-room.

"How are you this morning, Clytie?" he asked.

"Just fine, Gerald; how are you?"

"I'm going to the store," he said.

He sat down stiffly, and she laid a place on the table before him.

From above, Octavia screamed, "Where in the devil is my thimble, you stole my thimble, Clytie Farr, you carried it away, my little silver thimble!"

"It's started," said Gerald intensely. Clytie saw his fine, thin, almost black lips spread in a crooked line. "How can a man live in the house with women? How can he?"

He jumped up, and tore his napkin exactly in two. He walked out of the dining-room without eating the first bite of his breakfast. She heard him going back upstairs into his room.

"My thimble!" screamed Octavia.

She waited one moment. Crouching eagerly, rather like a little squirrel, Clytie ate part of her breakfast over the stove before going up the stairs.

At nine Mr Bobo, the barber, knocked at the front door.

Without waiting, for they never answered the knock, he let himself in and advanced like a small general down the hall. There was the old organ that was never uncovered or played except for funerals, and then nobody was invited. He went ahead, under the arm of the tiptoed male statue and up the dark stairway. There they were, lined up at the head of the stairs, and they all looked at him with repulsion. Mr Bobo was convinced that they were every one mad. Gerald, even, had already been drinking, at nine o'clock in the morning.

Mr Bobo was short and had never been anything but proud of it, until he had started coming to this house once a week. But he did not enjoy looking up from below at the soft, long throats, the cold, repelled, high-reliefed faces of those Farrs. He could only imagine what one of those sisters would do to him if he made one move. (As if he would!) As soon as he arrived upstairs, they all went off and left him. He pushed out his chin and stood with his round legs wide apart, just looking around. The upstairs hall was absolutely bare. There was not even a chair to sit down in.

"Either they sell away their furniture in the dead of night," said Mr

Bobo to the people of Farr's Gin, "or else they're just too plumb mean to use it."

Mr Bobo stood and waited to be summoned, and wished he had never started coming to this house to shave old Mr Farr. But he had been so surprised to get a letter in the mail. The letter was on such old, yellowed paper that at first he thought it must have been written a thousand years ago and never delivered. It was signed "Octavia Farr," and began without even calling him "Dear Mr Bobo." What it said was: "Come to this residence at nine o'clock each Friday morning until further notice, where you will shave Mr James Farr."

He thought he would go one time. And each time after that he thought he would never go back – especially when he never knew when they would pay him anything. Of course, it was something to be the only person in Farr's Gin allowed inside the house (except for the undertaker, who had gone there when young Henry shot himself, but had never to that day spoken of it). It was not easy to shave a man as bad off as Mr Farr, either – not anything like as easy as to shave a corpse or even a fighting-drunk field hand. Suppose you were like this, Mr Bobo would say: you couldn't move your face; you couldn't hold up your chin, or tighten your jaw, or even bat your eyes when the razor came close. The trouble with Mr Farr was his face made no resistance to the razor. His face didn't hold.

"I'll never go back," Mr Bobo always ended to his customers. "Not even if they paid me. I've seen enough."

Yet here he was again, waiting before the sick-room door.

"This is the last time," he said. "By God!"

And he wondered why the old man did not die.

Just then Miss Clytie came out of the room. There she came in her funny, sideways walk, and the closer she got to him the more slowly she moved.

"Now?" asked Mr Bobo nervously.

Clytie looked at his small, doubtful face. What fear raced through his little green eyes! His pitiful, greedy, small face – how very mournful it was, like a stray kitten's. What was it that this greedy little thing was so desperately needing?

Clytie came up to the barber and stopped. Instead of telling him that he might go in and shave her father, she put out her hand and with breath-taking gentleness touched the side of his face.

For an instant afterward, she stood looking at him inquiringly, and he stood like a statue, like the statue of Hermes.

Then both of them uttered a despairing cry. Mr Bobo turned and fled, waving his razor around in a circle, down the stairs and out the front door; and Clytie, pale as a ghost, stumbled against the railing. The terrible scent of bay rum, of hair tonic, the horrible moist scratch of an invisible beard, the dense, popping green eyes – what had she got hold of with her hand! She could hardly bear it – the thought of that face.

From the closed door to the sick-room came Octavia's shouting voice.

"Clytie! Clytie! You haven't brought Papa the rain-water! Where in the devil is the rain-water to shave Papa?"

Clytie moved obediently down the stairs.

Her brother Gerald threw open the door of his room and called after her, "What now? This is a madhouse! Somebody was running past my room, I heard it. Where do you keep your men? Do you have to bring them home?" He slammed the door again, and she heard the barricade going up.

Clytie went through the lower hall and out the back door. She stood beside the old rain barrel and suddenly felt that this object, now, was her friend, just in time, and her arms almost circled it with impatient gratitude. The rain barrel was full. It bore a dark, heavy, penetrating fragrance, like ice and flowers and the dew of night.

Clytie swayed a little and looked into the slightly moving water. She thought she saw a face there.

Of course. It was the face she had been looking for, and from which she had been separated. As if to give a sign, the index-finger of a hand lifted to touch the dark cheek.

Clytie leaned closer, as she had leaned down to touch the face of the barber.

It was a wavering, inscrutable face. The brows were drawn together as if in pain. The eyes were large, intent, almost avid, the nose ugly and discoloured as if from weeping, the mouth old and closed from any speech. On either side of the head dark hair hung down in a disreputable and wild fashion. Everything about the face frightened and shocked her with its signs of waiting, of suffering.

For the second time that morning, Clytie recoiled, and as she did so, the other recoiled in the same way.

Too late, she recognized the face. She stood there completely sick at heart, as though the poor, half-remembered vision had finally betrayed her.

"Clytie! Clytie! The water! The water!" came Octavia's monumental voice.

Clytie did the only thing she could think of to do. She bent her angular body further, and thrust her head into the barrel, under the water, through its glittering surface into the kind, featureless depth, and held it there.

When Old Lethy found her, she had fallen forward into the barrel, with her poor ladylike black-stockinged legs up-ended and hung apart like a pair of tongs.

The Pool

Daphne du Maurier

Location: Par, Cornwall.

Time: July, 1959.

Eyewitness Description: *"Suddenly the lightning forked again, and standing there, alive yet immobile, was the woman by the turnstile. She stared up at the windows of the house and Deborah recognised her. The turnstile was there, inviting entry and already the phantom figures, passing through it, crowded towards the trees beyond the lawn. The secret world was waiting . . ."*

Author: Daphne du Maurier (1907–89) has been credited with shifting the Gothic mode towards romantic fiction with her novel, *Rebecca* (1938) which built on the work of the Brontes and inspired a genre that has flourished ever since. For many years, du Maurier was one of the most popular novelists in the English-speaking world with her tales full of atmosphere, suspense and melodramatic situations, a trait she may well have developed as the granddaughter of George du Maurier, author of *Trilby* (1894), and daughter of the great English actor-manager, Sir Gerald du Maurier. She grew up in the world of theatrical excess, yet found her own way in the rugged isolation and mystery of Cornwall where she wrote a series of hugely successful novels, especially the "Gothics" that followed *Rebecca*: *Frenchman's Creek* (1941), *Hungry Hill* (1943) and *Mary Anne* (1954). Her short stories were equally impressive, notably "The Birds" (1952) and "Don't Look Now" (1966), which were both brilliantly filmed, and "The Pool" in which a typical du Maurier heroine, the pretty, sensitive young Deborah, on the verge of puberty, finds herself in a secret world of feelings and enchantment.

I

The children ran out on to the lawn. There was space all around them, and light, and air, with the trees indeterminate beyond. The gardener had cut the grass. The lawn was crisp and firm now, because of the hot sun through the day; but near the summer-house where the tall grass stood there were dew-drops like frost clinging to the narrow stems.

The children said nothing. The first moment always took them by surprise. The fact that it waited, thought Deborah, all the time they were away; that day after day while they were at school, or in the Easter holidays with the aunts at Hunstanton being blown to bits, or in the Christmas holidays with their father in London riding on buses and going to theatres – the fact that the garden waited for them was a miracle known only to herself. A year was so long. How did the garden endure the snows clamping down upon it, or the chilly rain that fell in November? Surely sometimes it must mock the slow steps of Grandpapa pacing up and down the terrace in front of the windows, or Grandmama calling to Patch? The garden had to endure month after month of silence, while the children were gone. Even the spring and the days of May and June were wasted, all those mornings of butterflies and darting birds, with no one to watch but Patch gasping for breath on a cool stone slab. So wasted was the garden, so lost.

"You must never think we forget," said Deborah in the silent voice she used to her own possessions. "I remember, even at school, in the middle of French" – but the ache then was unbearable, that it should be the hard grain of a desk under her hands, and not the grass she bent to touch now. The children had had an argument once about whether there was more grass in the world or more sand, and Roger said that of course there must be more sand, because of under the sea; in every ocean all over the world there would be sand, if you looked deep down. But there could be grass too, argued Deborah, a waving grass, a grass that nobody had ever seen, and the colour of that ocean grass would be darker than any grass on the surface of the world, in fields or prairies or people's gardens in America. It would be taller than trees and it would move like corn in a wind.

They had run in to ask somebody adult, "What is there most of in the world, grass or sand?", both children hot and passionate from the argument. But Grandpapa stood there in his old panama hat looking for clippers to trim the hedge – he was rummaging in the drawer full of screws – and he said, "What? What?" impatiently.

The boy turned red – perhaps it was a stupid question – but the girl thought, he doesn't know, they never know, and she made a face at her brother to show that she was on his side. Later they asked their grandmother, and she, being practical said briskly, "I should think sand. Think of all the grains," and Roger turned in triumph. "I told you so!" The grains. Deborah had not considered the grains. The magic of millions and millions of grains clinging together in the world and under the oceans made her sick. Let Roger win, it did not matter. It was better to be in the minority of the waving grass.

Now, on this first evening of summer holiday, she knelt and then lay full-length on the lawn, and stretched her hands out on either side like Jesus on the Cross, only face downwards, and murmured over and over again the words she had memorized from Confirmation preparation. "A full, perfect and sufficient sacrifice . . . a full, perfect and sufficient sacrifice . . . satisfaction, and oblation, for the sins of the whole world." To offer herself to the earth, to the garden, the garden that had waited patiently all these months since last summer, surely this must be her first gesture.

"Come on," said Roger, rousing himself from his appreciation of how Willis the gardener had mown the lawn to just the right closeness for cricket, and without waiting for his sister's answer he ran to the summer-house and made a dive at the long box in the corner where the stumps were kept. He smiled as he lifted the lid. The familiarity of the smell was satisfying. Old varnish and chipped paint, and surely that must be the same spider and the same cobweb? He drew out the stumps one by one, and the bails, and there was the ball – it had not been lost after all, as he had feared. It was worn, though, a greyish red – he smelt it and bit it, to taste the shabby leather. Then he gathered the things in his arms and went out to set up the stumps.

"Come and help me measure the pitch," he called to his sister, and looking at her, squatting in the grass with her face hidden, his heart sank, because it meant that she was in one of her absent moods and would not concentrate on the cricket.

"Deb?" he called anxiously. "You are going to play?"

Deborah heard his voice through the multitude of earth sounds, the heartbeat and the pulse. If she listened with her ear to the ground there was a humming much deeper than anything that bees did, or the sea at Hunstanton. The nearest to it was the wind, but the wind was reckless. The humming of the earth was patient. Deborah sat up, and her heart sank just as her brother's had done, for the same reason in reverse. The monotony of the game ahead would be like a great chunk torn out of privacy.

"How long shall we have to be?" she called.

The lack of enthusiasm damped the boy. It was not going to be any fun at all if she made a favour of it. He must be firm, though. Any concession on his part she snatched and turned to her advantage.

"Half-an-hour," he said, and then, for encouragement's sake, "You can bat first."

Deborah smelt her knees. They had not yet got the country smell, but if she rubbed them in the grass, and in the earth too, the white London look would go.

"All right," she said, "but no longer than half-an-hour."

He nodded quickly, and so as not to lose time measured out the pitch and then began ramming the stumps in the ground. Deborah went into the summer-house to get the bats. The familiarity of the little wooden hut pleased her as it had her brother. It was a long time now, many years, since they had played in the summer-house, making yet another house inside this one with the help of broken deckchairs; but, just as the garden waited for them a whole year, so did the summer-house, the windows on either side, cobweb-wrapped and stained, gazing out like eyes. Deborah did her ritual of bowing twice. If she should forget this, on her first entrance, it spelt ill-luck.

She picked out the two bats from the corner, where they were stacked with old croquet-hoops, and she knew at once that Roger would choose the one with the rubber handle, even though they could not bat at the same time, and for the whole of the holidays she must make do with the smaller one, that had half the whipping off. There was a croquet clip lying on the floor. She picked it up and put it on her nose and stood a moment, wondering how it would be if for evermore she had to live thus, nostrils pinched, making her voice like Punch. Would people pity her?

"Hurry," shouted Roger, and she threw the clip into the corner, then quickly returned when she was halfway to the pitch, because she knew the clip was lying apart from its fellows, and she might wake in the night and remember it. The clip would turn malevolent, and haunt her. She replaced him on the floor with two others, and now she was absolved and the summer-house at peace.

"Don't get out too soon," warned Roger as she stood in the crease he had marked for her, and with a tremendous effort of concentration Deborah forced her eyes to his retreating figure and watched him roll up his sleeves and pace the required length for his run-up. Down came the ball and she lunged out, smacking it in the air in an easy catch. The impact of ball on bat stung her hands. Roger missed the catch on purpose. Neither of them said anything.

"Who shall I be?" called Deborah.

The game could only be endured, and concentration kept, if Roger gave her a part to play. Not an individual, but a country.

"You're India," he said, and Deborah felt herself grow dark and lean. Part of her was tiger, part of her was sacred cow, the long grass fringing the lawn was jungle, the roof of the summer-house a minaret.

Even so, the half-hour dragged, and, when her turn came to bowl, the ball she threw fell wider every time, so that Roger, flushed and self-conscious because their grandfather had come out on to the terrace and was watching them, called angrily, "Do try."

Once again the effort at concentration, the figure of their grand-father — a source of apprehension to the boy, for he might criticize them — acting as a spur to his sister. Grandpapa was an Indian god, and tribute must be paid to him, a golden apple. The apple must be flung to slay his enemies. Deborah muttered a prayer, and the ball she bowled came fast and true and hit Roger's off-stump. In the moment of delivery their grandfather had turned away and pottered back again through the French windows of the drawing-room.

Roger looked round swiftly. His disgrace had not been seen. "Jolly good ball," he said. "It's your turn to bat again."

But his time was up. The stable clock chimed six. Solemnly Roger drew stumps.

"What shall we do now?" he asked.

Deborah wanted to be alone, but if she said so, on this first evening of the holiday, he would be offended.

"Go to the orchard and see how the apples are coming on," she suggested, "and then round by the kitchen garden in case the raspberries haven't all been picked. But you have to do it all without meeting anyone. If you see Willis or anyone, even the cat, you lose a mark."

It was these sudden inventions that saved her. She knew her brother would be stimulated at the thought of outwitting the garden-er. The aimless wander round the orchard would turn into a stalking exercise.

"Will you come too?" he asked.

"No," she said, "you have to test your skill."

He seemed satisfied with this and ran off towards the orchard, stopping on the way to cut himself a switch from the bamboo.

As soon as he had disappeared Deborah made for the trees fringing the lawn, and once in the shrouded wood felt herself safe. She walked softly along the alley-way to the pool. The late sun sent shafts of light between the trees and on to the alley-way, and a myriad insects webbed their way in the beams, ascending and descending like angels on Jacob's ladder. But were they insects, wondered Deborah, or particles of dust, or even split fragments of light itself, beaten out and scattered by the sun?

It was very quiet. The woods were made for secrecy. They did not recognize her as the garden did. They did not care that for a whole year she could be at school, or at Hunstanton, or in London. The woods would never miss her: they had their own dark, passionate life.

Deborah came to the opening where the pool lay, with the five alley-ways branching from it, and she stood a moment before advancing to the brink, because this was holy ground and required atonement. She crossed her hands on her breast and shut her eyes. Then she kicked off her shoes. "Mother of all things wild, do with me what you will," she said aloud. The sound of her own voice gave her a slight shock. Then she went down on her knees and touched the ground three times with her forehead.

The first part of her atonement was accomplished, but the pool demanded sacrifice, and Deborah had come prepared. There was a stub of pencil she had carried in her pocket throughout the school term which she called her luck. It had teeth marks on it, and a chewed piece of rubber at one end. This treasure must be given to the pool just as other treasures had been given in the past, a miniature jug, a crested button, a china pig. Deborah felt for the stub of pencil and kissed it. She had carried and caressed it for so many lonely months, and now the moment of parting had come. The pool must not be denied. She flung out her right hand, her eyes still shut, and heard the faint plop as the stub of pencil struck the water. Then she opened her eyes, and saw in mid-pool a ripple. The pencil had gone, but the ripple moved, gently shaking the water-lilies. The movement sym- bolized acceptance.

Deborah, still on her knees and crossing her hands once more, edged her way to the brink of the pool and then, crouching there beside it, looked down into the water. Her reflection wavered up at her, and it was not the face she knew, not even the looking-glass face which anyway was false, but a disturbed image, dark-skinned and ghostly. The crossed hands were like the petals of the water-lilies themselves, and the colour was not waxen white but phantom green. The hair too was not the live clump she brushed every day and tied back with ribbon, but a canopy, a shroud. When the image smiled it became more distorted still. Uncrossing her hands, Deborah leant forward, took a twig, and drew a circle three times on the smooth surface. The water shook in ever-widening ripples, and her reflection, broken into fragments, heaved and danced, a sort of monster, and the eyes were there no longer, nor the mouth.

Presently the water became still. Insects, long-legged flies and beetles with spread wings hummed upon it. A dragon-fly had all the magnificence of a lily leaf to himself. He hovered there, rejoicing. But when Deborah took her eyes off him for a moment he was gone. At the far end of the pool, beyond the clustering lilies, green scum had formed, and beneath the scum were rooted, tangled weeds. They were so thick, and had lain in the pool so long, that if a man walked into them from the bank he would be held and choked. A fly, though, or a beetle, could sit upon the surface, and to him the pale green scum would not be treacherous at all, but a resting-place, a haven. And if someone threw a stone, so that the ripples formed, eventually they came to the scum, and rocked it, and the whole of the mossy surface moved in rhythm, a dancing-floor for those who played upon it.

There was a dead tree standing by the far end of the pool. He could have been fir or pine, or even larch, for time had stripped him of identity. He had no distinguishing mark upon his person, but with grotesque limbs straddled the sky. A cap of ivy crowned his naked head. Last winter a dangling branch had broken loose, and this now lay in the pool half-submerged, the green scum dripping from the withered twigs. The soggy branch made a vantage-point for birds, and as Deborah watched a nestling suddenly flew from the under-growth enveloping the dead tree, and perched for an instant on the mossy filigree. He was lost in terror. The parent bird cried warningly from some dark safety, and the nestling, pricking to the cry, took off from the branch that had offered him temporary salvation. He swerved across the pool, his flight mistimed, yet reached security. The chitter from the undergrowth told of his scolding. When he had gone silence returned to the pool.

It was, so Deborah thought, the time for prayer. The water-lilies were folding upon themselves. The ripples ceased. And that dark hollow in the centre of the pool, that black stillness where the water was deepest, was surely a funnel to the kingdom that lay below. Down that funnel had travelled the discarded treasures. The stub of pencil had lately plunged the depths. He had now been received as an equal among his fellows. This was the single law of the pool, for there were no other commandments. Once it was over, that first cold headlong flight, Deborah knew that the softness of the welcoming water took away all fear. It lapped the face and cleansed the eyes, and the plunge was not into darkness at all but into light. It did not become blacker as the pool was penetrated, but paler, more golden-green, and the mud that people told themselves was there was only a defence against strangers. Those who belonged, who knew, went to the source at once, and there were caverns and fountains and rainbow-coloured seas. There were shores of the whitest sand. There was soundless music.

Once again Deborah closed her eyes and bent lower to the pool. Her lips nearly touched the water. This was the great silence, when she had no thoughts, and was accepted by the pool. Waves of quiet ringed themselves about her, and slowly she lost all feeling, and had no knowledge of her legs, or of her kneeling body, or of her cold, clasped hands. There was nothing but the intensity of peace. It was a deeper acceptance than listening to the earth, because the earth was of the world, the earth was a throbbing pulse, but the acceptance of the pool meant another kind of hearing, a closing in of the waters, and just as the lilies folded so did the soul submerge.

"Deborah . . .? Deborah . . .?" Oh, no! Not now, don't let them call me back now! It was as though someone had hit her on the back, or jumped out at her from behind a corner, the sharp and sudden clamour of another life destroying the silence, the secrecy. And then came the tinkle of the cowbells. It was the signal from their grand-mother that the time had come to go in. Not imperious and ugly with authority, like the clanging bell at school summoning those at play to lessons or chapel, but a reminder, nevertheless, that Time was all-important, that life was ruled to order, that even here, in the holiday home the children loved, the adult reigned supreme.

"All right, all right," muttered Deborah, standing up and thrusting her numbed feet into her shoes. This time the rather raised tone of "Deborah?", and the more hurried clanging of the cowbells, brought long ago from Switzerland, suggested a more imperious Grandmama than the tolerant one who seldom questioned. It must mean their supper was already laid, soup perhaps getting cold, and the farce of washing hands, of tidying, of combing hair, must first be gone through.

"Come on, Deb," and now the shout was close, was right at hand, privacy lost for ever, for her brother came running down the alley-way swishing his bamboo stick in the air.

"What *have* you been doing?" The question was an intrusion and a threat. She would never have asked him what he had been doing, had he wandered away wanting to be alone, but Roger, alas, did not claim privacy. He liked companionship, and his question now, asked half in irritation, half in resentment, came really from the fear that he might lose her.

"Nothing," said Deborah.

Roger eyed her suspiciously. She was in that mooning mood. And it meant, when they went to bed, that she would not talk. One of the best things, in the holidays, was having the two adjoining rooms and calling through to Deb, making her talk.

"Come on," he said, "they've rung," and the making of their grandmother into "they", turned a loved individual into something impersonal, showed Deborah that even if he did not understand he was on her side. He had been called from play, just as she had.

They ran from the woods to the lawn, and on to the terrace. Their grandmother had gone inside, but the cowbells hanging by the French window were still jangling.

The custom was for the children to have their supper first, at seven, and it was laid for them in the dining-room on a hot-plate. They served themselves. At a quarter-to-eight their grandparents had dinner. It was called dinner, but this was a concession to their status. They ate the same as the children, though Grandpapa had a savoury which was not served to the children. If the children were late for supper then it put out Time, as well as Agnes, who cooked for both generations, and it might mean five minutes' delay before Grandpapa had his soup. This shook routine.

The children ran up to the bathroom to wash, then downstairs to the dining-room. Their grandfather was standing in the hall. Deborah sometimes thought that he would have enjoyed sitting with them while they ate their supper, but he never suggested it. Grandmama had warned them, too, never to be a nuisance, or indeed to shout, if Grandpapa was near. This was not because he was nervous, but because he liked to shout himself.

"There's going to be a heat-wave," he said. He had been listening to the news.

"That will mean lunch outside tomorrow," said Roger swiftly. Lunch was the meal they took in common with the grandparents, and it was the moment of the day he disliked. He was nervous that his grandfather would ask him how he was getting on at school.

"Not for me, thank you," said Grandpapa. "Too many wasps."

Roger was at once relieved. This meant that he and Deborah would have the little round garden-table to themselves. But Deborah felt sorry for her grandfather as he went back into the drawing-room. Lunch on the terrace could be gay, and would liven him up. When people grew old they had so few treats.

"What do you look forward to most in the day?" she once asked her grandmother.

"Going to bed," was the reply, "and filling my two hot-water bottles." Why work through being young, thought Deborah, to this?

Back in the dining-room the children discussed what they should do during the heat-wave. It would be too hot, Deborah said, for cricket. But they might make a house, suggested Roger, in the trees by the paddock. If he got a few old boards from Willis, and nailed them together like a platform, and borrowed the orchard ladder, then they could take fruit and bottles of orange squash and keep them up there, and it would be a camp from which they could spy on Willis afterwards.

Deborah's first instinct was to say she did not want to play, but she checked herself in time. Finding the boards and fixing them would take Roger a whole morning. It would keep him employed. "Yes, it's a good idea," she said, and to foster his spirit of adventure she looked at his notebook, as they were drinking their soup, and approved of items necessary for the camp while he jotted them down. It was all part of the day-long deceit she practised to express understanding of his way of life.

When they had finished supper they took their trays to the kitchen and watched Agnes, for a moment, as she prepared the second meal for the grandparents. The soup was the same, but garnished. Little croûtons of toasted bread were added to it. And the butter was made into pats, not cut in a slab. The savoury tonight was to be cheese straws. The children finished the ones that Agnes had burnt. Then they went through to the drawing-room to say good night. The older people had both changed. Grandmama had a dress that she had worn several years ago in London. She had a cardigan round her shoulders like a cape.

"Go carefully with the bathwater," she said. "We'll be short if there's no rain."

They kissed her smooth, soft skin. It smelt of rose leaves. Grandpapa's chin was sharp and bony. He did not kiss Roger.

"Be quiet overhead," whispered their grandmother. The children nodded. The dining-room was underneath their rooms, and any jumping about or laughter would make a disturbance.

Deborah felt a wave of affection for the two old people. Their lives must be empty and sad. "We *are* glad to be here," she said. Grandmama smiled. This was how she lived, thought Deborah, on little crumbs of comfort.

Once out of the room their spirits soared, and to show relief Roger chased Deborah upstairs, both laughing for no reason. Undressing they forgot the instructions about the bath, and when they went into the bathroom – Deborah was to have first go – the water was gurgling into the overflow. They tore out the plug in a panic, and listened to the waste roaring down the pipe to the drain below. If Agnes did not have the wireless on she would hear it.

The children were too old now for boats or play, but the bathroom was a place for confidences, for a sharing of those few tastes they agreed upon, or, after quarrelling, for moody silence. The one who broke silence first would then lose face.

"Willis has a new bicycle," said Roger. "I saw it propped against the shed. I couldn't try it because he was there. But I shall tomorrow. It's a Raleigh."

He liked all practical things, and the trying of the gardener's bicycle would give an added interest to the morning of next day. Willis had a bag of tools in a leather pouch behind the saddle. These could all be felt and the spanners, smelling of oil, tested for shape and usefulness.

"If Willis died," said Deborah, "I wonder what age he would be."

It was the kind of remark that Roger resented always. What had death to do with bicycles? "He's sixty-five," he said, "so he'd be sixty-five."

"No," said Deborah, "what age when he got *there*."

Roger did not want to discuss it. "I bet I can ride it round the stables if I lower the seat," he said. "I bet I don't fall off."

But if Roger would not rise to death, Deborah would not rise to the wager. "Who cares?" she said.

The sudden streak of cruelty stung the brother. Who cared indeed . . . The horror of an empty world encompassed him, and to give himself confidence he seized the wet sponge and flung it out of the window. They heard it splosh on the terrace below.

"Grandpapa will step on it, and slip," said Deborah, aghast.

The image seized them, and choking back laughter they covered their faces. Hysteria doubled them up. Roger rolled over and over on the bathroom floor. Deborah, the first to recover, wondered why laughter was so near to pain, why Roger's face, twisted now in merriment, was yet the same crumpled thing when his heart was breaking.

"Hurry up," she said briefly, "let's dry the floor," and as they wiped the linoleum with their towels the action sobered them both.

Back in their bedrooms, the door open between them, they watched the light slowly fading. But the air was warm like day.

Their grandfather and the people who said what the weather was going to be were right. The heat-wave was on its way. Deborah, leaning out of the open window, fancied she could see it in the sky, a dull haze where the sun had been before; and the trees beyond the lawn, day-coloured when they were having their supper in the dining-room, had turned into night-birds with outstretched wings. The garden knew about the promised heat-wave, and rejoiced: the lack of rain was of no consequence yet, for the warm air was a trap, lulling it into a drowsy contentment.

The dull murmur of their grandparents' voices came from the dining-room below. What did they discuss, wondered Deborah. Did they make those sounds to reassure the children, or were their voices part of their unreal world? Presently the voices ceased, and then there was a scraping of chairs, and voices from a different quarter, the drawing-room now, and a faint smell of their grandfather's cigarette.

Deborah called softly to her brother but he did not answer. She went through to his room, and he was asleep. He must have fallen asleep suddenly, in the midst of talking. She was relieved. Now she could be alone again, and not have to keep up the pretence of sharing conversation. Dusk was everywhere, the sky a deepening black. "When they've gone up to bed," thought Deborah, "then I'll be truly alone." She knew what she was going to do. She waited there, by the open window, and the deepening sky lost the veil that covered it, the haze disintegrated, and the stars broke through. Where there had been nothing was life, dusty and bright, and the waiting earth gave off a scent of knowledge. Dew rose from the pores. The lawn was white.

Patch, the old dog, who slept at the end of Grandpapa's bed on a plaid rug, came out on to the terrace and barked hoarsely. Deborah leant out and threw a piece of creeper on to him. He shook his back. Then he waddled slowly to the flower-tub above the steps and cocked his leg. It was his nightly routine. He barked once more, staring blindly at the hostile trees, and went back into the drawing-room. Soon afterwards, someone came to close the windows – Grandmama, thought Deborah, for the touch was light. "They are shutting out the best," said the child to herself, "all the meaning, and all the point." Patch, being an animal, should know better. He ought to be in a kennel where he could watch, but instead, grown fat and soft, he preferred the bumpiness of her grandfather's bed. He had forgotten the secrets. So had they, the old people.

Deborah heard her grandparents come upstairs. First her grand-mother, the quicker of the two, and then her grandfather, more laboured, saying a word or two to Patch as the little dog wheezed his way up. There was a general clicking of lights and shutting of doors. Then silence. How remote, the world of the grandparents, undressing with curtains closed. A pattern of life unchanged for so many years. What went on without would never be known. "He that has ears to hear, let him hear," said Deborah, and she thought of the callousness of Jesus which no priest could explain. Let the dead bury their dead. All the people in the world, undressing now, or sleeping, not just in the village but in cities and capitals, they were shutting out the truth, they were burying their dead. They wasted silence.

The stable clock struck eleven. Deborah pulled on her clothes. Not the cotton frock of the day, but her old jeans that Grandmama disliked, rolled up above her knees. And a jersey. Sandshoes with a hole that did not matter. She was cunning enough to go down by the back stairs. Patch would bark if she tried the front stairs, close to the grandparents' rooms. The back stairs led past Agnes's room, which smelt of apples though she never ate fruit. Deborah could hear her snoring. She would not even wake on Judgement Day. And this led her to wonder on the truth of that fable too, for there might be so many millions by then who liked their graves – Grandpapa, for instance, fond of his routine, and irritated at the sudden riot of trumpets.

Deborah crept past the pantry and the servants' hall – it was only a tiny sitting-room for Agnes, but long usage had given it the dignity of the name – and unlatched and unbolted the heavy back door. Then she stepped outside, on to the gravel, and took the long way round by the front of the house so as not to tread on the terrace, fronting the lawns and the garden.

The warm night claimed her. In a moment it was part of her. She walked on the grass, and her shoes were instantly soaked. She flung up her arms to the sky. Power ran to her fingertips. Excitement was communicated from the waiting tree, and the orchard, and the paddock; the intensity of their secret life caught at her and made her run. It was nothing like the excitement of ordinary looking forward, of birthday presents, of Christmas stockings, but the pull of a magnet – her grandfather had shown her once how it worked, little needles springing to the jaws – and now night and the sky above were a vast magnet, and the things that waited below were needles, caught up in the great demand.

Deborah went to the summer-house, and it was not sleeping like the house fronting the terrace but open to understanding, sharing complicity. Even the dusty windows caught the light, and the cobwebs shone. She rummaged for the old lilo and the motheaten car rug that Grandmama had thrown out two summers ago, and bearing them over her shoulder she made her way to the pool. The alley-way was ghostly, and Deborah knew, for all her mounting tension, that the test was hard. Part of her was still body-bound, and afraid of shadows. If anything stirred she would jump and know true terror. She must show defiance, though. The woods expected it. Like old wise lamas they expected courage.

She sensed approval as she ran the gauntlet, the tall trees watching. Any sign of turning back, of panic, and they would crowd upon her in a choking mass, smothering protest. Branches would become arms, gnarled and knotty, ready to strangle, and the leaves of the higher trees fold in and close like the sudden furling of giant umbrellas. The smaller undergrowth, obedient to the will, would become a briary of a million thorns where animals of no known world crouched snarling, their eyes on fire. To show fear was to show misunderstanding. The woods were merciless.

Deborah walked the alley-way to the pool, her left hand holding the lilo and the rug on her shoulder, her right hand raised in salutation. This was a gesture of respect. Then she paused before the pool and laid down her burden beside it. The lilo was to be her bed, the rug her cover. She took off her shoes, also in respect, and lay down upon the lilo. Then, drawing the rug to her chin, she lay flat, her eyes upon the sky. The gauntlet of the alley-way over, she had no more fear. The woods had accepted her, and the pool was the final resting-place, the doorway, the key.

"I shan't sleep," thought Deborah. "I shall just like awake here all the night and wait for morning, but it will be a kind of introduction to life, like being confirmed."

The stars were thicker now than they had been before. No space in the sky without a prick of light, each star a sun. Some, she thought, were newly born, white-hot, and others wise and colder, nearing completion. The law encompassed them, fixing the riotous path, but how they fell and tumbled depended upon themselves. Such peace, such stillness, such sudden quietude, excitement gone. The trees were no longer menacing but guardians, and the pool was primeval water, the first, the last.

Then Deborah stood at the wicket-gate, the boundary, and there was a woman with outstretched hand, demanding tickets. "Pass through," she said when Deborah reached her. "We saw you coming." The wicket-gate became a turnstile. Deborah pushed against it and there was no resistance, she was through.

"What is it?" she asked. "Am I really here at last? Is this the bottom of the pool?"

"It could be," smiled the woman. "There are so many ways. You just happened to choose this one."

Other people were pressing to come through. They had no faces, they were only shadows. Deborah stood aside to let them by, and in a moment they had all gone, all phantoms.

"Why only now, tonight?" asked Deborah. "Why not in the afternoon, when I came to the pool?"

"It's a trick," said the woman. "You seize on the moment in time. We were here this afternoon. We're always here. Our life goes on around you, but nobody knows it. The trick's easier by night, that's all."

"Am I dreaming, then?" asked Deborah.

"No," said the woman, "this isn't a dream. And it isn't death, either. It's the secret world."

The secret world . . . It was something Deborah had always known, and now the pattern was complete. The memory of it, and the relief, were so tremendous that something seemed to burst inside her heart.

"Of course . . ." she said, "of course . . ." and everything that had ever been fell into place. There was no disharmony. The joy was indescribable, and the surge of feeling, like wings about her in the air, lifted her away from the turnstile and the woman, and she had all knowledge. That was it – the invasion of knowledge.

"I'm not myself, then, after all," she thought. "I knew I wasn't. It was only the task given," and, looking down, she saw a little child who was blind trying to find her way. Pity seized her. She bent down and put her hands on the child's eyes, and they opened, and the child was herself at two years old. The incident came back. It was when her mother died and Roger was born.

"It doesn't matter after all," she told the child. "You are not lost. You don't have to go on crying." Then the child that had been herself melted, and became absorbed in the water and the sky, and the joy of the invading flood intensified so that there was no body at all but only being. No words, only movements. And the beating of wings. This above all, the beating of wings.

"Don't let me go!" It was a pulse in her ear, and a cry, and she saw the woman at the turnstile put up her hands to hold her. Then there was such darkness, such dragging, terrible darkness, and the beginning of pain all over again, the leaden heart, the tears, the misunderstanding. The voice saying "No!" was her own harsh, worldly voice, and she was staring at the restless trees, black and ominous against the sky. One hand trailed in the water of the pool.

Deborah sat up, sobbing. The hand that had been in the pool was wet and cold. She dried it on the rug. And suddenly she was seized with such fear that her body took possession, and throwing aside the rug she began to run along the alley-way, the dark trees mocking and the welcome of the woman at the turnstile turned to treachery. Safety lay in the house behind the closed curtains, security was with the grandparents sleeping in their beds, and like a leaf driven before a whirlwind Deborah was out of the woods and across the silver soaking lawn, up the steps beyond the terrace and through the garden-gate to the back door.

The slumbering solid house received her. It was like an old staid person who, surviving many trials, had learnt experience. "Don't take any notice of them," it seemed to say, jerking its head – did a house have a head? – towards the woods beyond. "They've made no contribution to civilization. I'm man-made, and different. This is where you belong, dear child. Now settle down."

Deborah went back again upstairs and into her bedroom. Nothing had changed. It was still the same. Going to the open window she saw that the woods and the lawn seemed unaltered from the moment, how long back she did not know, when she had stood there, deciding upon the visit to the pool. The only difference now was in herself. The excitement had gone, the tension too. Even the terror of those last moments, when her flying feet had brought her to the house, seemed unreal.

She drew the curtains, just as her grandmother might have done, and climbed into bed. Her mind was now preoccupied with practical difficulties, like explaining the presence of the lilo and the rug beside the pool. Willis might find them, and tell her grandfather. The feel of her own pillow, and of her own blankets, reassured her. Both were familiar. And being tired was familiar too, it was a solid bodily ache, like the tiredness after too much jumping or cricket. The thing was, though – and the last remaining conscious thread of thought decided to postpone conclusion until the morning – which was real? This safety of the house, or the secret world?

2

When Deborah woke next morning she knew at once that her mood was bad. It would last her for the day. Her eyes ached, and her neck was stiff, and there was a taste in her mouth like magnesia.

Immediately Roger came running into her room, his face refreshed and smiling from some dreamless sleep, and jumped on her bed.

"It's come," he said, "the heat-wave's come. It's going to be ninety in the shade."

Deborah considered how best she could damp his day. "It can go to a hundred for all I care," she said. "I'm going to read all morning."

His face fell. A look of bewilderment came into his eyes. "But the house?" he said. "We'd decided to have a house in the trees, don't you remember? I was going to get some planks from Willis."

Deborah turned over in bed and humped her knees. "You can, if you like," she said. "I think it's a silly game."

She shut her eyes, feigning sleep, and presently she heard his feet patter slowly back to his own room, and then the thud of a ball against the wall. If he goes on doing that, she thought maliciously, Grandpapa will ring his bell, and Agnes will come panting up the stairs. She hoped for destruction, for grumbling and snapping, and everyone falling out, not speaking. That was the way of the world.

The kitchen, where the children breakfasted, faced west, so it did not get the morning sun. Agnes had hung up fly-papers to catch wasps. The cereal, puffed wheat, was soggy. Deborah complained, mashing the mess with her spoon.

"It's a new packet," said Agnes. "You're mighty particular all of a sudden."

"Deb's got out of bed the wrong side," said Roger.

The two remarks fused to make a challenge. Deborah seized the nearest weapon, a knife, and threw it at her brother. It narrowly missed his eye, but cut his cheek. Surprised, he put his hand to his face and felt the blood. Hurt, not by the knife but by his sister's action, his face turned red and his lower lip quivered. Deborah ran out of the kitchen and slammed the door. Her own violence distressed her, but the power of the mood was too strong. Going on to the terrace, she saw that the worst had happened. Willis had found the lilo and the rug, and had put them to dry in the sun. He was talking to her grandmother. Deborah tried to slip back into the house, but it was too late.

"Deborah, how very thoughtless of you," said Grandmama. "I tell you children every summer that I don't mind your taking the things from the hut into the garden if only you'll put them back."

Deborah knew she should apologize, but the mood forbade it. "That old rug is full of moth," she said contemptuously, "and the lilo has a rainproof back. It doesn't hurt them."

They both stared at her, and her grandmother flushed, just as

Roger had done when she had thrown the knife at him. Then her grandmother turned her back and continued giving some instructions to the gardener.

Deborah stalked along the terrace, pretending that nothing had happened, and skirting the lawn she made her way towards the orchard and so to the fields beyond. She picked up a windfall, but as soon as her teeth bit into it the taste was green. She threw it away. She went and sat on a gate and stared in front of her, looking at nothing. Such deception everywhere. Such sour sadness. It was like Adam and Eve being locked out of paradise. The Garden of Eden was no more. Somewhere, very close, the woman at the turnstile waited to let her in, the secret world was all about her, but the key was gone. Why had she ever come back? What had brought her?

People were going about their business. The old man who came three days a week to help Willis was sharpening his scythe behind the toolshed. Beyond the field where the lane ran towards the main road she could see the top of the postman's head. He was pedalling his bicycle towards the village. She heard Roger calling, "Deb? Deb . . .?" which meant that he had forgiven her, but still the mood held sway and she did not answer. Her own dullness made her own punishment. Presently a knocking sound told her that he had got the planks from Willis and had embarked on the building of his house. He was like his grandfather; he kept to the routine set for himself.

Deborah was consumed with pity. Not for the sullen self humped upon the gate, but for all of them going about their business in the world who did not hold the key. The key was hers, and she had lost it. Perhaps if she worked her way through the long day the magic would return with evening and she would find it once again. Or even now. Even now, by the pool, there might be a clue, a vision.

Deborah slid off the gate and went the long way round. By skirting the fields, parched under the sun, she could reach the other side of the wood and meet no one. The husky wheat was stiff. She had to keep close to the hedge to avoid brushing it, and the hedge was tangled. Foxgloves had grown too tall and were bending with empty sockets, their flowers gone. There were nettles everywhere. There was no gate into the wood, and she had to climb the pricking hedge with the barbed wire tearing her knickers. Once in the wood some measure of peace returned, but the alley-ways this side had not been scythed, and the grass was long. She had to wade through it like a sea, brushing it aside with her hands.

She came upon the pool from behind the monster tree, the hybrid whose naked arms were like a dead man's stumps, projecting at all angles. This side, on the lip of the pool, the scum was carpet-thick, and all the lilies, coaxed by the risen sun, had opened wide. They basked as lizards bask on hot stone walls. But here, with stems in water, they swung in grace, cluster upon cluster, pink and waxen white. "They're asleep," thought Deborah. "So is the wood. The morning is not their time," and it seemed to her beyond possibility that the turnstile was at hand and the woman waiting, smiling. "She said they were always there, even in the day, but the truth is that being a child I'm blinded in the day. I don't know how to see."

She dipped her hands in the pool, and the water was tepid brown. She tasted her fingers, and the taste was rank. Brackish water, stagnant from long stillness. Yet beneath . . . beneath, she knew, by night the woman waited, and not only the woman but the whole secret world. Deborah began to pray. "Let it happen again," she whispered. "Let it happen again. Tonight. I won't be afraid."

The sluggish pool made no acknowledgement, but the very silence seemed a testimony of faith, of acceptance. Beside the pool, where the imprint of the lilo had marked the moss, Deborah found a kirby-grip, fallen from her hair during the night. It was proof of visitation. She threw it into the pool as part of the treasury. Then she walked back into the ordinary day and the heat-wave, and her black mood was softened. She went to find Roger in the orchard. He was busy with the platform. Three of the boards were fixed, and the noisy hammering was something that had to be borne. He saw her coming, and as always, after trouble, sensed that her mood had changed and mention must never be made of it. Had he called, "Feeling better?", it would have revived the antagonism, and she might not play with him all the day. Instead, he took no notice. She must be the first to speak.

Deborah waited at the foot of the tree, then bent, and handed him up an apple. It was green, but the offering meant peace. He ate it manfully. "Thanks," he said. She climbed into the tree beside him and reached for the box of nails. Contact had been renewed. All was well between them.

3

The hot day spun itself out like a web. The heat haze stretched across the sky, dun-coloured and opaque. Crouching on the burning boards of the apple-tree, the children drank ginger beer and fanned themselves with dock-leaves. They grew hotter still. When the cowbells summoned them for lunch they found that their grandmother had drawn the curtains of all the rooms downstairs, and the drawing-room was a vault and strangely cool. They flung themselves into chairs. No one was hungry. Patch lay under the piano, his soft mouth dripping saliva. Grandmama had changed into a sleeveless linen dress never before seen, and Grandpapa, in a dented panama, carried a fly-whisk used years ago in Egypt.

"Ninety-one," he said grimly, "on the Air Ministry roof. It was on the one o'clock news."

Deborah thought of the men who must measure heat, toiling up and down on this Ministry roof with rods and tapes and odd-shaped instruments. Did anyone care but Grandpapa?

"Can we take our lunch outside?" asked Roger.

His grandmother nodded. Speech was too much effort, and she sank languidly into her chair at the foot of the dining-room table. The roses she had picked last night had wilted.

The children carried chicken drumsticks to the summer-house. It was too hot to sit inside, but they sprawled in the shadow it cast, their heads on faded cushions shedding kapok. Somewhere, far above their heads, an aeroplane climbed like a small silver fish, and was lost in space.

"A Meteor," said Roger. "Grandpapa says they're obsolete."

Deborah thought of Icarus, soaring towards the sun. Did he know when his wings began to melt? How did he feel? She stretched out her arms and thought of them as wings. The fingertips would be the first to curl, and then turn cloggy soft, and useless. What terror in the sudden loss of height, the drooping power . . .

Roger, watching her, hoped it was some game. He threw his picked drumstick into a flowerbed and jumped to his feet.

"Look," he said, "I'm a Javelin," and he too stretched his arms and ran in circles, banking. Jet noises came from his clenched teeth. Deborah dropped her arms and looked at the drumstick. What had been clean and white from Roger's teeth was now earth-brown. Was it offended to be chucked away? Years later, when everyone was dead, it would be found, moulded like a fossil. Nobody would care.

"Come on," said Roger.

"Where to?" she asked.

"To fetch the raspberries," he said.

"You go," she told him.

Roger did not like going into the dining-room alone. He was self-conscious. Deborah made a shield from the adult eyes. In the end he consented to fetch the raspberries without her on condition that she played cricket after tea. After tea was a long way off.

She watched him return, walking very slowly, bearing the plates of raspberries and clotted cream. She was seized with sudden pity, that same pity which, earlier she had felt for all people other than herself. How absorbed he was, how intent on the moment that held him. But tomorrow he would be some old man far away, the garden forgotten, and this day long past.

"Grandmama says it can't go on," he announced. "There'll have to be a storm."

But why? Why not for ever? Why not breathe a spell so that all of them could stay locked and dreaming like the courtiers in the *Sleeping Beauty*, never knowing, never waking, cobwebs in their hair and on their hands, tendrils imprisoning the house itself?

"Race me," said Roger, and to please him she plunged her spoon into the mush of raspberries but finished last, to his delight.

No one moved during the long afternoon. Grandmama went upstairs to her room. The children saw her at her window in her petticoat drawing the curtains close. Grandpapa put his feet up in the drawing-room, a handkerchief over his face. Patch did not stir from his place under the piano. Roger, undefeated, found employment still. He first helped Agnes to shell peas for supper, squatting on the back-door step while she relaxed on a lopsided basket chair dragged from the servants' hall. This task finished, he discovered a tin bath, put away in the cellar, in which Patch had been washed in younger days. He carried it to the lawn and filled it with water. Then he stripped to bathing-trunks and sat in it solemnly, an umbrella over his head to keep off the sun.

Deborah lay on her back behind the summer-house, wondering what would happen if Jesus and Buddha met. Would there be discussion, courtesy, an exchange of views like politicians at summit talks? Or were they after all the same person, born at separate times? The queer thing was that this topic, interesting now, meant nothing in the secret world. Last night, through the turnstile, all problems disappeared. They were non-existent. There was only the knowledge and the joy.

She must have slept, because when she opened her eyes she saw to her dismay that Roger was no longer in the bath but was hammering the cricket-stumps into the lawn. It was a quarter-to-five.

"Hurry up," he called, when he saw her move. "I've had tea."

She got up and dragged herself into the house, sleepy still, and giddy. The grandparents were in the drawing-room, refreshed from the long repose of the afternoon. Grandpapa smelt of eau-de-Cologne. Even Patch had come to and was lapping his saucer of cold tea.

"You look tired," said Grandmama critically. "Are you feeling all right?"

Deborah was not sure. Her head was heavy. It must have been sleeping in the afternoon, a thing she never did.

"I think so," she answered, "but if anyone gave me roast pork I know I'd be sick."

"No one suggested you should eat roast pork," said her grand-mother, surprised. "Have a cucumber sandwich, they're cool enough."

Grandpapa was lying in wait for a wasp. He watched it hover over his tea, grim, expectant. Suddenly he slammed at the air with his whisk. "Got the brute," he said in trumph. He ground it into the carpet with his heel. It made Deborah think of Jehovah.

"Don't rush around in the heat," said Grandmama. "It isn't wise. Can't you and Roger play some nice, quiet game?"

"What sort of game?" asked Deborah.

But her grandmother was without invention. The croquet mallets were all broken. "We might pretend to be dwarfs and use the heads," said Deborah, and she toyed for a moment with the idea of squatting to croquet. Their knees would stiffen, though, it would be too difficult.

"I'll read aloud to you, if you like," said Grandmama.

Deborah seized upon the suggestion. It delayed cricket. She ran out on to the lawn and padded the idea to make it acceptable to Roger.

"I'll play afterwards," she said, "and that ice-cream that Agnes has in the fridge, you can eat all of it. I'll talk tonight in bed."

Roger hesitated. Everything must be weighed. Three goods to balance evil.

"You know that stick of sealing-wax Daddy gave you?" he said. "Yes."

"Can I have it?"

The balance for Deborah too. The quiet of the moment in opposition to the loss of the long thick stick so brightly red.

"All right," she grudged.

Roger left the cricket stumps and they went into the drawing-room. Grandpapa, at the first suggestion of reading aloud, had disappeared, taking Patch with him. Grandmama had cleared away the tea. She found her spectacles and the book. It was *Black Beauty*. Grandmama kept no modern children's books, and this made common ground for the three of them. She read the terrible chapter where the stable-lad lets Beauty get overheated and gives him a cold drink and does not put on his blanket. The story was suited to the day. Even Roger listened entranced. And Deborah, watching her grandmother's calm face and hearing her careful voice reading the sentences, thought how strange it was that Grandmama could turn herself into Beauty with such ease. She *was* a horse, suffering there with pneumonia in the stable, being saved by the wise coachman.

After the reading, cricket was an anticlimax, but Deborah must keep her bargain. She kept thinking of Black Beauty writing the book. It showed how good the story was, Grandmama said, because no child had ever yet questioned the practical side of it, or posed the picture of a horse with a pen in its hoof.

"A modern horse would have a typewriter," thought Deborah, and she began to bowl to Roger, smiling to herself as she did so because of the twentieth-century Beauty clacking with both hoofs at a machine.

This evening, because of the heat-wave, the routine was changed. They had their baths first, before their supper, for they were hot and exhausted from the cricket. Then, putting on pyjamas and cardigans, they ate their supper on the terrace. For once Grandmama was indulgent. It was still so hot that they could not take chill, and the dew had not yet risen. It made a small excitement, being in pyjamas on the terrace. Like people abroad, said Roger. Or natives in the South Seas, said Deborah. Or beachcombers who had lost caste. Grandpapa, changed into a white tropical jacket, had not lost caste.

"He's a white trader," whispered Deborah. "He's made a fortune out of pearls."

Roger choked. Any joke about his grandfather, whom he feared, had all the sweet agony of danger.

"What's the thermometer say?" asked Deborah.

Her grandfather, pleased at her interest, went to inspect it.

"Still above eighty," he said with relish.

Deborah, when she cleaned her teeth later, thought how pale her face looked in the mirror above the wash-basin. It was not brown, like Roger's, from the day in the sun, but wan and yellow. She tied back her hair with a ribbon, and the nose and chin were peaky sharp. She yawned largely, as Agnes did in the kitchen on Sunday afternoons.

"Don't forget you promised to talk," said Roger quickly.

Talk . . . That was the burden. She was so tired she longed for the white smoothness of her pillow, all blankets thrown aside, bearing only a single sheet. But Roger, wakeful on his bed, the door between them wide, would not relent. Laughter was the one solution, and to make him hysterical, and so exhaust him sooner, she fabricated a day in the life of Willis, from his first morning kipper to his final glass of beer at the village inn. The adventures in between would have tried Gulliver. Roger's delight drew protests from the adult world below. There was the sound of a bell, and then Agnes came up the stairs and put her head round the corner of Deborah's door.

"Your Granny says you're not to make so much noise," she said.

Deborah, spent with invention, lay back and closed her eyes. She could go no further. The children called good night to each other, both speaking at the same time, from age-long custom, beginning with their names and addresses and ending with the world, the universe, and space. Then the final main "Good night", after which neither must ever speak, on pain of unknown calamity.

"I must try and keep awake," thought Deborah, but the power was not in her. Sleep was too compelling, and it was hours later that she opened her eyes and saw her curtains blowing and the forked flash light the ceiling, and heard the trees tossing and sobbing against the sky. She was out of bed in an instant. Chaos had come. There was no stars, and the night was sulphurous. A great crack split the heavens and tore them in two. The garden groaned. If the rain would only fall there might be mercy, and the trees, imploring, bowed themselves this way and that, while the vivid lawn, bright in expectation, lay like a sheet of metal exposed to flame. Let the waters break. Bring down the rain.

Suddenly the lightning forked again, and standing there, alive yet immobile, was the woman by the turnstile. She stared up at the windows of the house, and Deborah recognized her. The turnstile was there, inviting entry, and already the phantom figures, passing through it, crowded towards the trees beyond the lawn. The secret world was waiting. Through the long day, while the storm was brewing, it had hovered there unseen beyond her reach, but now that night had come, and the thunder with it, the barriers were down. Another crack, mighty in its summons, the turnstile yawned, and the woman with her hand upon it smiled and beckoned.

Deborah ran out of the room and down the stairs. Somewhere somebody called – Roger, perhaps, it did not matter – and Patch was barking; but caring nothing for concealment she went through the dark drawing-room and opened the French window on to the terrace. The lightning searched the terrace and lit the paving, and Deborah ran down the steps on to the lawn where the turnstile gleamed.

Haste was imperative. If she did not run the turnstile might be closed, the woman vanish, and all the wonder of the sacred world be taken from her. She was in time. The woman was still waiting. She held out her hand for tickets, but Deborah shook her head. "I have none." The woman, laughing, brushed her through into the secret world where there were no laws, no rules, and all the faceless phantoms ran before her to the woods, blown by the rising wind. Then the rain came. The sky, deep brown as the lightning pierced it, opened, and the water hissed to the ground, rebounding from the earth in bubbles. There was no order now in the alley-way. The ferns had turned to trees, the trees to Titans. All moved in ecstasy, with sweeping limbs, but the rhythm was broken up, tumultuous, so that some of them were bent backwards, torn by the sky, and others dashed their heads to the undergrowth where they were caught and beaten.

In the world behind, laughed Deborah as she ran, this would be punishment, but here in the secret world it was a tribute. The phantoms who ran beside her were like waves. They were linked one with another, and they were, each one of them, and Deborah too, part of the night force that made the sobbing and the laughter. The lightning forked where they willed it, and the thunder cracked as they looked upwards to the sky.

The pool had come alive. The water-lilies had turned to hands, with palms upraised, and in the far corner, usually so still under the green scum, bubbles sucked at the surface, steaming and multiplying as the torrents fell. Everyone crowded to the pool. The phantoms bowed and crouched by the water's edge, and now the woman had set up her turnstile in the middle of the pool, beckoning them once more. Some remnant of a sense of social order rose in Deborah and protested.

"But we've already paid," she shouted, and remembered a second later that she had passed through free. Must there be duplication? Was the secret world a rainbow, always repeating itself, alighting on another hill when you believed yourself beneath it? No time to think. The phantoms had gone through. The lightning, streaky white, lit the old dead monster tree with his crown of ivy, and because he had no spring now in his joints he could not sway in tribute with the trees and ferns, but had to remain there, rigid, like a crucifix.

"And now . . . and now . . . and now . . ." called Deborah.

The triumph was that she was not afraid, was filled with such wild acceptance . . . She ran into the pool. Her living feet felt the mud and the broken sticks and all the tangle of old weeds, and the water was up to her armpits and her chin. The lilies held her. The rain blinded her. The woman and the turnstile were no more.

"Take me too," cried the child. "Don't leave me behind!" In her heart was a savage disenchantment. They had broken their promise, they had left her in the world. The pool that claimed her now was not the pool of secrecy, but dank, dark brackish water choked with scum.

4

"Grandpapa says he's going to have it fenced round," said Roger. "It should have been done years ago. A proper fence, then nothing can ever happen. But barrow-loads of shingle tipped in it first. Then it won't be a pool, but just a dewpond. Dewponds aren't dangerous."

He was looking at her over the edge of her bed. He had risen in status, being the only one of them downstairs, the bearer of tidings good or ill, the go-between. Deborah had been ordered two days in bed.

"I should think by Wednesday," he went on, "you'd be able to play cricket. It's not as if you're hurt. People who walk in their sleep are just a bit potty."

"I did not walk in my sleep," said Deborah.

"Grandpapa said you must have done," said Roger. "It was a good thing that Patch woke him up and he saw you going across the lawn . . ." Then, to show his release from tension, he stood on his hands.

Deborah could see the sky from her bed. It was flat and dull. The day was a summer day that had worked through storm. Agnes came into the room with junket on a tray. She looked important.

"Now run off," she said to Roger. "Deborah doesn't want to talk to you. She's supposed to rest."

Surprisingly, Roger obeyed, and Agnes placed the junket on the table beside the bed. "You don't feel hungry, I expect," she said. "Never mind, you can eat this later, when you fancy it. Have you got a pain? It's usual, the first time."

"No," said Deborah.

What had happened to her was personal. They had prepared her for it at school, but nevertheless it was a shock, not to be discussed with Agnes. The woman hovered a moment, in case the child asked questions; but, seeing that none came, she turned and left the room.

Deborah, her cheek on her hand, stared at the empty sky. The heaviness of knowledge lay upon her, a strange, deep sorrow.

"It won't come back," she thought. "I've lost the key."

The hidden world, like ripples on the pool so soon to be filled in and fenced, was out of her reach for ever.

A Spot of Gothic

Jane Gardam

Location: Low Thwaite, North Yorkshire.
Time: Autumn, 1980.
Eyewitness Description: *"It was just after
what appeared to be the loneliest part of the
road that I took a corner rather faster than
I should and saw the woman standing in*
*her garden and waving at me with a slow decorous arm, a
queenly arm. You could see from the moonlight that her head
was piled up high with queenly hair . . ."*
Author: Jane Gardam (1928—) was born Jean Mary Pearson in
Coatham, North Yorkshire, read English at Bedford College
and worked for a travelling library before serving in editorial
positions on the *Weldon Ladies Journal* and the literary
weekly, *Time and Tide*. Her early fiction consisted of short
stories which won several literary prizes before her first adult
novel, *God on the Rocks* (1978), a coming-of-age story set in
the thirties, which was short-listed for the Booker Prize, won
the *Prix Baudelaire* in France and was adapted for television in
1992. Her interest in the supernatural has been evident in
several of her subsequent collections of short stories, in
particular *Going into a Dark House* (1994) and *Missing the
Midnight: Hauntings and Grotesques* (1997) and her novel,
The Queen of the Tambourine (1991), the haunting story of a
woman's fascination with a mysterious stranger, that won the
Whitbread Novel Award. "A Spot of Gothic" is, in essence, a
tribute to all those who have written gothic fiction, and
describes the eerie encounter of a "ghost feeler", Mrs
Bainbridge, in a remote corner of the country, that is so
contemporary it could have happened last night . . . or might
just happen this evening.

I was whizzing along the road out of Wensleydale through Low Thwaite beyond Naresby when I suddenly saw a woman at her cottage gate, waving at me gently like an old friend. In a lonely dale this is not very surprising, as I had found out. Several times I have met someone at a lane end flapping a letter that has missed the post in Kirby Thore or Hawes. "It's me sister's birthday tomorrow. I near forgot" or "It's the bill fort telephone. We'll be cut off next thing." The curious thing about this figure, so still and watchful, was that it was standing there waving to me in the middle of the night.

It was full moon. I had been out to dinner at Mealbeck. I had only been living in the North for two months and for one month alone. I had joined my husband near Catterick camp the minute he had found us a house, which was only a few days before he found that the regiment was being posted to Hong Kong. The house he had found was beautiful, old and tall in an old garden, on the edge of a village on the edge of the fell. It was comfortable and dark with a flagged floor and old furniture. Roses and honeysuckle were nearly strangling black hedges of neglected yew. There was nice work to be done.

It was the best army house we had ever found. The posting to Hong Kong promised to be a short one. I had been there before and hated it – I hate crowded places – and I decided to stay behind alone.

He said, "But you will be alone, mind. The camp is a good way off and most people will have gone with us. It's the North. You'll make no friends. They take ten years to do more than wag their heads at you in the street up here. Now, are you sure?"

I said I was and I stayed and found that he was quite wrong. Within days, almost within hours of my miserable drive home from Darlington Station to see him off, I found that I was behaving as if I'd always known the people here and they were doing the same to me. I got home from the station and stopped the car outside my beautiful front door and sat still, thinking, "He has gone again. Again he has gone. What a marriage. Always alone. Shall I forget his face again? Like last time? Shall I begin to brood? Over-eat? Drink by myself in the evenings – rather more every evening? Shall I start tramping about the lanes pretending I like long walks?" I sat there thinking and a great truculent female head with glaring eyes stuck itself through the car window.

"D'you want some *beans*?"

"Oh!"

"Some *beans*? Stick beans?"

"Oh I don't—? Can you spare—?"

"Beans, beans. Masses of beans. They're growin' out of me ears. Grand beans. Up to you."

"I'd love some beans."

A sheaf of them was dumped on the seat beside me. "There's plenty more. You've just to say. So 'e's off then? The Captain?"

"Yes."

"Well, yer not to fret. There's always a cup of tea at our place. Come rount back but wear yer wellies or you'll get in a slather int yard."

In the post office they asked kindly for news. Of how I was settling, of where I had come from. The vicar called. A man in a land-rover with a kind face – the doctor – waved his hat. A woman in the ironmonger's buying paraffin in gloves and a hat invited me to tea in a farmhouse the size of a mill with a ha-ha and a terrace at the back, gravel a foot thick and a thousand dahlias staked like artillerymen and luminous with autumn. The tea cups must have been two hundred years old.

I was asked to small places too – a farm so isolated that the sheep and cows looked up aghast when I found my way to it, and the sheep-dogs nearly garrotted themselves on the end of hairy ropes.

"You'll be missin the Captain," the farmer's wife said as she opened the door. Her accent was not the local one.

I said, "You talk differently," and she said, "Well, I would do. I come from Stennersceugh. It was a Danish settlement long since. It's all of ten miles off."

Never in my life had I had so much attention paid to me by strangers, nor been told so many intimate things from the heart – of marriages, love and death; of children or the lack of them, fears of sickness, pregnancy; of lost loves and desperate remedies. Three old ladies living by the church, I heard, drank three crates of sherry a week ("It's the chemist delivers"). A husband had "drowned 'isself in Ash Beck for fear of a thing growing out of the side of his head".

There seemed to be total classlessness, total acceptance, offence only taken if you gave yourself airs, offered money in return for presents or didn't open your door wide enough at the sound of every bell. There was a certain amount of derision at bad management – "She never gets out to the shops till twelve o'clock." "She hasn't had them curtains down in a twelve-month" – but I met no violence, no hatred. There were threats of "bringin me gun" to walkers on the fells with unleashed dogs, but not one farmer in ten possessed a gun or would have known how to use if he had. Language addressed to animals was foul and unrefined, ringing over the fells and sheep dips and clipping sheds – but bore no relation to conversation with humans or at any rate not with me. "Come ere yer bloody, buggerin little – 'ello there, Mrs Bainbridge, now. Grand day. Comin over for yer tea then?"

Alan had told me that when he came home I'd be used to my tea as my supper and then more tea just before bedtime and I would forget how to cook a steak. However he was wrong again, because it had been dinner I had been invited to at Mealbeck the night of the waving woman, and a much better dinner than I'd ever have got in Aldershot.

Mealbeck is the big Gothic house of two sisters – a magnificent cold, turretted, slightly idiotic house, something between the Brighton Pavilion and the Carpathians. We ate not in a corner of it but the corner of a corner, passing from the tremendous door, over flagged halls, a great polar-bear skin rug and down a long cold passage. At the end was a little room which must once have been the housekeeper's and crammed into it among the housekeeper's possessions – a clock, a set of bells, a little hat-stand, a photograph of servants like rows of suet dumplings, starched and stalwart and long ago dead – were a Thomas Lawrence, photographs by Lenare and haunted Ypres faces in 1914 khaki. On the housekeeper's old table where she must have handed out the wages were some fine silver and glasses fit for emperors.

Good wine, too. The sisters, Millicent and Gertie, knew their wine. They also knew their scotch and resorted to it wordlessly after the best pheasant and lemon pudding I think I've ever eaten.

I said, "Oh this has been lovely. Lovely." We stood under the green moon that did not so much light the fells as isolate them in the long clean lines of the faded day.

"You are from Sussex," said Millicent. "You must find this very bare."

"It's wonderful. I love it."

"I hope you'll stay the winter," said Gertie. "And I hope you'll come here soon again."

The two of them walked, not too steadily to the iron gates and I roared off in the little Fiat down the drive and out on to the fell, between the knobbly blocks of the stone walls flashing up in the car lights. I felt minute between the long lines snaking away, the long low undercorated horizon, the clear hard pencil lines cut with a very sharp hard point. Gigantic lamp-eyes of sheep now and then came shining into the headlights. It was midnight. I did not meet a single car between Mealbeck and Naresby and the road rippled up and down, narrow and sweeping and black and quiet. I thought of Alan in Hong Kong. It would be breakfast time. I wished he were with me.

Then I forgot him in the emptiness of the road under the moon and the great encircling ball of the stars.

I went flying through High Thwaite, hurtling through Low Thwaite and the same landscape spread out still in front of me – endlessly deserted, not a light in any cottage, not a dog barking, not a cry of a bird. It was just after what appeared to be the loneliest part of the road that I took a corner rather faster than I should and saw the woman standing in her garden and waving at me with a slow decorous arm, a queenly arm. You could see from the moonlight that her head was piled up high with queenly hair. I think I was about two miles on before I really took it in. I was so shaken by it that I stopped the car.

I was not many miles from home now – my village, my new house, my heavy safe front door. The road had dropped low to a humped bridge, and after a moment when I had switched off the engine I could hear the clear quick brown water running deep and noisy below it. I thought, "There can't have been anyone. I'm drunk."

I got out of the car and walked about. It was cold. I stood on the bridge. Apart from the noise of the beck everything was absolutely quiet. There was not a light from any house in any direction. Down here by the beck I could see no horizons, not the fell's edge, not even the sweet nibbled grass beside the road. The air smelled very clean like fresh sheets.

This was the pedlars' road. For five hundred years, they had walked it with packs of ribbons and laces and buttons and medicines, and a great many of them according to all the stories had been murdered for them or disappeared in the snow in winter – often not found until Martinmas. If my car doesn't start now, I thought, I shall be very much alone.

Had the woman been asking for help? I wondered whether to go back. I felt absolutely certain – and it is amazing how much even at midnight under only the palest moon the eye can know from the angle of a moving arm – that she hadn't.

She had been waving kindly. Not afraid. Not asking. Not even beckoning. She had been waving in some sort of recognition.

I had never been so frightened in my life.

"I went to Mealbeck last night."

"Y'd get a fair plateful there."

"Yes."

"And a fair skinful."

"We – yes. Lovely wine."

"Wine, eh? And mebbe a tot?"

"I had a lovely time. They're very nice. Very kind."

"That's right. They're kind. Home boozers. Did you get back safe? They say the police sits outside Mealbeck when there's entertaining. When they can spare't time."

"I'm not saying anything against them."

"That's right then." He – it was the farmer who had the demented dogs and whose wife came from the Danish settlement – he looked satisfied. I could see he had been wondering if I was too fancy to answer back. 'They're right. Old Gertie and Millicent. There's nowt amiss wi' them. Did you have a fair drive home?"

"Fair," I said. "One thing wasn't though. I passed a place—. I saw a ghost."

"Oh aye. Y'd see half a dozen after a night out at Mealbeck."

"No, I don't think it was that. I saw someone at a gate. It was a woman waving."

"Oh aye."

"Well – it was nearly one o'clock in the morning."

"Did yer stop?" He was clipping. The sheep was taut between his legs, its yellow eyes glaring. The clippers snapped deep into the dirty heathery wool.

"Well, no. I didn't believe it till I was miles past. It took a minute. Then I thought I'd dreamed. Dropped asleep."

"Woman was it? Dark-haired?"

"I didn't see the colour. Just the shape."

"Did yer go on back?"

"No – well. She didn't seem to be in trouble or anything. I hope I did right. Not going back."

He said nothing till the fleece of the sheep fell away and the animal sprang out of his clutches like a soul released and slithered dizzily light into the yard.

"Watch now or yer'll get yerself hiked," he said as I stood clear. "The Missus'll have a pot of tea if you fancy it."

"*Was* it a ghost?"

"Missus!"

She appeared at the door and looked pleased to see me – this really was a wonderfully friendly country – 'Kettle's on'', she called. "I hear yer've bin gallivanting at the Hall."

"Was it a ghost?" I asked again before I went into tea.

"I'd not think so," he said.

*   *   *

I went back along the road the very next day and at first I could find no
sign of the house at all. Or at any rate I could not decide which one it
was. The fell that had looked so bare at night, by daylight could be seen
to be dotted with crumpled, squat little stone farms, their backs turned
to the view, two trees to each to form a wind-break, grey with white
stone slabs to the window and only a tall spire of smoke to show they
were occupied. It was not the townsfolk-country-cottage belt so that
there was not much white paint about, lined curtains, urns on yard
walls – and any one of several little isolated farms could have been the
eerie one. In the end I turned back and found the bridge where I'd
stopped. I got out of the car again as I had before, and walked back a
mile or two until I came to a lane going alongside a garden end. All I
could see from the road was the garden end – a stone wall and a gate
quite high up above me and behind that a huge slab-stoned roof so low
that the farmhouse must have been built deep down in a dip.

Now nobody stood at the gate – more of a look-out post, a
signalling post above the road. There were tangled flowers behind it.
There was no excuse for me to go up the lane that must have led to
the house and it was not inviting. I thought of pretending to have lost
my way or asking for a drink of water but these things you grow out
of doing. I might perhaps just ask if there were eggs for sale. This was
quite usual. Yet I hung back because the lane was dark and overgrown. I sat down instead on a rickety milk platform meant for
churns but all stuck through with nettles and which hardly took my
weight. It must have been years since any churn was near it. I sat
there in the still afternoon and nobody passed.

Then I felt I was being watched. There was no sound or snapping
twig, no breathing and no branch stirred but I looked quickly up and
into a big bewildered face, mouth a little open, large bright mooning
eyes. The hair was waved deeply like an old *Vogue* photograph and
the neckline of the dress was rounded, quite high with a string of
pearls. The hands of the woman were on the wall and I think they
were gloved – neat pretty kid gloves. The trappings of the whole
figure were all the very soul of order and confidence. The figure itself,
however, almost yearned with uncertainty and loss.

"Whatever *time* is it?" she said.

"About three o'clock." I found I had stood up and turned to face
her. For all the misery in the face there were the relics of unswervable
good manners which demanded good manners back; as well as a
quite curious sensation, quite without visible foundation, that this
body, this dotty half-bemused memsahib had once commanded
respect, inspired good sense.

"It's just after three," I said again.

"Oh, good *gracious* – good gracious." She turned with a funny, bent movement feeling for the wall to support her as she moved away. The face had not been an old woman's but the stance, the tottering walk were ancient. The dreadful sense of loss, the melancholy, were so thick in the air that there was almost a smell, a sick smell of them.

She was gone, and utterly silently, as if I had slept for a moment in the sunshine and had a momentary dream. She had seemed like a shade, a classical Greek shade, though why I should think of ancient Greece in bleak North Westmorland I did not know.

As I stood looking up at the gate there was a muffled urgent plunging noise and round the bend of the road came sheep – a hundred of them with a shepherd and two dogs. The sheep shouldered each other, fussing, pushing, a stream of fat fleeces pressed together, eyes sharp with pandemonium. The dogs were happily tearing about. The shepherd walked with long steps behind. The sheep new-clipped filled the road like snow. They stopped when they saw me, then when they were yelled at came on careering drunkenly round me, surrounding me and I stood knee deep in them and the flat blank rattle of bleats, the smell of sheep dip and dog and man – and petrol, for when I looked beyond I found a land-rover had been crawling behind and at the wheel the doctor with the tweed hat was sitting laughing.

He said, "Well! You look terrified."

"They were so sudden."

"They'll not hurt you."

"No. I know – just they were so – quiet. They broke in—"

"Broke in?"

"To the silence. It's very – silent here, isn't it?" I was inane.

He got down from the car and came round near me. "You've not been here long, have you? We haven't been introduced. I'm the doctor."

"I know. I'm—"

"Yes. I know too. And we're to know each other better. We're both to go dining out at the good sisters' in a week or so. I gather we're not supposed to know it yet. We are both supposed to be lonely."

I said how could one be lonely here? I had made friends so fast.

"Some are," he said. "Who aren't born to it. Not many. It's always all right at first." We both looked together towards the high gate and he said, 'Poor Rose. My next patient. Not that I expect to be let in."

"Is she—?"

"A daughter of the regiment like yourself. Well, I mustn't discuss patients. I call on her now and then."

He walked up the side lane waving the tweed hat and left me. As he reached the point where the little lane bent out of sight he turned and cheerfully waved again, and I turned too and walked the two miles back to my car. As I reached it the land-rover passed me going very fast and the doctor made no signal and I could not see his face. I thought he must be reckless to drive at that lick on a sheep-strewn road but soon forgot it in the pleasure of the afternoon – the bright fire I'd light at home and the smell of wood smoke and supper with a book ahead. No telephone, thank God. As I turned into my yard I found I was very put out to see Mrs Metcalfe coming across it with yet another great basket of beans.

"Tek 'em or leave 'em," she said. 'But we've more than we'll ever want and they'll just get the worm in. Here, you could do wi' a few taties too from the look of you. Oh aye – and I've just heard. That daft woman up near Mealbeck. She's dead. The doctor's just left her. Or I hear tell. She hanged herself."

It was no story.

Or rather it is the most detestable, inadmissible story. For I don't yet know half the facts and I don't feel I want to invent any. It would be a story so easy to improve upon. There are half a dozen theories about poor Rose's hanging and half a dozen about the reason for her growing isolation and idleness and seclusion. There is only one view about her character though, and that is odd because the whole community in the fells and Dales survives on firmly-grounded assessment of motives and results; the gradations and developments of character are vital to life and give validity to passing years. Reputations change and rise and fall. But Rose – Rose had always been very well-liked and had very much liked living here. Gertie and Millicent said she had fitted in round here as if she were country born. She had been one of the few southerners they said who had seemed to belong. She had loved the house – a queer place. It had been the heart of a Quaker settlement. Panes of glass so thick you could hardly see out. She had grown more and more attached to it. She didn't seem able to leave it in the end.

"The marriage broke up after the War," said the doctor. We were sitting back after dinner in the housekeeper's room among the Thomas Lawrences. 'He was always on the move. Rose had no quarrel with him you know. She just grew – well, very taken with the place. It was – yes, possession. Greek idea – possession by local gods. The Romans were here you know. They brought a Greek legend or two with them."

I said, "How odd, when I saw her I thought of the Greeks, though I hadn't known what I meant. It was the way she moved – so old. And the way she held her hands out. Like, – well, sort of like on the walls of Troy."

"Not Troy," said the doctor. "More like hell, poor thing. She was quite gone. You know – these fells, all the little isolated houses, I'm not that sure how good for you they are, unless you're farming folk."

Millicent said rubbish.

"No," he said, "I mean it. D'you remember C. S. Lewis's hell? A place where people live in isolation unable to reach each other. Where the houses get further and further apart?"

"Everyone reaches each other here," I said. "Surely?"

The doctor was looking at me and I noticed he was looking at me very hard. He said, "What was it you said?"

"Everyone reaches each other—"

"No," he said. "You said you saw her."

"Yes I did. I saw her on the way home from here, the night before she died. Then I saw her again the next day, the very afternoon. That's what is so terrible. I must have seen her, just before she – did it. I must be the last person to have seen her."

"I wonder," he said, "if that could be true." Gertie and Millicent were busy with coffee cups. They turned away.

" 'Could be true?' But it is certainly true. I know exactly when. She asked me the time that afternoon. I told her. It was just after three. She seemed very – bewildered about it. You called upon her hardly a quarter of an hour later. She'd hardly been back in the house a quarter of an hour."

"She'd been in it longer than that," he said, "When I found her she'd been dead for nearly three weeks. Maybe since hay-time."

I went to Hong Kong.

5

Entertaining Spooks

Supernatural High Jinks

The Inexperienced Ghost

H. G. Wells

Location: The Mermaid Golf Club, Surrey.
Time: March, 1902.
Eyewitness Description: *"I came upon him,*
you know, in the long passage. His back
was towards me and I saw him first. Right
off I knew him for a ghost. He was
transparent and whitish; clean through his chest I could see the
glimmer of the little window at the end . . ."

Author: Herbert George Wells (1866–1946), the Bromley
shopkeeper's son who is now one of England's major literary
figures, has been credited with being the "Founding Father" of
Science Fiction and a significant influence on both the horror
and fantasy story. It would be a surprise, therefore, if he had
not contributed to the ghost story genre. Apart from the
haunted "The Red Room" (1896) and the unsettling "The
Presence by the Fire" (1918), "The Inexperienced Ghost" is one
of the earliest humorous ghost stories and was first published
in the *Strand* magazine, March 1902. (The earliest, though, are
probably the interjected tales in Charles Dickens' *Pickwick
Papers* (1836), "The Lawyer and the Ghost", "The Queer
Chair", "The Ghosts of the Mail" and the bizarre "Goblins
Who Stole a Sexton".) Wells' story of a golfer and the jaded
phantom he meets one night at his club has deservedly been
praised for its comic originality and was filmed in the movie,
Dead of Night (1945). It has also proved a template for many
subsequent humorous supernatural tales and admired by
authors from Jerome K. Jerome who spoofed the Victorian
tradition in *Told After Supper* (1891) to Terry Pratchett.

T he scene amidst which Clayton told his last story comes back very vividly to my mind. There he sat, for the greater part of the time, in the corner of the authentic settle by the spacious open fire, and Sanderson sat beside him smoking the Broseley clay that bore his name. There was Evans, and that marvel among actors, Wish, who is also a modest man. We had all come down to the Mermaid Club that Saturday morning, except Clayton, who had slept there overnight – which indeed gave him the opening of his story. We had golfed until golfing was invisible; we had dined, and we were in that mood of tranquil kindliness when men will suffer a story. When Clayton began to tell one, we naturally supposed he was lying. It may be that indeed he was lying – of that the reader will speedily be able to judge as well as I. He began, it is true, with an air of matter-of-fact anecdote, but that we thought was only the incurable artifice of the man.

"I say!" he remarked, after a long consideration of the upward rain of sparks from the log that Sanderson had thumped, "you know I was alone here last night?"

"Except for the domestics," said Wish.

"Who sleep in the other wing," said Clayton. "Yes. Well—" He pulled at his cigar for some little time as though he still hesitated about his confidence. Then he said, quite quietly, "I caught a ghost!"

"Caught a ghost, did you?" said Sanderson. "Where is it?"

And Evans, who admires Clayton immensely and has been four weeks in America, shouted, "*Caught* a ghost, did you, Clayton? I'm glad of it! Tell us all about it right now."

Clayton said he would in a minute, and asked him to shut the door.

He looked apologetically at me. "There's no eavesdropping, of course, but we don't want to upset our very excellent service with any rumours of ghosts in the place. There's too much shadow and oak panelling to trifle with that. And this, you know, wasn't a regular ghost. I don't think it will come again – ever."

"You mean to say you didn't keep it?" said Sanderson.

"I hadn't the heart to," said Clayton.

And Sanderson said he was surprised.

We laughed, and Clayton looked aggrieved. "I know," he said, with the flicker of a smile, "but the fact is it really *was* a ghost, and I'm as sure of it as I am that I am talking to you now. I'm not joking. I mean what I say."

Sanderson drew deeply at his pipe, with one reddish eye on Clayton, and then emitted a thin jet of smoke more eloquent than many words.

Clayton ignored the comment. "It is the strangest thing that has ever happened in my life. You know I never believed in ghosts or anything of the sort, before, ever; and then, you know, I bag one in a corner; and the whole business is in my hands."

He meditated still more profoundly and produced and began to pierce a second cigar with a curious little stabber he affected.

"You talked to it?" asked Wish.

"For the space, probably, of an hour."

"Chatty?" I said, joining the party of the sceptics.

"The poor devil was in trouble," said Clayton, bowed over his cigar-end and with the very faintest note of reproof.

"Sobbing?" someone asked.

Clayton heaved a realistic sight at the memory. "Good Lord!" he said, "yes." And then, "Poor fellow! yes."

"Where did you strike it?" asked Evans, in his best American accent.

"I never realized," said Clayton, ignoring him, "the poor sort of thing a ghost might be," and he hung us up again for a time, while he sought for matches in his pocket and lit and warmed to his cigar.

"I took an advantage," he reflected at last.

We were none of us in a hurry. "A character," he said, "remains just the same character for all that it's been disembodied. That's a thing we too often forget. People with a certain strength or fixity of purpose may have ghosts of a certain strength and fixity of purpose – most haunting ghosts, you know, must be as one-idea'd as mono-maniacs and as obstinate as mules to come back again and again. This poor creature wasn't." He suddenly looked up rather queerly, and his eye went round the room. "I say it," he said, "in all kindliness, but that is the plain truth of the case. Even at the first glance he struck me as weak."

He punctuated with the help of his cigar.

"I came upon him, you know, in the long passage. His back was towards me and I saw him first. Right off I knew him for a ghost. He was transparent and whitish; clean through his chest I could see the glimmer of the little window at the end. And not only his physique but his attitude struck me as being weak. He looked, you know, as though he didn't know in the slightest whatever he meant to do. One hand was on the panelling and the other fluttered to his mouth. Like – *so!*"

"What sort of physique?" said Sanderson.

"Lean. You know that sort of young man's neck that has two great flutings down the back, here and here – so! And a little, meanish head with scrubby hair and rather bad ears. Shoulders bad, narrower than the hips; turndown collar, ready-made short jacket, trousers baggy and a little frayed at the heels. That's how he took me. I came very quietly up the staircase. I did not carry a light, you know – the candles are on the landing table and there is that lamp – and I was in my list slippers, and I saw him as I came up. I stopped dead at that – taking him in. I wasn't a bit afraid. I think that in most of these affairs one is never nearly so afraid or excited as one imagines one would be. I was surprised and interested. I thought, 'Good Lord! Here's a ghost at last! And I haven't believed for a moment in ghosts during the last five-and-twenty years.'"

"Um," said Wish.

"I suppose I wasn't on the landing a moment before he found out I was there. He turned on me sharply, and I saw the face of an immature young man, a weak nose, a scrubby little moustache, a feeble chin. So for an instant we stood – he looking over his shoulder at me – and regarded one another. Then he seemed to remember his high calling. He turned round, drew himself up, projected his face, raised his arms, spread his hands in approved ghost fashion – came towards me. As he did so his little jaw dropped, and he emitted a faint, drawn-out 'Boo.' No, it wasn't – not a bit dreadful. I'd dined. I'd had a bottle of champagne, and being all alone, perhaps two or three – perhaps even four or five – whiskies, so I was as solid as rocks and no more frightened than if I'd been assailed by a frog. 'Boo!' I said. 'Nonsense. You don't belong to *this* place. What are you doing here?'

"I could see him wince. 'Boo – oo,' he said.

"'Boo – be hanged! Are you a member?' I said: and just to show I didn't care a pin for him I stepped through a corner of him and made to light my candle. 'Are you a member?' I repeated, looking at him sideways.

"He moved a little so as to stand clear of me, and his bearing became crestfallen. 'No,' he said, in answer to the persistent interrogation of my eye; 'I'm not a member – I'm a ghost.'

"'Well, that doesn't give you the run of the Mermaid Club. Is there anyone you want to see, or anything of that sort?' And doing it as steadily as possible for fear that he should mistake the carelessness of whisky for the distraction of fear, I got my candle alight. I turned on him, holding it. 'What are you doing here?' I said.

"He had dropped his hands and stopped his booing, and there he stood, abashed and awkward, the ghost of a weak, silly, aimless young man. 'I'm haunting,' he said.

" 'You haven't any business to,' I said in a quiet voice.

" 'I'm a ghost,' he said, as if in defence.

" 'That may be, but you haven't any business to haunt here. This is a respectable private club; people often stop here with nursemaids and children, and, going about in the careless way you do, some poor little mite could easily come upon you and be scared out of her wits. I suppose you didn't think of that?'

" 'No, sir,' he said, 'I didn't.'

" 'You should have done. You haven't any claim on the place, have you? Weren't murdered here, or anything of that sort?'

" 'None, sir; but I thought as it was old and oak-panelled—'

" 'That's *no* excuse.' I regarded him firmly. 'Your coming here is a mistake,' I said, in a tone of friendly superiority. I feigned to see if I had my matches, and then looked up at him frankly. 'If I were you I wouldn't wait for cock-crow – I'd vanish right away.'

"He looked embarrassed. 'The fact *is*, sir—' he began.

" 'I'd vanish,' I said, driving it home.

" 'The fact is, sir, that – somehow – I can't.'

" 'You *can't*?'

" 'No, sir. There's something I've forgotten. I've been hanging about here since midnight last night, hiding in the cupboards of the empty bedrooms and things like that. I'm flurried. I've never come haunting before, and it seems to put me out.'

" 'Put you out?'

" 'Yes, sir. I've tried to do it several times, and it doesn't come off. There's some little thing has slipped me, and I can't get back.'

"That, you know, rather bowled me over. He looked at me in such an abject way that for the life of me I couldn't keep up quite the high hectoring vein I had adopted. 'That's queer,' I said, and as I spoke I fancied I heard someone moving about down below. 'Come into my room and tell me more about it,' I said. I didn't, of course, understand this, and I tried to take him by the arm. But, of course, you might as well have tried to take hold of a puff of smoke! I had forgotten my number, I think; anyhow, I remember going into several bedrooms – it was lucky I was the only soul in that wing – until I saw my traps. 'Here we are,' I said, and sat down in the armchair; 'sit down and tell me all about it. It seems to me you have got yourself into a jolly awkward position, old chap.'

"Well, he said he wouldn't sit down; he'd prefer to flit up and down the room if it was all the same to me. And so he did, and in a little while we were deep in a long and serious talk. And presently, you know, something of those whiskies and sodas evaporated out of me, and I began to realize just a little what a thundering rum and weird business it was that I was in. There he was, semi-transparent – the proper conventional phantom, and noiseless except for his ghost of a voice – flitting to and fro in that nice, clean, chintz-hung old bedroom. You could see the gleam of the copper candlesticks through him, and the lights on the brass fender, and the corners of the framed engravings on the wall, and there he was telling me all about this wretched little life of his that had recently ended on earth. He hadn't a particularly honest face, you know, but being transparent, of course, he couldn't avoid telling the truth."

"Eh?" said Wish, suddenly sitting up in his chair.

"What?" said Clayton.

"Being transparent – couldn't avoid telling the truth – I don't see it," said Wish.

"*I* don't see it," said Clayton, with inimitable assurance. "But it *is* so, I can assure you nevertheless. I don't believe he got once a nail's breadth off the Bible truth. He told me how he had been killed – he went down into a London basement with a candle to look for a leakage of gas – and described himself as a senior English master in a London private school when that release occurred."

"Poor wretch!" said I.

"That's what I thought, and the more he talked the more I thought it. There he was, purposeless in life and purposeless out of it. He talked of his father and mother and his school-master, and all who had ever been anything to him in the world, meanly. He had been too sensitive, too nervous; none of them had ever valued him properly or understood him, he said. He had never had a real friend in the world, I think; he had never had a success. He had shirked games and failed examinations. 'It's like that with some people,' he said; 'whenever I got into the examination-room or anywhere everything seemed to go.' Engaged to be married, of course – to another over-sensitive person, I suppose – when the indiscretion with the gas escape ended his affairs. 'And where are you now?' I asked. 'Not in—?'

"He wasn't clear on that point at all. The impression he gave me was of a sort of vague, intermediate state, a special reserve for souls too non-existent for anything so positive as either sin or virtue. *I* don't know. He was much too egotistical and unobservant to give me any clear idea of the kind of place, kind of country, there is on the Other Side of Things. Wherever he was, he seems to have fallen in with a set of kindred spirits: ghosts of weak Cockney young men, who were on a footing of Christian names, and among these there was certainly a lot of talk about 'going haunting' and things like that.

Yes – going haunting! They seemed to think 'haunting' a tremendous adventure, and most of them funked it all the time. And so primed, you know, he had come."

"But really!" said Wish to the fire.

"These are the impressions he gave me, anyhow," said Clayton, modestly. "I may, of course, have been in a rather uncritical state, but that was the sort of background he gave to himself. He kept flitting up and down, with his thin voice going – talking, talking about his wretched self, and never a word of clear, firm statement from first to last. He was thinner and sillier and more pointless than if he had been real and alive. Only then, you know, he would not have been in my bedroom here – if he *had* been alive. I should have kicked him out."

"Of course," said Evans, "there *are* poor mortals like that."

"And there's just as much chance of their having ghosts as the rest of us," I admitted.

"What gave a sort of point to him, you know, was the fact that he did seem within limits to have found himself out. The mess he had made of haunting had depressed him terribly. He had been told it would be a 'lark': he had come expecting it to be a 'lark,' and here it was, nothing but another failure added to his record! He proclaimed himself an utter out-and-out failure. He said, and I can quite believe it, that he had never tried to do anything all his life that he hadn't made a perfect mess of – and through all the wastes of eternity he never would. If he had had sympathy, perhaps—He paused at that, and stood regarding me. He remarked that, strange as it might seem to me, nobody, not anyone, ever, had given him the amount of sympathy I was doing now. I could see what he wanted straight away, and I determined to head him off at once. I may be a brute, you know, but being the Only Real Friend, the recipient of the confidences of one of these egotistical weaklings, ghost or body, is beyond my physical endurance. I got up briskly. 'Don't you brood on these things too much,' I said. 'The thing you've got to do is to get out of this – get out of this sharp. You pull yourself together and *try*.' 'I can't,' he said. 'You try,' I said, and try he did."

"Try!" said Sanderson. "*How?*"

"Passes," said Clayton.

"Passes?"

"Complicated series of gestures and passes with the hands. That's how he had come in and that's how he had to get out again. Lord! what a business I had!"

"But how could *any* series of passes—" I began.

"My dear man," said Clayton, turning on me and putting a great emphasis on certain words, "you want *everything* clear. I don't know *how*. All I know is that you *do* – that *he* did, anyhow, at least. After a fearful time, you know, he got his passes right and suddenly disappeared."

"Did you," said Sanderson slowly, "observe the passes?"

"Yes," said Clayton, and seemed to think. "It was tremendously queer," he said. "There we were, I and this thin, vague ghost, in that silent room, in this silent, empty inn, in this silent little Friday-night town. Not a sound except our voices and a faint panting he made when he swung. There was the bedroom candle, and one candle on the dressing-table alight, that was all – sometimes one or other would flare up into a tall, lean, astonished flame for a space. And queer things happened. 'I can't,' he said; 'I shall never——!' And suddenly he sat down on a little chair at the foot of the bed and began to sob and sob. Lord! what a harrowing, whimpering thing he seemed!

"'You pull yourself together,' I said, and tried to pat him on the back, and . . . my confounded hand went through him! By that time, you know, I wasn't nearly so – massive as I had been on the landing. I got the queerness of it full. I remember snatching back my hand out of him, as it were, with a little thrill, and walking over to the dressing-table. 'You pull yourself together,' I said to him, 'and try.' And in order to encourage and help him I began to try as well."

"What!" said Sanderson, "the passes?"

"Yes, the passes."

"But——" I said, moved by an idea that eluded me for a space.

"This is interesting," said Sanderson, with his finger in his pipe-bowl. "You mean to say this ghost of yours gave way——"

"Did his level best to give away the whole confounded barrier? *Yes*."

"He didn't," said Wish; "he couldn't. Or you'd have gone there, too."

"That's precisely it," I said, finding my elusive idea put into words for me.

"That *is* precisely it," said Clayton, with thoughtful eyes upon the fire.

For just a little while there was silence.

"And at last he did it?" said Sanderson.

"At last he did it. I had to keep him up to it hard, but he did it at last – rather suddenly. He despaired, we had a scene, and then he got up abruptly and asked me to go through the whole performance, slowly, so that he might see. 'I believe,' he said, 'if I could *see* I should spot what was wrong at once.' And he did. '*I* know,' he said. 'What do you know?' said I. '*I* know,' he repeated. Then he said, peevishly, 'I *can't* do it, if you look at me – I really *can't*; it's been that, partly, all along. I'm such a nervous fellow that you put me out.' Well, we had a bit of an argument. Naturally I wanted to see; but he was as obstinate as a mule, and suddenly I had come over as tired as a dog – he tired me out. 'All right,' I said, '*I* won't look at you,' and turned towards the mirror, on the wardrobe, by the bed.

"He started off very fast. I tried to follow him by looking in the looking-glass, to see just what it was had hung. Round went his arms and his hands, so, and so, and so, and then with a rush came to the last gesture of all – you stand erect and open out your arms – and so, don't you know, he stood. And then he didn't! He didn't! He wasn't! I wheeled round from the looking-glass to him. There was nothing! I was alone, with the flaring candles and a staggering mind. What had happened? Had anything happened? Had I been dreaming? . . . And then, with an absurd note of finality about it, the clock upon the landing discovered the moment was ripe for striking *one*. So! – Ping! And I was as grave and sober as a judge, with all my champagne and whisky gone into the vast serene. Feeling queer, you know – confoundedly *queer*! Queer! Good Lord!"

He regarded his cigar-ash for a moment. "That's all that happened," he said.

"And then you went to bed?" asked Evans.

"What else was there to do?"

I looked Wish in the eye. We wanted to scoff, and there was something, something perhaps in Clayton's voice and manner, that hampered our desire.

"And about these passes?" said Sanderson.

"I believe I could do them now."

"Oh!" said Sanderson, and produced a pen-knife and set himself to grub the dottel out of the bowl of his clay.

"Why don't you do them now?" said Sanderson, shutting his pen-knife with a click.

"That's what I'm going to do," said Clayton.

"They won't work," said Evans.

"If they do—" I suggested.

"You know, I'd rather you didn't," said Wish, stretching out his legs.

"Why?" asked Evans.

"I'd rather he didn't," said Wish.

"But he hasn't got 'em right," said Sanderson, plugging too much tobacco into his pipe.

"All the same, I'd rather he didn't," said Wish.

We argued with Wish. He said that for Clayton to go through those gestures was like mocking a serious matter. "But you don't believe—?" I said. Wish glanced at Clayton, who was staring into the fire, weighing something in his mind. "I do – more than half, anyhow, I do," said Wish.

"Clayton," said I, "you're too good a liar for us. Most of it was all right. But that disappearance . . . happened to be convincing. Tell us, it's a tale of cock and bull."

He stood up without heeding me, took the middle of the hearth-rug, and faced me. For a moment he regarded his feet thoughtfully, and then for all the rest of the time his eyes were on the opposite wall, with an intent expression. He raised his two hands slowly to the level of his eyes and so began . . .

Now, Sanderson is a Freemason, a member of the lodge of the Four Kings, which devotes itself so ably to the study and elucidation of all the mysteries of Masonry past and present, and among the students of this lodge Sanderson is by no means the least. He followed Clayton's motions with a singular interest in his reddish eye. "That's not bad," he said, when it was done. "You really do, you know, put things together, Clayton, in a most amazing fashion. But there's one little detail out."

"I know," said Clayton. "I believe I could tell you which."

"Well?"

"This," said Clayton, and did a queer little twist and writhing and thrust of the hands.

"Yes."

"That, you know, was what *he* couldn't get right," said Clayton. "But how do *you*—?"

"Most of this business, and particularly how you invented it, I don't understand at all," said Sanderson, "but just that phase – I do." He reflected. "These happen to be a series of gestures – connected with a certain branch of esoteric Masonry. Probably you know. Or else— *How?*" He reflected still further. "I do not see I can do any harm in telling you just the proper twist. After all, if you know, you know; if you don't, you don't."

"I know nothing," said Clayton, "except what the poor devil let out last night."

"Well, anyhow," said Sanderson, and placed his church-warden very carefully upon the shelf over the fireplace. Then very rapidly he gesticulated with his hands.

"So?" said Clayton, repeating.

"So," said Sanderson, and took his pipe in hand again.

"Ah, *now*," said Clayton, "I can do the whole thing – right."

He stood up before the waning fire and smiled at us all. But I think there was just a little hesitation in his smile. "If I begin—" he said.

"I wouldn't begin," said Wish.

"It's all right!" said Evans. "Matter is indestructible. You don't think any jiggery-pokery of this sort is going to snatch Clayton into the world of shades. Not it! You may try, Clayton, so far as I'm concerned, until your arms drop off at the wrists."

"I don't believe that," said Wish, and stood up and put his arm on Clayton's shoulder. "You've made me half-believe in that story somehow, and I don't want to see the thing done."

"Goodness!" said I, "here's Wish frightened!"

"I am," said Wish, with real or admirably feigned intensity. "I believe that if he goes through these motions right he'll *go*."

"He'll not do anything of the sort," I cried. "There's only one way out of this world for men, and Clayton is thirty years from that. Besides . . . And such a ghost! Do you think—?"

Wish interrupted me by moving. He walked out from among our chairs and stopped beside the table and stood there. "Clayton," he said, "you're a fool."

Clayton, with a humorous light in his eyes, smiled back to him. "Wish," he said, "is right and all you others are wrong. I shall go. I shall get to the end of these passes, and as the last swish whistles through the air, Presto! – this hearthrug will be vacant, the room will be blank amazement, and a respectably dressed gentleman of fifteen stone will plump into the world of shades. I'm certain. So will you be. I decline to argue further. Let the thing be tried."

"*No*," said Wish, and made a step and ceased, and Clayton raised his hands once more to repeat the spirit's passing.

By that time, you know, we were all in a state of tension – largely because of the behaviour of Wish. We sat all of us with our eyes on Clayton – I, at least, with a sort of tight, stiff feeling about me as though from the back of my skull to the middle of my thighs my body had been changed to steel. And there, with a gravity that was imperturbably serene, Clayton bowed and swayed and waved his hands and arms before us. As he drew towards the end one piled up, one tingled in one's teeth. The last gesture, I have said, was to swing the arms out wide open, with the face held up. And when at last he swung out to this closing gesture I ceased even to breathe. It was ridiculous, of course, but you know that ghost-story feeling. It was after dinner, in a queer old shadowy house. Would he, after all—?

There he stood for one stupendous moment, with his arms open and his upturned face, assured and bright, in the glare of the hanging lamp. We hung through that moment as if it were an age, and then came from all of us something that was half a sigh of infinite relief and half a reassuring "*No!*" For visibly – he wasn't going. It was all nonsense. He had told an idle story, and carried it almost to conviction, that was all! . . . And then in that moment the face of Clayton changed.

It changed. It changed as a lit house changes when its lights are suddenly extinguished. His eyes were suddenly eyes that were fixed, his smile was frozen on his lips, and he stood there still. He stood there, very gently swaying.

That moment, too, was an age. And then, you know, chairs were scraping, things were falling, and we were all moving. His knees seemed to give, and he fell forward, and Evans rose and caught him in his arms . . .

It stunned us all. For a minute I suppose no one said a coherent thing. We believed it, yet could not believe it . . . I came out of a muddled stupefaction to find myself kneeling beside him, and his vest and shirt were torn open, and Sanderson's hand lay on his heart . . .

Well – the simple fact before us could very well wait our convenience; there was no hurry for us to comprehend. It lay there for an hour; it lies athwart my memory, black and amazing still, to this day. Clayton had, indeed, passed into the world that lies so near to and so far from our own, and he had gone thither by the only road that mortal man may take. But whether he did indeed pass there by that poor ghost's incantation, or whether he was stricken suddenly by apoplexy in the midst of an idle tale – as the coroner's jury would have us believe – is no matter for my judging; it is just one of those inexplicable riddles that must remain unsolved until the final solution of all things shall come. All I certainly know is that, in the very moment, in the very instant, of concluding those passes, he changed, and staggered, and fell down before us – dead!

Full Fathom Five

Alexander Woollcott

Location: Cape Cod, Massachusetts.
Time: October, 1908.
Eyewitness Description: *"On the spot in front of the fireplace where the apparition had seemed to stand, was a patch of water, a little circular pool that had issued from no crack in the floor . . ."*

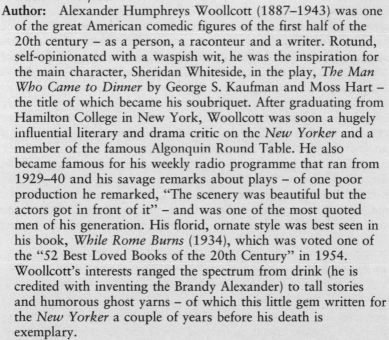

Author: Alexander Humphreys Woollcott (1887–1943) was one of the great American comedic figures of the first half of the 20th century – as a person, a raconteur and a writer. Rotund, self-opinionated with a waspish wit, he was the inspiration for the main character, Sheridan Whiteside, in the play, *The Man Who Came to Dinner* by George S. Kaufman and Moss Hart – the title of which became his soubriquet. After graduating from Hamilton College in New York, Woollcott was soon a hugely influential literary and drama critic on the *New Yorker* and a member of the famous Algonquin Round Table. He also became famous for his weekly radio programme that ran from 1929–40 and his savage remarks about plays – of one poor production he remarked, "The scenery was beautiful but the actors got in front of it" – and was one of the most quoted men of his generation. His florid, ornate style was best seen in his book, *While Rome Burns* (1934), which was voted one of the "52 Best Loved Books of the 20th Century" in 1954. Woollcott's interests ranged the spectrum from drink (he is credited with inventing the Brandy Alexander) to tall stories and humorous ghost yarns – of which this little gem written for the *New Yorker* a couple of years before his death is exemplary.

This is the story just as I heard it the other evening – a ghost story told me as true. It seems that one chilly October night in the first decade of the present century, two sisters were motoring along a Cape Cod road, when their car broke down just before midnight, and would go no further. This was in an era when such mishaps were both commoner and more hopeless than they are today.

For these two, there was no chance of help until another car might chance to come by in the morning and give them a tow. Of a lodging for the night there was no hope, except a gaunt, unlighted frame house which, with a clump of pine trees beside it, stood black in the moonlight, across a neglected stretch of frost-hardened lawn.

They yanked at its ancient bell-pull, but only a faint tinkle within made answer. They banged despairingly on the door panel only to awaken what at first they thought was an echo, and then identified as a shutter responding antiphonally with the help of a nipping wind. This shutter was around the corner, and the ground-floor window behind it was broken and unfastened.

There was enough moonlight to show that the room within was a deserted library, with a few books left on the sagging shelves and a few pieces of dilapidated furniture still standing where some departing family had left them, long before. The sweep of the flashlight which one of the women had brought with her showed them that on the uncarpeted floor the dust lay thick and trackless, as if no one had trod there in many a day.

They decided to bring their blankets in from the car and stretch out there on the floor until daylight, none too comfortable, perhaps, but at least sheltered from that salt and cutting wind.

It was while they were lying there, trying to get to sleep, while, indeed, they had drifted halfway across the borderland, that they saw – each confirming the other's fear by a convulsive grip of the hand – standing at the empty fireplace, as if trying to dry himself by a fire that was not there, the wraithlike figure of a sailor, come dripping from the sea.

After an endless moment, in which neither woman breathed, one of them somehow found the strength to call out, "Who's there?"

The challenge shattered the intolerable silence, and at the sound, muttering a little – they said afterwards that it was something between a groan and a whimper – the misty figure seemed to dissolve. They strained their eyes, but could see nothing between themselves and the battered mantelpiece.

Then, telling themselves (and, as one does, half believing it) that they had been dreaming, they tried again to sleep, and indeed did sleep until a patch of shuttered sunlight striped the morning floor. As they sat up and blinked at the gritty realism of the forsaken room, they would, I think, have laughed at their shared illusion of the night before, had it not been for something at which one of the sisters pointed with a kind of gasp.

There, in the still undisturbed dust, on the spot in front of the fireplace where the apparition had seemed to stand, was a patch of water, a little circular pool that had issued from no crack in the floor nor, as far as they could see, fallen from any point in the innocent ceiling. Near it in the surrounding dust was no footprint – their own or any other's – and in it was a piece of green that looked like seaweed. One of the women bent down and put her finger to the water, then lifted it to her tongue. The water was salty.

After that the sisters scuttled out and sat in their car, until a passer-by gave them a tow to the nearest village. In its tavern at breakfast they gossiped with the proprietress about the empty house among the pine trees down the road. Oh, yes, it had been just that way for a score of years or more. Folks did say the place was spooky, haunted by a son of the family who, driven out by his father, had shipped before the mast and been drowned at sea.

Some said the family had moved away because they could not stand the things they heard and saw at night.

A year later, one of the sisters told the story at a dinner party in New York. In the pause that followed a man across the table leaned forward.

"My dear lady," he said, with a smile, "I happen to be the curator of a museum where they are doing a good deal of work on submarine vegetation. In your place, I never would have left that house without taking the bit of seaweed with me."

"Of course you wouldn't," she answered tartly, "and neither did I."

It seems she had lifted it out of the water and dried it a little by pressing it against a window pane. Then she had carried it off in her pocket-book, as a souvenir. As far as she knew, it was still in an envelope in a little drawer of her desk at home. If she could find it, would he like to see it? He would. Next morning she sent it around by messenger, and a few days later it came back with a note.

"You were right," the note said, "this is seaweed. Furthermore, it may interest you to learn that it is of a rare variety which, as far as we know, grows only on dead bodies."

The Night the Ghost Got In

James Thurber

Location: Jefferson Avenue, Columbus, Ohio.
Time: 17 November, 1915.
Eyewitness Description: *"Instantly the steps begin again, circled the dining-room table like a man running and started up the stairs towards us, heavily two at a time. The light still shone palely down the stairs; we saw nothing coming; we only heard the steps . . ."*

Author: James Grover Thurber (1894–1961) was a contemporary of Alexander Woollcott at the *New Yorker* and left an even more remarkable legacy of humorous works and cartoons. Born in Columbus, Ohio, he studied at the Ohio State University and, after serving as a code clerk in France during World War One, joined the staff of the magazine where he made his name in 1927. Despite losing one eye due to a childhood injury, Thurber's perception of life and observation of the comedy of human beings was vividly illustrated in books like *The Seal in the Bedroom* (1932), the sixties TV series *My World and Welcome To It* and the enigmatic Walter Mitty. His interest in ghosts stemmed from his mother's fascination with the occult and living in a haunted house, 77, Jefferson Avenue, from 1912, which inspired this story. Initially, Thurber's friends dismissed the tale as just another example of his humour, but he insisted: "In his play, *The Potting Shed*, Graham Greene has a character say, 'No one who has ever experienced a ghost can be argued out of believing he did.' After laughing off my own ghost in my story, I now share with Greene the conviction that it *was* a supernatural phenomenon." Years later, Thurber discovered that a man who once lived in an upstairs room of his old home had shot and killed himself there.

The ghost that got into our house on the night of 17 November 1915, raised such a hullabaloo of misunderstandings that I am sorry I didn't just let it keep on walking, and go to bed. Its advent caused my mother to throw a shoe through a window of the house next door and ended up with my grandfather shooting a patrolman. I am sorry, therefore, as I have said, that I ever paid any attention to the footsteps.

They began about a quarter past one o'clock in the morning, a rhythmic, quick-cadenced walking around the dining-room table. My mother was asleep in one room upstairs, my brother Herman in another; grandfather was in the attic, in the old walnut bed which, as you will remember, once fell on my father. I had just stepped out of the bathtub and was busily rubbing myself with a towel when I heard the steps. They were the steps of a man walking rapidly around the dining-room table downstairs. The light from the bathroom shone down the back steps, which dropped directly into the dining-room; I could see the faint shine of plates on the plate-rail; I couldn't see the table. The steps kept going round and round the table; at regular intervals a board creaked, when it was trod upon. I supposed at first that it was my father or my brother Roy, who had gone to Indianapolis but were expected home at any time. I suspected next that it was a burglar. It did not enter my mind until later that it was a ghost.

After the walking had gone on for perhaps three minutes, I tiptoed to Herman's room. "Psst!" I hissed, in the dark, shaking

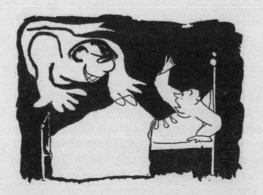

He always half suspected that
something would get him.

him. "Awp," he said, in the low, hopeless tone of a despondent beagle – he always half suspected that something would "get him" in the night. I told him who I was. "There's something downstairs!" I said. He got up and followed me to the head of the back staircase. We listened together. There was no sound. The steps had ceased. Herman looked at me in some alarm: I had only the bath towel around my waist. He wanted to go back to bed, but I gripped his arm. "There's something down there!" I said. Instantly the steps began again, circled the dining-room table like a man running, and started up the stairs toward us, heavily, two at a time. The light still shone palely down the stairs; we saw nothing coming; we only heard the steps. Herman rushed to his room and slammed the door. I slammed shut the door at the stairs top and held my knee against it. After a long minute, I slowly opened it again. There was nothing there. There was no sound. None of us ever heard the ghost again.

The slamming of the doors had aroused mother: she peered out of her room. "What on earth are you boys doing?" she demanded. Herman ventured out of his room. "Nothing," he said, gruffly, but he was, in color, a light green. "What was all that running around downstairs?" said mother. So she had heard the steps, too! We just looked at her. "Burglars!" she shouted, intuitively. I tried to quiet her by starting lightly downstairs.

"Come on, Herman," I said.

"I'll stay with mother," he said. "She's all excited."

I stepped back onto the landing.

"Don't either of you go a step," said mother. "We'll call the police." Since the phone was downstairs, I didn't see how we were going to call the police – nor did I want the police – but mother made one of her quick, incomparable decisions. She flung up a window of her bedroom which faced the bedroom windows of the house of a neighbor, picked up a shoe, and whammed it through a pane of glass across the narrow space that separated the two houses. Glass tinkled into the bedroom occupied by a retired engraver named Bodwell and his wife. Bodwell had been for some years in rather a bad way and was subject to mild "attacks". Most everybody we knew or lived near had *some* kind of attacks.

It was now about two o'clock of a moonless night; clouds hung black and low. Bodwell was at the window in a minute, shouting, frothing a little, shaking his fist. "We'll sell the house and go back to Peoria," we could hear Mrs Bodwell saying. It was some time before Mother "got through" to Bodwell. "Burglars!" she shouted.

"Burglars in the house!" Herman and I hadn't dared to tell her that it was not burglars but ghosts, for she was even more afraid of ghosts than of burglars. Bodwell at first thought that she meant there were burglars in his house, but finally he quieted down and called the police for us over an extension phone by his bed. After he had disappeared from the window, mother suddenly made as if to throw another shoe, not because there was further need of it but, as she later explained, because the thrill of heaving a shoe through a window glass had enormously taken her fancy. I prevented her.

The police were on hand in a commendably short time: a Ford sedan full of them, two on motorcycles, and a patrol wagon with about eight in it and a few reporters. They began banging at our front door. Flashlights shot streaks of gleam up and down the walls, across the yard, down the walk between our house and Bodwell's. "Open up!" cried a hoarse voice. "We're men from Headquarters!" I wanted to go down and let them in, since there they were, but mother wouldn't hear of it. "You haven't a stitch on," she pointed out. "You'd catch your death." I wound the towel around me again. Finally the cops put their shoulders to our big heavy front door with its thick beveled glass and broke it in: I could hear a rending of wood and a splash of glass on the floor of the hall. Their lights played all over the living-room and crisscrossed nervously in the dining-room, stabbed into hallways, shot up the front stairs and finally up the back. They caught me standing in my towel at the top. A heavy policeman bounded up the steps. "Who are you?" he demanded. "I live here," I said. "Well, whattsa matta, ya hot?" he asked. It was, as a matter of fact, cold; I went to my room and pulled on some trousers. On my way out, a cop stuck a gun into my ribs. "Whatta you doin' here?" he demanded. "I live here," I said.

The officer in charge reported to mother. "No sign of nobody, lady," he said. "Musta got away – whatt'd he look like?" "There were two or three of them," mother said, "whooping and carrying on and slamming doors." "Funny," said the cop. "All ya windows and doors was locked on the inside tight as a tick."

Downstairs, we could hear the tromping of the other police. Police were all over the place; doors were yanked open, drawers were yanked open, windows were shot up and pulled down, furniture fell with dull thumps. A half-dozen policemen emerged out of the darkness of the front hallway upstairs. They began to ransack the floor: pulled beds away from walls, tore clothes off hooks in the closets, pulled suitcases and boxes off shelves. One of them found an old zither that Roy had won in a pool tournament. "Looky here, Joe," he said, strumming it with a big paw. The cop named Joe took it and turned it over. "What is it?" he asked me. "It's an old zither our guinea pig used to sleep on," I said. It was true that a pet guinea pig we once had would never sleep anywhere except on the zither, but I should never have said so. Joe and the other cop looked at me a long time. They put the zither back on a shelf.

"No sign o' nuthin'," said the cop who had first spoken to mother. "This guy," he explained to the others, jerking a thumb at me, "was nekked. The lady seems historical." They all nodded, but said nothing; just looked at me. In the small silence we all heard a creaking in the attic. Grandfather was turning over in bed. "What's 'at?" snapped Joe. Five or six cops sprang for the attic door before I could intervene or explain. I realized that it would be bad if they burst in on grandfather unannounced, or even announced. He was going through a phase in which he believed that General Meade's men, under steady hammering by Stonewall Jackson, were beginning to retreat and even desert.

When I got to the attic, things were pretty confused. Grandfather had evidently jumped to the conclusion that the police were deserters from Meade's army, trying to hide away in his attic. He bounded out of bed wearing a long flannel nightgown over long woolen underwear, a nightcap, and a leather jacket around his chest. The cops must have realized at once that the indignant white-haired old man belonged in the house, but they had no chance to say so. "Back, ye cowardly dogs!" roared grandfather. "Back t' the lines, ye goddam lily-livered cattle!" With that, he fetched the officer who found the zither a flat-handed smack alongside his head that sent him sprawling. The others beat a retreat, but not fast enough; grandfather grabbed Zither's gun from its holster and let fly. The report seemed to crack the rafters; smoke filled the attic. A cop cursed and shot his hand to his shoulder. Somehow, we all finally got downstairs again and locked the door against the old gentleman. He fired once or twice more in the darkness and then went back to bed. "That was grandfather," I explained to Joe, out of breath. "He thinks you're deserters." "I'll say he does," said Joe.

The cops were reluctant to leave without getting their hands on somebody besides grandfather; the night had been distinctly a defeat for them. Furthermore, they obviously didn't like the "layout";

something looked – and I can see their viewpoint – phony. They began to poke into things again. A reporter, a thin-faced, wispy man, came up to me. I had put on one of mother's blouses, not being able to find anything else. The reporter looked at me with mingled suspicion and interest. "Just what the hell is the real lowdown here, Bud?" he asked. I decided to be frank with him. "We had ghosts," I said. He gazed at me a long time as if I were a slot machine into which he had, without results, dropped a nickel. Then he walked away. The cops followed him, the one grandfather shot holding his now-bandaged arm, cursing and blaspheming. "I'm gonna get my gun back from that old bird," said the zither-cop. "Yeh," said Joe. "You – and who else?" I told them I would bring it to the station house the next day.

"What was the matter with that one policeman?" mother asked, after they had gone. "Grandfather shot him," I said. "What for?" she demanded. I told her he was a deserter. "Of all things!" said mother. "He was such a nicc-looking young man."

Grandfather was fresh as a daisy and full of jokes at breakfast next morning. We thought at first he had forgotten all about what had happened, but he hadn't. Over his third cup of coffee, he glared at Herman and me. "What was the idee of all them cops tarryhootin' round the house last night?" he demanded. He had us there.

Sir Tristram Goes West

Eric Keown

Location: Ararat, Florida, USA.

Time: Autumn, 1934.

Eyewitness Description: *"The story goes that his father, a fire-eating old Royalist, got so bored at always finding his son mooning about in the library when he might have been out trailing Cromwell, that when he was dying he laid a curse on Tristram which can only be expunged by a single-handed act of valour . . ."*

Author: Eric Oliver Dilworth Keown (1860–1963) was born in Mobile, Alabama, where his family were involved in the oil industry. After majoring in literature at Alabama University, he began writing humorous stories and sketches for American magazines. At the turn of the century Keown moved to Britain, settled in the pretty Surrey village of Worplesdon and became a regular contributor to *Punch* magazine. He wrote numerous comic sketches, scripts for several British comedy films and biographies of two popular English actresses, Peggy Ashcroft and Margaret Rutherford. Keown's hilarious tale of a ghost being shipped across the Atlantic when the family mansion is transported to Florida was spotted in *Punch* in 1935 by producer Alexander Korda, fresh from his triumph filming H. G. Wells' *Things To Come*, and adapted for the screen as *The Ghost Goes West*. Directed by Rene Clair, the picture starred Robert Donat in the dual role of clan chief and ghost and Eugene Pallete as the American millionaire. The script by Geoffrey Kerr got in some sly digs at American imperialism and with Special Effects designer Ned Mann creating a series of convincing supernatural illusions, the result was a classic ghost movie, a big success at the box office and one still regularly reshown on late night TV.

Three men sat and talked at the long table in the library of Moat Place. Many dramatic conversations had occurred in that mellow and celebrated room, some of them radically affecting whole pages of English history; but none so vital as this to the old house itself. For its passport was being viséd to the United States.

Lord Mullion sighed gently. He was wondering whether, if a vote could be taken amongst his ancestors – most of whose florid portraits had already crossed the Atlantic – they would condemn or approve his action. Old Red Roger, his grandfather, would have burnt the place round him rather than sell an inch of it. But then Red Roger had never been up against an economic crisis. And at that moment, the afternoon sun flooding suddenly the great oriel window, a vivid shaft of light stabbed the air like a rapier and illuminated Mr Julius Plugg's chequebook, which was lying militantly on the table.

"Would you go to forty thousand?" asked Lord Mullion.

Mr Plugg's bushy eyebrows climbed a good half-inch. When they rose further a tremor was usually discernible in Wall Street.

"I'll say it's a tall price for an old joint," he said. "Well – I might."

Lord Mullion turned to the Eminent Architect. "You're absolutely certain that the house can be successfully replanted in Mr Plugg's back garden, like a damned azalea?"

The Eminent Architect, whose passion happened to be Moat Place, also sighed. "Bigger houses than this have been moved. It'll be a cracking job, but there's no real snag. I recommend that for greater safety the library be sent by liner. The main structure can go by cargo-boat."

The shaft of sunlight was still playing suggestively on the golden cover of the chequebook. Sadly Lord Mullion inclined his head.

"Very well, Mr Plugg. It's yours," he said.

A gasp of childish delight escaped the Pokerface of American finance. "That's well," he cried, "that's dandy! And, now it's fixed, would you give me the the low-down on a yarn I've heard about a family spook? Bunk?"

"On the contrary," said Lord Mullion, "he's quite the most amusing ghost in this part of the country. But I shouldn't think he'll bother you."

"Anyone ever seen him?"

"I saw him yesterday, sitting over there by the window."

Mr Plugg sprang round apprehensively. "Doing what?" he demanded.

"Just dreaming. He was a poet, you know."

"A poet? Hey, Earl, are you getting funny?"

"Not a bit. We know all about him. Sir Tristram Mullion, laid out by a Roundhead pike at Naseby. He must have been pretty absent-minded; probably he forgot about the battle until somebody hit him, and then it was too late. The story goes that his father, a fire-eating old Royalist, got so bored at always finding his eldest son mooning about the library when he might have been out trailing Cromwell that when he was dying he laid a curse on Tristram which could only be expunged by a single-handed act of valour. Tristram rode straight off to Naseby and got it in the neck in the first minute. So he's still here, wandering about this library, never getting a chance to do anything more heroic than a couplet. And he wasn't even a particularly good poet."

Mr Plugg had regained command of himself. "I seem to have read somewhere of a ghost crossing the Atlantic with a shack," he said, "but that won't rattle a tough baby like me, and I doubt if your spook and I'd have much in common. How about having the lawyers in and signing things up?"

The S.S. *Extravaganza* was carving her way steadily through the calm and moonlit surface of the Atlantic. The thousand portholes in her steep sides blazed, and the air was sickly with the drone of saxophones. It was as though a portion of the new Park Lane had taken to the water.

Down in the dim light of No. 3 Hold a notable event had just taken place. Sir Tristram Mullion had emerged from nowhere and was standing there, very nearly opaque with surprise and irritation. His activities had been confined to the Moat Place library for so long that he could think of no good reason why he should suddenly materialize in this strange dungeon. That it was a dungeon he had little doubt. Its sole furniture was a number of large packing-cases marked "JULIUS PLUGG, ARARAT, USA", and they were too high for even a ghost to sit upon with comfort. Tristram decided to explore.

The first person he encountered in the upper reaches of the ship was Alfred Bimsting, a young steward, who cried, "The Fancy Dress ain't on till tomorrow, Sir," and then pardonably fainted as he saw Tristram pass clean through a steel partition . . .

Sitting up on high stools at the bar, Professor Gupp, the historian, and an unknown Colonel were getting all argumentative over the *Extravaganza*'s special brown sherry.

"My dear fellow," the Professor was saying, "whatever you may say about Marston Moor, Naseby showed Rupert to be a very great cavalry leader. Very great indeed."

"Nonsense!" growled the Colonel. "A hot-headed young fool. Fairfax was the better soldier in every way."

"I tell you—" the Professor began when he became aware of a presence at his elbow – a handsome young man in the clothes of a Cavalier.

"Frightfully sorry to interrupt," said Tristram (for acquaintance with the young Mullions had kept his idiom level with the fashion), "but as a matter of fact I used to know Rupert and Fairfax pretty well, and you can take it from me they were a couple of insufferable bores. Rupert was a shockin' hearty, always slappin' you on the back, and Fairfax was a pompous old fool. As for Naseby, it was a hell of a mess."

Professor Gupp hiccupped. "Young man," he said reprovingly, "I am driven to conclude that you have been drinking to excess. It may interest you to know that I am the author of the standard monograph on Naseby."

"It may interest *you* to know," Tristram cried rather dramatically, "that I was killed there." And he faded through the black glass wall of the refrigerator with such startling ease that neither Professor Gupp nor the Colonel could ever face Very Old Solera again . . .

After the dazzle of strip-lights and chromium Tristram was glad to find himself out on the promenade deck, which was deserted. It was nearly three hundred years since he had been to sea, returning from the French Court in considerable disgrace, having lost his dispatches; but, aided by the traditional adaptability of the ghost and the aristocrat, he noted with unconcern the tremendous pace at which the waves were flying past and the vast scarlet funnels towering above, which seemed to him to salute the moon so insuitably (he was a poet, remember) with great streamers of heavy black smoke. As he paced the deck he meditated the opening rhymes of a brief ode to the heavens . . .

Meanwhile, in the the convenient shadow of Lifeboat 5, a stout politician was surprised to find himself proposing marriage to his secretary, who with a more practised eye had seen it coming ever since Southampton. He was warming up to it nicely. Not for nothing had he devoted a lifetime to the mastery of circumambient speech.

"And though I cannot offer you, my dear, either the frivolities of youth or the glamour of an hereditary title, I am asking you to share a position which I believe to carry a certain distinction—" Here he broke off abruptly as Tristram appeared in the immediate neighbourhood and leaned dreamily over the rail.

There was an embarrassing silence, of which the secretary took advantage to repair the ravages of the politician's first kiss.

"Would you oblige me, Sir, by going away?" he boomed in the full round voice that regularly hypnotised East Dimbury into electing him.

Tristram made no answer. He was trying hard to remember if "tune" made an impeccable rhyme to "moon".

"Confound you, Sir," cried the Politician, "are you aware that you are intruding upon a sacred privacy?"

Tristram genuinely didn't hear. He was preparing to let "boon" have it, or, if necessary, "loon".

The Politician heaved his bulk out of his deck chair and fetched Tristram a slap on the shoulder. But of course as you can't do that with a properly disembodied matured-in-the-wood ghost, all that happened was that the Politician's hand sank through Tristram like a razor through dripping and was severely bruised on the rail. It was left to the secretary to console him, for Tristram was gone.

And then, rumours of Tristram's strange interludes percolating through the ship, all at once he became the centre of a series of alarming enfilading movements. The young Tuppenny-Berkeleys and their friends, who had been holding a sausage-and-*peignoir* party in the swimming-bath, bore down upon him waving *Leberwursts* and crowing "Tally-ho! The jolly old Laughing Cavalier!" Cavalierly was the way he treated them. Sweeping off his hat to young Lady Catherine, he nodded coldly to the others and walked straight through his brother, a young Guardsman, who was to dine out on the experience for nearly half a century.

The main staircase was already blocked with excited passengers. At the top of it stood the Chief Stewardess, a vast and imposing figure. Just for fun (for he was beginning to enjoy his little outing – and so would you if you had been stuck in a mouldy library for three hundred years) Tristram flung his arms gallantly round her neck and cried, "Your servant, Madam!" The poor woman collapsed mountainously into the arms of a Bolivian millionaire, who consequently collapsed too, in company with the three poorer millionaires who were behind him.

At this point the Captain arrived and advanced majestically. To the delight of the company Tristram picked up a large potted palm and thrust it dustily into his arms* Then, with a courtly bow to the crowd and a valedictory gesture of osculation, he disappeared backwards through a massive portrait of Albert The Good.

* N.B. – Can't a ghost grip? I say it can.

On the way back to No. 3 Hold he sped through the Athenian Suite. In it the new lord of Moat Place lay on his bed in his pink silken underwear, pondering on the triumph with which in a few months he would spring upon the markets the child of his dreams, his new inhumane killer for demolishing the out-of-date buildings of the world, Plugg's Pneumatic Pulveriser.

Tristram took one look at him and disliked him at sight. On the bed table lay a basin of predigested gruel. Inverting it quickly over Mr Plugg's head, he passed on to disappear into the bowels of the ship.

Blowzy Bolloni and Redgat Ike sat at a marble-topped table sinking synthetic gin with quiet efficiency. They had spent the afternoon emptying several machine-guns into a friend, so they were rather tired.

"I've given Bug and Toledo the line-up," Bolloin said. "It's a wow. Toledo's in cahoots with one of Plugg's maids and she spilled the beans. The stuff's in his new safe in the library – see? Any hop-head could fetch it out. Is that oke?"

"Mebbe it'll mean a grand all round, eh?" asked Redgat.

"Or two." And Bolloni winked.

"That'll be mighty nice. You want my ukulele?"

"Yeah. But I got a hunch heaters'll be enough."

They called for another snort of hooch, testing its strength in the approved gangster way by dipping a finger in it. The nail remaining undissolved, they drank confidently.

In the library of the reassembled Moat Place, Julius Plugg squirmed on a divan and cursed his folly in not entrusting the secret plans of his Pulveriser to the strong-room of his factory. Only a simp would have asked for it by bringing them home, he told himself bluntly. But it was too late now to do anything about them, for he was roped down as tightly as a thrown steer. Also he was gagged with his own handkerchief, a circumstance which gave him literally a pain in the neck.

Mrs Plugg, similarly captive in the big armchair had shed her normal dignity in a way which would have startled the Ararat Branch of the Women's Watch and Ward Fellowship, over which she presided. Her head was completely obscured by a large wicker wastepaper-basket, and through it there filtered strange canine noises.

As for Hiram Plugg, the leader of sophomore fashion, he was lashed so firmly to the suit of armour in the corner that it positively hurt him to blink; for before the high rewards of ace-gunning had attracted Blowzy Bolloni to the civilization of the West he had helped his father with his fishing-nets in Sicily, and it was now his boast that he could tie a victim up quicker and more unpleasantly than any other gangster in the States.

At the back of the library Redgat Ike lounged gracefully on the table with a finger curled ready round the trigger of a Thompson sub-machine-gun, trained on the door. He grinned amiably as he thought how bug-house the servants had looked as they went down before his little chloroform-squirt, the cook clutching a rolling-pin and the butler muttering he'd rung the cops already – the poor bozo not knowing the wire had been cut an hour before. Oh, it was a couple of grands for nothing, a show like this. Redgat couldn't think why every one wasn't a gangster.

Bolloni and Toledo and the Bug, who had been searching the panels for signs of the safe, gave it up and gathered round the prostrate form of Mr Plugg, who snarled at them as fiercely as he could manage through his nose.

"Come on, Mister," said Bolloni, "we ain't playing Hunt the Slipper any more. You'd better squawk where that tin box is *and* its combination. Otherwise my boyfriend over there might kinda touch his toy by mistake, and that's goodbye to that teapot dome of yours." He smiled evilly at Redgat, who smiled back and swung the machine-gun into line with Mr Plugg's bald head.

"Have his comforter out and see what he says," suggested Toledo. But, shorn of much pungent criticism of the gangsters and their heredity, all Mr Plugg said was, "There's no safe here, you big bunch of saps."

Most sailormen are practical and many are crude. Bolloni was both. Replacing the gag in Mr Plugg's champing jaws, he drew from his pocket a twelve-bore shot-gun sawn off at the breech and pressed it persuasively against Mr Plugg's ample stomach. With his other hand he took a firm grip of the magnate's moustache and began to heave.

"When you sorta remember about the safe," he said, "give three toots on your nose."

Who would blame Mr Plugg? Gathering together his remaining breath, he let out a first toot which would have done honour to a Thames tug. He was filling up with air for a second one when suddenly the three gangsters sprang round as if stung. Painfully he turned his head, to see a strange figure standing by the bookshelves. (You've got it first guess. It *was*.)

Tristram hadn't noticed the others. He was poring over a set of Spenser when Redgat slid back his trigger, and it was not until a heavy .45 bullet tore the book from his hand that he realized that something was happening. A stream of lead was hurtling through him and turning a priceless edition of Boccaccio to pulp, but he felt nothing. He was filled only with resentment at such ill-mannered interruption.

None of the gangsters had ever seen a man take fifty bullets in the chest and remain perpendicular. The sight unnerved them. Redgat continued to fire as accurately as before, but the other three stood irresolute.

Before Bolloni could dodge him Tristram had picked up what was left of *The Faëry Queen* and brought it down with terrific force on his head, dropping him like a skittle. Boiling with rage, Tristram grabbed up *The Anatomy of Melancholy* and set about Toledo and the Bug. One of them discharged the shotgun full in his face, but not with any great hope – Gee! a ritzy guy in fancy-dress who only got fresher after a whole drum of slugs!

It was soon over. Redgat clung to his beloved machine-gun to the end, unable to believe that a second drum wouldn't take effect. But he, too, went down to a thundering crack on the jaw from an illustrated *Apocrypha* . . .

Tristram began to feel very odd. For a moment he surveyed the scene, not quite comprehending what it all meant. Mrs Plugg had swooned, which merely caused the wastepaper-basket on her head to drop from the vertical to the horizontal. Her son was clearly about to be sick. Julius Plugg, himself supine but undaunted, was making wild signals with his famous eyebrows to be released.

Then, something in his nebulous inside going queerly click, Tristram realized what was happening. At last he had been a hero. At last he was free. The hail of bullets had smashed up not only Boccaccio but his father's curse . . .

Debating, with the exquisite detachment of the poet, whether the Pluggs would be free before the gangsters recovered, he faded imperceptibly and left them to it.

Who or What Was It?

Kingsley Amis

Location: Fareham, Hertfordshire.

Time: August, 1971.

Eyewitness Description: *"I was very alarmed. Because the Green Man wasn't only the name of the pub in my book; it was also the name of a frightening creature, a sort of solid ghost conjured up out of tree branches and leaves and so on . . ."*

Author: Sir Kingsley Amis (1922–95) was born in Norwood, South London and educated at Norbury College, whose only other famous pupil, he liked to say, was Derek Bentley, who was hung for the murder of a policeman. In 1954, Amis wrote *Lucky Jim*, which won the Somerset Maugham Award and has since proved to be one of the great comic creations of 20th century fiction. In subsequent works, he has proved to be a master of invective and comedy as well as revealing his interest in the supernatural in several short stories and the chilling novel, *The Green Man* (1969) described by *The Times* as "an accomplished ghost story in the M. R. James style, under appreciated when it first came out, but winning some belated admiration when it became a television serial in 1990." A clubbable, generous-hearted, though often irascible man, Amis created a furore when he published this story in *Playboy* in 1972. It was written in its original form as a radio broadcast intended to make listeners believe it was a factual account. The whole idea backfired, however, when – like Machen before him – he found people, including close friends, believing it was *true*. Indeed, despite the fact he repeatedly stated it was "a lying narrative, fiction disguised as fact," this misapprehension, like the theme of the story, haunted Amis for the rest of his life.

I want to tell you about a very odd experience I had a few months ago, not so as to entertain you, but because I think it raises some very basic questions about, you know, what life is all about and to what extent we run our own lives. Rather worrying questions. Anyway, what happened was this.

My wife and I had been staying the weekend with her uncle and aunt in Westmorland, near a place called Milnethorpe. Both of us, Jane and I that is, had things to do in London on the Monday morning, and it's a long drive from up there down to Barnet, where we live, even though a good half of it is on the M6. So I said, Look, don't let's break our necks trying to get home in the light (this was in August), let's take it easy and stop somewhere for dinner and reckon to get home about half-past ten or eleven. Jane said okay.

So we left Milnethorpe in the middle of the afternoon, took things fairly easily, and landed up about half-past seven or a quarter to eight at the . . . the place we'd picked out of one of the food guides before we started. I won't tell you the name of the place, because the people who run it wouldn't thank me if I did. Please don't go looking for it. I'd advise you not to.

Anyway, we parked the car in the yard and went inside. It was a nice-looking sort of place, pretty old, built a good time ago I mean, done up in a sensible sort of way, no muzak and no bloody silly blacked-out lighting, but no olde-worlde nonsense either.

Well, I got us both a drink in the bar and went off to see about a table for dinner. I soon found the right chap, and he said, Fine, table for two in half an hour, certainly sir, are you in the bar, I'll get someone to bring you the menu in a few minutes. Pleasant sort of chap, a bit young for the job.

I was just going off when a sort of paunchy business type came in and said something about, Mr Allington not in tonight? and the young fellow said No sir, he's taken the evening off. All right, never mind.

Well, I'll tell you why in a minute, but I turned back to the young fellow, said Excuse me, but is your name Palmer? and he said Yes sir, and I said, Not David Palmer by any chance? and he said No sir, actually the name's George. I said, or rather burbled, A friend of mine was telling me about this place, said he'd stayed here, liked it very much, mentioned you, anyway I got half the name right, and Mr Allington is the proprietor, isn't he? That's correct, sir. See you later and all that.

I went straight back to the bar, went up to the barman and said, Fred? and he said Yes sir. I said, Fred Soames? and he said, Fred

Browning, sir. I just said, Wrong Fred, not very polite, but it was all I could think of. I went over to where my wife was sitting and I'd hardly sat down before she asked, What's the matter?

What was the matter calls for a bit of explanation. In 1969 I published a novel called *The Green Man*, which was not only the title of the book but also the name of a sort of classy pub, or inn, where most of the action took place, very much the kind of establishment we were in that evening.

Now the landlord of the Green Man was called Allington, and his deputy was called David Palmer, and the barman was called Fred Soames. Allington is a very uncommon name – I wanted that for reasons nothing to do with this story. The other two aren't, but to have got Palmer and Fred right, so to speak, as well as Allington was a thumping great coincidence, staggering in fact. But I wasn't just staggered, I was very alarmed. Because the Green Man wasn't only the name of the pub in my book; it was also the name of a frightening creature, a sort of solid ghost conjured up out of tree-branches and leaves and so on that very nearly kills Allington and his young daughter. I didn't want to find I was right about that, too.

Jane was very sensible, as always. She said stranger coincidences had happened and still been just coincidences, and mightn't I have come across an innkeeper called Allington somewhere, half forgotten about it and brought it up out of my unconscious mind when I was looking for a name for an innkeeper to put in the book, and now the real Allington's moved from wherever I'd seen him before to this place. And Palmer and Fred really are very common names. And I'd got the name of the pub wrong. I'm still not telling you what it's called, but one of the things it isn't called is the Green Man. And, my pub was in Hertfordshire and this place was . . . off the M6. All very reasonable and reassuring.

Only I wasn't very reassured. I mean, I obviously couldn't just leave it there. The thing to do was get hold of this chap Palmer and see if there was, well, any more to come. Which was going to be tricky if I wasn't going to look nosy or mad or something else that would shut him up. Neither of us ate much dinner, though there was nothing wrong with the food. We didn't say much, either. I drank a fair amount.

Then halfway through, Palmer turned up to do his everything-all-right routine, as I'd hoped he would, and as he would have done in my book. I said yes, it was fine, thanks, and then I asked him, I said we'd be very pleased if he'd join us for a brandy afterwards if he'd got time, and he said he'd be delighted. Jolly good, but I was still stuck with this problem of how to dress the thing up.

Jane had said earlier on, why didn't I just tell the truth, and I'd said, since Palmer hadn't reacted at all when I gave him my name when I was booking the table – see what I mean? – he'd only have my word for the whole story and might still think I was off my rocker, and she said of course she'd back me up, and I'd said he'd just think he'd got two loonies on his hands instead of one. Anyway, *now* she said, *Some* people who've read *The Green Man* must have mentioned it, – fancy that, Mr Palmer, you and Mr Allington and Fred are all in a book by somebody called Kingsley Amis. Obvious enough when you think of it, but like a lot of obvious things, you have got to think of it.

Well, that was the line I took when Palmer rolled up for his brandy, I'm me and I wrote this book and so on. Oh really? he said, more or less. I thought we were buggered, but then he said, Oh yes, now you mention it, I do remember some chap saying something like that, but it must have been two or three years ago – you know, as if that stopped it counting for much. I'm not much of a reader, you see, he said.

So. What about Mr Allington, I said, doesn't he read? Not what you'd call a reader, he said. Well, that was one down to me, or one up, depending on how you look at it, because *my* Allington was a tremendous reader, French poetry and all that. Still, the approach had worked after a fashion, and Palmer very decently put up with being cross-questioned on how far this place corresponded with my place, in the book.

Was Mrs Allington blonde? There wasn't a Mrs Allington any more; she'd died of leukemia quite a long time ago. Had he got his widowed father living here? (Allington's father, that is.) No, Mr Allington senior, and his wife, lived in Eastbourne. Was the house, the pub, haunted at all? Not as far as Palmer knew, and he'd been there three years. In fact, the place was only about two hundred years old, which completely clobbered a good half of my novel, where the ghosts had been hard at it more than a hundred years earlier still.

Nearly all of it was like that. Of course, there were some questions I couldn't ask, for one reason or another. For instance, was Allington a boozer, like my Allington, and even more so, had this Allington had a visit from God. In the book, God turns up in the form of a young man to give Allington some tips on how to deal with the ghosts, who he, God, thinks are a menace to him. No point in going any further into that part.

I said nearly all the answers Palmer gave me were straight negatives. One wasn't, or rather there were two points where I scored, so to speak. One was that Allington had a fifteen-year-old daughter called Marilyn living in the house. My Allington's daughter was thirteen and called Amy, but I'd come somewhere near the mark – too near for comfort.

The other thing was a bit harder to tie down. When I'm writing a novel, I very rarely have any sort of mental picture of any of the characters, what they actually look like. I think a lot of novelists would say the same. But, I don't know why, I'd had a very clear image of what my chap *David* Palmer looked like, and now I'd had a really good look at *George* Palmer, this one here, he was *nearly* the same as I'd imagined, not so tall, different nose, but still nearly the same. I didn't care for that.

Palmer, George Palmer, said he had things to see to and took off. I told Jane what I've just told you, about the resemblance. She said I could easily have imagined that, and I said I suppose I might. Anyway, she said, what do you think of it all?

I said it could still all be coincidence. What could it be if it isn't coincidence? she asked. I'd been wondering about that while we were talking to Palmer. Not an easy one. Feeling a complete bloody fool, I said I thought we could have strayed into some kind of parallel world that slightly resembles the world I made up, you know, like in a science-fiction story.

She didn't laugh or back away. She looked round and spotted a newspaper someone had left on one of the chairs. It was that day's *Sunday Telegraph*. She said, if where we are is a world that's parallel to the real world, it's bound to be different from the real world in all sorts of ways. Now you read most of the *Telegraph* this morning, the real *Telegraph*. Look at this one, she said, and see if it's any different. Well, I did, and it wasn't: same front page, same article on the trade unions by Perry, that's Peregrine Worsthorne, same readers' letters, same crossword down to the last clue. Well, that was a relief.

But I didn't stay relieved, because there was another coincidence shaping up. It was a hot night in August when all this happened – or did I mention that before? Anyway, it was. And Allington was out for the evening. It was on a hot night in August, after Allington had come back from an evening out, that the monster, the Green Man, finally takes shape and comes pounding up the road to tear young Amy Allington to pieces. That bit begins on page 225 in my book, if you're interested.

The other nasty little consideration was this. Unlike some novelists

I could name, I invent all my characters, except for a few minor ones here and there. What I mean is, I don't go in for just renaming people I know and bunging them into a book. But of course, you can't help putting *something* of yourself into all your characters, even if it's only, well, a surly bus-conductor who only comes in for half a page.

Right, obviously, this comes up most of all with your heroes. Now none of my heroes, not even old Lucky Jim, are me, but they can't help having pretty fair chunks of me in them, some more than others. And Allington in that book was one of the some. I'm more like him than I'm like most of the others; in particular, I'm more like my Maurice Allington in my book than the real Allington, who by the way turned out to be called John, seemed (from what I'd heard) to be like my Maurice Allington. Sorry to be long-winded, but I want to get that quite clear.

So: if, by some fantastic chance, the Green Man, the monster, was going to turn up here, he, or it, seemed more likely to turn up tonight than most nights. And, furthermore, I seemed sort of better cast for the part of the young girl's father, who manages in the book to save her from the monster, than this young girl's father did. You see that.

I tried to explain all this to Jane. Evidently I got it across all right, because she said straight away, We'd better stay here tonight, then. If we can, I said, meaning if there was a room. Well, there was, and at the front of the house too, which was important, because in the book that's the side the monster appears on.

While one of the blokes was taking our stuff out of the car and upstairs, I said to Jane, I'm not going to be like a bloody fool in a ghost story who insists on seeing things through alone, not if I can help it – I'm going to give Bob Conquest a ring. Bob's an old chum of mine, and about the only one I felt I could ask to come belting up all this way (he lives in Battersea) for such a ridiculous reason. It was just after ten by this time, and the Green Man wasn't scheduled to put in an appearance till after one a.m., so Bob could make it all right if he started straight away. Fine, except his phone didn't answer; I tried twice.

Jane said, Get hold of Monkey; I'll speak to him. Monkey, otherwise known as Colin, is her brother; he lives with us in Barnet. Our number answered all right, but I got my son Philip, who was staying the weekend there. He said Monkey was out at a party, he didn't know where. So all I could do was the necessary but not at all helpful job of saying we wouldn't be home till the next morning. So that was that. I mean, I just couldn't start getting hold of George Palmer and asking him to sit up with us into the small hours in case a ghost came along. Could any of you? I should have said that Philip hasn't got a car.

Well, we stayed in the bar until it closed. I said to Jane at one point, You don't think I'm mad, do you? Or silly or anything? She said, On the contrary, I think you're being extremely practical and sensible. Well, thank God for that. Jane believes in ghosts, you see. My own position on that is exactly that of the man who said, I don't believe in ghosts, but I'm afraid of them.

Which brings me to one of the oddest things about this whole business. I'm a nervous type by nature, I never go in an aeroplane, I won't drive a car (Jane does the driving), I don't even much care for being alone in the house. But, ever since we'd decided to stay the night at this place, all the uneasiness and, let's face it, the considerable fear I'd started to feel as soon as these coincidences started coming up, it all just fell away. I felt quite confident, I felt I knew I'd be able to do whatever might be required of me.

There was one other thing to get settled. I said to Jane, we were in the bedroom by this time, I said, If he turns up, what am I going to use against him? You see, in the book, Maurice Allington has dug up a sort of magic object that sort of controls the Green Man. I hadn't. Jane saw what I was driving at. She said she'd thought of that, and took off and gave me the plain gold cross she wears round her neck, not for religious reasons, it was her grandmother's. That'll fix him, I thought, and as before I felt quite confident about it.

Well, after that we more or less sat and waited. At one point a car drove up and stopped in the car park. A man got out and went in the front door. It must have been Allington. I couldn't see much about him except he had the wrong colour hair, but when I looked at my watch it was eight minutes to midnight, the exact time when the Allington in the book got back after his evening out the night he coped with the creature. One more bit of . . . call it confirmation.

I opened our bedroom door and listened. Soon I heard footsteps coming upstairs and going off towards the back of the house and then a door shutting, and then straight away the house seemed totally still. It can't have been much later that I said to Jane, Look, there's no point in me hanging round up here. He might be early, you never know. It's a warm night, I might as well go down there now. She said, Are you sure you don't want me to come with you? Absolutely sure, I said, I'll be fine. But I do want you to watch from the window here. Okay, she said. She wished me luck and we clung to each other for a bit, and then off I went.

I was glad I'd left plenty of time, because getting out of the place turned out to be far from straightforward. Everything seemed to be locked and the key taken away. Eventually I found a scullery door with the key still in the lock.

Outside it was quite bright, with a full moon or not far off, and a couple of fairly powerful lights at the corners of the house. It was a pretty lonely spot, with only two or three other houses in sight. I remember a car went by soon after I got out there, but it was the only one. There wasn't a breath of wind. I saw Jane at our window and waved, and she waved back.

The question was, where to wait. If what was going to happen – assuming something was – if it went like the book, then the young girl, the daughter, was going to come out of the house because she'd thought she'd heard her father calling her (another bit of magic), and then this Green Man creature was going to, from one direction or the other he was going to come running at her. I couldn't decide which was the more likely direction.

A bit of luck, near the front door there was one of those heavy wooden benches. I sat down on that and started keeping watch first one way, then the other, half a minute at a time. Normally, ten minutes of this would have driven me off my head with boredom, but that night somehow it was all right. Then, after some quite long time, I turned my head from right to left on schedule and there was a girl, standing a few yards away; she must have come round that side of the house. She was wearing light green pyjamas – wrong colour again. I was going to speak to her, but there was something about the way she was standing . . .

She wasn't looking at me, in fact I soon saw she wasn't looking at anything much. I waved my hand in front of her eyes, you know, the way they do in films when they think someone's been hypnotized or something. I felt a perfect idiot, but her eyes didn't move. Sleepwalking, presumably; not in the book. Do people walk in their sleep? Apparently not, they only pretend to, according to what a psychiatrist chum told me afterwards, but I hadn't heard that then. All I knew, or thought I knew, was this thing everybody's heard somewhere about it being dangerous to wake a sleepwalker.

So I just stayed close to the girl and went on keeping watch, and a bit more time went by, and then, sure enough, I heard, faintly but clearly, the sound I'd written about, the rustling, creaking sound of the movement of something made of tree-branches, twigs, and clusters of leaves. And there it was, about a hundred yards away, not really much like a man, coming up at a clumsy, jolting sort of jogtrot on the grass verge, and accelerating.

I knew what I had to do. I started walking to meet it, with the cross ready in my hand. (The girl hadn't moved at all.) When the thing was about twenty yards away I saw its face, which had fungus on it, and I heard another sound I'd written about coming from what I suppose you'd have to call its mouth, like the howling of wind through trees.

I stopped and steadied myself and threw the cross at it and it immediately vanished – immediately. That wasn't like the book, but I didn't stop to think about it. I didn't stop to look for the cross, either. When I turned back, the girl had gone. So much the better. I rushed back into the inn and up to the bedroom and knocked on the door – I'd told Jane to lock it after me.

There was a delay before she came and opened it. I could see she looked confused or something, but I didn't bother with that, because I could feel all the calm and confidence I'd had earlier, it was all just draining away from me. I sat her down on the bed and sat down myself on a chair and just rattled off what had happened as fast as I could. I must have forgotten she'd been meant to be watching.

By the time I'd finished I was shaking. So was Jane. She said, What made you change your mind? Change my mind? – what about? Going out there, she said; getting up again and going out. But, I said, I've been out there all the time. Oh no you haven't, she said, you came back up here after about twenty minutes, she said, and you told me the whole thing was silly and you were going to bed, which we both did. She seemed quite positive.

I was absolutely shattered. But it all really happened, I said, just the way I told you. It couldn't have, she said; you must have dreamed it. You certainly didn't throw the cross at anything, she said, because it's here, you gave it back to me when you came back the first time. And there it was, on the chain round her neck.

I broke down then. I'm not quite clear what I said or did. Jane got some sleeping pills down me and I went off in the end. I remember thinking rather wildly that somebody or other with a funny sense of humour had got me into exactly the same predicament, the same mess, as the hero of my book had been: seeing something that must have been supernatural and just not being believed. Because I knew I'd seen the whole thing; I knew it then and I still know it.

I woke up late, feeling terrible. Jane was sitting reading by the bed. She said, I've seen young Miss Allington. Your description of her fits and, she said, she used to walk in her sleep. I asked her how she'd found out and she said she just had; she's good at that kind of thing.

Anyway, I felt better straight away. I said it looked as if we'd neither of us been dreaming even if what I'd seen couldn't be reconciled with what she'd seen, and she agreed. After that we rather dropped the subject in a funny sort of way. We decided not to look for the cross I'd thrown at the Green Man. I said we wouldn't be able to find it. I didn't ask Jane whether she was thinking what I was thinking, that looking would be a waste of time because she was wearing it at that very moment. I'll come back to that point in a minute.

We packed up, made a couple of phone calls rearranging our appointments, paid the bill and drove off. We still didn't talk about the main issue. But then, as we were coming off the Mill Hill roundabout, that's only about ten minutes from home, Jane said, What do you think happened? – happened to sort of make it all happen?

I said, I think someone was needed there to destroy that monster. Which means I was guided there at that time, or perhaps the time could be adjusted, I said; I must have been, well, sent all that stuff about the Green Man and about Allington and the others.

To make sure you recognized the place when you got there and knew what to do, she said. Who did all the guiding and the sending and so on? she said. The same, the same chap who appeared in my book to tell Allington what he wanted done. Why couldn't he have fixed the monster himself? she said. There are limitations to his power. There can't be many, she said, if he can make the same object be in two places at the same time.

Yes, you see, she'd thought of that too. It's supposed to be a physical impossibility, isn't it? Anyway, I said probably the way he'd chosen had been more fun. More fun, Jane repeated. She looked very thoughtful.

As you'll have seen, there was one loose end, of a sort. Who or what was it that had taken on my shape to enter that bedroom, talk to Jane with my voice, and share her bed for at any rate a few minutes? She and I didn't discuss it for several days. Then one morning she asked me the question more or less as I've just put it.

Interesting point, I said; I don't know. It's more interesting than you think, she said; because when . . . whoever it was got into bed with me, he didn't just go to sleep.

I suppose I just looked at her. That's right, she said; I thought I'd better go and see John before I told you. (That's John Allison, our GP.)

It was negative, then, I said. Yes, Jane said.

Well, that's it. A relief, of course. But in one way, rather disappointing.

Another Fine Mess

Ray Bradbury

Location: Vendome Heights, Los Angeles.
Time: Midsummer, 1995.
Eyewitness Description: *"At first there was only a creaking of wheels down in the dark, like crickets, and then a moan of wood and a hum of piano strings, and then one voice lamenting about this job, and the other voice claiming it had nothing to do with it, and then the thumps as two derby hats fell . . ."*
Author: Ray Douglas Bradbury (1920—) was born in the small town of Waukegan, Illinois, but later moved with his family to Los Angeles where much of his fiction has reflected his interest in rural life and the wonder-world of films. His early stories were written for the legendary horror magazine, *Weird Tales* – several featuring the supernatural – but he later turned to Science Fiction to create the books that made his name, *The Martian Chronicles* (1950), *Fahrenheit 451* (1951) and *The Illustrated Man* (1951), all of which have been filmed with varying degrees of success. Few writers have better captured the magic of film making in Hollywood on paper than Ray, although his own experiences as a scriptwriter with producers and directors in trying to bring his imaginative words to the screen have often been fraught. His love of old movies and their stars is evident in many of his books and short stories, but rarely more deeply felt than in this ghost story first published in *The Magazine of Fantasy & Science Fiction* in April 1995. The title of Ray's story all but gives away the stars of this little comedy masterpiece – though nothing will prepare you for its moving and poignant finale.

The sounds began in the middle of summer in the middle of the night.

Bella Winters sat up in bed about three a.m. and listened and then lay back down. Ten minutes later she heard the sounds again, out in the night, down the hill.

Bella Winters lived in a first-floor apartment on top of Vendome Heights, near Effie Street in Los Angeles, and had lived there now for only a few days, so it was all new to her, this old house on an old street with an old staircase, made of concrete, climbing steeply straight up from the low-lands below, one hundred and twenty steps, count them. And right now . . .

"Someone's on the steps," said Bella to herself.

"What?" said her husband, Sam, in his sleep.

"There are some men out on the steps," said Bella. "Talking, yelling, not fighting, but almost. I heard them last night, too, and the night before, but . . ."

"What?" Sam muttered.

"Shh, go to sleep. I'll look."

She got out of bed in the dark and went to the window, and yes, two men were indeed talking out there, grunting, groaning, now loud, now soft. And there was another noise, a kind of bumping, sliding, thumping, like a huge object being carted up the hill.

"No one could be moving in at this hour of the night, could they?" asked Bella of the darkness, the window, and herself.

"No," murmured Sam.

"It sounds like . . ."

"Like what?" asked Sam, fully awake now.

"Like two men moving—"

"Moving what, for God's sake?"

"Moving a piano. Up those steps."

"At three in the *morning!?*"

"A piano and two men. Just listen."

The husband sat up, blinking, alert.

Far off, in the middle of the hill, there was a kind of harping strum, the noise a piano makes when suddenly thumped and its harp strings hum.

"There, did you *hear?*"

"Jesus, you're right. But why would anyone steal—"

"They're not stealing, they're delivering."

"A *piano?*"

"I didn't make the rules, Sam. Go out and ask. No, don't; I will."

And she wrapped herself in her robe and was out the door and on the sidewalk.

"Bella," Sam whispered fiercely behind the porch screen. "Crazy."

"So what can happen at night to a woman fifty-five, fat, and ugly?" she wondered.

Sam did not answer.

She moved quietly to the rim of the hill. Somewhere down there she could hear the two men wrestling with a huge object. The piano on occasion gave a strumming hum and fell silent. Occasionally one of the men yelled or gave orders.

"The voices," said Bella. "I know them from somewhere," she whispered and moved in utter dark on stairs that were only a long pale ribbon going down, as a voice echoed:

"Here's *another* fine mess you've got us in."

Bella froze. Where have I heard that voice, she wondered, a million *times!*

"Hello," she called.

She moved, counting the steps, and stopped.

And there was no one there.

Suddenly she was very cold. There was nowhere for the strangers to have gone to. The hill was steep and a long way down and a long way up, and they had been burdened with an upright piano, *hadn't* they?

How come I know *upright?* she thought. I only *heard.* But – yes, *upright!* Not only that, but inside a box!

She turned slowly and as she went back up the steps, one by one, slowly, slowly, the voices began to sound again, below, as if, disturbed, they had waited for her to go away.

"What *are* you doing?" demanded one voice.

"I was just—" said the other.

"*Give* me that!" cried the first voice.

That *other* voice, thought Bella, I know that, *too.* And I know what's going to be said next!

"Now," said the echo far down the hill in the night, "just don't stand there, *help* me!"

"Yes!" Bella closed her eyes and swallowed hard and half fell to sit on the steps, getting her breath back as black-and-white pictures flashed in her head. Suddenly it was 1929 and she was very small, in a theater with dark and light pictures looming above the first row where she sat, transfixed, and then laughing, and then transfixed and laughing again.

She opened her eyes. The two voices were still down there, a faint wrestle and echo in the night, despairing and thumping each other with their hard derby hats.

Zelda, thought Bella Winters. I'll call Zelda. She knows everything. She'll tell me what this is. Zelda, yes!

Inside, she dialed Z and E and L and D and A before she saw what she had done and started over. The phone rang a long while until Zelda's voice, angry with sleep, spoke half-way across L.A.

"Zelda, this is Bella!"

"Sam just *died?*"

"No, no, I'm sorry—"

"*You're* sorry?"

"Zelda, I know you're going to think I'm crazy, but . . ."

"Go ahead, be crazy."

"Zelda, in the old days when they made films around L.A., they used lots of places, right? Like Venice, Ocean Park . . ."

"Chaplin did, Langdon did, Harold Lloyd, sure."

"Laurel and Hardy?"

"What?"

"Laurel and Hardy, did *they* use lots of locations?"

"Palms, they used Palms lots, Culver City Main Street, Effie Street."

"*Effie* Street!"

"Don't yell, Bella."

"Did you say *Effie* Street?"

"Sure, and God, it's three in the morning!"

"Right at the *top* of Effie Street!?"

"Hey, yeah, the stairs. Everyone knows them. That's where the music box chased Hardy downhill and ran over him."

"Sure, Zelda, *sure!* Oh, God, Zelda, if you could *see*, hear, what *I* hear!"

Zelda was suddenly wide awake on the line. "What's going *on?* You *serious?*"

"Oh, God, yes. On the steps just now, and last night and the night before maybe, I heard, I hear – two men hauling a – a piano up the hill."

"Someone's pulling your leg!"

"No, no, they're there. I go out and there's nothing. But the steps are haunted, Zelda! One voice says: 'Here's another fine mess you've got us in.' You got to *hear* that man's voice!"

"You're drunk and doing this because you know I'm a nut for them."

"No, no. Come, Zelda. Listen. Tell!"

Maybe half an hour later, Bella heard the old tin lizzie rattle up the alley behind the apartments. It was a car Zelda, in her joy at visiting silent-movie theaters, had bought to lug herself around in while she wrote about the past, always the past, and steaming into Cecil B. DeMille's old place or circling Harold Lloyd's nation-state, or cranking and banging around the Universal backlot, paying her respects to the Phantom's opera stage, or sitting on Ma and Pa Kettle's porch chewing a sandwich lunch. That was Zelda, who once wrote in a silent country in a silent time for *Silver Screen*.

Zelda lumbered across the front porch, a huge body with legs as big as the Bernini columns in front of St. Peter's in Rome, and a face like a harvest moon.

On that round face now was suspicion, cynicism, skepticism, in equal pie-parts. But when she saw Bella's pale stare she cried:

"Bella!"

"You *see* I'm *not* lying!" said Bella.

"I *see!*"

"Keep your voice down, Zelda. Oh, it's scary and strange, terrible and nice. So come on."

And the two women edged along the walk to the rim of the old hill near the old steps in old Hollywood, and suddenly as they moved they felt time take a half turn around them and it was another year, because nothing had changed, all the buildings were the way they were in 1928 and the hills beyond like they were in 1926 and the steps, just the way they were when the cement was poured in 1921.

"Listen, Zelda. *There!*"

And Zelda listened and at first there was only a creaking of wheels down in the dark, like crickets, and then a moan of wood and a hum of piano strings, and then one voice lamenting about this job, and the other voice claiming he had nothing to do with it, and then the thumps as two derby hats fell, and an exasperated voice announced:

"Here's *another* fine mess you've got us in."

Zelda, stunned, almost toppled off the hill. She held tight to Bella's arm as tears brimmed in her eyes.

"It's a trick. Someone's got a tape recorder or—"

"No, I checked. Nothing but the steps, Zelda, the steps!"

Tears rolled down Zelda's plump cheeks.

"Oh, God, that *is* his voice! I'm the expert, I'm the mad fanatic, Bella. That's Ollie. And that other voice, Stan! And you're *not* nuts after all!"

The voices below rose and fell and one cried: "Why don't you do something to *help* me?"

Zelda moaned. "Oh, God, it's so *beautiful*."

"What does it mean?" asked Bella. "Why are they here? Are they really ghosts, and why would ghosts climb this hill every night, pushing that music box, night after night, tell me, Zelda, why?"

Zelda peered down the hill and shut her eyes for a moment to think. "Why do *any* ghosts go anywhere? Retribution? Revenge? No, not *those* two. Love maybe's the reason, lost loves or something. *Yes?*"

Bella let her heart pound once or twice and then said, "Maybe nobody *told* them."

"Told them *what?*"

"Or maybe they were told a lot but still didn't believe, because maybe in their old years things got bad, I mean they were sick, and sometimes when you're sick you forget."

"Forget *what!?*"

"How much we loved them."

"They *knew!*"

"*Did* they? Sure, we told each other, but maybe not enough of us ever wrote or waved when they passed and just yelled '*Love!*' you think?"

"Hell, Bella, they're on TV every *night!*"

"Yeah, but that don't count. Has anyone, since they left us, come here to these steps and *said?* Maybe those voices down there, ghosts or whatever, have been here every night for years, pushing that music box, and nobody thought, or tried, to just whisper or yell all the love we had all the years. Why not?"

"Why not?" Zelda stared down into the long darkness where perhaps shadows moved and maybe a piano lurched clumsily among the shadows. "You're right."

"If I'm right," said Bella, "and you say so, there's only one thing to do—"

"You mean you and *me?*"

"Who else? Quiet. Come on."

They moved down a step. In the same instant lights came on around them, in a window here, another there. A screen door opened somewhere and angry words shot out into the night:

"Hey, what's going *on?*"

"Pipe down!"

"You know what *time* it is?"

"My God," Bella whispered, "everyone *else* hears now!"

"No, no." Zelda looked around wildly. "They'll spoil everything!"

"I'm calling the cops!" A window slammed.

"God," said Bella, "if the cops come—"

"What?"

"It'll be all wrong. If anyone's going to tell them to take it easy, pipe down, it's gotta be us. We *care, don't* we?"

"God, yes, but—"

"No buts. Grab on. Here we go."

The two voices murmured below and the piano tuned itself with hiccups of sound as they edged down another step and another, their mouths dry, hearts hammering, and the night so dark they could see only the faint streetlight at the stair bottom, the single street illumination so far away it was sad being there all by itself, waiting for shadows to move.

More windows slammed up, more screen doors opened. At any moment there would be an avalanche of protest, incredible outcries, perhaps shots fired, and all this gone forever.

Thinking this, the women trembled and held tight, as if to pummel each other to speak against the rage.

"Say something, Zelda, quick."

"*What?*"

"Anything! They'll get hurt if we don't—"

"*They?*"

"You know what I mean. Save them."

"Okay. Jesus!" Zelda froze, clamped her eyes shut to find the words, then opened her eyes and said, "Hello."

"Louder."

"Hello," Zelda called softly, then loudly.

Shapes rustled in the dark below. One of the voices rose while the other fell and the piano strummed its hidden harp strings.

"Don't be afraid," Zelda called.

"That's good. Go on."

"Don't be afraid," Zelda called, braver now. "Don't listen to those others yelling. We won't hurt you. It's just us. I'm Zelda, you wouldn't remember, and this here is Bella, and we've known you forever, or since we were kids, and we love you. It's late, but we thought you should know. We've loved you ever since you were in the desert or on that boat with ghosts or trying to sell Christmas trees door-to-door or in that traffic where you tore the headlights off cars, and we still love you, right, Bella?"

The night below was darkness, waiting.

Zelda punched Bella's arm.

"Yes!" Bella cried, "what she *said*. We love you."

"We can't think of anything else to say."

"But it's enough, yes?" Bella leaned forward anxiously. "It's *enough?*"

A night wind stirred the leaves and grass around the stairs and the shadows below that had stopped moving with the music box suspended between them as they looked up and up at the two women, who suddenly began to cry. First tears fell from Bella's cheeks, and when Zelda sensed them, she let fall her own.

"So now," said Zelda, amazed that she could form words but managed to speak anyway, "we want you to know, you don't have to come back anymore. You don't have to climb the hill every night, waiting. For what we said just now is it, isn't it? I mean you wanted to hear it here on this hill, with those steps, and that piano, yes, that's the whole thing, it had to be that, didn't it? So now here we are and there you are and it's said. So rest, dear friends."

"Oh, there, Ollie," added Bella in a sad, sad whisper. "Oh, Stan, Stanley."

The piano, hidden in the dark, softly hummed its wires and creaked its ancient wood.

And then the most incredible thing happened. There was a series of shouts and then a huge banging crash as the music box, in the dark, rocketed down the hill, skittering on the steps, playing chords where it hit, swerving, rushing, and ahead of it, running, the two shapes pursued by the musical beast, yelling, tripping, shouting, warning the Fates, crying out to the gods, down and down, forty, sixty, eighty, one hundred steps.

And half down the steps, hearing, feeling, shouting, crying themselves, and now laughing and holding to each other, the two women alone in the night wildly clutching, grasping, trying to see, almost sure that they *did* see, the three things ricocheting off and away, the two shadows rushing, one fat, one thin, and the piano blundering after, discordant and mindless, until they reached the street, where, instantly, the one overhead streetlamp died as if struck, and the shadows floundered on, pursued by the musical beast.

And the two women, abandoned, looked down, exhausted with laughing until they wept and weeping until they laughed, until suddenly Zelda got a terrible look on her face as if shot.

"My God!" she shouted in panic, reaching out. "Wait. We didn't mean, we don't want – don't go *forever!* Sure, go, so the neighbors here sleep. But once a year, you *hear?* Once a year, one night a year from tonight, and every year after that, come back. It shouldn't bother anyone so much. But we got to tell you all over again, huh? Come back and bring the box with you, and we'll be here waiting, won't we, Bella?"

"Waiting, yes."

There was a long silence from the steps leading down into an old black-and-white, silent Los Angeles.

"You think they heard?"

They listened.

And from somewhere far off and down, there was the faintest explosion like the engine of an old jalopy knocking itself to life, and then the merest whisper of a lunatic music from a dark theater when they were very young. It faded.

After a long while they climbed back up the steps, dabbing at their eyes with wet Kleenex. Then they turned for a final time to stare down into the night.

"You know something?" said Zelda. "I think they *heard*."

6

Christmas Spirits

Festive Season Chillers

Only A Dream . . .

Rider Haggard

Location: Ditchingham, Norfolk.

Time: October, 1905.

Eyewitness Description: *"There it is again – a dreadful sound; it makes the blood turn chill and yet has something familiar about it. It is a woman's voice calling round the house. There, she is at the window now, and rattling it, and, great heavens she is calling me . . ."*

Author: Sir Henry Rider Haggard (1856–1925) was an innovator as well as one of the greatest adventure story writers whose classic novel *King Solomon's Mines* (1885) has continued to influence the genre to the present day. Born in Norfolk, he was educated at Ipswich Grammar School, but spent much of his early life in South Africa, which was to fire his imagination with its mysteries and strange peoples. After the success of his most famous lost-race story, he wrote several sequels and short stories about the hero, Allan Quatermain, and revealed an increasing interest in the supernatural as he grew older in titles like *The Wizard* (1896), *The Ghost Kings* (1908), which he plotted with his friend, Rudyard Kipling, and *Love Eternal* (1918), about spiritualism, which owes more than a nod to Sir Arthur Conan Doyle. Haggard was also an early enthusiast of the "story for Christmas" tradition that grew rapidly in the popular illustrated magazines of the 20th century. His curious tale of a haunted man on the day before his marriage – which has been said to stand comparison with the stories of M. R. James – must have made startling reading for his admirers as they huddled round their fires and opened their edition of the popular writer and illustrator *Harry Furniss's Christmas Annual* in December 1905.

Footprints – footprints – the footprints of one dead. How ghastly they look as they fall before me! Up and down the long hall they go, and I follow them. *Pit, pat* they fall, those unearthly steps, and beneath them starts up that awful impress. I can see it grow upon the marble, a damp and dreadful thing.

Tread them down; tread them out; follow after them with muddy shoes, and cover them up. In vain. See how they rise through the mire! Who can tread out the footprints of the dead?

And so on, up and down the dim vista of the past, following the sound of the dead feet that wander so restlessly, stamping upon the impress that will not be stamped out. Rave on, wild wind, eternal voice of human misery; fall, dead footsteps, eternal echo of human memory; stamp, miry feet; stamp into forgetfulness that which will not be forgotten.

And so on, on to the end.

Pretty ideas these for a man about to be married, especially when they float into his brain at night like ominous clouds into a summer sky, and he is going to be married tomorrow. There is no mistake about it – the wedding, I mean. To be plain and matter-of-fact, why there stand the presents, or some of them, and very handsome presents they are, ranged in solemn rows upon the long table. It is a remarkable thing to observe when one is about to make a really satisfactory marriage how scores of unsuspected or forgotten friends crop up and send little tokens of their esteem. It was very different when I married my first wife, I remember, but then that marriage was not satisfactory – just a love-match, no more.

There they stand in solemn rows, as I have said, and inspire me with beautiful thoughts about the innate kindness of human nature, especially the human nature of our distant cousins. It is possible to grow almost poetical over a silver teapot when one is going to be married tomorrow. On how many future mornings shall I be confronted with that teapot? Probably for all my life; and on the other side of the teapot will be the cream jug, and the electro-plated urn will hiss away behind them both. Also, the chased sugar basin will be in front, full of sugar, and behind everything will be my second wife.

"My dear," she will say, "will you have another cup of tea?" and probably I shall have another cup.

Well, it is very curious to notice what ideas will come into a man's head sometimes. Sometimes something waves a magic wand over his being, and from the recesses of his soul dim things arise and walk. At unexpected moments they come, and he grows aware of the issues of his mysterious life, and his heart shakes and shivers like a lightning-shattered tree. In that drear light all earthly things seem far, and all unseen things draw near and take shape and awe him, and he knows not what is true and what is false, neither can he trace the edge that marks off the Spirit from the Life. Then it is that the footsteps echo, and the ghostly footprints will not be stamped out.

Pretty thoughts again! and how persistently they come! It is one o'clock and I will go to bed. The rain is falling in sheets outside. I can hear it lashing against the window panes, and the wind wails through the tall wet elms at the end of the garden. I could tell the voice of those elms anywhere; I know it as well as the voice of a friend. What a night it is; we sometimes get them in this part of England in October. It was just such a night when my first wife died, and that is three years ago. I remember how she sat up in her bed.

"Ah! those horrible elms," she said; "I wish you would have them cut down, Frank; they cry like a woman," and I said I would and just after that she died, poor dear. And so the old elms stand, and I like their music. It is a strange thing; I was half broken-hearted, for I loved her dearly, and she loved me with all her life and strength, and now – I am going to be married again.

"Frank, Frank, don't forget me!" Those were my wife's last words; and, indeed, though I am going to be married again tomorrow, I have not forgotten her. Nor shall I forget how Annie Guthrie (whom I am going to marry now) came to see her the day before she died. I know that Annie always liked me more or less, and I think that my dear wife guessed it. After she had kissed Annie and bid her a last goodbye, and the door had closed, she spoke quite suddenly: "There goes your future wife, Frank," she said; "You should have married her at first instead of me; she is very handsome and very good, and she has two thousand a year; *she* would never have died of a nervous illness." And she laughed a little, and then added:

"Oh, Frank dear, I wonder if you will think of me before you marry Annie Guthrie. Wherever I am I shall be thinking of you."

And now that time which she foresaw has come, and Heaven knows that I have thought of her, poor dear. Ah! those footsteps of one dead that will echo through our lives, those woman's footprints on the marble flooring which will not be stamped out. Most of us have heard and seen them at some time or other, and I hear and see them very plainly tonight. Poor dead wife, I wonder if there are any doors in the land where you have gone through which you can creep out to look at me tonight? I hope that there are none. Death must indeed be a hell if the dead can see and feel and take measure of the forgetful faithlessness of their beloved. Well, I will go to bed and try to get a little rest. I am not so young or so strong as I was, and this wedding wears me out. I wish that the whole thing were done or had never been begun.

What was that? It was not the wind, for it never makes that sound here, and it was not the rain, since the rain has ceased its surging for a moment; nor was it the howling of a dog, for I keep none. It was more like the crying of a woman's voice; but what woman can be abroad on such a night or at such an hour – half-past one in the morning?

There it is again – a dreadful sound; it makes the blood turn chill, and yet has something familiar about it. It is a woman's voice calling round the house. There, she is at the window now, and rattling it, and, great heavens! she is calling me.

"Frank! Frank! Frank!" she calls.

I strive to stir and unshutter that window, but before I can get there she is knocking and calling at another.

Gone again, with her dreadful wail of "Frank! Frank!" Now I hear her at the front door, and, half mad with a horrible fear, I run down the long, dark hall and unbar it. There is nothing there – nothing but the wild rush of the wind and the drip of the rain from the portico. But I can hear the wailing voice going round the house, past the patch of shrubbery. I close the door and listen. There, she has got through the little yard, and is at the back door now. Whoever it is, she must know the way about the house. Along the hall I go again, through a swing door, through the servants' hall, stumbling down some steps into the kitchen, where the embers of the fire are still alive in the grate, diffusing a little warmth and light into the dense gloom.

Whoever it is at the door is knocking now with her clenched hand against the hard wood, and it is wonderful, though she knocks so low, how the sound echoes through the empty kitchen.

There I stood and hesitated, trembling in every limb; I dared not open the door. No words of mine can convey the sense of utter desolation that overpowered me. I felt as though I were the only living man in the whole world.

"*Frank! Frank!*" cried the voice with the dreadful familiar ring in it. "Open the door; I am so cold. I have so little time."

My heart stood still, and yet my hands were constrained to obey. Slowly, slowly I lifted the latch and unbarred the door, and, as I did so, a great rush of air snatched it from my hands and swept it wide.

The black clouds had broken a little overhead, and there was a patch of blue, rain-washed sky and with just a start or two glimmering in it fitfully. For a moment I could only see this bit of sky, but by degrees I made out the accustomed outline of the great trees swinging furiously against it, and the rigid line of the coping of the garden wall beneath them. Then a whirling leaf hit me smartly on the face, and instinctively I dropped my eyes on to something that as yet I could not distinguish – something small and black and wet.

"What are you?" I gasped. Somehow I seemed to feel that it was not a person – I could not say, Who are you?

"Don't you know me?" wailed the voice, with the far-off familiar ring about it. "And I mayn't come in and show myself. I haven't the time. You were so long opening the door, Frank, and I am so cold – oh, so bitterly cold! Look there, the moon is coming out, and you will be able to see me. I suppose that you long to see me, as I have longed to see you."

As the figure spoke, or rather wailed, a moonbeam struggled through the watery air and fell on it. It was short and shrunken, the figure of a tiny woman. Also it was dressed in black and wore a black covering over the whole head, shrouding it, after the fashion of a bridal veil. From every part of this veil and dress the water fell in heavy drops.

The figure bore a small basket on her left arm, and her hand – such a poor thin little hand – gleamed white in the moonlight. I noticed that on the third finger was a red line, showing that a wedding-ring had once been there. The other hand was stretched towards me as though in entreaty.

All this I saw in an instant, as it were, and as I saw it, horror seemed to grip me by the throat as though it were a living thing, for as the voice had been familiar, so was the form familiar, though the churchyard had received it long years ago. I could not speak – I could not even move.

"Oh, don't you know me yet?" wailed the voice; "and I have come from so far to see you, and I cannot stop. Look, look," and she began to pluck feverishly with her poor thin hand at the black veil that enshrouded her. At last it came off, and, as in a dream, I saw what in a dim frozen way I had expected to see – the white face and pale yellow hair of my dead wife. Unable to speak or to stir, I gazed and gazed. There was no mistake about it, it was she, ay, even as I had last seen her, white with the whiteness of death, with purple circles round her eyes and the grave-cloth yet beneath her chin. Only her eyes were wide open and fixed upon my face; and a lock of the soft yellow hair had broken loose, and the wind tossed it.

"You know me now, Frank – don't you, Frank? It has been so hard to come to see you, and so cold! But you are going to be married tomorrow, Frank; and I promised – oh, a long time ago – to think of you when you were going to be married wherever I was, and I have kept my promise, and I have come from whence I am and brought a present with me. It was bitter to die so young! I was so young to die and leave you, but I had to go. Take it – take it; be quick, I cannot stay any longer. *I could not give you my life, Frank, so I brought you my death – take it!*"

The figure thrust the basket into my hand, and as it did so the rain came up again, and began to obscure the moonlight.

"I must go, I must go," went on the dreadful, familiar voice, in a cry of despair. "Oh, why were you so long opening the door? I wanted to talk to you before you married Annie; and now I shall never see you again – never! never! *never!* I have lost you for ever! ever! *ever!*"

As the last wailing notes died away the wind came down with a rush and a whirl and the sweep as of a thousand wings, and threw me back into the house, bringing the door to with a crash after me.

I staggered into the kitchen, the basket in my hand, and set it on the table. Just then some embers of the fire fell in, and a faint little flame rose and glimmered on the bright dishes on the dresser, even revealing a tin candlestick, with a box of matches by it. I was well-nigh mad with the darkness and fear, and, seizing the matches, I struck one, and held it to the candle. Presently it caught, and I glanced round the room. It was just as usual, just as the servants had left it, and above the mantelpiece the eight-day clock ticked away solemnly. While I looked at it it struck two, and in a dim fashion I was thankful for its friendly sound.

Then I looked at the basket. It was of very fine white plaited work with black bands running up it, and a chequered black-and-white handle. I knew it well. I have never seen another like it. I bought it years ago at Madeira, and gave it to my poor wife. Ultimately it was washed overboard in a gale in the Irish Channel. I remember that it was full of newspapers and library books, and I had to pay for them. Many and many is the time that I have seen that identical basket standing there on that very kitchen table, for my dear wife always used it to put flowers in, and the shortest cut from that part of the garden where her roses grew was through the kitchen. She used to gather the flowers, and then come in and place her basket on the table, just where it stood now, and order the dinner.

All this passed through my mind in a few seconds as I stood there with the candle in my hand, feeling indeed half dead, and yet with my mind painfully alive, I began to wonder if I had gone asleep, and was the victim of a nightmare. No such thing. I wish it had only been a nightmare. A mouse ran out along the dresser and jumped on to the floor, making quite a crash in the silence.

What was in the basket? I feared to look, and yet some power within me forced me to it. I drew near to the table and stood for a moment listening to the sound of my own heart. Then I stretched out my hand and slowly raised the lid of the basket.

"I could not give you my life, so I have brought you my death!" Those were her words. What could she mean – what could it all mean? I must know or I should go mad. There it lay, whatever it was, wrapped up in linen.

Ah, heaven help me! It was a small bleached human skull!

A dream! After all, only a dream by the fire, but what a dream. And I am to be married tomorrow.

Can I be married tomorrow?

The Haunted House

Edith Nesbit

Location: Ormehurst Rectory, Crittenden, Kent.
Time: December, 1913.
Eyewitness Description: *"I did not say it was a ghost. I only say that there is something about this house which is not ordinary. Several of my assistants have had to leave, the thing got on their nerves . . ."*

Author: Edith Nesbit (1858–1924) was another innovator who, like her friend Rider Haggard, became a popular contributor to the Christmas issues of the *Strand* magazine. Her work is also regarded as having been an influence on a number of writers, notably J. K. Rowling, who has admitted that Nesbit's classic fantasies *The Phoenix and the Carpet* (1904), *The Story of the Amulet* (1907) and *The Enchanted Castle* (1908) delighted her in childhood and helped to inspire her to write the phenomenally successful Harry Potter series. Born in Kennington, Edith apparently lived in two haunted houses as child, which undoubtedly gave her a good grounding for some of her later stories and novels. It was, however, a non-fantasy children's book, *The Railway Children* (1904), that made her famous and her future seemed secure. Unhappily, the collapse of her marriage brought about by her husband's philandering meant she had to earn her living by the pen. She followed Rider Haggard's lead by writing "The Haunted House" for the Christmas 1913 number of the *Strand*. The story is set in Kent – a county which she loved – and it is interesting to wonder if there is anything of either of the two real haunted houses in which she lived in the sinister Ormehurst Rectory.

It was by the merest accident that Desmond ever went to the Haunted House. He had been away from England for six years, and the nine months' leave taught him how easily one drops out of one's place.

He had taken rooms at The Greyhound before he found that there was no reason why he should stay in Elmstead rather than in any other of London's dismal outposts. He wrote to all the friends whose addresses he could remember, and settled himself to await their answers.

He wanted someone to talk to, and there was no one. Meantime he lounged on the horsehair sofa with the advertisements, and his pleasant grey eyes followed line after line with intolerable boredom. Then, suddenly, "Halloa!" he said, and sat up. This is what he read:

A HAUNTED HOUSE. Advertiser is anxious to have phenomena investigated. Any properly-accredited investigator will be given full facilities. Address, by letter only, Wildon Prior, 237, Museum Street, London.

"That's rum!" he said. Wildon Prior had been the best wicket-keeper in his club. It wasn't a common name. Anyway, it was worth trying, so he sent off a telegram.

WILDON PRIOR, 237, MUSEUM STREET, LONDON. MAY I COME TO YOU FOR A DAY OR TWO AND SEE THE GHOST? – WILLIAM DESMOND

On returning the next day from a stroll there was an orange envelope on the wide Pembroke table in his parlour.

DELIGHTED – EXPECT YOU TODAY. BOOK TO CRITTEN-DEN FROM CHARING CROSS. WIRE TRAIN – WILDON PRIOR, ORMEHURST RECTORY, KENT.

"So that's all right," said Desmond, and went off to pack his bag and ask in the bar for a time-table. "Good old Wildon; it will be ripping, seeing him again."

A curious little omnibus, rather like a bathing-machine, was waiting outside Crittenden Station, and its driver, a swarthy, blunt-faced little man, with liquid eyes, said, "You a friend of Mr Prior, sir?" shut him up in the bathing-machine, and banged the door on him. It was a very long drive, and less pleasant than it would have been in an open carriage.

The last part of the journey was through a wood; then came a churchyard and a church, and the bathing-machine turned in at a gate under heavy trees and drew up in front of a white house with bare, gaunt windows.

"Cheerful place, upon my soul!" Desmond told himself, as he tumbled out of the back of the bathing-machine.

The driver set his bag on the discoloured doorstep and drove off. Desmond pulled a rusty chain, and a big-throated bell jangled above his head.

Nobody came to the door, and he rang again. Still nobody came, but he heard a window thrown open above the porch. He stepped back on to the gravel and looked up.

A young man with rough hair and pale eyes was looking out. Not Wildon, nothing like Wildon. He did not speak, but he seemed to be making signs; and the signs seemed to mean, "Go away!"

"I came to see Mr Prior," said Desmond. Instantly and softly the window closed.

"Is it a lunatic asylum I've come to by chance?" Desmond asked himself, and pulled again at the rusty chain.

Steps sounded inside the house, the sound of boots on stone. Bolts were shot back, the door opened, and Desmond, rather hot and a little annoyed, found himself looking into a pair of very dark, friendly eyes, and a very pleasant voice said: "Mr Desmond, I presume? Do come in and let me apologize."

The speaker shook him warmly by the hand, and he found himself following down a flagged passage a man of more than mature age, well dressed, handsome, with an air of competence and alertness which we associate with what is called "a man of the world". He opened a door and led the way into a shabby, bookish, leathery room.

"Do sit down, Mr Desmond."

"This must be the uncle, I suppose," Desmond thought, as he fitted himself into the shabby, perfect curves of the armchair. "How's Wildon?" he asked, aloud. "All right, I hope?"

The other man looked at him. "I beg your pardon," he said, doubtfully.

"I was asking how Wildon is?"

"I am quite well, I thank you," said the other man, with some formality.

"I beg your pardon" – it was now Desmond's turn to say it – "I did not realise that your name might be Wildon, too. I meant Wildon Prior."

"I am Wildon Prior," said the other, "and you, I presume, are the expert from the Psychical Society?"

"Good Lord, no!" said Desmond. "I'm Wildon Prior's friend, and, of course, there must be two Wildon Priors."

"You sent the telegram? You are Mr Desmond? The Psychical Society were to send an expert, and I thought—"

"I see," said Desmond; "and I thought you were Wildon Prior, an old friend of mine – a young man," he said, and half rose.

"Now, don't," said Wildon Prior. "No doubt it is my nephew who is your friend. Did he know you were coming? But of course he didn't. I am wandering. But I'm exceedingly glad to see you. You will stay, will you not? If you can endure to be the guest of an old man. And I will write to Will tonight and ask him to join us."

"That's most awfully good of you," Desmond assured him. "I shall be glad to stay. I was awfully pleased when I saw Wildon's name in the paper, because—" and out came the tale of Elmstead, its loneliness and disappointment.

Mr Prior listened with the kindest interest. "And you have not found your friends? How sad! But they will write to you. Of course, you left your address?"

"I didn't, by Jove!" said Desmond. "But I can write. Can I catch the post?"

"Easily," the elder man assured him. "Write your letters now. My man shall take them to the post, and then we will have dinner, and I will tell you about the ghost."

Desmond wrote his letters quickly, Mr Prior just then reappearing.

"Now I'll take you to your room," he said, gathering the letters in long, white hands. "You'll like a rest. Dinner at eight."

The bed-chamber, like the parlour, had a pleasant air of worn luxury and accustomed comfort.

"I hope you will be comfortable," the host said, with courteous solicitude. And Desmond was quite sure that he would.

Three covers were laid, the swarthy man who had driven Desmond from the station stood behind the host's chair, and a figure came towards Desmond and his host from the shadows beyond the yellow circles of the silver-sticked candles.

"My assistant, Mr Verney," said the host, and Desmond surrendered his hand to the limp, damp touch of the man who had seemed to say to him, from the window of the porch, "Go away!" Was Mr Prior perhaps a doctor who received "paying guests", persons who were, in Desmond's phrase, "a bit balmy"? But he had said "assistant".

"I thought," said Desmond, hastily, "you would be a clergyman.

The Rectory, you know – I thought Wildon, my friend Wildon, was staying with an uncle who was a clergyman."

"Oh no," said Mr Prior. "I rent the Rectory. The rector thinks it is damp. The church is disused, too. It is not considered safe, and they can't afford to restore it. Claret to Mr Desmond, Lopez." And the swarthy, blunt-faced man filled his glass.

"I find this place very convenient for my experiments. I dabble a little in chemistry, Mr Desmond, and Verney here assists me."

Verney murmured something that sounded like "only too proud", and subsided.

"We all have our hobbies, and chemistry is mine," Mr Prior went on. "Fortunately, I have a little income which enables me to indulge it. Wildon, my nephew, you know, laughs at me, and calls it the science of smells. But it's absorbing, very absorbing."

After dinner Verney faded away, and Desmond and his host stretched their feet to what Mr Prior called a "handful of fire", for the evening had grown chill.

"And now," Desmond said, "won't you tell me the ghost story?"

The other glanced round the room.

"There isn't really a ghost story at all. It's only that – well, it's never happened to me personally, but it happened to Verney, poor lad, and he's never been quite his own self since."

Desmond flattered himself on his insight.

"Is mine the haunted room?" he asked.

"It doesn't come to any particular room," said the other, slowly, "nor to any particular person."

"Anyone may happen to see it?"

"No one sees it. It isn't the kind of ghost that's seen or heard."

"I'm afraid I'm rather stupid, but I don't understand," said Desmond, roundly. "How can it be a ghost, if you neither hear it nor see it?"

"I did not say it was a ghost," Mr Prior corrected. "I only say that there is something about this house which is not ordinary. Several of my assistants have had to leave; the thing got on their nerves."

"What became of the assistants?" asked Desmond.

"Oh, they left, you know; they left," Prior answered, vaguely. "One couldn't expect them to sacrifice their health. I sometimes think – village gossip is a deadly thing, Mr Desmond – that perhaps they were prepared to be frightened; that they fancy things. I hope that that Psychical Society's expert won't be a neurotic. But even without being a neurotic one might – but you don't believe in ghosts, Mr Desmond. Your Anglo-Saxon common sense forbids it."

"I'm afraid I'm not exactly Anglo-Saxon," said Desmond. "On my father's side I'm pure Celt; though I know I don't do credit to the race."

"And on your mother's side?" Mr Prior asked, with extraordinary eagerness; an eagerness so sudden and disproportioned to the question that Desmond stared. A faint touch of resentment as suddenly stirred in him, the first spark of antagonism to his host.

"Oh," he said lightly, "I think I must have Chinese blood, I get on so well with the natives in Shanghai, and they tell me I owe my nose to a Red Indian great grandmother."

"No negro blood, I suppose?" the host asked, with almost discourteous insistence.

"Oh, I wouldn't say that," Desmond answered. He meant to say it laughing, but he didn't. "My hair, you know – it's a very stiff curl it's got, and my mother's people were in the West Indies a few generations ago. You're interested in distinctions of race, I take it?"

"Not at all, not at all," Mr Prior surprisingly assured him; "but, of course, any details of your family are necessarily interesting to me. I feel," he added, with another of his winning smiles, "that you and I are already friends."

Desmond could not have reasoningly defended the faint quality of dislike that had begun to tinge his first pleasant sense of being welcomed and wished for as a guest.

"You're very kind," he said; "it's jolly of you to take in a stranger like this."

Mr Prior smiled, handed him the cigar-box, mixed whisky and soda, and began to talk about the history of the house.

"The foundations are almost certainly thirteenth century. It was a priory, you know. There's a curious tale, by the way, about the man Henry gave it to when he smashed up the monasteries. There was a curse; there seems always to have been a curse—"

The gentle, pleasant, high-bred voice went on. Desmond thought he was listening, but presently he roused himself and dragged his attention back to the words that were being spoken.

"– that made the fifth death . . . There is one every hundred years, and always in the same mysterious way."

Then he found himself on his feet, incredibly sleepy, and heard himself say: "These old stories are tremendously interesting. Thank you very much. I hope you won't think me very uncivil, but I think I'd rather like to turn in; I feel a bit tired, somehow."

"But of course, my dear chap."

Mr Prior saw Desmond to his room.

"Got everything you want? Right. Lock the door if you should feel nervous. Of course, a lock can't keep ghosts out, but I always feel as if it could," and with another of those pleasant, friendly laughs he was gone.

William Desmond went to bed a strong young man, sleepy indeed beyond his experience of sleepiness, but well and comfortable. He awoke faint and trembling, lying deep in the billows of the feather bed; and lukewarm waves of exhaustion swept through him. Where was he? What had happened? His brain, dizzy and weak at first, refused him any answer. When he remembered, the abrupt spasm of repulsion which he had felt so suddenly and unreasonably the night before came back to him in a hot, breathless flush. He had been drugged, he had been poisoned!

"I must get out of this," he told himself, and blundered out of bed towards the silken bell-pull that he had noticed the night before hanging near the door.

As he pulled it, the bed and the wardrobe and the room rose up round him and fell on him, and he fainted.

When he next knew anything someone was putting brandy to his lips. He saw Prior, the kindest concern in his face. The assistant, pale and watery-eyed. The swarthy manservant, stolid, silent, and expressionless. He heard Verney say to Prior: "You see it was too much – I told you—"

"Hush," said Prior, "he's coming to."

Four days later Desmond, lying on a wicker chair on the lawn, was a little disinclined for exertion, but no longer ill. Nourishing foods and drinks, beef-tea, stimulants, and constant care – these had brought him back to something like his normal state. He wondered at the vague suspicions, vaguely remembered, of that first night; they had all been proved absurd by the unwavering care and kindness of everyone in the Haunted House.

"But what caused it?" he asked his host, for the fiftieth time. "What made me make such a fool of myself?" And this time Mr Prior did not put him off, as he had always done before by begging him to wait till he was stronger.

"I am afraid, you know," he said, "that the ghost really did come to you. I am inclined to revise my opinion of the ghost."

"But why didn't it come again?"

"I have been with you every night, you know," his host reminded him. And, indeed, the sufferer had never been left alone since the ringing of his bell on that terrible first morning.

"And now," Mr Prior went on, "if you will not think me inhospitable, I think you will be better away from here. You ought to go to the seaside."

"There haven't been any letters for me, I suppose?" Desmond said, a little wistfully.

"Not one. I suppose you gave the right address? Ormehurst Rectory, Crittenden, Kent?"

"I don't think I put Crittenden," said Desmond. "I copied the address from your telegram." He pulled the pink paper from his pocket.

"Ah, that would account," said the other.

"You've been most awfully kind all through," said Desmond, abruptly.

"Nonsense, my boy," said the elder man, benevolently. "I only wish Willie had been able to come. He's never written, the rascal! Nothing but the telegram to say he could not come and was writing."

"I suppose he's having a jolly time somewhere," said Desmond, enviously; "but look here – do tell me about the ghost, if there's anything to tell. I'm almost quite well now, and I *should* like to know what it was that made a fool of me like that."

"Well" – Mr Prior looked round him at the gold and red of dahlias and sunflowers, gay in the September sunshine – "here, and now, I don't know that it could do any harm. You remember that story of the man who got this place from Henry VIII and the curse? That man's wife is buried in a vault under the church. Well, there were legends, and I confess I was curious to see her tomb. There are iron gates to the vault. Locked, they were. I opened them with an old key – and I couldn't get them to shut again."

"Yes?" Desmond said.

"You think I might have sent for a locksmith; but the fact is, there is a small crypt to the church, and I have used that crypt as a supplementary laboratory. If I had called anyone in to see to the lock they would have gossiped. I should have been turned out of my laboratory – perhaps out of my house."

"I see."

"Now the curious thing is," Mr Prior went on, lowering his voice, "that it is only since that grating was opened that this house has been what they call 'haunted'. It is since then that all the things have happened."

"What things?"

"People staying here, suddenly ill – just as you were. And the attacks always seem to indicate loss of blood. And—" He hesitated a moment. "That wound in your throat. I told you you had hurt yourself falling when you rang the bell. But that was not true. What *is* true is that you had on your throat just the same little white wound that all the others have had. I wish" – he frowned – "that I could get that vault gate shut again. The key won't turn."

"I wonder if I could do anything?" Desmond asked, secretly convinced that he *had* hurt his throat in falling, and that his host's story was, as he put it, "all moonshine". Still, to put a lock right was but a slight return for all the care and kindness. "I'm an engineer, you know," he added, awkwardly, and rose. "Probably a little oil. Let's have a look at this same lock."

He followed Mr Prior through the house to the church. A bright, smooth old key turned readily, and they passed into the building, musty and damp, where ivy crawled through the broken windows, and the blue sky seemed to be laid close against the holes in the roof. Another key clicked in the lock of a low door beside what had once been the Lady Chapel, a thick oak door grated back, and Mr Prior stopped a moment to light a candle that waited in its rough iron candlestick on a ledge of the stonework. Then down narrow stairs, chipped a little at the edges and soft with dust. The crypt was Norman, very simply beautiful. At the end of it was a recess, masked with a grating of rusty ironwork.

"They used to think," said Mr Prior, "that iron kept off witchcraft. This is the lock," he went on, holding the candle against the gate, which was ajar.

They went through the gate, because the lock was on the other side. Desmond worked a minute or two with the oil and feather that he had brought. Then with a little wrench the key turned and re-turned.

"I think that's all right," he said, looking up, kneeling on one knee, with the key still in the lock and his hand on it.

"May I try it?"

Mr Prior took Desmond's place, turned the key, pulled it out, and stood up. Then the key and the candlestick fell rattling on the stone floor, and the old man sprang upon Desmond.

"Now I've got you," he growled, in the darkness, and Desmond says that his spring and his clutch and his voice were like the spring and the clutch and the growl of a strong savage beast.

Desmond's little strength snapped like a twig at his first bracing of it to resistance. The old man held him as a vice holds. He had got a rope from somewhere. He was tying Desmond's arms.

Desmond hates to know that there in the dark he screamed like a caught hare. Then he remembered that he was a man, and shouted "Help! Here! Help!"

But a hand was on his mouth, and now a handkerchief was being knotted at the back of his head. He was on the floor, leaning against something. Prior's hands had left him.

"Now," said Prior's voice, a little breathless, and the match he struck showed Desmond the stone shelves with long things on them – coffins he supposed. "Now, I'm sorry I had to do it, but science before friendship, my dear Desmond," he went on, quite courteous and friendly. "I will explain to you, and you will see that a man of honour could not act otherwise. Of course, you having no friends who know where you are is most convenient. I saw that from the first. Now I'll explain. I didn't expect you to understand by instinct. But no matter. I am, I say it without vanity, the greatest discoverer since Newton. I know how to modify men's natures. I can make men what I choose. It's all done by transfusion of blood. Lopez – you know, my man Lopez – I've pumped the blood of dogs into his veins, and he's my slave – like a dog. Verney, he's my slave, too – part dog's blood and partly the blood of people who've come from time to time to investigate the ghost, and partly my own, because I wanted him to be clever enough to help me. And there's a bigger thing behind all this. You'll understand me when I say" – here he became very technical indeed, and used many words that meant nothing to Desmond, whose thoughts dwelt more and more on his small chance of escape.

To die like a rat in a hole, a rat in a hole! If he could only loosen the handkerchief and shout again!

"Attend, can't you?" said Prior, savagely, and kicked him. "I beg your pardon, my dear chap," he went on suavely, "but this is important. So you see the elixir of life is really the blood. The blood is the life, you know, and my great discovery is that to make a man immortal, and restore his youth, one only needs blood from the veins of a man who unites in himself blood of the four great races – the four colours, black, white, red, and yellow. Your blood unites these four. I took as much as I dared from you that night. I was the vampire, you know." He laughed pleasantly. "But your blood didn't act. The drug I had to give you to induce sleep probably destroyed the vital germs. And, besides, there wasn't enough of it. Now there is going to be enough!"

Desmond had been working his head against the thing behind him, easing the knot of the handkerchief down till it slipped from head to neck. Now he got his mouth free, and said, quickly: "That was not

true what I said about the Chinamen and that. I was joking. My
mother's people were all Devon."

"I don't blame you in the least," said Prior, quietly. "I should lie
myself in your place."

And he put back the handkerchief. The candle was now burning
clearly from the place where it stood – on a stone coffin. Desmond
could see that the long things on the shelves *were* coffins, not all of
stone. He wondered what this madman would do with his body
when everything was over. The little wound in his throat had broken
out again. He could feel the slow trickle of warmth on his neck. He
wondered whether he would faint. It felt like it.

"I wish I'd brought you here the first day – it was Verney's doing,
my tinkering about with pints and half-pints. Sheer waste – sheer
wanton waste!"

Prior stopped and stood looking at him.

Desmond, despairingly conscious of growing physical weakness,
caught himself in a real wonder as to whether this might not be a
dream – a horrible, insane dream – and he could not wholly dismiss
the wonder, because incredible things seemed to be adding themselves to the real horrors of the situation, just as they do in dreams.
There seemed to be something stirring in the place – something that
wasn't Prior. No – nor Prior's shadow, either. That was black and
sprawled big across the arched roof. This was white, and very small
and thin. But it stirred, it grew – now it was no longer just a line of
white, but a long, narrow, white wedge – and it showed between the
coffin on the shelf opposite him and that coffin's lid.

And still Prior stood very still looking down on his prey. All
emotion but a dull wonder was now dead in Desmond's weakened
senses. In dreams – if one called out, one awoke – but he could not
call out. Perhaps if one moved – But before he could bring his
enfeebled will to the decision of movement – something else moved.
The black lid of the coffin opposite rose slowly – and then suddenly
fell, clattering and echoing, and from the coffin rose a form, horribly
white and shrouded, and fell on Prior and rolled with him on the
floor of the vault in a silent, whirling struggle. The last thing
Desmond heard before he fainted in good earnest was the scream
Prior uttered as he turned at the crash and saw the white-shrouded
body leaping towards him.

"It's all right," he heard next. And Verney was bending over him
with brandy. "You're quite safe. He's tied up and locked in the
laboratory. No. That's all right, too." For Desmond's eyes had

turned towards the lidless coffin. "That was only me. It was the only way I could think of, to save you. Can you walk now? Let me help you, so. I've opened the grating. Come."

Desmond blinked in the sunlight he had never thought to see again. Here he was, back in his wicker chair. He looked at the sundial on the house. The whole thing had taken less than fifty minutes.

"Tell me," said he. And Verney told him in short sentences with pauses between.

"I tried to warn you," he said, "you remember, in the window. I really believed in his experiments at first – and – he'd found out something about me – and not told. It was when I was very young. God knows I've paid for it. And when you came I'd only just found out what really had happened to the other chaps. That beast Lopez let it out when he was drunk. Inhuman brute! And I had a row with Prior that first night, and he promised me he wouldn't touch you. And then he did."

"You might have told me."

"You were in a nice state to be told anything, weren't you? He promised me he'd send you off as soon as you were well enough. And he *had* been good to me. But when I heard him begin about the grating and the key I *knew* – so I just got a sheet and—"

"But why didn't you come out before?"

"I didn't dare. He could have tackled me easily if he had known what he was tackling. He kept moving about. It had to be done suddenly. I counted on just that moment of weakness when he really thought a dead body had come to life to defend you. Now I'm going to harness the horse and drive you to the police-station at Crittenden. And they'll send and lock him up. Everyone knew he was as mad as a hatter, but somebody had to be nearly killed before anyone would lock him up. The law's like that, you know."

"But you – the police – won't they—"

"It's quite safe," said Verney, dully. "Nobody knows but the old man, and now nobody will believe anything he says. No, he never posted your letters, of course, and he never wrote to your friend, and he put off the Psychical man. No, I can't find Lopez; he must know that something's up. He's bolted."

But he had not. They found him, stubbornly dumb, but moaning a little, crouched against the locked grating of the vault when they came, a prudent half-dozen of them, to take the old man away from the Haunted House. The master was dumb as the man. He would not speak. He has never spoken since.

The Light in the Garden

E. F. Benson

Location: West Riding, Yorkshire.

Time: July, 1921.

Eyewitness Description: *"A shadow seemed to cross the window looking on to the gardens; on the road a light had appeared as if carried by some nocturnal passenger; and somehow the two seemed to have a common source, as if some presence that hovered about the place was striving to manifest itself . . ."*

Author: Edward Frederic Benson (1867–1940) was the middle of the three literary Benson brothers and also the most famous, largely due to the huge success of his shocking novel, *Dodo* (1893), mocking society and "its lies and swank". Like his brothers, he was classically educated and formed a deep interest in archaeology, although he had no desire to settle for the life of a scholar as they had done. He was, though, invited to M. R. James' first Christmas reading in 1893 and soon afterwards was busy creating the supernatural stories which he said were "deliberately written to frighten": a number of them having subsequently become the favourites of anthologists, particularly the nauseating "Caterpillars" (1912) and his two gruesome vampire tales, "The Room in the Tower" (1912) and "Mrs Amworth" (1922). The majority of Benson's stories were later collected into popular volumes, *Visible and Invisible* (1923), *Spook Stories* (1928) and *More Spook Stories* (1934), but a few, like "The Light in the Garden" which he wrote for the Christmas 1921 issue of *Eve: The Lady's Pictorial*, escaped the net and it is now brought back into print as another reminder of the grisly fare being offered – even to female readers – around Edwardian fireplaces at the Festive season.

The house and the dozen areas of garden and pasture-land surrounding it, which had been left me by my uncle, lay at the top end of one of those remote Yorkshire valleys carved out among the hills of the West Riding. Above it rose the long moors of bracken and heather, from which flowed the stream that ran through the garden, and, joining another tributary, brawled down the valley into the Nidd, and at the foot of its steep fields lay the hamlet – a dozen of houses and a small grey church. I had often spent half my holidays there when a boy, but for the last twenty years my uncle had become a confirmed recluse, and lived alone, seeing neither kith nor kin nor friends from January to December,

It was, therefore, with a sense of clearing old memories from the dust and dimness with which the lapse of years had covered them that I saw the dale again on a hot July afternoon in this year of drought and rainlessness. The house, as his agent had told me, was sorely in need of renovation and repair, and my notion was to spend a fortnight here in personal supervision. I had arranged that the foreman of a firm of decorators in Harrogate should meet me here next day and discuss what had to be done. I was still undecided whether to live in the house myself or let or sell it. As it would be impossible to stay there while painting and cleaning and repairing were going on, the agent had recommended me to inhabit for the next fortnight the lodge which stood at the gate on to the high road. My friend, Hugh Grainger, who was to have come up with me, had been delayed by business in London, but he would join me to-morrow.

It is strange how the revisiting of places which one has known in youth revives all sorts of memories which one had supposed must have utterly faded from the mind. Such recollections crowded fast in upon me, jostling each other for recognition and welcome, as I came near to the place. The sight of the church recalled a Sunday of disgrace, when I had laughed at some humorous happening during the progress of the prayers: the sight of the coffee-coloured stream recalled memories of trout fishing: and, most of all, the sight of the lodge, built of brown stone, with the high wall enclosing the garden, reawoke the most vivid and precise recollections. My uncle's butler, of the name of Wedge – how it all came back! – lived there, coming up to the house of a morning, and going back there with his lantern at night, if it was dark and moonless, to sleep; Mrs Wedge, his wife, had the care of the locked gate, and opened it to visiting or outgoing vehicles. She had been rather a formidable figure to a small boy, a dark, truculent woman, with a foot curiously malformed, so twisted that it pointed outwards and at right angles to the other. She scowled at you when you knocked at the door and asked her to open the gate, and came hobbling out with a dreadful rocking movement. It was, in fact, worth the trouble of going round by a path through the plantation in order to avoid an encounter with Mrs Wedge, especially after one occasion, when, not being able to get any response to my knockings, I opened the door of the lodge and found her lying on the floor, flushed and tipsily snoring. . . . Then the last year that I ever came here Mrs Wedge went off to Whitby or Scarborough on a fortnight's holiday. Wedge had not waited at breakfast that morning, for he was said to have driven the dogcart to take Mrs Wedge to the station at Harrogate, ten miles away. There was something a little odd about this, for I had been early abroad that morning, and thought I had seen the dogcart bowling along the road with Wedge, indeed, driving it, but no wife beside him. How odd, I thought now, that I should recollect that, and even while I wondered that I should have retained so insignificant a memory, the sequel, which made it significant, flashed into my mind, for a few days afterwards Wedge was absent again, having been sent for to go to his wife, who was dying. He came back a widower. A woman from the village was installed as lodge-keeper, a pleasant body, who seemed to enjoy opening the gate to a young gentleman with a fishing-rod. . . . Just at that moment my rummaging among old memories ceased, for here was the agent, warned by the motor-horn, coming out of the brown stone lodge.

There was time before sunset to stroll up to the house and form a general idea of what must be done in the way of decoration and repair, and not till we had got back to the lodge again did the thought of Wedge re-occur to me.

"My uncle's butler used to live here," I said. "Is he alive still? Is he here now?"

"Mr Wedge died a fortnight ago," said the agent. "It was of the suddenest; he was looking forward to your coming and to attending to you, for he remembered you quite well."

Though I had so vivid a mental picture of Mrs Wedge, I could not recall in the least what Wedge looked like.

"I, too, can remember all about him," I said. "But I can't remember him. What was he like?"

Mr Harkness described him to me, of course, as he knew him, an old man of middle height, grey-haired and much wrinkled, with the habit of looking round quickly when he spoke to you; but his description roused no response whatever in my memory. Naturally, the grey hair and the wrinkles, and, for that matter, perhaps the habit of "looking round quickly," delineated an older man than he was when I knew him, and anyhow, among so much that was vivid in recollection, the appearance of Wedge was to me not even dim, but had no existence at all.

I found that Mr Harkness had made thoughtful arrangements for my comfort in the lodge. A woman from the village and her daughter were to come in early every morning for cooking and housework, and leave again at night after I had had my dinner. I was served with an excellent plain meal, and presently, as I sat watching the fading of the long twilight, there came past my open window the figures of the woman and the girl going home to the village. I heard the gate clang as they passed out, and knew that I was alone in the house. To cheerful folk fond of solitude, such as myself, that is a rare but pleasant sensation; there is the feeling that by no possibility can one be interrupted, and I prepared to spend a leisurely evening over a book that had beguiled my journey and a pack of patience cards. It was fast growing dark, and before settling down I turned to the chimney-piece to light a pair of candles. Perhaps the kindling of the match cast some momentary shadow, for I found myself looking quickly across to the window, under the impression that some black figure had gone past it along the garden path outside. The illusion was quite momentary, but I knew that I was thinking about Wedge again. And still I could not remember in the least what Wedge was like.

My book that had begun so well in the train proved disappointing in its development, and my thoughts began to wander from the printed page, and presently I rose to pull down the blinds which till now had remained unfurled. The room was at an angle of the cottage: one window looked on to the little high-walled garden, the other up the road towards my uncle's house. As I drew down the blind here I saw up the road the light as of some lantern, which bobbed and oscillated as if to the steps of someone who carried it, and the thought of Wedge coming home at night when his work at the house was done re-occurred to my memory. Then, even as I watched, the light, whatever it was, ceased to oscillate, but burned steadily. At a guess, I should have said it was about a hundred yards distant. It remained like that a few seconds and then went out, as if the bearer had extinguished it. As I pulled down the blind I found that my breath came quick and shallow, as if I had been running.

It was with something of an effort that I sat myself down to play Patience, and with an effort that I congratulated myself on being alone and secure from interruptions. I did not feel quite so secure now, and I did not know what the interruption might be. . . . There was no sense of any presence but my own being in the house with me, but there was a sense, deny it though I might, of there being some presence outside. A shadow had seemed to cross the window looking on to the garden; on the road a light had appeared, as if carried by some nocturnal passenger, as if somehow the two seemed to have a common source, as if some presence that hovered about the place was striving to manifest itself. . . .

At that moment there came on the door of the house, just outside the room where I sat, a sharp knock, followed by silence, and then once more a knock. And instantaneous, as a blink of lightning, there flashed unbidden into my mind the image of the lantern-bearer who, seeing me at the window, had extinguished his light, and in the darkness had crept up to the house and was now demanding admittance. I knew that I was frightened now, but I knew also that I was hugely interested, and, taking one of the candles in my hand, I went quietly to the door. Just then the knocking was renewed outside, three raps in quick succession, and I had to wait until mere curiosity was ascendant again over some terror that came welling up to my forehead in beads of moisture. It might be that I should find outside some tenant or dependant of my uncle, who, unaware of my advent, wondered who might have business in this house lately vacated, and in that case my terror would vanish; or I should find outside either nothing or some figure as yet unconjecturable, and my curiosity and interest would flame up again. And then, holding the candle above my head so that I could look out undazzled, I pulled back the latch of the door and opened it wide.

Though but a few seconds ago the door had sounded with the knockings, there was no one there, neither in front of it nor to the right or left of it. But though to my physical eye no one was visible, I must believe that to the inward eye of soul or spirit there was apparent that which my grosser bodily vision could not perceive. For as I scrutinised the empty darkness it was as if I was gazing on the image of the man whom I had so utterly forgotten, and I knew what Wedge was like when I had seen him last. "In his habit as he lived" he sprang into my mind, his thick brown hair not yet tinged with grey, his hawk-like nose, his thin, compressed mouth, his eyes set close together, which shifted if you gave him a straight gaze. No less did I know his low, broad shoulders and the mole on the back of his left hand, his heavy watch-chain, his dark striped trousers. Externally and materially my questing eyes saw but the empty circle of illumination cast by my candle, but my soul's vision beheld Wedge standing on the doorstep. It was his shadow that had passed the window as I lit my lights after dinner, his lantern that I had seen on the road, his knocking that I had heard.

Then I spoke to him who stood there so minutely seen and yet so invisible.

"What do you want with me, Wedge?" I asked. "Why are you not at rest?"

A draught of wind came round the corner, extinguishing my light. At that a gust of fear shook me, and I slammed to the door and bolted it. I could not be there in the darkness with that which indubitably stood on the threshold.

The mind is not capable of experiencing more than a certain degree of any emotion. A climax arrives, and an assuagement, a diminution follows. That was certainly the case with me now, for though I had to spend the night alone here, with God knew what possible visitations before day, the terror had reached its culminating point and ebbed away again. Moreover, that haunting presence, which I now believed I had identified, was without and not within the house. It had not, to the psychical sense, entered through the open door, and I faced my solitary night with far less misgiving than would have been mine if I had been obliged now to fare forth into the darkness. I slept and woke again, and again slept, but never with panic of nightmare, or with the sense, already once or twice familiar to me, that there was any presence in the room beside my own, and when finally I dropped into a dreamless slumber I woke to find the cheerful day already bright, and the dawn-chorus of the birds in full harmony.

My time was much occupied with affairs of restorations and repairs that day, but I did a little private thinking about Wedge, and made up my mind that I would not tell Hugh Grainger any of my experiences on the previous evening. Indeed, they seemed now of no great evidential value: the shape that had passed my window might so easily have been some queer shadow cast by the kindling of my match; the lantern-light I had seen up the road – if, indeed, it was a lantern at all – might easily have been a real lantern, and who knew whether those knocks at the door might not have been vastly exaggerated by my excitement and loneliness, and be found only to have been the tapping of some spray of ivy or errant creeper? As for the sudden recollection of Wedge, which had eluded me before, it was but natural that I should sooner or later have recaptured the memory of him. Besides, supposing there was anything supernormal about these things, and supposing that they or similar phenomena appeared to Hugh also, his evidence would be far more weighty, if it was come at independently, without the prompting of suggestions from me. He arrived, as I had done the day before, a little before sunset, big and jovial, and rather disposed to reproach me for holding out trout-fishing as an attraction, when the stream was so dwindled by the drought.

"But there's rain coming," said he. "Can't you smell it?"

The sky certainly was thickly overcast and sultry with storm, and before dinner was over the shrubs outside began to whisper underneath the first drops. But the shower soon passed, and while I was busy with some estimate which I had promised the contractor to look at before he came again next morning, Hugh strolled out along the road up to the house for a breath of air. I had finished before he came back, and we sat down to picquet. As he cut, he said:

"I thought you told me the house above was unoccupied. But I passed a man apparently coming down from there, carrying a lantern."

"I don't know who that could be," said I. "Did you see him at all clearly?"

"No, he put out his lantern as I approached; I turned immediately afterwards, and caught him up, and passed him again."

There came a knock at the front door, then silence, and then a repetition.

"Shall I see who it is while you are dealing?" he said.

He took a candle from the table, but, leaving the deal incomplete, I followed him, and saw him open the door. The candlelight shone out into the darkness, and under Hugh's uplifted arm I beheld, vaguely and indistinctly, the shape of a man. Then the light fell full on to his face, and I recognised him.

"Yes, what do you want?" said Hugh, and just as had happened last night a puff of wind blew the flame off the candle-wick and left us in the dark.

Then Hugh's voice, suddenly raised, came again.

"Here, get out," he said. "What do you want?"

I threw open the door into the sitting-room close at hand, and the light within illuminated the narrow passage of the entry. There was no one there but Hugh and myself.

"But where's the beggar gone?" said Hugh. "He pushed in by me. Did he go into the sitting-room? And where on earth is he?"

"Did you see him?" I asked.

"Of course I saw him. A little man, hook-nosed, with eyes close together. I never liked a man less . . . Look here, we must search through the house. He did come in."

Together, not singly, we went through the few rooms which the cottage contained, the two living rooms and the kitchen below, and the three bedrooms upstairs. All was empty and quiet.

"It's a ghost," said Hugh; and then I told him my experience on the previous evening. I told him also all that I knew of Wedge, and of his wife, and of her sudden death when on her holiday. Once or twice as I spoke I saw that Hugh put up his hand as if to shade the flame of the candle from shining out into the garden, and as I finished he suddenly blew it out and came close to me.

"I thought it was the reflection of the candle-light on the panes," he said, "but it isn't. Look out there."

There was a light burning at the far end of the garden, visible in glimpses through a row of tall peas, and there was something moving beside it. A piece of an arm appeared there, as of a man digging, a shoulder and head . . .

"Come out," whispered Hugh. "That's our man. And what is he doing?"

Next moment we were gazing into blackness: the light had vanished.

We each took a candle and went out through the kitchen door. The flames burned steady in the windless air as in a room, and in five minutes we had peered behind every bush, and looked into every cranny. Then suddenly Hugh stopped.

"Did you leave a light in the kitchen?" he asked.

"No."

"There's one there now," he said, and my eye followed his pointing finger.

There was a communicating door between our bedrooms, both of which looked out on to the garden, and before getting into bed I made myself some trivial excuse of wanting to speak to Hugh, and left it open. He was already in bed.

"You'd like to fish tomorrow?" I asked.

Before he could answer the room leaped into light, and simultaneously the thunder burst overhead. The fountains of the clouds were unsealed, and the deluge of the rain descended. I took a step across to the window with the idea of shutting it, and across the dark streaming cave of the night outside, again, and now unobscured from the height of the upper floor, I saw the lantern light at the far end of the garden, and the figure of a man bending and rising again as he plied his secret task . . . The downpour continued; sometimes I dozed for a little, but through dozing and waking alike, my mind was

delving and digging as to why out there in the hurly-burly of the
storm, the light burned and the busy figure rose and fell. There was
haste and bitter urgency in that hellish gardening, which recked
nothing of the rain.

I awoke suddenly from an uneasy doze, and felt the skin of my
scalp grow tight with some nameless terror. Hugh apparently had lit
his candle again, for light came in through the open door between
our rooms. Then came the click of a turned handle, and the other
door into the passage slowly opened. I was sitting up in bed now with
my eyes fixed on it, and round it came the figure of Wedge. He
carried a lantern, and his hands were black with mould. And at that
sight the whole of my self-control was shattered.

"Hugh!" I yelled. "Hugh! He is here."

Hugh came hurrying in, and for one second I turned my eyes to
him.

"There by the door!" I cried.

When I looked back again the apparition was no longer there. But
the door was open, and on the floor by it fragments of mud and
soaked soil . . .

The sequel is soon told. Where we had seen the figure digging in the
garden was a row of lavender bushes. These we pulled up, and three
feet below came on the huddled remains of a woman's body. The
skull had been beaten in by some crashing blow; fragments of
clothing and the malformation of one of the feet were sufficient
to establish identification. The bones lie now in the churchyard close
by the grave of her husband and murderer.

The Prescription

Marjorie Bowen

Location: Verrall Hall, Sunford, Bucks.
Time: Christmas Eve, 1928.
Eyewitness Description: *"We got, however, our surprise and our shock because Mrs Mahogany began suddenly to writhe into ugly contortions and called out in a loud voice, quite different from the one that she had hitherto used: 'Murder!' . . ."*

Author: Marjorie Bowen (1886–1952) was no relation of Elizabeth Bowen: she had been born Gabrielle Margaret Long to a poor family on Hayling Island in Hampshire where she spent the early years of her career writing prolifically to support her extravagant mother and sister. She used a variety of pen names to conceal her huge output of over 150 novels, using the Bowen pseudonym on her supernatural stories, starting with *Black Magic* (1909), which was a best seller. She also used the name on *The Haunted Vintage* (1921); but chose Robert Paye for the eerie *Julia Roseing Rave* (1933); and Joseph Shearing for *The Spectral Bride* (1942), based on a real Victorian case. Despite this productivity, the best of her books brilliantly conjure up haunted landscapes along with a unique mixture of cruelty and pathos among her characters. The best of the Bowen short stories – or "twilight tales," as she liked to call them – were collected in several volumes between 1917 and 1932, her own favourites appearing in *The Bishop of Hell* (1949). However, "The Prescription", which was originally published in the Christmas issue of the *London Magazine* in 1928, did not find a place in any of these – an undeserved fate for a story about a professional medium by a writer recently described by Jack Sullivan unequivocally as "one of the great supernatural writers of the 20th century."

John Cuming collected ghost stories; he always declared that this was the best that he knew, although it was partially second-hand and contained a mystery that had no reasonable solution, while most really good ghost stories allow of a plausible explanation, even if it is one as feeble as a dream, excusing all; or a hallucination or a crude deception. Cuming told the story rather well. The first part of it at least had come under his own observation and been carefully noted by him in the flat green book which he kept for the record of all curious cases of this sort. He was a shrewd and a trained observer; he honestly restrained his love of drama from leading him into embellishing facts. Cuming told the story to us all on the most suitable possible occasion – Christmas Eve – and prefaced it with a little homily.

"You all know the good old saw – 'The more it changes the more it is the same thing' – and I should like you to notice that this extremely up-to-date ultra-modern ghost story is really almost exactly the same as the one that might have puzzled Babylonian or Assyrian sages. I can give you the first start of the tale in my own words, but the second part will have to be in the words of someone else. They were, however, most carefully and scrupulously taken down. As for the conclusion, I must leave you to draw that for yourselves – each according to your own mood, fancy and temperament; it may be that you will all think of the same solution, it may be that you will each think of a different one, and it may be that everyone will be left wondering."

Having thus enjoyed himself by whetting our curiosity, Cuming settled himself down comfortably in his deep armchair and unfolded his tale:

It was about five years ago. I don't wish to be exact with time, and of course I shall alter names – that's one of the first rules of the game, isn't it? Well, whenever it was, I was the guest of a – Mrs Janey we will call her – who was, to some extent, a friend of mine; an intelligent, lively, rather bustling sort of woman who had the knack of gathering interesting people about her. She had lately taken a new house in Buckinghamshire. It stood in the grounds of one of those large estates which are now so frequently being broken up. She was very pleased with the house, which was quite new and had only been finished about a year, and seemed, according to her own rather excited imagination, in every way desirable. I don't want to emphasize anything about the house except that it *was* new and did stand on the verge, as it were, of this large old estate, which had belonged to one of those notable English families now extinct and completely forgotten. I am no antiquarian or connoisseur in architecture, and the rather blatant modernity of the house did not offend me. I was able to appreciate its comfort and to enjoy what Mrs Janey rather maddeningly called "the old-world garden", which were really a section of the larger gardens of the vanished mansion which had once commanded this domain. Mrs Janey, I should tell you, knew nothing about the neighbourhood nor anyone who lived there, except that for the first it was very convenient for town and for the second she believed that they were all "*nice*" people, not likely to bother one. I was slightly disappointed with the crowd she had gathered together at Christmas. They were all people whom either I knew too well or whom I didn't wish to know at all, and at first the party showed signs of being extremely flat. Mrs Janey seemed to perceive this too, and with rather nervous haste produced, on Christmas Eve, a trump card in the way of amusement – a professional medium, called Mrs Mahogany, because that could not possibly have been her name. Some of us "believed in", as the saying goes, mediums, and some didn't; but we were all willing to be diverted by the experiment. Mrs Janey continually lamented that a certain Dr Dilke would not be present. He was going to be one of the party, but had been detained in town and would not reach Verrall, which was the name of the house, until later, and the medium, it seemed, could not stay; for she, being a personage in great demand, must go on to a further engagement. I, of course, like everyone else possessed of an intelligent curiosity and a certain amount of leisure, had been to mediums before. I had been slightly impressed, slightly disgusted, and very much bewildered, and on the whole had decided to let the matter alone, considering that I really preferred the more direct old-fashioned method of getting in touch with what we used to call "the Unseen". This sitting in the great new house seemed rather banal. I could understand in some haunted old manor that a clairvoyant, or a clairaudient, or a trance-medium might have found something interesting to say, but what was she going to get out of Mrs Janey's bright, brilliant and comfortable dwelling?

Mrs Mahogany was a nondescript sort of woman – neither young nor old, neither clever nor stupid, neither dark nor fair, placid, and not in the least self-conscious. After an extremely good luncheon (it was a gloomy, stormy afternoon) we all sat down in a circle in the cheerful drawing-room; the curtains were pulled across the dreary prospect of grey sky and grey landscape, and we had merely the light of the fire. We sat quite close together in order to increase "the power", as Mrs Mahogany said, and the medium sat in the middle, with no special precautions against trickery; but we all knew that trickery would have been really impossible, and we were quite prepared to be tremendously impressed and startled if any manifestations took place. I think we all felt rather foolish, as we did not know each other very well, sitting round there, staring at this very ordinary, rather common, stout little woman, who kept nervously pulling a little tippet of grey wool over her shoulders, closing her eyes and muttering, while she twisted her fingers together. When we had sat silent for about ten minutes Mrs Janey announced in a rather raw whisper that the medium had gone into a trance. "Beautifully," she added. I thought that Mrs Mahogany did not look at all beautiful. Her communication began with a lot of rambling talk which had no point at all, and a good deal of generalisation under which I think we all became a little restive. There was too much of various spirits who had all sorts of ordinary names, just regular Toms, Dicks and Harrys of the spirit world, floating round behind us, their arms full of flowers and their mouths full of good will – all rather pointless. And though, occasionally, a Tom, a Dick, or a Harry was identified by some of us, it wasn't very convincing and, what was worse, not very interesting. We got, however, our surprise and our shock, because Mrs Mahogany began suddenly to writhe into ugly contortions and called out in a loud voice, quite different from the one that she had hitherto used:

"Murder!"

This word gave us all a little thrill, and we leant forward eagerly to hear what further she had to say. With every sign of distress and horror Mrs Mahogany began to speak:

"He's murdered her. Oh, how dreadful. Look at him! Can't somebody stop him? It's so near here too. He tried to save her. He was sorry, you know. Oh, how dreadful! Look at him – he's borne it as long as he can, and now he's murdered her! I see him mixing it in a glass. Oh, isn't it awful that no one could have saved her – and he was so terribly remorseful afterwards. Oh, how dreadful! How horrible!"

She ended in a whimpering of fright and horror, and Mrs Janey, who seemed an adept at this sort of thing, leant forward and asked eagerly:

"Can't you get the name – can't you find out who it is? Why do you get that here?"

"I don't know," muttered the medium; "it's somewhere near here – a house, an old dark house, and there are curtains of mauve velvet –

do you call it mauve? – a kind of blue-red at the windows. There's a garden outside with a fish-pond and you go through a low doorway and down stone steps."

"It isn't near here," said Mrs Janey decidedly; "all the houses are new."

"The house is near here," persisted the medium. "I am walking through it now; I can see the room, I can see that poor woman, and a glass of milk—"

"I wish you'd get the name," insisted Mrs Janey, and she cast a look, as I thought not without suspicion, round the circle. "You can't be getting this from my house, you know, Mrs Mahogany," she added decidedly, "it must be given out by someone here – something they've read or seen, you know," she said, to reassure us that our characters were not in dispute.

But the medium replied drowsily, "No, it's somewhere near here. I see a light dress covered with small roses. If he could have got help he would have gone for it, but there was no one; so all his remorse was useless . . ."

No further urging would induce the medium to say more; soon afterwards she came out of the trance, and all of us, I think, felt that she had made rather a stupid blunder by introducing this vague piece of melodrama, and if it was, as we suspected, a cheap attempt to give a ghostly and mysterious atmosphere to Christmas Eve, it was a failure.

When Mrs Mahogany, blinking round her, said brightly, "Well, here I am again! I wonder if I said anything that interested you?" we all replied rather coldly, "Of course it has been most interesting, but there hasn't been anything definite." And I think that even Mrs Janey felt that the sitting had been rather a disappointment, and she suggested that if the weather was really too horrible to venture out of doors we should sit round the fire and tell old-fashioned ghost stories. "The kind," she said brightly, "that are about bones and chairs and shrouds. I really think that is the most thrilling kind of all." Then, with some embarrassment, and when Mrs Mahogany had left the room, she suggested that not one of us should say anything about what the medium had said in her trance.

"It really was rather absurd," said our hostess, "and it would make me look a little foolish if it got about; you know some people think these mediums are absolute fakes, and anyhow the whole thing, I am afraid, was quite stupid. She must have got her contacts mixed. There is no old house about here and never has been since the original Verrall was pulled down, and that's a good fifty years ago,

I believe, from what the estate agent told me; and as for a murder, I never heard the shadow of any such story."

We all agreed not to mention what the medium had said, and did this with the more heartiness as we were not any of us impressed. The feeling was rather that Mrs Mahogany had been obliged to say something, and had said that . . .

"Well" [said Cuming comfortably], "that is the first part of my story, and I dare say you'll think it's dull enough. Now we come to the second part":

Latish that evening Dr Dilke arrived. He was not in any way a remarkable man, just an ordinary successful physician, and I refuse to say that he was suffering from overwork or nervous strain; you know, that is so often put into this kind of story as a sort of excuse for what happens afterwards. On the contrary, Dr Dilke seemed to be in the most robust of health and the most cheerful frame of mind, and quite prepared to make the most of his brief holiday. The car that fetched him from the station was taking Mrs Mahogany away, and the doctor and the medium met for just a moment in the hall. Mrs Janey did not trouble to introduce them, but without waiting for this Mrs Mahogany turned to the doctor and, looking at him fixedly, said: "You're very psychic, aren't you?" And upon that Mrs Janey was forced to say hastily: "This is Mrs Mahogany, Dr Dilke, the famous medium."

The physician was indifferently impressed: "I really don't know," he answered, smiling. "I have never gone in for that sort of thing. I shouldn't think I am what you call 'psychic' really, I have had a hard scientific training, and that rather knocks the bottom out of fantasies."

"Well, you are, you know," said Mrs Mahogany. "I felt it at once; I shouldn't be at all surprised if you had some strange experiences one of these days."

Mrs Mahogany left the house and was duly driven away to the station. I want to make the point very clear that she and Dr Dilke did not meet again and that they held no communication except those few words in the hall spoken in the presence of Mrs Janey. Of course Dr Dilke got twitted a good deal about what the medium had said; it made quite a topic of conversation during dinner and after dinner, and we all had queer little ghost stories or incidents of what we considered "psychic" experiences to trot out and discuss. Dr Dilke remained civil, amused, but entirely unconvinced. He had what he called a material, or physical, or medical explanation for almost everything that we said, and, apart from all these explanations, he added, with some justice, that human credulity was such that there was always someone who would accept and embellish anything, however wild, unlikely or grotesque it was.

"I should rather like to hear what you would say if such an experience happened to you," Mrs Janey challenged him; "whether you use the ancient terms of 'ghost', 'witches', 'black magic', and so on, or whether you speak in modern terms like 'medium', 'clairvoyance', 'psychic contacts', and all the rest of it; well, it seems one is in a bit of a tangle, anyhow, and if any queer thing ever happens to you—"

Dr Dilke broke in pleasantly: "Well, if it ever does I will let you all know about it, and I dare say I shall have an explanation to add at the end of the tale."

When we all met again the next morning we rather hoped that Dr Dilke *would* have something to tell us – some odd experience that might have befallen him in the night, new as the house was and banal as was his bedroom. He told us, of course, that he had passed a perfectly good night.

We most of us went to the morning service in the small church that had once been the chapel belonging to the demolished mansion, and which had some rather curious monuments inside and in the church-yard. As I went in I noticed a mortuary chapel with niches for the coffins to be stood upright, now whitewashed and used as a sacristy. The monuments and mural tablets were mostly to the memory of members of the family of Verrall – the Verralls of Verrall Hall, who appeared to have been people of little interest or distinction. Dr Dilke sat beside me, and I, having nothing better to do through the more familiar and monotonous portions of the service, found myself idly looking at the mural tablet beyond him. This was a large slab of black marble deeply cut with a very worn Latin inscription which I found, unconsciously, I was spelling out. The stone, it seemed, commemorated a woman who had been, of course, the possessor of all the virtues; her name was Philadelphia Carwithen, and I rather pleasantly sampled the flavour of that ancient name – Philadelphia. Then I noticed a smaller inscription at the bottom of the slab, which indicated that the lady's husband also rested in the vault; he had died suddenly about six months after her – of grief at her loss, no doubt, I thought, scenting out a pretty romance.

As we walked home across the frost-bitten fields and icy lanes Dr Dilke, who walked beside me, as he had sat beside me in church, began to complain of cold; he said he believed that he had caught a chill. I was rather amused to hear this old-womanish expression on the lips of a successful physician, and I told him that I had been taught in my more enlightened days that there was no such thing as "catching a chill". To my surprise he did not laugh at this, but said:

"Oh, yes, there is, and I believe I've got it – I keep on shivering; I think it was that slab of black stone I was sitting next. It was as cold as ice, for I touched it, and it seemed to me exuding moisture – some of that old stone does, you know; it's always, as it were, sweating; and I felt exactly as if I were sitting next a slab of ice from which a cold wind was blowing; it was really as if it penetrated my flesh."

He looked pale, and I thought how disagreeable it would be for us all, and particularly for Mrs Janey, if the good man was to be taken ill in the midst of her already not too successful Christmas party. Dr Dilke seemed, too, in that ill-humour which so often presages an illness; he was quite peevish about the church and the service, and the fact that he had been asked to go there.

"These places are nothing but charnel-houses after all," he said fretfully; "one sits there among all those rotting bones, with that damp marble at one's side. . . ."

"It is supposed to give you 'atmosphere'," I said. "The atmosphere of an old-fashioned Christmas . . . Did you notice who your black stone was erected 'to the memory of?'" I asked, and the doctor replied that he had not.

"It was to a woman – a young woman, I took it, and her husband: 'Philadelphia Carwithen', I noticed that, and of course there was a long eulogy of her virtues, and then underneath it just said that he had died a few months afterwards. As far as I could see it was the only example of that name in the church – all the rest were Verralls. I suppose they were strangers here."

"What was the date?" asked the doctor, and I replied that really I had not been able to make it out, for where the Roman figures came the stone had been very worn.

The day ambled along somehow, with games, diversions, and plenty of good food and drink, and towards the evening we began to feel a little more satisfied with each other and our hostess. Only Dr Dilke remained a little peevish and apart, and this was remarkable in one who was obviously of a robust temperament and an even temper. He still continued to talk of a "chill", and I did notice that he shuddered once or twice, and continually sat near the large fire which Mrs Janey had rather laboriously arranged in imitation of what she would call "the good old times."

That evening, the evening of Christmas Day, there was no talk whatever of ghosts or psychic matters; our discussions were entirely topical and of mundane affairs, in which Dr Dilke, who seemed to have recovered his spirits, took his part with ability and agreeableness. When it was time to break up I asked him, half in jest, about his mysterious chill, and he looked at me with some surprise and appeared to have forgotten that he had ever said he had got such a thing; the impression, whatever it was, which he had received in the church had evidently been effaced from his mind. I wish to make that quite clear.

The next morning Dr Dilke appeared very late at the breakfast table, and when he did so his looks were matter for hints and comment; he was pale, distracted, troubled, untidy in his dress, absent in his manner, and I, at least, instantly recalled what he had said yesterday, and feared he was sickening for some illness.

On Mrs Janey putting to him some direct question as to his looks and manner, so strange and so troubled, he replied rather sharply: "Well, I don't know what you can expect from a fellow who's been up all night. I thought I came down here for a rest."

We all looked at him as he dropped into his place and began to drink his coffee with eager gusto; I noticed that he continually shivered. There was something about this astounding statement and his curious appearance which held us all discreetly silent. We waited for further developments before committing ourselves; even Mrs Janey, whom I had never thought of as tactful, contrived to say casually:

"Up all night, doctor. Couldn't you sleep then? I'm so sorry if your bed wasn't comfortable."

"The bed was all right," he answered, "that made me the more sorry to leave it. Haven't you got a local doctor who can take the local cases?" he added.

"Why, of course we have; there's Dr Armstrong and Dr Fraser – I made sure about that before I came here."

"Well, then," demanded Dr Dilke angrily, "why on earth couldn't one of them have gone last night?"

Mrs Janey looked at me helplessly, and I, obeying her glance, took up the matter.

"What do you mean, doctor? Do you mean that you were called out of your bed last night to attend a case?" I asked deliberately.

"Of course I was – I only got back with the dawn."

Here Mrs Janey could not forbear breaking in.

"But, whoever could it have been? I know nobody about here yet, at least, only one or two people by name, and they would not be aware that you were here. And how did you get out of the house? It's locked every night."

Then the doctor gave his story in rather, I must confess, a confused fashion, and yet with an earnest conviction that he was speaking the simple truth. It was broken up a good deal by ejaculations and comments from the rest of us, but I give it you here shorn of all that and exactly as I put it down in my note-book afterwards:

"I was awoken by a tap at the door. I was instantly wide awake and I said: 'Come in.' I thought immediately that probably someone in the house was ill – a doctor, you know, is always ready for these emergencies. The door opened at once and a man entered holding a small ordinary storm-lantern. I noticed nothing peculiar about the man. He had a dark great-coat on, and appeared extremely anxious. 'I am sorry to disturb you,' he said at once, 'but there is a young woman dangerously ill. I want you to come and see her.' I, somehow, did not think of arguing or of suggesting that there were other medical men in the neighbourhood, or of asking how it was he knew of my presence at Verrall. I dressed myself quickly and accompanied him out of the house. He opened the front door without any trouble, and it did not occur to me to ask him how it was he had obtained either admission or egress. There was a small carriage outside the door, such a one as you may still see in isolated country places, but such a one as I was certainly surprised to see here. I could not very well make out either the horse or the driver for, though the moon was high in the heavens, it was frequently obscured by clouds. I got into the carriage and noticed, as I have often noticed before in these ancient vehicles, a most repulsive smell of decay and damp. My companion got in beside me. He did not speak a word during the whole of the journey, which was, I have the impression, extremely long, and yet I could not say how long. I had also the sense that he was in the greatest trouble, anguish, and almost despair; I do not know why I did not question him. I should tell you that he had drawn down the blinds of the carriage and we travelled in darkness, yet I was perfectly aware of his presence and seemed to see him in his heavy dark great-coat turned up round his chin, his black hair low on his forehead, and his anxious, furtive dark eyes.

"I think I may have gone to sleep in the carriage, I was tired and cold. I was aware, however, when it stopped, and of my companion opening the door and helping me out. We went through a garden, down some steps and past a fish-pond; I could see by the moonlight the silver and gold shapes of fishes slipping in and out of the black water. We entered the house by a side-door – I remember that very distinctly – and went up what seemed to be some secret or seldom-used stairs, and into a bedroom. I was by now quite alert, as one is when one gets into the presence of the patient, and I said to myself, 'What a fool I've been, I've brought nothing with me'; and I tried to remember, but could not quite do so, whether or not I had brought anything with me – my cases and so on – to Verrall.

"The room was very badly lit, but a certain illumination, I could not say whether it came from any artificial light within the room or merely from the moonlight through the open window, draped with mauve velvet curtains, fell on the bed, and there I saw my patient. She was a young woman who, I surmised, would have been, when in health, of considerable though coarse charm. She was now in great suffering, twisted and contorted with agony, and in her struggles of anguish had pulled and torn the bedclothes into a heap. I noticed that she wore a dress of some light material spotted with small roses, and it occurred to me at once that she had been taken ill during the daytime and must have lain thus in great pain for many hours, and I turned with some reproach to the man who had fetched me and demanded why help had not been sought sooner. For answer he wrung his hands – a gesture that I do not remember having noticed in any human being before; one hears a great deal of hands being wrung but one does not so often see it. This man, I remember distinctly, wrung his hands, and muttered, 'Do what you can for her – do what you can!' I feared that this would be very little. I endeavoured to make an examination of the patient, but owing to her half-delirious struggles this was very difficult; she was, however, I thought, likely to die, and of what malady I could not determine.

"There was a table nearby on which lay some papers – one I took to be a will – and a glass in which there had been milk. I do not remember seeing anything else in the room – the light was so bad. I endeavoured to question the man, whom I took to be the husband, but without any success. He merely repeated his monotonous appeal for me to save her. Then I was aware of a sound outside the room – of a woman laughing, perpetually and shrilly laughing. "Pray stop that,' I cried to the man; 'who have you got in the house – a lunatic?' But he took no notice of my appeal, merely repeating his own hushed lamentations. The sick woman appeared to hear that demoniacal laughter outside, and, raising herself on one elbow, said, 'You have destroyed me and you may well laugh!'

"I sat down at the table on which were the papers and the half-full glass of milk, and wrote a prescription on a sheet torn out of my note-book. The man snatched it eagerly. 'I don't know when and where you can get that made up,' I said, 'but it's the only hope.' At this he seemed wishful for me to depart, as wishful as he had been for me to come. 'That's all I want,' he said. He took me by the arm and led me out of the house by the same back stairs. As I descended I still heard those two dreadful sounds – the thin laughter of the woman I had not seen, and the groans, becoming every moment fainter, of the young woman whom I had seen. The carriage was waiting for me and I was driven back by the same way I had come. When I reached the house and my room I saw the dawn just breaking. I rested till I heard the breakfast gong. I suppose some time had gone by since I returned to the house, but I wasn't quite aware of it; all through the night I had rather lost the sense of time."

When Dr Dilke had finished his narrative, which I give here badly – but, I hope, to the point – we all glanced at each other rather uncomfortably, for who was to tell a man like Dr Dilke that he had been suffering from a severe hallucination? It was, of course, quite impossible that he could have left the house and gone through the peculiar scenes he had described, and it seemed extraordinary that he could for a moment have believed that he had done so. What was even more remarkable was that so many points of his story agreed with what the medium, Mrs Mahogany, had said in her trance. We recognized the frock with the roses, the mauve velvet curtains, the glass of milk, the man who had fetched Dr Dilke sounded like the murderer, and the unfortunate woman writhing on the bed sounded like the victim; but how had the doctor got hold of these particulars? We all knew that he had not spoken to Mrs Mahogany and each suspected the other of having told him what the medium had said, and that this having wrought on his mind he had the dream, vision, or hallucination he had just described to us. I must add that this was found afterwards to be wholly false; we were all reliable people and there was not a shadow of doubt we had all kept our counsel about Mrs Mahogany. In fact, none of us had been alone with Dr Dilke the previous day for more than a moment or so save myself, who had walked with him home from the church, when we had certainly spoken of nothing except the black stone in the church and the chill which he had said emanated from it . . . Well, to put the matter as briefly as possible, and to leave out a great deal of amazement and wonder, explanation and so on, we will come to the point when Dr Dilke was finally persuaded that he had not left Verrall all the night. When his story was taken to pieces and put before him, as it were, in the raw, he himself recognized many absurdities; how could the man have come straight to his bedroom?

How could he have left the house? – the doors were locked every night, there was no doubt about that. Where did the carriage come from and where was the house to which he had been taken? And who could possibly have known of his presence in the neighbourhood? Had not, too, the scene in the house to which he was taken all the resemblance of a nightmare? Who was it laughing in the other room? What was the mysterious illness that was destroying the young woman? Who was the black-browed man who had fetched him? And, in these days of telephone and motor-cars, people didn't go out in old-fashioned one-horse carriages to fetch doctors from miles away in the case of dangerous illness.

Dr Dilke was finally silenced, uneasy, but not convinced. I could see that he disliked intensely the idea that he had been the victim of an hallucination, and that he equally intensely regretted the impulse which had made him relate his extraordinary adventure of the night. I could only conclude that he must have done so while still, to an extent, under the influence of his delusion, which had been so strong that never for a moment had he questioned the reality of it. Though he was forced at last to allow us to put the whole thing down as a most remarkable dream, I could see that he did not intend to let the matter rest there, and later in the day (out of good manners we had eventually ceased discussing the story) he asked me if I would accompany him on some investigation in the neighbourhood.

"I think I should know the house," he said, "even though I saw it in the dark. I was impressed by the fish-pond and the low doorway through which I had to stoop in order to pass without knocking my head."

I did not tell him that Mrs Mahogany had also mentioned a fish-pond and a low door.

We made the excuse of some old brasses we wished to discover in a nearby church to take my car and go out that afternoon on an investigation of the neighbourhood in the hope of discovering Dr Dilke's dream house.

We covered a good deal of distance and spend a good deal of time without any success at all, and the short day was already darkening when we came upon a row of almshouses in which, for no reason at all that I could discern, Dr Dilke showed an interest and insisted on stopping before them. He pointed out an inscription cut in the centre gable, which said that these had been built by a certain Richard Carwithen in memory of Philadelphia, his wife.

"The people whose tablet you sat next to in the church," I remarked.

"Yes," murmured Dr. Dilke, "when I felt the chill," and he added, "when I *first* felt the chill. You see the date is 1830. That would be about right."

We stopped in the little village, which was a good many miles from Verrall, and after some tedious delays because everything was shut up for the holidays we did discover an old man who was willing to tell us something about the almshouses, though there was nothing much to be said about them. They had been founded by a certain Mr Richard Carwithen with his wife's fortune. He had been a poor man, a kind of adventurer, our informant thought, who had married a wealthy woman; they had not been at all happy. There had been quarrels and disputes, and a separation (at least, so the gossip went, as his father had told it to him). Finally, the Carwithens had taken a house here in this village of Sunford – a large house it was, and it still stood. The Carwithens weren't buried in this village though, but at Verrall, she had been a Verrall by birth – perhaps that's why they came to this neighbourhood – it was the name of a great family in those days you know . . . There was another woman in the old story, as it went, and she got hold of Mr Carwithen and was for making him put his wife aside; and so, perhaps, he would have done, but the poor lady died suddenly, and there was some talk about it, having the other woman in the house at the time, and it being so convenient for both of them . . . But he didn't marry the other woman, because he died six months after his wife . . . By his will he left all his wife's money to found these almshouses.

Dr Dilke asked if he could see the house where the Carwithens had lived.

"It belongs to a London gentleman," the old man said, "who never comes here. It's going to be pulled down and the land sold in building lots; why, it's been locked up these ten years or more. I don't suppose it's been inhabited since – no, not for a hundred years."

"Well, I'm looking for a house round about here. I don't mind spending a little money on repairs if that house is in the market."

The old man didn't know whether it was in the market or not, but kept repeating that the property was to be sold and broken up for building lots.

I won't bother you with all our delays and arguments, but merely tell you that we did finally discover the lodge-keeper of the estate, who gave us the key. It was not such a very large estate, nothing to be compared to Verrall, but had been, in its time, of some pretension. Builders' boards had already been raised along the high road frontage. There were some fine old trees, black and bare, in a little park. As we turned in through the rusty gates and motored towards the house it was nearly dark, but we had our electric torches and the powerful head-lamps of the car. Dr Dilke made no comment on what we had found, but he reconstructed the story of the Carwithens whose names were on that black stone in Verrall church.

"They were quarrelling over money, he was trying to get her to sign a will in his favour; she had some little sickness perhaps – brought on probably by rage – he had got the other woman in the house, remember. I expect he was no good. There was some sort of poison about – perhaps for a face wash, perhaps as a drug. He put it in the milk and gave it to her."

Here I interrupted: "How do you know it was in the milk?"

The doctor did not reply to this. I had now swung the car round to the front of the ancient mansion – a poor, pretentious place, sinister in the half-darkness.

"And then, when he had done it," continued Dr Dilke, mounting the steps of the house, "he repented most horribly; he wanted to fly for a doctor to get some antidote for the poison with the idea in his head that if he could have got help he could have saved her himself. The other woman kept on laughing. He couldn't forgive that – that she could laugh at a moment like that! He couldn't get help. He couldn't find a doctor. His wife died. No one suspected foul play – they seldom did in those days as long as the people were respectable, you must remember the state in which medical knowledge was in 1830. He couldn't marry the other woman, and he couldn't touch the money; he left it all to found the almshouses; then he died himself, six months afterwards, leaving instructions that his name should be added on that black stone. I dare say he died by his own hand. Probably he loved her through it all, you know – it was only the money, that cursed money, a fortune just within his grasp, but which he couldn't take!"

"A pretty romance," I suggested as we entered the house; "I am sure there is a three-volume novel in it of what Mrs Janey would call 'the good old-fashioned' sort."

To this Dr Dilke answered: "Suppose the miserable man can't rest? Supposing he is still searching for a doctor?"

We passed from one room to another of the dismal, dusty, dismantled house. Dr Dilke opened a damaged shutter which concealed one of the windows at the back, and pointed out in the waning light a decayed garden with stone steps and a fish-pond – dry now, of course, but certainly once a fish-pond; and a low gateway, to pass through which a man of his height would have to stoop. We could just discern this in the twilight. He made no comment. We went upstairs.

Here Cuming paused dramatically to give us the full flavour of the final part of his story. He reminded us, rather unnecessarily, for somehow he had convinced us, that this was all perfectly true:

I am not romancing; I won't answer for what Dr Dilke said or did, or his adventure of the night before, or the story of the Carwithens as he constructed it, but *this* is actually what happened . . . We went upstairs by the wide main stairs. Dr Dilke searched about for and found a door which opened on to the back stairs, and then he said: "This must be the room." It was entirely devoid of any furniture, and stained with damp, the walls stripped of panelling and cheaply covered with decayed paper, peeling, and in parts fallen.

"What's this?" said Dr Dilke.

He picked up a scrap of paper that showed vivid on the dusty floor and handed it to me. It was a prescription. He took out his note-book and showed me the page where this fitted in.

"This page I tore out last night when I wrote that prescription in this room. The bed was just there, and there was the table on which were the papers and the glass of milk."

"But you couldn't have been here last night," I protested feebly, "the locked doors – the whole thing! . . ."

Dr Dilke said nothing. After a while neither did I. "Let's get out of the place," I said. Then another thought struck me. "What is your prescription?" I asked.

He said: "A very uncommon kind of prescription, a very desperate sort of prescription, one that I've never written before, nor I hope shall again – an antidote for severe arsenical poisoning."

"I leave you," smiled Cuming, "to your various attitudes of incredulity or explanation."

Christmas Honeymoon

Howard Spring

Location: Falmouth, Cornwall.
Time: Christmas Eve, 1938.
Eyewitness Description: *"The remarkable thing about what happened to me and Ruth was simply that* Nothing *happened. If you have never come up against* Nothing *you have no idea how it can scare you out of your wits . . ."*

Author: Howard Spring (1889–1965) was born in Cardiff, the son of a poor jobbing gardener, and had to leave school at the age of 12 when his father died. He alleviated his tough life as an office boy in the Cardiff docks by taking Evening Classes at the local university and achieved his dream of becoming a newspaper reporter. After learning his trade on several provincial newspapers, Spring landed a job on the London *Evening Standard* where his descriptive prose and astute literary reviews lead to him achieving an international success with one of his first novels *My Son, My Son*, which was filmed in 1940. That same year he wrote *Fame is the Spur*, about a labour leader's rise to power, that established his reputation. During the years of the Second World War, he continued to demonstrate his understanding of contemporary human character in books such as *Hard Facts* (1944) and *Dunkerley's* (1946). He and his wife settled in Falmouth where he produced three volumes of fascinating autobiography, half a dozen more novels and several short stories: a number of which evoked the supernatural in a completely new way. "Christmas Honeymoon", which appeared in the 24 December 1940 issue of the *Standard*, is arguably the best of these and also believed to be based on personal experience.

W e were married on 22 December, because we had met on the
21st. It was as sudden as that. I had come down from
Manchester to London. Londoners like you to say that you come
up to London; but we Manchester people don't give a hoot what
Londoners like. We know that we, and the likes of us, lay the eggs,
and the Londoners merely scramble them. That gives us a sense of
superiority.

Perhaps I have this sense unduly. Certainly I should never have
imagined that I would marry a London girl. As a bachelor, I had
survived thirty Manchester summers, and it seemed unlikely to me
that, if I couldn't find a girl to suit me in the north, I should find one
in London.

I am an architect, and that doesn't make me love London any the
more. Every time I come down to the place I find it has eaten another
chunk of its own beauty, so as to make more room for the fascias of
multiple shops.

All this is just to show you that I didn't come to London looking
for a bride; and if I had been looking for a bride, the last place I
would have investigated would be a cocktail party. But it was at a
cocktail party in the Magnifico that I met Ruth Hutten.

I had never been to a cocktail party in my life before. We don't go
in much for that sort of thing in Manchester: scooping a lot of people
together and getting rid of the whole bang shoot in one do. It seems
to us ungracious. We like to have a few friends in, and give them a cut
off the joint and something decent to drink, and talk in a civilised
fashion while we're at it. That's what we understand by hospitality.
But these cocktail parties are just a frantic St Vitus gesture by people
who don't want to be bothered.

I shouldn't have been at this party at all if it hadn't been for Claud
Tunstall. It was about half-past six when I turned from the lunatic
illumination of Piccadilly Circus, which is my idea of how hell is lit
up, and started to walk down the Haymarket. I was wondering in an
absent-minded sort of way how long the old red pillars of the
Haymarket Theatre would be allowed to stand before some bright
lad thought what fun it would be to tear them down, when Claud
turned round from reading one of the yellow playbills, and there we
were, grinning and shaking hands.

Claud had something to grin about, because the author's name on
the play-bill was his. It was his first play, and it looked as though it
wouldn't matter to Claud, so far as money went, if it were his last.
The thing had been running for over a year; companies were touring
it in the provinces and Colonies; and it was due to open in New York

in the coming year. No wonder Claud was grinning; but I think a spot of the grin was really meant for me. He was the same old Claud who had attended the Manchester Grammar School with me and shared my knowledge of its smell of new exercise books and old suet pudding.

Claud was on his way to this party at the Magnifico, and he said I must come with him. That's how these things are: there's no sense in them; but there would have been no sense either in trying to withstand Claud Tunstall's blue eyes and fair tumbling hair and general look of a sky over a cornfield.

That's going some, for me, and perhaps the figure is a bit mixed, but I'm not one for figures at any time. Anyway, it explains why, five minutes later, I was gritting my teeth in the presence of great boobies looking like outsizes in 18th-century footmen, yelling names and looking down their noses.

We stood at the door of a room, and I was aware of the gold blurs of chandeliers, and a few dozen apparent football scrums, and a hot blast of talk coming out and smacking our faces, so I deduced this was the party all right. One of the boobies yelled: "Mr Claud Tunstall and Mr Edward Oldham," and from what happened it might just as well have been "The Archangel Gabriel and one Worm". Because, the moment we were over the threshold, all the scrums loosened up and girls descended on Claud like a cloud of bright, skitering, squawking parrakeets, flashing their red nails at him, unveiling their pearly portals in wide grins, and bearing him off towards a bar where a chap in white was working overtime among all the sweet accessories of Sin. I never saw him again.

Well, as I say, I might have been a worm, no use at all to parrakeets, but that lets in the sparrows. I was just turning slowly on my own axis, so to speak, in the space that was miraculously cleared round me, when I saw a girl looking at me with an appreciative gleam in her brown eye. She was the brownest girl I ever saw – eyes, skin, and hair – homely as a sparrow, and just as alert.

As our eyes met, there came fluting out of one of the scrums a high-pitched female voice: "No, Basil, I'm teetotal, but I can go quite a long way on pahshun fruit."

The pronunciation of that *pahshun* was indescribable; it seemed the bogus essence of the whole damn silly occasion; and the brown girl and I, looking into one another's eyes, twinkled, savouring together the supreme idiocy. Instinctively we moved towards one another, the twinkle widening to a smile, and I found myself getting dangerously full of similes again, for when she smiled the teeth in her brown face were like the milky kernel of a brown nut.

We sat together on a couch at the deserted end of the room, and I said: "Let me get you something to drink. What would you like? Though whatever it is, it would taste nicer in civilised surroundings."

"I agree," she said simply. "Come on."

And so, ten minutes after I had entered the Magnifico, I was outside again, buttoning my overcoat warmly about me, and this girl was at my side. It was incredible. This is not the sort of thing I usually do; but it had happened so spontaneously, and to be out there in the street, with a little cold wind blowing about us, was such a relief after that gaudy Bedlam, that the girl and I turned to one another and smiled again. I could see she was feeling the same about it as I was.

Our eyes were towards the dazzle of Piccadilly Circus, when she turned and said, "Not that way," so we went the other way, and down those steps where the Duke of York's column towers up into the sky, and then we were in the park. To be walking there, with that little wind, and the sky full of stars huddling together in the cold, and the bare branches of the trees standing up against the violet pulsing of the night – this was indescribable, incredible, coming within a few minutes upon that screeching aviary.

Ruth Hutten was a typist – nothing more. Her father had been one of those old fogies who rootle for years and years in the British Museum to prove that Ben Jonson had really inserted a semi-colon where the 1739 edition or what not has a full-stop. Things like that. Somehow he had lived on it, like a patient old rat living on scraps of forgotten and unimportant meat. Ruth had lived with him – just lived, full of admiration for the old boy's scholarship, typing his annual volume, which usually failed to earn the publisher's advance.

When he died, the typewriter was all she had; and now she typed other people's books. She had been typing a long flaming novel about Cornwall by Gregoria Gunson; and Gregoria (whom I had never heard of before, but who seemed a decent wench) had said, "I'll take you along to a party. You'll meet a lot of people there. Perhaps I can fix up some work for you."

So there Ruth Hutten was, at the Magnifico, feeling as much out of it as I did, and as glad to escape.

She told me all this was we walked through the half-darkness of the park, and I, as naturally, told her all about myself. She was hard up, but I had never known anyone so happy. And I don't mean gay, bubbling, effervescent. No; you can keep that for the Magnifico.

I mean something deep, fundamental; something that takes courage when you're as near the limit as Ruth was.

To this day I don't know London as well as Londoners think everyone ought to know the place. I don't know where we had supper; but it was in a quiet place that everybody else seemed to have forgotten. There was a fire burning, and a shaded lamp on the table. The food was good and simple, and no one seemed to care how long we stayed. I wanted to stay a long time. I had a feeling that once Ruth got outside the door, shook hands, and said "Good night," I should be groping in a very dark place.

I crumbled a bit of bread on the table, and without looking at her I said: "Ruth, I like you. I've never liked anyone so much in my life. Will you marry me?"

She didn't answer till I looked up, and when our glances met she said, "Yes. If you and I can't be happy together, no two people on earth ever could."

This was five years ago. We have had time to discover that we didn't make a mistake.

We were married at a registry office the next morning. The taxi-driver, who looked like one of the seven million exiled Russian princes, and the office charwoman, who had a goitre and a hacking cough, were the witnesses. I tipped them half a sovereign each. I cling to these practical details because I find them comforting in view of the mad impracticality of what was to follow. Please remember that I am an unromantic northerner who couldn't invent a tale to save his life. If I tried to do so, I should at once begin to try and fill it with this and that – in short with Something. The remarkable thing about what happened to me and Ruth was simply that Nothing happened. If you have never come up against Nothing you have no idea how it can scare you out of your wits. When I was a child I used to be afraid of Something in the dark. I know now that the most fearful thing about the dark is that we may find Nothing in it.

It was Ruth's idea that we should spend the few days of our honeymoon walking in Cornwall. Everything was arranged in a mad hurry. Not that there was much to arrange. We bought rucksacks, stuffed a change of under-clothing into them, bought serviceable shoes and waterproofs, and we were ready to start.

Walking was the idea of both of us. This was another bond: you could keep all the motor-cars in the world so far as we were concerned, and all the radio and daily newspapers, too; and we both liked walking in winter as much as in summer.

Cornwall was Ruth's idea. She had Cornwall on the brain. Her father had done some learned stuff on Malory; and her head was full of Merlin and Tintagel and the Return of Arthur. Gregoria Gunson's novel helped, too, with its smugglers and romantic inns and the everlasting beat of surf on granite coasts. So Cornwall it was – a place in which neither of us had set foot before.

We made our first contact with Cornwall at Truro. Night had long since fallen when we arrived there on our wedding day. I have not been there since, nor do I wish ever to return. Looking back on what happened, it seems appropriate that the adventure should have begun in Truro. There is in some towns something inimical, irreconcilable. I felt it there. As soon as we stepped out of the station, I wished we were back in the warm, lighted train which already was pulling out on its way to Penzance.

There was no taxi in sight. To our right the road ran slightly uphill; to our left, downhill. We knew nothing of the town, and we went to the left. Soon we were walking on granite. There was granite everywhere: grey, hard, and immemorial. The whole town seemed to be hewn out of granite. The streets were paved with it, enormous slabs like the lids of ancestral vaults. It gave me the feeling of walking in an endless graveyard, and the place was silent enough to maintain the illusion. The streets were lit with grim economy. Hardly a window had a light, and when, here and there, we passed a public-house, it was wrapped in a pall of decorum which made me wonder whether Cornishmen put on shrouds when they went in for a pint.

It did not take us long to get to the heart of the place, the few shopping streets that were a bit more festive, gay with seasonable things; and when we found an hotel, it was a good one. I signed the book, "Mr and Mrs Edward Oldham, Manchester," and that made me smile. After all, it was something to smile about. At this time last night, Ruth and I had just met, and now "Mr and Mrs Edward Oldham."

Ruth had moved across to a fire in the lounge. She had an arm along the mantelpiece, a toe meditatively tapping the fender. She looked up when I approached her and saw the smile. But her face did not catch the contagion. "Don't you hate this town?" she asked.

"I can put up with it," I said, "now that I'm in here, and now that you're in here with me."

"Yes," she answered, "this is all right. But those streets! They gave me the creeps. I felt as if every stone had been hewn out of a cliff that the Atlantic had battered for a thousand years and plastered with wrecks. Have you ever seen Tewkesbury Abbey?"

The irrelevant question took me aback. "No," I said.

"I've never seen stone so saturated with sunlight," said Ruth. "It looks as if you could wring summers out of it. The fields about it, I know, have run with blood, but it's a happy place all the same. This place isn't happy. It's under a cold enchantment."

"Not inside these four walls," I said, "because they enclose you and me and our supper and bed."

We fled from Truro the next morning. Fled is the word. As soon as breakfast was over we slung our rucksacks on to our backs and cleared out of the granite town as fast as our legs would take us. 23 December, and utterly unseasonable weather. The sky was blue, the sun was warm, and the Christmas decorations in the shops had a farcical and inappropriate look. But we were not being bluffed by these appearances. We put that town behind us before its hoodoo could reimpose itself upon our spirits.

And soon there was nothing wrong with our spirits at all. We were travelling westward, and every step sunk us deeper into a warm enchantment. Ruth had spoken last night of a cold enchantment. Well, this was a warm enchantment. I hadn't guessed that, with Christmas only two days ahead, any part of England could be like this. We walked through woods of evergreens and saw the sky shining like incredible blue lace through the branches overhead. We found violets blooming in warm hedge bottoms, and in a cottage garden a few daffodils were ready to burst their sheaths. We could see the yellow staining the taut green. We had tea at that cottage, out of doors! I thought of Manchester, and the fog blanketing Albert Square, and the great red trams going through it, slowly, like galleons, clanging their warning bells. I laughed aloud at the incredible, the absurd things that could happen to a man in England. One day Manchester. The next London. The next marriage, Truro, and the cold shudders. The next – this! I said all this to Ruth, who was brushing crumbs off the table to feed the birds that hopped tamely round her feet. "It makes me wonder what miracle is in store for tomorrow," I said. "And, anyway, what is Cornwall? I've always thought it was beetling cliffs and raging seas, smugglers, wreckers, and excisemen."

We entered the cottage to pay the old woman, and I went close up to the wall to examine a picture hanging there. It was a fine bit of photography: spray breaking on wicked-looking rocks. "That's the Manacles," the old girl said. "That's where my husband was drowned."

The Manacles. That was a pretty fierce name, and it looked a pretty fierce place. The woman seemed to take it for granted. She made no further comment. "Good-bye, midear," she said to Ruth. "Have a good day."

We did, but I never quite recaptured the exaltation of the morning. I felt that this couldn't last, that the spirit which had first made itself felt in the hard grey streets of Truro had pounced again out of that hard grey name: the Manacles. It sounded like a gritting of gigantic teeth. We were being played with. This interlude in fairyland, where May basked in December, was something to lure us on, to bring us within striking reach of – well, of what? Isn't this England? I said to myself. Isn't Cornwall as well within the four walls of Britain as Lancashire?

We breasted a hill, and a wide estuary lay before us, shining under the evening sun. Beyond it, climbing in tier upon tier of streets, was Falmouth. I liked the look of it. "This is where we stay tonight," I said to Ruth. "We shall be comfortable here."

A ferry took us across the harbour. Out on the water it was cold. Ruth pointed past the docks, past Pendennis Castle standing on the hill. "Out there is the way to Land's End," she said.

I looked, and low down on the water there was a faint grey smudge. Even a Manchester man would know that that was fog, creeping in from the Atlantic.

All night long we heard the fog-horns moaning, and it was very cold.

I hate sleeping in an airless room, but by midnight the white coils of fog, filling every crevice, and cold as if they were the exhalation of icebergs, made me rise from bed and shut the window. Our bedroom hung literally over the sea. The wall of the room was a deep bay, and I had seen how, by leaning out of the window, one could drop a stone to the beach below. Now I could not see the beach. I could not see anything. If I had stretched my arm out into the night the fingers would have been invisible. But though I could not see, I could hear. The tide had risen, and I could hear the plash of little waves down there below me. It was so gentle a sound that it made me shudder. It was like the voice of a soft-spoken villain. The true voice of the sea and of the night was that long, incessant bellow of the fog-horns. The shutting of the window did nothing to keep that out.

I drew the curtains across the window, and, turning, saw that a fire was laid in the grate. I put a match to it. Incredible comfort! In ten minutes we felt happier. In twenty we were asleep.

There seemed nothing abnormal about Falmouth when we woke in the morning. A fairly stiff wind had sprung up. The fog was torn to pieces. It hung here and there in dirty isolated patches, but these were being quickly swept away. There was a run on the water. It was choppy and restless, and the sky was a rag-bag of fluttering black and grey. Just a normal winter day by the seaside: a marvellous day for walking, Ruth said.

At the breakfast-table we spread out the map and considered the day's journey. This was going to be something new again. There had been the grey in hospitality of Truro; the Arcadian interlude; the first contact with something vast and menacing. Now, looking at the map, we saw that, going westward, following the coast, we should come to what we had both understood Cornwall to be: a sparsely populated land, moors, a rock-bound coast. It promised to be something big and hard and lonely, and that was what we wanted.

We put sandwiches into our rucksacks, intending to eat lunch out of doors. We reckoned we should find some sort of inn for the night.

A bus took us the best part of ten miles on our westward journey. Then it struck inland, to the right. We left it at that point, climbed a stile, walked through a few winter-bare fields, and came to a path running with the line of the coast.

Now, indeed, we had found traditional Cornwall. Here, if anywhere, was the enchanted land of Merlin and of Arthur – the land that Ruth dreamed about. Never had I found elsewhere in England a sense so overpowering both of size and loneliness. To our left was the sea, down there at the foot of the mighty cliffs along whose crest we walked. The tide was low, and the reefs were uncovered. In every shape of fantastic cruelty they thrust out towards the water, great knives and swords of granite that would hack through any keel, tables of granite on which the stoutest ship would pound to pieces, jaws of granite that would seize and grind and not let go. Beyond and between these prone monsters was the innocent yellow sand, and, looking at the two – the sand and the reefs – I thought of the gentle lapping of the water under my window last night, and the crying of the fog-horns, the most desolate crying in the world.

Southward and westward the water stretched without limit; and inland, as we walked steadily forward all through the morning, was now a patch of cultivation, now the winter stretch of rusty moor with gulls and lapwings joining their lamentations as they glided and drooped across it, according to their kind. From time to time a cluster of trees broke the monotony of the inland view, and I remember rooks fussing among the bare boughs. Rooks, lapwings, and gulls: those were the only birds we saw that day.

It was at about one o'clock that we came to a spot where the cliff path made a loop inland to avoid a deep fissure into which we peered. In some cataclysm the rocks here had been torn away, tumbling and piling till they made a rough giant's stairway down which we clambered to the beach below. We ended up in a cove so narrow that I could have thrown a stone across it, and paved with sand of an unbelievable golden purity. The sun came through the clouds, falling right upon that spot. It was tiny, paradisal, with the advancing tide full of green and blue and purple lights. We sat on the sand, leaned against the bottom-most of the fallen granite blocks, and ate our lunch.

We were content. This was the loveliest thing we had found yet. Ruth recalled a phrase from the novel she had typed for Miss Gregoria Gunson. "And you will find here and there a paradise ten yards wide, a little space of warmth and colour set like a jewel in the hard iron of that coast." Farfetched, I thought, but true enough.

It was while we were sitting there, calculating how long that bit of sun could last, that Ruth said, "We wanted a lonely place, and we've found it, my love. Has it struck you that we haven't seen a human being since we got off the bus?"

It hadn't, and it didn't seem to me a matter of concern. I stretched my arms lazily towards the sun. "Who wants to see human beings?" I demanded. "I had enough human beings at the Magnifico to last me a very long time."

"So long as we find some human beings to make us a bit of supper tonight . . ."

"Never fear," I said. "We'll do that. There! Going . . . Going . . . Gone."

The sun went in. We packed up, climbed to the cliff top, and started off again.

At three o'clock the light began to go out of the day. This was Christmas Eve, remember. We were among the shortest days of the year. It was now that a little uneasiness began to take hold of me. Still, I noticed, we had seen no man or woman, and, though I kept a sharp lookout on the country inland, we saw no house, not a barn, not a shed.

We did not see the sun again that day, but we witnessed his dying magnificence. Huge spears of light fanned down out of the sky and struck in glittering points upon the water far off. Then the clouds turned into a crumble and smother of dusky red, as though a city were burning beyond the edge of the world, and when all this began to fade to grey ashes I knew that I was very uneasy indeed.

Ruth said: "I think we ought to leave this cliff path. We ought to strike inland and find a road – any road."

I thought so, too, but inland now was nothing but moor. Goodness knows, I thought, where we shall land if we embark on that.

"Let us keep on," I said, "for a little while. We may find a path branching off. Then we'll know we're getting somewhere."

We walked for another mile, and then Ruth stopped. We were on the brink of another of those deep fissures, like the one we had descended for lunch. Again the path made a swift right-hand curve. I knew what Ruth was thinking before she said it. "In half an hour or so the light will be quite gone. Suppose we had come on this in the dark?"

We had not found the path we were seeking. We did not seek it any more. Abruptly, we turned right and began to walk into the moor. So long as we could see, we kept the coast behind our backs. Soon we could not see at all. The night came on, impenetrably black and there would be no moon.

It was now six o'clock. I know that because I struck a match to look at the time, and I noticed that I had only three matches left. This is stuck in my mind because I said, "We must be careful with these. If we can't find food, we'll find a smoke a comfort."

"But, my love," said Ruth, and there was now an undoubted note of alarm in her voice, "we *must* find food. Surely, if we just keep on we'll see a light, or hear a voice, or come to a road—"

She stopped abruptly, seized my arm, held on to prevent my going forward. I could not see her face, but I sensed her alarm. "What is it?" I asked.

"I stepped in water."

I knelt and tested the ground in front of me with my hands. It was a deep oozy wetness; not the clear wetness of running water. "Bog," I said; and we knew we could go forward no longer. With cliff on the one hand and the possibility of stumbling into a morass on the other, there seemed nothing for it but to stay where we were till heaven sent us aid or the dawn came up.

I put my arm round Ruth and felt that she was trembling. I want to put this adventure down exactly as it happened. It would be nice to write that her nerves were steady as rock. Clearly they weren't, and I was not feeling very good either. I said as gaily as I could, "This is where we sit down, smoke a cigarette, and think it out."

We went back a little so as to be away from the bog, and then we plumped down among the heather. We put the cigarettes to our lips and I struck a match. It did not go out when I threw it to the ground. In that world of darkness the little light burning on the earth drew our eyes, and simultaneously we both stood up with an exclamation of surprised delight. The light had shown us an inscribed stone, almost buried in the heather. There were two matches left. Fortunately, we were tidy people. We had put our sandwich papers into the rucksacks. I screwed these now into little torches. Ruth lit one and held it to the stone while I knelt to read. It seemed a stone of fabulous age. The letters were mossy and at first illegible. I took out a penknife and scraped at them. "2 Miles—" we made out, but the name of this place two miles off we do not know to this day. I scraped away, but the letters were too defaced for reading, and just as the last of the little torches flared to extinction the knife slipped from my hand into the heather. There was nothing to do but leave it there.

We stood up. Two miles. But two miles to where, and two miles in what direction? Our situation seemed no happier, when suddenly I saw the stones.

I had seen stones like them on the Yorkshire moors, round about the old Brontë parsonage. But were they the same sort of stones, and did they mean the same thing? I was excited now. "Stay here," I said to Ruth, and I stepped towards the first stone. As I had hoped, a third came into view in line with the second, and, as I advanced, a fourth in line with the third. They were the same: upright monoliths set to mark a path, whitewashed half-way up so that they would glimmer through the dark as they were doing now, tarred on their upper half to show the way when snow was on the ground. I shouted in my joy: "Come on! Supper! Fires! Comfort! Salvation!" but Ruth came gingerly. She had not forgotten the bog.

But the stones did not let us down. They led us to the village. It must have been about nine o'clock when we got there.

Half-way through that pitch-black two-mile journey we were aware that once more we were approaching the sea. From afar we could hear its uneasy murmur growing louder, and presently threaded with a heart-darkening sound: the voice of a bell-buoy tolling its insistent warning out there on the unseen water.

As the murmur of the sea and the melancholy clangour of the bell came clearer we went more warily, for we could not see more than the stone next ahead; and presently there was no stone where the next stone should be. We peered into the darkness, our hearts aching for the light which would tell us that we were again among houses and men. There was no light anywhere.

"We have one match," I said. "Let us light a cigarette apiece and chance seeing something that will help us."

We saw the wire hawser: no more than the veriest scrap of it, fixed by a great staple into the head of a post and slanting down into darkness. I first, Ruth behind me, we got our hands upon it, gripping for dear life, and went inching down towards the sound of water.

So we came at last to the village. Like many a Cornish village, it was built at the head of a cove. The sea was in front; there was a horse-shoe of cliffs; and snuggling at the end was a half-moon of houses behind a seawall of granite.

All this did not become clear to us at once. For the moment, we had no other thought than of thankfulness to be treading on hard cobbles that had been laid by human hands, no other desire than to bang on the first door and ask whether there was in the place an inn or someone who would give us lodging for the night.

Most of the cottages were whitewashed; their glimmer gave us the rough definition of the place; and I think already we must have felt some uneasy presage at the deathly mask of them, white as skulls with no light in their eyes.

For there was no living person, no living thing, in the village. That was what we discovered. Not so much as a dog went by us in the darkness. Not so much as a cock crowed. The tolling from the water came in like a passing bell, and the sea whispered incessantly, and grew to a deep-throated threatening roar as the tide rose and billows beat on the sand and at last on the seawall; but there was no one to notice these things except ourselves; and our minds were almost past caring, so deeply were we longing for one thing only – the rising of the sun.

There was nothing wrong with the village. It contained all the apparatus of living. Bit by bit we discovered that. There was no answer to our knocking at the first door we came to. There was nothing remarkable in that, and we went on to the next. Here, again, there was no welcome sound of feet, no springing up of a light to cheer us who had wandered for so long in the darkness.

At the third house I knocked almost angrily. Yes; anger was the feeling I had then: anger at all these stupid people who shut down a whole village at nine o'clock, went to their warm beds, and left us standing there, knocking in the cold and darkness. I thudded the knocker with lusty rat-tat-tats; and suddenly, in the midst of that noisy assault, I stopped, afraid. The anger was gone. Plain fear took its place. At the next house I *could* not knock, because I knew there was no one to hear me.

I was glad to hear Ruth's voice. She said, surprisingly, "It's no good knocking. Try a door."

I turned the handle and the door opened. Ruth and I stepped over the threshold, standing very close together. I shouted, "Is there anyone at home?" My voice sounded brutally loud and defiant. Nothing answered it.

We were standing in the usual narrow passageway of a cottage. Ruth put out her hand and knocked something to the floor from a little table. "Matches," she said; and I groped on the floor and found them. The light showed us a hurricane lantern standing on the table. I lit it, and we began to examine the house, room by room.

This was a strange thing to do, but at the time it did not seem strange. We were shaken and off our balance. We wanted to reassure ourselves. If we had found flintlocks, bows and arrows, bronze hammers, we might have been reassured. We could have told ourselves that we had wandered, bewitched, out of our century. But we found nothing of the sort. We found a spotless cottage full of contemporary things. There was a wireless set. There was last week's *Falmouth Packet*. There were geraniums in a pot in the window; there were sea-boots and oilskins in the passage. The bed upstairs was made, and there was a cradle beside it. There was no one in the bed, no child in the cradle.

Ruth was white. "I want to see the pantry," she said, inconsequentially I thought.

We found the pantry, and she took the cloth off a breadpan and put her hand upon a loaf. "It's warm," she said. "It was baked today." She began to tremble.

We left the house and took the lantern with us. Slowly, with the bell tolling endlessly, we walked through the curved length of the village. There was one shop. I held up the light to its uncurtained window. Toys and sweets, odds and ends of grocery, all the stock-in-trade of a small general store, were there behind the glass. We hurried on.

We were hurrying now, quite consciously hurrying; though where we were hurrying to we did not know. Once or twice I found myself looking back over my shoulder. If I had seen man, woman, or child I think I should have screamed. So powerfully had the death of the village taken hold of my imagination that the appearance of a living being, recently so strongly desired, would have affected me like the return of one from the dead.

At the centre of the crescent of houses there was an inn, the Lobster Pot, with climbing geraniums ramping over its front in the way they do in Cornwall; then came more cottages; and at the farther tip of the crescent there was a house standing by itself. It was bigger than any of the others; it stood in a little garden. In the comforting daylight I should have admired it as the sort of place some writer or painter might choose for a refuge.

Now I could make it out only bit by bit, flashing the lantern here and there; and, shining the light upon the porch, I saw that the door was open. Ruth and I went in. Again I shouted, "Is anyone here?" Again I was answered by nothing.

I put the lantern down on an oak chest in the small square hall, and that brought my attention to the telephone. There it was, standing on the chest, an up-to-date microphone in ivory white. Ruth saw it at the same moment, and her eyes asked me, "Do you dare?"

I did. I took up the microphone and held it to my ear. I could feel at once that it was dead. I joggled the rest. I shouted, "Hallo! Hallo!" but I knew that no one would answer. No one answered.

We had stared through the windows of every cottage in the village. We had looked at the shop and the inn. We had banged at three doors and entered two houses. But we had not admitted our extraordinary situation in words. Now I said to Ruth, "What do you make of it?"

She said simply, "It's worse than ghosts. Ghosts are something. This is nothing. Everything is absolutely normal. That's what seems so horrible."

And, indeed, a village devastated by fire, flood, or earthquake would not have disturbed us as we were disturbed by that village which was devastated by nothing at all.

Ruth shut the door of the hall. The crashing of the sea on granite, the tolling of the bell, now seemed far off. We stood and looked at one another uneasily in the dim light of the hurricane lamp. "I shall stay here," said Ruth, "either till the morning or till something happens."

She moved down the hall to a door which opened into a room at the back. I followed her. She tapped on the door, but neither of us expected an answer, and there was none. We went in.

Nothing that night surprised us like what we saw then. Holding the lantern high above my head, I swung its light round the room. It was a charming place, panelled in dark oak. A few fine pictures were on the walls. There were plenty of books, some pieces of good porcelain. The curtains of dark-green velvet fringed with gold were drawn across the window. A fire was burning on the hearth. That was what made us start back almost in dismay – the fire.

If it had been a peat fire – one of those fires that, once lit, smoulder for days – we should not have been surprised. But it was not. Anyone who knew anything about fires could see that this fire had been lit within the last hour. Some of the coals were still black; none had been consumed. And the light from this fire fell upon the white smooth texture of an excellent linen cloth upon the table. On the table was supper, set for one. A chair was placed before the knife and fork and plates. There was a round of cold beef waiting to be cut, a loaf of bread, a jar of pickles, a fine cheese, a glass, and a jug containing beer.

Ruth laughed shrilly. I could hear that her nerves were strained by this last straw. "At least we shan't starve," she cried. "I'm nearly dying of hunger. I suppose the worst that could happen would be the return of the bears, demanding 'Who's been eating my beef? Who's been drinking my beer?' Sit down. Carve!"

I was as hungry as she was. As I looked at the food the saliva flowed in my mouth, but I could as soon have touched it as robbed a poor-box. And Ruth knew it. She turned from the table, threw herself into an easy chair by the fire, and lay back, exhausted. Her eyes closed. I stood behind the chair and stroked her forehead till she slept. That was the best that could happen to her.

That, in a way, was the end of our adventure. Nothing more happened to us. Nothing *more*? But, as you see, nothing at all had happened to us. And it was this nothingness that made my vigil over Ruth sleeping in the chair the most nerve-destroying experience of all my life. A clock ticking away quietly on the chimney-piece told me that it was half-past nine. A tear-off calendar lying on a writing-table told me that it was 24 December. Quite correct. All in order.

The hurricane-lamp faded and went out. I lit a lamp, shaded with green silk, that stood on the table amid the waiting supper. The room became cosier, even more human and likeable. I prowled about quietly, piecing together the personality of the man or woman who lived in it. A man. It was a masculine sort of supper, and I found a tobacco jar and a few pipes. The books were excellently bound editions of the classics, with one or two modern historical works. The pictures, I saw now, were Medici reprints of French Impressionists, all save the one over the fireplace, which was an original by Paul Nash.

I tried, with these trivial investigations, to divert my mind from the extraordinary situation we were in. It wouldn't work. I sat down and listened intently, but there was nothing to hear save the bell and the water – water that stretched, I reminded myself, from here to America. This was one of the ends of the world.

At one point I got up and locked the door, though what was there to keep out? All that was to be feared was inside me.

The fire burned low, and there was nothing for its replenishment. It was nearly gone, and the room was turning cold, when Ruth stirred and woke. At that moment the clock, which had a lovely silver note, struck twelve. "A merry Christmas, my darling," I said.

Ruth looked at me wildly, taking some time to place herself. Then she laughed and said, "I've been dreaming about it. It's got a perfectly natural explanation. It was like this . . . No . . . It's gone. I can't remember it. But it was something quite reasonable."

I sat with my arm about her. "My love," I said, "I can think of a hundred quite reasonable explanations. For example, every man in the village for years has visited his Uncle Henry at Bodmin on Christmas Eve, taking wife, child, dog, cat, and canary with him. The chap in this house is the only one who hasn't got an Uncle Henry at Bodmin, so he laid the supper, lit the fire, and was just settling down for the evening when the landlord of the Lobster Pot thought he'd be lonely, looked in, and said: 'What about coming to see *my* Uncle Henry at Bodmin?' And off they all went. That's perfectly reasonable. It explains everything. Do you believe it?"

Ruth shook her head. "You must sleep," she said. "Lay your head on my shoulder."

We left the house at seven o'clock on Christmas morning. It was slack tide. The sea was very quiet, and in the grey light, standing in the garden at the tip of the crescent, we could see the full extent of the village with one sweep of the eye, as we had not been able to do last night.

It was a lovely little place, huddled under the rocks at the head of its cove. Every cottage was well cared for, newly washed in cream or white, and on one or two of them a few stray roses were blooming, which is not unusual in Cornwall at Christmas.

At any other time, Ruth and I would have said, "Let's stay here." But now we hurried, rucksacks on backs, disturbed by the noise of our own shoes, and climbed the path down which we had so cautiously made our way the night before.

There were the stones of black and white. We followed them till we came to the spot where we found the stone with the obliterated name. "And, behold, there was no stone there, but your lost pocket-knife was lying in the heather," said a sceptical friend to whom I once related this story.

That, I suppose, would be a good way to round off an invented tale if I were a professional story-teller. But, in simple fact, the stone *was* there, and so was my knife. Ruth took it from me, and when we came to the place where we had left the cliff path and turned into the moor, she hurled it far out and we heard the faint tinkle of its fall on the rocks below.

"And now," she said with resolution, "we go back the way we came, and we eat our Christmas dinner in Falmouth. Then you can inquire for the first train to Manchester. Didn't you say there are fogs there?"

"There are an' all," I said broadly.

"Good," said Ruth. "After last night, I feel a fog is something substantial, something you can get hold of."

South Sea Bubble

Hammond Innes

Location: Sumburgh Head, Shetland.
Time: September, 1973.
Eyewitness Description: *"Every now and then I had the sense of a presence on board. It was so strange at times that when I came back from telephoning or collecting parts or stores, I would find myself looking about me as though expecting somebody to be waiting for me . . ."*

Author: Ralph Hammond Innes (1914–98), who became one of the century's most popular novelists with over thirty novels of high adventure, was born in Horsham, Sussex and after being educated at Cranbrook School in Kent became a journalist on the *Financial Times*. During the Second World War he served in the Royal Artillery, eventually rising to the rank of Major, and also began writing the type of books based on personal experience and exhaustive research that made his name, notably *Attack Alarm* (1941), based on his experiences as an Anti-Aircraft Gunner during the Battle of Britain. After the war he began his regular schedule of six months' travelling and six months' writing to produce an annual novel for his publishers, several of which were filmed, including *Hell Below Zero* (1954), *Campbell's Kingdom* (1957) and *The Wreck of the Mary Deare* (1959). His interest in the supernatural at sea had been evident in his very first book, *The Doppelganger* (1937), and continued through his career as well as in one of his best short stories, "South Sea Bubble", written for the Christmas 1973 issue of *Punch* Magazine. Innes' knowledge of the sea as an experienced yachtsman and his fascination with its mysteries are very evident.

S he lay in Kinlochbervie in the north-west of Scotland, so cheap I should have known there was something wrong. I had come by way of Lairg, under the heights of Arkle, and four miles up the road that skirts the north shores of Loch Laxford I turned a corner and there she was – a ketch painted black and lying to her own reflection in the evening sun.

Dreams, dreams . . . dreams are fine, as an escape, as a means of counteracting the pressures of life in a big office. But when there is no barrier between dream and reality, what then? Draw back, create another dream? But one is enough for any man and this had been mine; that one day I would find the boat of my dream and sail her to the South Seas.

Maybe it was the setting, the loneliness of the loch, the aid of Nordic wildness with the great humped hills of Sutherland as back-cloth and the mass of Arkle cloud-capped in splendour. Here the Vikings had settled. From here men only just dead sailed open boats south for the herring. Even her name seemed right – *Samoa*.

I bought her, without a survey, without stopping to think. And then my troubles started.

She was dry when I bought her. Nobody told me the agents had paid a man to pump her out each day. If my wife had been alive I would never have been such a fool. But it was an executor's sale. The agents told me that. Also that she had been taken in tow off Handa Island by a Fraserburgh trawler and was the subject of a salvage claim. With her port of registry Kingston, Jamaica, it explained the low asking price. What they didn't tell me was that the trawler had found her abandoned, drifting water-logged without a soul on board. Nor did they tell me that her copper sheathing was so worn that half her underwater planking was rotten with toredo.

"A wee bit of a mystery," was the verdict of the crofter who helped me clean her up and pump the water out of her. Nobody seemed to know who had sailed her across the Atlantic, how many had been on board, or what had happened to them.

The first night I spent on board – I shall always remember that; the excitement, the thrill of ownership, of command, of being on board a beautiful ship that was also now my home. The woodwork gleamed in the lamp-light (yes, she had oil lamps as well as electric light), and lying in the quarter berth I could look up through the open hatch to the dark shape of the hills black against the stars. I was happy in spite of everything, happier than I had been for a long time, and when I finally went to sleep it was with a picture of coral islands in my mind

– white sands and palm trees and proas scudding across the pale green shadows of warm lagoons.

I woke shivering, but not with cold. It was a warm night and the cold was inside me. I was cold to my guts and very frightened. It wasn't the strangeness of my new habitation, for I knew where I was the instant I opened my eyes. And it wasn't fear of the long voyage ahead. It was something else, something I didn't understand.

I shifted to one of the saloon berths, and as I slept soundly the rest of the night I put it down to nerves. It was a nervous breakdown that had led to my early retirement, enabling me to exchange my small suburban house for the thing I had always dreamed of. But I avoided the quarter berth after that, and though I was so tired every night that I fell asleep almost instantly, a sense of uneasiness persisted.

It is difficult to describe, even more difficult to explain. There was no repetition of the waking cold of that first night, but every now and then I had the sense of a presence on board. It was so strong at times that when I came back from telephoning or collecting parts or stores I would find myself looking about me as though expecting somebody to be waiting for me.

There was so much to do, and so little time, that I never got around to making determined enquiries as to whether the previous owner had been on that ill-fated voyage. I did write to his address in Kingston, but with no reply I was left with a sense of mystery and the feeling that whatever it was that had happened, it had become imprinted on the fabric of the boat. How else to explain the sense of somebody, something, trying to communicate?

It was August when I bought her, late September when I sailed out of Kinlochbervie bound for Shetland. It would have been more sensible to have headed south to an English yard, for my deadline to catch the trades across the Atlantic was December. But Scalloway was cheaper. And nearer.

I left with a good forecast, and by nightfall I was motoring north in a flat calm with Cape Wrath light bearing 205° and beginning to dip below the dark line of the horizon. My plan to install larger batteries, an alternator and an automatic pilot had had to be shelved. The money for that was now earmarked for new planking. I stayed on deck, dozing at the helm and watching for trawlers. I was tired before I started and I was tireder now.

A hand touched my shoulder and I woke with a start to complete silence. It was pitch dark, clammily cold. For a moment I couldn't think where I was. Then I saw the shadowy outline of the mainsail above my head. Nothing else – no navigation lights, no compass light, the engine stopped and the boat sluggish. I switched on my torch and the beam shone white on fog. The sails, barely visible, were drawing and we were moving slowly westward, out into the Atlantic.

I pressed the self-starter, but nothing happened, and when I put the wheel over she took a long time to come back on course. I went below then and stepped into a foot or more of water. Fortunately I had installed a powerful, double-action pump. Even so, it took me the better part of four hours to get the water level below the cabin sole. By then it was daylight and the fog had cleared away to the west, a long bank of it looking like a smudge of smoke as the sun glimmered through the damp air.

I tried swinging the engine, but it was no good. Just as well perhaps, because it must have been the prolonged running of the engine that had caused her to take in so much water. Without it the leaks in the planking seemed no worse than when she had been at anchor. I cooked myself a big breakfast on the paraffin stove and it was only when I was sitting over coffee and a cigarette that I remembered how I had woken to the feel of a hand on my shoulder.

I put it out of my mind, not wanting to know about it, and switched to consideration of whether to go on or turn back. But I was already nearly halfway to Shetland and the wind settled the matter by coming from the south-west. I eased sheets and for the next hour we were sailing at almost 6 knots.

The wind held steady all day at Force 3–4, and though there were occasional fog patches I did manage to catch a glimpse of Orkney away to the south-east. Sail trimming and pumping took most of my time, but in the afternoon, when the pump at last sucked dry, I was able to give some thought to navigation.

The tides run strong in the waters between Orkney and Shetland, up to 10 knots in the vicinity of the major headlands, and I had an uneasy feeling I was being carried too far to the east. Just before midnight I sighted what looked like the loom of a light almost over the bows, but my eyes were too tired to focus clearly. I pumped until the bilges sucked dry again, checked the compass and the log, then fell into the quarter berth, still with my oilskins on, not caring whether it was a light or a ship, or whether the boat held her course or not.

I was utterly exhausted and I came out of a dead sleep to see the shadowy figure of a man standing over me. He had something in his hand, and as his arm came up, I rolled off the bunk, hit the floorboards and came up crouched, the hair on my neck prickling, my body trembling.

Maybe I dreamed it; there was nothing there, and the only sound on board the slatting of the sails. But still my body trembled and I was cold with fright. I had a slug of whisky and went up on deck to find the log line hanging inert, the ship drifting in circles; no wind and the fog like a wet shroud.

I stayed on deck until it got light – a ghostly, damp morning, everything dripping. I pumped the bilges dry, cooked breakfast, attended to the navigation. But though I was fully occupied, I couldn't get it out of my head that I wasn't alone on the ship. Now, whatever I was doing, wherever I was on the boat, I was conscious of his presence.

I know I was tired. But why had my reflexes been so instantaneous? How had I known in the instant of waking that the man standing over me was bent on murder?

The day dragged, the wind coming and going, my world enclosed in walls of fog. The circle of sea in which I was imprisoned was never still, enlarging and contracting with the varying density of the fog, and it was cold. Hot tea, exercise, whisky – nothing seemed to dispel that cold. It was deep inside me, a brooding fear.

But of what?

Shetland was getting close now. I knew it would be a tricky landfall, in fog and without an engine. The tidal stream, building up against the long southern finger of the islands, causes one of the worst races in the British Isles. Roost is the local name and the Admiralty Pilot warned particularly of the roost off Sumburgh Head. It would only require a small error of navigation . . . And then, dozing at the helm, I thought I saw two figures in the bows.

I jerked awake, my vision blurred with moisture, seeing them vaguely. But when I rubbed my eyes they were gone. And just before dusk, when I was at the mainmast checking the halyards, I could have sworn there was somebody standing behind me. The fog, tiredness, hallucinations – it is easy not to rationalize. But the ever-present feeling that I was not alone on the boat, the sense of fear, of something terrible hanging over me – that's not so easy to explain.

Night fell, the breeze died and the damp blanket of fog clamped down. I could feel the wetness of it on my eyeballs, my oilskins clammy with moisture and water dripping off the boom as though it were raining. I pumped the bilges dry and had some food. When I came up on deck again there was the glimmer of a moon low down, the boat's head swinging slowly in an eddy. And then I heard it, to the north of me, the soft mournful note of a diaphone – the fog signal on Sumburgh Head.

The tide had just started its main south-easterly flow and within an hour the roost was running and I was in it. The sea became lumpy, full of unpredictable hollows. Sudden overfalls reared up and broke against the top-sides. The movement grew and became indescribable, exhausting, and above the noise of water breaking, the sound of the sails slatting back and forth.

I was afraid of the mast then. I had full main and genoa up. I don't know how long it took me to get the headsail down and lashed, the boat like a mad thing intent on pitching me overboard. An hour maybe. And then the main. I couldn't lash it properly, the movement of the boom was too violent. Blood was dripping from a gash in my head where I had been thrown against a winch, my body a mass of bruises. I left the mainsail heaped on deck and wedged myself into the quarter berth. It was the only safe place, the saloon a shambles of crockery and stores, locker doors swinging, the contents flying.

I was scared. The movement was so violent I couldn't pump. I couldn't do anything. I must have passed out from sheer exhaustion when I suddenly saw again the figure standing over the quarter berth, and the thing in his hand was a winch handle. I was seeing it vaguely now, as though from a long way away. I saw the man's arm come up. The metal of the winch handle gleamed. I saw him strike, and as he struck the figure in the bunk moved, rolling out on to the floorboards and coming up in a crouch, his head gashed and blood streaming. There was fear there. I can remember fear then as something solid, a sensation so all-pervading it was utterly crushing, and then the winch handle coming up again and the victim's reaching out to the galley where a knife lay, the fingers grasping for it.

I opened my eyes and a star streaked across the swaying hatch. I was on the floor, in a litter of galley equipment, and I had a knife in my hand. As I held it up, staring at it, dazed, the star streaked back across the hatch, the bottom of the mizzen sail showing suddenly white. The significance of that took a moment to sink in, so appalled was I by my experience. The star came and went again, the sail momentarily illumined; then I was on my feet, clawing my way into the cockpit.

The sky was clear, studded with stars, and to the north the beam of Sumburgh Light swung clear. The fog had gone. There was a breeze from the east now. Somehow I managed to get the genoa hoisted, and inside of half an hour I was sailing in quiet waters clear of the roost.

I went below then and started clearing up the mess. The quarter berth was a tumbled pile of books from the shelf above, and as I was putting them back, a photograph fell to the floor. It showed a man and a woman and two children grouped round the wheel. The man was about 45, fair-haired with a fat, jolly face, his eyes squinting against bright sunlight. I have that picture still, my only contact with the man who had owned *Samoa* before me, the man whose ghostly presence haunted the ship.

By nightfall I was in Scalloway, tied up alongside a trawler at the pier. I didn't sell the boat. I couldn't afford to. And I didn't talk about it. Now that I had seen his picture, knew what he looked like, it seemed somehow less disturbing. I made up my mind I would have to live with it, whatever it was.

I never again used the quarter berth – in fact, I ripped it out of her before I left Scalloway. Sailing south I thought a lot about him in the long night watches. But though I speculated on what must have happened, and sometimes felt he was with me, I was never again identified with him.

Maybe I was never quite so tired again. But something I have to add. From the Azores I headed for Jamaica, and as soon as I arrived in Kingston the boat was the focus of considerable interest. She had apparently been stolen. At least, she had disappeared, and her owner with her. Hi-jacked was the word his solicitors used, for a merchant seaman named O'Sullivan, serving a six-year sentence for armed robbery, had escaped the night before and had never been heard of since. The police now believed he had boarded the boat, hi-jacked her and her owner and sailed her across the Atlantic, probably with Ireland as his objective.

I didn't attempt to see his wife. My experience – what I thought I now knew – could only add to her grief. I sailed at once for the Canal. But though I have tried to put it out of my mind, there are times when I feel his presence lingering. Maybe writing this will help. Maybe it will exorcise his poor, frightened ghost from my mind – or from the boat – whichever it is.

Ringing in the Good News

Peter Ackroyd

Location: Acton, London.
Time: Christmas Eve, 1985.
Eyewitness Description: *"He stared at her. 'Kevin, darling, have you gone deaf?' And as he looked at her grey mouth he wondered whose voice it was he had heard, a voice which in memory no longer seemed human at all . . ."*

Author: Peter Ackroyd (1949–) is a graduate of that hothouse of the ghost story, Cambridge University, where he attended Clare College. After further study at Yale, he worked for the *Spectator*, serving as literary editor and film critic. Since his first publication *Ouch* in 1971, Ackroyd has written a series of inventive biographies and diverse fiction that has often revolved around the city of London: haunted and animated by its past and its characters, real and imaginary. This is evident in *Hawksmoor* (1985), about a 300-year-old doppelganger; the story of the famous Elizabethan alchemist, *The House of Doctor Dee* (1993); and *Dan Leno and the Limehouse Golem* (1994) in which the ghosts of music hall characters are mingled with a series of grisly East End murders. Ackroyd's admiration for Charles Dickens as a master of the supernatural can be traced through his novel, *The Great Fire of London* (1982), a reworking of *Little Dorritt*; his controversial biography of the author published in 1990; and also his perceptive foreword to *The Haunted House* (2003). It seems hardly surprising, therefore, that he should have chosen to continue Dickens's practice of a ghost story for Christmas with one of his own for *The Times*, 24 December 1985, "Ringing in the Good News", about a new father haunted by mysterious phone calls that repeatedly announce the birth of his son.

. . . the army of spirits, once so near, has been receding farther and farther from us, banished by the magic wand of science from hearth and home.

— J. G. Frazer, *The Golden Bough*

Kevin returned home from the hospital in a state of mild imbecility; his wife, Claire, had been about to give birth for the past 12 hours and he had not slept or eaten as he waited. He blamed the delay upon his mother-in-law, Vera, whose presence always seemed to reduce his wife to a kind of nursery torpor. And it had been Vera who had eventually ordered him away.

"Kevin, darling," she had said, patting her hair into shape (for the occasion she had tied it behind her head in a bun as if, Kevin thought, she were a nurse in a field hospital), "Kevin, darling, do go home. We can manage perfectly well." It was the voice of the professional organizer; it never varied at weddings or at funerals, at christenings or at cocktail parties. He had been hearing it all his life and, as usual, he obeyed.

The telephone rang and he was so tired that he gazed at it incuriously before going towards it. "Kevin darling." It was Vera again, her voice higher so that it seemed both more peremptory and more triumphant than ever. "It's boy! It's a lovely boy!" He said nothing in reply but when he replaced the receiver, those words still echoed in his head as he noticed how warm it was for the early autumn.

He had been hoping that, before Christmas came to end another year, he might have a child – it seemed to represent his real purpose in the world, a duty he felt bound to undertake. But now that it had happened it was more like a wonderful gift – a gift both to him and to Claire but, more mysteriously, also their gift to others. He took the telephone and danced with it in a small circle. "It's a boy," he whispered. "It's a boy!"

The memory of that first exhilaration did not leave him until they returned with the baby. Then he saw how pale and tired his wife was, how bright and plump his son – in that respect, at least, the infant already resembled Vera whose energy had redoubled as that of her daughter began to fade. In sympathy with Claire, Kevin began to feel very tired as well. "Is there," he said, "anything I can do? Shall I boil some water?"

"Kevin, darling, what on earth would we need boiling water for? This isn't the 19th century. Why don't you be a poppet and see to Claire's things?"

"I only thought. . . ." He looked enquiringly at his wife, who was presenting the child to Vera. Then she said, "Mummy's got it all arranged".

The telephone rang and, in his confusion, Kevin picked it up without saying anything. There was someone talking faintly at the other end, and he heard the word "joy" or "toy" before putting down the receiver. "There must be a crossed line," he told them, almost apologetically but they were not listening to him. Vera was holding the baby in the air while Claire gazed at it solemnly. So my child, he thought, has become one more reason why they can ignore me.

The dusk of early winter cast its thin gloom over Kevin as he tried without success to read Benjamin Spock's *The First Year of Baby's Life*, and when the telephone rang he rose to answer it with a certain relief; his mood of pleasurable anticipation changed to one of incredulity, however, when he heard Vera saying softly but quite distinctly, "It's a boy. It's a lovely boy . . ." It was the fact that she was whispering which really disturbed him. "Vera?" The dialling tone returned and he was already blushing when he called her back. "Vera?"

"Kevin, angel. I'm already out of the door. Tell Claire to wait."

"Did you just talk to me?"

"Of course not. Why should I talk to you?" But she added: "Is there anything the matter with the baby?"

"No. Nothing's the matter. I'll tell Claire to expect you." When he put down the telephone he crept to the foot of the stairs, and listened intently as his wife whispered to the child.

As the rockets of Guy Fawkes' Day exploded above his head Kevin hurried home through the darkness, worried in case his wife already missed him; when he opened the front door he heard the telephone ringing. He raced towards it and, with his coat half-falling from his shoulders, picked it up to hear Vera shouting at him, "It's a boy! It's a lovely boy!" With a sudden rush of anxiety he slammed down the receiver, and stood panting in the middle of the room.

He climbed the stairs slowly, as if in pain, and found Claire lying on the bed beside the baby's cot. "I thought it must be you," she said without rising to greet him. "What were you doing?"

He was still breathing heavily. "I think I was talking to Vera."

She immediately raised herself into a sitting position, and piled the pillows around her. "Oh, what did Mummy want? Did she get that book on breastfeeding?" He was about to explain what in fact had occurred when a bell rang – for one moment Kevin thought it was the telephone again, and gave a start which was perceptible to Claire. But it was the front door, and when he went down to open it Vera was waiting for him on the threshold, dangling some keys. "Oh, Kevin, darling, can you be an angel and get Claire's book from the car for me? You can't miss it."

"Of course." He could not look at her, but stared down at his shoes as she passed in front of him and went upstairs to her daughter. With a nervous gesture he examined his watch: it was now 6.15. And when he returned with the book he lingered in the bedroom doorway to scrutinize Vera; she was laughing, her head deliberately thrown back as if the world were being asked to witness her good humour, but she seemed neither ill nor deranged. And yet she must have telephoned him just before coming to the door. "There, there," she was saying now as she took the infant from its cot. "Come to lovely Vera. She could eat you, you're so gorgeous." And the baby, apparently fascinated by this sudden access to his grandmother's face, stuck his tiny fingers in her open mouth.

It was an evening in late November. Kevin was turning on the television at six o'clock when the telephone rang; and as he watched the screen fill with light, casting vague shadows upon the walls, he picked up the receiver and heard Vera shrieking, "It's a boy! It's a lovely boy!"

"Vera, I'm sorry if this is a joke but . . ."

"It's a boy! It's a lovely boy!" To Kevin the voice now seemed hysterical, with an additional ferocity which both alarmed and angered him. He was about to shout back in panic when he looked up and saw Vera's face at the window, her mouth flattened against the glass and rendered a luminous grey by the light from the television. He dropped the telephone. "Let me in, darling!" she was saying. "Your bell isn't working!" He stared at her. "Kevin, darling, have you gone deaf?" And as he looked at her grey mouth he wondered whose voice it was he had heard, a voice which in memory no longer seemed human at all.

A week later, at the same time, he heard it again; he had thought of little else except those disembodied sounds, and he wanted to test his theory that Vera had somehow arranged a recording. He was quite calm but, when he picked up the receiver, his calmness disappeared. "It's a boy! It's a lovely boy!" He remembered what he had to say. "Can you repeat that, please?" There was a slight pause. "It's a boy!

It's a lovely boy!" So there *was* someone there, listening to him, hearing his quick breathing and the sudden intake of that breath. He put down the telephone and hurried upstairs; for some reason he now feared that some terrible harm might befall either Claire or the child.

She looked defiantly at him as he entered the bedroom. "Mummy told me to rest, so I'm resting. It's good for my milk." But she was clearly puzzled. "Are you all right? You look as if you've seen a ghost."

"It was the phone."

"Anyone I know?"

"No. I don't think so." The baby gave a fat gurgle of satisfaction from the cot beside her.

He went downstairs and, in order to calm himself, noted down the time and day of this latest call. But he did not need to look at his own scrawled handwriting to know that the telephone always rang at six o'clock on Tuesday evenings. This was the time when Vera had originally called him from the hospital with news of the birth. And who could have known that? Only Vera and Claire, naturally. He put his hands to the sides of his head. Then, he thought, perhaps the baby knew . . .

When the following week the telephone rang again he snatched up the receiver and shouted, "Who are you? Who put you up to this?" There was a pause, almost out of politeness, and then it began again, "It's a boy! It's a lovely boy!" It seemed to Kevin that these harmless words had become threatening, even sinister, like an incantation designed to raise the dead. The voice seemed about to break into laughter: he could not bear the thought of that, and slammed down the receiver just before Claire entered the room. She looked at him curiously, and in that moment they realized how ill at ease they had become with each other.

"I thought I heard voices."

"It was the phone." He dared not look down at it, but pointed his finger.

"Oh? I didn't hear it ring."

"They rang off quickly," he replied without thinking about what he was saying.

"Who were *they?*"

"Oh, I don't know. Just the usual." She said nothing, but he noticed that she was biting the inside of her mouth as she stood uncertainly in the middle of the room.

When she left him, he sat down sighing – only to spring to his feet with the thought that perhaps the telephone had never rung, that the voice was only within his own head. All at once he saw himself as the centre of an illness which might infect his wife and child. He went over to the telephone and began minutely to examine it; he did not know what he was looking for, but he wanted to feel its weight and bulk in his now trembling hands. Then suddenly it rang again and with a yell he dropped it to the floor; from the spilled receiver he could hear Vera's voice oozing out. He wanted to scream abuse at it but instead he carefully picked it up, holding it a little way from his ear.

"Kevin, poppet. What *is* the matter? What was that bloody noise?"

"Nothing." He cleared his throat. "It's just the phone."

But apparently she had not heard him, since she began hurriedly to discuss the arrangements which she had made for them all at Christmas. Oh God, he thought as she talked at him, will I be able to endure all this until Christmas?

On the following Tuesday, at six o'clock, it rang again; but he remained seated and would not answer it. Claire and her mother were shopping for presents, and the noise of the bell seemed to fill the house. But he sat very still.

When at last it stopped, he went to the cupboard under the stairs, took out a can of paint, a brush, and then began solemnly to daub the telephone until it was entirely blue – a bright blue. For some reason this exercise calmed and satisfied him. It had become a battle of wills, the next round of which would be fought on the following Tuesday, which was Christmas Eve.

They were all sitting together on that day, Vera rocking the baby in her arms, Claire watching her, and Kevin pretending to doze. At six o'clock, the telephone rang. He looked up at them quickly to see if they had heard it, too, and when Claire muttered, "Now who can *that* be?" he got up from his chair in relief. "It may be for you," he said to his mother-in-law, "Why don't you answer it?"

"Don't be silly, darling, with a baby?"

"Could you get it then, Claire?" He coughed. "I've got a frog in my throat."

She glanced at her mother before slowly picking up the telephone. And then there came the voice again: "It's a boy! It's a lovely boy!" Kevin stiffened and stared down at his infant son, not daring to say anything. But Claire laughed. She handed the receiver to her mother: "Oh Mummy it's you!" Vera listened as the baby tried to grasp the telephone and the voice came again. She laughed also, but clearly she was abashed. "I didn't realize," she said, "how *military* I sound. I'm sorry."

Kevin was astonished at their response, and even more so when his wife walked forward to embrace him. "What a wonderful Christmas present! I knew you wouldn't forget baby's anniversary! Is it like a singing telegram?"

"No." He didn't really know what to say. "Not exactly."

Vera was smiling at him. "So that's why you painted the phone. We thought you were going dotty, darling."

And Kevin laughed with them, for all at once he realized that the voice had been neither menacing nor inhuman. His suspicions had been absurd; the only evil had resided in his own fear. It was Vera's voice, but, somehow, it had never left the telephone and had become an echo of that joyful mood he had experienced at the first news of his infant son. "So you don't mind?" he asked his wife.

"Why should I mind? I was waiting for you to show some sign."

"Sign?"

"You know." It was her turn to become abashed. "About little Tom."

Tom was laughing now, and Kevin took him from Vera's arms to hold him up to the light. The two women rested the telephone between them, listening once more to the refrain, "It's a boy! It's a lovely boy!" as Kevin realized that these words also represented the spirit of Christmas itself. And at each Christmas they returned.

7

Haunting Times

Tales of Unease

Smoke Ghost

Fritz Leiber

Location: Chicago, USA.

Time: October, 1941.

Eyewitness Description: *"I mean a ghost from the world today, with the soot of the factories on its face and the pounding of machinery in its soul. The kind that would haunt coal yards and slip around at night through deserted office buildings."*

Author: Fritz Reuter Leiber (1910–92) deserves the accolade as the writer who introduced the ghost of the tough city centre. His stories postulated a modern post-industrial aesthetic of horror, emerging spontaneously from the urban landscape. In a 1940 essay he argued: "The supernatural beings of a modern city would be different from the ghosts of yesterday, because each culture creates its own ghosts." The son of a noted Shakespearean actor, Fritz toured with his father's road company for several years and secured parts in a few films before turning to authorship in the Forties. He hit a rich vein of form with tales about the supernatural in contemporary America, notably *Conjure Wife* (1943), about witchcraft in a modern university, and a series of short stories, "The Automatic Pistol" (1940), "The Girl With Hungry Eyes" (1949) and "Smoke Ghost" (1941) with its grimy phantom. He later reworked this concept into a novel, *Our Lady of Darkness* (1977), set in San Francisco and proffering reasons why so many of the city's coterie of writers, including Ambrose Bierce and Jack London, had met such tragic deaths. Several critics regard this work as Leiber's homage to the horror of Edgar Allan Poe and the supernaturalism of M. R. James. Here, though, is the original short story that created a new niche for the ghost story.

Miss Millick wondered just what had happened to Mr Wran. He kept making the strangest remarks when she took dictation. Just this morning he had quickly turned around and asked, "Have you ever seen a ghost, Miss Millick?" And she had tittered nervously and replied, "When I was a girl there was a thing in white that used to come out of the closet in the attic bedroom when I slept there, and moan. Of course it was just my imagination. I was frightened of lots of things." And he had said, "I don't mean that kind of ghost. I mean a ghost from the world today, with the soot of the factories on its face and the pounding of machinery in its soul. The kind that would haunt coal yards and slip around at night through deserted office buildings like this one. A real ghost. Not something out of books." And she hadn't known what to say.

He'd never been like this before. Of course he might be joking, but it didn't sound that way. Vaguely Miss Millick wondered whether he mightn't be seeking some sort of sympathy from her. Of course, Mr Wran was married and had a little child, but that didn't prevent her from having daydreams. The daydreams were not very exciting, still they helped fill up her mind. But now he was asking her another of those unprecedented questions.

"Have you ever thought what a ghost of our times would look like, Miss Millick? Just picture it. A smoky composite face with the hungry anxiety of the unemployed, the neurotic restlessness of the person without purpose, the jerky tension of the high-pressure metropolitan worker, the uneasy resentment of the striker, the callous opportunism of the scab, the aggressive whine of the panhandler, the inhibited terror of the bombed civilian, and a thousand other twisted emotional patterns. Each one overlying and yet blending with the other, like a pile of semitransparent masks?"

Miss Millick gave a little self-conscious shiver and said, "That would be terrible. What an awful thing to think of."

She peered furtively across the desk. She remembered having heard that there had been something impressively abnormal about Mr Wran's childhood, but she couldn't recall what it was. If only she could do something – laugh at his mood or ask him what was really wrong. She shifted the extra pencils in her left hand and mechanically traced over some of the shorthand curlicues in her notebook.

"Yet, that's just what such a ghost or vitalized projection would look like, Miss Millick," he continued, smiling in a tight way. "It would grow out of the real world. It would reflect the tangled, sordid, vicious things. All the loose ends. And it would be very grimy. I don't think it would seem white or wispy, or favor graveyards. It wouldn't moan. But it would mutter unintelligibly, and twitch at your sleeve. Like a sick, surly ape. What would such a thing want from a person, Miss Millick? Sacrifice? Worship? Or just fear? What could you do to stop it from troubling you?"

Miss Millick giggled nervously. There was an expression beyond her powers of definition in Mr Wran's ordinary, flat-cheeked, thirtyish face, silhouetted against the dusty window. He turned away and stared out into the gray down-town atmosphere that rolled in from the railroad yards and the mills. When he spoke again his voice sounded far away.

"Of course, being immaterial, it couldn't hurt you physically – at first. You'd have to be peculiarly sensitive to see it, or be aware of it at all. But it would begin to influence your actions. Make you do this. Stop you from doing that. Although only a projection, it would gradually get its hooks into the world of things as they are. Might even get control of suitably vacuous minds. Then it could hurt whomever it wanted."

Miss Millick squirmed and read back her shorthand, like the books said you should do when there was a pause. She became aware of the failing light and wished Mr Wran would ask her to turn on the overhead. She felt scratchy, as if soot were sifting down on to her skin.

"It's a rotten world, Miss Millick," said Mr Wran, talking at the window. "Fit for another morbid growth of superstition. It's time the ghosts, or whatever you call them, took over and began a rule of fear. They'd be no worse than men."

"But" – Miss Millick's diaphragm jerked, making her titter inanely – "of course, there aren't any such things as ghosts."

Mr Wran turned around.

"Of course there aren't, Miss Millick," he said in a loud, patronizing voice, as if she had been doing the talking rather than he. "Science and common sense and psychiatry all go to prove it."

She hung her head and might even have blushed if she hadn't felt so all at sea. Her leg muscles twitched, making her stand up, although she hadn't intended to. She aimlessly rubbed her hand along the edge of the desk.

"Why, Mr Wran, look what I got off your desk," she said, showing him a heavy smudge. There was a note of clumsily playful reproof in her voice. "No wonder the copy I bring you always gets so black. Somebody ought to talk to those scrubwomen. They're skimping on your room."

She wished he would make some normal joking reply. But instead he drew back and his face hardened.

"Well, to get back," he rapped out harshly, and began to dictate.

When she was gone, he jumped up, dabbed his finger experimentally at the smudged part of the desk, frowned worriedly at the almost inky smears. He jerked open a drawer, snatched out a rag, hastily swabbed off the desk, crumpled the rag into a ball and tossed it back. There were three or four other rags in the drawer, each impregnated with soot.

Then he went over to the window and peered out anxiously through the dusk, his eyes searching the panorama of roofs, fixing on each chimney and water tank.

"It's a neurosis. Must be. Compulsions. Hallucinations," he muttered to himself in a tired, distraught voice that would have made Miss Millick gasp. "It's that damned mental abnormality cropping up in a new form. Can't be any other explanation. But it's so damned real. Even the soot. Good thing I'm seeing the psychiatrist. I don't think I could force myself to get on the elevated railway tonight." His voice trailed off, he rubbed his eyes, and his memory automatically started to grind.

It had all begun on the elevated. There was a particular little sea of roofs he had grown into the habit of glancing at just as the packed car carrying him homeward lurched around a turn. A dingy, melancholy little world of tar-paper, tarred gravel and smoky brick. Rusty tin chimneys with odd conical hats suggested abandoned listening posts. There was a washed-out advertisement of some ancient patent medicine on the nearest wall. Superficially it was like ten thousand other drab city roofs. But he always saw it around dusk, either in the smoky half-light, or tinged with red by the flat rays of a dirty sunset, or covered by ghostly windblown white sheets of rain-splash, or patched with blackish snow; and it seemed unusually bleak and suggestive; almost beautifully ugly though in no sense picturesque; dreary, but meaningful. Unconsciously it came to symbolize for Catesby Wran certain disagreeable aspects of the frustrated, frightened century in which he lived, the jangled century of hate and heavy industry and total wars. The quick daily glance into the half darkness became an integral part of his life. Oddly, he never saw it in the morning, for it was then his habit to sit on the other side of the car, his head buried in the paper.

One evening toward winter he noticed what seemed to be a shapeless black sack lying on the third roof from the tracks. He did not think about it. It merely registered as an addition to the well-known scene and his memory stored away the impression for further reference. Next evening, however, he decided he had been mistaken in one detail. The object was a roof nearer than he had thought. Its color and texture, and the grimy stains around it, suggested that it was filled with coal dust, which was hardly reasonable. Then, too, the following evening it seemed to have been blown against a rusty ventilator by the wind – which could hardly have happened if it were at all heavy. Perhaps it was filled with leaves. Catesby was surprised to find himself anticipating his next daily glance with a minor note of apprehension. There was something unwholesome in the posture of the thing that stuck in his mind – a bulge in the sacking that suggested a misshaped head peering around the ventilator. And his apprehension was justified, for that evening the thing was on the nearest roof, though on the farther side, looking as if it had just flopped down over the low brick parapet.

Next evening the sack was gone. Catesby was annoyed at the momentary feeling of relief that went through him, because the whole matter seemed too unimportant to warrant feelings of any sort. What difference did it make if his imagination had played tricks on him, and he'd fancied that the object was slowly crawling and hitching itself closer across the roofs? That was the way any normal imagination worked. He deliberately chose to disregard the fact that there were reasons for thinking his imagination was by no means a normal one. As he walked home from the elevated, however, he found himself wondering whether the sack was really gone. He seemed to recall a vague, smudgy trail leading across the gravel to the nearer side of the roof, which was masked by a parapet. For an instant an unpleasant picture formed in his mind – that of an inky, humped creature crouched behind the parapet, waiting.

The next time he felt the familiar grating lurch of the car, he caught himself trying not to look out. That angered him. He turned his head quickly. When he turned it back, his compact face was definitely pale. There had been only time for a fleeting rearward glance at the escaping roof. Had he actually seen in silhouette the upper part of a head of some sort peering over the parapet? Nonsense, he told himself. And even if he had seen something, there were a thousand explanations which did not involve the supernatural or even true hallucination. Tomorrow he would take a good look and clear up the whole matter. If necessary, he would visit the roof personally, though he hardly knew where to find it and disliked in any case the idea of pampering a silly fear.

He did not relish the walk home from the elevated that evening, and visions of the thing disturbed his dreams, and were in and out of his mind all next day at the office. It was then that he first began to relieve his nerves by making jokingly serious remarks about the supernatural to Miss Millick, who seemed properly mystified. It was on the same day, too, that he became aware of a growing antipathy to grime and soot. Everything he touched seemed gritty, and he found himself mopping and wiping at his desk like an old lady with a morbid fear of germs. He reasoned that there was no real change in his office, and that he'd just now become sensitive to the dirt that had always been there, but there was no denying an increasing nervousness. Long before the car reached the curve, he was straining his eyes through the murky twilight, determined to take in every detail.

Afterward he realized he must have given a muffled cry of some sort, for the man beside him looked at him curiously, and the woman ahead gave him an unfavourable stare. Conscious of his own pallor and uncontrollable trembling, he stared back at them hungrily, trying to regain the feeling of security he had completely lost. They were the usual reassuringly wooden-faced people everyone rides home with on the elevated. But suppose he had pointed out to one of them what he had seen – that sodden, distorted face of sacking and coal dust, that boneless paw which waved back and forth, unmistakably in his direction, as if reminding him of a future appointment – he involuntarily shut his eyes tight. His thoughts were racing ahead to tomorrow evening. He pictured this same windowed oblong of light and packed humanity surging around the curve – then an opaque monstrous form leaping out from the roof in a parabolic swoop – an unmentionable face pressed close against the window, smearing it with wet coal dust – huge paws fumbling sloppily at the glass—

Somehow he managed to turn off his wife's anxious inquiries. Next morning he reached a decision and made an appointment for that evening with a psychiatrist a friend had told him about. It cost him a considerable effort, for Catesby had a well-grounded distaste for anything dealing with psychological abnormality. Visiting a psychiatrist meant raking up an episode in his past which he had never fully described even to his wife. Once he had made the decision, however, he felt considerably relieved. The psychiatrist, he told himself, would clear everything up. He could almost fancy him saying, "Merely a bad case of nerves. However, you must consult the oculist whose name I'm writing down for you, and you must take two of these pills in water every four hours," and so on. It was almost comforting, and made the coming revelation he would have to make seem less painful.

But as the smoky dusk rolled in, his nervousness had returned and he had let his joking mystification of Miss Millick run away with him until he had realized he wasn't frightening anyone but himself.

He would have to keep his imagination under better control, he told himself, as he continued to peer out restlessly at the massive, murky shapes of the downtown office buildings. Why, he had spent the whole afternoon building up a kind of neo-medieval cosmology of superstition. It wouldn't do. He realized then that he had been standing at the window much longer than he'd thought, for the glass panel in the door was dark and there was no noise coming from the outer office. Miss Millick and the rest must have gone home.

It was then he made the discovery that there would have been no special reason for dreading the swing around the curve that night. It was, as it happened, a horrible discovery. For, on the shadowed roof across the street and four stories below, he saw the thing huddle and roll across the gravel and, after one upward look of recognition, merge into the blackness beneath the water tank.

As he hurriedly collected his things and made for the elevator, fighting the panicky impulse to run, he began to think of hallucination and mild psychosis as very desirable conditions. For better or for worse, he pinned all his hopes on the psychiatrist.

"So you find yourself growing nervous and . . . er . . . jumpy, as you put it," said Dr Trevethick, smiling with dignified geniality. "Do you notice any more definite physical symptoms? Pain? Headache? Indigestion?"

Catesby shook his head and wet his lips. "I'm especially nervous while riding in the elevated," he murmured swiftly.

"I see. We'll discuss that more fully. But I'd like you first to tell me about something you mentioned earlier. You said there was something about your childhood that might predispose you to nervous ailments. As you know, the early years are critical ones in the development of an individual's behavior pattern."

Catesby studied the yellow reflections of frosted globes in the dark surface of the desk. The palm of his left hand aimlessly rubbed the thick nap of the armchair. After a while he raised his head and looked straight into the doctor's small brown eyes.

"From perhaps my third to my ninth year," he began, choosing the words with care, "I was what you might call a sensory prodigy."

The doctor's expression did not change. "Yes?" he inquired politely.

"What I mean is that I was supposed to be able to see through walls, read letters through envelopes and books through their covers, fence and play ping-pong blindfolded, find things that were buried, read thoughts." The words tumbled out.

"And could you?" The doctor's voice was toneless.

"I don't know. I don't suppose so," answered Catesby, long-lost emotions flooding back into his voice. "It's all confused now. I thought I could, but then they were always encouraging me. My mother . . . was . . . well . . . interested in psychic phenomena. I was . . . exhibited. I seem to remember seeing things other people couldn't. As if most opaque objects were transparent. But I was very young. I didn't have any scientific criteria for judgment."

He was reliving it now. The darkened rooms. The earnest assemblages of gawking, prying adults. Himself alone on a little platform, lost in a straight-backed wooden chair. The black silk handkerchief over his eyes. His mother's coaxing, insistent questions. The whispers. The gasps. His own hate of the whole business, mixed with hunger for the adulation of adults. Then the scientists from the university, the experiments, the big test. The reality of those memories engulfed him and momentarily made him forget the reason why he was disclosing them to a stranger.

"Do I understand that your mother tried to make use of you as a medium for communicating with the . . . er . . . other world?"

Catesby nodded eagerly.

"She tried to, but she couldn't. When it came to getting in touch with the dead, I was a complete failure. All I could do – or thought I could do – was see real, existing, three-dimensional objects beyond the vision of normal people. Objects anyone could have seen except for distance, obstruction, or darkness. It was always a disappointment to mother."

He could hear her sweetish, patient voice saying, "Try again, dear, just this once. Katie was your aunt. She loved you. Try to hear what she's saying." And he had answered, "I can see a woman in a blue dress standing on the other side of Dick's house." And she had replied, "Yes, I know, dear. But that's not Katie. Katie's a spirit. Try again. Just this once, dear." The doctor's voice gently jarred him back into the softly gleaming office.

"You mentioned scientific criteria for judgment, Mr Wran. As far as you know, did anyone ever try to apply them to you?"

Catesby's nod was emphatic.

"They did. When I was eight, two young psychologists from the university got interested in me. I guess they did it for a joke at first, and I remember being very determined to show them I amounted to something. Even now I seem to recall how the note of polite superiority and amused sarcasm drained out of their voices. I suppose they decided at first that it was very clever trickery, but somehow they persuaded mother to let them try me out under controlled conditions. There were lots of tests that seemed very businesslike after mother's slipshod little exhibitions. They found I was clairvoyant – or so they thought. I got worked up and on edge. They were going to demonstrate my supernormal sensory powers to the university psychology faculty. For the first time I began to worry about whether I'd come through. Perhaps they kept me going at too hard a pace, I don't know. At any rate, when the test came, I couldn't do a thing. Everything became opaque. I got desperate and made things up out of my imagination. I lied. In the end I failed utterly, and I believe the two young psychologists got into a lot of hot water as a result."

He could hear the brusque, bearded man saying, "You've been taken in by a child, Flaxman, a mere child. I'm greatly disturbed. You've put yourself on the same plane as common charlatans. Gentlemen, I ask you to banish from your minds this whole sorry episode. It must never be referred to." He winced at the recollection of his feeling of guilt. But at the same time he was beginning to feel exhilarated and almost light-hearted. Unburdening his long-respressed memories had altered his whole viewpoint. The episodes on the elevated began to take on what seemed their proper proportions as merely the bizarre workings of overwrought nerves and an overly suggestible mind. The doctor, he anticipated confidently, would disentangle the obscure subconscious causes, whatever they might be. And the whole business would be finished off quickly, just as his childhood experience – which was beginning to seem a little ridiculous now – had been finished off.

"From that day on," he continued, "I never exhibited a trace of my supposed powers. My mother was frantic and tried to sue the university. I had something like a nervous breakdown. Then the divorce was granted, and my father got custody of me. He did his best to make me forget it. We went on long outdoor vacations and did a lot of athletics, associated with normal matter-of-fact people. I went to business college eventually. I'm in advertising now. But," Catesby paused, "now that I'm having nervous symptoms, I've wondered if there mightn't be a connection. It's not a question of whether I was really clairvoyant or not. Very likely my mother taught me a lot of unconscious deceptions, good enough to fool even young psychology instructors. But don't you think it may have some important bearing on my present condition?"

For several moments the doctor regarded him with a professional frown. Then he said quietly, "And is there some . . . er . . . more specific connection between your experiences then and now? Do you by any chance find that you are once again beginning to . . . er . . . see things?"

Catesby swallowed. He had felt an increasing eagerness to unburden himself of his fears, but it was not easy to make a beginning, and the doctor's shrewd question rattled him. He forced himself to concentrate. The thing he thought he had seen on the roof loomed up before his inner eye with unexpected vividness. Yet it did not frighten him. He groped for words.

Then he saw that the doctor was not looking at him but over his shoulder. Color was draining out of the doctor's face and his eyes did not seem so small. Then the doctor sprang to his feet, walked past Catesby, threw up the window and peered into the darkness.

As Catesby rose, the doctor slammed down the window and said in a voice whose smoothness was marred by a slight, persistent gasping, "I hope I haven't alarmed you. I saw the face of . . . er . . . a Negro prowler on the fire escape. I must have frightened him, for he seems to have gotten out of sight in a hurry. Don't give it another thought. Doctors are frequently bothered by *voyeurs* . . . er . . . Peeping Toms."

"A Negro?" asked Catesby, moistening his lips.

The doctor laughed nervously. "I imagine so, though my first odd impression was that it was a white man in blackface. You see, the color didn't seem to have any brown in it. It was dead-black."

Catesby moved toward the window. There were smudges on the glass. "It's quite all right, Mr Wran." The doctor's voice had acquired a sharp note of impatience, as if he were trying hard to reassume his professional authority. "Let's continue our conversation. I was asking you if you were" – he made a face – "seeing things."

Catesby's whirling thoughts slowed down and locked into place. "No, I'm not seeing anything that other people don't see, too. And I think I'd better go now. I've been keeping you too long." He disregarded the doctor's half-hearted gesture of denial. "I'll phone you about the physical examination. In a way you've already taken a big load off my mind." He smiled woodenly. "Goodnight, Dr Trevethick."

Catesby Wran's mental state was a peculiar one. His eyes searched every angular shadow, he glanced sideways down each chasm-like alley and barren basement passage-way, and kept stealing looks at the irregular line of the roofs, yet he was hardly conscious of where he was going. He pushed away the thoughts that came into his mind, and kept moving. He became aware of a slight sense of security as he turned into a lighted street where there were people and high buildings and blinking signs. After a while he found himself in the dim lobby of the structure that housed his office. Then he realized why he couldn't go home, why he daren't go home – after what had happened at the office of Dr Trevethick.

"Hello, Mr Wran," said the night elevator man, a burly figure in overalls, sliding open the grille-work door to the old-fashioned cage. "I didn't know you were working nights now, too."

Catesby stepped in automatically. "Sudden rush of orders," he murmured inanely. "Some stuff that has to be gotten out."

The cage creaked to a stop at the top floor. "Be working very late, Mr Wran?"

He nodded vaguely, watched the car slide out of sight, found his keys, swiftly crossed the outer office, and entered his own. His hand went out to the light switch, but then the thought occurred to him that the two lighted windows, standing out against the dark bulk of the building, would indicate his whereabouts and serve as a goal toward which something could crawl and climb. He moved his chair so that the back was against the wall and sat down in the semidarkness. He did not remove his overcoat.

For a long time he sat there motionless, listening to his own breathing and the faraway sounds from the streets below: the thin metallic surge of the crosstown streetcar, the farther one of the elevated, faint lonely cries and honkings, indistinct rumblings. Words he had spoken to Miss Millick in nervous jest came back to him with the bitter taste of truth. He found himself unable to reason critically or connectedly, but by their own volition thoughts rose up into his mind and gyrated slowly and rearranged themselves with the inevitable movement of planets.

Gradually his mental picture of the world was transformed. No longer a world of material atoms and empty space, but a world in which the bodiless existed and moved according to its own obscure laws or unpredictable impulses. The new picture illuminated with dreadful clarity certain general facts which had always bewildered and troubled him and from which he had tried to hide: the inevitability of hate and war, the diabolically timed mischances which wreck the best of human intentions, the walls of willful misunderstanding that divide one man from another, the eternal vitality of cruelty and ignorance and greed. They seemed appropriate now, necessary parts of the picture. And superstition only a kind of wisdom.

Then his thoughts returned to himself and the question he had asked Miss Millick, "What would such a thing want from a person? Sacrifices? Worship? Or just fear? What could you do to stop it from troubling you?" It had become a practical question.

With an explosive jangle, the phone began to ring. "Cate, I've been trying everywhere to get you," said his wife. "I never thought you'd be at the office. What are you doing? I've been worried."

He said something about work.

"You'll be home right away?" came the faint anxious question. "I'm a little frightened. Ronny just had a scare. It woke him up. He kept pointing to the window saying, 'Black man, black man.' Of course it's something he dreamed. But I'm frightened. You will be home? What's that, dear? Can't you hear me?"

"I will. Right away," he said. Then he was out of the office, buzzing the night bell and peering down the shaft.

He saw it peering up the shaft at him from the deep shadows three floors below, the sacking face pressed against the iron grille-work. It started up the stair at a shockingly swift, shambling gait, vanishing temporarily from sight as it swung into the second corridor below.

Catesby clawed at the door to the office, realized he had not locked it, pushed it in, slammed and locked it behind him, retreated to the other side of the room, cowered between the filing cases and the wall. His teeth were clicking. He heard the groan of the rising cage. A silhouette darkened the frosted glass of the door, blotting out part of the grotesque reverse of the company name. After a little the door opened.

The big-globed overhead light flared on and, standing inside the door, her hand on the switch, was Miss Millick.

"Why, Mr Wran," she stammered vacuously, "I didn't know you were here. I'd just come in to do some extra typing after the movie. I didn't . . . but the lights weren't on. What were you—"

He stared at her. He wanted to shout in relief, grab hold of her, talk rapidly. He realized he was grinning hysterically.

"Why, Mr Wran, what's happened to you?" she asked embarrassedly, ending with a stupid titter. "Are you feeling sick? Isn't there something I can do for you?"

He shook his head jerkily and managed to say, "No, I'm just leaving. I was doing some extra work myself."

"But you *look* sick," she insisted, and walked over toward him. He inconsequentially realized she must have stepped in mud, for her high-heeled shoes left neat black prints.

"Yes, I'm sure you must be sick. You're so terribly pale." She sounded like an enthusiastic, incompetent nurse. Her face brightened with a sudden inspiration. "I've got something in my bag, that'll fix you up right away," she said. "It's for indigestion."

She fumbled at her stuffed oblong purse. He noticed that she was absent-mindedly holding it shut with one hand while she tried to open it with the other. Then, under his very eyes, he saw her bend back the thick prongs of metal locking the purse as if they were tinfoil, or as if her fingers had become a pair of steel pliers.

Instantly his memory recited the words he had spoken to Miss Millick that afternoon. "It couldn't hurt you physically – at first . . . gradually get its hooks into the world . . . might even get control of suitably vacuous minds. Then it could hurt whomever it wanted." A sickish, cold feeling grew inside him. He began to edge toward the door.

But Miss Millick hurried ahead of him.

"You don't have to wait, Fred," she called. "Mr Wran's decided to stay a while longer."

The door to the cage shut with a mechanical rattle. The cage creaked. Then she turned around in the door.

"Why, Mr Wran," she gurgled reproachfully, "I just couldn't think of letting you go home now. I'm sure you're terribly unwell. Why, you might collapse in the street. You've just got to stay here until you feel different."

The creaking died away. He stood in the center of the office, motionless. His eyes traced the coal-black course of Miss Millick's footprints to where she stood blocking the door. Then a sound that was almost a scream was wrenched out of him, for it seemed to him that the blackness was creeping up her legs under the thin stockings.

"Why, Mr Wran," she said, "You're acting as if you were crazy. You must lie down for a while. Here, I'll help you off with your coat."

The nauseously idiotic and rasping note was the same; only it had been intensified. As she came toward him he turned and ran through the storeroom, clattered a key desperately at the lock of the second door to the corridor.

"Why, Mr Wran," he heard her call, "are you having some kind of a fit? You must let me help you."

The door came open and he plunged out into the corridor and up the stairs immediately ahead. It was only when he reached the top that he realized the heavy steel door in front of him led to the roof. He jerked up the catch.

"Why, Mr Wran, you mustn't run away. I'm coming after you."

Then he was out on the gritty gravel of the roof. The night sky was clouded and murky, with a faint pinkish glow from the neon signs. From the distant mills rose a ghostly spurt of flame. He ran to the edge. The street lights glared dizzily upward. Two men were tiny round blobs of hat and shoulders. He swung around.

The thing was in the doorway. The voice was no longer solicitous but moronically playful, each sentence ending in a titter.

"Why, Mr Wran, why have you come up here? We're all alone. Just think, I might push you off."

The thing came slowly toward him. He moved backward until his heels touched the low parapet. Without knowing why, or what he was going to do, he dropped to his knees. He dared not look at the face as it came nearer, a focus for the worst in the world, a gathering point for poisons from everywhere. Then the lucidity of terror took possession of his mind, and words formed on his lips.

"I will obey you. You are my god," he said. "You have supreme power over man and his animals and his machines. You rule this city and all others. I recognize that."

Again the titter, closer. "Why, Mr Wran, you never talked like this before. Do you mean it?"

"The world is yours to do with as you will, save or tear to pieces," he answered fawningly, the words automatically fitting themselves together in vaguely liturgical patterns. "I recognize that. I will praise, I will sacrifice. In smoke and soot I will worship you for ever."

The voice did not answer. He looked up. There was only Miss Millick, deathly pale and swaying drunkenly. Her eyes were closed. He caught her as she wobbled toward him. His knees gave way under the added weight and they sank down together on the edge of the roof.

After a while she began to twitch. Small noises came from her throat and her eyelids edged open.

"Come on, we'll go downstairs," he murmured jerkily, trying to draw her up. "You're feeling bad."

"I'm terribly dizzy," she whispered. "I must have fainted, I didn't eat enough. And then I'm so nervous lately, about the war and everything, I guess. Why, we're on the roof! Did you bring me up here to get some air? Or did I come up without knowing it? I'm awfully foolish. I used to walk in my sleep, my mother said."

As he helped her down the stairs, she turned and looked at him. "Why, Mr Wran," she said, faintly, "you've got a big black smudge on your forehead. Here, let me get it off for you." Weakly she rubbed at it with her handkerchief. She started to away again and he steadied her.

"No, I'll be all right," she said. "Only I feel cold. What happened, Mr Wran? Did I have some sort of fainting spell?"

He told her it was something like that.

Later, riding home in the empty elevated railway car, he wondered how long he would be safe from the thing. It was a purely practical problem. He had no way of knowing, but instinct told him he had satisfied the brute for some time. Would it want more when it came again? Time enough to answer that question when it arose. It might be hard, he realized, to keep out of an insane asylum. With Helen and Ronny to protect, as well as himself, he would have to be careful and tightlipped. He began to speculate as to how many other men and women had seen the thing or things like it.

The elevated slowed and lurched in a familiar fashion. He looked at the roofs near the curve. They seemed very ordinary, as if what made them impressive had gone away for a while.

The Ghost

A. E. Van Vogt

Location: Agan, Gatineau Hills, Ottawa.
Time: August, 1942.
Eyewitness Description: *"Was this alien creature a mind reader as well as a seer and ghost? An old, worn-out brain that had taken on automaton qualities and reacted almost entirely to thoughts that trickled in from other minds . . ."*

Author: Alfred Elton Van Vogt (1912–2000) was among the group of young writers in the Thirties who transformed fantasy and science fiction into a new "Golden Age" of imaginative writing – "the literature of ideas", as it has been described. Born in Canada, Van Vogt moved to America where, with other authors like Fritz Leiber and Ray Bradbury, he used his talents to explore new avenues of supernaturalism. His novels cut new pathways with their variety from *Slan* (1940), featuring a small boy able to read minds, to *The Weapon Shops of Isher* (1942), about a retail chain store operating inter-dimensionally. With *Asylum* (1942), he offered an adroit new twist on the vampire theme. Van Vogt turned his attention to ghosts after reading *An Experiment With Time* by J. W. Dunne – originally written in 1927 and revised several times – in which the English engineer and author expounded his theories about the nature of time to justify his conviction that dreams are often precognitive. From this came the brilliantly complex "The Ghost" – which acknowledges Dunne – and it was introduced on first publication in the August 1942 *Unknown Worlds* by editor John W. Campbell as, "One of the most unusual tales of haunting and ghosts we've read – and one that might explain what ghosts *really* are."

"Four miles," Kent thought, "four miles from the main-line town of Kempster to the railwayless village of Agan." At least, he remembered that much.

He remembered the hill, too, and the farm at the foot of it. Only it hadn't been deserted when he saw it last.

He stared at the place as the hotel car edged down the long hill. The buildings showed with a curious, stark bleakness. All the visible windows of the farmhouse itself were boarded up. And great planks had been nailed across the barn door.

The yard was a wilderness of weeds and – Kent experienced an odd sense of shock – the tall, dignified old man who emerged abruptly from behind the house, seemed as out of place in that desolate yard as . . . as life itself.

Kent was aware of the driver leaning toward him, heard him say above the roar of the ancient engine:

"I was wondering if we'd see the ghost, as we passed; and yep, there he is, taking his morning walk."

"The ghost!" Kent echoed.

It was as if he had spoken a key word. The sun burst brilliantly from behind an array of dark clouds and flooded the valley with warm light. The blaze of it illuminated the drab old buildings – and wrought changes. The over-all grayness of the house showed in that bright illumination as a faded green.

The old man walked slowly toward the gate that led to the main highway. Nearer now, he seemed taller, thinner, a gaunt caricature of a human being; his black frock coat glinted in the sun.

Kent found his voice. "Ghost!" he said again. "Why, that's old Mr Wainwright. He doesn't look a day older than when I left this part of the world fifteen years ago."

The old, square-fronted car ground queasily to a stop before the farm gate. The driver turned. It struck Kent that the man was smugly enjoying the moment.

"See that gate?" the fellow asked. "Not the big one; the little one. It's padlocked, eh?"

Kent nodded. "What about it?"

"Watch!"

The old man stood fumbling at the gate less than ten feet away. It was like gazing at a pantomime, Kent thought; for the man paid no attention to the padlock, but seemed absorbed with some simpler catch.

Abruptly, the patriarch straightened, and pushed at the gate. Kent had no real sense of alienness. Without having given the matter any thought, he believed it was the gate that was going to open, and that it was some unusual aspect of the opening that he had been admonished to watch.

The gate didn't. It did not so much as stir; not a creak came from its rusty hinges. It remained solid, held in position by the uncompromising padlock.

The old man walked through it.

Through it! Then he turned, seemed to push at some invisible counterpart of the gate and, once again, stood there, as if manipulating a hidden catch.

Finally, apparently satisfied, he faced the car again; and, for the first time, saw it and its occupants. His long, finely wrinkled face lighted.

"Hello, there!" he said.

Kent hadn't expected speech. The words caught him like a blow. He felt a chill; his mind whirled with a queer, twisting motion that momentarily wrecked the coherence of his thought. He half leaned, half fell back against the seat because his muscles wouldn't support him.

"Ghost," he thought finally, dizzily. Good heavens, what was going on here?

The world began to right itself. The land and the horizon straightened; and there was the house and the barn, an almost colorless, utterly lifeless background to the beanpole of an old, old man and the magic gate through which he had stepped.

"Hello!" Kent said shakily. "Hello!"

The old man came nearer, peered; and an expression of surprise flitted across his face. "Why, it's Mr Kent. I thought you'd left the Agan Hotel."

"Eh!" Kent began.

Out of the corner of his eyes he saw the driver make a sharp movement with one hand. The man whispered hastily:

"Don't act surprised at anything the ghost says. It confuses him."

Ghost! There it was again. Kent swallowed hard. "Am I mad?" he thought. "The last time I saw this old fellow was when I was twenty. He didn't know my name then. How—"

The old man was speaking again, in bewilderment: "I distinctly remember Mr Jenkins, the proprietor, informing me that you had found it necessary to leave at once. He said something about a prophecy coming out exactly to the day, 17 August. People are always talking to me about prophecies. But that was the date he said it was, 17 August."

He looked up, unscrewing the frown from his thin, worn face. "I beg your pardon, young sir. It is very remiss of me to stand here mumbling to myself. May I say that I am glad that the report was untrue, as I have very much enjoyed our several conversations."

He raised his hat. "I would invite you in for tea, but Mrs Carmody is not in the best of moods this morning. Poor woman! Looking after an old man must be a great trial; and I dare not add to her afflictions. Good morning to you, Mr Kent. Good morning, Tom."

Kent nodded, unable to speak. He heard the driver say:

"S'long, Mr Wainwright."

Kent watched, as the tall, frail figure walked slowly across the road behind the car, and moved unhurriedly across the open pasture land to the south. His mind and gaze came back to the car, as the driver, Tom, said:

"Well, Mr Kent, you're lucky. You know how long you're staying at the Agan Hotel."

"What do you mean?"

"Mr Jenkins will have your bill ready for you 17 August."

Kent stared at him, uncertain whether he ought to laugh, or — what! "You're not trying to tell me that the ghost also tells the future. Why, today's only 8 July, and I intend to stay till the end of Septem—"

He stopped. The eyes that were staring into his were utterly earnest, humorless: "Mr Kent, there never was anyone like Mr Wainwright in the world before. When he tells the future, it happens; it was that way when he was alive, and it's the same now that he's dead.

"The only thing is that he's old. He's over ninety, and weak in the head. He gets confused; he always mixes the future with the past. To him it is the past, and it's all equally blurred. But when he says anything as clear as a date, it's so. You wait and see."

There were too many words; and the concreteness of them, the colloquial twang of them on the still air, built an oddly insubstantial picture. Kent began to feel less startled. He knew these country folk; and the conviction was suddenly strong in him that, in some obscure way, he was being made the victim of a practical joke.

It wouldn't do, of course, to say so. Besides, there was the unaccountable episode of the gate.

"This Mrs Carmody," he said finally. "I don't recall her. Who is she?"

"She came to look after the farm when her sister-in-law, the old man's grand-daughter, died. No blood relation, but—" The driver drew a deep breath, tried hard to look casual, and said: "She's the one, you know, who murdered old Wainwright five years ago. They put her in the crazy house at Peerton for doing it."

"Murdered!" Kent said. "What is this – the local ghost story?" He paused; then: "Just a minute. He talked as if he was still living with her."

"Look, Mr Kent" – the man was pitying – "let's not go into why the ghost says what he says. People have tried figuring out what's going on, and have ended with their brains twisted into seventeen knots."

"There must be a natural explanation."

The driver shrugged. "Well, then, you find it." He added: "I was the one who drove Mrs Carmody and her two kids from Kempster to the farm here. Maybe you'd like to hear as much of the story as I can tell you the rest of the way to the hotel."

Kent sat quietly as gears shifted; and the machine moved heavily off. He turned finally to look at the farm. It was just passing out of sight behind a long spread of trees.

That last look showed – desolation, deadness. He shuddered involuntarily, and did not look again. He said: "This story . . . what about it?"

The woman saw the farm as the car slowed at the lip of the hill. She was dimly aware that the car was in low gear, with brakes on, slithering down the loose gravel of the steep incline.

The farm, she thought with a greedy intensity that shook her heavy body; safety at long, long last. And only a senile old man and a girl standing between her and possession.

Between her – and the hard, sordid years that stretched behind her. Years of being a widow with two children in a tenement house, with only an occasional job to eke out the income from the relief department.

Years of hell!

And here was heaven for the taking. Her hard blue eyes narrowed; her plump, hard body grew taut – if she couldn't take the treasure of security that was here, she'd better—

The thought faded. Fascinated, she stared at the valley farm below, a green farmhouse, a great red barn and half a dozen outhouses. In the near distance a vast field of wheat spread; tiny wheat, bright green with a mid-spring greenness.

The car came down to the level of the valley; and trees hid the distant, rolling glory of the land. The automobile came to a stop, its shiny front pointed at the gate; and, beside her, the heavily built boy said:

"This it, ma?"

"Yes, Bill!" The woman looked at him anxiously. All her ultimate plans about this farm centered around him. For a moment she was preternaturally aware of his defects, his sullen, heavy, yet not strong face. There was a clumsiness of build in his chunky, sixteen-year-old body that made him something less than attractive.

She threw off that brief pattern of doubt; she ventured: "Isn't it wonderful?"

"Naw!" The thick lips twisted. "I'd rather be in the city." He shrugged. "But I guess I know what's good for us."

"That's right." She felt relieved. "In this world it's what you get, not what you want. Remember that, Bill . . . what is it, Pearl?"

She spoke impatiently. It was the way her daughter always affected her. What good was a pasty-faced, twelve-year-old, too plump, too plain, and without the faintest promise of ever being pretty. With an even sharper annoyance, the woman repeated:

"What is it?"

"There's a skinny old man coming across the field. Is that Mr Wainwright, ma?"

Mrs Carmody turned slowly and stared in the direction Pearl was pointing. And, after a moment, a current of relief surged through her. Until this instant she had felt a sharp edge of worry about the old man. Old, her sister-in-law had written in her occasional letter. But she hadn't imagined he'd be this old. Why, he must be ninety, a hundred; utterly no danger to her at all.

She saw that the driver had opened the gate, and was coming back to drive the car through. With a new confidence she raised her voice at him:

"Wait!" she said, "wait for the old man. He's been out for a walk, and he'll be tired. Give him a lift to the house."

Might as well make a good first impression, she thought. Politeness was the watchword. Iron hands within velvet gloves.

It struck her that the driver was staring at her peculiarly; the man said: "I wouldn't count on him driving with us. He's a queer old duck, Mr Wainwright is. Sometimes he's deaf and blind, and he don't pay attention to no one. And he does a lot of queer things."

The woman frowned. "For instance?"

The man sighed. "Well, ma'am, it's no use trying to explain. You might as well start learning by experience, now as later. Watch him."

The long, thin figure came at an even, slow pace across the pasture to the south. He crossed the road, passing the car less than three feet from the fenders, seemingly completely blind to its presence. He headed straight for the gate.

Not the open gate, wide enough for the car to go through, but the narrow, solidly constructed wooden gate for human beings. He seemed to fumble at some hidden catch. And then—

The gate did not open, but he stepped through as if it had.

Stepped through the solid wooden gate.

For a long second Mrs Carmody was aware of a harsh woman's voice screaming. With a terrible shock, she realized it was her own voice.

The effort to choke that wild cry was so horrible that she fell back against the seat, the blood hammering at her temples. She sagged there, sick, cold as ice, her vision blurred, her throat ash dry, every muscle in her body jumping with tiny, painful surges of nervous convulsion; and, for a long moment, her mind wouldn't hold thoughts.

"Just a minute!" Kent interrupted the driver. "I thought you told me the old man was alive at this time. How come he walked through the gate?"

His narrator stared at him strangely: "Mr Kent, the only reason that old man hasn't made us all crazy these past twelve years is that he's harmless. He walked through gates when he was alive just as he does now. And not only gates. The difference is that we know we buried him. Maybe he's always been a ghost, and killing him don't do no good. All we know is, he's harmless. That's enough, isn't it?"

Kent nodded, but there was a world of doubt in his voice as he said:

"I suppose so; anyway, go on."

The dark blur of fear in the woman's mind yielded to an awareness of tugging at her arm; and then she realized that the driver was speaking:

"It's all right, ma'am, he's just a queer, harmless old man. Nothing to get excited about."

It was not the driver, but the boy beside her, whose words pulled her together; the boy saying rather scornfully:

"Gee, ma, you sure take on. I seen a trick like that on the stage last year, only it was better than that. It don't mean a thing."

The woman began to feel better. Bill was such a solid, practical boy, she thought gratefully. And of course he was right. Some trick, of course, and – what was that stupid little fool of a girl saying. She found herself repeating the question out loud:

"What did you say, Pearl?"

"He sees us, ma – look!" the girl said.

The woman saw that the old man was peering at her over the gate. A thin, long, gentle, wrinkled face it was, bright with gathering interest. He said with an astonishingly crisp voice for one so old:

"You're back from town rather early, Mrs Carmody. Does that mean an early dinner?"

He paused politely; then: "I have no objection naturally. I am only too happy to fit myself into any routine you desire."

The deadly thought that came to her was that she was being made ridiculous in some way. Her face grew taut, her eyes narrowed, then she mustered an uncertain smile, and tried to force her mind past his words. The fierce whisper of the driver rescued her from that developing confusion:

"Begging your pardon, ma'am," the man said hurriedly, "don't let on you're new here. He's got the gift of seeing, and he's been acting for months as if you were already here, and, if you contradict him, it only puzzles him. Toward the end, he was actually calling Mrs Wainwright by your name. He's just a queer old man."

Mrs Carmody sat a very still, her blue eyes brighter, wide with abrupt calculation. The thrill that came was warm along her nerves. Expected!

One of the several things she had feared was this moment of her arrival; but now – expected!

All her careful preparation would go over smoothly. The letter she had forged so painstakingly, in which the dead woman, the old man's granddaughter, *asked* her to come to look after her daughter, Phyllis – that prize letter would merely be a confirmation of something which had already been accepted as inevitable. Though how—

The woman shook herself firmly. This was no time to worry about the curious actions of an old man. She had a farm to take over; and the quicker that problem was solved, the better.

She smiled again, her thick face smirking a little with the comfortable glow of her inner triumph.

"Won't you ride to the house with us, Mr Wainwright? You must be tired after your walk."

The old fellow nodded alertly. "Don't mind if I do, madam. I was all the way to Kempster, and I'm a little tired. Saw your sister there, by the way."

He had come through the gate, this time the one that was standing open for the car, and he was heading for the front door of the machine when Mrs Carmody managed heavily:

"My – sister?"

"*Sssshh!*" hissed the driver. "Pay no attention. He's mixed up in his head. He thinks everyone of us has a living image, and he's always meeting them. He's been like this for years, perfectly harmless."

It was easier to nod this time. The episode of the gate was a vague unreality in her mind, becoming dimmer by the minute. She smiled her smile as the old man politely lifted his hat, watched as he climbed into the front seat beside the driver.

The car puffed along the yard road, rounded the house and drew up before the veranda. A girl in a white dress came to the screen door, and stood there very quietly staring at them.

She was a pretty, fragile thing, Mrs Carmody noted with a sharp eye to detail, slim, with yellow hair, about fifteen or sixteen, and – the woman's mind tightened – not very friendly.

The woman smiled sweetly. "Hello, Phyllis," she said, "I'm so glad to see you."

"Hello," said Phyllis; and the older woman smiled comfortably at the reluctant greeting. Because – it *had* been a greeting. It was acceptance of a sort.

The woman smiled a thin smile to herself. This simple country girl was going to learn how impossible it was to fight a friendly approach, backed by an iron purpose.

She could see the whole future smoothly fitting in with her wishes. First, to settle down; then to set about throwing Bill and Phyllis together, so that they'd consider marriage a natural and early conclusion to their relationship. And then—

It was night; and she had blown out the lamp in the master bedroom before she thought again of the old man, and the astounding things he had said and done.

She lay in the darkness, nestling into the special comfort of the great bed, frowning. Finally, sleepily, she shrugged. Harmless, the driver had said. Well, he'd better stay that way, the old coot.

Mrs Carmody wakened the following morning to the sounds of movement downstairs. She dressed hurriedly with a sense of having been outmaneuvered on her first day; and that empty feeling became conviction when she saw the old man and Phyllis eating breakfast. There were three other plates set with bowls of cereal; and Mrs

Carmody sank down before one of them in a dead silence. She saw that the girl had a notebook open in front of her; and she clutched at the straw of conversation it offered.

"Doing your homework?" she asked in her friendliest voice.

"No!" said the girl, closing the notebook and getting up from the table.

Mrs Carmody sat very still, fighting the surge of dull color that crept up into her cheeks. No use getting excited, she thought. The thing was, somehow – somehow she had to make friends with this quiet girl.

And besides, there was some information she had to have – about food, about the house, about – money.

Abruptly, breakfast was a meaningless, tasteless act. She got up from her half-finished cereal; in the kitchen she found Phyllis washing the dishes.

"Let me wash," said the woman, "you dry."

She added: "Pretty hands like yours shouldn't be in dish water."

She sent a swift glance at the girl's face, and spoke for the third time: "I'm rather ashamed of myself for getting up so late. I came here to work, not to rest."

"Oh, you'll get used to it," said the girl; and Mrs Carmody smiled her secret smile. The dangerous silence strike was over. She said:

"What about food? Is there any particular store where you buy it? Your mother didn't mention such details in her letter. I—"

She stopped, startled in spite of herself at that mention of the letter. She stood for a moment, hands rigid in the hot water; then forced on:

"Your poor mother! It was such a tired letter she wrote. I cried when I read it."

From under half-closed eyes she saw that the girl's lips were trembling – and she knew her victory. She had a brief blazing exultation at the way every word, every mood of this moment was under her control. She said swiftly:

"We can talk about those details later."

The girl said tearfully: "We have a charge account at Graham's General Store in Agan. You can phone up. He delivers this far."

The woman walked hurriedly into the dining room to get the dishes that were still there, and to hide the irrepressible light of triumph in her eyes. A charge account! The problem of obtaining control of the money had actually made her feel sick, the consciousness that legal steps might be necessary, the conviction that she must first establish herself in the household and in the community.

And here was her stepping-stone: a charge account! Now, if this

Graham's store would only accept her order – what was the girl saying?

"Mrs Carmody, I want to apologize for not answering your question about my notebook at breakfast. You see, the neighbors always want to know what great-grandfather says about them; so, at breakfast, when he's strongest, I ask him questions, and take notes. I pretend to him that I'm going to write a book about his life when I grow up. I couldn't explain all that in front of him, could I?"

"Of course not," said the woman. She thought sharply: So the neighbors were interested in the old man's words about them. They'd be interested and friendly with anyone who kept them supplied with the latest titbits of news. She'd have to keep her ears open, and perhaps keep a notebook herself.

She grew aware that the girl was speaking again: "I've been wanting to tell you, great-grandpa really has the gift of seeing. You won't believe that yet, but—"

The girl's eyes were bright, eager; and the woman knew better than to let such enthusiasm pass.

"Why, of course, I believe it," she said. "I'm not one of these skeptics who won't face facts. All through history there have been people with strange powers; and besides, didn't I see with my own eyes Mr Wainwright step through a solid gate. I—"

Her voice faltered; her own words describing that incredible action brought a vivid return of reality, and she could only finish weakly: "Of course, I believe it."

"What I meant, Mrs Carmody," the girl was saying, "don't be offended if he seems to say something unpleasant. He always thinks he's talking about events that have already happened, and then, of course, there's the way he talks about your sister, if you're a woman, and your brother if you're a man. It's really you he means."

Really you—

The woman's mind spun curiously; and the memory of the words stayed with her after the girl had ridden off to school, even after Graham's accepted her order on behalf of the Wainwright farm with a simple, utterly effective: "Oh, yes, Mrs Carmody, we know about you."

It was not until nearly noon that she went out onto the porch, where the old man was sitting, and asked the question that had been quivering in her mind:

"Mr Wainwright, yesterday you mentioned you had seen my sister in Kempster. W-what did she have to say?"

She waited with a tenseness that startled her; and there was the queer thought that she was being utterly ridiculous. The old man took his long pipe out of his mouth, thoughtfully. He said:

"She was coming out of the courthouse, and—"

"Courthouse!" said Mrs Carmody.

The old man was frowning to himself. "She didn't speak to me, so I cannot say what she was doing there." He finished politely: "Some little case, no doubt. We all have them."

Kent was aware of the car slowing. The driver nodded at a two-story wooden building with a veranda, and said:

"That's the hotel. I'll have to leave you now and do some chores. I'll finish that story for you some other time. Or, if I'm too busy, just ask anyone. The whole district knows all about it."

The following morning the sun peered with dazzling force into his hotel room. Kent walked to the window and stared out over the peaceful village.

For a moment there was not a sound audible. The little spread of trees and houses lay almost dreamily under the blue, blue sky.

Kent thought quietly: He had made no mistake in deciding to spend the rest of the summer here, while, in a leisurely fashion, he carried on negotiations for the sale of the farm his parents had left him. Truth was he had been overworking.

He went downstairs and amazed himself by eating two eggs and four slices of bacon in addition to cereal and toast. From the dining room he walked to the veranda – and there was the ghost sitting in one of the wicker chairs.

Kent stopped short. The tiny beginning of a chill formed at the nape of his spine; then the old man saw him and said:

"Good morning, Mr Kent. I should take it very kind if you would sit down and talk with me. I need cheering up."

It was spoken with an almost intimate pathos; and yet Kent had a sudden sense of being beyond his depth. Somehow the old man's friendliness of the day before had seemed unreal.

Yet here it was again.

He shook himself. After all, part of the explanation at least was simple. Here was an old man – that ghost part was utterly ridiculous, of course – an old man, then, who could foretell the future. Foretell it in such a fashion that, in the case of Mrs Carmody, he, the old man, had actually had the impression that she had been around for months before she arrived.

Apparently, he had had the same impression about Kent. Therefore –

"Good morning, Mr Wainwright!" Kent spoke warmly as he seated himself. "You need cheering up, you say. Who's been depressing you?"

"Oh!" The old man hesitated, his finely lined face twisted into a faint frown. He said finally, slowly. "Perhaps, it is wrong of me to have mentioned it. It is no one's fault, I suppose. The friction of daily life, in this case Mrs Carmody pestering me about what her sister was doing in court."

Kent was silent, astounded. The reference of the old man to the only part of the story that he, Kent, knew, was – shattering. His brain recoiled from the coincidence into a tight, corded layer of thoughts:

Was this – alien – creature a mind reader as well as seer and ghost? An old, worn-out brain that had taken on automaton qualities, and reacted almost entirely to thoughts that trickled in from other minds? Or –

He stopped, almost literally pierced by the thought that came: Or was this reference to Mrs Carmody, this illusion that Mrs Carmody was still looking after him, one of those fantastic, brain-chilling re-enactments of which the history of haunted houses was so gruesomely replete?

Dead souls, murderess and murdered, doomed through all eternity to live over and over again their lives before and during the crime!

But that was impossible. Mrs Carmody was still alive; in a madhouse to be sure, but *alive*.

Kent released carefully the breath of air he had held hard in his lungs for nearly a minute. "Why don't you tell her," he said finally, "to ask her sister about what she was doing in court!"

The thin, gray, old face wrinkled into puzzlement. The old man said with a curious dignity:

"It is more complicated than that, Mr Kent. I have never quite understood the appearance of so many twins in the world during the recent years of my life; and the fact that so many of them are scarcely on speaking terms with each other is additionally puzzling."

He shook his head. "It is all very confusing. For instance, this courtroom appearance of Mrs Carmody's sister – I seem to remember having heard something else about it, but it must have struck me as unimportant at the time, for I cannot rightly recollect the details. It's not a pleasant situation for a harmless old man to handle."

Harmless! Kent's eyes narrowed involuntarily. That was what

people kept saying about – the ghost. First, the driver, Tom; then, according to Tom's story, the girl Phyllis, and now the old man himself.

Harmless, harmless, harmless. Old man, he thought tensely, what about the fact that you drove a woman to murder you? What *is* your purpose? What—

Kent loosened the tight grip his fingers had taken on the arms of the chair. What was the matter with him, letting a thing like this get on his nerves?

He looked up. The sky was as blue as ever; the summer day peaceful, perfect. All was well with the world of reality.

There was silence, a deep, peaceful quiet during which Kent studied that long, aged face from half-closed eyes. The old man's skin was of a normal grayish texture with many, very many criss-cross lines. He had a lean, slightly hawklike nose, and a thin, rather fine mouth.

Handsome, old man; only – that explained nothing, and—

He saw that the old man was rising; he stood for a moment very straight, carefully adjusting his hat on his head; then:

"I must be on my way. It is important, in view of our strained relations, that I do not keep Mrs Carmody waiting for lunch. I shall be seeing you again, Mr Kent."

Kent stood up, a little, fascinated thought in his mind. He had intended to walk over to the farm that had belonged to his parents and introduce himself to the tenants. But that could wait.

Why not go with the – ghost – to the deserted Wainwright place, and –

What?

He considered the question blankly; then his lips tightened. After all, this mysterious business was on his mind. To let it go would be merely to have a distraction at the back of his head, sufficient perhaps to interfere with anything he might attempt. Besides, there was no rush about the business. He was here for a rest and change as much as anything.

He stood there, still not absolutely decided, chilled by a dark miasma of mind stuff that welled up inside him:

Wasn't it perhaps dangerous to accompany a ghost to a hide-out in an isolated, old house?

He pressed the clammy fear out of his system because – it wasn't Mrs Carmody who had been killed. She was out of her head, yes; but the danger was definitely mental, not physical, and—

His mind grew hard, cool. No sudden panic, no totality of

horrendous threats or eerie menaces would actually knock his reason off its base. Therefore—

Kent parted his lips to call after the old man, who was gingerly moving down the wooden walk to the wooden sidewalk. Before he could speak, a deep voice beside him said:

"I noticed you were talking to the ghost, Mr Kent."

Kent turned and faced a great, gross fat man whom he had previously noticed sitting in a little office behind the hotel desk. Three massive chins quivered as the man said importantly:

"My name is Jenkins, sir, proprietor of the Agan Hotel."

His pale, deep-set eyes peered at Kent. "Tom was telling me that you met our greatest local character yesterday. A very strange, uncanny case. Very uncanny."

The old man was farther up the street now, Kent saw, an incredibly lean, sedately moving figure, who vanished abruptly behind a clump of trees. Kent stared after him, his mind still half on the idea of following as soon as he could reasonably break away from this man.

He took another look at the proprietor; and the man said heavily:

"I understand from Tom that he didn't have time to finish the story of what happened at the Wainwright farm. Perhaps I could complete the uncanny tale for you."

It struck Kent that the word "uncanny" must be a favorite with this dark mountain of flesh.

It struck him, too, that he would have to postpone his visit to the ghost farm, or risk offending his host.

Kent frowned and yielded to circumstances. It wasn't actually necessary to trail the old man today. And it might be handy to have all the facts first, before he attempt to solve the mystery. He seated himself after watching the fat man wheeze into a chair. He said:

"Is there any local theory that would explain the" – he hesitated – "uncanny appearance of the ghost. You do insist that he is a ghost, in spite of his substantial appearance."

"Definitely a ghost!" Jenkins grunted weightily. "We buried him, didn't we? And unburied him again a week later to see if he was still there; and he was, dead and cold as stone. Oh, yes, definitely a ghost. What other explanation could there be?"

"I'm not," said Kent carefully, "not exactly – a believer – in ghosts."

The fat man waved the objection aside with a flabby hand. "None of us were, sir, none of us. But facts are facts."

Kent sat silent; then: "A ghost that tells the future. What kind of future? Is it all as vague as that statement of his to Mrs Carmody about her sister coming out of the courthouse?"

Sagging flesh shook as Mr Jenkins cleared his throat. "Mostly local events of little importance, but which would interest an old man who lived here all his life."

"Has he said anything about the war?"

"He talks as if it's over, and therefore acts as if the least said the better." Mr Jenkins laughed a great husky, tolerant laugh. "His point about the war is amazement that prices continue to hold up. It confuses him. And it's no use keeping after him, because talking tires him easily, and he gets a persecuted look. He did say something about American armies landing in northern France, but" – he shrugged – "we all know that's going to happen, anyway."

Kent nodded. "This Mrs. Carmody – she arrived when?"

"In 1933, nearly nine years ago."

"And Mr Wainwright has been dead five years?"

The fat man settled himself deeper into his chair. "I shall be glad," he said pompously, "to tell you the rest of the story in an orderly fashion. I shall omit the first few months after her arrival, as they contained very little of importance—"

The woman came exultantly out of the Wholesale Marketing Co. She felt a renewal of the glow that had suffused her when she first discovered this firm in Kempster two months before.

Four chickens and three dozen eggs – four dollars cash.

Cash!

The glow inside her dimmed. She frowned darkly. It was no use fooling herself; now that the harvesting season was only a week away, this makeshift method of obtaining money out of the farm couldn't go on— Her mind flashed to the bank book she had discovered in the house, with its tremendous information that the Wainwrights had eleven thousand seven hundred thirty-four dollars and fifty-one cents in the Kempster Bank.

An incredible fortune, so close yet so far away—

She stood very still in front of the bank finally, briefly paralyzed by a thought dark as night. If she went in – in minutes she'd know the worst.

This time it wouldn't be an old, old man and a young girl she'd be facing. It would be—

The banker was a dapper little fellow with horn-rimmed glasses, behind which sparkled a large pair of gray eyes.

"Ah, yes, Mrs Carmody!" The man rubbed his fingers together. "So it finally occurred to you to come and see me."

He chuckled. "Well, well, we can fix everything; don't worry. I think between us we can manage to look after the Wainwright farm to the satisfaction of the community and the court, eh?

Court! The word caught the woman in the middle of a long, ascending surge of triumph. So this was it. This was what the old man had prophesied. And it was good, not bad.

She felt a brief, ferocious rage at the old fool for having frightened her so badly – but the banker was speaking again:

"I understand you have a letter from your sister-in-law, asking you to look after Phyllis and the farm. It is possible such letter is not absolutely necessary, as you are the only relative, but in lieu of a will it will constitute a definite authorization on the basis of which the courts can appoint you executrix."

The woman sat very still, almost frozen by the words. Somehow, while she had always felt that she would in a crisis produce the letter she had forged, now that the terrible moment was there—

She felt herself fumbling in her purse, and there was the sound of her voice mumbling some doubt about the letter still being around. But she knew better.

She brought it out, took it blindly from the blank envelope where she had carefully placed it, handed it toward the smooth, reaching fingers – and waited her doom.

As he read, the man spoke half to himself, half to her: "Hm-m-m, she offers you twenty-five dollars a month over and above expenses—"

The woman quivered in every muscle of her thick body. The incredibly violent thought came that she must have been mad to put such a thing in the letter. She said hurriedly: "Forget about the money. I'm not here to—"

"I was just going to say," interrupted the banker, "that it seems an inadequate wage. For a farm as large and wealthy as that of the Wainwrights', there is no reason why the manager should not receive fifty dollars, at least, and that is the sum I shall petition the judge for."

He added: "The local magistrate is having a summer sitting this morning just down the street, and if you'll step over there with me we can have this all settled shortly."

He finished: "By the way, he's always interested in the latest predictions of old Mr Wainwright."

"I know them all!" the woman gulped.

She allowed herself, a little later, to be shepherded onto the sidewalk. A brilliant, late July sun was pouring down on the pavement. Slowly, it warmed the chill out of her veins.

It was three years later, three undisturbed years. The woman stopped short in the task of running the carpet sweeper over the living-room carpet, and stood frowning. Just what had brought the thought into her mind, she couldn't remember, but—

Had she seen the old man, as she came out of the courthouse that July day three years before, when the world had been handed to her without a struggle.

The old man had predicted that moment. That meant, in some way, he must have seen it. Had the picture come in the form of a vision? Or as a result of some contact in his mind across the months? Had he in short been physically present; and the scene had flashed back through some obscure connection across time?

She couldn't remember having seen him. Try as she would, nothing came to her from that moment but a sort of blurred, enormous contentment.

The old man, of course, thought he'd been there. The old fool believed that everything he ever spoke about was memory of his past. What a dim, senile world that past must be.

It must spread before his mind like a road over which shifting tendrils of fog drifted, now thick and impenetrable, now thin and bright with flashing rays of sunlight – and pictures.

Pictures of events.

Across the room from her she was vaguely aware of the old man stirring in his chair. He spoke:

"Seems like hardly yesterday that Phyllis and that Couzens boy got married. And yet it's—"

He paused; he said politely: "When was that, Pearl? My memory isn't as good as it was, and—"

The words didn't actually penetrate the woman. But her gaze, in its idle turning, fastened on plump Pearl – and stopped. The girl sat rigid on the living-room couch, where she had been sprawling. Her round, baby eyes were wide.

"Ma!" she shrilled. "Did you hear that? Grandpa's talking like Phyllis and Charlie Couzens are married."

There was a thick, muffled sound of somebody half choking. With a gulp the woman realized that it was she who had made the sound. Gasping, she whirled on the old man and loomed over him, a big, tight-lipped creature, with hard blue eyes.

For a moment, her dismay was so all-consuming that words wouldn't come. The immensity of the catastrophe implied by the old man's statement scarcely left room for thought. But—

Marriage!

And she had actually thought smugly that Bill and Phyllis – Why, Bill had told her and—

Marriage! To the son of the neighboring farmer. Automatic end to her security. She had nearly a thousand dollars, but how long would that last, once the income itself stopped?

Sharp pain of fear released the explosion that, momentarily, had been dammed up by the sheer fury of her thoughts:

"You old fool, you!" she raged. "So you've been sitting here all these years while I've been looking after you, scheming against me and mine. A trick, that's what it is. Think you're clever, eh, using your gift to—"

It was the way the old man was shrinking that brought brief, vivid awareness to the woman of the danger of such an outburst after so many years of smiling friendliness. She heard the old man say:

"I don't understand, Mrs Carmody. What's the matter?"

"Did you say it?" She couldn't have stopped the words to save her soul.

"Did I say what?"

"About Phyllis and that Couzens boy—"

"Oh, them!" He seemed to forget that she was there above him. A benign smile crept into his face. He said at last quietly: "It seems like hardly yesterday that they were married—"

For a second time he became aware of the dark, forbidding expression of the woman who towered above him.

"Anything wrong?" he gasped. "Has something happened to Phyllis and her husband?"

With a horrible effort the woman caught hold of herself. Her eyes blazed at him with a slate-blue intensity.

"I don't want you to talk about them, do you understand? Not a word. I don't want to hear a word about them."

The old man stirred, his face creasing into a myriad extra lines of bewilderment. "Why, certainly, Mrs Carmody, if you wish, but my own great-granddaughter—"

He subsided weakly as the woman whipped on Pearl: "If you mention one word of this to Phyllis, I'll . . . you know what I'll do to you."

"Oh, sure, ma," Pearl said. "You can trust me, ma."

The woman turned away, shaking. For years there had been a dim plan in the back of her mind, to cover just such a possibility as Phyllis wanting to marry someone else.

She twisted her face with distaste and half fear, and brought the ugly thing out of the dark brain corridor where she had kept it hidden.

Her fingers kept trembling as she worked. Once she saw herself in the mirror over the sink – and started back in dismay at the distorted countenance that reflected there.

That steadied her. But the fear stayed, sick surge after sick surge of it. A woman, forty-five, without income, in the depths of the depression. There was Federal relief, of course, but they wouldn't give that to her till the money was gone. There was old-age pension – twenty-five years away.

She drew a deep breath. Actually, those were meaningless things, utter defeats. Actually, there was only her desperate plan – and that required the fullest co-operation from Bill.

She studied Bill when he came in from the field at lunch. There had been a quietness in him this last year or so that had puzzled her. As if, at twenty, he had suddenly grown up.

He looked like a man; he was strongly built, of medium height with lines of dark passion in his rather heavy face.

That was good, that passion; undoubtedly, he had inherited some of her own troubled ambition – and there was the fact that he had been caught stealing just before they left the city, and released with a warning.

She hadn't blamed him then, felt only his bitter fury against a world that lashed out so cruelly against boys ruthlessly deprived by fate of spending money.

That was all over, of course. For two years he had been a steady, quiet worker, pulling his full share with the other hired men. Nevertheless—

To get Phyllis, that earlier, harder training would surely rise up once more – and win for all of them.

Slyly, she watched as, out of the corner of his eyes, he took one of his long, measured glances at Phyllis, where she sat across the table slantwise from him. For more than a year now, the woman had observed him look at Phyllis like that – and besides she had asked him, and—

Surely, a young man of twenty would fight to get the girl he loved. Fight unscrupulously. The only thing was—

How did a mother tell her son the particular grim plan that was in her mind? Did she . . . she just tell him?

After lunch, while Phyllis and Pearl were washing the dishes, the woman softly followed Bill up to his room. And, actually, it was easier than she had thought.

He lay for a while, after she had finished, staring at the ceiling; his heavy face was quiet almost placid. Finally:

"So the idea is that this evening you take Pearl in to Kempster to a movie; the old man, of course, will sleep like a log. But after Phyllis goes to bed at her usual time, I go into her room – and then she'll have to marry me."

It was so baldly put that the woman shrank, as if a mirror had been held up to her; and the image was an incredibly evil, ravaged thing. The cool voice went on:

"If I do this it means we'll be able to stay on the farm, is that right?"

She nodded, because no words would come. Then, not daring to stay a moment longer, she turned and left the room.

Slowly, the black mood of that interview passed. It was about three o'clock in the afternoon when she came out into the veranda; and the old man looked up from his chair, and said:

"Terrible thing," he said, "your sister hanged. They told me at the hotel. Hanged. Terrible, terrible; you've been right to have nothing to do with her."

He seemed to forget her, simply sat there staring into space.

The whole thing was utterly unreal, and, after a moment, quite unthinkably fantastic. The woman stared at him with a sudden, calm, grim understanding of the faint smile that was creeping back into his face, a serene smile.

So that was his plan, she thought coolly. The mischievous old scoundrel intended that Phyllis should not marry Bill. Therefore, knowing his own reputation for prophecy, he had cleverly told her that Phyllis and Charlie Couzens—

That was his purpose. And now he was trying to scare her into doing nothing about it. Hanging indeed. She smiled, her thick face taut with inward anger.

He was clever – but not clever enough.

In the theater she had a curious sense of chattering voices and flickering lights. Too much meaningless talk, too much light.

Her eyes hurt and, afterward, when they came out onto the pale dimness of Kempster's main street, the difference – the greater darkness – was soothing.

She must have said, "Pearl, let's go in and have a banana split."

She must have said that or agreed to it because after a while they were sitting at a little table; and the ice cream was cold as it went into her mouth; and there was a taste of banana.

Her mind held only a variation of one tense thought: If she and Bill could put this over, the world was won. Nothing thereafter could ever damage them to the same dreadful degree as this could.

"Aw, gee, ma, I'm sleepy. It's half past eleven."

The woman came to reality with a start. She looked at her watch; and it was true. "Goodness gracious!" she exclaimed with artifical amazement. "I didn't realize—"

The moon was shining, and the horse anxious to get home. Coming down the great hill, she could see no light anywhere in the house. The buildings loomed silent in the moonlit darkness, like great semiform-less shapes against the transparent background of the land.

She left Pearl to unhitch the animal and, trembling, went into the house. There was a lamp in the kitchen turned very low. She turned it into brightness, but the light didn't seem to help her feet on the stairs. She kept stumbling, but she reached the top, reached Bill's door. Ever so softly, she knocked.

No answer.

She opened the door. The pale, yellow light of the lamp poured onto the empty bed – and it was only the sound of Pearl coming into the kitchen downstairs that made her close hastily the door of Bill's room. Pearl came up, yawning, and disappeared instantly into her own room.

The fat man stopped abruptly as a distant telephone thrummed. He rolled apologetically out of his seat. "I'll be right back," he said.

"One question," Kent asked hastily. "What about this prophecy of hanging? I thought Mrs Carmody was in a madhouse, very much alive."

"She is." The vast bulk of the hotel proprietor filled the door. "We figured out that the old man was definitely trying to put something over."

The minutes dragged. Kent took his note-book and wrote with the elaborate ornateness of vague purpose.

An old man
Who can tell the future
Who caused a woman to murder him
But still lives
Who walks through solid objects
Who reads minds (possibly)

He sat thoughtful, then added to the list:

 A senile ghost

For long minutes he stared at the combination. Finally he laughed ruefully – and simultaneously grew aware of the clicking of pool balls inside.

He stood up, peered through the door – and smiled sardonically as he saw that fat Jenkins was playing a game of snooker with a chunky man of his own age.

Kent shrugged; and, turning, went down the steps. It was obvious that he would have to get the rest of this story piecemeal, here and there over the countryside: obvious, too, that he'd better write Miss Kincaid to send him some books on ghosts and seers, the folklore as well as anything remotely scientific.

He'd need everything he could lay his hands on if he was going to solve the mystery of – the ghost!

The books kept trickling in over a period of four weeks. Miss Kincaid sent ghost stories, compilations of true ghost tales, four books on psychic phenomena, a history of magic, a treatise on astrology and kindred arts, the works of Charles Fort; and, finally, three thin volumes by one J. W. Dunne, on the subject of time.

Kent sat on the veranda in the early morning just after the arrival of the mail that had brought them, and read the three books in one sitting, with an excitement that gathered at every page.

He got up at last, shaky, and half convinced that he had the tremendous answer; and yet – there were things to clear up—

An hour later he was lying in a little wooded dell that overlooked the house and yard, waiting. It was almost time for the – ghost – to come out, if he intended to take his morning walk—

At noon Kent returned to the hotel, thinking tensely: The old man must have gone somewhere else today . . . somewhere else—

His mind nearly came out of his head from contemplating that somewhere else. The following morning, eight o'clock found him in his little copse, waiting. Again, the old man failed to appear.

The third morning, Kent's luck was better. Dark, threatening clouds rode the sky as he watched the thin, tall figure move from behind the house and slowly approach the gate. The old man came across the field; Kent showed himself in plenty of time, striding along out of the bush as if he, too, was out for a walk.

"Hello, there, Mr Wainwright," he said.

The old man came closer without answering, and Kent saw that the man was peering at him curiously. The old man stopped.

"Do I know you, young sir?" he asked politely.

For the barest moment Kent was thrown mentally off balance; and then—

"Good heavens!" he thought excitedly, "even this fits. It *fits*. There had to be a time when he met me."

Aloud, he explained patiently that he was the son of Angus Kent, and that he had come back to the district for a visit. When he had finished the old man said:

"I shall be glad to come to the hotel and talk about your father. It is a pleasure to have met you."

He walked off. The moment he was out of sight, Kent started toward the gate. The first drops of rain fell as he crawled laboriously under the wire. He stood just inside the gate, hesitant. It was important that he get inside the house before the old man, driven by the rain, returned.

The question was, would he have time?

He hurried toward the buildings, glancing over his shoulders every few seconds, expecting to see that long form come into sight.

The house stood quietly under the soft, glinting rain. The weight of the neglected years lay heavily on its wooden walls. A burst of rain whipped into Kent's face, and then thudded dully on the wood as he ducked into the shelter of the building.

He stood there waiting for the blast to die down. But, as the seconds passed, and there was no abatement, he peered around the corner and saw the veranda.

He reached the safety it offered; and then, more leisurely, investigated the two boarded windows and the boarded door. They were solid, and, though he had expected it, the reality brought a stab of disappointment.

Getting inside was going to be a tough job.

The rain became a thin splatter; and he went hastily down the steps, and saw that there was an open balcony on the second floor. It was hard work climbing, but the effort proved its worth.

A wide, loose board on one of the two balcony windows came off with a jerk, and made it easy to tear off the rest. Beyond was a window, locked.

Kent did not hesitate. He raised one of the boards and, with a single sharp blow, struck. The glass shattered with a curious, empty tinkling sound.

He was inside. The room was empty, dusty, dark, unfurnished. It led out onto a long, empty hallway, and a line of empty, dark rooms.

Downstairs it was the same; empty rooms, unlived in. The basement was dark, a cemented hole. He fumbled around it hurriedly, lighting matches; and then hurriedly went back to the ground floor. There were some cracks in the boards that covered the downstairs windows and, after locating the likeliest ones, he stationed himself at the one that faced the gate – and waited.

It didn't take long.

The old man came through the gate, toward the house. Kent shifted to a window at the side of the house, then at the back; and each time the old man came into view after a moment.

Kent raced to the crack he had selected in the veranda window, expecting to see the old man come into sight.

Ten minutes passed; and that tall figure had still to come around the back corner of the house. Slowly, Kent went upstairs, and out onto the balcony.

It was simple hammering the boards back into position, not so simple easing down to the ground.

But he had his fact. Somewhere at the rear of the house the ghost vanished. The problem was – how to prevent that disappearance.

How did one trap the kind of – ghost – that the long-dead Mr Wainwright had become?

It was the next day, nearly noon. Kent lay well into the field south of the farmhouse. Earlier, he had watched the old man emerge from the gate, and go past his hiding place along the valley. Now—

Through his field glasses Kent watched the long, straight form coming toward him, toward the farm.

Kent emerged casually from the wood and walked along as if he had not seen the other. He was wondering just what his verbal approach should be when the old man hailed him:

"Hello there, Mr Kent. Out for a walk?"

Kent turned and waited for the aged man to come up to him. He said: "I was just going to go in to Mrs Carmody, and ask for a drink of water, before heading on to the hotel. If you don't mind, I'll walk with you."

"Not at all, sir," said the old man.

They walked along, Kent consciously more erect, as he tried to match that superb straightness of body. His mind was seething. What *would* happen at the gate? Somewhere along here the old man's body would become less substantial, but—

He couldn't hold the thought. Besides, he'd better start laying his groundwork. He said tautly:

"The farm looks rather deserted from here, does it not, Mr Wainwright?"

Amazingly, the old man gulped; he said almost swiftly: "Have you noticed it, too, Mr Kent? I have long thought it an illusion on my part, and I have felt rather uneasy about my vision. I have found that the peculiar desolated appearance vanishes as soon as I pass through the gate."

So it was the gate where the change began – He jerked his soaring thought back to earth, listened as the old man said in evident relief:

"I am glad that we both share this illusion, Mr Kent. It has had me worried."

Kent hesitated, and then very carefully took his field glasses out of their case; and handed them to the old man.

"Try a look through these," he said casually. "Perhaps they will help to break the illusion."

The moment he had given the instrument over, compunction came, a hard, bright pity for the incredible situation he was forcing.

Compunction passed; pity yielded to an almost desperate curiosity. From narrowed eyes he stared at that lined face as the man's thin, bony hands held the glasses up to his face and slowly adjusted the lens.

There was a harsh gasp; and Kent, who had expected it, leaped forward and caught the glasses as they fell toward the ground.

"Why," the old man was quavering, "it's impossible. Windows boarded up, and" – a wild suspicion leaped into his eyes – "has Mrs Carmody gone so swiftly?"

"What's wrong, sir?" Kent said, and felt like a villain. But – he *couldn't* let this go now.

The old man was shaking his head. "I must be mad. My eyes . . . my mind . . . not what they used to be—"

"Let's go over," Kent suggested. "I'll get my drink and we'll see what's wrong."

It was important that the old man retain in his wandering mind that he had a companion. The patriarch straightened, said quietly:

"By all means, you shall have your drink, Mr Kent."

Kent had a sick feeling as he walked beside that tall form across the road to the gate, the empty feeling that he had meddled in human tragedy.

He watched, almost ill with his victory, as the trembling non-agenarian fumbled futilely with the padlocked gate.

He thought, his mind as tight as a drum: For perhaps the first time since this strange, strange phenomena had started, the old man had failed to walk *through* the gate.

"I don't understand it!" the old man said. 'This gate locked – why, this very morning, I—'

Kent had been unwinding the wire that held the large gate. "Let's go in here," he said gently.

The dismay of the old man was so pitiful it was dreadful. He stopped and peered at the weeds. Incredulously, he felt the black old wood that was nailed, board on board of it, over one of the windows. His high shoulders began to sag. A haunted expression crept into his face. Paradoxically, he looked suddenly *old*.

He climbed the faded veranda steps with the weariness of un-utterable age. And then—

The flashing, terrible realization of the truth struck at Kent in that last instant, as the old man stepped timidly, almost blindly, toward the nailed door.

"Wait!" he shrilled. "Wait!"

His piercing voice died. Where the old man had been was – nothingness.

A thin wind howled with brief mournfulness around the house, rattling the eaves.

He stood alone on that faded, long-unused veranda. Alone with the comprehension that had, in one dreadful kaleidoscope of mind picture, suddenly cleared up – everything.

And, dominating everything else, was the dreadful fear that he would be too late.

He was running, his breath coming in great gulps. A tiny wind caught the dust that his shoes kicked up from the soft road-bed, and whipped it in little, unpleasant gusts around his nostrils.

The vague thought came that it was lucky he had done so much walking the past month; for the exercise had added just enough strength to bring the long, long mile and a half to the hotel within his powers—

A tangy, unpleasant taste of salt was in his mouth as he staggered up the steps. Inside, he was blurrily aware of the man, Tom, staring at him across the counter. Kent gasped:

"I'll give you five dollars if you can pack my things and get me to Kempster in time to catch the twelve-o'clock train. And tell me how to get to the insane asylum at Peerton. For Heaven's sake, make it fast."

The man goggled. "I had the maid pack your things right after breakfast, Mr Kent. Don't you remember, this is 17 August."

Kent glared at him with a blank horror. *That* prophecy come true. Then what about the other, more awful one—

On the way to Kempster he was vaguely aware of the driver speaking, something about Peerton being a large town, and he'd be able to get a taxi at the station—

From the taxi the asylum showed as a series of long, white buildings, a green, tree-filled inclosure, surrounded by a high iron fence. He was led through an endless, quiet corridor; his mind kept straining past the sedate, white-clothed woman ahead of him. Couldn't she realize this was life and death?

The doctor sat in a little, bright cozy room. He stood up politely as Kent entered, but Kent waited only for the woman to close the door as she went out.

"Sir, you have a woman here named Mrs Carmody." He paused a fraction of a second to let the name sink in, then rushed on: "Never mind if you can't remember her name. It's true."

The fine, strong face of the white-haired doctor cleared. "I remember the case."

"Look!" said Kent desperately. "I've just found out the truth about that whole affair; and this is what you've got to do – at once:

"Take me to the woman, and I'll assure her, and you assure her, that she has been found innocent, and will be freed. Do you understand?"

"I think," said the doctor quietly, "that you had better begin at the beginning."

Kent had a frantic sense of walls rising up between him and his purpose. "For Heaven's sake, sir, believe me, there's no time. I don't know just how it is supposed to happen, but the prediction that she would be hanged can only come true in—"

"Now, Mr Kent, I would appreciate—"

"Don't you understand?" Kent yelled. "If that prophecy is not to be fulfilled, you must act. I tell you I have information that will release this woman. And, therefore, *the next few minutes* are the vital ones."

He stopped because the man was frowning at him. The doctor said: "Really, Mr Kent, you will have to calm down. I am sure everything will be all right."

The strained wonder came to Kent, if all sane, be-calm people seemed as maddening as this quiet-spoken doctor.

He thought shakily: "He'd better be careful or they'd be keeping him in here with the rest of the lunatics."

He began to speak, to tell what he'd heard and seen and done. The man kept interrupting him with incisive questions; and, after a while, it came to Kent, that he would actually have to begin at the beginning to fill in the gaps of this fellow's knowledge.

He stopped, sat shaky for a moment, struggling to clear his brain, and then with a tense quietness, began again.

He found himself, as the minutes dragged, listening to his own voice. Every time his words speeded up, or rose in crescendo, he would deliberately slow down and articulate every syllable. He reached the point where the Dunne books came into the story, and—

His mind paused in a wild dismay: Good heavens, would he have to explain the Dunne theory of time with its emphasis on time as a state of mind. The rest was unimportant, but that part—

He grew aware that the doctor was speaking, saying: "I've read several volumes by Mr Dunne. I'm afraid I cannot accept his theory of multi-dimensional time. I—"

"Listen," said Kent in a tight voice, "picture an old man in his dotage. It's a queer, incoherent mind-world he lives in; strange, frequently unassociated ideas are the normal condition; memory, particularly memory, is unutterably mixed up. And it is in that confused environment that somehow *once* a variation of the Dunne phenomena operated.

"An old man whose time sense has been distorted by the ravages of senility, an old man who walks as easily into the future as you and I walk into the next room."

"*What!*"

The doctor was on his feet, pacing the rugged floor. He stared at Kent finally.

"Mr Kent, this a most extraordinary idea. But still I fail to see why Mrs Carmody—"

Kent groaned, then with a terrible effort pulled himself together. "Do you remember the murder scene?"

"Vaguely. A domestic tragedy, I believe."

"Listen. Mrs Carmody woke up the morning after she thought she'd made everything right for herself and her family, and found a note on her dressing table. It had been lying there all night, and it was from her son, Bill.

"In it, he said he couldn't go through with her plan. Besides, he didn't like the farm, so he was going immediately to the city – and in fact he walked to Kempster and caught the train while she was in the theater.

"Among other things, he said in his note that a few days before the old man had acted surprised at seeing him, Bill, still around. The old man talked as if he thought Bill had gone to the city—"

That was what kept stabbing into the woman's mind. The old man, the interfering old man—

He had, in effect, told Bill that he, Bill, had gone to the city, and so in a crisis Bill had gone.

Gone, gone, gone – and all hope with him. Phyllis would marry Charlie Couzens; and what then? What would become of a poor, miserable woman of forty-five?

The old man, she thought, as she went down the stairs from her room, the old man planned it all. Fiendish old man! First, telling Bill about the city, then suggesting who Phyllis was to marry, then trying to scare *her* with that hanging—

Hanging—

The woman stopped short in the downstairs hallway, her blue eyes stark, a strange, burning sensation in her brain. Why—

If all the rest came true, then—*hanging!*

Her mind whirled madly. She crouched for a moment like an animal at bay, cunning in her eyes. They couldn't hang you unless you murdered someone, and—

She'd see that she didn't pull anything so stupid.

She couldn't remember eating breakfast. But there was a memory of her voice asking monotonously:

"Where's Mr Wainwright?"

"He's gone for a walk, ma. Hey, ma, are you ill?"

Ill! Who asked a silly question like that. It was the old man who'd be ill when she got through with him.

There was a memory, too, of washing the dishes, but after that a strange, dark gap, a living, evil night flooding her mind . . . gone . . . hope . . . Bill . . . damned old man—

She was standing at the screen door for the hundredth time, peering malignantly at the corner of the house where the old man would come into sight – when it happened.

There was the screen door and the deserted veranda. That was one instant. The next, the old man materialized out of the thin air two feet away. He opened the screen door, and then half fell against the door, and slowly crumbled to the ground, writhing, as the woman screamed at him, meaningless words—

* * *

"That was her story," Kent said wearily, "that the old man simply fell dead. But the doctor who came testified that Mr Wainwright died of choking, and besides, in her hysteria, Mrs Carmody told everything about herself, and the various facts taken together combined to discredit her story."

Kent paused, then finished in a queer voice: "It is medically recognized, I believe, that very old people can choke themselves to death by swallowing saliva the wrong way, or by a paralysis of the throat produced by shock—"

"Shock!" The doctor sank back into his chair from which he had half risen. "Man!" he gasped, "are you trying to tell me that your interference with the old man that day caused his abrupt appearance before Mrs Carmody, and that it was the shock of what he had himself gone through that—"

"I'm trying to tell you," said Kent, "that we've got minutes to prevent this woman from hanging herself. It could only happen if she did do it with her own hands; and it could only happen today, for if we can get there in time to tell her, why, she'll have no incentive. Will you come . . . for Heaven's sake, man—"

The doctor said: "But the prophecy. If this old man actually had this incredible power, how can we hope to circumvent the inevitable?"

"Look!" said Kent, "I influenced the past by an act from the future. Surely, I can change the future by – *but come along!*"

He couldn't take his eyes off the woman. She sat there in her bright little room, and she was still smiling, as she had been when they first came in, a little more uncertainly now, as the doctor talked.

"You mean," she said finally, "that I am to be freed, that you're going to write my children, and they'll come and get me."

"Absolutely!" Kent spoke heartily, but with just the faintest bit of puzzlement in his voice. "I understand your son, Bill, is working in a machine factory, and that he's married now, and that your daughter is a stenographer for the same company."

"Yes, that's true." She spoke quietly—

Afterward, while the doctor's maid was serving Kent a warmed-up lunch, he said frowningly: "I can't understand it. I ought to feel that everything is cleared up. Her children have small jobs, the girl Phyllis is married to that Couzens chap, and is living in his family home. As for Mrs Carmody – and this is what gets me – I had no impression that she was in danger of hanging herself. She was cheerful; she had her room fixed with dozens of little fancily sewed things, and—"

The doctor said: "The records show that she's been no trouble while she's been here. She's been granted special privileges; she does a lot of sewing – What's the matter?"

Kent wondered grimly if he looked as wild as the thought that had surged into his mind. "Doctor!" he gasped, "there's a psychological angle here that I forgot completely."

He was on his feet. "Doctor, we've got to get to that woman again, tell her she can stay here, tell her—"

There was the sound of a door opening violently, then running footsteps. A man in uniform burst in.

"Doctor, there's a woman just hanged herself, a Mrs Carmody. She cut her dress into strips and using the light fixture—"

They had already cut her down when Kent and the doctor arrived. She lay stiff in death, a dark, heavily built woman. A faint smile was fixed on her rigid lips— Kent was aware of the doctor whispering to him:

"No one's to blame, of course. How could we sane people remember that the greatest obsession in her life was security, and that here in this asylum was that security she craved."

Kent scarcely heard. He felt curiously cold; the room seemed remote. In his mind's eye he could see the Wainwright house, empty, nailed-up; and yet for years an old, old man would come out of it and wander over the land before he, too, sank forever into the death that had long ago struck him down.

The time would come when the – ghost – would walk no more.

The Party

William F. Nolan

Location: Manhattan Apartment, New York.
Time: April, 1967.
Eyewitness Description: *"The place was pretty wild: ivory tables with serpent legs; tall, figured screens with chain-mail warriors cavorting across them; lamps with jewel— eyed dragons looped at the base. And, at the far end of the room, an immense bronze gong suspended between a pair of demon-faced swordsmen. A thing to wake the dead . . ."*
Author: William Francis Nolan (1928–) is a former racing driver, commercial artist and cartoonist, and now multi-award winning author: having twice won the Edgar Allan Poe Special Award, been voted "Living Legend in Dark Fantasy" by the International Horror Guild and "Author Emeritus" by the SF Writers of America. He became famous with *Logan's Run* (1967), about a future world where a youth culture has taken over and orders the death of all those over 21 to avoid over-population, which inspired a movie, TV series and two sequels, *Logan's World* (1977) and *Logan's Search* (1980). Nolan has written a number of contemporary ghost stories, though none have received higher praise than "The Party", published by *Playboy* in April 1967. The following year, *Newsweek* named the story as one of the seven most effective horror tales of the century ("The Monkey's Paw" by W. W. Jacobs and Saki's "The Open Window" were two of the others). The story was bought for the American TV series, *Darkroom*, but the programme was cancelled before it could be filmed. A highly visual tale with mounting tension, this decision is *almost* as puzzling as the situation in which partygoer David Ashland finds himself.

Ashland frowned, trying to concentrate in the warm emptiness of the thickly carpeted lobby. Obviously, he had pressed the elevator button, because he was alone here and the elevator was blinking its way down to him, summoned from an upper floor. It arrived with an efficient hiss, the bronze doors clicked open, and he stepped in, thinking *blackout. I had a mental blackout.*

First the double vision. Now this. It was getting worse. Just where the hell was he? Must be a party, he told himself. Sure. Someone he'd met, whose name was missing along with the rest of it, had invited him to a party. He had an apartment number in his head: 9E. That much he retained. A number – nothing else.

On the way up, in the soundless cage of the elevator, David Ashland reviewed the day. The usual morning routine: work, then lunch with his new secretary. A swinger – but she liked her booze; put away three martinis to his two. Back to the office. More work. A drink in the afternoon with a writer. ("Beefeater. No rocks. Very dry.") Dinner at the new Italian joint on West Forty-Eighth with Linda. Lovely Linda. Expensive girl. Lovely as hell, but expensive. More drinks, then – nothing. Blackout.

The doc had warned him about the hard stuff, but what else can you do in New York? The pressures get to you, so you drink. Everybody drinks. And every night, somewhere in town, there's a party, with contacts (and girls) to be made . . .

The elevator stopped, opened its doors. Ashland stepped out, uncertainly, into the hall. The softly lit passageway was long, empty, silent. No, not silent. Ashland heard the familiar voice of a party: the shifting hive hum of cocktail conversation, dim, high laughter, the sharp chatter of ice against glass, a background wash of modern jazz . . . All quite familiar. And always the same.

He walked to 9E. Featureless apartment door. White. Brass button housing. Gold numbers. No clues here. Sighing, he thumbed the buzzer and waited nervously.

A smiling fat man with bad teeth opened the door. He was holding a half-filled drink in one hand. Ashland didn't know him.

"C'mon in fella," he said. "Join the party."

Ashland squinted into blue-swirled tobacco smoke, adjusting his eyes to the dim interior. The rising-falling sea tide of voices seemed to envelop him.

"Grab a drink, fella," said the fat man. "Looks like you need one!"

Ashland aimed for the bar in one corner of the crowded apartment. He *did* need a drink. Maybe a drink would clear his head, let him get this all straight. Thus far, he had not recognized any of the faces in the smoke-hazed room.

At the self-service bar a thin, turkey-necked woman wearing paste jewelry was intently mixing a black Russian. "Got to be exceedingly careful with these," she said to Ashland, eyes still on the mixture. "Too much vodka craps them up."

Ashland nodded. "The host arrived?" *I'll know him, I'm sure.*

"Due later – or sooner. Sooner – or later. You know, I once spilled three black Russians on the same man over a thirty-day period. First on the man's sleeve, then on his back, then on his lap. Each time his suit was a sticky, gummy mess. My psychiatrist told me that I did it unconsciously, because of a neurotic hatred of this particular man. He looked like my father."

"The psychiatrist?"

"No, the man I spilled the black Russians on." She held up the tall drink, sipped at it. "Ahhh . . . still too weak."

Ashland probed the room for a face he knew, but these people were all strangers.

He turned to find the turkey-necked woman staring at him.

"Nice apartment," he said mechanically.

"Stinks. I detest pseudo-Chinese decor in Manhattan brownstones." She moved off, not looking back at Ashland.

He mixed himself a straight Scotch, running his gaze around the apartment. The place *was* pretty wild: ivory tables with serpent legs; tall, figured screens with chain-mail warriors cavorting across them; heavy brocade drapes in stitched silver; lamps with jewel-eyed dragons looped at the base. And, at the far end of the room, an immense bronze gong suspended between a pair of demon-faced swordsmen. Ashland studied the gong. A thing to wake the dead, he thought. Great for hangovers in the morning.

"Just get here?" a girl asked him. She was red-haired, full-breasted, in her late twenties. Attractive. Damned attractive. Ashland smiled warmly at her.

"That's right," he said, "I just arrived." He tasted the Scotch; it was flat, watery. "Whose place is this?"

The girl peered at him above her cocktail glass. "Don't you know who invited you?"

Ashland was embarrassed. "Frankly, no. That's why I—"

"My name's Viv. For Vivian. I drink. What do you do? Besides drink?"

"I produce. I'm in television."

"Well, *I'm* in a dancing mood. Shall we?"

"Nobody's dancing," protested Ashland. "We'd look – foolish."

The jazz suddenly seemed louder. Overhead speakers were sending out a thudding drum solo behind muted strings. The girl's body rippled to the sounds.

"Never be afraid to do anything foolish," she told him. "That's the secret of survival." Her fingers beckoned him. "C'mon . . ."

"No, really – not right now. Maybe later."

"Then I'll dance alone."

She spun into the crowd, her long red dress whirling. The other partygoers ignored her. Ashland emptied the watery Scotch and fixed himself another. He loosened his tie, popping the collar button. *Damn!*

"I train worms."

Ashland turned to a florid-faced little man with bulging, feverish eyes. "I heard you say you were in TV," the little man said. "Ever use any trained worms on your show?"

"No . . . no, I haven't."

"I breed 'em, train 'em. I teach a worm to run a maze. Then I grind him up and feed him to a dumb, untrained worm. Know what happens? The dumb worm can run the maze! But only for twenty-four hours. Then he forgets – unless I keep him on a trained-worm diet. I defy you to tell me that isn't fascinating!"

"It is, indeed." Ashland nodded and moved away from the bar. The feverish little man smiled after him, toasting his departure with a raised glass. Ashland found himself sweating.

Who was his host? Who had invited him? He knew most of the Village crowd, but had spotted none of them here . . .

A dark, doll-like girl asked him for a light. He fumbled out some matches.

"Thanks," she said, exhaling blue smoke into blue smoke. "Saw that worm guy talking to you. What a lousy bore *he* is! My ex-husband had a pet snake named. Baby and he fed it worms. That's all they're good for, unless you fish. Do you fish?"

"I've done some fishing up in Canada."

"My ex-husband hated all sports. Except the indoor variety." She giggled. "Did you hear the one about the indoor hen and the outdoor rooster?"

"Look, miss—"

"Talia. But you can call me Jenny. Get it?" She doubled over, laughing hysterically, then swayed, dropping her cigarette. "Ooops! I'm sick. I better go lie down. My tum-tum feels awful."

She staggered from the party as Ashland crushed out her smoldering cigarette with the heel of his shoe. *Stupid bitch!*

A sharp handclap startled him. In the middle of the room, a tall man in a green satin dinner jacket was demanding his attention. He clapped again. "You," he shouted to Ashland. "Come here."

Ashland walked forward. The tall man asked him to remove his wristwatch. "I'll read your past from it," the man said. "I'm psychic. I'll tell you about yourself."

Reluctantly, Ashland removed his watch, handed it over. He didn't find any of this amusing. The party was annoying him, irritating him.

"I thank you most kindly, sir!" said the tall man, with elaborate stage courtesy. He placed the gold watch against his forehead and closed his eyes, breathing deeply. The crowd noise did not slacken; no one seemed to be paying any attention to the psychic.

"Ah. Your name is David. David Ashland. You are successful, a man of big business . . . a producer . . . and a bachelor. You are twenty-eight . . . young for a successful producer. One has to be something of a bastard to climb that fast. What about that, Mr. Ashland, *are* you something of a bastard?"

Ashland flushed angrily.

"You like women," continued the tall man. "A lot. And you like to drink. A lot. Your doctor told you—"

"I don't have to listen to this," Ashland said tightly, reaching for his watch. The man in green satin handed it over, grinned amiably, and melted back into the shifting crowd.

I ought to get the hell out of here, Ashland told himself. Yet curiosity held him. When the host arrived, Ashland would piece this evening together; he'd know why he was here, at this particular party. He moved to a couch near the closed patio doors and sat down. He'd wait.

A soft-faced man sat down next to him. The man looked pained. "I shouldn't smoke these," he said, holding up a long cigar. "Do you smoke cigars?"

"No."

"I'm a salesman. Dover Insurance. Like the White Cliffs of, ya know. I've studied the problems involved in smoking. Can't quit, though. When I do, the nerves shrivel up, stomach goes sour. I worry a lot – but we all worry, don't we? I mean, my mother used to worry about the earth slowing down. She read somewhere that between 1680 and 1690 the earth lost twenty-seven hundredths of a second. She said that meant something."

Ashland sighed inwardly. What is it about cocktail parties that causes people you've never met to unleash their troubles?

"You meet a lotta fruitcakes in my dodge," said the pained-looking insurance salesman. "I sold a policy once to a guy who lived in the woodwork. Had a ratty little walk-up in the Bronx with a foldaway bed. Kind you push into the wall. He'd *stay* there – I mean, inside the wall – most of the time. His roommate would invite some friends in and if they made too much noise the guy inside the wall would pop out with his Thompson. BAM! The bed would come down and there he was with a Thompson submachine gun aimed at everybody. Real fruitcake."

"I knew a fellow who was *twice* that crazy."

Ashland looked up into a long, cadaverous face. The nose had been broken and improperly reset; it canted noticeably to the left. He folded his long, sharp-boned frame onto the couch next to Ashland. "This fellow believed in falling grandmothers," he declared. "Lived in upper Michigan. 'Watch out for falling grandmothers,' he used to warn me. 'They come down pretty heavy in this area. Most of 'em carry umbrellas and big packages and they come flapping down out of the sky by the thousands!' This Michigan fellow swore he saw one hit a postman. 'An awful thing to watch,' he told me. 'Knocked the poor soul flat. Crushed his skull like an egg.' I recall he shuddered just telling me about it."

"Fruitcake," said the salesman. "Like the guy I once knew who wrote on all his walls and ceilings. A creative writer, he called himself. Said he couldn't write on paper, had to use a wall. Paper was too flimsy for him. He'd scrawl these long novels of his, a chapter in every room, with a big black crayon. Words all over the place. He'd fill up the house, then rent another one for his next book. I never read any of his houses, so I don't know if he was any good."

"Excuse me, gentlemen," said Ashland. "I need a fresh drink."

He hurriedly mixed another Scotch at the bar. Around him, the party rolled on inexorably, without any visible core. What time was it, anyway? His watch had stopped.

"Do you happen to know what time it is?" he asked a long-haired Oriental girl who was standing near the bar.

"I've no idea," she said. "None at all." The girl fixed him with her eyes. "I've been watching you, and you seem horribly *alone*. Aren't you?"

"Aren't I what?"

"Horribly alone?"

"I'm not with anyone, if that's what you mean."

The girl withdrew a jeweled holder from her bag and fitted a cigarette in place. Ashland lit it for her.

"I haven't been really alone since I was in Milwaukee," she told him. "I was about – God! – fifteen or something, and this creep wanted me to move in with him. My parents were both dead by then, so I was all alone."

"What did you do?"

"Moved in with the creep. What else? I couldn't make the being-alone scene. Later on, I killed him."

"You *what?*"

"Cut his throat." She smiled delicately. "In self-defense, of course. He got mean on the bottle one Friday night and tried to knife me. I had witnesses."

Ashland took a long draw on his Scotch. A scowling fellow in shirt-sleeves grabbed the girl's elbow and steered her roughly away.

"I used to know a girl who looked like that," said a voice to Ashland's right. The speaker was curly-haired, clean-featured, in his late thirties. "Greek belly dancer with a Jersey accent. Dark, like her, and kind of mysterious. She used to quote that line of Hemingway's to Scott Fitzgerald – you know the one."

"Afraid not."

"One that goes, 'We're all bitched from the start.' Bitter. A bitter line."

He put out his hand. Ashland shook it.

"I'm Travers. I used to save America's ass every week on CBS."

"Beg pardon?"

"Terry Travers. The old *Triple Trouble for Terry* series on channel nine. Back in the late fifties. Had to step on a lotta toes to get that series."

"I think I recall the show. It was—"

"Dung. That's what it was. Cow dung. Horse dung. The *worst*. Terry Travers is not my real name, natch. Real one's Abe Hock-statter. Can you imagine a guy named Abe Hockstatter saving America's ass every week on CBS?"

"You've got me there."

Hockstatter pulled a brown wallet from his coat, flipped it open. "There I am with one of my other rugs on," he said, jabbing at a photo. "Been stone bald since high school. Baldies don't make it in showbiz, so I have my rugs. Go ahead, tug at me."

Ashland blinked. The man inclined his head. "*Pull* at it. Go on – as a favor to me!"

Ashland tugged at the fringe of Abe Hockstatter's curly hairpiece.

"Tight, eh? Really *snug*. Stays on the old dome."

"Indeed it does."

"They cost a fortune. I've got a wind-blown one for outdoor scenes. A stiff wind'll lift a cheap one right off your scalp. Then I got a crew cut and a Western job with long sideburns. All kinds. Ten, twelve . . . all first-class."

"I'm certain I've seen you," said Ashland. "I just don't—"

" 'S'awright. Believe me. Lotta people don't know me since I quit the *Terry* thing. I booze like crazy now. You an' me, we're among the nation's six million alcoholics."

Ashland glared at the actor. "Where do you get off linking me with—"

"Cool it, cool it. So I spoke a little out of turn. Don't be so touchy, chum."

"To hell with you!" snapped Ashland.

The bald man with curly hair shrugged and drifted into the crowd.

Ashland took another long pull at his Scotch. All these neurotic conversations . . . He felt exhausted, wrung dry, and the Scotch was lousy. No kick to it. The skin along the back of his neck felt tight, hot. A headache was coming on; he could always tell.

A slim-figured, frosted blonde in black sequins sidled up to him. She exuded an aura of matrimonial wars fought and lost. Her orange lipstick was smeared, her cheeks alcohol-flushed behind flaking pancake make-up. "I have a theory about sleep," she said. "Would you like to hear it?"

Ashland did not reply.

"My theory is that the world goes insane every night. When we sleep, our subconscious takes charge and we become victims to whatever it conjures up. Our conscious mind is totally blanked out. We lie there, helpless, while our subconscious flings us about. We fall off high buildings, or have to fight a giant ape, or we get buried in quicksand . . . We have absolutely no control. The mind whirls madly in the skull. Isn't that an unsettling thing to consider?"

"Listen," said Ashland. "Where's the host?"

"He'll get here."

Ashland put down his glass and turned away from her. A mounting wave of depression swept him toward the door. The room seemed to be solid with bodies, all talking, drinking, gesturing in the milk-thick smoke haze.

"Potatoes have eyes," said a voice to his left. "I really *believe* that." The remark was punctuated by an ugly, frog-croaking laugh.

"Today is tomorrow's yesterday," someone else said.

A hot swarm of sound:

"You can't get prints off human skin."

"In China, the laborers make sixty-five dollars a year. How the hell can you live on sixty-five dollars a year?"

"So he took out his Luger and blew her head off."

"I knew a policewoman who loved to scrub down whores."

"Did you ever try to live with eight kids, two dogs, a three-legged cat and twelve goldfish?"

"Like I told him, those X rays destroyed his white cells."

"They found her in the tub. Strangled with a coat hanger."

"What I had, exactly, was a grade-two epidermoid carcinoma at the base of a seborrheic keratosis."

Ashland experienced a sudden, raw compulsion: somehow he had to stop these voices!

The Chinese gong flared gold at the corner of his eye. He pushed his way over to it, shouldering the partygoers aside. He would strike it – and the booming noise would stun the crowd; they'd have to stop their incessant, maddening chatter.

Ashland drew back his right first, then drove it into the circle of bronze. He felt the impact, and the gong shuddered under his blow. *But there was no sound from it!*

The conversation went on.

Ashland smashed his way back across the apartment.

"You can't stop the party," said the affable fat man at the door.

"I'm leaving!"

"So go ahead," grinned the fat man. "Leave."

Ashland clawed open the door and plunged into the hall, stumbling, almost falling. He reached the elevator, jabbed at the DOWN button.

Waiting, he found it impossible to swallow; his throat was dry. He could feel his heart hammering against the wall of his chest. His head ached.

The elevator arrived, opened. He stepped inside. The doors closed smoothly and the cage began its slow, automatic descent.

Abruptly, it stopped.

The doors parted to admit a solemn-looking man in a dark blue suit.

Ashland gasped "Freddie!"

The solemn face broke into a wide smile. "Dave! It's great to see you! Been a long time."

"But – you can't be Fred Baker!"

"Why? Have I changed so much?"

"No, no, you look – exactly the same. But that car crash in Albany. I thought you were . . ." Ashland hesitated, left the word unspoken.

He was pale, frightened. Very frightened. "Look, I'm – I'm late. Got somebody waiting for me at my place. Have to rush . . . He reached forward to push the LOBBY button.

There was none.

The lowest button read FLOOR 2.

"We use this elevator to get from one party to another," Freddie Baker said quietly, as the cage surged into motion. "That's all it's good for. You get so you need a change. They're all alike, though – the parties. But you learn to adjust, in time."

Ashland stared at his departed friend. The elevator stopped.

"Step out," said Freddie. "I'll introduce you around. You'll catch on, get used to things. No sex here. And the booze is watered. Can't get stoned. That's the dirty end of the stick."

Baker took Ashland's arm, propelled him gently forward.

Around him, pressing in, David Ashland could hear familar sounds: nervous laughter, ice against glass, muted jazz – and the ceaseless hum of cocktail voices.

Freddie thumbed a buzzer. A door opened.

The smiling fat man said, "C'mon in fellas. Join the party."

Underground

J. B. Priestley

Location: Northern Line, London Underground.
Time: December, 1974.
Eyewitness Description: *"Through the gap,
he saw for the first time a small figure
sitting down. It had the face of an old-
looking boy or rather a young-looking
dwarf. He stared at this creature, who then met his stare with a
widening of the eyes, old eyes, yellowish . . ."*
Author: John Boynton Priestley (1894–1984) was another of the
20th century's most popular novelists and playwrights whose
work, like that of A. E. Van Vogt, was influenced by the
theories of J. W. Dunne. Initially a critic and journalist, he
enjoyed a great success with *The Good Companions* (1929), a
picaresque novel about English life and then broadened his
output to include fantasy, science fiction and the supernatural.
Two of his major plays, *Dangerous Corner* (1932) and *Time
and the Conways* (1937) utilized Dunne's theories with
"timelines" opening up destructive events. He took the idea
further in *The Other Place* (1953) and a non-fiction discussion,
Man and Time (1964). Priestley's novel, *Benighted* (1929)
about a young couple forced to seek refuge in a haunted
mansion, was made into a classic movie, *The Old Dark House*,
in 1932, starring Boris Karloff and directed by James Whale of
Frankenstein fame. It, in turn, inspired a whole series of "old
dark house" films set in isolated rural properties plagued by
ghosts. Priestley wrote several short stories with supernatural
themes, including "Mr Strenberry's Tale" (1930), "The Grey
Ones" (1953) and, perhaps most unnerving of all, this next
story written in 1974 about a ride on the underground that
turns, inexorably, into a living nightmare.

Ray Aggarstone took the Northern Line from Leicester Square. It was some time since he had gone anywhere by Underground. Either he had used his car or had taken taxis for shorter journeys. But now that he was almost ready for what he liked to call, to himself but not to anybody else, the *Big Getaway*, he had sold his car for just over four hundred quid. Just showed you how useful it could be to chat somebody up, in this case that stupid sod who was always in the Saloon bar of the King's Arms. While waiting on the crowded platform at Leicester Square, Ray told himself once again that he was careful as well as very clever. For instance, after that car deal and with a few drinks inside them, some fellows would have boasted about the Brazilian setup and the flight to Rio, but not Ray – not on your life! He had told this stupid sod exactly the same story he had told his mother and his wife, Cherry, now waiting for him some- where near the end of this Northern Line. "Going to France, old man – Nice actually – where I've bought into a very promising property deal. Smart work, if I may say so."

But of course he hadn't shown him the letters he'd concocted to show his Mum and Cherry, now ready to part with eight thousand between them, about all they had. They were both so excited about his plan for them to join him at Nice within the next two or three weeks, like a pair of idiotic kids, they left *business* entirely to him, Mum's clever handsome son, Cherry's dominating, fascinating if occasionally unfaithful husband. Serve them right when he vanished with the two cheques he was going to collect – the silly cows!

No train yet but more people arriving on the platform. He changed his place, bumping and shoving a bit, if only to show these types what he thought about them. A run-down lot in a running-down country! He could never come back of course, not after those two women finally decided he'd robbed them blind, but he didn't want to anyhow. He'd had it here all right – finish! He couldn't blame Rita and Karl for sneering and jeering, even though now and again they got his goat, specially Karl. But that was early on, before they began to talk business.

The train came along, already more than half full. And because he hadn't stood near the platform edge, though he pushed and shoved as hard as anybody, perhaps a bit harder than most, of course he didn't get a seat – not a hope! So there he was, standing and swaying, wedged in with a lot of fat arses, smelly underclothes and bad breath. Looking around, disgusted, he couldn't imagine now what had made him come down here when he might have hired a car, travelled in comfort and also impressed Mum and Cherry. So, to stop cursing himself, he began thinking about Rita and Karl again. After all he'd be meeting them in Rio in two or three days, and he began to wonder how things would work over there. Every time Karl, who was her husband all right, had gone to Manchester or Leeds and had stayed the night, he'd had Rita, a hot brunette if there ever was one, who'd start moaning if a finger touched a tit. Did Karl know, just guess, not care – or what? Anyhow, what Karl, a real businessman in the German-Swedish style, did know was that his friend, smart Ray Aggarstone, would be shortly financing most of the deal they'd worked out. Moreover, there must be plenty of hot moaning brunettes in Brazil.

Tottenham Court Road and people, dreary bloody people, pushing their way out and pushing their way in. And off again – sway, rattle, bang, bang, rattle, sway. A long thin woman, loaded with parcels, dug an elbow into his ribs, and he used his own elbow, with some force, to knock it away. She glared at him over her parcels, but all he did was to raise his eyebrows at her. After a moment or two she was able to move away a few inches. It was then that a curious thing happened. Through the gap she had left between them he saw for the first time a small figure sitting down. It had the face of an old-looking boy or a rather young-looking dwarf. He stared at this creature, who then met his stare with a widening of the eyes, odd eyes, yellowish. Next, the little oddity closed his eyes and moved his head slowly from side to side, almost as if he was giving a "No-no-no" signal. As soon as the eyes opened again, Ray gave them a hard scowling look. But now there was no sign of recognition in them. It was just as if Ray was no longer there at all. The boy-or-dwarf might have been looking *through him*. A silly idea. Ray began to think how he would deal with Mum and Cherry.

At Euston there was a lot more pushing out and shoving in, twerps on the move. The little monster had gone, and in his place was a fat suet-faced woman who stared angrily at anything or nothing, just to prove she had a right to a seat. Rattling and swaying on again, Ray told himself how he ought to deal with Mum and Cherry this time. Very different, he decided, from last time when he'd been all solemn, very much the business man, explaining again why Cherry had to stay with Mum, now that he'd got rid of their flat, and why he was staying in an hotel to be near the two Frenchmen who'd agreed to let him buy into the big property development just outside Nice. This time, everything being settled now they were giving him their cheques, there'd be no point in going on with the solemn business thing. It would have to be all merry chit-chat about Nice and the

Riviera, how they'd be joining him down there quite soon, how he'd be arranging their flights, booking a posh double-bedded room with bath for Cherry and him, with a good single nearby for Mum, and at least one balcony the three could use for breakfast – all that bullshit. Yes, there he'd be, egging them on, the stupid cows, maybe taking them out to a pub if Mum hadn't got anything in to drink.

Somebody touched his arm. This was deliberate. A woman was smiling at him. She was an oldish woman, white-haired but with a plump red-cheeked face and bright blue eyes; and he'd seen her before somewhere. "You're Ray Aggarstone, aren't you?" she said, smiling away.

It seemed as if he hadn't time to think before he heard himself saying, "No, I'm not." He said it sharply too, as if really telling her to mind her own dam' business.

It wiped the smile off her face and narrowed and darkened her eyes, almost turning her into another person. "I think you *are* Ray Aggarstone, y'know," she said; and though the train was making a lot of noise, somehow she managed to say it quietly. "And you must remember me. I'm an old friend of your mother's."

She must have been too, he realized now. But he hadn't to be bothered with her, when he was busy with his own thoughts and plans. He shook his head at her. "Got this all wrong." And he had to shout because the train might have been grinding its way through rocks, the noise it was making. "I don't know you. And you don't know me."

"Yes, I do. Or I did do, once," she went on steadily. "She thought the world of you, Ray. Her only son – so good-looking, so clever!"

He found a snarl coming out of him this time. "Do you mind! Just turn it up!" And he looked away, to get rid of her. But when he turned his head again, she was still there, though not quite so close, having managed to back away from him a little. And now she seemed a lot older and was giving him a long sad look. He couldn't return it – he suddenly felt he had nothing to return it with, not even a scowl – so he looked away again and was relieved to find the train was stopping at Camden Town. This time not many got in, but then not many got out, so he was still forced to stand, even though he'd a bit more space round him. And this suited him all right because if there was one thing he didn't like it was being jammed among all these idiotic, bloody disgusting people, staring old cows, smelly bitches and stupid buggers of all ages and sizes. When he got to Brazil and the money was rolling in, as Karl swore it would, he'd work it so that there was no more of this horrible caper. The only people allowed near him would be the ones he could enjoy seeing, hearing, smelling and touching.

As the train started rattling and banging off again, he started thinking again. Working out how he'd deal with Cherry and his mother, chatting them up about life on the Riviera, breakfasts on balconies, drinks to welcome the wonderful new life, laughs and hugs and kisses and all that female crap, he realised he'd overdone it, not for them but for himself. For what he'd gone and done, if only for a minute or two, was to go soft and feel a bit sorry for both of them, considering that he was about to skin them down to their last fifty quid each. No time for that tonight! He'd got to be as sensible and hard as he'd been when he worked out the plan. Serve 'em right for not having more sense! He'd to look after himself, so they could look after themselves – and women always managed somehow. And he began to remember and light up every grievance he'd ever had against the pair of 'em. He'd deal with them the way he'd planned, pretending to be as silly as they were, and when they laughed then he'd laugh too, even, just for a private giggle, bringing out and flourishing his wallet, which already had in it his Air France ticket to Rio.

It was just past Chalk Farm when the man tapped him on the shoulder. He was a tall man, so tall he had to bend over Ray, and he had very sharp grey eyes and a long chin.

"Better get out at Hampstead," the man said, almost in Ray's ear.

"Can't do," Ray told him briskly. "Going as far as Hendon Central. Unless of course I have to change. Is that it?"

"You might say that's it." A solemn reply.

This sounded idiotic to Ray. "I don't know what you're talking about." This tall fellow didn't look a chump, but then, like so many people now, he might be round the bend.

Two women pushed past them, getting ready for Belsize Park. The man waited but then he tapped Ray on the shoulder again and bent closer to his ear. "Just a last word. Most people think this line's at its deepest at Hampstead. What they don't know – and I don't suppose you do – is that there's a second line, starting at Hampstead, that goes deeper still – on and on, deeper and deeper—"

"Oh – come off it!" Ray was impatient now. This was obviously a crackpot.

"I'm not on it." The man gave a short crackpot's laugh. "But you may be *if* you don't get out at Hampstead and then take a taxi or a bus – *and go back*."

"That's enough," Ray told him. "I'll mind my own business and you mind yours."

"No, it's not as simple as that," said the tall man quite mildly. "You're part of my business now. That's why I'm telling you – not asking you, *telling* you – to forget Hendon Central and get out at Hampstead—"

Ray lost his temper. "And I'm *telling* you – not asking you – to piss off."

The train was slowing up. Belsize Park now. There were sufficient people getting out to push between Ray and the tall man, but then there was quite a gap between them now. Only a few got on, and Ray saw that he could have a seat at last if he wanted one. But somehow he didn't. Perhaps he felt he might go soft again if he sat down. Better to keep on standing and be hard and tough. The tall man, easily seen, had moved down and was now near the far door, ready to get out at Hampstead, where the big daft sod thought everybody ought to get out. All these mental hospitals and yet a crackpot pest like this was allowed to wander around loose, making a bloody nuisance of himself! Anyhow, as soon as the train pulled up at Hampstead, out the chap went, followed by nearly everybody else. This left the carriage almost empty. Ray could have taken as many seats as he wanted now, but he didn't make a move, not for the moment trusting himself to let go of the strap he was clinging to, for he had to admit that he felt a bit faint, probably because of all the clattering and swaying and what so many stinking people had done to the air had combined to make him feel faint.

This was an unusually long wait. He closed his eyes, just for a few moments, and when he opened them again he was both surprised and alarmed to discover that he had the whole long carriage to himself. Nobody else at all in sight. Had they shouted, "Hampstead – all change!" and he'd missed it? Even dim as he felt, he was about to make for the door when, with an unpleasant jerk, the train started again. Then two things, equally unpleasant, happened together. There were several loud bangs and the lights went out. Badly shaken, there in the dark with the train obviously gathering speed, he made up his mind he would get out at the next stop, which would be Golders Green, and find a taxi to take him up to Mum's place. The lights came on again, and though they seemed bright enough at first, after the dark, he soon realized that in fact they were much lower than they'd been before. Ten to one some powercut frigging nonsense!

Then quite suddenly – and it came like a hammer-blow at the heart – he *knew* that this train was going nowhere near Golders Green. At the same time he felt that it wasn't moving like all the others, which went more or less level or climbed a bit to rush out into the open air. No, it was *going down and down*. And what had that tall crackpot said? Something about a second line going deeper still – *on and on, deeper and deeper* – ? He tried to forget this but he couldn't, and he began to wish there was somebody else with him who could explain what was happening. The train went rattling on, faster now than the usual underground train. There was nothing to be seen of course, and with this poor lighting he could hardly catch a glimpse of his own reflection. He tried cursing and blinding, to stop himself feeling frightened; but it didn't work.

However, bringing a flood of relief, something happened he never remembered seeing before on an underground train. Some sort of conductor chap, wearing a dark uniform, had come through a door at the far end of the carriage and was now walking towards him – that is, if you could call this slow shuffle a walk. Enjoying his relief, Ray took a seat at last and began rehearsing the indignant questions he would ask. "Now look here," he called out, "what the hell's the idea –?" But there he stopped, terrified. He was staring at something out of a nightmare. The man hadn't a face, just eyes like a couple of blackcurrants, and nothing else – no mouth, no nose, no ears. In his terror Ray huddled into his seat and shut his eyes tight, hoping feverishly that the lard-faced monster wouldn't stop, even to put a finger on him, but would go shuffling past him. And this indeed he did, so that when Ray risked opening his eyes he was alone again. That was something, and what happened next was better still. At last the train was slowing down. There must be a station soon – certainly not Golders Green – but whatever the station was, however far it might be from Hendon Central, it was where he would get out of this nightmare train.

He caught glimpses of an enormous packed platform. As soon as the train stopped he reached the door, but even then it was too late. He was swept back by a solid mass of people, who pushed and shoved like maniacs and closed round him so that he couldn't move and felt he could hardly breathe. And what people! All the faces he'd ever looked away from, disgust blotting out compassion, seemed to be here, and the train was already moving again. He felt he was hemmed in by ulcers, abscesses, half-blind eyes, rotting noses, gangrenous mouths and chins. And how far, how long? Even out of the depths of his nausea, he'd have to say something.

He put his question to the face nearest to him, a twisted slobbery caricature of a face, but all he got in reply was a senseless gabble.

"No use asking him," a voice said over his shoulder. "He's

forgotten how to talk. What you want to know?" The voice belonged
to a bull of a man with a face like a volcanic eruption.

"Where—" and it was a shaky question, "where are we going?"

"Where we going?" the bull roared. "We're not going anywhere,
you silly sod." Now he roared louder still. "Time to push around,
shove about, all you bastards!"

Ray found at his elbow an old creature whose nose and chin nearly
met: she could have been a witch out of an ancient fairy tale. "I'll tell
you where you're *not* going, young man," she said, cackling and
spitting. "*He-he-he!* You're not going to Rio in Brazil. Not now and
not ever. *He-he-he!*"

His heart turning into ice-water, he understood at last that he
might never know anything again except this underground journey
to nowhere, wedged beyond any chance of escape among these
malicious jeering monstrosities . . .

. . . "Full name's Raymond Geoffrey Aggarstone, but liked to call
himself just *Ray*," said the first man. "Got that? Okay. Now – effects.
Silver cigarette case, inscribed *Darling Ray from his loving Cherry*
. . . Posh lighter . . . Diary, gold pencil, three fivers and four pound
notes in small notecase in one inside pocket. . . ."

"Not too fast," said the second man. "And what about trousers
pockets – keys and change and all that?"

"Come to them in a minute, chum," said the first man. "And if I'm
going too fast, why ask for more? . . . Wallet in right inside pocket.
. . . Contains credit cards, two letters, and something from Air
France—"

"Hold it! Yes, sir?" But this query was addressed to the new
arrival. He was a tall man, with a long chin and sharp grey eyes,
and he was obviously top brass authority, not the kind of bloke to
be asked what he was doing there and where was his warrant
card.

"I'll take the two letters," this tall man said pleasantly but with
assured authority. "Not needed for the next of kin. I must look at
that Air France booking too. Thank you!" He examined it, took out
a pen and made an alteration. "Yes, as I thought. There's a mistake
here. Should have been Nice not Rio. Here you are, ready for the next
of kin, but I'll keep the two letters, they'd only bewilder a couple of
miserable women." He gave the two men a sombre look. "You
know, this is a world where the guilty all too often go unpunished
and the innocent are increasingly victimized, robbed, ruined, maimed
or murdered."

"That's true enough, sir," said the first man. "As I've said more than once to the wife and kids."

"Well, now and again," the tall man told him, "we have the chance to change that. Just now and again. By the way, what are the facts here?"

"Found unconscious in the Northern Line train at Hampstead, sir. Major heart attack. Never recovered consciousness. In fact, died in the ambulance, sir. Finish!"

"Thank you! Possibly *finish* – possibly not. We don't know, do we? Goodnight!" And he left them so quickly, he might almost have vanished, a trick some of these top blokes seem to have mastered.

Haunted

Joyce Carol Oates

Location: Minton Farm, Elk Creek.
Time: Summer, 1987.
Eyewitness Description: *"There weren't such things as ghosts, they told us. They were just superstition. But we could injure ourselves tramping around where we weren't wanted – and you never knew who you might meet up with in an old house or barn that's supposed to be empty . . ."*

Author: Joyce Carol Oates (1938—) is one of the most prolific contemporary US female writers and her vision of the dark side of American life has been compared to that of Honoré de Balzac, "whose feverish productivity she has more than matched," according to John Clute. Born and raised in the rural countryside around Lockport, New York, she has combined the roles of teacher and author, writing over 75 books that have forged new directions in psychological realism and taken the supernatural tale into new and unexpected paths. Among Oates' highly rated novels are *Wonderland* (1971), about a dreadful life haunted by doubles; *A Bloodsmoor Romance* (1982), a Gothic tale of spiritualism; and *Mysteries of Winterburn* (1984), in which detective Xavier Kilgarvan investigates a series of supernatural cases. She has acknowledged her admiration for Henry James, William Faulkner and D. H. Lawrence in, respectively, her short story, "Accursed Inhabitants of the House of Bly" (1972); the southern novel, *Bellefleur* (1980) and the essays in *Contraries* (1981). "Haunted" draws a little from all three as well as her rural upbringing to relate a story of crime, punishment and the inexplicable that lures the narrator – and with her, the reader – into a situation of almost unbearable terror.

Haunted houses, forbidden houses. The old Medlock farm. The Erlich farm. The Minton farm on Elk Creek. *No Trespassing* the signs said, but we trespassed at will. *No Trespassing No Hunting No Fishing Under Penalty of Law* but we did what we pleased because who was there to stop us?

Our parents warned us against exploring these abandoned properties: the old houses and barns were dangerous, they said. We could get hurt, they said. I asked my mother if the houses were haunted and she said, Of course not, there aren't such things as ghosts, you know that. She was irritated with me; she guessed how I pretended to believe things I didn't believe, things I'd grown out of years before. It was a habit of childhood – pretending I was younger, more childish, than in fact I was. Opening my eyes wide and looking puzzled, worried. Girls are prone to such trickery; it's a form of camouflage when every other thought you think is a forbidden thought and with your eyes open staring sightless you can sink into dreams that leave your skin clammy and your heart pounding – dreams that don't seem to belong to you that must have come to you from somewhere else from someone you don't know who knows *you*.

There weren't such things as ghosts, they told us. That was just superstition. But we could injure ourselves tramping around where we weren't wanted – the floorboards and the staircases in old houses were likely to be rotted, the roofs ready to collapse, we could cut ourselves on nails and broken glass, we could fall into uncovered wells – and you never knew who you might meet up with, in an old house or barn that's supposed to be empty. "You mean a bum? – like somebody hitch-hiking along the road?" I asked. "It could be a bum, or it could be somebody you know," Mother told me evasively. "A man, or a boy – somebody you know—" Her voice trailed off in embarrassment and I knew enough not to ask another question.

There were things you didn't talk about, back then. I never talked about them with my own children; there weren't the words to say them.

We listened to what our parents said, we nearly always agreed with what they said, but went off on the sly and did what we wanted to do. When we were little girls: my neighbor Mary Lou Siskin and me. And when we were older, ten, eleven years old, tomboys, roughhouses our mothers called us. We liked to hike in the woods and along the creek for miles; we'd cut through farmers' fields, spy on their houses – on people we knew, kids we knew from school – most of all we liked to explore abandoned houses, boarded-up houses if we could break in; we'd scare ourselves thinking the houses might be haunted though really we knew they weren't haunted, there weren't such things as ghosts. Except—

I am writing in a dime-store notebook with lined pages and a speckled cover, a notebook of the sort we used in grade school. *Once upon a time* as I used to tell my children when they were tucked safely into bed and drifting off to sleep. *Once upon a time* I'd begin, reading from a book because it was safest so: the several times I told them my own stories they were frightened by my voice and couldn't sleep and afterward I couldn't sleep either and my husband would ask what was wrong and I'd say, Nothing, hiding my face from him so he wouldn't see my look of contempt.

I write in pencil, so that I can erase easily, and I find that I am constantly erasing, wearing holes in the paper. Mrs Harding, our fifth grade teacher, disciplined us for handing in messy notebooks: she was a heavy, toad-faced woman, her voice was deep and husky and gleeful when she said, "You, Melissa, what have you to say for yourself?" and I stood there mute, my knees trembling. My friend Mary Lou laughed behind her hand, wriggled in her seat she thought I was so funny. Tell the old witch to go to hell, she'd say, she'll respect you then, but of course no one would every say such a thing to Mrs Harding. Not even Mary Lou. "What have you to say for yourself, Melissa? Handing in a notebook with a ripped page?" My grade for the homework assignment was lowered from A to B, Mrs Harding grunted with satisfaction as she made the mark, a big swooping B in red ink, creasing the page. "More is expected of you, Melissa, so you disappoint me more," Mrs Harding always said. So many years ago and I remember those words more clearly than words I have heard the other day.

One morning there was a pretty substitute teacher in Mrs Harding's classroom. "Mrs Harding is unwell, I'll be taking her place today," she said, and we saw the nervousness in her face; we guessed there was a secret she wouldn't tell and we waited and a few days later the principal himself came to tell us that Mrs Harding would not be back, she had died of a stroke. He spoke carefully as if we were much younger children and might be upset and Mary Lou caught my eye and winked and I sat there at my desk feeling the strangest sensation, something flowing into the top of my head, honey-rich and warm making its way down my spine. *Our Father Who art in Heaven* I whispered in the prayer with the others my head bowed and my hands clasped tight together but my thoughts were somewhere else leaping wild and crazy somewhere else and I knew Mary Lou's were too.

On the school bus going home she whispered in my ear, "That was because of us, wasn't it! – what happened to that old bag Harding. But we won't tell anybody."

Once upon a time there were two sisters, and one was very pretty and one was very ugly. . . . Though Mary Lou Siskin wasn't my sister. And I wasn't ugly, really: just sallow-skinned, with a small pinched ferrety face. With dark almost lashless eyes that were set too close together and a nose that didn't look right. A look of yearning, and disappointment.

But Mary Lou *was* pretty, even rough and clumsy as she sometimes behaved. That long silky blond hair everybody remembered her for afterward, years afterward. . . . How, when she had to be identified, it was the long silky white-blond hair that was unmistakable. . . .

Sleepless nights, but I love them. I write during the nighttime hours and sleep during the day, I am of an age when you don't require more than a few hours sleep. My husband has been dead for nearly a year and my children are scattered and busily absorbed in their own selfish lives like all children and there is no one to interrupt me no one to pry into my business no one in the neighborhood who dares come knocking at my door to see if I am all right. Sometimes out of a mirror floats an unexpected face, a strange face, lined, ravaged, with deep-socketed eyes always damp, always blinking in shock or dismay or simple bewilderment – but I adroitly look away. I have no need to stare.

It's true, all you have heard of the vanity of the old. Believing ourselves young, still, behind our aged faces – mere children, and so very innocent!

Once when I was a young bride and almost pretty my color up when I was happy and my eyes shining we drove out into the country for a Sunday's excursion and he wanted to make love I knew, he was shy and fumbling as I but he wanted to make love and I ran into a cornfield in my stockings and high heels, I was playing at being a woman I never could be, Mary Lou Siskin maybe, Mary Lou whom my husband never knew, but I got out of breath and frightened, it was the wind in the cornstalks, that dry rustling sound, that dry terrible rustling sound like whispering like voices you can't quite identify and he caught me and tried to hold me and I pushed him away sobbing and he said, What's wrong? My God what's wrong? as if he really loved me as if his life was focused on me and I knew I could never be equal to it, that love, that importance, I knew I was only Melissa the ugly one the one the boys wouldn't give a second glance, and one day he'd understand and know how he'd been cheated. I pushed him away, I said, Leave me alone! don't touch me! You disgust me! I said.

He backed off and I hid my face, sobbing.

But later on I got pregnant just the same. Only a few weeks later.

Always there were stories behind the abandoned houses and always the stories were sad. Because farmers went bankrupt and had to move away. Because somebody died and the farm couldn't be kept up and nobody wanted to buy it – like the Medlock farm across the creek. Mr Medlock died aged seventy-nine and Mrs Medlock refused to sell the farm and lived there alone until someone from the country health agency came to get her. Isn't it a shame, my parents said. The poor woman, they said. They told us never, never to poke around in the Medlocks' barns or house – the buildings were ready to cave in, they'd been in terrible repair even when the Medlocks were living.

It was said that Mrs Medlock had gone off her head after she'd found her husband dead in one of the barns, lying flat on his back his eyes open and bulging, his mouth open, tongue protruding, she'd gone to look for him and found him like that and she'd never gotten over it they said, never got over the shock. They had to commit her to the state hospital for her own good (they said) and the house and the barns were boarded up, everywhere tall grass and thistles grew wild, dandelions in the spring, tiger lilies in the summer, and when we drove by I stared and stared narrowing my eyes so I wouldn't see someone looking out one of the windows – a face there, pale and quick – or a dark figure scrambling up the roof to hide behind the chimney—Mary Lou and I wondered was the house haunted, was the barn haunted where the old man had died, we crept around to spy, we couldn't stay away, coming closer and closer each time until something scared us and we ran away back through the woods clutching and pushing at each other until one day finally we went right up to the house to the back door and peeked in one of the windows. Mary Lou led the way, Mary Lou said not to be afraid, nobody lived there any more and nobody would catch us, it didn't matter that the land was posted, the police didn't arrest kids our ages.

We explored the barns, we dragged the wooden cover off the well and dropped stones inside. We called the cats but they wouldn't come close enough to be petted. They were barn cats, skinny and diseased-looking, they'd said at the country bureau that Mrs Medlock had let a dozen cats live in the house with her so that the house was filthy from their messes. When the cats wouldn't come we got mad and threw stones at them and they ran away hissing – nasty dirty things, Mary Lou said. Once we crawled up on the tar-paper roof over the Medlocks' kitchen, just for fun, Mary Lou wanted to climb up the big roof too to the very top but I got frightened and said, No, no please don't, no Mary Lou please, and I sounded so strange Mary Lou looked at me and didn't tease or mock as she usually did. The roof was so steep, I'd known she would hurt herself. I could see her losing her footing and slipping, falling, I could see her astonished face and her flying hair as she fell, knowing nothing could save her. You're no fun, Mary Lou said, giving me a hard little pinch. But she didn't go climbing up the big roof.

Later we ran through the barns screaming at the top of our lungs just for fun for the hell of it as Mary Lou said, we tossed things in a heap, broken-off parts of farm implements, leather things from the horses' gear, handfuls of straw. The farm animals had been gone for years but their smell was still strong. Dried horse and cow droppings that looked like mud. Mary Lou said, "You know what – I'd like to burn this place down." And she looked at me and I said, "Okay – go on and do it, burn it down." And May Lou said, "You think I wouldn't? Just give me a match." And I said, "You know I don't have any match." And a look passed between us. And I felt something flooding at the top of my head, my throat tickled as if I didn't know would I laugh or cry and I said, "You're crazy—" and Mary Lou said with a sneering little laugh, "*You're* crazy, dumbbell. I was just testing you."

By the time Mary Lou was twelve years old Mother had got to hate her, was always trying to turn me against her so I'd make friends with other girls. Mary Lou had a fresh mouth, she said. Mary Lou didn't respect her elders – not even her own parents. Mother guessed that Mary Lou laughed at her behind her back, said things about all of us. She was mean and snippy and a smart-ass, rough sometimes as her brothers. Why didn't I make other friends? Why did I always go running when she stood out in the yard and called me? The Siskins weren't a whole lot better than white trash, the way Mr Siskin worked that land of his.

In town, in school, Mary Lou sometimes ignored me when other girls were around, girls who lived in town, whose fathers weren't farmers like ours. But when it was time to ride home on the bus she'd sit with me as if nothing was wrong and I'd help her with her homework if she needed help, I hated her sometimes but then I'd forgive her as soon as she smiled at me, she'd say, "Hey 'Lissa are you mad at me?" and I'd make a face and say no as if it was an insult, being asked. Mary Lou was my sister I sometimes pretended, I told myself a story about us being sisters and looking alike, and Mary Lou said sometimes she'd like to leave her family her goddamned family and come live with me. Then the next day or the next hour she'd get moody and be nasty to me and get me almost crying. All the Siskins had mean streaks, bad tempers, she'd tell people. As if she was proud.

Her hair was a light blond, almost white in the sunshine, and when I first knew her she had to wear it braided tight around her head – her grandmother braided it for her, and she hated it. Like Gretel or Snow White in one of those damn dumb picture books for children, Mary Lou said. When she was older she wore it down and let it grow long so that it fell almost to her hips. It was very beautiful – silky and shimmering. I dreamt of Mary Lou's hair sometimes but the dreams were confused and I couldn't remember when I woke up whether I was the one with the long blond silky hair, or someone else. It took me a while to get my thoughts clear lying there in bed and then I'd remember Mary Lou, who was my best friend.

She was ten months older than I was, and an inch or so taller, a bit heavier, not fat but fleshy, solid and fleshy, with hard little muscles in her upper arms like a boy. Her eyes were blue like washed glass, her eyebrows and lashes were almost white, she had a snubbed nose and Slavic cheekbones and a mouth that could be sweet or twisty and smirky depending upon her mood. But she didn't like her face because it was round – a moon face she called it, staring at herself in the mirror though she knew damned well she was pretty – didn't older boys whistle at her, didn't the bus driver flirt with her? – calling her "Blondie" while he never called me anything at all.

Mother didn't like Mary Lou visiting with me when no one else was home in our house: she didn't trust her, she said. Thought she might steal something, or poke her nose into parts of the house where she wasn't welcome. That girl is a bad influence on you, she said. But it was all the same old crap I heard again and again so I didn't even listen. I'd have told her she was crazy except that would only make things worse.

Mary Lou said, "Don't you just hate them? – your mother, and mine? Sometimes I wish—"

I put my hands over my ears and didn't hear.

*　　*　　*

The Siskins lived two miles away from us, farther back the road where the road got narrower. Those days, it was unpaved, and never got plowed in the winter. I remember their barn with the yellow silo, I remember the muddy pond where the dairy cows came to drink, the muck they churned up in the spring. I remember Mary Lou saying she wished all the cows would die – they were always sick with something – so her father would give up and sell the farm and they could live in town in a nice house. I was hurt, her saying those things as if she'd forgotten about me and would leave me behind. Damn you to hell, I whispered under my breath.

I remember smoke rising from the Siskins' kitchen chimney, from their wood-burning stove, straight up into the winter sky like a breath you draw inside you deeper and deeper until you begin to feel faint.

Later on, that house was empty too. But boarded up only for a few months – the bank sold it at auction. (It turned out the bank owned most of the Siskin farm, even the dairy cows. So Mary Lou had been wrong about that all along and never knew.)

As I write I can hear the sound of glass breaking, I can feel glass underfoot. *Once upon a time there were two little princesses, two sisters, who did forbidden things.* That brittle terrible sensation under my shoes – slippery like water – "Anybody home? Hey – anybody home?" and there's an old calendar tacked to a kitchen wall, a faded picture of Jesus Christ in a long white gown stained with scarlet, thorns fitted to His bowed head. Mary Lou is going to scare me in another minute making me think that someone is in the house and the two of us will scream with laughter and run outside where it's safe. Wild frightened laughter and I never knew afterward what was funny or why we did these things. Smashing what remained of windows, wrenching at stairway railings to break them loose, running with our heads ducked so we wouldn't get cobwebs in our faces.

One of us found a dead bird, a starling, in what had been the parlor of the house. Turned it over with a foot – there's the open eye looking right up calm and matter-of-fact. *Melissa*, that eye tells me, silent and terrible, *I see you.*

That was the old Minton place, the stone house with the caved-in roof and the broken steps, like something in a picture book from long ago. From the road the house looked as if it might be big, but when we explored it we were disappointed to see that it wasn't much bigger than my own house, just four narrow rooms downstairs, another four upstairs, an attic with a steep ceiling, the roof partly caved in. The barns had collapsed in upon themselves; only their stone foundations remained solid. The land had been sold off over the years to other farmers, nobody had lived in the house for a long time. The old Minton house, people called it. On Elk Creek where Mary Lou's body was eventually found.

In seventh grade Mary Lou had a boyfriend she wasn't supposed to have and no one knew about it but me – an older boy who'd dropped out of school and worked as a farmhand. I thought he was a little slow – not in his speech which was fast enough, normal enough, but in his way of thinking. He was sixteen or seventeen years old. His name was Hans; he had crisp blond hair like the bristles of a brush, a coarse blemished face, derisive eyes. Mary Lou was crazy for him she said, aping the older girls in town who said they were "crazy for" certain boys or young men. Hans and Mary Lou kissed when they didn't think I was watching, in an old ruin of a cemetery behind the Minton house, on the creek bank, in the tall marsh grass by the end of the Siskins' driveway. Hans had a car borrowed from one of his brothers, a battered old Ford, the front bumper held up by wire, the running board scraping the ground. We'd be out walking on the road and Hans would come along tapping the horn and stop and Mary Lou would climb in but I'd hang back knowing they didn't want me and the hell with them: I preferred to be alone.

"You're just jealous of Hans and me," Mary Lou said, unforgivably, and I hadn't any reply. "Hans is sweet. Hans is nice. He isn't like people say," Mary Lou said in a quick bright false voice she'd picked up from one of the older, popular girls in town. "He's . . ." And she stared at me blinking and smiling not knowing what to say as if in fact she didn't know Hans at all. "He isn't *simple*," she said angrily, "he just doesn't like to talk a whole lot."

When I try to remember Hans Meunzer after so many decades I can see only a muscular boy with short-trimmed blond hair and protuberant ears, blemished skin, the shadow of a moustache on his upper lip – he's looking at me, eyes narrowed, crinkled, as if he understands how I fear him, how I wish him dead and gone, and he'd hate me too if he took me that seriously. But he doesn't take me that seriously, his gaze just slides right through me as if nobody's standing where I stand.

There were stories about all the abandoned houses but the worst story was about the Minton house over on the Elk Creek Road about three miles from where we lived. For no reason anybody ever discovered Mr Minton had beaten his wife to death and afterward killed himself with a .12-gauge shotgun. He hadn't even been drinking, people said. And his farm hadn't been doing at all badly, considering how others were doing.

Looking at the ruin from the outside, overgrown with trumpet vine and wild rose, it seemed hard to believe that anything like that had happened. Things in the world even those things built by man are so quiet left to themselves . . .

The house had been deserted for years, as long as I could remember. Most of the land had been sold off but the heirs didn't want to deal with the house. They didn't want to sell it and they didn't want to raze it and they certainly didn't want to live in it so it stood empty. The property was posted with *No Trespassing* signs layered one atop another but nobody took them seriously. Vandals had broken into the house and caused damage, the McFarlane boys had tried to burn down the old hay barn one Halloween night. The summer Mary Lou started seeing Hans she and I climbed in the house through a rear window – the boards guarding it had long since been yanked away – and walked through the rooms slow as sleepwalkers our arms around each other's waists our eyes staring waiting to see Mr Minton's ghost as we turned each corner. The inside smelled of mouse droppings, mildew, rot, old sorrow. Strips of wallpaper torn from the walls, plasterboard exposed, old furniture overturned and smashed, old yellowed sheets of newspaper underfoot, and broken glass, everywhere broken glass. Through the ravaged windows sunlight spilled in tremulous quivering bands. The air was afloat, alive: dancing dust atoms. "I'm afraid," Mary Lou whispered. She squeezed my waist and I felt my mouth go dry for hadn't I been hearing something upstairs, a low persistent murmuring like quarreling like one person trying to convince another going on and on and on but when I stood very still to listen the sound vanished and there were only the comforting summer sounds of birds, crickets, cicadas; birds, crickets, cicadas.

I knew how Mr Minton had died: he'd placed the barrel of the shotgun beneath his chin and pulled the trigger with his big toe. They found him in the bedroom upstairs, most of his head blown off. They found his wife's body in the cistern in the cellar where he'd tried to hide her. "Do you think we should go upstairs?" Mary Lou asked, worried. Her fingers felt cold; but I could see tiny sweat beads on her forehead. Her mother had braided her hair in one thick clumsy braid, the way she wore it most of the summer, but the bands of hair were loosening. "No," I said, frightened. "I don't know." We hesitated at the bottom of the stairs – just stood there for a long time. "Maybe not," Mary Lou said. "Damn stairs'd fall in on us."

In the parlor there were bloodstains on the floor and on the wall – I could see them. Mary Lou said in derision, "They're just waterstains, dummy."

I could hear the voices overhead, or was it a single droning persistent voice. I waited for Mary Lou to hear it but she never did.

Now we were safe, now we were retreating, Mary Lou said as if repentant, "Yeah – this house *is* special."

We looked through the debris in the kitchen hoping to find something of value but there wasn't anything – just smashed china-ware, old battered pots and pans, more old yellowed newspaper. But through the window we saw a garter snake sunning itself on a rusted water tank, stretched out to a length of two feet. It was a lovely coppery color, the scales gleaming like perspiration on a man's arm; it seemed to be asleep. Neither one of us screamed, or wanted to throw something – we just stood there watching it for the longest time.

Mary Lou didn't have a boyfriend any longer; Hans had stopped coming around. We saw him driving the old Ford now and then but he didn't seem to see us. Mr Siskin had found out about him and Mary Lou and he'd been upset – acting like a damn crazy man Mary Lou said, asking her every kind of nasty question then interrupting her and not believing her anyway, then he'd put her to terrible shame by going over to see Hans and carrying on with him. "I hate them all," Mary Lou said, her face darkening with blood. "I wish—"

We rode our bicycles over to the Minton farm, or tramped through the fields to get there. It was the place we liked best. Sometimes we brought things to eat, cookies, bananas, candy bars; sitting on the broken stone steps out front, as if we lived in the house really, we were sisters who lived here having a picnic lunch out front. There were bees, flies, mosquitoes, but we brushed them away. We had to sit in the shade because the sun was so fierce and direct, a whitish heat pouring down from overhead.

"Would you ever like to run away from home?" Mary Lou said. "I don't know," I said uneasily. Mary Lou wiped at her mouth and gave me a mean narrow look. "'I don't know,'" she said in a falsetto voice, mimicking me. At an upstairs window someone was watching us – was it a man or was it a woman – someone stood there listening hard and I couldn't move feeling so slow and dreamy in the heat like a fly caught on a sticky petal that's going to fold in on itself and swallow him up. Mary Lou crumpled up some wax paper and threw it into the weeds. She was dreamy too, slow and yawning. She said, "Shit – they'd just find me. Then everything would be worse."

I was covered in a thin film of sweat but I'd begun to shiver. Goose bumps were raised on my arms. I could see us sitting on the stone steps the way we'd look from the second floor of the house, Mary Lou sprawled with her legs apart, her braided hair slung over her shoulder, me sitting with my arms hugging my knees my backbone tight and straight knowing I was being watched. Mary Lou said, lowering her voice, "Did you ever touch yourself in a certain place, Melissa?" "No," I said, pretending I didn't know what she meant. "Hans wanted to do that," Mary Lou said. She sounded disgusted. Then she started to giggle. "I wouldn't let him, then he wanted to do something else – started unbuttoning his pants – wanted me to touch *him*. And . . ."

I wanted to hush her, to clap my hand over her mouth. But she just went on and I never said a word until we both started giggling together and couldn't stop. Afterward I didn't remember most of it or why I'd been so excited my face burning and my eyes seared as if I'd been staring into the sun.

On the way home Mary Lou said, "Some things are so sad you can't say them." But I pretended not to hear.

A few days later I came back by myself. Through the ravaged cornfield: the stalks dried and broken, the tassels burnt, that rustling whispering sound of the wind I can hear now if I listen closely. My head was aching with excitement. I was telling myself a story that we'd made plans to run away and live in the Minton house. I was carrying a willow switch I'd found on the ground, fallen from a tree but still green and springy, slapping at things with it as if it were a whip. Talking to myself. Laughing aloud. Wondering was I being watched.

I climbed in the house through the back window and brushed my hands on my jeans. My hair was sticking to the back of my neck.

At the foot of the stairs I called up, "Who's here?" in a voice meant to show it was all play; I knew I was alone.

My heart was beating hard and quick, like a bird caught in the hand. It was lonely without Mary Lou so I walked heavy to let them know I was there and wasn't afraid. I started singing, I started whistling. Talking to myself and slapping at things with the willow switch. Laughing aloud, a little angry. Why was I angry, well I didn't know, someone was whispering telling me to come upstairs, to walk on the inside of the stairs so the steps wouldn't collapse.

The house was beautiful inside if you had the right eyes to see it. If you didn't mind the smell. Glass underfoot, broken plaster, stained wallpaper hanging in shreds. Tall narrow windows looking out onto wild weedy patches of green. I heard something in one of the rooms but when I looked I saw nothing much more than an easy chair lying on its side. Vandals had ripped stuffing out of it and tried to set it afire. The material was filthy but I could see that it had been pretty once – a floral design – tiny yellow flowers and green ivy. A woman used to sit in the chair, a big woman with sly staring eyes. Knitting in her lap but she wasn't knitting just staring out the window watching to see who might be coming to visit.

Upstairs the rooms were airless and so hot I felt my skin prickle like shivering. I wasn't afraid! – I slapped at the walls with my springy willow switch. In one of the rooms high in a corner wasps buzzed around a fat wasp's nest. In another room I looked out the window leaning out the window to breathe thinking this was my window, I'd come to live here. She was telling me I had better lie down and rest because I was in danger of heatstroke and I pretended not to know what heatstroke was but she knew I knew because hadn't a cousin of mine collapsed haying just last summer, they said his face had gone blotched and red and he'd begun breathing faster and faster not getting enough oxygen until he collapsed. I was looking out at the overgrown apple orchard, I could smell the rot, a sweet winey smell, the sky was hazy like something you can't get clear in your vision, pressing in close and warm. A half mile away Elk Creek glittered through a screen of willow trees moving slow glittering with scales like winking.

Come away from that window, someone told me sternly.

But I took my time obeying.

In the biggest of the rooms was an old mattress pulled off rusty bedsprings and dumped on the floor. They'd torn some of the stuffing out of this too, there were scorch marks on it from cigarettes. The fabric was stained with something like rust and I didn't want to look at it but I had to. Once at Mary Lou's when I'd gone home with her after school there was a mattress lying out in the yard in the sun and Mary Lou told me in disgust that it was her youngest brother's mattress – he'd wet his bed again and the mattress had to be aired out. As if the stink would ever go away, Mary Lou said.

Something moved inside the mattress, a black glittering thing, it was a cockroach but I wasn't allowed to jump back. Suppose you have to lie down on that mattress and sleep, I was told. Suppose you can't go home until you do. My eyelids were heavy, my head was pounding with blood. A mosquito buzzed around me but I was too tired to brush it away. Lie down on that mattress, Melissa, she told me. You know you must be punished.

I knelt down, not on the mattress, but on the floor beside it. The smells in the room were close and rank but I didn't mind, my head was nodding with sleep. Rivulets of sweat ran down my face and sides, under my arms, but I didn't mind. I saw my hand move out slowly like a stranger's hand to touch the mattress and a shiny black cockroach scuttled away in fright, and a second cockroach, and a third – but I couldn't jump up and scream.

Lie down on that mattress and take your punishment.

I looked over my shoulder and there was a woman standing in the doorway – a woman I'd never seen before.

She was staring at me. Her eyes were shiny and dark. She licked her lips and said in a jeering voice, "What are you doing here in this house, miss?"

I was terrified. I tried to answer but I couldn't speak.

"Have you come to see me?" the woman asked.

She was no age I could guess. Older than my mother but not old-seeming. She wore men's clothes and she was tall as any man, with wide shoulders, and long legs, and big sagging breasts like cows' udders loose inside her shirt not harnessed in a brassiere like other women's. Her thick wiry gray hair was cut short as a man's and stuck up in tufts that looked greasy. Her eyes were small, and black, and set back deep in their sockets; the flesh around them looked bruised. I had never seen anyone like her before – her thighs were enormous, big as my body. There was a ring of loose soft flesh at the waistband of her trousers but she wasn't fat.

"I asked you a question, miss. Why are you here?"

I was so frightened I could feel my bladder contract. I stared at her, cowering by the mattress, and couldn't speak.

It seemed to please her that I was so frightened. She approached me, stooping a little to get through the doorway. She said, in a mock-kindly voice, "You've come to visit with me – is that it?"

"No," I said.

"No!" she said, laughing. "Why, of course you have."

"No. I don't know you."

She leaned over me, touched my forehead with her fingers. I shut my eyes waiting to be hurt but her touch was cool. She brushed my hair off my forehead where it was sticky with sweat. "I've seen you here before, you and that other one," she said. "What is her name? The blond one. The two of you, trespassing."

I couldn't move, my legs were paralyzed. Quick and darting and buzzing my thoughts bounded in every which direction but didn't take hold. "Melissa is *your* name, isn't it," the woman said. "And what is your sister's name?"

"She isn't my sister," I whispered.

"What is her name?"

"I don't know."

"You don't know!"

"– don't know," I said, cowering.

The woman drew back half sighing half grunting. She looked at me pityingly. "You'll have to be punished, then."

I could smell ashes about her, something cold. I started to whimper started to say I hadn't done anything wrong, hadn't hurt anything in the house, I had only been exploring – I wouldn't come back again . . .

She was smiling at me, uncovering her teeth. She could read my thoughts before I could think them.

The skin of her face was in layers like an onion, like she'd been sunburnt, or had a skin disease. There were patches that had begun to peel. Her look was wet and gloating. Don't hurt me, I wanted to say. Please don't hurt me.

I'd begun to cry. My nose was running like a baby's. I thought I would crawl past the woman I would get to my feet and run past her and escape but the woman stood in my way blocking my way leaning over me breathing damp and warm her breath like a cow's breath in my face. Don't hurt me, I said, and she said, "You know you have to be punished – you and your pretty blond sister."

"She isn't my sister," I said.

"And what is her name?"

The woman was bending over me, quivering with laughter.

"Speak up, miss. What is it?"

"I don't know—" I started to say. But my voice said, "Mary Lou."

The woman's big breasts spilled down into her belly, I could feel her shaking with laughter. But she spoke sternly saying that Mary Lou and I had been very bad girls and we knew it her house was forbidden territory and we knew it hadn't we known all along that others had come to grief beneath its roof?

"No," I started to say. But my voice said, "Yes."

The woman laughed, crouching above me. "Now, miss, 'Melissa'

as they call you – your parents don't know where you are at this very
moment, do they?"

"I don't know."

"Do they?"

"No."

"They don't know anything about you, do they? – what you do,
and what you think? You and 'Mary Lou.'"

"No."

She regarded me for a long moment, smiling. Her smile was wide
and friendly.

"You're a spunky little girl, aren't you, with a mind of your own,
aren't you, you and your pretty little sister. I bet your bottoms have
been warmed many a time," the woman said, showing her big
tobacco-stained teeth in a grin, ". . . your tender little asses."

I began to giggle. My bladder tightened.

"Hand that here, miss," the woman said. She took the willow
switch from my fingers – I had forgotten I was holding it. "I will now
administer punishment: take down your jeans. Take down your
panties. Lie down on that mattress. Hurry." She spoke briskly now,
she was all business. "Hurry, Melissa! *And* your panties! Or do you
want me to pull them down for you?"

She was slapping the switch impatiently against the palm of her left
hand, making a wet scolding noise with her lips. Scolding and teasing.
Her skin shone in patches, stretched tight over the big hard bones of her
face. Her eyes were small, crinkling smaller, black and damp. She was
so big she had to position herself carefully over me to give herself proper
balance and leverage so that she wouldn't fall. I could hear her hoarse
eager breathing as it came to me from all sides like the wind.

I had done as she told me. It wasn't me doing these things but they
were done. Don't hurt me, I whispered, lying on my stomach on the
mattress, my arms stretched above me and my fingernails digging
into the floor. The coarse wood with splinters pricking my skin.
Don't hurt me O please but the woman paid no heed her warm wet
breath louder now and the floorboards creaking beneath her weight.
"Now, miss, now 'Melissa' as they call you – this will be our secret
won't it . . ."

When it was over she wiped at her mouth and said she would let me
go today if I promised never to tell anybody if I sent my pretty little
sister to her tomorrow.

She isn't my sister, I said, sobbing. When I could get my breath.

*   *   *

I had lost control of my bladder after all, I'd begun to pee even before the first swipe of the willow switch hit me on the buttocks, peeing in helpless spasms, and sobbing, and afterward the woman scolded me saying wasn't it a poor little baby wetting itself like that. But she sounded repentant too, stood well aside to let me pass, Off you go! Home you go! And don't forget!

And I ran out of the room hearing her laughter behind me and down the stairs running running as if I hadn't any weight my legs just blurry beneath me as if the air was water and I was swimming I ran out of the house and through the cornfield running in the cornfield sobbing as the corn stalks slapped at my face *Off you go! Home you go! And don't forget!*

I told Mary Lou about the Minton house and something that had happened to me there that was a secret and she didn't believe me at first saying with a jeer, "Was it a ghost? Was it Hans?" I said I couldn't tell. Couldn't tell what? she said. Couldn't tell, I said. Why not? she said.

"Because I promised."

"Promised who?" she said. She looked at me with her wide blue eyes like she was trying to hypnotize me. "You're a goddamned liar."

Later she started in again asking me what had happened what was the secret was it something to do with Hans? did he still like her? was he mad at her? and I said it didn't have anything to do with Hans not a thing to do with him. Twisting my mouth to show what I thought of him.

"Then who –?" Mary Lou asked.

"I told you it was a secret."

"Oh shit – what kind of a secret?"

"A secret."

"A secret *really?*"

I turned away from Mary Lou, trembling. My mouth kept twisting in a strange hurting smile. "Yes. A secret *really*," I said.

The last time I saw Mary Lou she wouldn't sit with me on the bus, walked past me holding her head high giving me a mean snippy look out of the corner of her eye. Then when she left for her stop she made sure she bumped me going by my seat, she leaned over to say, "I'll find out for myself, I hate you anyway," speaking loud enough for everybody on the bus to hear, "– I always have."

Once upon a time the fairy tales begin. But then they end and often you don't know really what has happened, what was meant to happen, you only know what you've been told, what the words suggest. Now that I have completed my story, filled up half my notebook with my handwriting that disappoints me, it is so shaky and childish – now the story is over I don't understand what it means. I know what happened in my life but I don't know what has happened in these pages.

Mary Lou was found murdered ten days after she said those words to me. Her body had been tossed into Elk Creek a quarter mile from the road and from the old Minton place. Where, it said in the paper, nobody had lived for fifteen years.

It said that Mary Lou had been thirteen years old at the time of her death. She'd been missing for seven days, had been the object of a countrywide search.

It said that nobody had lived in the Minton house for years but that derelicts sometimes sheltered there. It said that the body was unclothed and mutilated. There were no details.

This happened a long time ago.

The murderer (or murderers as the newspaper always said) was never found.

Hans Meunzer was arrested of course and kept in the county jail for three days while police questioned him but in the end they had to let him go, insufficient evidence to build a case it was explained in the newspaper though everybody knew he was the one wasn't he the one? – everybody knew. For years afterward they'd be saying that. Long after Hans was gone and the Siskins were gone, moved away nobody knew where.

Hans swore he hadn't done it, hadn't seen Mary Lou for weeks. There were people who testified in his behalf said he couldn't have done it for one thing he didn't have his brother's car any longer and he'd been working all that time. Working hard out in the fields – couldn't have slipped away long enough to do what police were saying he'd done. And Hans said over and over he was innocent. Sure he was innocent. Son of a bitch ought to be hanged my father said, everybody knew Hans was the one unless it was a derelict or a fisherman – fishermen often drove out to Elk Creek to fish for black bass, built fires on the creek bank and left messes behind – sometimes prowled around the Minton house too looking for things to steal. The police had records of automobile license plates belonging to some of these men, they questioned them but nothing came of it. Then there was that crazy man, that old hermit living in a tar-paper shanty near the Shaheen dump that everybody'd said ought to have been committed to the state hospital years ago. But everybody knew really it was Hans and Hans got out as quick as he could, just disappeared and not even his family knew where unless they were lying which probably they were though they claimed not.

Mother rocked me in her arms crying, the two of us crying, she told me that Mary Lou was happy now, Mary Lou was in Heaven now, Jesus Christ had taken her to live with Him and I knew that didn't I? I wanted to laugh but I didn't laugh. Mary Lou shouldn't have gone with boys, not a nasty boy like Hans, Mother said, she shouldn't have been sneaking around the way she did – I knew that didn't I? Mother's words filled my head flooding my head so there was no danger of laughing.

Jesus loves you too you know that don't you Melissa? Mother asked hugging me. I told her yes. I didn't laugh because I was crying.

They wouldn't let me go to the funeral, said it would scare me too much. Even though the casket was closed.

It's said that when you're older you remember things that happened a long time ago better than you remember things that have just happened and I have found that to be so.

For instance I can't remember when I bought this notebook at Woolworth's whether it was last week or last month or just a few days ago. I can't remember why I started writing in it, what purpose I told myself. But I remember Mary Lou stooping to say those words in my ear and I remember when Mary Lou's mother came over to ask us at suppertime a few days later if I had seen Mary Lou that day – I remember the very food on my plate, the mashed potatoes in a dry little mound. I remember hearing Mary Lou call my name standing out in the driveway cupping her hands to her mouth the way Mother hated her to do, it was white trash behavior.

"'Lissa!" Mary Lou would call, and I'd call back, "Okay, I'm coming!" *Once upon a time.*

Video Nasty

Philip Pullman

Location: Oxford, England.

Time: November, 1994.

Eyewitness Description: *"David looked at the strange boy. His eyes were wide and fixed intently on the screen, and his lips were moving unconsciously with the words. David felt queer. He knew now very strongly that he didn't want to watch the film at all . . ."*

Author: Philip Pullman (1946–) is the author of *His Dark Materials* (1995–2000), the biggest-selling and most controversial trilogy of modern times in which he has challenged Christian faith and attacked the constraints of dogmatism. Born in Norwich, but educated at Harlech and Exeter College, Oxford, Pullman says that he started telling stories as soon as he knew what they were and formed a life-long fascination with the supernatural. He recalled recently, "I used to enjoy frightening myself and my friends with the tales I read and I liked making up stories about the tree in the woods we used to call the Hanging Tree. My friends and I would creep past it in the dark and shiver as we looked at the bare, sinister outline against the sky. I still enjoy ghost stories, even though I don't think I believe in ghosts any more." Pullman began writing while he was working as a teacher, but the popularity of his children's titles such as *Count Karlstein* (1982), *Frankenstein* (1990) and the Sally Lockhart series of modern "penny dreadfuls", followed by the phenomenal acclaim for his trilogy, has enabled him to devote himself entirely to the art of storytelling. "Video Nasty" is one of his few short stories, contemporary, unsettling and, as the title indicates, dealing with *something* very unpleasant.

It was a cold grey afternoon in November, and the three boys had been hanging around the shopping precinct since mid-morning. They'd had some chips at midday, and Kevin had nicked a couple of Mars bars from the newsagent's, so they weren't hungry. And until they were thrown out of Woolworth's they weren't cold either; but by half-past three they were cold and fed up, and almost wished they'd gone to school.

"How much longer we got to wait?" said David, the youngest boy, to Martin, the oldest.

Martin was fourteen, thin and dark and sharper than the other two by a long way. He looked at his watch. "Oh, come on," he said. "Let's go and see if it's ready."

He hunched himself inside his anorak and led the way out of the precinct and down one of the old streets that led towards the canal. The cold wind blew crisp packets and old newspapers around their ankles. The boys turned around two corners and stopped outside a little newsagent's, where one of the windows was filled with a display of video cassettes.

"See if there's anyone in there, Kev," said Martin.

Kevin opened the door, which jangled loudly. The street was empty, apart from an abandoned Datsun without any wheels that stood in a scatter of broken glass half on and half off the pavement. After a few seconds Kevin came out and said, "'S okay."

The other two went in. The place smelled like all newsagents – a bit chocolatey, a bit smokey, a bit like old comics. There was nothing unusual about it, but David felt his stomach tightening. He pretended to be unconcerned and picked up a paperback that said AQUARIUS: Your Horoscope For 1994. He didn't know if he was Aquarius or what, but he had to look cool.

An old man had come out from the back. He was carrying a mug of tea, and sipped at it before he spoke.

"Yes, lads?" he said.

Martin went up to the counter. "You got that video in yet?" he said. "The one you told me about last week?"

The old man took another sip, and narrowed his eyes.

"What one's that? I don't remember you."

"You said it'd be in today. *Snuff Park*. You told me about it."

Recognition came into the old man's eyes, and he smiled carefully.

"Course I remember," he said. "You got to be careful, that's all. Wait there."

He put his mug on a shelf and shuffled out. Kevin's frowning, short-sighted eyes flickered to the sweets, but Martin put his hand on his arm, and shook his head. No-one spoke.

After a minute the old man came back with a video cassette, which he put in a brown paper bag. Martin passed over the money; David put back his book and opened the jangling door.

"Bye, lads," said the old man. "Enjoy the film."

"Let's have a look," said Kevin, once they were outside.

Martin took out the cassette, but there was no picture. There was just a plain white label with "SNUFF PARK. 112 mins" typed in the centre.

"What's mins?" said Kevin.

"Minutes, you berk. That's how long it lasts," said Martin, putting it back. "Come on, let's get a cup of tea. I'm perished."

"Can't we go to your place?"

"Not yet. I told you. They ain't going out till six. We got to hang about till then."

As they walked past the abandoned Datsun, one of the doors creaked open. David jumped back out of the way. A thin boy of about his age, wearing torn jeans and trainers and a dirty anorak, was sitting in the driver's seat, with his feet on the pavement. He said something quietly and Martin stopped.

"What?" he said.

"What cassette you got?" said the boy. His voice sounded like the sound your feet make in dry leaves.

"What you want to know for?" said Martin.

The boy shrugged. David thought he could smell him: sharp and dirty and somehow cold. Kevin had his hand on the car door.

"*Snuff Park*," said Martin after a moment. "You seen it?"

The boy shrugged again, and said "Yeah". He wasn't looking at any of them, but down at the pavement. He scuffed the broken glass with one foot.

No-one else spoke, so Martin turned and walked off. The other two followed. David looked back at the boy in the car, but he hadn't moved. Just before they turned the corner, he shut the car door.

In the cafeteria, Martin paid for three cups of tea and brought them to the table by the window where Kevin and David had found a place. David didn't know where Martin got his money from; he assumed Martin's parents gave it to him. He always seemed to have plenty, but he never boasted about stealing it, as Kevin would have done.

He stirred sugar into his tea and watched his reflection in the glass. It was nearly dark outside already.

"What's it about, *Snuff Park?*" said Kevin. "Sounds crummy."

"Well it ain't," said Martin. "It's a real snuff movie."

"What's one of them?"

Martin sighed. "Tell him, Dave," he said.

David felt a glow of pride at being called Dave.

"It's where they kill someone," he said. "Ain't it, Martin?"

Martin nodded and sipped the hot tea.

"What d'you mean?" said Kevin. "I seen plenty of them."

"No you ain't," said Martin. "They stopped 'em years back. You can't get 'em no more. 'Cept if you know how."

"I seen all sorts," said Kevin. "I seen *Forest of Blood* and *Sawmill.* You seen *Sawmill?*"

"That ain't a snuff movie. You're a berk, you are. This is real. There's someone really killed on this. You see it being done. You ain't never seen that."

David again felt his stomach lift. He hoped desperately that he wouldn't be sick in front of Martin when the time came. Even thinking about it . . .

"There's that kid again," said Kevin.

He pointed to the brightly-lit doorway of an electricity board showroom opposite. Sandwich-makers, microwave ovens, cookers, heaters, freezers, and in the doorway gazing in, the thin huddled figure from the car. As they looked he wandered away from there and stared through the window of the supermarket next door.

Martin looked away.

"If you're scared, you needn't watch it," he said.

"Course I ain't scared," said Kevin. "I seen *Sawmill* and I weren't scared of that."

"This is different," said Martin.

David looked out of the window again, but the other boy had gone.

Martin turned the key and opened the door. The house was full of darkness and the smell of chips and tobacco smoke. David felt the warmth on his cheeks. He'd never been to Martin's house before, and he looked around curiously as Martin put the hall light on. There was a really smart carpet, and a mirror with all gold round it, and a TV phone. He felt reassured. It was so nice that you couldn't imagine anything horrible happening there. *Snuff Park* might not be all that bad. And he could always close his eyes.

"You going to put it on then?" said Kevin. "Where's the telly?"

"No hurry. I want something to eat first. Ain't you hungry?"

"What you got to eat?"

"Dunno. Fish and chips'll do. You better eat it now 'cause you won't want to after, will he, Dave?"

"No," said David. "Not after."

"Here," said Martin to David, handing him a ten-pound note. "Go round the chippy. Cod and chips three times, all right?"

"Ta, Martin," said David, and added "Don't start it without me."

The chip shop was just around the corner. On his way back, with the soft hot bundles clutched to his chest, David suddenly stopped. The boy from the car was standing outside Martin's front door.

"What do you want?" said David, before he could stop himself.

"You going to watch the video?" said the boy.

David could hardly hear what he said. He supposed the boy had got a cold, or asthma, like David's sister.

"Yeah," he said.

"Can I watch it?"

"I dunno. It ain't mine, it's my mate's."

The two boys stood still, not looking at each other.

"I'll ask him," said David finally, and rang the bell.

When Martin opened the door David said "I got 'em. Three cod and chips. And this kid was there outside the house. He says he wants to watch the video."

Martin twisted his mouth. Kevin, behind him, said, "He'll never take it. He'll never take the pressure."

"All right, let's see if he does," said Martin. "Let him in, then."

The strange boy came in after David and stood in the living-room while they ate their fish and chips. David offered him some, but he just said, "No, I don't want none." After a minute or two he sat down. The others didn't say anything, but ate quickly, and dropped their papers in the fireplace. David could smell the strange boy again. The room was hot, and he dropped his anorak on the thick red carpet, but the strange boy kept his on, and sat with his hands in his pockets, unmoving.

"All right then?" said Martin. "I'll put it on."

He fitted the cassette into the machine and sprawled back in a big leather armchair with the remote control. David and Kevin were sitting on the settee, and the other boy was on a dining chair by the table. Martin turned the TV on.

"Smart telly," said Kevin.

It was a 48-inch. The big screen lifted itself out of the console and filled with colour.

"You seen a snuff picture before?" said Martin to the strange boy.

"Yeah. I seen this one." They had to strain to hear him.

"This one?" It was plain that Martin didn't believe him. "You know what happens?"

"Yeah. I seen it hundreds of times."

"Hundreds? Get lost."

"Here," said Kevin. "Let's watch it with the light out."

"Stay there," said Martin. "Watch this."

He pressed a button on the remote control, and the big centre light above them faded into darkness. Now the only light came from the screen.

"Smart!" said Kevin.

They found themselves watching a suburban street from the windscreen of a moving car. It was a sunny day. There were lots of trees covered in leaves, and the houses looked nice and big, with lots of space between them.

Then the commentary began.

"Just an ordinary road in an ordinary English town," said a man's voice. It was a strong deep voice, warm and concerned. "An ordinary summer's day. But for one woman nothing will be the same again. There will never be another summer's day for her."

David looked at the strange boy. His eyes were wide and fixed intently on the screen, and his lips were moving unconsciously with the words. David felt queer. He knew now very strongly that he didn't want to watch the film at all. He let his eyes go back to the screen, but tried to make them out of focus so that he couldn't see clearly.

A few minutes passed. There was no more commentary from the film, but suddenly the strange boy said something.

"What?" said Martin.

"I says it's a nice house, ain't it?" said the boy.

Kevin, frowning concentratedly, took no notice. Martin grunted, but David looked at the boy again. Anything to get his eyes off the screen; but nothing had happened yet.

"Must be nice living there," said the boy, still staring. But his expression was strange; David couldn't understand it.

"Yeah," he said to the boy.

There was a woman on the screen. She was doing normal things, like washing up and ironing. She was talking to the camera about housework or something. David felt full of fear, almost ready to be sick, because it was all so ordinary, and you knew she was real, and you knew it had really happened, like this, and you knew you were going to see her murdered.

"This is boring," said Kevin. "What's she on about?"

"Shut up," said Martin. "They got the camera in there to get her confidence."

"But there ain't nothing happening," said Kevin. "She's just bloody talking."

"She's pretty, ain't she?" said the boy.

The other two fell silent, and turned to him for a moment. Even David sensed it was an odd thing to say.

"Eh?" said Martin.

"I says she's pretty, ain't she. She's really nice."

"What d'you mean?" said Kevin.

"She's my mum," said the boy.

There was another silence then. Everything had suddenly changed, and David felt it, but didn't know how or why.

"Eh?" said Martin.

"I says she's my mum. She loves me and I love her."

The boys shifted in their seats. The pictures on the screen had changed. It was night-time, and the camera was outside the house looking in through the kitchen window. The room was warmly lit; the woman was moving about, alone, watering some big green plants. She bent down and picked up a little baby from what must have been a carry-cot, and cuddled it. But none of the three boys were taking this in: they were paralysed by what the strange boy had said. No-one said that sort of thing.

"He's mad," said Kevin uneasily.

"Hey, what's your name?" said Martin.

There was no reply. Instead the commentary began again:

"*Alone. There is no-one to help. Little does she know that an unseen hand has cut the phone wire. And now . . . the fear begins.*"

The boy was mouthing the words as if he knew them by heart. Suddenly from the darkness a stone shattered the kitchen window, and the woman gasped and turned wildly, clutching the baby to her. Her wide-eyed face stared out at them, and then they all saw at once that she *was* his mother.

She was bending now, putting the baby down swiftly. And then another window shattered, and she jumped and cried out.

David's heart was beating like a captured bird.

"Martin—" he started to say, but Martin himself spoke at the same time, loudly, sitting up tensely in his chair and turning to the strange boy.

"What d'you want?" he cried. "What you come here for?"

Kevin was shifting himself next to David, making himself look small and inconspicuous, like he did in class. Martin's face was twisted and full of hate.

"Just wanted to see—" began the strange boy, but his dry rustling voice was drowned by a scream from the TV. David flicked a sideways look at the screen: a man with a stocking mask had burst into the kitchen. There was a blur in the sound, as if two pieces of film had been joined carelessly, and then the camera was suddenly inside the kitchen with them.

"Martin!" cried David.

"What's the matter?" shouted Martin. He was shaking, glaring at the screen, staring wildly, gripping the remote control. "You scared? You seen enough?" He pressed the volume switch, and terrible sounds flooded the room. David put his hands over his ears. Kevin was still watching, but he'd curled up very small, and he was holding his fists in front of his mouth.

And the strange boy was still gazing at the screen. The woman was speaking, gabbling desperately, and the boy's eyes followed her and his lips moved with her words.

"Shut up!" Martin yelled. "Shut up!"

He jumped up and dropped the remote control. The picture faded at once, and the last thing David saw was Martin's face, wet with sweat.

They were in darkness.

No one moved.

David heard Martin gulping and breathing heavily. He felt sick with fear and shame.

The strange boy said, "It ain't finished."

"Shut up!" said Martin fiercely. "Get out!"

"I can't till it's finished. I always see the end."

"What you want to watch it for?"

"I always watch it. That's the only time I see her. I like seeing my mum."

In the darkness his voice sounded more than ever distant, and cold, and strange. David's skin was crawling. Everything was horrible. It had been horrible all day, but this was worse than anything. He thought of his own mum, and nearly sobbed out loud, but stifled it just in time.

"And the baby." The strange boy spoke again. "It's a nice baby, ain't it? It looks nice. It must be nice being picked up like that, like what she does. I wish I could remember."

"What d'you mean?" said Martin hoarsely.

The boy's voice was even quieter now: hardly more than dead leaves falling.

"They killed her and then they set fire to the house. It all burnt up, the baby and all. That was me, that was, that baby. I burnt up all with my mum. But I didn't stop growing up, getting older, like. It must be the video. Sort of kept me going. I seen it hundreds of times. The best bit is where she picks me up. I reckon she must have loved me a lot. That's all I do, watch that video. There ain't nothing else . . ."

He stopped.

Martin stumbled to the door and felt for the light-switch. The room sprang into being around them, all solid and bright, but there was no-one else there. Only a sharp, distant smell remained, and that dwindled after a moment and then vanished completely as if it had never existed. The boy was gone.

My Beautiful House

Louis de Bernières

Location: Abbots Notwithstanding, Surrey.
Time: December, 2004.
Eyewitness Account: *"The house is alive. It watches over me always, and it's watching me now as I sit here, not feeling the cold, looking at it from the end of the garden . . ."*

Author: Louis de Bernières (1954–) has been named one of the most outstanding British novelists of his generation and the international success of his novel, *Captain Corelli's Mandolin* (1994), has transformed his life. Born in London, he joined the Army but dropped out of the 2nd Queen's Dragoon Guards and led something of a hippie lifestyle in countless jobs – including mechanic, motorcycle messenger and *gaucho* in Argentina – before succeeding as a writer. Supplementing his income restoring old guitars and mandolins, he hit on the idea of writing about the German and Italian occupying forces on the Greek island of Cephalonia. The story of the troubled captain was the result and apart from generating huge sales, was made into a movie and turned the island into a tourist hot spot. With each of his subsequent works, de Bernières has set himself a new challenge: most recently delving into the ghost story genre with "Mrs Mac" (1997) and "My Beautiful House" written for *The Times* in December 2004. It is a wonderfully evocative, beautifully crafted and chilling tale in the very best supernatural tradition and proves, if any such proof is necessary, that the ghost story is alive and well and certain to hold its interest for readers as successfully in the 21st century as it has done in the past one. No doubt developing, entertaining and *surprising* us all, too.

I love it at Christmas. I just sit here at the end of the garden on top of the rockery, like a garden gnome. I don't find the stones uncomfortable. I sit here and look at the house. It's very beautiful, I always did think so. I grew up here, and I am still here now, although I spend much of my time out in the garden just looking.

Other people may not think it beautiful, but it's beautiful to me mainly because I always loved it. I loved my childhood in this house, and I loved it when I had to go abroad on military service, because it represented everything I was fighting for, and I loved it when I came back to Notwithstanding from Korea, and settled into the life I was born to. Here is the clump of bamboos behind which I used to conceal myself when playing hide and seek with my brothers and sister. Further up there on the left is a bird-table that I made when I was at school. It's amazing that it hasn't rotted away by now. The lawn isn't very smooth, there's too much couch grass, but we used to set up a putting green on it in the summer, and it ruined my father's scores at the real golf course because he kept hitting the ball a long way past the hole. Here is the big apple tree that was so easy to climb, and produced great Bramleys that my mother made into pies. One year we tried to make cider, but it was very sharp. We had rabbits in the orchard, in a big wire enclosure that was movable. They kept the grass mown if you remembered to move the cage around. Of course they'd escape quite often by burrowing underneath, and they'd go and raid the vegetable patch, but they came when you called them anyway. The cage started life as a chicken run, but we found them too ill-natured. There used to be a modest fruit cage just here as well, and I often had to go into it to free the robins and blackbirds that got stuck inside. They would fly about in a silly panic, and didn't know you were trying to be helpful. "Funny kind of fruit-cage," my father used to say. "Keeps birds in instead of out."

The house isn't very old. It's Edwardian, and it's made of nice red brick with tiles coming half way down the walls, in the Surrey farmhouse style. I remember when the Virginia creeper and the wistaria were planted, and now they're all over the walls. I don't know who the architect was, but it's a very conventional design. Most of the other family houses around here are quite similar. The first people to live here came down from the North. I think they were in textiles. Then it belonged to a writer who was quite famous in his time, but now no one's even heard of him. Then it belonged to a retired naval officer and his wife, and then it was ours. I have so many happy memories. I don't ever want to leave.

Inside there were about five bedrooms. My parents had the one at the back. Mine was above the kitchen. Every morning the smell of frying eggs and sausages would get me out of bed in a good mood. My room wasn't big, but it was big enough for my model aeroplanes to hang from the ceiling on string, and for my toy soldiers to have decent-sized battles. I had a little cannon that worked on a spring, and you could put ball-bearings or matches into it, pull back the lever, release it, and mow down the troops. When I grew up I would find little ball-bearings all over the place.

My brother Michael shared a room with my other brother Sebastian. They were twins, but not identical. My sister Catherine had the room opposite my parents, and sometimes I would creep into her room at night with a sheet over my head, and give her a fright, or I'd listen for when she went to the loo, and I'd lie down at the corner of the corridor and grab her ankle as she went past in the dark. It worked every time. Then my mother told me to stop doing it, because it was unnerving being woken up by screaming in the middle of the night. Catherine used to get revenge by leaning over the banisters of the landing, and spitting on my head when I was underneath in the hallway. It's hard to imagine that she grew up to be so beautiful and refined, and married a baronet.

On the top floor up the back stairs, under the roof, is a lovely big dusty attic. I think it had been fitted out for a servant to live in, because it had a proper little fireplace, and the rafters were all boarded in. I spent hours up there. I fixed a dartboard to the wall, and I threw darts at it, backhand, underarm, over my shoulder, every possible way. I got very good at it. It was one of my party tricks. I used to go up there when I was miserable as well, because no one would know I was weeping.

I always liked the bells. You'd press a button on the wall in any room, and it would ring in the pantry, and a little brown semaphore would wave back and forth in a box above the door, and indicate which room you were ringing from. Catherine and I used to push the buttons to make my mother go to the front door and find nobody there. Once we did it, and my mother went to the door, and when she opened it, the cat was sitting there on the mat in the porch, looking up at her as if he'd pressed it himself. The cat just walked past her into the hallway, and my mother was astonished for a short time, until she realised that it couldn't possibly have been Tobermory that rang the bell. Tobermory was named after a talking cat in a story that my father read to us once. The moral of the story was that if you can talk, it's better not to tell the truth.

Our phone number was 293, amazing when you consider how long the numbers are nowadays.

I love sitting here at Christmas time, at the end of the garden. I don't

feel the cold. I like to sit here because the house looks so wonderful with
the Christmas tree behind the french windows. There's a full moon, and
I can see everything around me with perfect clarity. The stars are out,
and I can never remember which ones are the planets. Perhaps they're
the very bright ones. Sebastian used to point them out to me, but I don't
know how he knew. I used to point them out to girlfriends when I was
being romantic, but I was bluffing. I knew that they didn't know either.
The house and the garden and the sky look like something out of a
Christmas card, appropriately enough. The only thing missing is snow.
I only ever remember one white Christmas, when it snowed as we came
out of church, and Catherine was wearing a lilac coat with a hood that
had a lining of white rabbit fur that framed her face and made me think
that she was the prettiest sister that anyone ever had. Everything is silver
and shadow now, except for the Christmas tree, which is glowing with
all sorts of different coloured lights, that reflect off the tinsel and the
glass balls.

It reminds me, it can't be helped, of that dreadful night of the fire. We
had little candles in those days, little candles that sat on cups that clipped
to the branches of the Christmas tree, along with all the tatty taffeta
angels that we'd inherited. It looked magical, but it wasn't ever a good
idea. The trees dry out, and they're full of resin. They go up like a torch.

We all went to midnight Mass, and when we got home we had a
nightcap. We talked about plans for Christmas Day. My father used
to like to go shooting, but my mother more or less forbade him. She
said it wasn't nice to go round bowling over rabbits and blasting
birds out of the sky on the day when our Saviour was born to bring
peace and harmony to the world. We decided we'd all walk to
Abbot's Notwithstanding and back again before lunch, but my
mother would have to drop out because someone had to baste
the goose. I think she was probably relieved, because she wasn't a
great one for unnecessary exercise.

The whole family were there, including the baronet. We liked the
baronet. He didn't put on any airs, and he didn't have any side. He
had a quiet charm and a confidence. He gave up the army for
Catherine's sake, because she didn't want to have to be sent off all
over the world at a moment's notice. It was decent of him because he
was a Coldstreamer, he was doing well, and he obviously loved it. He
and Catherine came down from Cambridgeshire in the Riley to be
with us for Christmas. Sebastian and Michael came down from
Merton, and I was living at home anyway, because I'd always loved
that house, and didn't want to move anywhere else, not unless I
married, and anyway I'd found a decent job in Guildford. I paid rent

to my mother without my father knowing, which seemed the best thing. Knowing her, she spent the money on shoes.

That night, what with us being tired and having a tot of whisky inside us, we forgot to put out the candles on the tree, just as anyone might, but the next thing I knew, I woke up choking. I got out of bed, hacking and coughing, and I groped about in the smoke, but I couldn't find the lightswitch, and there was a terrible pain in my lungs, and I was coughing so much that it was agony. I felt that I was vomiting my lungs up. My eyes stung so badly from the smoke that I couldn't open them, and even so they were still streaming with tears. I remember the pain, the coughing, the stinging in my eyes, and the insuperable fear, the not knowing where I was in the room, the roaring noise, and then it was as if my chest and my brain were full of molten lead, and I must have passed out. I don't really know what happened next.

As I sit here at the end of the garden, on the rockery, looking at the Christmas tree with its electric lights, it's hard to believe that the house was almost gutted. The tree must have set the curtains alight, and so on. Anyway, it's all been repaired, and you'd never know that anything happened. It's part of the wonder of the house. It doesn't die, it just keeps on evolving. The house is alive. It watches over me always, and it's watching me now as I sit here, not feeling the cold, looking at it from the end of the garden.

The house may be alive, but my family aren't. They all perished in the fire, from inhaling the smoke, every one of them, including the cat. Even so, it doesn't stop them turning up. Just now my father put his hand on my shoulder, and said: "Come on, my boy." Death hasn't changed him at all. He's just as solid, he's still got the same voice and even the same smell of Three Nuns Navy Cut pipe tobacco. He still smokes a pipe. He wears the plus fours and long socks and brogues that I used to find so embarrassing and old-fashioned. Every time I sit here, he comes and asks me to leave. I wish he wouldn't. I love him, but he isn't entitled to tell me what to do any more.

They're all here now, as solid and real as when they were alive. There's Catherine and her baronet, hand in hand, and Sebastian and Michael looking at me pityingly. There's even the cat. It's not Tobermory. This one is Gerald, and he was two cats later. Gerald used to drink from the dripping tap in the bathroom basin, whereas Tobermory would get under the sofa, stick his claws into the hessian underneath, and drag himself along on his back as fast as he could go. Gerald settles on his haunches and looks up at me with interest, as if I were an experiment.

My mother is here too. She reaches out a hand to try to take mine, and says: "Please, darling, please," but I take my hand away, not roughly, but gently. I know she loves me, you see, and I don't want to cause her any hurt. She implores me with her eyes, and still holds out, her hand.

"Come on, you big fool," says Sebastian, grinning like a big schoolboy, and Michael thumps me on the shoulder with the same old fraternal violence, and says: "Come on, old thing. You've been here quite long enough."

"I'm watching the house," I say.

The baronet lights a cigarette, and when he throws the match to the ground, it disappears. "Look," he says, "I know I'm not strictly family and whatnot, only being married in, as it were, but you've got to give it up one of these days, this watching over the house lark."

"It's really the house watching over me," I say. "Anyway, you're all dead."

"When are you going to understand?" asks Catherine, shaking her head.

"What's wrong with staying here?" I say.

"Please," says my mother.

After a while they leave, one by one, as they always do. My mother and Catherine give me a gentle kiss on the cheek. It's surprising how you can distinctly feel the kiss of someone who is dead. My father once surprised me by taking my head between his hands and kissing me on the forehead. He would never have done that when he was alive, and he hasn't done it since. Michael and Sebastian subject me to more claps between the shoulderblades. They all turn and wave modestly before they fade away not far from where the bonfire always used to be. Only Gerald stays a little while. He winds himself around my legs a few times, and reaches up to touch a claw to my hand, as he used to when he suspected that it contained a morsel of cheddar cheese. After a while he wanders away after the rest of them.

I don't understand why they keep coming back. I am glad to see them, of course, but they are dead. I keep telling them, but they don't seem to be able to take it in. They don't seem to understand why I won't go with them. Perhaps death makes you less perceptive.

Anyway, I am perfectly contented here, sitting atop this rockery by moonlight, not even feeling the cold, looking at the tree sparkling with so many colours in the french window. I love it here. I love this beautiful house, I love the way it holds me as if it had hands and I was cupped inside them. I sit here and it watches over me, I feel absolute happiness, and there's nothing I'd rather do.

Appendix

A Century of Ghost Novels
1900–2000

1902: *THE HAUNTED MAJOR* by Robert Marshall

Inspired by the new craze for golf that had developed at the dawn of the 20th century, this comic story recounts the efforts of sports-mad Major Gore to beat Lindsay, a young golf champion. The Major receives supernatural assistance in his cause from the ghost of Cardinal Smeaton, a Scottish renaissance figure who is still nursing a grudge against his opponent's family.

1904: *THE GREY WORLD* by Evelyn Underhill

When little Cockney Jimmy Rogers dies of typhoid fever he finds himself in a grey world of wraith-like beings. Here he learns that it is possible to return to the real world and reincarnates himself into another quite different person whose behaviour leads him into the path of mysticism and a series of bizarre encounters.

1907: *THE GHOST* by Arnold Bennett

In pursuit of Rosetta Rose, a beautiful singer, Carl Foster survives a series of disasters: a train crash, a shipwreck and even attempted murder. On each occasion he sees a sinister figure, who proves to be the ghost of Lord Clarenceux, once in love with Rosa and now deeply jealous of his rival. It takes the intervention of the girl herself to enable Carl's love to succeed.

1907: *ALICE FOR SHORT* by William De Morgan

A beautiful woman in 18th century clothes and a man with a sword repeatedly re-enact a murder haunt in an old house in Soho. The arrival of little orphan Alice Kavanagh eventually leads to the discovery of the woman's bones buried in the basement as well as a surprising revelation about the child's ancestry.

1909: *THE GHOST PIRATES* by William Hope Hodgson

The old ship, the *Mortzestus*, is beset by mysterious phenomena – shadowy figures emerging from the sea, men hurled from aloft by invisible hands and the vessel itself seemingly trapped in a world of mist. The horrors reach a climax when ghost pirates swarm aboard to sink the ship and only one man survives to tell the story.

1911: *AN EXCHANGE OF SOULS* by Barry Pain

Dr Daniel Myas is carrying out experiments in order to transfer human souls. When the doctor dies suddenly from an overdose of drugs, his special apparatus transfers him to the body of his fiancée, Alice. The girl herself dies shortly afterwards in a train crash and the ghosts of the two endeavour to resolve their endless future.

1911: *THE WHITE PEOPLE* by Frances Hodgson Burnett

Isobel Muircarrie grows up in the Scottish Highlands where her gift of "Second Sight" enables her to see the phantom White People and communicate with a ghost child. When she moves to London as an adult and falls in love with a stricken young man, Hector MacNairn, who dies shortly afterwards of a heart attack, her ability enables her to "see" him as a spirit.

1911 *THE HAUNTED PYJAMAS* by Francis Perry Elliott

After spending three years in England, the Harvard educated narrator returns to America with a pair of pyjamas said to be over 4,000 years old. These can transform the wearer into a phantom-like figure and the young man uses them in a number of seductive exploits with very unexpected results.

1912 *THE GODS OF THE DEAD* by Winifred Graham

Matilda Turnus has inherited the poise and beauty of an Egyptian princess as well as ancient supernatural powers that she uses to great effect. Aware of a ghostly figure hovering over her in moments of crisis, she uses her ability to fend off unwanted suitors and advance the career of her young lover into the highest echelons of society.

1918 *THE GHOST GARDEN* by Amelia Rives

The ghost of a wilful and vicious young woman, Melany Horse-manden, haunts a house in colonial Virginia. When, years later, another young girl named Melany settles in the house and attracts a lover, the spirit of the deceased woman intervenes to frustrate their courtship. Ultimately, only the power of love can overcome the vampire-like powers of the undead.

1919 *SINISTER HOUSE* by Leland Hall

The ghosts of a man and woman haunt the new housing develop-ment at Forsby near Boston, sapping the vitality of a young wife, Julia Grier. They are identified as the former owners of the land who have been tricked out of their property by fraud. It requires a cruel revelation and the fortitude of Julia to finally lay the two spirits to rest.

1920 *FROM THE VASTY DEEP* by Marie Belloc Lowndes

A ghost that is initially seen only by the servants disturbs a house party at Wyndfell Hall. However, when the spirit appears more distinctly to several of the guests, it is recognised as the deceased owner of the property. Holding a séance provides the resolution to an old and terrible crime.

1921 *THE HAUNTING* by Catherine Dawson-Scott

Set in 19th-century Cornwall, Gale and Pascoe Corylon are half-brothers drawn together in an uneasy alliance carrying out shady deals in which both suspect the other of making more profit. When Gale poisons Pascoe, he suffers a series of hauntings that finally drive him to seek a desperate solution in a sea cave.

1921 *THE SHADOW OF FEAR* by Nina Toye

An old abbey reputed to be haunted and a swamp that lures unsuspecting victims to their death, play upon the emotions of an ill-matched couple who live nearby. The neurotic wife gradually succumbs to the supernatural powers and is only just prevented from killing her husband by the new love in his life.

1922 *THE HAUNTED WOMAN* by David Lindsay

Runhill Court is situated over an ancient Saxon burial ground and haunted by supernatural forces. When Henry Judge inherits the property it brings him into contact with lovely Isobel Loment and together they delve into the mystery of a secret stairway, the adventure putting their lives at risk while also causing them to fall in love.

1924 *COLD HARBOUR* by Francis Brett Young

The small Worcestershire inn that Ronald and Evelyn Wake stumble on when their car breaks down proves to be beset by poltergeist phenomena. The open-minded couple are intrigued and try to get to the bottom of the supernatural presence, ultimately deciding that the area is still in the grip of an ancient evil from Roman times that requires exorcism.

1925 *THE GREEN ROOM* by Walter de la Mare

In the back room of an old bookshop, a young man sees the ghost of a woman reading some papers. It transpires that she is the author of a manuscript of poems recording her love for a previous owner of the building. When the young man finds the poetry and decides to publish it, he quickly discovers the ghost's reaction very different to the one he had expected.

1926 *THE NEW TERROR* by Gaston Leroux

After his marriage to the beautiful Cordelia, the narrator discovers that a portrait of his bride painted by a mystical English artist seems to be obsessing her. He comes to realize his wife is so haunted by the picture that only by killing the painter can he free her – but by doing so he fatally threatens Cordelia's life.

1926 *TOPPER* by Thorne Smith

Classic novel in which harmless American banker Cosmo Topper is haunted by a group of immoral ghosts who turn him on to the delights of alcohol, drugs and sexual freedom. His riotous escapades with the spirits and everyone they come in contact with inspired a popular film and an equally successful sequel, *Topper Takes A Trip* (1932).

1928 *THE GENERAL'S RING* by Selma Lagerlof

The town of Hedby is badly haunted by the ghost of an old general. Although the descendants of the military man take the story rather casually, his grandson believes there is some truth in it. The young man has to survive being put into a trance by the powerful spirit, but manages to find the ring which is the cause of the haunting and return it to the old soldier's grave.

1931 *THE JEALOUS GHOST* by L. A. G. Strong

Middle-aged Stewart finds when he returns to his ancestral home near Skye that things have changed in many respects. But the ability to fall in love has not, and he falls for a local girl much younger than himself. His infatuation is, however, dashed when another girl, a ghost from his past, warns him off.

1931 *THE LADY WHO CAME TO STAY* by Robin Spencer

When widowed Katherine and her little daughter move in with her late husband's wealthy maiden sisters, she soon becomes the object of their enmity and dies. The abuse continues against the child, but Katherine is able to return as a ghost and protect her daughter as well as bringing an end to the evil ways of the old sisters.

1935 *BEGINNING AT DUSK* by Ross Williamson

Every year, on Midsummer Eve, the ghosts of Kitzbrook rise and mingle with the living. Among them are two lovers, Hedwig and Stefan, who cause a commotion in the spirit world by carrying out erotic escapades, involving people in the real world. The pair prove to have an honourable intention: to avenge a murder before they can live in peace – in the grave – together.

1936 *THE CROQUET PLAYER* by H. G. Wells

The inhabitants of Cainmarsh are suffering from breakdowns and fear, which leads to an outbreak of violence and crime. A young doctor, Finchatton, recognizes the symptoms as being caused by shadows from the past affecting the minds of susceptible individuals. There is no hope of the haunting ending, the doctor declares, unless mankind changes its warlike ways.

1937 *NIGHTMARE FARM* by Jack Mann

An elemental ghost with vicious powers, which has already killed one person, is haunting an old house in Knightsmere in Shropshire. Occult detective Gees investigates and discovers that the terrible manifestation is located in a secret compartment of the building. His attempts to dislodge the ghost involve a near fatal attack on his life and the necessity to exorcise a spirit from a young woman.

1940 *MISS HARGREAVES* by Frank Baker

While on a visit to Ireland, the critic Norman Hunter finds himself pursued by the ghost of an octogenarian poet, Miss Hargreaves, who he has made the mistake of describing as "imaginary". When the lady follows him back to England, the hapless young man has to find a way of luring her across the Irish Sea to lay her peacefully to rest.

1940 *CASTLE COTTAGE* by Horace Horsnell

Miss Lavinia Bligh, a retired maid, discovers that the Regency-style Castle Cottage she is asked to look after is haunted by a pair of ghosts from the Napoleonic period. They are obviously lovers denied happiness by the young man's death during the conflict. The kind-hearted Lavinia tries to unite the two spirits, but finds that she must destroy the cottage to achieve her objective.

1941 *UNEASY FREEHOLD* by Dorothy Macardle

A house on the Bristol Channel appears to be the ideal location for Roderick Fitzgerald to write his new play. But when he and his sister settle in, they are soon being subjected to the depredations of two warring ghosts and after séances and physic researchers have failed to drive the pair away, the couple are forced to create a dramatic confrontation of their own.

1941 *THE GHOST OF MR BROWN* by Ashley Sampson

Mr Brown is a ghost and condemned to haunt a house for no apparent reason he can deduce. He tries to make contact with the occupants and even falls in love with one of the female tenants. However, when the girl gets engaged to another man, Mr Brown is overcome with rage, kills her and finds himself even more damned than before.

1941 *THE REMARKABLE ANDREW* by Dalton Trumbo

A young book-keeper, Andrew Jackson Long, of Shale City, Colorado discovers a plot to defraud the city. When he feels himself being sucked into the conspiracy, he is able to summon up the spirit of his great ancestor along with a number of other ghosts including George Washington and Ben Franklin. Together they lure the conspirators into a confession and clear Andrew's name.

1944 *THE NIGHT OF THE WORLD* by Frederick Rose

Ken Favery is blown up while fighting a desperate action with the British forces in North Africa. He wakes to find himself surrounded by the ghosts of soldiers killed during the battle and is so moved by their terrible accounts of the foolishness of war that he vows to write down his thoughts and hope that they are found with his body.

1945 *ALL HALLOWS' EVE* by Charles Williams

Two young women who have died in a plane crash find themselves as spirits in London where they are able to intervene in the lives of both their friends and adversaries. They become embroiled in a great act of magic where their own supernatural powers are tested to the fullest before the self-defeating nature of evil is exposed.

1945 *THE GHOST AND MRS MUIR* by R. A. Dick

The recently widowed Mrs Muir takes a little house near the English Channel that is haunted by its previous owner, Captain Gregg, an old sea dog who does not welcome the new tenant. She is made of sterner stuff, though, and after a series of exchanges, they both agree to share the property – until Mrs Muir dies and joins the Captain on the Other Side.

1946 *DEATH INTO LIFE* by Olaf Stapledon

While flying over Germany, the crew of a British bomber are shot down and killed. Almost immediately, the ghost of the rear-gunner rises above the wreckage and begins a journey of discovery that reveals the futility of war and enables him to grow spiritually before he is finally reunited with his comrades.

1947 *THE MEMOIRS OF A GHOST* by George W. Stonier

During a German bombing raid over London, the narrator is killed and finds himself turned into a ghost able to see and hear everything while remaining unseen by everyone else in the city. Gradually, however, his energy begins to diminish as the war draws to a close and he becomes no more than a memory.

1947 *A NAME FOR EVIL* by Andrew Lytle

When Brent buys a rundown plantation in the American South, his attempts to make the property viable are hampered by the intransigence of his workforce and their fear of the ghost of a former owner. Brent soon finds his young wife is also being subjected to the attentions of the evil phantom and has to wage a desperate battle to keep her from being spirited away.

1947 *THE MASTER OF THE MACABRE* by Russell Thorndike

In the days of Richard I, the ghost of a lewd and wicked monk weaves itself into an ancient cup that once belonged to Mohammed. Centuries later, the cup is obtained by the mysterious "Master of the Macabre" and almost at once finds himself embroiled in a dangerous plot by a group of Orientals to reclaim the relic.

1948 *THE HAUNTING OF TOBY JUGG* by Dennis Wheatley

The supernatural manifestations that plague Toby Jugg while he is convalescing in Wales prove to be only the start of a plot involving black magicians determined to bring about the downfall of his huge industrial empire. Visions of a giant spider and the Face of Astoroth also cross Toby's path as he struggles to outwit and smash the diabolists.

1950 *BRIMSTONE IN THE GARDEN* by Elizabeth Cadell

A trio of ghosts, Frobisher, Telemachus and Captain Verlander haunt Elinor Stirling's house in a small West Country English village. When she invites a group of relatives and friends to stay with her, they have to compete with the attentions of the phantoms as well as their own mixed emotions about one another in order to resolve the situation.

1954 *BRIEF CANDLES* by Francis Gaite

Jeremy and Sally Latimer are visiting a district of France where two of their forebears were killed in 1870. Their presence activates the ghosts of the long-dead man and woman and a series of phenomena convince the couple that the spirits are trying to pass on a message. It is only when Jeremy and Sally discover the location of a lost family treasurer that peace can be restored.

1954 *MY LIFE IN THE BUSH OF GHOSTS* by Amos Tutuola

A child, who has escaped from slave traders stalking the African bush, finds himself in "The Bush of Ghosts" where he goes through a succession of terrible experiences that prepare him for manhood. Eventually, with the help of a pair of native ghosts, he returns home and there creates "The Secret Society of Ghosts", dedicated to ending the persecution of his people.

1957 *THE STRANGE CASE OF MR PELHAM* by Anthony Armstrong

Pelham, an innocuous little book-keeper, becomes increasingly unnerved when friends report seeing him at places he has never visited and with people he has never met. When he is accused of seducing his secretary and orchestrating a series of dubious business deals, Pelham sets about tracking down his "double" and finds "him" to be a spirit of incredible power.

1957 *AMOROUS GHOST* by Pierre Bessand-Massenet

A young writer, Michel Panouche, is living in an old office building in Paris when he discovers it was once part of a Royal Palace and is haunted by the ghosts of a group of courtesans. One of these, the pretty Rosette, falls in love with him and it takes all the feminine wiles of Panouche's real-life lover, Annik, to break the spell and free her man.

1958 *A STIR OF ECHOES* by Richard Matheson

Tom Wallace has lived an ordinary life until the day he is hypnotized by a friend and begins to "hear" the thoughts of everyone around him. His existence becomes a living nightmare when he starts to receive haunting messages from an entity beyond the grave and finds himself compelled to try and solve a crime of almost unthinkable violence.

1959 *THE HAUNTING OF HILL HOUSE* by Shirley Jackson

Arguably the finest ghost novel of the century. Hill House has a reputation for being plagued by spirits and has changed very little since the 1880s. A psychic researcher invites a group of people to stay in the property to test his theories about the manifestations. Messages smeared in blood, bumps in the night and horrifying phenomena crowd one upon another until a finger of suspicion begins to point at one of the guests.

1960 *A FINE AND PRIVATE PLACE* by Peter Beagle

Jonathan Rebeck lives in a tomb in the Bronx where he has learned to see and talk to ghosts. Some of his most interesting conversations are with Michael Morgan, who claims his wife murdered him, and a beautiful young woman named Laura. When the beguiling widow, Mrs Klapper, induces Jonathan to leave the cemetery, he has to first find time for a little matchmaking between his ethereal friends.

1969 *THE GREEN MAN* by Kingsley Amis

Maurice Allingham, the owner of a medieval coaching inn, finds his life of debauchery and drinking suddenly affected by the malevolent reappearance of the ghost of Dr Thomas Underhill, a notorious 17th-century practitioner of black magic. Driven by curiosity and a desire to save his own sanity, Allingham has to uncover the secret to the doctor's evil purpose.

1973 *BURNT OFFERINGS* by Robert Marasco

The Rolfe family from New York are hoping for a happy summer in a beautiful, secluded country mansion with a pool and private beach on Long Island. But it does not take the four people long to realize that the place is haunted by terror and they are plunged into a nightmare from which there seems to be no escape.

1975 *JULIA* by Peter Straub

Julia Lufting is still mourning the death of her only child and hoping against hope that the future will bring her better luck. Then her nights begin to be haunted by the ghost of a child. Not her own lost infant, apparently, but a quite terrifying little girl, and Julia finds herself driven to discover the unspeakable way in which the youngster died.

1977 *SWEETHEART, SWEETHEART* by Bernard Taylor

To all intents and purposes Gerrard's Hill Cottage, deep in the English countryside surrounded by meadows, trees and rose bushes, is an idyllic spot, promising rest and relaxation to anyone who visits. Instead, just beneath the surface, a malevolent female spirit is at large weaving an aura of murder, madness and betrayal around those who cross the threshold.

1977 *THE SHINING* by Stephen King

Snowbound Overlook Hotel is intended to be a home-away-from home for writer Jack Torrance, his wife Wendy and their son Danny, when Jack accepts the post of janitor for the winter. But their stay turns to madness when ghosts of the past start to come to life and those gifted with the "shining" have to do battle with the darkest evils.

1978 *THE HOUSE NEXT DOOR* by Anne Rivers Siddons

It seems like such a good idea for Walter and Colquitt Kennedy to buy the piece of land adjoining their house and build their "dream home" on it. But once work begins, mishaps start to occur with wildlife being killed, pets going missing and strange sights in the neighbourhood. The couple's conviction they may have created a "haunted house" moves rapidly from suspicion to terrifying reality.

1979 *GHOST STORY* by Peter Straub

There is a secret never mentioned when the five life-long friends in Milburn, NY meet each week as "The Chowder Society" to swap ghost stories. The mystery concerns Eva, a young girl the group accidentally killed in a car and dumped in the local lake when they were teenagers. Now a shape-shifting ghost has begun to haunt all their dreams and kill them one by one unless drastic action is taken.

1982 *THE WOMAN IN BLACK* by Susan Hill

Arthur Kipps is a junior solicitor in Victorian England who attends the funeral of a client and during the service glimpses a mysterious woman in black. Later in the day, he sees the figure again and also hears the terrifying sounds of an adult and child sinking into a quicksand. To resolve the mystery he has to remain overnight in ancient Eel Marsh House and face the greatest horror of all.

1988 *HAUNTED* by James Herbert

Ghost hunter David Ash is invited to investigate the hauntings taking place in an old house called Edbrook. Three nights the young man spends in the gloomy property with maleficent and blood-chilling events occurring one after another. On the third night, David has to face the enigma of his own past before the secret of Edbrook itself is revealed.

1991 *THE MIST IN THE MIRROR* by Susan Hill

Sir James Monmouth is obsessed with the life and career of a mysterious traveller named Conrad Vane whose ghost has been seen about London. Monmouth's research establishes that Vane was a man of evil deeds involving terrible cruelty to children. Now his curse threatens the lives of all those who become drawn to his legend.

1993 *GHOSTS* by Noel Hynd

Following two unexplained deaths on sleepy Nantucket Island, a number of ghostly disturbances have started to upset the residents and visitors. Timothy Brooks, a detective assigned to investigate the killings, begins to suspect the ghost may be that of a stage actor killed in the 1920s and the deaths are in some way connected to him. It takes a mixture of sleuthing and "ghost-busting" to solve the mystery.

1994 *THE GHOSTS OF SLEATH* by James Herbert

A second enquiry for ghost hunter David Ash takes him to the quiet and peaceful village of Sleath in the Chiltern Hills. This calm has been disturbed by reports of ghost sightings and some frighteningly bizarre events. Once again Ash has to confront secrets from his own past on a night of horror when awesome and malignant forces are unleashed on the helpless community.

1994 *REVENANT* by Melanie Tem

The ghost town of Revant is where spirits congregate: the mother who talks to her dead children, the father with an image of his son before a fatal accident and a girl mourning her phantom aborted baby. But there is also a presence in Revenant, ancient, powerful and hungry waiting to feed on the souls in torment and free more terrifying spirits into the darkness.

1996 *A FACE AT THE WINDOW* by Dennis McFarland

A man who is sober after years of alcohol abuse undergoes a mid-life crisis while staying in a haunted hotel. There he encounters several ghosts: a violent drunken man, an unpleasant small boy and an adolescent girl with a split personality. However, when he becomes engrossed in the details of the girl's former life he is unaware that he is also endangering his own life and that of his family.

1996 *NAZARETH HILL* by Ramsey Campbell

Amy is an unhappy teenager whose mother died when she was a child and now lives with her controlling father in newly renovated Nazareth Hill. When she begins to see and hear strange sights and sounds, Amy realizes the secret behind the events lies somewhere in her childhood. Her attempts to discover the truth, however, drive her father increasingly nasty and turn Nazareth Hill into a hell on earth.

1996 *THE HOUSE THAT JACK BUILT* by Graham Masterton

Despite the fact that the old mansion, Valhalla, is known to echo with the sounds of terrible sobbing, Craig Bellman is determined to live there. His frightened wife hires a spiritualist to try and rid the place of its fearsome vibrations. But even when death and injury continue to disturb Valhalla, Bellman's obsession drives him relentlessly towards a terrible conclusion.

1997 *FOG HEART* by Thomas Tessier

When two couples are haunted by, respectively, the father of one wife and messages from the dead daughter of the other, they consult a powerful young medium named Oona. The four people and their guide have to endure a number of psychic attacks and sadistic disturbances before Oona's conviction that the four are somehow connected finally enables them to resolve the frightening situation.

1998 *BAG OF BONES* by Stephen King

Mike Noonan has mourned for his beloved wife Jo for some time when he meets a young widow, Mattie and her daughter, Kyra. He agrees to help them in a custody case being brought by Mattie's wealthy father-in-law and soon finds himself being haunted by a vengeful ghost. The spirit is that of a black woman gang-raped and forced to witness the murder of her child and it is through her that the custody case is won.

1999 *SUSPICION* by Barbara Rogan

Ghost story writer Emma Roth hopes that the old Victorian house on the North Shore of Long Island will help her work. Instead, cruel remarks begin appearing on her computer, her manuscript is tampered with and there is every indication the house is haunted. But Emma remains sceptical and begins to wonder whether she is losing her mind or – perhaps – someone very close is trying to destroy her.

2000 *MISCHIEF* by Douglas Clegg

Harrow Academy is a private boy's school located in an old haunted mansion. Young Jim Hook is in his first year when the ghost of his brother, recently killed in a car accident with their father, visits him one night with a warning. A secret group of students try to induct Jim into their Cadaver Society and he has a powerful battle to wage against them and the other even more powerful force that inhabits the building before his life can return to normal. Clegg has written two further titles to complete the Harrow Academy series: *The Infinite* (2001) and *Nightmare House* (2003).